MW01632273

HUNGER

THE COMPLETE TRILOGY

WORKS BY JEREMY ROBINSON

The Didymus Contingency
Raising The Past
Beneath
Antarktos Rising
Kronos
Pulse
Instinct
Threshold
Callsign: King
Callsign: Queen
Callsign: Rook
Callsign: King 2 – Underworld
Callsign: Bishop
Callsign: Knight
Callsign: Deep Blue
Callsign: King 3 – Blackout
Torment
The Sentinel
The Last Hunter – Descent
The Last Hunter – Pursuit
The Last Hunter – Ascent
The Last Hunter – Lament
The Last Hunter – Onslaught
The Last Hunter – Collected Edition
Insomnia
SecondWorld
Project Nemesis
Ragnarok
Island 731
The Raven
Nazi Hunter: Atlantis
Prime
Omega
Project Maigo
Refuge
Guardian
Human After All
Savage
Flood Rising
Project 731
Cannibal
Endgame
MirrorWorld
Herculean
Project Hyperion
Patriot
Apocalypse Machine
Empire
Unity
Project Legion
The Distance
The Last Valkyrie
Centurion
Infinite
Helios
Viking Tomorrow
Forbidden Island
The Divide
The Others
Space Force
Alter
Flux
Tether
Tribe
NPC
Exo-Hunter
Infinite²
The Dark
Mind Bullet
The Order
Khaos
Singularity
Hunger – The Complete Trilogy

HUNGER

THE COMPLETE TRILOGY

JEREMY ROBINSON

BREAKNECK MEDIA

Jacket design by Damonza.
Case art, title page art, layout, and design by Jeremy Robinson.

Visit Jeremy Robinson on the World Wide Web at: www.bewareofmonsters.com.

BOOK ONE:

HUNGER

1

New Mexico

"What the hell am I looking at, Jeff?" A surge of annoyance threatened to overwhelm Dr. Ella Masse's practiced serenity. She was the lead geneticist heading up ExoGen's GMO division. She worked with hundreds of people, from hard laborers, to farmers, to marketing gurus and her fellow geneticists. Of all the people she encountered, it was her own ilk that burrowed under her skin and scratched at her nerves. The more brilliant the scientist, the more frustrating she found them. And Jeff Sexton topped the charts in both brilliance and irritating habits, the worst of which was his inability to give a straight answer.

"You tell me," he said, wiping dirt from the knees of his white cleansuit. Like most of the gene-hackers working for ExoGen, Sexton didn't just work in a sterile lab. He got in the dirt, observing growth patterns and rates, and water consumption and crop yield. They could have had cheap labor work the dirt, but Masse wanted her people to feel connected to the job. To care about it. When that happened, people worked harder, and in a field ruled by the mind, that meant her staff was working even when not at work. They woke up with new ideas. Beat her to the office. Finished ahead of schedule.

And that was how they were going to beat the competition, which in ExoGen's David and Goliath scenario, was just Sancio. Of course, they had Sancio to thank for the relaxed regulations on genetically modified foods. The corporation had pretty much paved the way for (and paid for) the laws that gave ExoGen the freedom to modify food however they saw fit. Most of the time it was exciting, groundbreaking work with the potential to alter the fate of the human race. But during moments like this...

"I see corn."

"Use your eyes, Ell." She shot him a look over the top of her narrow glasses. "Dr. Masse," Sexton corrected as he bounced on his feet, a belled hat away from acting like a court jester. She'd never seen the man so worked up before.

Maybe this will be worthwhile, if I can figure out what put the ants in his pants.

She stepped into the hundred-foot-long greenhouse. The sky above was bold and blue, the sun blazing down on them. The curved glass ceiling would have been all but invisible if not for the white support structure. The room looked more like it belonged on a space station, except for the corn. Rows of it.

She stepped up to the nearest ear, gripped the husk and peeled it down, revealing a grid of bright yellow, bulbous corn kernels.

"*Zea mays indenta*," she said, identifying the Dent strain of corn used for feed, processed foods, and industrial products, meaning it was some of the most common corn on the planet. Nothing special. "If it's been modified from our Dent-Y strain, I'm not seeing how."

"Then maybe you should use your nose," he said.

"Seriously?"

The man just jounced around, waiting for her to stumble upon his discovery.

She smelled the corn through the filter in her suit. Nothing special. She snapped off the ear and tossed it deeper into the greenhouse, then wheeled around on Sexton. Her lungs filled with pressure, preparing to vent, but then she noticed a different smell. She paused, turned back to the corn, and sniffed.

She could smell the corn. Lots of it. The odor had become so familiar to her that she rarely ever ate the stuff. Nose lifted, she stepped deeper inside the greenhouse and quickly became aware of a second sensation. Her skin prickled from dry heat. Her eyes began to sting.

Before realizing what she was doing, Masse crouched down into the shade of the corn stalks. But even in that twilight shadow, she could see there was something wrong with the soil.

It wasn't soil at all.

It was sand.

She stood as though electrocuted, wheeling around toward Sexton. "How much water have you given them?"

He smiled.

"Not a drop."

She looked at the lush corn. "That's not possible."

"It's the roots," he said. "They're deep."

"How deep?"

Sexton cleared his throat with a smile. "Twenty feet."

With wide eyes, she turned to the corn again. The parts of the plants she could see were just a small tip of the whole, with the rest being underground, stretching down to the water table, which in this part of New Mexico, was deep. *Twenty feet deep, apparently.*

As the initial surprise and wonder began to ebb, Masse caught sight of the number on the greenhouse door: C-8. "Eight? I thought you were working in Seven. Not like you to make mistakes."

His smile looked wide enough to lift the top half of his head clean off. "Come with me."

They entered the decontamination unit, which was essentially a manmade whirlwind pulling any dust, seeds, pollen or other potential contaminants off their clean suits, and sucking it away. This prevented one crop from contaminating another, making sure their observations were accurate and reliable. There were a hundred greenhouses in all, dedicated to the world's ten most common and important crops—corn, rice, wheat, soybeans, potatoes, cassava, sweet potatoes, sorghum, yams, and alfalfa.

Each of the ten greenhouses in a grouping were arranged around a central hub, spokes without a wheel. From the hub, each single crop's greenhouse could be reached. But to visit a different crop without returning to the hub, you had to head outside, into the heat. Most of the ExoGen staff had no reason to visit multiple crops. The gene hackers all had their own specialty crops. Masse was one of the unlucky few who found herself wandering the arid plain, working up a sweat once a week for inspections and progress reports. Sexton was her first visit today, and if he'd managed to develop a strain of corn capable of growing in the desert...well, she'd cancel the rest of her day and order some champagne. This was the kind of worldchanging stuff ExoGen wanted, and it would put them on the map, side by side with Sancio.

They moved through the hub, a fifty-foot-wide circular space that was Sexton's lab. His eager-eyed team of three men and two women looked up in silence, watching them pass through, in on the joke's punch line. *But this isn't a joke,* she told herself. *Sexton would never joke about this. First, because he cares, and second, because he has no sense of humor.*

She barely heard the fans whipping the air around her inside of greenhouse C-7's decontamination chamber. Her eyes were on the glass door, beyond which was the access door to the greenhouse. When Sexton opened the door, she hurried past, punched in the four-digit code that gave her access to every room in the facility, and pulled open the door.

Corn.

Rows of it.

Visually, the crop was identical to what she had seen in C-8, but it smelled of rich soil, manure, and moisture. These were the elements that had been missing from C-8, and yet the result was the same.

"You did it," she said. "A single crop that can grow in multiple environments."

"In nearly any environment with a permeable floor," he said. "Resistant to freezing, heat, insects, disease, and drought."

Masse felt her knees go weak. He was talking about the mother of all GMOs. This wasn't comparable to striking oil, this was like striking all of it, at once. She bent forward, hands on her knees. "Tell me you haven't developed a sick sense of humor."

"Not at all," he said, and bent down to look her in the eyes. "But I'm not done yet, either."

She stood up again. "What else could there be?"

"You were right," he said. "I was working in C-7. As per usual, the plan was to plant the crop under optimal conditions. Then move on to the next greenhouse and change the conditions."

She nodded. That was standard protocol when trying to develop crops that thrived in multiple environs.

Sexton swept his hand out to the crop. "This was the first crop of Dent I planted, modified with a variety of genes, but most recently with RC-714. I planted it—"

"—thirty days ago." The gene sequence meant nothing to her. They worked with thousands of genes that came and went, and keeping track of them was next to impossible. But crop plantings were far less common and something she tracked with great interest. She looked at the fully grown crop. "It grows faster, too?"

"Aggressively so," Sexton said.

"So, you moved on to the second stage...when? I never gave approval for a second crop."

"I didn't know about the second crop," he admitted. "The greenhouse hadn't even been prepped yet. The barren earth in C-8 is the same as the desert surrounding the facility. I found the crop when I opened the door this morning."

"Who planted it?"

"No one," he said, but then shook his head. "Technically, I did. In C-7."

The first real clue of what he was revealing began to resolve, her eyes widening in time with the revelation. "It *spread?* How?"

"Remember the twenty-foot roots?"

"Underground?"

"Near as I can tell, the plants are interconnected, but separate, like the Great Barrier Reef...of corn. Looking at the amount of growth, I've estimated that it spread to five of the ten greenhouses in the last few weeks, with the farthest away in C-5 being a week's growth behind C-6, and C-6 a week behind C-7. Like I said, it's aggressive. The only thing keeping it inside the greenhouse system is the perimeter concrete foundation, which is ten feet deep. The foundation between greenhouses is just two feet deep. The corn follows the path of least resistance."

Once again pitched over, hands on knees, the vast implications of everything Sexton revealed crashed down on Masse with a tidal force, roaring in her ears, adding weight to her body, and then washing away. "How long?"

"For what?"

"Until it gets out."

She knew Sexton would have seen the eventual outcome. Once the corn spread through the remaining five greenhouses, if it was as aggressive as he thought, it would eventually work its way outside.

"Two months," he said. "Three at the most. The foundation should slow it down."

"That's not much time," she said.

"For what?"

"We need to get this gene of yours in the other crops."

His brow furrowed. "To what end?"

She smiled. "We're going to feed the world."

2

Five Years Later

"Sometimes I hate my life," Kevin Travis said, as he looked through his pair of forward-looking infrared (FLIR) thermal binoculars. He tracked a blob of heat moving through the field. From a distance, it looked like one massive organism, but he knew the truth, even before zooming in. They moved like a shoal of fish, shifting one way and then the other, all following the few individuals in the lead. They would stop to feast on the endless sea of food before moving on, sometimes sticking to the wilderness, but most often heading back to where they were most comfortable: the city.

"Could be worse," his understudy, Cliff Foster, said. Foster was a glass-half-full kind of guy, but that was just because he'd only been on the job for a few weeks. Travis had been at it, waging a war no one would ever see or know about—if everything went right—for the last three years. And every year, he lost ground, just like the hundreds of other exterminators now in the employ of ExoGen.

At least it pays well, Travis thought, focusing on the blob's head. He zeroed in on a single target and confirmed its identity.

A rat.

There were more than a thousand of them.

In the years following what was now called the Farm Bomb, several things had happened. ExoGen's aggressive GMO crops—more than two hundred varieties of fruits, vegetables, fungi, and legumes—had spread across the country, and then the world. The plants grew everywhere there wasn't pavement, concrete, or steel. The company had been the target of countless lawsuits, first from competitors, and then from landowners and governments. But that stopped when it had become clear that ExoGen had solved one of humanity's impending humanitarian crises before it began.

Hunger was no more.

No one would ever starve again.

That was when the counter-suits began, and thanks to the legislation already passed and the lawsuits against farmers already won by Sancio, anyone who grew and ate ExoGen's food—everyone—owed them a small monthly fee. The company kept the payments low so that even the poorest people could afford it, and ExoGen quickly became the most powerful corporation in the world. After the food problem, they tackled fossil fuels, their endless corn and sugarcane crops making ethanol production efficient and cheap. While all farms and seed companies were put out of business, their skilled laborers were absorbed into ExoGen and were paid better than they had been before. Few people complained. The world had been remade into a prosperous place for everyone and everything.

Animal populations boomed.

At first, this was seen as a drawback because vehicle collisions increased, but then the federal government removed the hunting season restrictions. Every day of the year was fair game for prey animals. And a year later, when the predator population increased, all animals became targets. As a result, a large number of people went off the grid, living solitary lives in the woods, surrounded by endless food.

But there were still some problems no one wanted to face. Like rats. Who hunted rats? No one. Unless they were paid for it, like Travis and Foster.

"I think it's fun," Foster said. "Aside from the military, where else can you get paid to throw grenades and use flamethrowers?"

"The military doesn't use flamethrowers anymore," Travis said, lowering the FLIR binoculars. He glanced at Foster with a grin. "Though you do make a good point."

"Hell, yes, I do." Foster pulled a shock grenade from his vest. The device wasn't designed to kill rats, though the overpressure wave would certainly kill those closest to the device. Its primary function was to knock the rodents unconscious. For a group this large, they'd probably have to lob four grenades in an even spread. Some of the critters would probably escape, but most would fall to the ground, motionless if not lifeless, and that's when it would be time to move in with the flamethrowers. The surrounding crop would burn as well, but they had extinguishers to prevent its spread. And even if it did spread, there were large fires all the time now. A few C-130s loaded with water could be called in to douse the fire before it really got legs.

"You were in the military, weren't you?" Foster asked. "It's why you have the buzz cut and the serious personality, yeah?"

Travis's smile faded. He *had* been in the military. An Army Ranger. But he didn't like to talk about it. "The new world doesn't have much need for soldiers. Best it stays that way. Now, let's get this done."

He put the FLIR back up to his eyes and tracked the pack of rats through the stalks of corn. They were headed toward a patch of raspberries a hundred yards ahead, no doubt their intended meal, but the thorny brambles would make their job harder. "Let's hit them before they—"

Travis stopped as he panned between the raspberry patch and the rodents. There was a single heat signature. A lone rabbit. While rabbits were now one of the most common animals on the planet, they rarely ventured into cities, making them a lower priority than the rats. But they were still an approved target. What was odd about this rabbit was that it was alone.

Not for long, he thought, as the rat horde closed in.

The rabbit seemed oblivious to their approach. Or perhaps it just didn't care? The species shared the same habitat, and there was more than enough food to go around.

He watched the rabbit lift its head, ears straight up.

It can hear them, he thought. The rabbit hopped out of the pack's path, but the rodents adjusted, following the hare.

"What the...?" Foster saw it, too. "Are they chasing the rabbit?"

"Rats are territorial," Travis said, "but usually only when food is scarce. But it's possible that—"

The rats launched themselves at the rabbit, which sprang up into the air at the last moment, avoiding the rodent cascade. It then outpaced them, running in wide circles. The tactic wouldn't work for long, though. The rat pack was breaking up, spreading apart and flanking it.

"This is more like watching lions hunt," Foster observed. "Rats don't do this normally, right?"

"Not that I've seen."

Travis was locked in place. He could see how it would end. The rabbit had maybe ten seconds before it was surrounded by the now loosely packed rat horde. And then what?

They're going to kill it.

"Holy Watership Down," Foster said, watching the scene unfold through the lines of corn stalks. They were just a hundred feet away from the action, close enough to lob their shock grenades and put an end to all of this, but they remained rooted, fixated, and distracted.

And that was when everything changed.

"What's that?" Foster asked. "On the hill."

The flat plain, where the rats pursued the rabbit, was fringed by rolling hills topped with fruit trees. A moment before, those hills had been a cool blue in the FLIR's thermal vision. They were now a torrent of heat, moving downward, toward the rats.

Travis zeroed in on a single heat signature, tracking it. It took just a moment to recognize the shape. Rabbits. Thousands of them. "They set a trap."

Foster lowered his binoculars. "What?"

"The rabbits set a trap. For the rats."

He watched through the FLIR as the horde of rats, now detecting the onrushing rabbits, changed course, heading uphill, while the solo rabbit stopped running and engaged a single rat. The two heat signatures meshed for a moment, wriggling and twitching, and then, a hot red spray of blood burst into the air, followed by the first rabbit, as it launched itself into the fray.

The two lines of small furry mammals collided like two medieval armies, hacking and slashing, killing and maiming.

Travis lowered the FLIR. He couldn't watch.

There was something unsettling about this behavior. Rats and rabbits didn't wage wars on each other. They didn't use the hunting tactics of lions or wolves.

"This is bad," he said.

Foster was still watching the fight, a smile on his face. "This is *awesome*."

"You don't understand," Travis said. "They shouldn't be acting this way. Something is wrong."

"All I know is that they're doing our job for us in the most entertaining way. This is something I can tell my kids about. Hell, this is something I can tell my grandkids!"

Travis was about to switch on his phone and call it in, when he heard a hiss. He recognized the sound. You couldn't move through a corn field without the large dry leaves rattling against your body. But it was the volume that was strange.

He looked behind them and saw nothing but corn. "Foster, who's winning the fight?"

"Looks like a draw so far. Man, so much blood."

Travis put the FLIR to his eyes and looked behind them again. Fifty feet away, the base of the cool field was lined with a writhing mass of heat closing in on them, and on the rats, from the far side. The rabbits had flanked them.

"Foster!" Travis shouted, getting to his feet.

The younger man spun around, FLIR to his eyes, and saw the rabbits swarming toward them. "Oh, fu—"

He fumbled with the shock grenade in his hand, pulling the pin and cocking his arm back to throw it. It wasn't a bad strategy. The concussion might have given them time to get out of the small army's path...if he'd thrown it just a few seconds sooner. The first of the rabbits to reach them launched itself in the air, landing on Foster's chest and burying its long incisors in his neck.

A flash of *Monty Python and the Holy Grail* shot into Travis's mind, but it was wiped clear when the dropped shock grenade detonated. The blast instantly killed Foster, liquefying his insides. But Travis, who had begun to run, was simply knocked to the ground, unconscious.

He woke, five minutes later, his body wracked by unimaginable pain. Shock set in quickly, numbing his agony, but fogging his mind. He tried to stand, but couldn't.

What's wrong with me?

He remembered the grenade.

Had the pressure wave snapped his back?

He tried moving his arms to his pocket and the phone, but he couldn't feel either limb. With rising anxiety about being paralyzed, he lifted his head and looked down.

"Oh no... Oh, God, no..."

The rabbits feasting on his gut looked up, their muzzles coated in blood and bits of his entrails. Beyond them he saw his legs, gnawed down to the bones.

One of the rabbits stepped onto his chest, its white fur coated in blood, its red eyes gleaming with menace. Its nose twitched a few times, and Travis remembered a time, as a kid, watching a rabbit's nose and thinking it was the most adorable thing he'd seen. Then the rabbit pounced, landing atop his face, muffling his scream, and feasting on his nose.

3

One Year Later

Bacon sizzled in a black, cast-iron pan. A whole pound of it. The sweet and salty scent filled the small, two-bedroom apartment. Dressed in overly tight sweatpants with the word 'Juicy' across her backside, Jenn Waters danced back and forth, humming a tune of her own creation. Her tightly pulled-back ponytail swished back and forth. She watched the twitching, pink and white, marbled meat, leaning her face over the particles of steam rising up, absorbing it.

Until six months ago, she'd been a vegetarian. Not because meat disgusted her, but because of the way animals were treated—kept in crates, force fed antibiotic-laced food, and abused in ways that no civilized world should tolerate. But then, literally overnight, her taste for meat overpowered her revulsion.

There had never been a better time to be a vegetarian. The world was overflowing with food, and for years, she had devoured her fair share of the crops, happily paying her $8 a month fee to ExoGen. But now...it was like that saying: too much of a good thing. In high school, she'd been obsessed with Cinnamon Toast Crunch. Ate it every morning for breakfast, for nearly four years. Until one day the smell of it made her gag. She couldn't even eat real cinnamon toast. That was how she saw fruit and vegetables now. Not quite as repulsive, but if she was going to even consider eating a green bean or apple, there'd better be a steak next to it.

Rare, thank you very much.

Lost in thought, she let out a whispered curse when she saw the bacon start to crisp. Like her steaks, she liked her bacon chewy and meaty. If bacteria weren't a real concern, she might even try it raw. But she knew better, even though there were few smells more intoxicating to her now than a freshly opened package of ground beef.

She turned off the stove and plucked the wriggling bacon from the pan, depositing the slices onto a plate. She then poured the hot grease over the top. Later, when it congealed, she'd scrape the plate with a fork, leaving nothing behind.

With the crackling bacon silenced, she could hear the TV again. The shouting voice of some newscaster instantly set her nerves on edge.

"You left the TV on!" She picked up a slice of bacon, almost too hot to hold, and put it in her mouth, slurping the long strand inside and licking the grease from her lips. She chewed and chewed, letting out a moan of delight. How she had been a vegetarian for so long she'd never know. There were few things in this world more pleasurable than animal fat.

After swallowing, she shouted, "Hey asshole! The TV!"

When no reply came, she gripped the kitchen counter and squeezed. Logically, she knew this wasn't a big deal, but it was just one of many recent irritations. Tony, her boyfriend, was really getting under her skin. They'd been fighting all month. In fact, she'd been bickering with most everyone she knew. The world had become full of assholes, but chief among them was Tony.

When she let go of the island, the hair on the back of her neck stood up. If Tony didn't shut that damn TV off, she was going to crack him over the head with the cast-iron pan. *One good whack, and he'll shut the hell up forever.* She looked at the pan, considering it, but then realized there would be cool grease to eat later on, if she let it be.

Consoled by that knowledge, she picked up the plate with her pound of bacon and stepped out of the kitchen and into the living room. Tony was nowhere in sight. He wasn't even watching the damn thing.

"Tony!"

Silence.

"So help me God, Tony, if you don't—"

The images on screen caught her attention. Two men fighting. But there was something off about it. This wasn't news footage of a brawl or a foiled burglary—this was happening in the studio. She recognized the two men. One was the morning host along with a woman who wasn't on camera at the moment. The other man was the weatherman. And they weren't just trading punches like most men fought, they were tearing into each other, clawing, biting, drawing blood.

A smile spread across her bacon juice-laced lips. "This is more like it."

She sat on the edge of the couch, slurping up long strands of bacon, reveling in the twin guilty pleasures of meat and violence.

Some distant and quiet part of her mind thought, *Who am I? How did I get like this?* But then the weatherman bit off the host's finger. Blood sprayed. The host cocked his head back and screamed in pain. And then... the weatherman swallowed.

Oh my God, he ate that guy's finger!

She wondered how it tasted, and then she shoved more bacon in her mouth.

Then the host kicked himself free and caught the weatherman with a right cross that shattered his nose. She stood up. "Kick his ass!"

As the weatherman reeled back, the host picked up a laptop computer, yanked it from its cord and then brought it down on the stunned weatherman's bloody head. The force of the blow broke the laptop in two at the joint. Keyboard keys launched into the air.

Waters took a handful of bacon, crushing it between her fingers before shoving the mass of flesh into her mouth. She chewed, moaning, swaying back and forth, waiting to see what would happen next.

The host let the laptop fall to the floor and stood over the weatherman. He seemed confused or stunned.

Probably because he's missing a finger, she thought, but then she understood what held the man in place.

Indecision.

"Do it!" she shouted at the TV, a chunk of bacon slipping out only to be slurped back in. "Freaking eat him!"

The host dropped to his knees and lifted the weatherman's arm. He looked it over the way one might select a steak from the butcher's. Then he opened his mouth and—a woman dressed in a blood-soaked power suit ran into the frame, dive-tackling the host.

Waters flinched back in surprise.

The woman's face was covered in thick, tacky blood. A tendril of gore—meat dangling from connective tissue, hung from between her teeth. With a primal roar, the woman dove for the host's jugular, biting deep, unleashing a spray of thirst-quenching blood.

That was when the power went out.

"What. The. Fuck!" Waters screamed at no one and everyone. She nearly threw the plate, but noticed the few remaining bacon slices. Energized by the carnage she'd just witnessed, she shoved the remaining bacon in her mouth, swallowed without chewing and then licked the cooling fat from the plate with fervent urgency, like it might suddenly disappear. When she was done, the rage and a new kind of hunger, returned.

She screamed and flung the plate. It struck the living room window, shattering it, letting in the sounds of the city.

Sirens blared.

Tires screeched. People screamed.

A high-pitched wail rose up from the street below. She ran to the window and looked down. Two men were in the street. The man on top tore at the man below, while a pool of blood formed around them.

She recognized the man on top. "Tony!"

"Fuck off!" he shouted back.

"The fuck did you just say?" Her voice became shrill. Tony did *not* talk to her like that. He didn't dare.

Tony never turned around, but lifted one hand back behind his head and flipped her off.

He's dead, she thought, and she charged to the apartment door. In the hallway, she could hear other arguments under way. A crash from above tugged at her interest, but—

Tony...that asshole.

He was going to pay for talking to her like that. She took the stairs two at a time, never thinking twice about the fact that she was barefoot, wearing 'Juicy' pants and a tight tank top with no bra. She hit the lower landing, and without losing her stride, she pushed through the front door.

She could sense chaos around her. The world coming undone. But she remained solely focused on her prey.

"Tony," she said, following up the word with something close to a growl.

Her boyfriend didn't reply. Instead, his six-foot, muscular form worked over the dead man beneath him. When his hands came up clutching coils of intestine, she didn't flinch. Didn't slow. Instead, she hooked her fingers, only casually noticing that her fake nails had fallen away to be replaced by longer, thicker, black talons.

"Baby," she said, looking at his muscular arm, licking her lips. "Don't you ever—"

Tony dove forward with surprising speed and agility. He rolled over, spun around, low to the ground, on his hands and feet. His face was covered in chunky gore. He hissed at her, circling the dead body.

"It's mine," he said, glancing at the body.

"I don't want it," she replied, moving around the body, hunched forward, ready to spring.

He squinted at her, then licked his lips. He tilted his head to the side, making a show of checking out her ass. He grinned. "You *are* looking juicy, aren't you?"

With a roar, Waters sprang forward, stepping in the dead man's open gut to reach Tony. She lashed out her hooked fingers, lacerating her boyfriend's cheek and then tackling him to the ground. Inhuman shrieks rose up from the pair as they rolled over the pavement, snapping jaws, scratching, gouging, and eventually—for one of them—feasting.

4

Kansas
Two Years Later

"Hey. Wake up."

"Already?"

The bed creaked as Peter Crane sat down beside his son, Jakob. "Sun's up. That means you are, too."

Jakob groaned and sat up. "Have I told you how much I hate this?"

"Every day," Peter said, smiling. "But the farm's not going to tend itself."

Jakob stood, dressed in boxers. The wood floor would be cold beneath his feet, but he didn't seem to mind. Probably helped him wake up. He stepped up to the hermetically sealed window, a modification Peter had made six years ago, back when the world was mostly normal. Back when his mother was still alive.

Peter watched his son, wondering how long the two of them could eke out a living this way, in this place. Alone. Waiting for the inevitable.

He stepped up next to his son, looking at the endless field of wheat. Seven years ago, the view was much the same. The difference was that back then, he put the seeds in the ground and harvested the crop. Now... You couldn't even eat the stuff.

No one could.

But most everyone had. Only the staunchest opponents to GMO foods—organic farmers, homesteaders, and the subculture of 'crunchy' eaters—had resisted the plump crops' siren song. Those who had the means built biodome greenhouses. Those who didn't either found someone who did, or eventually they gave in.

By the time people figured out what was driving the smallest creatures on the planet insane, it was too late. And it wasn't that the small mammals and insects that ate the crops were gripped by some kind of madness. They simply became predatory. With an instinct to hunt and kill, their taste in food changed as well. The planet was covered in food, but those who had been eating it no longer had a taste for it. At first, the affected creatures kept to their own kind, eating, attacking, and warring with other species. But eventually they turned on each other. Survival of the fittest at its most gruesome.

When larger species of animals began to hunger for meat instead of plants, people realized two truths: it was the food causing it, and they were next. But it was worse than anyone had anticipated. While herbivores turned predatory, animals that were already predators—canines, cats, bears, birds of prey, reptiles—became super-predators, changing physically as much as mentally. The higher up the food chain, the more dangerous they became.

The human population, which had exploded thanks to an over-abundance of food, hacked, chewed, and swallowed itself down to a more manageable size. It had been a year since Peter and Jakob had seen another person, and that was fine by them.

But how long could they live like this, trapped inside a sealed farmhouse attached to a football-field-sized biodome? It was a closed system, protecting them from the dangers lurking outside, both animal and plant, but it wasn't a perfect system. Something would eventually give out. A water filter. An air scrubber. Something.

"You think anyone is left out there?" Jakob asked.

"I'm sure someone is."

They'd been in touch with other biodomes around the country up until six months ago, when the generator ran out of propane. They still had power for the essentials—water and air—thanks to six solar panels on the roof, but the battery didn't hold much juice. Using it for anything more than it was intended for put them at risk. So, they'd gone silent and dark. They could have tried to find more propane. No one else was using it now. But Peter didn't want to take the risk. They could survive without electricity.

For a few more months anyway. When winter returned, they'd need to find propane. It wouldn't be hard to find, but Peter hoped that a few more months would mean fewer predators.

They could eat each other into extinction.

That was as close to a long-term plan as he had. For now, it was business as usual.

Jakob on the other hand... "When can we look? For others."

Peter read between the lines. Before the power had gone out, Jakob had met a sixteen-year-old girl, Alia, who was just a year younger than him, via the radio. Since the cell-phone network and the Internet had already become relics of the past, the only real way to communicate was via locally powered radio. They spoke for hours on end, and though they'd never actually seen each other in person, or knew what the other looked like, Peter could tell his son had feelings for the girl.

But it wasn't time. The world was still too dangerous. If Alia's parents were smart, they'd understand that as well. She'd be there when the world became safe again.

If the world became safe.

"Eventually."

"Why not now?"

"You know why."

Jakob glowered at the field of wheat. "Can't we just burn it all?"

"It's a temporary fix," Peter said. "The fire just makes the ground more fertile, and since the roots are—"

"Yeah. I know. I just want to burn it. To do something."

"A symbolic gesture?"

Jakob nodded. "A big 'fuck you,' to mother nature."

"I'm pretty sure it's mother nature who's most offended by what we did."

Jakob turned away from the window and began dressing.

"We didn't do anything."

"The human race." Peter leaned against the sill, looking at the golden field, undulating in the wind. He longed to feel that breeze again. To taste unfiltered air. To hear the rasp of nature. The dry, stale air inside the house had become stifling. The greenhouse was better, but the pungent smell of trapped vegetation served as a constant reminder of what had been lost.

Not the world.

Screw the world.

He missed Kristen.

"Dad," Jakob said loudly, and Peter realized the boy had been speaking to him.

Without looking away from the wheat field, Peter said, "Yeah?"

"What's that?"

As his thoughts cleared, Peter not only heard his son's question, but also the trepidation in his voice. His eyes, which had been lost in a memory, focused on the present.

Jakob pointed toward the field. "'Bout a half mile out."

"I see it," Peter said. The one benefit of being surrounded by endless, tightly packed wheat was that anyone or anything moving through it was instantly revealed. Right now, there was a single line, pointed straight at the house.

Something was coming.

"I'll keep watch on it," Peter said. "You get some breakfast."

"But–"

"You know there's nothing out there that can get in here." Peter hoped he sounded more convincing than he felt.

"Fine," Jakob left the room, his bare feet slapping over the hardwood floor.

"Jake," Peter called. "Put your shoes on. Just in case."

Jakob stood silent for a moment before saying, "Yeah."

The sound of defeat in his son's voice filled Peter with anguish. This was not the kind of life he had wanted for his son, trapped in a farmhouse, motherless, and surrounded by death.

"Hey, Jake," Peter called again.

He heard his son stop without reply.

"We'll burn the field tonight."

"Thanks," Jakob said, and he continued down the stairs, where a breakfast of potatoes and green beans awaited. When he was sure the boy was gone, Peter headed for his bedroom, a place he rarely slept since Kristen... He stopped in front of the closet.

While he'd done what he could to make the bedroom emotionally bearable to him, hiding her trinkets and belongings, the inside of the closet was something different. He put his hand on the metal knob and turned it slowly, fueled by the knowledge that something was closing the distance to their refuge. With a deep breath, he yanked the door open, pulling the air inside the closet, out. It washed over him, still smelling faintly of orange, the oil she put on her skin, which, over time, had become infused in all her clothing.

The smell triggered a cascade of unbidden memories. He could hear her voice again. Feel her touch. Her closeness. Had she been alive now, he might have been content to stay in this farmhouse forever.

Why did you go outside?

Why did you do it?

His hands fumbled through the dark closet and found what he was looking for. He took the shotgun and a box of shells, flung himself back out of the closet, and slammed the door shut behind him, gasping for air. At some point, he'd held his breath without realizing it.

Perched on the side of the bed, Peter caught his breath. His hands shook. But with each breath of stale, filtered, farmhouse air, the memories of Kristen and her passing faded back into the recesses, replaced by the more pressing question. *What the hell is outside the house?*

He loaded the 12-gauge, pump-action shotgun with eight shells into the magazine tube, then gave the pump a quick pull, chambering a round into the breach. He loaded one more round into the tube. All that was left to do was aim and pull the trigger. If they ran into trouble, he'd be able to fire nine shots before needing to reload, and super predators or not, there wasn't anything short of a whale that could take nine shotgun shells and keep going.

Nothing he'd seen, at least.

Feeling a little more secure, he stood and walked to the bedroom window. He quickly found the line of approach through the wheat and noted the change. Whatever was out there had turned at a ninety-degree angle and was now walking perpendicular to the house. As long as it kept on going, he was happy to let it go. But if it breached the wheat field and stepped onto the fifty-foot concrete barrier he'd poured around the home and the biodome, he'd put a shell in it, no questions asked.

He watched the line moving to the side. "Just keep on going."

The line stretched another thirty feet and then made another ninety-degree turn, bringing it toward the front of the home.

Shit.

What's it doing?

He followed the line as it traced a path across the front of the house, a half mile out, never wavering in its route. He listened as Jakob went about his chores downstairs, seeing to the kitchen before heading into the dome, where he'd tend to the plants and animals.

When the line turned again, keeping its distance, and carving a path along the far side of the house from where it began, Peter understood. *It's scoping out the house. Looking for weaknesses.* It seemed the predators hadn't just gotten bigger and meaner, they'd also gotten smarter.

5

"Anything yet?" Jakob asked. They were in the biodome, the younger Crane feeding the three pigs scraps of vegetation inedible to the two men. The pigs themselves weren't for eating. Their manure, when added to the compost and allowed to rot and get hot enough to kill any E.coli, Salmonella, or parasites, kept the plants growing.

Peter stood atop a stepladder, peering through the large, domed greenhouse window with a pair of binoculars. The line of trampled wheat continued around the property, methodical and patient. "Nothing," he said, though he felt their visitor's behavior was foreboding, to say the least. "But let's keep a low profile. No candles tonight. If it looks like no one is home, I think it will move on."

He didn't really believe that. But he could hear the slowly rising fear in his son's voice, and he didn't want to concern him...until there was definitely a reason for it. The last time they'd faced the horrors wrought by the genetically modified predators patrolling the planet, their lives had been changed forever. Jakob was finally sleeping through the night again, though Peter still struggled. He told his son that their low profile had kept them from attracting attention, but he really thought they'd just been lucky. The world was big, and they were far from any of the former population centers. What reason would a predator have to wade through the miles of wheat that separated them from the nearest road or wooded area?

The pigs squealed with delight, devouring their secondhand meal.

"Are they being too loud?" Jakob asked.

Peter shook his head, losing sight of their visitor's path. "We're sealed up tight, and the glass is thick." The biodome wasn't designed to be soundproof; it just was, which turned out to be a benefit when the world started eating everything that made noise.

"Are you going to watch it all day?"

"Until it goes away," Peter replied. "Yeah."

"Might want to stop using the binoculars then."

Peter lowered the lens and turned to face his son, who now stood below him, arms crossed. "And why is that?"

Jakob pointed to the East, where the lurker was headed. "The sun will reflect off the lens. Give you away. Give *us* away."

Peter looked at the sun. It was still low enough in the sky to strike the binoculars. Would be until noon. *I'm getting rusty*, he thought, chiding himself for not noticing what his son had. He put the binocular strap over his head and let them hang. "Who taught you that?"

"Battlefield 3."

"The video game?"

"Turns out games were good training for the apocalypse." Jakob looked unsure for a moment, but then he took a breath and said, "I think I should have a gun, too."

"Video games didn't prepare you for that. The real thing is different. And you don't need one in here."

"Is that why you have the shotgun out?"

Peter stood statue-like for a moment. There was no way to win that argument. Jakob was right. Having the shotgun nearby made him feel a little safer. It took the edge off. "Noticed that, did you?"

"Not much changes in here," Jakob said. "Putting a shotgun behind a curtain that hasn't moved in a year is kind of easy to spot." When Peter said nothing, Jakob added, "So?"

"Jake... We don't..."

"You have a handgun," Jakob said. "Beretta M9, right?"

Peter was stunned. How could his son, who hadn't shown any real interest in weaponry, for hunting or target practice, identify the pistol hidden behind the bottom drawer of his dresser?

"Before you ask," Jakob said. "Battlefield 3. And it's the preferred weapon of the U.S. Marines, which you were, once upon a time, before you decided to become a farmer."

Peter didn't so much decide to become a farmer as retreat from the world, where loud noises—screeching tires, backfiring cars, screaming kids—triggered his mild PTSD. The farm had been a retreat, and a return to the skills taught to him by his own father, before Peter had joined the Marines and went on to become a CSO—Critical Skills Operator—the most elite special ops units in the Corps.

"Also, before you ask," Jakob continued, "I'm a teenage boy trapped in a house without a whole lot to do. It's safe to assume you don't have any secrets left aside from what's in your head."

Peter smiled. "Good to know. Found my leopard print thong, did you?"

Jakob laughed. "What!"

"Kidding," Peter said, though he wasn't. Kristen had bought him the leopard print garment as a joke. But he'd never dug it out of the underwear drawer and thrown it out. Jakob's reaction told him there might still be a few secrets left hidden. Or, at least, one. Perhaps the biggest of them all.

"So," Jakob said. "Can I?"

"A weapon is a big responsibility. Knowing how to shoot it, which you've only done in video games, is only half the equation. The other half is knowing *when* to shoot it." Peter turned back to the window, finding the line in the wheat, which was slowly wrapping around to the rear of the house. "Some would say that a gun gives man a god-like power to take life. But for those who have done it..." He looked his son in the eyes. "For those who have fired a gun and ended a life...there's nothing god-like about it. That kind of power, in the hands of men, is far darker."

"But what about self-defense? Or a justified war?"

"All life is precious, now more than ever."

"Except for what's out there," Jakob added.

Peter nodded. He'd feel no remorse for killing whatever predator lurked outside. But he hoped to never have to kill a human being again. That cup of remorse had been filled to overflowing long ago. Enemy combatants or not, humans weren't meant to take each other's lives. It left a stain on the soul. He hoped it was something his son would never have to experience.

But how many people were really left? Odds were, if Jakob needed a gun, it wouldn't be against anything human. Previously human, maybe, but a genuine human being? They were an endangered species put on the brink of extinction by their own hubris.

Peter watched the still-moving visitor, hidden in the tall wheat. Its presence filled him with dread. They were the prey now, but prey who could fight back. "Go ahead."

"For real?" Jakob sounded stunned. All this time, he hadn't expected his argument to work.

"The M9 isn't loaded, but there's—"

"Three magazines and a box of 9mm ammo." Jakob practically spat the words. "Not great stopping power, but it will do in a pinch."

Peter chuckled. His son's military education had come from a video game, and so far, it was spot on. Peter had gone through basic training, years of service and then seven months of the Individual Training Course program to become a CSO, and his son's knowledge of armaments matched his own.

But could he handle himself with a weapon?

There was no way to find out, and he wasn't about to turn the biodome into a gun range. The first time Jakob fired a gun, it would be in defense of his life.

"Go ahead. Bring it all to the kitchen table. I'll show you how to load the magazines, switch them out, and chamber a round. But there'll be no shooting, understood?"

"Yes, sir," Jakob said with a sarcastic salute that would have gotten him a tooth knocked out by a drill instructor. Then he was gone, back into the house.

Peter returned his gaze to the ominous line in the wheat.

What the hell are you?

He knew very little about the thing outside, only that it was there and was making a slow circle around the house. But why? What kind of predator behaved in this way? None that he could think of. But the world was full of predators beyond imagining. The truth was, they'd been squirreled away for so long that they didn't know *what* was out there.

The human race had changed. He knew that much. Longer canine teeth. Sharp, hooked claws. A penchant for scurrying on all fours. And a hunger for meat...and the hunt. But had they continued to change? Had everything else? He'd seen one of the first cows to change. It was on the news just a few months before the human race became affected. Despite the cow's size, the copious amount of food it ate triggered the change earlier. Its legs had thickened, its body slimming to a more agile shape, and its teeth...like daggers. The cow was found in a pig pen, having slaughtered and devoured three swine, chewing a cud of pig flesh, over and over, the way cows used to eat grass. It made headlines as a freak of nature. The whole herd had been slaughtered the next day as a precautionary measure, the CDC guessing it was some kind of new Mad Cow disease. If only they'd realized the true source... *No,* Peter thought, *it would have been too late.* The human race had already crossed the tipping point.

Show yourself, he thought at the Etch-a-Sketch line tracing its way through the field. *Let me put an end to your hunger.*

The line just kept on moving, pausing every now and again, but clearly headed all the way around the house. When the line reached the spot where it began, the predator outside would be able to move around the house without detection. And maybe that was the point? Once the circle was complete, and night fell, it could approach the house with less chance of being spotted. It was a full moon tonight, but Peter couldn't keep watch over every side of the large home and biodome.

And that's if there's only one of them.

For all he knew, there was a whole pride of things out there.

The thought made him even more sure that giving Jakob the gun was the right thing to do. Odds were, he'd have to use it sooner than later, with sooner being nightfall and later being morning. One way or the other, Peter or the thing outside was going to lose patience and take action before the sun had a chance to rise again.

The orange sphere of the sun hung on the horizon like some kind of ancient protector, illuminating the world for as long as possible. But even the mighty Sol couldn't stop the Earth from rotating. Night came like a shroud, plunging the world outside into a bleak darkness. Peter couldn't see his hand in front of his face, let alone the world outside.

Moving slowly, feeling his way through the home, he entered the biosphere. On his way toward the stepladder, which he would climb to look at more nothing, he glanced up. The view made him stop.

The Milky Way hung over his head like a soft, shearling blanket. The fog of lights, so densely packed with stars he could see and worlds he couldn't, transported him through time. He hadn't given the universe much thought in his life, as a kid preoccupied with sports or on the battlefield. But then, he'd never really seen the nighttime sky. Kristen had shown it to him one night, after a windstorm that had cut the power. He'd resisted, arguing he needed to set up the generator, but she had pulled him outside, taken his chin in her small hand and turned his head skyward. It was then that he'd realized he'd never seen the night sky without modern life getting in the way. He'd been in many locations around the world that didn't have electricity, but he'd never really looked up. He was always too busy looking out for an enemy.

Like I should be right now.

For all the good it's doing.

Peter found the short ladder, climbed to the top and looked out over the field. After a moment, he thought he detected motion. His heart beat hard, but then he realized it was just the wheat, undulating in the wind.

The moon was rising. The sun had been defeated but was redirecting its light to them via the moon. Twenty minutes passed, and the full moon had cleared the horizon, illuminating the field and the circular path that led all the way around it.

Hours later, he still moved around the moonlit greenhouse, taking the stepladder with him, peering out over the field, searching for signs of approach or egress. When the view from the biodome revealed nothing new, he headed back to the house, which, with its shades pulled, was still pitch black. He opened what once was the back door and now separated home from greenhouse, and stepped inside, colliding with something that should not have been there.

Peter sprawled back, lifting his shotgun, but holding his fire.

"Shit!" It was Jakob. "Dad?"

"The hell are you doing down here?"

"You told me to come get you if I saw anything."

Peter had the boy watching the fields from the home's second floor. 'Your callsign is: Overwatch,' he'd told the boy. 'Keep an eye out from above. Get me if you see anything.' But he could tell by the groggy sound of Jakob's voice that Overwatch had fallen asleep. He couldn't blame him. It had to be 1:00am, and they had to sleep eventually.

"What did you see?" Peter asked.

"Out front," Jakob said, and he led the way through the dark. They both knew the space as well as blind people might their own home. With nothing new coming into the home, and everything already there having a place, the pair moved through the kitchen and living room without a sound, reaching the shade-covered front windows in seconds.

Jakob poked a finger behind the shade and lifted it away slightly. "Right there." He stood aside and let Peter have a look.

The farmer's porch, unused for years and coated with dirt and peeling white paint, was empty. As was the fifty feet of concrete between the porch and the field. But the field... Where there had been a wall of wheat when the sun went down, there was now a wall of wheat divided by a two-foot-wide patch of flattened stalks. Their visitor had closed the distance to the house in the cover of darkness.

It hadn't breached the house. There was no way to do that without making a lot of noise, but it could be anywhere. Right outside the window for all they knew.

Jakob slipped his finger out from under the window shade, letting it slowly close.

"I'm afraid we won't be sleeping for the rest of the night," Peter said.

If Jakob nodded, Peter couldn't see it.

But he heard his son's whispered voice. "Where do you want me? Overwatch?"

"Stay with me," he said and sat in a living room chair. "We know it's coming now. We'll have a better chance of..." *Of what? Surviving?* Could he say that to his son? Could he imply they might die tonight? *He's not stupid,* Peter decided. *He knows we might die. No need to sugarcoat it.* "...surviving."

Jakob sat on the couch. Peter couldn't see him, but he heard the distinctive pop of the spring Jakob had broken years ago when jumping on the couch was still a fun thing to do. "And here I thought you were going to say, 'kicking ass.'"

Peter huffed out a laugh. "That probably would have been better, huh?"

"Hells to the yes."

"Is that a pop-culture version of 'hell yes?'"

"I'm one of few teenagers left alive, right? I think that makes everything I do and say the new pop-culture. Okay, Cream Cheese?"

"Cream-what?"

"Your callsign," he said. "You called me Overwatch. I'm calling you Cream Cheese."

"Like hell you are."

"Okay, then. You tell me what to call you. You had a callsign, right?"

"Yeah..."

"Annnd?"

"Ricochet."

"You named yourself Ricochet?"

"Callsigns are given, not chosen. I was Ricochet...because bullets bounced off me. Which wasn't true. The enemy just had really bad aim."

"Huh," Jakob said. "That's kind of awesome."

"You wouldn't think so if you were the one being shot at enough to get the name."

"I supp—"

Three loud knocks sounded from the front door.

Both men held their breath. Peter stood slowly and moved to the window, shotgun in hand. When he peeked out, the porch was empty.

What the hell?

"What is it?" Jakob asked.

"Nothing's there."

"Seriously? We're being ding-dong ditched?"

While the answer was technically 'yes,' Peter didn't like the implications. A predator...*an animal*...would never think to do this, formerly human or not. But a person...

Peter let the shade shut. "I'm going out."

"What? Why? That's obviously what they want, right?"

"But not what they'll expect." Peter realized that they were both now using the plural for whoever was outside. He had no idea what was waiting outside the door, but he'd rather face it head on, in the open, instead of waiting for it, or them, to barge their way in. Opening the door now wasn't that big a deal. The wheat outside was still flowering. Would be for a few more days until it hit the ripening stage, shed its seeds into the wind, and started all over again. It was a cycle the crop went through *monthly*. Like the post office, the world's crops weren't stopped by snow, nor rain, nor heat, nor gloom of night, nor pretty much anything. The roots were just too deep.

But if the outer shell of the house was compromised, and seeds made it inside, they'd pretty much be screwed without the power to run the fans in the decontamination room, at the biodome's entryway. The powerful turbines would be more than the solar-panel battery could handle.

"Come over here," Peter said, standing at the front door. When Jakob joined him, he continued, "The moment I say so, I want you to turn on the front floods. The light will stun and blind whatever's out there."

"Won't that drain the solar battery?"

"We have enough water stored for a week. We'll survive one day without running water, and there's more than enough air for us to breathe. We're only going to get a few minutes out of the halogens, so wait until I say so, and shut it off the second we're all clear."

"Okay," Jakob said, but there was a quiver in his voice.

Real life was nothing like video games. Jakob would learn that lesson tonight, but he needed the boy at ease, or at least not freaking out.

"You have my six, Overwatch?"

"Copy that, Ricochet."

Peter saw the hint of white from Jakob's smile.

"Let's do this," Peter said. "On the count of three. One."

The door rattled with three loud knocks. Both men held their breath while Jakob gripped his father's arm. He was no doubt terrified, but the fact that he hadn't screamed at the knock meant he had potential. There were three things every soldier needed. Brains, which could be taught. Physical ability, which could be honed. And nerves of steel, which you were either born with, or not.

"Two," Peter whispered.

Jakob pulled his hand away from his father's arm and stood to the side.

"Three."

7

The heavy front door swung inward, forcing Peter to take a step back before stepping out. Floodlights cut through the night. Peter lunged through the door, leading with the shotgun, finger on the trigger. The deep thud of his work boots striking the wooden porch felt foreign, like a nearly forgotten sound from the past. And the air... It was intoxicating. He hadn't realized just how bad the house smelled—of rot, dirt, and body odor—until that moment.

But none of these stimuli distracted him. He swept the shotgun from side to side, searching for a target, but finding nothing. Jakob's footfalls on the porch alerted Peter to his son's approach.

"Get back inside."

"But I don't see anything," the boy argued.

"That's the problem." Peter motioned to the left and right. "Could be just below our line of sight." He motioned his head up to the farmer's porch ceiling. "Or above us."

"Above us? Could people really—"

Peter held his open palm up to Jakob, silencing him. His son was right—people couldn't get on the roof that fast—but they might not be dealing with a person. Then again... *What kind of predator knocks on doors? The human kind.* Unaltered person or not, that didn't make them safe. He was about to send Jakob back in, but he realized that might start an argument, which would distract and endanger both of them. So, he just glanced back to make sure Jakob had his weapon at the ready and pointed in the right direction, which was anywhere but toward Peter. He was surprised and impressed to find his son wielding the weapon in a two-hand grip, finger on the trigger, but with the barrel pointed down and away. With nothing to aim at, the boy was keeping the weapon at the ready, but in a safe position.

"Take the right side," Peter said. "I'll clear the left."

When Jakob stepped next to him, they took the three stairs to the flat concrete barrier and swept their weapons in opposite directions.

With nothing ahead of him, Peter asked, "Anything?"

"Clear," Jakob said.

"Check the far end and then meet back—"

A dry rustle of wheat snapped Peter's attention back to the slit of an opening, fifty feet away. Whatever had knocked on the door had apparently retreated back to the field. Assuming it was alone. He took a step forward. "Watch our six. Anything moves, it's not friendly. Pull the trigger and talk when it's dead."

He hated talking to his son in such blunt terms, but this was life or death. They'd been sheltered for so long, any sugar coating could get them both killed. And while he had trained Jakob to fight, it was against another person, and didn't involve guns. It became clear to him, as he stepped further toward the darkness at the edge of the floodlight's reach, that he would have to step up his son's training, holding nothing back.

If they survived the night.

Peter stopped, looking down the barrel of his shotgun. "Show yourself."

Wheat stalks rustled as a wind carrying the scent of flowers wafted over the field. Peter couldn't help but breathe more deeply. The air invigorated him. And a week later, when the wheat released its seeds to the breeze, the air outside the house would seal their fate. Opening the front door as briefly as they... Did they close the door behind them? Was it locked? He couldn't stop himself from looking. The door was shut, which was good. But was it locked? If so, it wouldn't be the deadbolt. They could break back in without damaging the door.

Attention back on the field, Peter shouted, "I've got nine shots. If you're not out here in five seconds, I'm going to fire a spread into the field. At this range, some of the buckshot will find you. Five!"

"Don't shoot."

The voice was raw. Feminine. And weak. Hardly threatening, but it could be a ruse.

"Step out," Peter said. "Slowly."

A figure limped out of the field. If this was the woman who spoke, he couldn't tell. The figure was clad in a black cloak coated with vegetation, like a homemade ghillie suit, the preferred camouflage of snipers. The figure carried a large, black duffle bag, similarly camouflaged. Whatever was in there, it was heavy, weighing the figure down.

"Hands," Peter said.

"Too heavy," the newcomer said. It *was* the woman. Her face was hidden, partly by the hood, partly by the smear of dried mud caked over her skin. She was gripping the bag like it contained something precious.

Peter's gaze moved between the woman and the bag. He spotted blood stains. Some of it long since dried. Some of it fresh. Still tacky. The sight of it raised his guard.

"Who are you?" Peter asked.

"I think she's hurt," Jakob said.

"Why are you here? Why did you walk around the house?"

"I wanted to be sure it was you," she said.

Me?

"That it was you living here. The house was dark. I...didn't think..." The woman stumbled forward, her knees grinding against the concrete floor. She somehow kept the bag from striking the ground and placed it down beside her. Then she wept.

Jakob stepped toward the woman, but Peter held him back. "Unearned trust is a weakness. It can get you killed."

"She needs help," Jakob said. "I think she knows you."

Peter agreed on both counts, but he meant what he'd said about trust, and this woman, whoever she was, hadn't earned it yet.

"Who are you?" Peter asked. "It's the last time I'll ask."

The woman's head sagged. "You really don't recognize me, Peter?"

When his name, spoken by the woman, reached his ear, the familiarity of it unleashed a torrent of memories and emotions that had been locked away for more than a decade. "E-Ella?"

The shotgun lowered.

The figure nodded.

"Who's Ella?" Jakob asked.

Peter didn't hear him. Didn't hear anything. Didn't smell anything. The hunched-over figure concealed beneath a mass of cloth and old vegetation, remained his sole focus. He tried to see the woman he knew underneath it all but failed. Her voice, though, was undeniable.

This was Ella Masse, the woman who had destroyed the world, and nearly destroyed his marriage.

He almost rushed forward without thought but stopped. He hadn't survived this long by being stupid. "How did you get here?"

"Walked."

"From California?"

A nod.

The more important question came next. "What did you eat?"

"There are still things in this world that grow without RC-714, and creatures who specialize in eating only those plants. There is edible food in the world, if you know where to look...and have a mental list of the more than two hundred plant species you shouldn't eat."

That last bit of knowledge confirmed that this was Ella Masse. Few people knew the ID number of the gene that had transformed the world.

"If you're wondering how I got here alive... I'm not sure I did." She lifted her cloak, revealing a white shirt beneath. There were four long tears, claw marks, framed by bright red, still-fresh blood. With this final revelation, Ella fell forward and collapsed to the concrete.

"Take this," Peter said, handing the shotgun to Jakob. He hurried to Ella's side and rolled her over. He peeled the cloak apart, revealing the torn shirt. He then slipped his fingers between the shirt's buttons and yanked. The buttons popped, revealing her belly and four gouges. He probed the flesh with his fingers, looking for signs of exposed muscle or organs, but found none. Still, she'd been a half inch from being eviscerated.

"Will she die?" Jakob asked.

"She's lost a lot of blood." Peter got his hands under Ella's back and knees. He paused before lifting. The duffle bag would weigh them down. But he suspected, by the way she'd clutched the bundle, that it contained something important. "Take the bag."

Jakob worked the long strap over Ella's arm and head. He lifted it with obvious strain. When he hefted it over his back, the bag moaned. Or rather, what was inside the bag moaned. Startled, Jakob dropped the bag and jumped away. He started to raise his pistol, too, but then the bag started crying.

"What the hell?" Jakob said.

Peter was frozen in place. "Open it."

"But—"

"Now, damn it." Peter's patience was worn razor thin, not because of anything Jakob had done, but because Ella had been carrying a person around in a bag. A young person by the sound of it.

Peter stood, lifting the unconscious woman with a grunt. While Peter was strong and Ella small, the camouflage she wore...*the camouflage*. It was covered in vegetation. Covered in seeds. In pollen.

"Dad..." Jakob said, as he unzipped the bag, revealing an unconscious girl, no older than twelve. Her hair and face were matted with mud, like Ella's, and her clothing was covered in blood. These two had been through a torturous journey. "Should I take her inside?"

"Yeah," Peter said, looking at the door to the house. If any seeds got inside... Even if they stopped in the foyer, the RC-714 laden crops could take root in a rug. In a dusty corner. And once they took root, sending shoots down through the floor, through the basement, there would be no stopping them.

"Take off her clothes," Peter said, lowering Ella to the ground and following his own order.

Jakob's eyebrows rose as he locked in place. Peter met his eyes. "It's the seeds."

"But—"

"Take off everything."

"Aren't we contaminated now, too?" Jakob asked.

Peter looked down as his clothing covered in loose, dry bits of grass and dangles of nature. He quickly peeled off his flannel shirt and tossed it away. Then took off his T-shirt. "Let's do this quick, son. It will be a lot less awkward for everyone if we're all dressed when they wake up."

If they wake up.

The pair quickly removed their clothing and then the women's. Carrying their weapons and visitors, they hurried back to the house and out of the night, neither one of them aware that they were being watched...

That they were being hunted.

8

Ella Masse opened her eyes, and for a moment, she forgot she was responsible for the deaths of seven billion people, give or take a million. While she hadn't developed RC-714 personally, she'd overseen the man who had. She had taken it to her superiors, lauded it as the miracle gene they'd all been searching for, and pushed it through to mass production. While the blame technically fell on ExoGen, she didn't buy the whole 'corporations are people' scapegoat. Real people worked behind the corporate names, making decisions that affected the world, or in her case, killed it.

But for a moment, looking at the sun filtering through a shade, illuminating flecks of dust dancing on breezes too subtle to detect, she felt human again. Protected. Safe.

Pain pulled her from the daydream. Her gut was on fire. But pain meant she was alive. Meant her encounter the night before hadn't been a hallucination brought on by exhaustion.

We made it, she thought. *We found Peter.*

She looked around the bedroom but saw nothing familiar. She'd never been in this house. Her eyes settled on a photo on the bedside table. She recognized Peter right away, and the woman standing next to him—his wife, Kristen. A boy stood between them. His son. Jakob. The last time she'd seen him, he was just six. Her eyes lingered on Kristen. Coming here had been a gamble. She didn't know if Kristen would welcome her or put a bullet in her head. But it seemed the sins of old had been forgiven. Otherwise, she wouldn't be lying in the woman's bed—Ella lifted the comforter—or wearing the woman's clothes.

She'd been dressed in a matching set of white underwear and a white tank top. For a moment, she felt violated. Without granting permission, she'd been stripped naked by a man she hadn't seen in twelve years, and his son. She chastised herself a moment later. If Peter Crane was anything, it was honorable, and the only glaring flaw in his character had been her. Plus, she'd been covered in vegetation, both natural and the ExoGenetic variety. She wouldn't be surprised if the clothing had been incinerated. She tugged up her shirt to find her stomach wrapped in tight bandages. There wasn't a trace of blood showing through, which told her two things: the bleeding had stopped, but only because Peter had sewn her up, putting his old military field experience to good use.

Agony swept through her when she tried to sit up, her muscles pushing against the line holding her gut together. But she couldn't stay in bed. Couldn't stay stationary. There was too much to do. Too much at stake.

And she needed to check on her daughter.

Rolling slowly to her side, Ella grunted and pushed herself up, careful to have her right arm, which was toned, strong and uninjured, do all the work. Sitting up, she had a better view of the room around her. It looked almost unused.

She spotted a note on the dresser in front of her. She could read the text on the folded sheet of paper from a distance.

You should probably stay in bed,
but I know you better than that.
Help yourself to some clothing.
I think it will fit.

Standing wiped the slight grin from her face, her present pain replacing ancient memories. The movement shifted the air over her head and sent a shiver through her body. Why did her head feel cold? She put a hand up to her hair and felt the short, stubby scratch of a recent shave. *He shaved my head!* She nearly got angry, but quickly understood why. It was the same reason he'd gotten rid of the clothing. They had arrived at his doorstep contaminated.

She headed toward the dresser and opened the top drawer. Underwear and bras. She looked down at her chest. Peter hadn't dressed her with a bra, probably because she was two cup sizes smaller than his wife. But that didn't matter, she'd gone without one for so long, the underwire and foam cups would probably irk her.

She closed the drawer and opened the next.

She found a black t-shirt and exchanged it with the white one she'd been dressed in, not because she liked black or wanted to outwardly express the condition of her soul, but because it would help her blend in with the darkness. The third drawer down contained pants. Mostly sweats, but buried at the bottom was a pair of dark green cargo pants. The tags still on them. She imagined Peter buying them for Kristen, never to be worn. She was a far too fashionable woman. For a time, Ella was too, but function was far more important than fashion these days.

The pants fit, but she snugged them in place with a belt from the top drawer, careful not to squeeze her belly too tightly. For shoes, she went to the closet, pushing aside Peter's old suits, and dresses that hadn't been worn in years. She found a pair of hiking boots on the floor, but didn't put them on. Clothes were one thing, but she'd need to ask about the boots. Supporting her weight on the doorframe, she bent down, wincing in pain and plucked up the boots.

When she stood, waves of pain echoed through her core and out to her extremities. She steeled herself with a deep breath, and then headed for the bedroom door.

The wood floor in the hallway creaked underfoot. She froze, listening for hints of predators who might have been alerted to her presence. *Calm down,* she told herself. *You're in a house. With a locked door.*

It won't be enough.

Deal with that later.

The warring sides of her conscience were silenced by a high-pitched sound that was alarming and unfamiliar. She reached for her machete, but the weapon—along with the rest—was missing. But then the true nature of the sound was identified by her scientist's mind: laughter.

She took the stairs cautiously, untrusting of the world, unbelieving in the lighthearted atmosphere. But what would the point of that be? And the person laughing wasn't Peter or Jakob. She stepped out of the stairwell and looked into the dining room. It was her daughter, Anne.

Jakob sat beside her, still chuckling. His voice was silenced when he looked up and saw Ella. "Oh. Uh, hi."

Ella said nothing, but stepped further into the room, eyeing a piece of paper lying on the table. Colored pencils, some worn down to nubs, surrounded the page, which Anne was now leaning over, blocking from her mother's view. Feeling a surge of protectiveness, Ella craned her head around for a better look. When Anne hid the page, Ella's hand shot out like a striking snake, snatching the piece of paper from the table.

"Sorry, Dr. Masse," Jakob blurted out. "I—I didn't think it would—"

"What is this?" Ella asked, looking at the page. She couldn't really tell what she was looking at. A page of TCAG genetic code would make more sense than this.

"What am I looking at?"

"It's a drawing," Anne said.

Ella gave her daughter a once-over. The girl had a bandage around her now shaved head and a second on her right forearm. They looked as professional as the one around her own waist. Like Ella, Anne was dressed in new clothes, except they were too big, and masculine. She was wearing the boy's clothes, perhaps from two years ago, when everyone on Earth had stopped buying anything. She glanced back at Jakob and confirmed that his clothing was too tight on him. He'd be in his father's clothes before long.

"It's a Stalker," Anne said. "You're holding it upside down."

Ella cringed at the word, but turned the page around. Then she saw it. The human-like head, the slender body, powerful legs, and arms. The long tail ending in what looked like a stalk of wheat. It was a Stalker, all right, but something had been hastily added to the image. Two large lumps that looked like... She looked up, trying not to smile. "Is this a butt?" She turned to Jakob. "Did you add a butt?"

Jakob burst out laughing, and Anne joined in. The annoyance Ella felt about trivializing something like a Stalker quickly melted away as the pair of kids—who were just *being* kids—laughed harder.

"It's got a big booty," Anne said, the laughter pushing tears from her eyes.

"Shake, shake, shake," Jakob sang, and Anne joined in, "Shake, shake, shake. Shake your booty."

Ella shook her head at the uproarious laughter that followed. "You'll be lucky if one of these doesn't hear you two."

Anne's laughter cut short immediately.

Jakob's faded more gradually, but ended more glumly.

"Are you serious? I thought they were nocturnal?"

"Used to be," Ella said. "And even if they are hiding from the sun right now, it doesn't mean they can't hear you. There isn't much making noise out there these days, and the—"

"Walls are thick." It was Peter, standing in the second door to the dining room. He carried a basket of veggies, the likes of which Ella hadn't eaten in months. "We're locked up tight. Nothing outside can hear us in here."

Anne and Jakob looked instantly relieved.

Peter put the basket on the table. "You're just in time for breakfast."

Anne eyed the vegetables. "Are these ExoGenetic?"

Jakob huffed, plucked a carrot from the basket, and snapped off a bite. "Yeah, right."

Anne didn't wait for permission. She dove right in, grabbing handfuls of pea pods, carrots, and broccoli.

While the kids ate, Ella slowly rounded the table toward Peter, who stood waiting, a sheepish grin on his face. "You kept the seeds out."

"Until last night, it was pretty easy. Sorry about your clothes."

She shrugged, looking over his shoulder. "Where's—"

A sudden, hard glare in his eyes stopped the question from leaving her lips and simultaneously answered it for Ella.

Kristen wasn't here. She was dead.

Trying to ignore her rising emotions, Ella put on the boots, tying them tightly, while Peter watched in silence. When she finished, tears welled in her eyes. Peter took a step back, and then another, leading her out of the room. She followed, meeting him in the hall. For a moment, they just stood there, looking at each other. Then his arms moved. Just a slight gesture. An invitation, which she accepted, slowly stepping into his embrace. His touch was light at first, but then, as she squeezed her head into his chest, his arms wrapped around her, squeezing, shielding, and sparking ancient memories.

When he leaned down and kissed the top of her shaved head, all the walls she'd erected, to keep her sane and moving and motivated, came crashing down. He quickly closed the dining room door as she sobbed against him and collapsed into his arms.

"I'm sorry," she said.

"For what?"

"For coming here. For ruining what you have."

"Ella," he said. "There is no one else on the planet I'm more happy to—"

His body went rigid. He understood. They'd brought danger with them. She looked up into his light brown eyes, as sharp as ever, and said, "We can't stay here. They're following us."

The mix of emotions roiling through Peter was almost disorienting. His joy at seeing other living people dulled the knowledge that danger followed in their wake. That one of those people was Ella Masse had further muddled his thoughts. Her presence here was either a gift meant to ease his pain, or a cruel twist of fate, designed to open old wounds. Of course, either option meant that some higher power was guiding the events playing out on planet Earth, and he didn't buy into that. If there was a God, he was shaking his head at what Ella and ExoGen had done to his world. Maybe that's why she was alive still. Retribution.

We all have sins to pay for, Peter thought, squeezing the source of his biggest folly against him. His resurgence of feelings for Ella surprised him. It had been so long. But then, their relationship had a long list of starts and stops. He'd known her since fourth grade. Loved her since seventh. They had become high school sweethearts separated by college. The relationship rekindled briefly post-college, but was separated again by careers—his in the military, hers in the sciences. When they found themselves living in the same town, a fluke or by fate, the relationship had flared once more, but that time with consequences. Ella's work had suffered, and Peter's marriage had nearly broken apart. The light they had always brought each other had become a darkness. He hadn't seen her since.

Ella's voice, fresh in his ear again, was like hearing music for the first time. But then her words finally sank in. "Who is following you?"

Ella stepped back and wiped her tears away with the cuff of her sleeve wrapped around her knuckles. "Stalkers."

"The thing Anne drew?"

She nodded.

"How many?"

Ella leaned her head to the door. The kids could be heard, still talking and laughing. Not listening. "Too many to count."

"They're hunting in packs?" The last predators he'd seen were so vicious they would turn on each other.

"They're adapting," she said. "Quickly. Competition is fierce. But what's following us is less of a pack and more like a herd. Upwards of fifty."

Peter's confidence plummeted. He could manage a handful of most anything. But over fifty? He didn't have that many shotgun shells. He headed for the kitchen. Poured two glasses of water from a pitcher full of peppermint leaves. A sprinkle of sugar, which was nearly gone, went in each. He mixed them and pushed one glass across the island. Ella accepted the glass and sat down across from him.

She sipped the water and smiled. "Tastes like a candy cane."

"Only because you haven't had candy recently." He took a swig from his glass, the mint waking him up and making the water feel cooler than it was. "Tell me about them. The Stalkers."

Ella placed her glass on the island. "We should just leave now."

"I want to know what we're up against. I'll decide if we need to leave." Peter leaned on his elbows and raised his eyebrows. He wasn't going anywhere without answers. "Tell me about the Stalkers."

Ella sighed and rubbed her hand over her stubbly head.

"It's a good look on you," he said. "Like Sigourney Weaver in *Alien 3*."

"Never saw it."

He shrugged. "I'll wait until you're ready."

"Persistent as ever."

"I get what I want."

She looked him in the eyes. "Not always." They stared at each other for several seconds, neither wavering. Then Ella cleared her throat and leaned back. "They're hairless. Black eyes. No noses to speak of. Sharp teeth, of course. Skin covered in jagged plates that jut out from their spines, like oversized spinous processes. They might be defensive, or for attracting mates. I don't know. They're fast. And smart."

"How smart?"

"They strategize, like lions used to, using natural camouflage, and setting traps. They range in size from a hundred pounds to three hundred. Long arms. Strong legs. They run on all fours, twice as fast as you or I could manage, but they can also stand upright."

Something about Ella's description unnerved him, but he couldn't quite peg what it was. The creatures she was describing sounded horrible, but it was something else about them. Something inferred, but not yet said.

"Corn and wheat crops are their preferred hunting grounds. They have long, thin tails—not prehensile, thank God—that look like stalks gone to seed. You could look at a field of wheat, like yours, and see a hundred of them, tails raised in the air, and not know it. Not until they rattled."

"Rattled?"

"They shake their tails before attacking. What look like seeds are actually hollow, hard nubs of skin that make a racket when shaken."

"But why warn prey of an attack?"

"It's not a warning. It's a strategy."

"Ahh." Peter understood. The sound was meant to flush the prey into a trap. Again, horrible, but she hadn't touched on what was bothering him. "What were they? Before?"

The way Ella paused before answering told him what he feared, even before she spoke the words.

"Human," she said. "And you can see it in their faces. But they're mostly monsters now."

"How is that possible?"

"RC-714," she said.

"How could a single gene make all those changes in the human body?" He'd seen people go savage, with longer teeth and claws. It was horrifying to witness. Even worse to be on the receiving end of an attack, and mind-numbingly painful to watch it happen to someone you loved. But those changes were minimal and mostly in the mind. What she was describing now was something different. A species transformation.

"The gene doesn't carry any information regarding specific traits," she said.

When she paused, he thought for sure she was going to say he wouldn't understand. But she knew him better than that. CSOs weren't just the most physically fit or deadly soldiers the Marines had to offer, they were also the smartest. And he'd spent enough time with her in the past to understand genetics better than the average layman.

She sipped her water. "It's more like a key."

"A key to what?" he asked.

"The human race evolved over millions of years."

"Which is why the rapid evolution you're talking about doesn't seem possible."

She held up her hands, beseeching patience. "We'll get to that. Most would say that it took the human race 160 million years to evolve into what we are today, starting with small squirrel-like insectivores like haramiyids. While creatures like the haramiyids might be distant ancestors of the human race, they didn't emerge from the primordial soup, or even from the oceans for that matter. They evolved from therapsids, which were mammal-like reptiles living at the end of the Triassic Period, 210 million years ago. And the therapsids..."

"Evolved from reptiles. From Triassic dinosaurs. That's what you're saying?"

She nodded. "As species evolve, adapt, and diversify, new genetic code is written, while the no longer useful code becomes pseudogenes. They're like backup copies of old genes that have lost their protein-coding ability and biological function. Ninety-eight point five percent of all genes in people, and animals, have been deemed 'junk' DNA. While it's likely that some of them serve some function we don't understand, most of them are pseudogenes, going back to the beginning of genes, containing all the adaptations, abilities, and mutations of millions of individual species that resulted in the human race." She paused to look Peter in the eyes. "RC-714 unlocked those genes, making them available."

"Fuck."

"Exactly."

"But why did everyone and everything become predatory?"

"Not everything did. There are a few species that remain docile, but are certainly more capable of defending themselves. Others haven't changed at all, like bees, still feeding on flowers unaltered by RC-714. But the main reason for the change was hunger. The release of all those genes created an insatiable hunger—for protein. That was the instigating external force that pushed those species to adapt, first into predators, and then into specialized predators dealing with competition. Over the past two years, new species have evolved without reproducing at all. What used to take millions of years can now happen in weeks."

"Leaving us with Stalkers."

"Tip of the iceberg, I'm afraid."

Peter's body had gone rigid with tension, but Ella's iceberg comment twisted the muscles in his back into tight balls. "What do you mean?"

"Apply the same junk DNA scenario to other species. Not just mankind. Not just predators. And not just mammals."

"What, like fish?" There were already giant killers in the ocean, and the Blue Whale was the largest animal to ever exist on the planet. While an ocean full of predators wasn't a pleasant thought, they were smack dab in the middle of the country, thousands of miles from the nearest shore.

Ella shook her head. "Birds."

"Birds?" The first thing he realized upon speaking the word, was that he hadn't actually seen a bird in a long time. That realization sparked his imagination. The first bird that came to mind was the extinct, South American Phorusrhacos. He'd seen a documentary about the giant, flightless bird. Eight feet tall, three hundred pounds and predatory. But it didn't sound much worse than the Stalkers she had described. He pictured the large bird and thought it looked a lot like a... "Dinosaur."

Ella gave him a sheepish grin, confirming the hypothesis.

He felt incredulous. "There are *dinosaurs* out there?"

Thankfully, she shook her head. "But there are animals with dinosaur traits. Remember, all genes going back to the beginning of life on Earth have been unlocked. The genetic Pandora's Box has been opened. If a dinosaur trait is advantageous, a species—or even an individual—will quickly adopt it. Rapid evolution. And that's what really makes them so dangerous. Once you find a way to beat them, they'll change. That's why we need to leave before they get here."

"Because you've been in this situation before?"

"Twice."

"Other biodomes?" When Ella had contacted him all those years ago, telling him to not eat the food, to build a biodome, he heeded her warning and allowed a crew, hired by her, to build the structure. Kristen had hated the idea, mostly because it had come from Ella, but he knew Ella wouldn't lie. Even if he had become untrustworthy because of Ella, his trust *in* her was implicit. Part of him wanted to believe she was merely looking out for him, because of what they'd had. But now it seemed there had been an alternate reason. "You're moving from one dome to the next, aren't you?"

She didn't even try to deny it. "There's a network of domes around the country, most built using funds I made from ExoGen. I am stopping at some I come across on the way, but I didn't build them for that purpose. Especially yours. If it weren't for Anne, I wouldn't have come here. But..."

"But what?"

"I knew you would protect her. It's selfish, I know. But I can't do this without you."

"Do what?"

"Turn the key the other way."

"How? Where?"

"There's a lab, off the coast of Boston. I had it built, but the world fell apart before I could get there."

"And you want me, and *my son*, to escort you there?" His words were nearly a growl "You want us to risk my family's life? I already lost Kristen, and now you–"

"Your family is already at risk," Ella said.

"We are *now*," he said.

Ella shook her head. "I wasn't talking about you. Or Jakob."

Peter's heart skipped a beat. Were Ella's feelings for him still so fresh that she was talking about herself? He considered it and realized it might be possible. His own feelings for her, forged over a lifetime, hadn't changed much. But then she simultaneously revealed the truth and secured his aid.

"It's Anne. She's your daughter."

10

If there was one thing Peter Crane was good at, it was preparing for the unknown, whether that be a bad crop year, an enemy ambush or even Ella's Stalkers. But the bombshell she just dropped hit him with the shock and awe of Hiroshima's atomic blast. He stood up straight, as though electrified, stumbled back, and caught himself on the kitchen counter. Ella's reappearance into his life was always tumultuous, but this...

Attempting to concisely express his mixed feelings about the revelation, he condensed it all into a single word. "Bullshit."

Ella looked aghast. Then angry. "Bullshit? *Bullshit?* I tell you that we, that *you* and *I*, have a daughter and that's your response? Bullshit?"

"Yes," he said. "I don't buy it."

"You think I'm just telling you that to...what? To guilt you into helping us?"

"It would work," he said. "And you know that."

"Whether or not the knowledge forces you to help us, doesn't make it a lie."

"How did you raise her?" he asked, knowing she'd understand the context. She was a busy woman in a powerful position at a growing company. She worked late. Sometimes she didn't go home. She lived her work. How could she have a baby, let alone raise a daughter?

"I was in the office when I went into labor," she said. "Took a week off to recover. Worked remotely for another week. And then I went back. I wasn't a good mother. Anne was raised by daycare, school, and nannies. I've only really gotten to know her in the past two years. Is that what you wanted to hear? Does it ease your guilt, knowing that I was a shitty parent?"

"Guilt?" he said. "I didn't even know she existed. Had you told me, I would have—"

"Taken her," Ella said. "You would have come back to New Mexico and taken her. You would have done right by her. You'd have raised her, with Kristen. And I...I would have let you. I'd have lost her to Kristen, just like I lost you."

That took the wind out of his sails. But it didn't prove his stance wrong.

"I still don't believe you."

Ella closed her eyes. Rubbed circles into her temples with her fingers. "Telling you about her was not meant to coax you into helping me."

"Prove it."

She stood up, rounded the island, and stabbed a finger at his face. "You already know I'm telling the truth, because both you and I know that you would have helped me regardless. Because that's who you are to me and who I am to you. It's who we've always been. Other relationships didn't change that. Distance never changed that. Time never changed that. I could have come here by myself, and you would have come with me. I'm telling you about her because I want you to protect her first. Before me. The only way to get you to do that was to tell you the truth about her."

Peter could feel his blood pressure dropping. She was right about him. About them. But did that mean she was telling the truth about Anne? The girl was the right age, but the verdict was still out. He'd try to see it in the girl's face. In her eyes. Believing he had a daughter, and adjusting to that idea, would take time. Time they didn't have. If they made it to Boston and the lab waiting for Ella, maybe he'd request a paternity test. It'd be a dick move, but Maury Povich made a living from such revelations, not just because men are dogs, but because the connection between a father and his bloodline was a powerful thing.

"How much time do we have?" he asked. "Do they hunt in the day?"

"They do," she said. "But only when agitated or ravenous. Most of the species I've seen still operate this way, so moving during the day is still the safest course..."

"I'm sensing a 'but' coming."

"But...these Stalkers. They hold a grudge. They've been following us for two weeks. We managed to avoid them by crossing rivers—they don't like water, but eventually they find their way across—and by hiding in trees. They're horrible climbers. They nearly had us two days ago, but I used the last of my C4 to bring down a train tunnel."

"Is that when this happened?" he asked, pointing at the bandaged claw marks.

She nodded. "One of them made it through before I detonated the explosive. I killed it with the machete."

"You've changed." He looked her up and down.

She was certainly more solidly built than she had been twelve years previous. Harder.

But he still had trouble picturing her blowing up train tunnels with C4 and fighting monsters with a machete.

"Yeah, well, I hope you haven't. Look, best guess, the ones that survived, made their way back out and around, are a day behind us."

"You've already been here fourteen hours," he pointed out.

"And that's a guess. They could be closer, especially if they're moving through the daylight."

This was all happening too fast. To make the kind of decision she was asking him to make, to uproot and endanger his son, he couldn't be rushed. Not without good cause. "So, what's the plan, then? Continue across the country, holing up in biodomes you had built, until you reach Boston? Find this lab and 'turn the key' back?"

"Essentially, yes."

"Without a map?"

"You know I don't need one."

Ella had an uncanny memory. If she set herself to the task of memorizing something, like a map of the United States and the locations of biodomes—locations that she had chosen—he believed she was capable. "What about the science? Is it possible to turn the key? And before you answer, you should know that you're standing above a bunker that has nothing to do with the biodome you had built, which is strong enough to withstand a nuclear blast, not to mention a hundred of your Stalkers—"

"They're not *my* Stalkers."

"—and that's if they could even find the entrance. So, for me to seriously consider what you're saying, it better be damn convincing. Now... is it possible to reverse this? To put things back the way they were?"

"Anything is possible," she said. "I think we've proven that. But if you're asking if this is something I've already made progress on, then no. Is there anyone else left alive that has any chance of undoing this hell? The answer to that question is an absolute 'no.' This is a Hail Mary play. I get it. But it's either that, or wait for the seeds to get inside, or for something hungry to come knocking. I wouldn't be doing this...wouldn't be putting Anne at risk, if I didn't think it was possible. You understand risk assessment. Is a world full of edible food and free of ExoGenetic predators worth the risk of dying a little sooner than fate has already scheduled? You tell me."

The best answer he could come up with was silence. But someone else gave an answer for him. "I think it is."

Peter turned to find Jakob and Anne standing in the dining room doorway. Seeing them standing together, Jakob was a foot and a half taller than the girl. Peter looked from one face to the other. Their eyes, dark brown, matched each other's. Matched his.

Two kids...

Under other circumstances he'd have been thrilled. Even if Kristen had still been alive. *A daughter? Holy shit.* But it also meant he had even more to risk. Also more to gain. If they could undo the genetic modifications unleashed on the world, then their children might not just have their lives, they might have futures.

"Did you hear me?" Jakob asked. "I'm tired of sitting here and doing nothing. If we can do something about it, we have to."

"It's not that easy," Peter said.

Jakob crossed his arms. "Why not? Because it's dangerous? Believing we're safe here means pretending that Mom didn't—"

"Enough," Peter said, his voice stern, not because he was angry at the boy, but because he didn't want to open that can of worms. Not with Ella, and not right now. He took a moment to collect himself, and then said, "If we do this, every single one of you does exactly what I say, at all times, without questioning and without hesitation." He looked at Ella.

"I don't care if you've survived out there for months, or a year, or however long you've been traveling; you can't do what I can do."

"But—" Anne said, before Ella silenced her with a raised hand.

Ella turned to Peter.

"Fine. We'll do things your way."

"For as long as it works," Anne said, eyebrows raised in challenge.

Peter had to fight his smile. He saw himself in her with every passing second. "Okay, then. Now let's—"

"The wheat is moving." It was Anne again, but all the toughness had left her voice. She sounded like a little girl again. Her eyes were fixated on the field outside the kitchen window above the sink.

Peter kept everyone else from moving by holding out his hand, and tip-toeing to the window. He leaned out slowly, looking through the window, which was covered by a sheer shade. He could see the wheat fifty feet away, but the fabric reduced the detail, making it a silhouette. The wheat was indeed moving, bending with the wind. He was about to say so when he noticed a subtle aberration. While most of the wheat stalks gave way to the breeze, some of them remained rigid and upright.

Not as smart as they think.

He stepped back from the window. "How long do we have?"

"They're here already?"

"What's here?" Jakob asked.

"Big booties," Anne whispered.

Jakob's eyes widened. "Stalkers? You mean, they're real?"

Peter put his hands on Ella's arms. "Ell, how long?"

The answer to his question didn't come from Ella, it came from the front door, as something large and heavy threw itself against the wood.

11

"Take them to the basement," Peter said to Jakob.

"Huddle?" Jakob asked, and Ella realized he was speaking in code.

Peter shook his head. "Extra points."

Code based on football.

Great.

Plan or not, retreating to a basement, fortified or not, sounded like a horrible idea to Ella. As strategically smart as Peter was, locking themselves below ground would only prolong their demise. The Stalkers were persistent, and patient. She opened her mouth to say as much, but he cut her short.

"Not a word," he said, pushing her toward Jakob, who was leading Anne to the back of the house.

"But—" was all Ella managed to say.

"I might not know very much about them." He motioned to the door, which received and withstood another impact. "But they know *nothing* about me. And if we're being honest, your knowledge in that regard is also fairly outdated."

"That works both ways," she argued.

"Agreed," he said. "But this is my house. You're just going to get in the way."

Jakob opened the basement door, stepped inside and motioned Anne to follow. The girl looked to her mother for the go ahead, but when the door shuddered once more, she made up her own mind, following Jakob down the stairs.

"We don't have much time," Peter said.

The door was hit again. This time, the distinct sound of cracking wood merged with the wall shaking like a rattle. Peter and Ella leaned into the hall. There was a hairline crack at the center of the door, but it was still in one piece, still dead-bolted and barricaded with a thick hardwood plank. But it wouldn't last. She'd seen stronger blockades fall to a continued barrage. The Stalker leading the attack was always the largest male, but when he didn't have any luck, he'd call in help from the real hunters—the females. Working together, the female Stalkers would make short work of the door. She was almost out of time.

Ella took Peter's arm in her hand. "You'll protect your daughter?"

Peter looked her in the eyes, and she saw that same, deep earnest gaze she'd fallen in and out of love with for decades.

"No one is going to die here today," he said. "But you have to listen to me. Go. *Now*."

She kissed his cheek and ran for the basement door. To her surprise, he ran in the opposite direction, heading upstairs. She felt herself pulled back, wanting to help. To fight. She'd stood her ground so often and fought her way across the country... She was unaccustomed to letting someone else fight her battles. But she knew this was a losing fight. If Peter had an ace up his sleeve, she had to let him play it.

The front door shook again, the sound of it chasing her around the basement door. She nearly shouted in surprise as Jakob's face emerged from the dark stairwell below her. Anne was behind him, lower on the stairs. Behind her was a metal door with a metal wheel, like something from a submarine.

"Dad's upstairs?" Jakob asked. When Ella nodded, he lifted his wrist and started a countdown. "He'll be down in forty-five seconds."

The boy moved past Anne, spun the wheel, and opened the metal door to absolute darkness. To Ella's surprise and relief, he flipped the light switch, illuminating the space beyond. "Let's go," he said, waving them on.

"Won't that exhaust the battery?" Ella asked, pointing at the light.

"Doesn't matter," he said and stepped onto the basement's concrete floor.

She followed Jakob into the basement. Her eyes went wide. The space was massive, at least twice the footprint of the house above, constructed beneath the concrete barricade outside. The walls were lined with shelves covered in canned goods, dehydrated food, and various supplies. Enough for two people to live for years. And it all looked untouched. In the past two years, neither father nor son had eaten anything but what the biodome had provided. The more she observed Jakob, the more she saw his father in him. Confident. Disciplined. Compassionate.

Jakob hurried across the broad open space, moving past cots and crates, heading for the back of the room. He held Anne's hand, whispering to her. Ella couldn't make out the words, but the tone was calm and consoling.

Just like his father.

From upstairs, she heard the front door crack again.

"Should I close this?"

"Leave it open," Jakob said. "Dad will be here in twenty seconds. And hurry up."

Another impact set her in motion. The frequency of attacks on the front door was increasing, and the hits were harder. The females had joined the assault. Twenty seconds might be too long. *C'mon Pete, hurry up.*

Ella rushed across the room, running past shelves intercut by large barrels. She passed the first few without a second glance. Then she noticed the label: *ammonium nitrate.* Then she noticed the wires connecting all the barrels. Her run slowed to a jog, and then to a stop. "Holy shit, is this...?"

A shotgun blast made her jump.

A second blast, along with Jakob's shouted, "C'mon!" spurred her onward.

When she reached the far end of the room, she found Jakob lifting a garage door. *A garage door in a basement?* But this wasn't just any garage door. It was thick and solid, windowless steel. Like the basement door. Jakob was pushing it up, but only with the help of grinding gears. As the door rose higher, the lights began to fade, sucking the remaining battery life to raise the heavy slab of metal.

Footsteps spun her around. It was Peter—she hoped—coming down the stairs. The booming footfalls were chased by a warbling shriek she recognized, and it made the tiny spires of hair atop her head prickle. Anne took hold of her hand and squeezed. Ella reached her free hand down for her machete, but it wasn't there. The weapon was still outside, laying in a heap with all the clothing and supplies that had taken her this far.

Peter, wearing a single backpack, leapt into the basement, spinning around, and slammed the metal door shut, but not before three long, brown, talon-tipped fingers reached through and pushed. Peter started sliding back, but before the Stalker could open the door wide enough to enter, Peter shoved his shotgun into the stairwell and pulled the trigger. The cacophonous boom was followed by a wailing shriek. The brown fingers snapped back as the force of the shot shoved the creature back into the stairwell.

Peter moved to shut the metal door again, but his eyes went wide, and he dove to the side instead. The metal door smashed open, clanging against the stairwell wall. A female Stalker hit the floor awkwardly, falling sideways and slamming into the wall. The stunned creature looked like all the others Ella had seen, its once human face lacking a nose. Black eyes blinked. Its long tail thrashed back and forth, rattling, guiding the others no doubt already flooding into the house. Its long arms and legs scrabbled at the smooth floor, claws digging gouges.

Before the monster could right itself, Peter, who had turned his dive into a roll, came up, spun around, and pulled the shotgun trigger again. The Stalker's head was turned inside out and splattered against the wall. Peter turned and ran as the lights dimmed to almost nothing. Screeching and thundering footsteps chased him from the stairwell. Ella saw them emerge a moment before the lights went out. The grinding gears stopped.

For a moment, the world was just sound. Jakob moving behind her, breathing hard. Peter feeling his way through the wide-open space. The Stalkers, smashing everything around them. Screaming for their prey. Giving chase. While Peter couldn't see, the Stalkers had excellent night vision. When the lights went out, the basement became the perfect hunting ground for the nocturnal predators.

A flashlight came on with a click. The light cut through the darkness from Peter's position.

"How much time?" Peter shouted.

"Ten seconds behind," Jakob replied. Ella glanced back. On the other side of the mostly open garage door was a large Dodge Ram, reinforced with plates of metal, and covered in spikes and barb wire. It looked like something from a Mad Max movie. Jakob had the door open and was helping Anne climb into the back seat.

When Jakob leaned over the front seat and turned the key, the truck roared to life, its rear lights casting beams of red. Ella looked back to Peter. He was just thirty feet away, waving her on. But he wasn't alone. A single Stalker had closed the distance, nearly within striking range. The rest were still fifty feet back, clumsily careening through the maze of contents in the room.

"Look out!" Ella shouted, as the nearest Stalker leaped forward, its long legs extended, claws open wide.

Peter dove forward, flipping over to land and slide on his back. He brought the shotgun up, fired—and missed. Instead of putting a hole in the Stalker, he simply took a chunk out of the ceiling. The Stalker landed on Peter's arms, pinning them to his sides. With a snarl that revealed its gleaming white teeth—now pink in the truck's light—the Stalker lunged for Peter's neck.

With a war cry, Ella stepped forward and drove a kick into the side of the Stalker's head. "Weapon!" Ella shouted back to Jakob. He leaned out of the truck, eyes going wide at the sight of his pinned father. While the Stalker hissed at Ella, Jakob drew his pistol and flung it to Ella. She caught the weapon and with surprising swiftness, spun around, and pulled the trigger, putting a single round in the Stalker's head.

The monster fell limp atop Peter.

The mob closed in.

Ella bent down and took Peter's arm with one hand, helping him to escape the Stalker's girth. With the other hand, she calmly raised the pistol, found her targets, and pulled the trigger. The rhythmic pop...pop... pop of the handgun was followed by pain-filled shrieks and toppling supplies, as the struck creatures thrashed and flailed on the floor.

Peter didn't offer any thanks when he got back to his feet. He simply shouted. "Time!"

"Thirty seconds back!" Jakob yelled.

Ella let out a shout of surprise when Peter's arm wrapped around her waist, lifted her off the ground and carried her into the garage. She was hefted up and flung over the flatbed hatch, landing hard on the metal floor. She was about to complain when Peter dove over after her. He slapped his palm on the metal floor twice and shouted, "Go, go, go!"

Tires screeched.

Peter sat up with the shotgun, but he didn't aim at the horde of Stalkers nearly at the door. Instead, he turned the weapon to the side and pulled the trigger. Sparks flew as the buckshot struck metal, destroying whatever support had held the large door in place. The door, a large sheet of metal, dropped. The fastest of the Stalkers dove forward and slid through, losing its tail to the door. The second in line had its head crushed. The rest slammed against the other side of the metal wall, attacking it with audible savagery.

As the truck raced away through the darkness, Ella sighted the tailless Stalker, which had gotten back to its feet, and she pulled the trigger. The monster twitched and fell, just as darkness claimed it again. The truck shifted gears and accelerated to what seemed like a dangerous speed.

He needs to slow down, Ella thought. *We're safe. We're...*

Peter and Jakob's shouted numbers mixed with her vision of the barrels of ammonium nitrate, and then clicked. It was a countdown. Audible. They'd rigged the whole place to explode.

She looked Peter in the eyes, his face lit by the flashlight he held. Shouting over the roar of the engine, which was amplified by the tunnel's confines, she asked, "Are we going to make it?"

When he replied, she was surprised to find he'd learned how to sugarcoat bad news. "It will be close."

The sudden, blinding light pursuing them through the tunnel, racing faster than the sound of the explosion that generated it, answered her more honestly, with a resolute and resounding, 'No.'

12

Ella felt heat on her back, but it was quickly smothered by Peter, who threw himself atop her and shouted, "Hold on!"

I can't even move, she thought at him, but said nothing. She felt the truck jolt and pitch upwards. At first, she thought they'd struck something and gone airborne, but the angle never changed.

We're heading up a ramp. Back to the surface.

And then she learned that Peter's shouted warning and his body pinning her down had nothing to do with the heat, sound, and pressure wave pursuing them. It had everything to do with their exit from the tunnel. Wood shattered with the crack of an explosion. The armored truck slammed through a floor, bursting out of the tunnel, this time actually catching air. As the vehicle bounced back to its wheels, she got a view past Peter's shoulder.

It was a glimpse of a barn interior. Old beams. A hay loft. The tang of animals long since deceased reached her nose, complementing the image and triggering memories of an easier time, when human beings were at the top of the food chain, rather than somewhere closer to the bottom.

Her father had been a lot like Peter, a Vietnam Vet turned farmer. She often wondered if Peter's entry into the military hadn't been to impress him. She hoped not, especially when circumstances had pulled them apart. But he'd taken to the life well enough. It had suited him. And her father had approved of Peter. Only Peter. When she had told him about Peter's marriage to Kristen, she could have sworn there were tears in the man's eyes. But by then she was more interested in genetics than in men. That's what she had told herself...until fate had brought them back into geographic proximity.

Who was it that said women fall for men like their fathers? Probably Freud. Whoever it was, he was right. At least about Peter.

The truck shattered a second wooden barrier, casting aside large, faded red planks like a rhino charging through balsa wood. A shower of large red paint flecks fluttered around them for a moment, butterflies in flight, and then they were left behind.

The engine roared louder. The wheels buzzed over the clear concrete keeping the ExoGenetic fields at bay. Peter rolled away, sitting up and looking back, his eyes squinting. Expectant.

She sat up to join him, shrugging away when he put a hand on her shoulder to keep her down. Her protest was cut short by the reason for their pell-mell drive through the tunnel and out the barn. She saw it in the distance first. An orange ball, framed by fluttering debris that used to be a house.

Peter's house. He destroyed it because of me. All those memories...

As the fiery tumult rose higher, three hundred yards behind the barn, the explosion, which had chased them down the tunnel, compressed and accelerated, reaching the barn. A roaring cough of fire burst from the tunnel's throat like some ancient, buried dragon, and the flames rose up into the barn. The old walls gave way and lifted skyward, propelled by the explosion. The pressure wave hit the truck, knocking them at an angle, just as they hit the wheat field.

Jakob righted the truck's course, but they were still in the field, surrounded by the hiss of wheat being shredded, leaving clouds of dust and young seeds in their wake.

"Shit," Peter said. His voice was impossibly calm, but his eyebrows were twisted up, following the course of his eyes, as debris was launched up and over them. He shuffled to the front of the truck bed, leaning on a long box covered by a tarp. He tapped on the window twice.

Anne flinched at the sound, but when she saw Peter, she opened the small sliding window. "Debris is falling from above. Floor it, but keep us straight unless something falls in your path."

"I'm already flooring it!" Jakob shouted back.

Peter turned back and up, eyes widening. He crouched down low, clinging to the side of the truck. Ella followed his eyes and saw a hay bale, trailing bits of loose hay like a comet's tail, descending toward them.

The hay landed just feet behind the truck, where they had been a fraction of a second before. It exploded with a cloud of old, rotted grass that no modern, man-eating cow could find remotely interesting.

Wood came next. While some of the stuff fluttered in the air, carried by the heat rising from the explosion, thicker support beams were thrown free like colossal javelins. Ella nearly fell from the truck bed as Jakob jerked the wheel. Peter caught her, reeling her back in just as they passed the long wooden beam now jutting out of the earth. Had Jakob not turned, they would have crashed. Had Peter not pulled her back in, she would have been decapitated. Despite having survived in the wilds on her own, she was quickly seeing how these two men would help keep her and Anne alive.

She just hoped it was worth it, and that everything she'd told Peter wasn't a lie. The lab was real, but she hadn't heard from the people there in a year. The place could be overrun by now. Maybe the people had changed. Maybe predators had made the swim from the mainland. Or maybe something from the water had adapted to live on land. The possibilities were as endless as they were horrible.

The truck carved a zig-zag path through the field as debris fell all around. Ella and Peter flattened themselves to the truck bed floor, watching the cloud of debris fly past overhead and falling around them, and in the case of a pair of shears, puncture the tarp-covered case above their heads.

But then they were clear, and all the debris was falling behind them. The truck bounced. Tires squealed. They had reached the road. Jakob cranked the steering wheel hard to the left, but they still overshot the road, plowing back into the field on the other side. Spewing gouts of dirt, the truck nearly completed a fishtailing circle, but then they found the road again. Slowing, Jakob pulled onto the pavement and continued forward at a manageable pace.

"Keep it straight and steady," Peter said. "If you have to turn, honk first."

The boy looked back and nodded, his eyes wide, but still in control.

Like father, like son.

Peter stood, one foot on the truck bed, the other on the tarp-covered container. He gripped the fog lights atop the truck's roof for balance and looked back. The way the sun caught his rugged features and the wind caught his flannel shirt, he looked like a model in an L. L. Bean catalog, but his face was all wrong. Instead of eye-squinching confidence, she saw regret.

She followed his eyes to the rising column of smoke. The home where his son had been born, and if she was right, where he had buried his wife.

"I'm sorry," she said, but her voice was carried away by the breeze, and she didn't bother repeating it. Because while she felt bad, she wasn't sorry. Not really. True, within fourteen hours of taking her and Anne in, he'd lost everything of the life he had known before, but most people on Earth had lost that years ago. It was only because of her warning, and wealth, that his family had managed to survive. That didn't change the fact that her work had caused all this, and for that she was sorry. But she needed his help. And if this was what it took to get it, so be it. He might have helped her anyway, especially after she told him about Anne, but now there would be no looking back. No doubt that anywhere but forward was the right direction. She needed that from him, because looking forward was hard to do when constantly looking over your shoulder.

She stood next to him, looking ahead. The road was crumbling on the side, giving way to the long roots of the aggressive wheat. In a few more years, the road would be overgrown. A few errant stalks of wheat were already rising from the cracks.

Her eyes turned skyward. They were headed east, covering more ground every minute than she had been covering in an hour. Traveling on foot meant leaving false trails, walking silently, and resting frequently, especially with a twelve-year-old girl. Anne was a good traveler. Had learned how to survive. But she had her limits.

Everyone did.

Ella looked up at Peter and wondered what his were, hoping she'd never have to find out.

"Hey, Dad," Jakob called from the front.

Peter lowered his head.

"You want me to pull over so you can drive?" Jakob asked.

"You're doing fine," Peter replied.

"But—"

"Son," Peter said.

Jakob's mouth clamped shut, knowing his father was about to speak.

"Pick up the pace. Stay on the road. If anything gets in front of you—"

"I'll go around it," Jakob said.

"Actually, I want you to run it down."

Jakob flinched as though slapped. "They're still back there?"

Peter nodded, maintaining his absolute calm. While Jakob returned to the task of driving, the engine revving faster, Peter turned to Anne, who was seated in the back seat. "Hey, honey. There's a case under the seat in front of you."

Anne bent, found the case, and pulled it free. It was too big to pass back.

"Open it up," Peter instructed. "Inside are two black bands with hooks on either side." Anne dug through the case, finding the bands. "Those are the ones. Thanks." He sat on the tarp, quickly untangling the two hooked bands. When he was done, he handed one to Ella.

"What's this for?" she asked.

He tied his around his waist, and then clipped either end into holes on the sides of the bed. The band held him rooted in place. "Things are going to get bumpy." He pointed to the field, behind and to the right. "The field is chasing us."

Her head snapped around. He was right. Wisps of what looked like wheat, were pursuing them through the field. Some of the Stalkers had survived. A dozen by the looks of it. Maybe more. "We can outrun them in the truck."

"In about a mile, the wheat field is going to end, and the road is going to get all kinds of bendy. If they're as persistent as you say, they'll catch up. Now, before you buckle up, open the crate behind me and give me what's inside."

Ella threw the tarp off the large wooden crate. It wasn't locked, so she lifted the top and looked in. The crate was full of gear and supplies, but she quickly understood which item Peter was interested in—the heavy looking tripod, folded down and compact, to which a drum-fed light machine gun was attached.

Having fled the Stalkers for months, eking out the worst kind of living, slogging through deplorable conditions to avoid the hunting grounds of other predators, she lifted the big gun with a grunt and a grin. *This is more like it,* she thought, too eager to see the Stalkers' demise to remember that the noise wasn't going to go unnoticed.

13

It took just a minute to talk Ella through bolting the tripod to the truck bed, but it felt like time had slowed, shifting hours with each tick of the clock. After the first bolt, she moved quickly, securing the tripod, and mounting the M249 drum-fed machine gun, transforming the truck into what the military called a 'Technical,' which was just a fancy word for 'improvised fighting vehicle.' The slowness came from the knowledge that they might be attacked at any second, and if he fired the heavy weapon before it was secure, his aim would flounder with each kickback.

After firing the last bolt through the hole in the tripod's foot and into the metal floor, Ella clipped the hooks of her own security band to the sides of the truck, a few feet behind him. They could be tossed and bounced and smashed all about, but they wouldn't be flung free, which was a good thing—most of the time.

"Where did you get this thing?" Ella asked. "Weren't they illegal?"

"Older machine guns were legal," Peter replied, speaking loudly over the wind rushing past. "But not this one. It came from a National Guard Depot. There are a lot of unguarded weapons in the world now."

Peter kept the gun barrel level and pointed straight back, ready to whip it to either side. Wheat streaked back, a blur of brown lines. And among it, shaking wildly, the tall tails of running Stalkers. The formerly human monsters were falling steadily behind, unable to keep up with the Ram's acceleration. He considered letting the weapon rip into the field, but he'd be firing blind. The drum held one hundred rounds, but with a sustained fire rate of one hundred rounds per minute, he'd burn through the entire chain far too quickly. With only one replacement drum, he'd have to pick his targets carefully.

He squeezed the grip as the first signs of an adrenaline spike set in, his hands shaking. It didn't concern him. He'd felt it many times in the past, though it had been a while. The adrenaline surging through his body made him hyper-aware, sped up his reaction time, and increased his tolerance for pain, but it also took a toll on his body. When the action slowed, his muscles would quiver and twitch all over with unused chemical energy until the adrenaline was reabsorbed by his system. That he experienced larger adrenaline dumps than most people made him a good Marine, but it also made recovering from a battle that much more strenuous. And after today, they'd all need to crash.

Hard. But was that even possible out here?

Is this what life outside the house is like all the time?

If so, how did Ella and Anne survive?

He tried to picture the two of them, always on the run, fighting Stalkers and foraging for the non-ExoGenetic flora that still existed. He couldn't do it. He glanced back at Ella as he was bounced side to side, held in place by the thick rubber band. He'd been treating her like the woman he knew long ago, the woman who had spent most of her life in a laboratory. Her eyes were hard, gazing out at the field of wheat, focused, seeking out danger. She'd changed. But how much?

The whoosh of passing trees snapped him out of his thoughts. The wheat field fell into the distance, blocked by tall leafy trees, sentinels of the former, non-GMO ruled world. And yet, even here, where the sun was held at bay by a leafy canopy and the temperature dropped, ExoGenetic berry crops flourished. Tangles of thorny raspberry and blackberry bushes covered the forest floor. Passing through on foot would be laborious and torturous. The long flowing vines were covered in thick fruits, the blackberries hidden in shadow, the raspberries glowing like red beacons, juicy, delicious, and deadly.

Berries, berries everywhere and not a bite to eat, Peter thought, butchering Samuel Coleridge's 'The Rime of the Ancient Mariner.' And yet, he knew that the sailors of old never had it this bad. If they had, no one would have bothered sailing to the far parts of the world, and Europe would have still been dependent on the Silk Road to get its iPhones from China. Not that anyone was using cell phones anymore. Paperweights, all.

Their speed fell by half when they reached the first bend in the road. Tires squealed around the corner, tearing through the strands of raspberry bushes stretching out over the pavement. Peter and Ella tipped sideways, but the rubber bands held them upright. Peter tried to keep the machine gun barrel straight back, but it swiveled to the side. Aiming on the curvy road would be hell.

As they rounded a bend in the opposite direction, the truck slowed even more, forced to stay on the road by large rocks and trees lining the sides. Over the lessening roar of the big truck's engine, Peter heard a high pitched, warbling cry, like a giant turkey being plucked alive.

"They're getting organized," Ella said. "For the hunt."

Peter listened to the sound of crashing vegetation and snapping branches. The Stalkers were moving through the forest behind them, but he hadn't seen one yet.

"We're already moving, so I don't think they'll try to trap us. They're inhuman, but they still have limits. They get tired. They'll probably charge in unison. Try to bring down the larger prey as a group."

For a moment, he was confused about the 'larger prey' comment, but then he realized the Stalkers might see the big truck as a single target.

"They'll stay low to the ground as they approach," Ella continued, "but they leap when attacking."

"That's when I'll get them," Peter said more to himself than Ella.

"Right," she said. "Or when they'll get us."

"Pessimism doesn't suit you," he said, once again thinking about the woman he knew, who had believed anything was possible if you set your mind to it.

"Realism keeps us alive."

He was about to tell her it was a horrible way to live, when the words brought him back in time. He'd said the very same thing to her in regard to surviving an ambush in Afghanistan. He'd done things to survive that he had tried to forget since, but he knew he would do them again if he needed to. The very blunt way he'd told her about those events, and his unflinching acceptance of them, had led to her questioning his sometimes cold outlook on life. *Realism keeps me alive*, he'd said.

He'd been right then, and she was right now. War was hell, and he'd survived it, but this was something worse.

"Two o'clock," Ella said.

Peter reacted to the statement with unflinching swiftness, which had been instilled in him long ago. He rotated the gun barrel to the right, finding the target a hundred feet back, tearing through the thorn laden bushes like they were made of fluff. Even from a distance, he could see the streaks of red blood running down the creature's gray skin, from a thousand razor-thin cuts. *They're monsters*, he thought, *but not invincible and not without limits*. He pulled the trigger.

Five 5.56×45 mm NATO rounds spewed from the barrel, one of them a bright orange tracer, showing the spread's path. Not that he needed the tracer round to see where the bullets hit. Tree bark exploded in the air. Getting a round through the forest streaking past and hitting a target moving just as quickly through the trees, would be nearly impossible.

He'd have to wait until they were closer.

"What's happening?" Anne called from the window.

Peter didn't look back but heard Ella reply. "Jakob, keep us moving and stable. That's more important than speed right now."

"What?" Jakob said. "Why?"

The fear in his son's voice broke his heart.

Ella shared some more of her newfound blunt realism. "Because we can't outrun them. Our only chance is to outgun them, and your father can't do that if we're swerving all over the road."

"Okay," Jakob said, and the vehicle slowed a little more. Peter was about to ask for more gas, when he realized the machine gun was much easier to control. He aimed at the single creature again, holding a bead on it. He pulled the trigger in quick jerks, spacing out the shots. The first two struck trees. The third squeezed through two tall trunks, shredded a blackberry, and then struck home, piercing the Stalker's broad chest. The creature coughed and fell, careening head over heels in a tangle of thorns.

Then a second took its place. And another. And another. They spread out through the woods, running with reckless abandon, focused solely on their prey. This kind of behavior, this desperate hunger, was what separated predators of the old world from the new. A lion wouldn't go after an animal it thought might injure it. In the wild, any injury could lead to death, by infection or by simply weakening the animal so it was susceptible to competitors. A lion that couldn't fend off hyenas because of an injured limb, was typically a dead lion.

He picked targets, squeezing off single rounds when he had a clear line of sight. He missed far more than he hit, and the mob of Stalkers was closing the distance. He'd counted a dozen at first, but he'd reduced the number to nine. Although he'd used twenty-five rounds to do so, and the math said he'd have to change ammo drums to kill them all. The long reload time would leave them wide open to attack.

Peter swung the barrel to the left as the truck swung around a bend to the right. He tracked five of the Stalkers, leaping across the open road. *If they flank us, we're screwed,* he thought, and he pulled the trigger. The spray of bullets and glowing tracer rounds ate into the group, empty bullet casings clanging to the truck bed, but the creatures at the back were protected from the fusillade by those in the front. After unleashing twenty-five more rounds, three of the Stalkers stumbled and slid across the pavement. The other three made it to the relative safety of the forest on the other side. The two sets of Stalkers advanced on either side, peeling away, deeper into the forest, fully flanking the truck.

At this point, they're going to overtake us and set that trap Ella warned us about.

But they didn't. Instead, after a series of squawking cries, both groups turned inward at once. He wasn't sure just how intelligent the Stalkers were, but he was pretty sure they knew three of them were sacrificing themselves, while the other three...they'd have a feast.

14

Peter fought the urge to swing the barrel around at the three Stalkers charging from the right. He knew they were still coming. Could hear their squeaking pants as they neared. But the three monsters on the left were closer. And airborne.

The stalkers led with their long hind legs extended, claws splayed wide. If they made contact with prey, the talons would sink into the flesh underneath as the full weight of the creature slammed into the victim. If the unlucky prey wasn't killed by the impact, the claws would finish the job.

He made momentary eye contact with the Stalker leading the way. He saw intelligence in its gaze, but it was masked by rage and hunger. If the creature was smart enough to understand what the machine gun could do, its raw emotions kept it from really comprehending the consequences for its actions.

Or maybe it did understand?

Maybe all this rage and hate seething from the thing was because it could remember what it once was and loathed him for it. His very existence might mock them. He didn't think the creature could comprehend all this, but back in the part of its brain that was once human, it might remember, and feel...

For a moment, he pitied the thing.

And then he shot it, punching three holes in the center of its gray chest, which was lined with bulging ribs. The shots kicked the monster back, flipping it over through a cloud of pink gore. The tumbling body stumbled the two Stalkers behind it, and Peter cheered inwardly as he turned the gun barrel to the right.

Too late.

He pulled the trigger, but the angle of the gun barrel was blocked by a Stalker's body as it landed on the side of the truck, the hot metal sizzling against the creature's skin. The truck shook and skidded from the impact, but Jakob managed to keep it moving and on the road. Somewhere in the back of Peter's mind, he heard Anne screaming. Or was it Ella? He couldn't tell, but then his voice joined the chorus.

He shouted in surprise and abject horror as the Stalker clinging to the side of the truck stretched out its sinewy neck, opened its needle tooth-filled maw large enough to clamp down on his head like a bear trap and lunged for him. Peter leaned away from the gaping jaws, but the elastic holding him in the truck also kept him from diving away.

The jaws snapped just an inch from his nose with such force that the colliding teeth snapped, spraying his face with bits of enamel and spittle.

Peter winced, but years of training and field operations—though now distant memories—had honed his reactions into something closer to instinct. Action without thought. He dropped back, letting his weight stretch the elastic band back until the stored potential force in the band propelled him back up. As his feet rose first, he kicked hard with both legs, catching the Stalker in the chest. He felt ribs break. The monster roared in pain. But it held on, a look of determination on its face...until a shotgun blast removed the expression, along with the rest of its bald head.

As the shotgun blast rang in Peter's ear, he felt glad that Ella had remembered his discarded weapon and had the wherewithal to use it. Not many people would have thought or moved as quickly. Of course, anyone unable to do so was probably already dead. The world was now a twisted version of Herbert Spencer's survival of the fittest. Now it was survival of the most savage, which didn't bode well for his son's future... or his daughter's.

The shotgun-propelled gore blasted back and slapped a second Stalker in the face, blinding it before the creature could lunge forward. But the third monster leapt up to take the now headless beast's place. The first thing it did was demonstrate its intelligence by slapping away the shotgun before Ella could chamber another shell. Then with a quick swipe of its claw, the Stalker severed Peter's rubber band. The black band, freed from one side of the truck, snapped away, striking Peter in the gut while the side of the cord, still wrapped around his waist, yanked him off his feet and slammed his head into the bed's side wall.

Vision spinning, Peter tried to right himself, but the loose floor of spent bullet casings rolled under his feet. There was nothing he could do to help Ella, who was still held in place by her rubber band, and she wasn't heavy enough to lean back very far.

And then, in a flash of vicious motion, everything he thought he knew about Ella changed. With a battle cry she reached forward, meeting the Stalker's reaching head, and as the creature tried to sever her head with its teeth, she clung to its face and buried her thumbs into its eyes. There was no hesitation in the action, no squeamish flinching. The motion was fluid. Practiced. Without remorse or revulsion.

The Stalker shrieked, twisting its head upward. Ella's thumbs slipped out of the ruined eye sockets with wet pops. And still, she didn't stop. While the monster had its head turned skyward, letting out a tortured wail, Ella punched the thing in the throat, connecting with what once might have been an Adam's apple. There was a crunch of cartilage and flesh that cut the Stalker's cry short and left it thrashing and gasping. Ella ducked as the creature's writhing claws passed over her head. And then it was gone, spinning over the pavement behind them.

As he stared at Ella, bewildered by what he'd just witnessed, she turned down to him, gazing hard at him, and shouted, "Ten o'clock!" The words snapped Peter back into action. There were still three Stalkers left. While Ella stretched against her rubber band, trying to recover the shotgun, Peter found his feet, latched onto the machine gun, and swung the barrel left to ten o'clock.

He pulled the trigger, unleashing four rounds, but the nearest Stalker had anticipated the attack, ducking and dodging to the side faster than he could track. While he followed it, the second moved in for the kill, leaping up to be met with a hail of buckshot. At a distance of fifteen feet, Ella couldn't miss. However, as the buckshot dispersed, it also lacked the lethal efficiency of a close range shot. The metal balls punched into the Stalker in a wide spread, creating many small, non-lethal wounds rather than a big hole. But the impact and pain generated by the shot caused the Stalker to fall short of the truck and stumble upon landing, craning its head down to look at the rivulets of blood now running down its body. In the long run, the wounds could prove lethal from infection, but in the short run... The wounded Stalker rejoined the chase, lagging behind, less of a threat, but determined to join the feast.

Peter fired a second volley at the Stalker to his left, missing once again, but forcing the monster to retreat into the trees. There were four of them now. Another had joined the hunt. Two on the right, one on the left and the injured creature, slowly falling behind.

Maybe some of the buckshot pierced a lung?

The situation was improved, but he was also dangerously low on ammo.

He'd lost count, but knew there wasn't enough to miss again. He swung the barrel right as the two Stalkers closed in. He lined up the shot, prepared to send a single round in the head of the nearest Stalker, but then the truck rounded a corner. No longer held in place by the rubber band, Peter was flung to the side. Instinctively, he gripped the machine gun to stay upright, but that also meant squeezing the trigger.

Bullets raged into the air as casings rattled to the truck bed. Peter tried to pry his finger away, but his falling weight had wedged it in tight, nearly to breaking. Ella ducked as the barrel swept over her head, narrowly avoiding the chaotic barrage. The only thing that saved Jakob and Anne from being mowed down by their father was that the machine gun ran out of ammunition.

Ella stood back up, lifted the shotgun, fired, pumped, and fired again.

Peter pulled with his arms, using the mounted machine gun to lift himself up. He expected a Stalker to be leaping at him, but found the two on the right lying in the road, separated by fifteen feet.

"You got the first one," Ella said, revealing his accidental barrage had yielded at least a small measure of success. It also implied that she'd killed the second, and he wondered if she might be more fit to lead this cross-country expedition through hell.

Movement pulled his vision back to the left, where the still healthy Stalker paralleled the truck, staying in the trees. Peter looked ahead and saw an approaching right turn. *That's where it's going to hit us,* he realized, and he saw the second Stalker, perhaps sensing the impending kill, charging up behind them, no longer slowed by its wounds.

The *shk-chk* of a shotgun being pumped turned his eyes back to Ella. She frowned. "It's spent."

He had shotgun shells in the backpack on his shoulders and shirked it off, but he already knew it was too late. Neither of them could reload in time.

Ella must have realized this, too, because she said, "Go for the eyes and throat. If it gets on top of you, and is a male, a kick in the nuts still does the job."

In the moment before the attack, something in the air changed. The crashing of the Stalker charging through bushes was joined by a rumbling. It was subtle at first, but then it rose through the air like an impending tsunami. If the Stalker heard the sound, it either didn't register a threat or was lost in bloodlust.

"What is it?" he asked.

Ella just shook her head.

The truck reached the turn, tires screeching. The Stalker moving parallel dove out over the road, which brought it right in front of them. The truck swerved hard to the left, but not far enough. Peter thought Jakob might have been trying to swerve away from it, but when a flash of pink moved past them on the right, he realized the boy had just been avoiding something else in the road.

Something massive.

Something hungry.

The source of the rumble charged past with something akin to a squeal of delight, high-pitched, but with the volume of a foghorn. For a moment, it appeared the object had collided with the airborne Stalker, but the notion was obliterated when the giant creature stopped and shook the already dead Stalker in its mouth. The new creature was the size of an elephant, with thick pink skin sprouting tufts of wiry black hair. Its tubular body led to a neckless head with a long snout, which was tipped by a beak that now severed the Stalker in two. A shield of flesh-covered bone rose up behind its eyes, giving it the appearance of a hornless triceratops. Peter noted the scars lining that shield and didn't like what they implied. The new monster pinned the Stalker's torso to the ground with its cloven hooves, split in two, the black halves looking more like over-sized spear tips.

The second, wounded Stalker, wisely skidded to a stop, its claws scratching against the pavement.

Without pausing to watch, it turned tail and ran. There was no meal here, and the Stalker knew it.

Predator had suddenly become the prey.

As the monster devoured the Stalker on the ground, now little more than shredded meat, Peter caught sight of a pattern on the muscular side of its hind thigh. For a moment, he thought it might be a scar or birth mark of some kind, but then he recognized it.

The truck rounded the bend, leaving the horror behind, or at least out of sight. Feeling numb, Peter lowered himself to the crate, sat down, and looked into the window. Anne had buried herself between the seats, head down. Jakob, hands on the wheel, ten and two, kept them on course, but the boy's arms were shaking.

"You did great," Peter said. "Take us a few more miles. If nothing is chasing us, I'll take over."

Jakob just nodded.

When Peter stood again, he set himself to the task of switching out the machine gun's ammo drum. He pointed to the backpack. "Shotgun shells are in there."

Ella quickly opened the pack and took out the box, pausing when she saw what was below. "What's this?"

"A change of clothes and gear for you and Anne," he said, discarding the empty drum. "Packed it last night."

"You knew this would happen?" she asked, surprised.

"If I was certain, I wouldn't have shaved your heads. But I like to be prepared." He allowed himself a grin. "You always were trouble."

She shook her head. "I have no idea what that was, by the way. The pink thing."

"I do," he said, meeting her eyes. "It had a brand on its hind leg, from a farm not far from here."

She raised her eyebrows, waiting.

"That...was a pig."

15

Jakob drove for three miles, after narrowly avoiding what his father had identified as a pig. It was six miles before his heart stopped racing and the muscles in his thighs, forearms, and chest stopped twitching. His body was exhausted, but his mind... It was spinning with the tumultuous urgency of a carnival Tilt-A-Whirl. It was still before noon, but he didn't think he'd be able to sleep later that night. Maybe not for days.

If we live that long.

Jakob understood what had happened to the world. His father had told him the details, holding nothing back, including the involvement of the woman they'd rescued the previous night. Ella. He couldn't remember her last name, but he had vague memories of his mother cursing it. But as much as his mother had loathed this woman, his father clearly felt differently. Despite having not seen each other in a decade, his father and Ella were comfortable with each other. *Old friends*, Jakob decided, then realized the truth: *they had been more than friends.*

Whatever they had been in the past, whatever they were now, he didn't really care. Ella and her daughter were real, living, breathing human beings. Since losing contact with other survivors, Jakob had been afraid that he and his father were all that was left. Now he knew differently, and the knowledge gave him hope. The pig on the other hand...

"Let's call it a Swine," Anne said. She sat beside him in the Ram's back seat. It was a little cramped for Jakob, who had become lanky in the past year, but he preferred the backseat to the driver's seat. His father had told him, more than once, what a good job he had done. Despite his success behind the wheel, though, he had no desire to repeat the experience.

"Fits," Ella said from the front passenger's seat.

"I was thinking something more like Giant Pink Asshole," Jakob said without thinking, his exhaustion switching off his verbal filter.

Anne burst out laughing.

Ella turned around, but didn't look upset by his language. She looked at Anne, a mix of happiness and sadness. Tears filled her eyes. She glanced at Jakob and mouthed, 'Thank you.'

Peter on the other hand... "*Jake.* Watch your mouth."

Ella put her hand on Peter's arm and said, "It's not like there's a society left to deem which words are wholesome and which are not. There are better things to be offended by, and if it makes her laugh—" She glanced back at Jakob again, "—he can say whatever he wants."

"Gives a whole new meaning to having a 4.0 GPA," Jakob said, encouraged by Ella's support. He spoke in a deep voice, saying, "What'd you get on your report card, son?" Then in a higher voice, "A 2.5 GPA, Daddy." And again in a deep voice, he said, "Son, I expect at least a 3.5 Giant Pink Asshole."

Anne was laughing so hard by the end of Jakob's corny shtick that her tears matched those of her mother. Jakob was happy to see his father's shoulders bouncing as he joined in, expelling the tension that had gripped them since the Stalkers and the Swine had fallen away behind them.

When the laughing died down, Peter turned to Ella and asked, "So, how is this going to work? We have thousands of miles to cover, which we can do in a few days in the truck, but..."

"The truck is going to attract attention," she finished. "If we drive steady and slow, during the day, we might do okay. On foot will draw less attention, but could increase the risk simply because we'll be exposed for months rather than for days. I say we take our chances with the truck until it's no longer an option. But what about gas? This beast must guzzle it."

"We can find gas along the way," Peter said. "There's a hand pump in the back for siphoning and two jugs of PRI to restore the old gas. Assuming there are hardware stores between here and Boston, we should have no trouble finding more if we need it."

"What's PRI?" Anne asked.

"You add it to the fuel," Jakob explained. "Old gas separates. Gets water in it. The PRI sucks it up. Or something. Makes it safe to use again." It had been more than a year since his father had explained it to him, and he'd only been half listening at the time, more concerned with when he would speak to Alia again.

Jakob's eyes widened as he thought about the girl. "Are we headed through Kentucky?"

Ella turned back. "We need to find a map. Plot a route. But it's possible. There are two biodomes in the state. Why?"

"He has a friend in one of them," Peter said.

"Alia." Jakob's stomach began twitching again. The idea of reaching Alia, after all this time, triggered an adrenaline spike that suddenly overcame him with nausea. The truck's AC was running, but he cracked the window and took several deep breaths. The air was full of sweet scents. Luckily, the endless stores of food that had destroyed the world was safe enough to smell. As his nerves settled, he looked out the window.

Banana trees.

In Kansas.

They'd grown fast, overtaking former grazing lands, producing fruit all year round. Mounds of the uneaten stuff littered the forest floor. New trees sprouted from the rot, joined by random tufts of corn, wheat, fruit bushes, and crops he didn't recognize. The vegetation seemed hell bent on taking up every inch of available soil.

They'll grow until it's impossible to get around, until the world is choked.

Or they are.

"Will the ExoGenetic plants ever exhaust the soil?"

"Not where the growth is mixed," his father said. "Like here. The bananas rot and add nutrients for the ground crops, while the ground crops go through their growth cycles monthly, adding nutrients for the trees. It's a fairly balanced circle of life."

"Hakuna matata," Anne said.

Jakob chuckled. "Hardly. And for the record, I hated that movie."

"Simba would have, like, three faces and wings by now," Anne said, giggling.

"It's not a perfect system, though," Ella said. "The crops will eventually use up the natural resources. It's why crop rotation works. The mix of plants might help sustain them, and the ExoGenetic plants don't need much in the way of nutrients, which is why they can grow on rooftops, or rugs, or really anything permeable. But there is a limit."

"That...sounds good," Jakob said.

"It's thousands of years away," Ella said. "At least."

Jakob frowned, eyeing the blur of plants streaking by. "What about the crops that aren't mixed? Like the wheat around our house?"

"It will deplete the land much sooner. Probably in our lifetimes, but the land will be taken over by another crop, or..."

This got Peter's attention. He glanced from the road to Ella just long enough to ask, "Or?"

"They'll adapt."

"Meaning?" Peter asked.

"They'll find other ways of getting what they need to survive, just like everything else on the planet does. But faster."

The truck slowed as Peter once again turned toward Ella. "How fast?"

But it was Anne who answered. "A tree ate our friend."

"A *what* did *what* now?" Jakob was horrified. As screwed up as the world had become, trees did *not* eat people.

"Anne," Ella chided, but then she sighed and explained. "We were camped beneath a lemon tree. During the night, the...roots... They came up through the ground. Well, use your imagination."

"The ExoGenetic plants are becoming *carnivorous*?" Peter asked.

"When conditions require it, yes. They're adapting. It's what they were designed to do."

"What you designed them to do," Jakob said, and he quickly regretted it. He liked Anne a lot, and her mother had been nice to them so far. She probably felt horrible about it already.

"What my company designed them to do," she said without a trace of humor, or regret. "Yes. In that regard, they're a success. The error was believing the genes wouldn't be passed on to anything consuming the plants. But testing for that would have taken years, and by then, the competition might have developed their own strains. It was a risk. A big one.

"But the company was protected by the long-term GMO Protection Act, passed thanks to generous campaign contributions and an army of lobbyists. Did you know the bill passed because it was attached to an education bill? Voting against it would have meant voting against America's future, and no politician on either side of the aisle could have afforded to do that. Of course, if any of them actually read the rider that was tacked on, none of them really understood the ramifications. They gave GMO companies an endless deck of get-out-of-jail-free cards. Without oversight, we could have made any genetic modifications to food, released that food, and regardless of the negative outcome, we couldn't be held liable for the results."

"It wouldn't have mattered," Jakob said.

"What wouldn't?" Ella asked.

"The bill protecting ExoGen. There's no one left to sue them, and no one left to sue."

"That's...not entirely correct." She spoke to Peter. "ExoGen has a secure location just outside San Francisco. When they realized what I had warned them about was true, they built a vast facility, similar to the biodomes I had built, where they could 'weather the storm.' But they're not interested in undoing the damage. For the group that's left, who are safe from harm, the world is more like a big Petri dish now."

"That's why you left?" Peter asked.

Ella nodded. "A group of us. What we couldn't do in San Francisco, we'd do in Boston."

"How many did you start with?" Jakob asked.

"Twenty-seven," Anne replied. "Including Ed, Mom's boyfriend."

Jakob watched his father for a reaction to this revelation—the death toll and the boyfriend—but his father's cool eyes betrayed nothing. When he spoke, the question caught Jakob off guard. "Are they dangerous?"

Jakob was about to ask who he was talking about, but Ella understood. "Maybe...yes. They came after us the following day. They have helicopters. Weapons. A security force. Three of our people were captured. I don't know what happened to them. Two who fought back were killed. We haven't seen them since, but it's possible they're still looking."

"And the other twenty...they died out here?"

She nodded. "Every one of them. Yes."

16

Rotor blades snapped through the air, shoving swirls of black smoke away from the helicopter. The vehicle hovered over a scene of carnage so vast that human involvement was guaranteed. As self-destructive as the world had become, nothing could blow shit up like the human race. The helicopter made a slow circle around the blackened earth. The remnants of a farmhouse's concrete foundation could be seen, like some ancient, uncovered ruin. The house had also been surrounded by a fifty-foot-wide circle of concrete, an interesting way of keeping the crops from encroaching. At the back side of the home, a long oval extended out, its glass dome shattered and missing, white framing hanging limp. The biodome was in ruins, but still recognizable now that Edward Kenyon had seen a few of them, each one surrounded by death.

Of course, the corpses here were different from the other locations. For starters, they were burned to a crisp rather than torn apart and partially consumed. But the biggest difference was that the bodies littering the concrete surrounding the foundation weren't human. The monsters Ella called Stalkers lay about in twisted, smoldering heaps.

Whoever Ella had found in this house was a dangerous son-of-a-bitch.

"Sir," the pilot's voice in his headphones came through clearly over the roar of the rotor. "We're not seeing anything on the FLIR. Overwatch says we're clear."

Overwatch was the third helicopter in their squadron of three. It was a mile up, watching for movement in all directions. The job was made easier thanks to the ring of fire eating up the vast wheat field. It was two miles out now and still burning, creating a large safezone. It was safe partly because their line of sight was extended, but also because most living creatures on Earth, ExoGenetic or not, still ran from fire.

"Take us down. I want a sweep for human casualties." While he couldn't see any bodies from the air, that didn't mean there weren't bits and pieces strewn about. The explosion that took down the house had been vast. They'd been slowly tracking Ella's flight across the country, gained ground with each discovery, but the column of smoke rising into the air had been like a beacon. They had arrived too late, but they'd never been so close. Their best estimate was that the explosion had taken place two hours ago. If there were survivors, they were likely long gone by now. But there would be a trail to follow, and if Ella was still alive, he knew that trail would be headed east.

But first they had to do their due diligence and make sure her body wasn't lying among the ashes.

And if it was... He closed his eyes, pushing the image from his thoughts. He'd lost her devotion, but that could be regained, especially when she realized he was still alive.

The blue, Black Hawk helicopter touched down beside the first, which had landed just moments before, the ten soldiers within spreading out, clearing the area, and seeking out the dead. As he opened the sliding door on the side of his helicopter, a man named Doug Hutchins approached. Of the thirty men making up the ranks of Field Expedition Alpha, Hutchins was the only one Kenyon considered a friend. Unlike these other grunts, who had been U.S. Military before the world went to shit, he and Doug had led the ExoGen security team for the past fifteen years. While he had gone along with Ella's expedition, to see where it would lead, when things had gone south and people started dying, it was Hutchins who had found him, clinging to a tree, surrounded by Stalkers.

"What's the plan, Ed?" Hutchins asked. "This place looks like a real shake n' bake."

Kenyon shook his head.

"Thanks."

Hutchins knew the story. Knew why Kenyon pushed for this mission, despite the odds. ExoGen wanted Ella back. Believed the future depended on her return. But they didn't want her nearly as bad as Kenyon. So, when he had suggested this long-distance expedition, taking three helicopters that would require scrounging fuel from airports large and small, scattered across the county, ExoGen had been apprehensive. But Kenyon had been persuasive. Passionate. If the mission ended in failure, or worse, death, Kenyon would be crushed.

"Sorry," Hutchins said. "But I think whoever did this had a way out."

Kenyon nodded. "The second site."

They'd seen evidence of a secondary explosion not far from the house, but they had to clear the main residence before moving on. "Double-time the search," he shouted to the soldiers spreading out. "We're in the clear, so focus on searching for bodies."

When they'd conducted similar searches at the ruins of previous biodomes, they'd had to keep their guard up, because some Stalkers tended to linger behind, looking for scraps. But here...that problem had been taken care of. Decisively.

"All I'm seeing is Rattletails, sir," a soldier called out from the side of the house.

"Same here," said another from the opposite side.

Kenyon spun his finger in the air. "Full perimeter, and then inside. You know the drill."

The men were never happy about being on the ground, especially where evidence of ExoGens was clear. But this was their job. Why they were allowed to stay in San Francisco. Why they were alive at all. So, they'd do their job, even if it was something Kenyon couldn't bring himself to do. It wasn't the idea of finding a dead body that spooked him, it was the idea of finding *her* dead body.

And if they did find her here, he'd make damn sure to find whoever blew this place apart and make them pay. He'd gone too far, fought too hard, and lost too many men on finding Ella to return to San Francisco without anything to show for it.

A soldier jogged over. "There's nothing here, sir."

"Nothing?"

"Nothing human, sir. That's what you wanted to know, right?"

The man was right, but that didn't make other details insignificant. "How many Stalkers?"

The man looked confused, so Kenyon used the term preferred by the soldiers. "Rattletails."

"Counted thirty outside the house. Hard to say how many were in the basement when—"

"The Stalkers were *inside* the house?"

"In the basement. Fifty or more."

"Shit," Hutchins whispered. "The most we've ever killed was..." He just shook his head.

"Fewer," Kenyon said. "A lot fewer." Whoever had lived here had prepared for the worst and blown the shit out of the place. Alpha would have to proceed with caution.

"Sir," the voice was in his earbud. It was Mackenzie, his third in command, and the only soldier among the lot he respected, reporting in from Overwatch. "We're over the second site now. No signs of dead, human or ExoGen. Looks like it was a barn. It's blown apart, but not like the house. The debris field is scattered over nearly a mile. Looks like it was shredded from the inside, but it's only slightly singed."

Kenyon eyed the basement, searching the blackened and crumbling walls. His eyes locked on a large square of metal, bent inward to expose a dark recess, but how far did it go? "Drop down closer. Look inside the barn. What do you see?"

"Hold on," Mackenzie said.

While he waited, Kenyon shut off his throat mic and shouted to his crew. "Pack it up! We're moving!"

The soldiers dutifully hurried back to their helicopter, more eager to be inside the secure cab than obedient.

"Sir," Mackenzie said, "Looks like there might be a tunnel inside the barn. Leads back toward the house."

That's how they got out, Kenyon thought. *Advanced tactics for a civilian.*

"Looks like the explosion vented through the tunnel. Tore the barn apart. There are tire tracks leading away from the barn."

Kenyon toggled his throat mic. "Which direction?" he asked, though he already knew the answer.

"Headed east, sir."

Kenyon headed for his Black Hawk. "Pack it up. There's nothing for us here, and we're not far behind now."

17

Peter glanced in the back seat. The adrenaline hangover that beat on the inside of his skull and tugged on his eyelids had claimed the two children an hour ago. They'd fought it for a time, exchanging stories—Anne's were far more disturbing—and keeping watch, but the endlessly monotonous crops walling them in on the road, and the white, dashed line of Interstate 64 fading along with the rest of civilization's remnants, had lulled them to sleep. Anne first. Then Jakob.

They'd driven in silence since then, but Peter needed to stem the tide of his own rising weariness. With no coffee, he settled for conversation. "So," he said. "A boyfriend?"

Ella leaned up, rubbing her prickly head, and then her eyes. "Yeah. Ed."

"Good guy?" Peter didn't really want to know, but the emotions brewing inside him were already chasing the sandman away.

He was surprised when she shrugged and said, "Good company. Funny." She turned sideways, leaning back against the door.

Probably to watch my facial expressions, he thought. *See if I care.*

"When the world has come to an end, and you're partly responsible for it, any attention is welcome."

He didn't know what to say to that.

"So...he was...what? Your post-apocalyptic comfort man?"

"That pretty much sums it up," she said, but she was frowning now, looking out the front window. "He wasn't the brightest...but he was brave. A fighter. Like you."

Was.

"He came with you?" Peter asked.

She kept her eyes facing out the windshield. "And died for it. More than a month ago. I didn't love him—"

Peter felt annoyed with himself for feeling relieved by this. He'd been married to Kristen, who he loved. He'd had a son with her. Had chosen his marriage over Ella. But as far as he knew, he'd been Ella's only real love. The one who got away. It was selfish—what his son would call a 'dick move'—but he couldn't deny feeling pleased that her feelings for the man were only skin deep. Deeper down, a darker part of him felt glad the guy was dead.

"—if that's what you're wondering. I'm surprised you want to know."

"Just trying to stay awake," he admitted.

"I'm afraid the details of our relationship aren't scintillating enough for that." He glanced at Ella to find her watching him again, a slight smile on her lips. "Though the relief on your face is adorable, in comparison to the rest of the world, anyway."

"*Ebola* is adorable, compared to the rest of the world," he said.

Ella barked out a laugh and clamped a hand over her mouth.

The sound, like a jolt from the past, freed a memory.

Teenagers. They sat in the back of a pickup truck at a drive-in. Classic make-out scenario. But the movie, *Spaceballs*, had had Ella in stitches, and all of his best moves were met with laughter and movie quotes. Despite getting nothing more than a kiss goodnight, it was one of his fondest memories from his teen years. One of the nights that had bonded them for life, despite distance and relationships.

As Ella's stifled laughter was squelched, she craned her head around and looked at the sky. "We've made good time. Should probably pack it in for the night."

Peter looked at his watch. "It's only four. We have hours of daylight still."

"Any predators still hiding from the sun will be most active at dusk, while the sun is still on the horizon. And where are we?"

"Missouri. A hundred fifty miles from the border. I think."

"Know what town?"

"Saw a sign for Mt. Vernon a ways back, but I don't think we've passed through. Never been there."

"Right. The point is, we need to find someplace secure to spend the night, in a town we've never been to, and we only have a few hours to get that done. And by secure, I mean like a bomb shelter."

"That how you do it every night?" he asked.

"Since the lemon tree," she said, and she didn't need to elaborate. "But it doesn't always work out." She glanced back at Anne, still sleeping. "The two of us spent more nights outside than in. Had some close calls, but the camouflage suits kept us hidden. With those things over us, there wasn't much that could see or smell us."

"Except the Stalkers?"

"They couldn't see or smell us at night, but they're smart. They tracked us. And when they figured out we were moving during the day, they switched hunting patterns."

"What about now?" he asked. "Think they're still following us?"

She shrugged.

"If they are, they're going to need to find a car."

"Right," he said. "They have limits."

"Not human limits, but they can't drive trucks. And they can't run all day and all night without stopping."

"Unless..." he said, but he wasn't sure if he should continue.

"Go on," she said.

"You said the ExoGenetic creatures are adapting fast, right?"

"Yeah."

"How fast?"

"Generations of change can take place in hours."

"So," he said. "It wouldn't be impossible for the Stalkers to adapt... bigger lungs, stronger legs or less of a need for sleep, say, overnight?"

"You see, this is what Ed never could do for me. No one crushes my spirit like you."

Her smile said she was joking, but he felt the underlying truth in her words.

And it stung.

"Then it's possible?" he asked.

"If there are any left alive, it's not just possible, it's probable. The problem is that we can't keep on going—even if they are still trailing us—because there are other things out here that are just as hungry. Just because other predators haven't adapted to eating people yet, doesn't mean they can't. And then there's the challenge of our lack of adaptability. Humans can correct most problems if given enough time. We don't need to evolve fur coats to survive a winter. We can make them. But there's nothing we can do about our biology. We still need to eat, and drink, and sleep. You're already driving all over the road. If we drove through the night, you'd probably careen into a tree long before the Stalkers ever found us."

"Point taken." He pointed ahead. "There's an exit."

"Take it," she said.

"You sure?"

She nodded. "Larger cities are tempting, but lots of places to hide for us means lots of places to hide for...whatever is out here. Last thing we need is to kick open the door on some predator's den."

"Okay then, navigator. Where to?"

She pointed to a rectangular, blue sign fifty feet ahead of the exit. It read, 'Pierce Creek Baptist Church.' "Yea, though I walk through the valley of the shadow of death... Churches have basements, right?"

"Most," he said, knowing without a doubt that she was asking because she'd never been in one. Her parents, despite being Midwest farmers, were also atheists. "I'm surprised you know the verse."

"When the residents of ExoGen's bio-refuge in San Francisco packed, not many of them brought books to read. But someone brought a handful of Bibles."

He steered the armored truck off the highway and turned left onto a double-yellow-lined road. He was surprised to have a decent view of the distance, no trees or tall crops rising up around them. Instead, for miles around, there was a carpet of cabbage. The plants looked like stemless, oversized green flowers. He'd never grown cabbage himself, but he had seen enough to recognize it. What was unfamiliar, however, was the way it grew. Instead of well-organized rows, ready to be harvested, the land was covered in a vibrant green carpet of cabbage.

"There's the church," Ella said.

It was easy to see the white steeple rising up over the endless green, like a beacon. He stopped short of considering it a symbol of hope; that well had gone dry after Kristen... But as the building came into view, it looked solid and undamaged, resting on a concrete foundation. *A new church,* he decided, *built just in time for the end of days.*

Is that what this is? he wondered. *Some kind of biblical prophecy coming true?*

He didn't hear any trumpets announcing the arrival of a returning savior, though it wouldn't be hard to argue the appearance of the White, Red, Black, and Pale Horsemen. And he wouldn't be surprised if there was a multi-headed dragon roaming the Earth. He didn't know his Bible well, not nearly as well as Ella now did, but he didn't think the biological apocalypse, started in part by the woman sitting next to him, qualified.

If he were a believer, that might give him hope. Because if the Bible was right, and the end hadn't arrived, it meant humanity would rebuild again...before the end. He turned his mind back to the church, trying to escape his fire-and-brimstone thought process, but the building made the mental transition impossible.

He stopped the truck in front of where the church's parking lot should have been and shut the engine off, conserving every drop of gas he could. "They must not have paved."

"This isn't going to work," Ella said.

He was about to ask why when he figured it out, chiding himself for not thinking of it first. He'd been pampered in that house for too long. "The cabbage will show where we went."

"That only matters with Stalkers," Anne said, her voice groggy. "They're not going to catch us. Even if they change."

Peter wasn't sure if Anne had been awake and listening or if she just thought like her mother, but the girl was probably right. Probably.

"We don't know what's out here," Ella said. "It's not impossible that there could be other intelligent predators."

"Have you seen anything out here?" Anne asked. "We're in the middle of nowhere. The population would have been slim, before."

"Meaning?" Peter asked.

"Big population areas produce pack hunters," Ella said. "Which are generally more intelligent. Sparsely populated areas generate...bigger predators."

"—and dumber," Anne added.

"And dumber," Ella agreed.

"So, we could stay here," Jakob said, sitting up. "I wouldn't mind getting out of the truck."

Ella rolled down her window and sniffed the air.

Is she really smelling the air for signs of nearby predators?

Peter got his answer when she leaned back in and said, "Seems clear."

But then a sound blared across the open landscape. Chills covered Peter's arms, as what sounded like a trumpet blare resounded around them.

The sound's source drew Peter's eyes to Ella's open window. What he saw made his stomach lurch.

"Nobody. Move."

18

Seated behind his father, Jakob had a similar view through the passenger side windows, so when he turned his head, he saw exactly what had caused his father to whisper those two fear-fueled words: 'Nobody. Move.'

Beyond turning his head, Jakob did as instructed, freezing in place. He nearly shouted an exclamation though, stopping at the last moment when he saw the thing's ears. Ella, with her back to the window, couldn't see what he could, but Anne... The girl slowly turned her head toward the window.

He expected a scream. At least a flinch of surprise. But the girl remained still, then she leaned over and spoke, her whispering words slurred together like they were nothing more than a breeze, which Jakob realized was her intention—and way too quick of thinking for a twelve-year-old girl.

"Fifteen feet tall," Anne said. "Light brown fur. Mammalian. Short hind legs. Long arms...twelve feet to the elbow...walks on the elbows..."

Her description was accurate and detailed, but was she just trying to inform her mother? Maybe identify the creature that stalked the cabbage field, three hundred feet away?

"The lower arms are like...spears...no hands...large ears, like bowls..." She held her breath when the distant monster stopped its loping walk across the field and cocked its head to the side. It let out a trumpet blast, the sound rolling past—

—and bouncing off us, Jakob thought. He leaned in close, whispering the way Anne had. "It was a bat. Using echolocation."

"It's an Echo," Anne said, putting her stamp of approval on the name.

Ella's hand slid down to the truck's old fashioned window roller. She slowly cranked the knob, silently rolling up the window. With the window shut, blocking at least some of the sound from within, Ella slid around in her seat, looking out the window. Like Anne, she showed no reaction to the monster, which was now looking straight at them.

But it's not really looking at us, Jakob realized, because the thing—the Echo—had no eyes. What it did have was a large, squashed in nose, massive ears atop its head and a mouth full of long, needle-like teeth. Its jaw went slack and then snapped shut, sending more sound out around it, reverberating through the landscape, bouncing auditory images back to the predator's mind.

The Echo didn't have eyes, but it could still see them—if they made noise, or if it echolocated while they were moving. Looking at the large flaring nostrils, he thought it might be able to smell them, too. It probably had heard the truck come in. Maybe smelled the fumes. In a world overrun by the smells of nature, the Ram's exhaust would stand out. It might not smell like lunch, but different enough to pique a predator's interest.

Ella turned around and delivered her assessment, whispering, "It's an Apex."

"Apex?" Jakob asked.

"Lone predator," Anne said. "One on one, they're top of the food chain. Pack hunters like the Stalkers can take care of them, but solo, they're the most dangerous, and evolved."

"It also means that it was a predator before the ExoGenetic changes. Apex Predators are typically more specialized and evolved than something that started out eating grass. Bats weren't big, but they were skilled and agile hunters."

"So, if it started as a bat, why is it out there now, in broad daylight?" Jakob asked.

Ella glanced out the window, watching the Echo. "It's malnourished. Desperate. Prey must be scarce in this area."

"Making it even more dangerous," Peter said, his grim gaze fixed on the Echo.

"We can't stay here," Jakob said.

Ella shook her head. "We can't leave. It would make short work of the truck. But we also can't stay here. We're too exposed. When the sun goes down, there will be other predators out."

Jakob's stomach soured like acid had just been poured down his throat.

His mind and body were still recovering from the Stalker's assault, not to mention the destruction of his childhood home.

"You want to go out there?"

"To the church," Ella said. "Quietly."

By default, Jakob looked to his father for the final say. He knew what his father had done for a living before becoming a farmer. If someone had a better plan for this situation, it would be him. J

akob's stomach felt like it would melt away when his father answered, "Sounds like a plan. Backpacks, the handgun, and shotgun. Anything that makes noise, leave it behind."

He demonstrated by reaching into his shirt and removing his dog tags.

Jakob checked himself, finding only the carabineer he kept clipped to his belt loop, a childhood habit turned fashion statement. He unclipped it and put it on the seat. There were two backpacks inside the cab. The third, packed for Ella and Anne was still in the truck bed.

"We'll open just one door," Peter said, looking back at Jakob and Anne. "So, you two will have to climb over the seat. They both nodded. "If it comes at us, you guys get under the truck." Two more nods.

Peter looked at Ella, and she gave him a nod. Moving slowly, he put his hand on the door handle and gently pulled. With his other hand, he held the door tightly so it wouldn't clunk open. The latch pulled away with the tiniest of thumps, but everyone in the truck froze, slowly turning to see if the Echo had noticed. Its head was turned away from them, rotating slowly. When Peter pushed the door open a crack, another trumpet blast of echolocation pulsed through the air, freezing them again.

Jakob had done nothing but sit still, but his heart was pounding like he was running a race. Adrenaline surged anew, narrowing his vision, heightening his senses, and boosting his anxiety. When the sound fell away, his father resumed opening the door, seemingly unfazed. How men like him went to war and came back with their humanity intact, Jakob had no idea. He didn't think he had that kind of strength. But here were Ella and Anne, who had endured horrors of their own, and they still seemed normal. Of course, he'd known them for less than 24 hours, and a good portion of that time was spent asleep, but they were more well-adjusted than a lot of people he knew before the ExoGen apocalypse.

Peter slid out of his seat, his boots hitting the pavement without a sound. Ella followed, crawling across the front seat like she was moving through honey. When she reached the pavement, she leaned back in, lifted the shotgun out by the barrel and waved at Anne to follow. The girl moved with surprising grace and unbelievable silence, testing each handhold and foot placement before fully committing, keeping three points of contact at all times. She looked like a spider. Like a predator.

This isn't the first time she's done something like this, Jakob thought, and he was suddenly struck by the realization that despite being a strong, fast, and smart teenage boy, he was the weak link in the quartet. Of all of them, he'd never had to fight for his survival before. Well, once, but never before and not since.

Had Jakob's eyes been closed, he would never have known that Anne had left. She slipped out of the car, moved to the rear wheel, and crouched down, disappearing from view. When it was his turn, he reached up and grabbed the back of the front seat. The leather creaked in his shaking hand.

Peter leaned into the cab. "Just move slow. Take your time. Think about each movement. We're not in a rush."

Jakob got his feet under him and lifted his body up. The seat squeaked under his hand again. *How did Anne do this so quietly?* he wondered, and then he remembered how light she had felt in his arms the night before. She was a wiry little kid and probably malnourished, while Jakob had eaten well and weighed one sixty—just twenty-five pounds shy of his father.

"Just like that," Peter said. "One foot at a time. Distribute the—"

Jakob froze.

His father was looking past him, through the passen-ger's side, at the Echo. "What?"

Peter raised an open palm. *Wait.*

The trumpet blast was so powerful that Jakob flinched, nearly losing his grip on the seat. His father put a hand on his back, steadying him, eyes never leaving the window.

Peter turned his hand around and waved Jakob on, uttering just a single word. "Faster."

Three points of contact, Jakob told himself. *Stay quiet. Move faster!*

He heard the Echo's clomping lower jaw sending pulses of noise toward them, and he tried to stop for each, but failed for most. When he found himself fully in the front seat, he felt a measure of relief. The rest was easy. But it was then that he saw fear creep into his father's eyes. Jakob knew the man wasn't worried about himself.

He's worried about me.

Jakob chanced a look back. The Echo was just a hundred feet away now, approaching slowly, its long forelimbs crunching into the bed of cabbage with each step, its gait awkward but menacing. He spun forward just as the thing unleashed another trumpet blast. The sound hurt his ears, making him flinch again, and as he reached forward, his hand missed the seat.

Jakob sucked in a breath as he sprawled forward, out of the truck, his face rushing toward the pavement.

His arms blasted with pain as what felt like two pit bulls clamped down on his shoulders. He nearly shouted but didn't. Instead, he snapped to a stop, his face just inches from the pavement. His father had caught him by the shoulders. Peter lowered Jakob's hands to the pavement, until he was supporting his own weight. When his father let go, Jakob remained rooted in place.

He looked under the truck, his view of the Echo upside down. He could only see its smooth, black limbs, but they weren't moving.

It heard me, he thought. *It's looking for us, but the truck has it confused.*

A sudden tug on Jakob's waist nearly caused him to shout out again. He pictured the Echo's long arm reaching over the truck, the spear-like tip punching through his gut. But it was just his father, lifting him out of the truck and giving him the world's first apocalyptic wedgie.

The Echo let out a series of loud jaw snaps. Peter stopped moving, holding Jakob's rear end off the ground. The boy's face burned with embarrassment, but this was the life of the weakest link. *I practically rang the dinner bell. This is what I get.* And it was a price he would gladly pay if it meant none of them got eaten. But as his father lowered him to the ground and the Echo took another stride forward, he didn't think all of them would make it out of this alive. And since Ella and Peter were fighters, and Anne was a little girl—and protected—he thought that someone would be him.

Back on solid ground, Jakob looked for Anne and found her missing. He turned toward the church and found Anne and Ella—her backpack over her shoulders—already crab walking in their weird, totally silent way, in clear view to anything with eyes, but invisible to the Echo.

Peter ducked next to him and motioned for the cabbage with his head.

Jakob shook his head. He couldn't climb over a seat without making noise, how could he crawl across an open field of densely packed cabbage? It was a death sentence.

Peter took Jakob's chin in his hand and burrowed into the boy's mind with his stern eyes, telling him that if he didn't move now, they were both going to die. And he was right. So, Jakob carefully stepped toward the cabbage, leaned out over it, and planted his hands onto one of the green balls, palming it like he might a basketball. The vegetation, growing larger and denser than the former non-GMO variety ever could, was firm, holding his weight with ease. He brought his foot forward, stepping on another plant with equal success.

I can do this, he told himself, freezing when a trumpet blast sounded out from just behind the truck. He flinched, but remained rooted in place, a frozen object unmoving in the Echo's auditory gaze.

That was when Anne slipped and fell forward. He saw the movement during the height of the Echo's cry. It was subtle. Barely anything.

But it was enough.

She'd been seen.

19

The Echo galloped around the truck. Its long forelimbs gave it the appearance of a running, short-legged man with forearm crutches, the legs moving triple-time to keep up with the longer gaited arms. It moved with frantic urgency, its rib cage flexing with each hurried breath. But it didn't charge after Anne. Instead, it stopped next to the truck, turning its head back and forth, listening.

It lost her, Peter thought.

For that brief moment, the Echo had registered the girl's sudden movement, but she was invisible once more, wisely lying still on the bed of cabbage.

While the Echo might not be smart enough to remember where it detected the movement, it understood that it was not alone. *It can smell us,* Peter realized, watching the big nose twitch. *But it's not like a bloodhound. It can't get a direction from smell alone. It's dependent on its hearing for that. For now. Until it adapts.*

He understood the Echo's evolution. Most creatures would run away from something as large and deadly as this. Other Apexes might attack. Either way, its prey would be moving and making noise. It wasn't accustomed to the silent treatment.

When the Echo stepped forward, what they believed was its elbow, landed just a foot away from his crouched form. It had two wide feet tipped with four digits, each with short black claws. But it was the hands that held his attention. At the end of the long black arms, what he thought was the elbow, was actually a wrist. Four fingers sprouted from the joint, each sporting long talons, but it was the thumb that was pointed upward, forming the four-foot-long, black spear tip.

The Echo breathed deeply through its nose, smelling them, but not targeting them. It exhaled and clomped its jaws shut. Peter tried to imagine what the thing could see when the sound bounced back. Could it see their shapes? He thought so, but there hadn't been people in this part of the world—in most of the world—for so long, it might not recognize them as living things by shape alone.

A trumpet blast nearly sent Peter's hands to his ears, but that was the kind of reaction the monster was looking for. When the sound faded down to a rumble in the Echo's chest, Peter's ears continued to ring.

Thankfully, no one reacted to the sound. But their luck would eventually run out. Ella was frozen in place, her hands and feet holding her body above the cabbage bed, but she couldn't hold that position indefinitely. Her arms were bent and the muscles in her chest would eventually cramp. He thought he detected a quiver in her arms already, the strength wavering. She had become a hardened woman, tough and resourceful, but she'd been through hell and was no doubt in severe pain from the wounds on her stomach. He'd stitched them as best he could, but he wasn't a doctor. Too much strain and the stitches would give.

He glanced to his side, not moving his head. Jakob was on his knees, seated and still. He could stay there for hours if needed. Anne, too. The girl lay atop the cabbage. Her low profile might not even register with the Echo's auditory sight. He evaluated himself next. His legs were starting to burn from the crouched position, but he could hold the pose for another hour before needing to shift, and then he could inch himself down without making a sound.

It's going to find Ella, he decided.

There was no avoiding it. And she was smart enough to realize it, too. He tried to picture what she'd do, what he'd do. *She's going to run. Put distance between herself and Anne. Sacrifice herself so her child can live.* That's what he would do.

But that's not what she did. Not even close.

Peter watched in silence as Ella lifted the fingers of her right hand, bending them up. During the silence between jaw snaps, Anne turned her head toward her mother, watching. Ella moved the digits just a few times, and he saw Anne give the slightest of nods. They were communicating, but what were they saying?

He deciphered part of the message when Ella rapidly stabbed her index finger toward the church twice. *She's telling her to run for the church. But why? That will just get her killed.*

Unless the thing was preoccupied.

Realizing what was coming, Peter risked turning his head toward Jakob, making eye contact. He mouthed the words, "Get ready. Run for the church." Jakob looked horrified by the suggestion but gave a nod. When Peter looked back to Ella, she was already counting down with her fingers, lowering one at a time. Peter held up three fingers and quickly lowered one, letting Jakob know about the countdown. He mirrored Ella's finger drop, down to one, but was still surprised by what came next.

"Now!" Ella shouted. The sound instantly drew the Echo's attention. It trumpeted in response, lunging toward Ella, straight through the path Jakob would take toward the church. The monster wasn't the only one in motion, though. Anne got to her feet and bolted for the church.

The girl's movement during the trumpet blast registered with the Echo. Perhaps finally recognizing the flight of prey, it turned its attention and body toward Anne, kicking up a confetti of green cabbage leaves as its claws hacked through the plants.

But the next sound, a *shk-chk* followed by an explosion, changed everything. Buckshot struck the side of the Echo's head, punching small holes in its ears, but doing no real damage. It did, however, get the Echo's attention. It trumpeted again, straight toward Ella, who was standing on her feet, clutching the shotgun. The monster veered away from Anne, heading toward the larger prey that had caused it pain.

Peter snapped his finger at Jakob and pointed toward Anne and the church. "Go!"

Jakob looked mortified, remaining locked in place, unable to move. Peter was frustrated by his son's inaction, but he couldn't blame the boy. This was too much.

The shotgun roared again, pulling Peter's attention back to the action. The Echo flinched as the cloud of metal pellets struck it, head on, but it didn't slow. The creature's tightly packed, coarse fur and thick, leathery skin shielded it from the brunt of the weapon's lethal force. The pellets would hurt, but they wouldn't kill with anything short of a point-blank shot—and Ella didn't have time to pump the weapon again.

Moving like a gunslinger, Peter drew his handgun and squeezed off three rounds at the Echo's head. The first round missed, but the second round struck the side of its head, ricocheting off the skull, but carving a red line that sprayed blood. The third round punched a clean hole through the left ear, close to the base. The effect was minimal, causing the Echo to shake its head, but the slight distraction was all Ella needed. She dived to the side just as the Echo thrust one of its spear thumbs forward, impaling a head of cabbage.

When Ella hit the cabbage floor, she shouted in pain, attempting to roll over and fire. But she was slowed, and when she made it onto her back, the spreading deep red on her stomach revealed the source of her pain. The wounds had opened and were bleeding through the bandage and her shirt.

Without thought, Peter charged, stepping up onto the unsteady cabbage crop and firing his weapon. The bullets punched against the Echo's back as it raised an arm, long thumb poised to stab Ella. If the rounds hurt the Echo, the creature didn't show it, flinching with each impact, but not reacting.

Bullets can't solve all problems, Peter thought, remembering the words of a drill instructor, and dropping the gun. *Sometimes you need to use a knife.* He drew the blade from the sheath on his belt. It was sharpened to a microscopic edge, capable of cutting most anything. He threw himself at the Echo's back, putting all the energy he could muster into the blow.

There was a moment of resistance and then the blade sank, all four inches slipping into the monster's back, driving between two of the monstrous ribs pushing up against the taut skin. The Echo trumpeted again, but this time, higher pitched, expressing pain. The thumb-spear still stabbed toward Ella, but the aim was off as the creature spun around with such force that Peter, knife in hand, was flung away. He landed on the cabbage beside Ella. Incensed, the Echo raised both arms, aiming its long thumbs at the pair. Ella fired another shot, but this time the Echo didn't even flinch. The pain in its back blinded it to the irritating shotgun blast. This close, Peter could see the pellets lodged in the Echo's thick skin.

Some simply fell away. But all were useless.

"Put it against the skin!" Peter shouted. "Point blank!"

But even as he spoke the words, the Echo, standing above them like an executioner, thrust the twin javelins down, its aim unwavering.

20

Ella closed her eyes. After all this time, fighting through the new wilds of an ExoGenetic America, she had finally met her match—an oversized Apex bat with spear thumbs. She had survived worse. The Stalkers, with their large numbers, were worse. But things had changed. She and Anne were no longer alone, and as she waited for death, she wondered if stopping at Peter's biodome and enlisting his help had been the right choice. If she hadn't, Peter and his son would still be safe and fed, while she and Anne...

Part of her would have liked to think they would have made it this far and silently crossed the distance without trouble, but she knew it wasn't true. When Peter found her the night before, she'd been on her last leg. And she wasn't feeling much better now. If not for the truck carrying them the distance, she didn't think she would have made it more than a few miles before collapsing.

Either way, she decided, *I was going to die.* The problem she had was that she'd also sentenced Peter and his son to die with her. Anne might survive the day. Maybe even a few days. But eventually, the girl would be caught, and would die horribly. The image of her daughter being chewed pulled a scream from her lips, as she watched the black spear thrust toward her already bleeding gut. But the sound of her voice was blotted out by the cacophonous staccato roar of something more powerful than the shotgun's blast or the Echo's sonar cry.

Ella's eyes blinked open as the Echo arched its back, pulling the spear up and away from her belly. Holes opened up in its chest as its inside burst outward, showering her and Peter in gore. Large bullets punched through the body like a swarm of savage bees, buzzing through flesh and slaying the beast. As the already dead Echo fell to its knees, the bullets continued to tear at it, tracing a line up its chest and to its face, which opened up, and disgorged a mass of white, red and gray material. It wasn't until this very visible sign of defeat that the bullets stopped flying.

She and Peter rolled away in opposite directions as the Echo fell forward, splashing its soupy insides all over the cabbage. She winced as her flexing abs stressed the stitches in her gut even further. She'd felt a few of them tear her skin earlier, but most were still intact. Lying on her back, she picked up her head and looked back at the armored truck. Jakob stood behind the smoking machine gun, eyes wide and frozen on the carnage he'd wrought. When Peter sat up, the boy's focus shifted.

"Are you okay?" the boy shouted.

His father gave a thumbs up. "Nice shooting."

Ella agreed. Jakob had saved them both and proven her fears about him wrong, but there wasn't time to say so. She climbed to her feet, clutching her stomach. "Anything living within a few miles is already headed in our direction. Once they smell the blood..."

A clank of metal announced the opening of the church's front door. Anne leaned out. "The first floor is clear. C'mon!" She disappeared inside, letting the door swing shut.

Peter gave a nod and shouted to Jakob. "Take what you can. Get inside."

As the boy set to work, taking supplies from the back of the pickup, Peter turned to her. Pointed to her stomach. "How bad is it?"

"Just a few stitches. It can wait." She peeled off her shirt, which was covered in her blood and the Echo's, oblivious to her naked torso.

Peter, on the other hand, noticed. "What are you doing?"

"Anything that finds this body with its nose will have no trouble sniffing us out, too, especially if we smell like a recent meal. We need to ditch the clothes. Leave them with the body.

Peter sighed but stripped. He turned to his son, who was already averting his eyes as he walked past carrying a box of supplies. "We need to change. We'll be in soon."

Ella tried to give Peter the same privacy that his son was granting them both, but her eyes wandered as he removed his pants. He was in the same staggering shape she remembered, muscles twitching just beneath the skin. She often wondered what life would have been like if he had stayed, but she always got hung up on the idea of being a homewrecker. In the long run, he'd made the right choice, morally, for his wife and his son, but that didn't stop her from wishing he hadn't.

Peter glanced up and looked surprised, caught in the act of peeking, but then he squinted, no doubt realizing she'd already been watching him. She deflected attention from her wandering eyes by saying, "Your boxers look clean."

"Yours, too," he said. She was wearing women's boxer briefs that ended just below her butt. Not exactly sexy, but not hiding any curves. Stepping away from the giant corpse, the two put on fresh clothes. Peter put on cargo shorts and a T-shirt while Ella dressed in jeans but held her T-shirt. Both shirts were black, but the blue jeans and beige shorts wouldn't do much to conceal them.

Partially dressed and carrying bloodied boots, Ella said, "We need water."

Peter led her to the truck and took out two sealed gallons of water. She popped the cap and handed it to him. "Pour it over my head. We need all the blood off."

She leaned forward and Peter slowly poured the water over her head. She scrubbed her bristly bald head, thankful that her hair wasn't long. Washing the blood out would have been impossible. She rubbed her hands over her face and finished by washing the blood from her hands.

She then took the gallon and poured water over the boots, rinsing away the blood. When she was done, she said, "Your turn." Peter repeated the steps, washing himself and then his boots.

Free of the creature's blood and its scent, Ella said, "Duct tape?"

Peter grinned. "Of course."

He fetched the roll from the storage crate and handed her the black tape. As he held it out, she noticed his hand shaking. She took hold of his hand, steadying it. "You get used to it."

"I know."

"Sorry, I sometimes forget who you were."

"Still am," he said. "Just a little rusty." He turned his hand over, depositing the tape in her fingers. The connection was brief, but it let her feel human again, for a moment. But just a moment. What she was about to do would require all the toughness she'd developed over the past years.

She peeled off strips of tape, gently sticking them one at a time to the side of the truck bed. When she had ten five-inch strips, she put the tape down and peeled off the now blood-soaked gauze Peter had placed over her wound. She tossed the red square away, picked up a gallon of water.

"Here," Peter said, holding out a bandana. She took it, soaked it, and wiped her stomach clean. Blood continued to seep through the opened stitches, but not fast, and in a moment, it wouldn't matter.

"Let me do it," Peter said.

Ella scoured the area around them, looking for motion. She had a clear view, nearly to the horizon in most directions. She saw nothing. That didn't mean they were alone, just that she couldn't see what was there. Still, she thought they had time. "Be quick."

"First time you said that," Peter said, getting a laugh that would have been more forceful if it didn't pull at the stitches. She laid down on the open truck bed hatch, aware of her nakedness, but uncaring. Peter had seen her naked before. Not quite so skinny and muscle toned, but under much more romantic circumstances. True to form, Peter was all business, peeling the duct tape from the truck, pinching her skin together and then sealing it with the tape. Once the open stitches were back in place, he attacked the rest, layering and wrapping her stomach with an armored plate of duct tape.

"It's going to hurt like hell when it comes off," he said, stepping away, "but it won't need to come off until it's healed...or if infection sets in. And if you feel that—"

"I'll tell you, doctor. Thanks." She sat up and put on her shirt. She hopped down from the truck, trying to look stronger than she felt. She wanted to fall into his arms. To be supported. But she'd learned that the only person she could rely on was herself. Relaxing that rule could lead to mistakes, and mistakes to death—hers or Anne's. "Now comes the fun part. Have a bucket?"

He squinted at her, but climbed into the truck bed, rummaged through the storage crate, and pulled out a bucket full of tools.

"Ditch the tools."

He did as she asked and stepped back down with an empty five-gallon bucket. By the time he rejoined her, she'd already torn three heads of cabbage out of the ground and put them aside.

"You're not planning on eating those?"

She didn't justify the stupid question with a reply. Instead, she dug her hands into the soil, lifted up two heaping handfuls, and smeared it around on the front of her shirt.

"Ahh," he said, dropping to his knees, following her lead. He dug his hands into the dirt and slathered his body. While they weren't covered in blood anymore, they still smelled like themselves, like human animals. To survive, to remain undetected by whatever heightened senses the next predator had, they would have to smell like the land itself.

After Peter finished coating his body, Ella rubbed some dirt between her fingers and applied it to his cheeks. Her hands stopped, and for a moment, she just held him.

"We should head in," Peter whispered after a moment.

Ella sniffed and turned away, her cheeks turning red. She dug more dirt and flung it into the bucket. "For the kids," she said, and Peter helped her. With the bucket filled, Peter stood and helped Ella to her feet. Standing once more, Ella felt exposed and did a scan of the area once more.

Nothing.

After all that noise, nothing.

She wasn't buying it.

The world wasn't yet that devoid of life. Moving in silence, it was possible to avoid other living things for weeks, but after that racket... She was expecting dinner guests. And since there wasn't any sign of them yet, that meant one of two things—they were small, or they were smart—and she knew from experience that neither were good things.

"Let's get inside," she said. "The sun is going down."

21

Anne pushed on the church's metal front door. The green paint still looked new, and the white-painted wood around it hadn't yet started to show signs of chipping. She slipped inside, pursued by yet another trumpet blast from the Echo. Part of her felt guilty for fleeing into the church while the others faced the creature, but she knew there was nothing she could do to help, and that one way or the other, she had to determine whether the building was safe. So while the others struggled with the Echo, she stepped into the dim foyer and let the door close behind her.

She glanced back at the window beside the door, seeing movement through the sheer shade, but she didn't move toward it. She hoped they survived, but if they didn't, she didn't want to see it. The prospect of living without them horrified her, but her mother had been preparing her for that potential fate for months. After all, she was important. She had to survive.

"Even if it means leaving you behind?" she'd asked Ella two months ago.

Her mother had put her hands on Anne's cheeks, fire in her eyes. "If things look bad, you leave me behind. No goodbyes. No tears. You have to be strong. If I survive, I'll find you. If not, you know what to do."

And she did know what to do, but that didn't make it easy. Since that time, they'd had several close calls, but nothing like this, nothing leading her to take her mother's advice and leave her behind. Not that she was going far, but she was acutely aware that her mother was facing death outside, while she was safe inside the church.

But how safe was she?

If the others died, would the Echo come for her? Would it remember seeing her enter the church?

Be brave, she told herself. *Be smart. Find someplace secure. Someplace to hide. For everyone.*

They're going to survive. They have to.

The sunlight streaking through the foyer windows cast her shadow on the thin, blue industrial carpet, while revealing swirls of dust kicked up by her entrance. Two separate double doors blocked the way ahead. To the left was a winding staircase leading up and down. And to the right, men's and women's bathrooms.

The basement was her goal, and her eyes lingered on the steps leading down, but heading down there before checking the rest of the church could be a deadly mistake. 'Know your surroundings first,' her mother had taught her. 'Then settle in. Even if you're wounded. Sleeping in a predator's den is a quick way to die.'

So, she checked the bathrooms first, ignoring the muffled trumpet blast outside. She opened the doors a crack, peeking inside. Both were immaculate, smelling faintly of ancient sanitary chemicals. She moved to the double doors next, pushing through into a wide-open sanctuary. Two rows of long wooden pews separated by an aisle stretched down the room to a small stage. There was no podium, but there was a collection of dusty musical instruments and microphone stands.

She moved silently over the ruby red rug lining the aisle. She'd never been in a church before, and she knew very little about the concept of God taught in them. She knew her mother staunchly opposed any kind of religion, though, so she moved to the back of the room without any kind of emotional response besides fearing what might lurk behind the next door, which was to the left of the stage.

She paused at the door, her hand on the knob. *Please be empty.* The knob spun without a sound, but a sudden thunderous roar made her jump, yanking her hand back. It took a moment for her to recognize the sound. Gunfire. A lot of it. And loud. The machine gun on the truck.

They killed it, she thought. The Echo was certainly dead, but who was left alive? Spurred by the question, she shoved the door open and found an empty office lined with shelves of thick books. The only decoration on the wall was a framed poster of footprints in the sand. A heavy wooden desk held a lone book, left open.

Glancing back at the sanctuary, she stepped inside the room and looked at the book. At the top of the page, it said LUKE. She recognized the book as the one her mother always read, but never let her look at. The forbidden fruit nearly proved too much to resist. She wanted to read that book, mostly because her mother didn't want her to, but it could wait. She retreated from the office and ran back through the sanctuary.

Back in the foyer, she shoved the front door open and was relieved to see a dead Echo and her mother alive—Jakob and Peter, too. "The first floor is clear," she shouted to the group. "C'mon!"

She ducked back inside the foyer, once again on the lookout for trouble inside the building. But knowing she'd soon have company, she waited. Jakob arrived two minutes later, a box in his hands full of supplies, including a small propane stove.

"As much as I like hot food," she said, "heating it up makes it smell stronger. Attracts attention."

"Right," The boy said, looking a little shell shocked and dejected. "No more hot food. Great."

"Haven't been outside much?" she asked.

"Try not at all."

Anne felt simultaneously sorry for and envious of Jakob. He'd lived in safety for the past two years, but it had left him unprepared for life outside, where ExoGenetic predators lurked. "Life out here, on the run, it sucks. But you'll get used to it."

"If I don't get us killed first," he said.

"Hey." She gripped his arm hard, garnering his unwavering attention. "You got us away from the Stalkers and avoided hitting that Swine. That wasn't easy. I couldn't have done it, and I doubt my mother could have, either. *And* you just saved both our parents. Killed an Apex on your first try. So, you don't know all the tricks of surviving out here. Big deal. I do."

He grinned. "You going to teach me?"

"Everything I know," she said. "Well, not everything. You're not *that* smart."

Jakob laughed. "Okay, kid. So, tell me, what next?"

She looked at the ceiling. "Next, we clear the second floor. And then the basement."

"Lead the way, Master Yoda."

"Master who?" she asked.

Jakob looked as confused as Anne felt, but answered, "*Star Wars*. It's a movie. A bunch of movies. But I guess you're too young to remember. Or something."

Anne rolled her eyes. "Or something. I've never even seen a movie."

"Geez. Well, that sucks. Of course, there isn't much that *doesn't* suck anymore. But still...no *Star Wars*?" Jakob said, heading for the stairs, taking the lead after all. "So, what should I look for? To clear the floor? Aside from things trying to eat my face, I mean."

"Best way to tell if you're not alone is smell, especially in a place like this, which is pretty much odor-free. If you smell anything animal, fecal, or earthy, you're probably not alone."

Jakob started up the rugged stairs. "Fecal, huh?"

"Shit," she said.

"I know what it is. It's just a weird way for a twelve-year-old to say it." Jakob paused on the top step, looking into a hallway with two doors on the right side. Large windows lined the walls, giving them clear views of the nursery and the Sunday School rooms that were conjoined by a doorway. Despite being empty, Jakob led the way inside the Sunday School room. Anne followed him in, taking in the array of brightly colored objects that she knew were designed for children, but with which she had no experience. A round table sat in the middle of the floor. Small chairs surrounded it. A large picture of a wooden boat, full of animals was tacked to the wall. A man stood on the boat, holding a dove that clutched a small green plant in its mouth. The man was smiling. A rainbow arched up over the scene. In each line of the rainbow were words. She read them aloud. "Never again will I punish the Earth for the sinful things its people do. All of them have evil thoughts from the time they are young, but I will never destroy everything that breathes, as I did this time. As long as the Earth remains, there will be planting and harvest, cold and heat; winter and summer, day and night."

"Well," Jakob said, standing at the window looking out at the road. "He got the planting and harvest part right. Not so much with not destroying everything."

"Who did?" she asked.

"God."

"Was he a teacher?"

Jakob chuckled. "Some people think so. Part of him, anyway. But for this story, God is the...guy or whatever, who created the Earth. The whole universe. And everyone in it."

"God didn't make me. I came from my mother" Anne said, revolted by the idea that some strange person might have made her. Someone who had once destroyed 'everything that breathes.' "But...if it *were* true, then you'd be wrong to blame him for killing everyone this time. My mother did that, too."

"I suppose," Jakob said, and he opened the window's curtain a little further. "What are they doing?"

Anne joined him at the window. Their parents knelt by the road, rubbing dirt over their bodies. "Hiding their scent. Don't worry, they'll bring some dirt for us, too."

Jakob shook his head. "Never had any doubt."

Anne sensed he was about to leave. "Is your father a nice man?"

"Nicest I know," Jakob said with a smirk, then added, "But yeah, he's a good guy. Trustworthy."

"Are you sure?" Anne asked.

Jakob turned from the window, looking at Anne. "Why?"

"Just want to be sure my mother chose the right person."

"For what?"

Anne was quiet for a moment.

She wasn't sure how to answer that question.

It was complicated. There were layers. Too many. So, she said, "Look at them."

Outside the window, framed by an armored Dodge Ram and a dead ExoGenetic Apex predator, Ella rubbed dirt on Peter's cheek. Her hands moved in gentle circles while the pair stared into each other's eyes.

"I think they were good friends," Anne said. "From before."

"Yeah," Jakob said, stepping away from the window and heading for the door. "I think they were, too."

She stopped him in the door by asking, "Maybe we can be friends?"

Jakob smiled back at her. "I think we already are. But not like them."

Anne looked back out the window. The affection her mother felt for Jakob's father was clear, and as far as she was concerned, unfounded, whether or not they had been friends before. She'd never spoken of him. He couldn't be that important. "Definitely not."

"C'mon," Jakob said. "Let's go check downstairs, cover ourselves in dirt, and spend the night cowering in a basement."

Anne let the curtain fall back into place, sighed, and said, "If we're lucky."

22

Peter took first watch. He sat alone in the Sunday School room over-looking what should have been a parking lot but was just an endless field of moonlit cabbage. The plants took on a dark blue hue at night, visible, but distorted by shadow, like ocean waves frozen in place. He could see the truck beyond, parked in the middle of the road, light from the half moon glinting off the side mirror.

The dead Echo was a dark silhouette, blotting out a part of the field, the details of its demise concealed by the darkness.

How did it come to this? he wondered.

He knew the answer. Understood the science and the sequence of events that had led to disaster. The reality that was the world was old news. What he couldn't fathom was how the people in charge, at ExoGen and in the Government, had missed the gene-altering capabilities of RC-714. Even more, he didn't understand how Ella had missed it.

Never had.

She was smarter than that. But she was also ambitious. But not selfishly so. As long as he'd known her, she'd been concerned about starving people. *Feeding the hungry masses had always been a pipe dream for you, Ella.* But then she grew up and saw a path to eradicating hunger, through genetics. It was a noble cause, but in the end, it had blinded her.

That was what he told himself, because the alternative, that she had knowingly released the gene-altering crops that resulted in the destruction of mankind, was unthinkable. And yet, someone had known. Someone had loaded that gun and pulled the trigger with the same lethal intent of a firing squad.

"Wine still make you sleepy?" Ella asked from the doorway.

Peter's heart slammed against his chest, but he managed to hide how badly she'd startled him. She was lucky he hadn't spun around and shot her.

"It does," he confessed.

She stepped into the dull moonlight filtering through the window. Like him, she was covered in grime, bits and pieces of soil clinging to her body. She smelled of earth and the outdoors. It wasn't unpleasant, at least not to a farmer. Good dirt meant life, or at least it used to.

Ella lifted an open bottle of wine and poured the dark liquid into a plastic cup. "Found it in the kitchen. The canned food is too new to eat, but the wine is from 2000." She finished pouring and turned the bottle around so he could see the vintage on the label.

"Old school communion," Peter said, taking the cup. "I thought only Catholics did that."

"I wouldn't know," Ella said.

Peter placed the cup on the short, round table without taking a drink. "I can't drink it, though."

"It's 2:00 am," she said. "I've got second watch. Anne will take over at five."

"*Anne* is going to keep watch?" Peter's surprise was impossible to hide. The kid was twelve years old. How could she have the discipline to stay awake while the sun was still down? He wouldn't trust Jakob with the job.

The boy could fall asleep standing up.

"It's been just the two of us for a long time," Ella said. "We're used to splitting the night watch fifty-fifty, so this is a treat."

When Peter didn't look convinced, Ella put her hand on his shoulder. The touch sent his stomach swirling. *Knock it off,* he told himself. *Stay focused. She might not be the person you remember, or even the person you thought she was.*

"I checked the doors. Still locked. Still barricaded. Nothing is getting inside. At least not without making a hell of a lot of noise and getting a face full of shotgun." She hoisted the shotgun off her shoulder and leaned it against the wall beneath the window. Her small frame, silhouetted by the moonlight, looked fragile. In need of protection. But that wasn't the case. Not at all. She was a stronger person than he'd have ever believed. And capable of more than he could imagine.

"Did you know?" he asked.

She turned toward him. "Know what?"

"What RC-714 would do to the human race."

He couldn't see her frown, but something in her silhouetted body language got the message across. "I warned you about it."

"Before then," he said. "Before it was released."

"*What?*"

The sudden swell of anger made Peter lean back, but he took it as a good sign.

"You think I knowingly released this hell on the world? Peter, you know me. You know—"

"I *knew* you," he said. "You're different."

"I've been fighting for my life. For my, for *our*, daughter's life. You don't think I'd rather be tucked away in a lab? Why would I choose this life for anyone? I wanted to save the world, not kill it." She turned away from him. "When did you become an asshole?"

Peter picked up the cup of wine and stood beside Ella. He looked out the window for a moment, took a sip of wine and let their emotions settle. "Here's the thing. Someone knew what would happen. Probably several someones. You might have missed it, and I really hope that's the case—that you wanted to feed the world so badly that you made a mistake. I'm willing to believe that because...I think I still know you. But someone knew. Someone at ExoGen. Someone still alive in San Francisco."

Silence returned as the pair kept watch.

After several minutes, Ella took a swig from the wine bottle. "Doesn't make me sleepy. A slut, maybe, but not sleepy."

Peter said nothing. His silence kept the conversation from being derailed.

"I didn't know," she said again, "but you're right."

Despite being confident in his assessment, Peter still felt surprised. He turned his head toward her. She stared out the window, her face cast in pale blue light.

"I don't know how many of them knew," she said, "but it's likely most of the board knew...the government liaisons, some of the security staff. Phil McKay, the CEO...he knew, for sure. The rest is speculation. I figured it out eventually. It was stupid, really." She shook her head, exasperated by what she was about to reveal. "I was in an elevator at the ExoGen bio-dome. I was alone. And bored. So, I read the old, out-of-date inspection certificate left on the elevator wall. I read it three times before a detail jumped out. The certificate was dated just five months after we discovered RC-714. Just two months after it had been released into the world."

"So, the ExoGen bio-dome hadn't been built in response to the global metamorphosis—"

"Or even my discovery of what consuming RC-714 would eventually lead to, a month after that."

"It was built in preparation for it," Peter concluded.

"That's what I realized, too."

"Did you talk to anyone about it?"

She huffed out a laugh. "The atmosphere in the facility is...oppressive. Strict rules. Anyone breaking rules or causing problems is sent outside. If they survive a week, they can come back. No one ever came back. But once I knew, I began to see the course of events in reverse, and I understood. The development and release of RC-714 was a genocidal attack. A purge.

"It's why I started looking for a way to undo the damage done. It's why I left."

"But you weren't alone," Peter said.

"I told people I trusted, and over time, we developed an escape plan."

Peter felt dubious.

"Including a cross-country trek to a lab on George's Island?"

"I didn't say it was a good plan, but it was only a matter of time before they found out and cast us out, unprepared. When we left, we had survival gear, weapons, even protection."

"From Ed?"

"And others," she said. "The point is, when we left...when we escaped, we thought we were prepared for what we'd find. But none of us knew the changes that... Traits observed two years ago continued to evolve. We were prepared for predators, not...what we found."

"The Stalkers."

She shook her head. "There were others before the Stalkers. Apex predators. Other Betas. Packs of horrible things. The Stalkers were the worst though."

"And the Echo?"

"I've never seen anything like it before," she confessed. "Thank God there was just one of them."

"How many are there?" he asked. "How many new species?"

"There's no way to know, but there's one thing I'm sure of; while the overall population of life on Earth has dropped significantly, the biodiversity of what is left, is at an all-time high. Take two of the same animal species, separated by just a few miles, give them a year and some ExoGenetic food, and you'll have two totally different sets of adaptations. A dog living in the desert might adapt camel-like humps to retain water, while a dog living in the forest might develop hooked claws and larger pectoral muscles for climbing trees. Adaptation has been super-charged, and creatures are changing every day. In another year, I'm not sure we'll even be able to tell what species the ExoGens started out as."

"But you can undo it, right?"

"Not exactly," she said. "We can't change people back into people. But we can keep future generations from changing. The ExoGenetic crops can still feed the planet."

Peter spoke quietly. The shadows outside were moving now. "I'm not sure that more genetic tinkering is the solution."

"I see them," Ella said, whispering, and then continued the conversation. "Altering humanity's genetic code is the *only* solution. Humanity can make a comeback, but we're going to have to fight for it. And to fight, we have to be fed. You'll learn that in the next few weeks."

Peter wanted to argue the point, but the sound of crunching bones announced the arrival of predators and the start of a feast. His belly growled.

Maybe she's right, he thought, and he put down the wine glass. Death waited for them just outside the church. Sleep could wait.

23

Despite the sounds of rending flesh and breaking bones lasting a full hour, the night passed without incident. At 4:00 am, Peter had finally relinquished his post to Ella and had joined the kids in the basement kitchen.

Jakob had heard his father come in, and having a good sense of time, even in the middle of the night, he had known it was late. So, as he crouched over his father now, he felt bad about having to wake him up. But it was 6:30. The sun was officially up and would continue its daylong arc across the sky, with or without Peter. Ella's words.

She had already organized and inventoried the supplies, packed the truck, and reloaded weapons. All that was left for their journey to continue was for Jakob to rouse his father...after just two and half hours of sleep.

Sorry, Dad, he thought, and then he placed his hand on his father's shoulder. "Dad..."

Without flinching or opening his eyes, Peter said. "Three feet back."

"W-what?"

Peter opened his eyes. "Next time you wake me up, do it from three feet back. And don't touch me."

The tone in his father's voice disturbed him. Deep, gravelly, and tired, the man lying on the linoleum floor didn't sound much like his father. Covered in dirt, he didn't really look like him either.

"Why?"

Peter rolled from his side to his back, revealing a knife in his hand. Then he pushed himself up. The handgun was under his arm. He lifted the knife and slowly traced a line through the air, stopping short of Jakob's neck. The message was clear: *I couldn't slit your throat if you were three feet back.*

"You think you might become one of them? An ExoGen?"

Peter shook his head.

"Old reflexes are coming back. If you spend enough time in enemy territory, you'll develop them, too. It's just a precaution. Had I been in the middle of nightmare..."

"I get it," Jakob said, and he did. He'd woken from enough nightmares about his mother, kicking and punching, to know anyone around him might have received a fat lip. "But what about the gun?"

Peter sat up and slid the weapon into its holster. "Takes more than a knee-jerk reaction to lift a gun, aim, and pull the trigger. Not much more. And I've been trained to never fire a weapon without confirming my target first."

"So, I shouldn't sleep with a gun?"

Peter grinned. "You'd probably shoot yourself in your sleep." Jakob took his father's hand and helped him off the floor. He knew his father didn't really need help, but the contact reaffirmed their relationship. Despite the horrors of the past two days, and the horrible lesson his father just gave him, they were still a team.

"Same rule applies to Ella and Anne," Peter said. "They've both been out here for some time. Give them a wide berth when they're sleeping."

Jakob's mind drifted to the previous night. After Peter had returned to the kitchen and fallen asleep, Anne had snuggled up beside Jakob, looped her arm in his and fallen back asleep. There was nothing weird about it. Nothing romantic. The contact provided comfort, for them both, but apparently even comfort could be deadly now. "Good to know."

Peter looked around the empty kitchen. "Where are they?"

"Ella sent me to get you. She's packed the truck. Organized it, too."

Peter chuckled as he sheathed his knife. "Sounds like Ella."

Jakob's stomach twisted.

He'd been waiting to ask his father about her, and he might not get another chance for a while. He wasn't sure he really wanted to know the truth about her. The subject shook the foundations of his reality, which was already on shaky ground. Want or not, he needed to know. So, he said, "Tell me about Ella. Who is she to you? Why do you trust her?"

The discomfort washing over his father's face looked more intense than when they were fleeing from the Stalkers. He walked in a tight circle, rubbing his hands over his head, and then his face.

Before Peter could reply, Jakob added, "And don't sugar-coat it. You've probably been trained to lie, and I probably wouldn't see through it, but I'm old enough to handle the truth, and I think you owe it to me."

Peter stopped walking in circles, leaned against the dusty counter and said, "Ella is my oldest friend."

"*No lies,*" Jakob said.

Peter held up his hands, a placating gesture. "That's the truth. I've known her for most of my life. Since I was nine. Until High School, we were inseparable."

His father paused, so Jakob filled the gap, determined to keep the narrative moving. It wouldn't be long before Ella or Anne came down to find out what was taking so long.

"And during high school?"

"Puberty," Peter said. "You remember that. What happened next was probably inevitable. She...was my life. And then, we drifted. College took us apart. But we came back together, somehow ending up in the same place, again and again."

"Including after you were married."

Peter's eyes locked on the floor. The nod was nearly impossible to see, but the shame his father felt was palpable.

"That's why Mom hated her."

"Yes." Peter blinked his eyes and turned away from Jakob. "I think she knew that even though I loved her and chose her—and you—that I could never really stop loving Ella. Even if I loved your mom. Even if Ella loved someone else. She's...a part of me. A part of my soul, I guess, if you want total honesty."

"Sounds a little fruity for a Marine, if you ask me," Jakob said.

Peter laughed and wiped his eyes before turning back around. "We still good?"

"I already figured most of this," Jakob said. "But I wanted to hear it from you. Wanted to really understand who they were to you."

Jakob was surprised to see his father sag, as though air had just been let out of a balloon man. "There's more."

Unable to imagine what more there could be, Jakob just waited.

"Anne," his father said. "She might be your sister. Half-sister."

The swirling caldron of emotions that struck Jakob stumbled him back. He leaned against the wall, beside the door, then slid down to his butt. Sister... *A sister! Holy shit.* As confusion gave way to understanding and excitement about the idea, Peter's wording struck him. "What do you mean, 'might?'"

"Right now, all we have is Ella's word that she's mine."

"Does the timing fit?" Jakob asked. "Were you...with her twelve years ago? Is that when it happened?"

Peter nodded and said, "That doesn't make it real."

"But you trust her, right?"

"I want to," Peter said.

"But...?"

"It's not easy to trust someone after they helped kill the planet, intentionally or not."

"Right," Jakob said. "That."

"That."

"Does Anne know?"

"I don't think so," Peter said. "And it's probably her mother's place to tell her, not ours."

"She looks a little like you," Jakob said. He realized he'd already gone from skeptical to accepting and hopeful. A sister meant his family had grown, and he'd given up believing things like that were possible.

"I saw that, too," Peter said, "but in case you haven't noticed, Ella and I look a lot alike, too. Dark hair. Dark eyes. When we were kids, people thought we were siblings. Some thought we were twins. Anne looks more like Ella than anything. Like how I remember Ella as a kid."

Jakob hadn't realized how alike Ella and his father looked.

But now that he mentioned it... "I guess I see it. So how will you decide? It's not like you can take a DNA test."

"When I decide I can trust Ella again. Fully trust her, I mean." Peter helped Jakob to his feet, once again reestablishing the bond of father and son. "Until then, there's no reason to not accept them. Life outside the house is hard. Dangerous. But I think their presence in our lives is a blessing. A possible future."

"A family," Jakob said.

"We'll see," Peter said, and stepped into the doorway. "But best to not get your hopes up. This is a harsh world. You told me not to lie to you, so I'm not going to. Not ever. The odds of all four of us reaching Boston alive are... Well, they're not good."

Jakob had already come to the same conclusion, and expected himself to be the first to fall, but now that he might have a sister... The temptation to hope for a new, safer life, was significant. "Okay, C3PO. Thanks for the pick-me-up. Maybe don't tell me the odds."

"If that's what you want, Captain Solo." Peter led them out of the kitchen, arm around his son. They walked up the stairs, side by side, heading for the front door. "By the way, nice shooting yesterday. You'd have made a good Marine."

Peter pushed through the door, squinting in the morning sun. But he stopped short of exiting, saying, "What the hell?"

24

Peter stared at the field separating the church's front door from the road. What looked like a pixelated section of the cabbage crop—exactly where the Echo and its remains had lain, was missing. In its place was barren soil, which would hold new cabbage plants inside a month, if not sooner. But for now, it was a geometric scar of the previous day's violence.

His hand went for his gun, but he didn't draw it. Ella and Anne waited by the armored pickup, looking alert, but relaxed. Peter crept over the cabbage, the leafy green balls crunching under his feet. When he got close enough to the truck that he didn't need to shout, he asked, "Did you do this?"

"Found it like this," Ella said. She leaned against the truck bed, one leg propped up on the wheel behind her, arms crossed. Closer now, Peter could see the tension in her eyes. "There isn't a single drop of blood left. Every plant that was soiled has been removed and taken away. No sign of what did it. No prints. No scat. I've never seen this kind of behavior before."

Peter stepped onto the dirt. The softness of it underfoot felt foreign, but familiar. A taste of his old life. When he had been a farmer, working the fields. When he had been an active duty CSO, deployed in one part of the world or another. The land underfoot was always dirt. Always soft. Since crops had covered the world, there wasn't much barren soil left. The clearings were either pavement or concrete.

He walked to the center of the dirt patch and crouched. He put his hand into the soil and lifted it up. The earth was cool, damp, and dark, like rich chocolate cake. He smelled it and realized it smelled exactly like he did. Like they all did since rubbing themselves in dirt. He worked his thumb through the soil, separating clumps. When he saw wriggling pink, he flinched.

A worm.

I haven't seen a worm since... But is it even still a worm?

He separated the small creature from the soil and held it in his open palm. Its body pulsed, sliding across his skin, leaving a thin trail of slick goo behind.

Just a worm.

"The soil's not contaminated yet," he said.

"And it won't be." Ella pushed off the truck. "The DNA breaks down with the rest of the plant as it decays. By the time it reaches the worms, there's nothing left but nutrients."

That the land was still able to be worked gave Peter a small measure of hope. The damage could be undone...if they could get rid of the Exo-Genetic plants. But that wasn't even the plan, was it? *Why change the world back, when the human race could adapt? When we could eat the unlimited GMO crops without becoming monsters?*

Peter dropped the soil and looked over the clearing. "You're right about the prints; there aren't any. But there *are* tracks." He pointed to the nearly invisible crisscrossing lines covering the soil, the kind made when a branch is dragged over the earth to erase footprints. "The question isn't what did this—it's *who*."

"We know," Ella said, opening the door to the truck and climbing in behind the steering wheel. "Why don't you tell him about it, Anne?"

Anne bounded up in front of Peter, bouncing from foot to foot. The action seemed playful in a way Peter hadn't seen since the Change. She switched from bouncing to running in place and waving her arms around.

"What are you doing?" Jakob asked, trying not to laugh, but failing.

"Looking natural," Anne said. "So, they won't know we're talking."

Peter was instantly on guard, his eyes scouring the area for signs of company, but any signs of his vigilance were hidden by a phony laugh. He clapped, as though cheering her on.

Jakob just stood there, stunned by the behavior.

"Why don't you get in the truck," Peter said to his son, just a flicker of seriousness in his eyes. Jakob suddenly grasped the secret messages being passed back and forth, and added his own horribly fake laugh to the mix, waving his arms at the pair like they were ridiculous and walking, stiff-legged, to the truck.

"Don't reply," Anne said, her voice jolting as she continued to bounce. "They might see you. And don't look straight when I—"

Peter lowered his head, hiding his mouth from any would-be lip readers watching them. "I was doing things like this before you were born."

"Right." Anne stopped moving, raised her hands and made a show of touching her toes. When she came back up, she said, "My five o'clock." Toe touch and back up. "Two miles out, not far from the horizon."

Peter raised his hands, laughing. "Okay, okay. I get it. You can stop now." His arms came up in a stretch, bending behind his head. As he slowly extended his arms, he rolled his head, snapping his eyes to five o'clock for a moment. In that brief observation, he saw a faint flicker of light, the tell-tale sign of an amateur watching through a spy glass, oblivious to the sun's reflection. He finished the faux stretch with a real yawn and said, "Let's get this show on the road."

With the casualness of a family continuing a cross-country vacation, Peter and Anne headed back to the truck and climbed inside. Peter had never sat in the passenger's seat of his truck, and he was momentarily uncomfortable, but a second glance at the reflection across the barren field made him forget about riding shotgun. He put on his seatbelt and turned to Ella, who started the engine.

"Part of me wants to drive across the field and run them down," Ella said.

"Why shouldn't we?" Jakob asked.

"For starters," Peter said, "our intel is limited. Non-existent. All we really know is that something intelligent, most likely human—" He glanced at Ella and saw her nodding, "—was here last night. We don't know how many there are. What they have for weapons. Or what their intentions are. All we really know is that they know we're here. That reflection out in the field could be a trap. Or a distraction. The variables are endless, and few of them are good. So, our best course of action is to—"

"Get the hell out," Anne said.

"And hope they don't have a way to follow us," Peter added.

Ella put the truck in gear and performed a fast three-point turn. Within a minute, they were back on the highway. Peter kept watch, but he saw no signs of pursuit.

"I've got two pieces of bad news," Ella said, dashing Peter's hopes that they'd managed to escape. "First..." she pointed ahead.

Cars filled the road in the distance. The remnants of a pile-up that had happened when civilization had gone to hell. Cars, trucks, and eighteen-wheelers filled both sides of the freeway, the shoulder, and the woods beyond, forming an impenetrable wall of twisted metal.

"Second," Ella said. "We're low on gas."

Peter leaned over, looking at the gas gauge, which was hovering over 'E.' He could have sworn they'd had at least a quarter of a tank the previous night.

"But there's a silver lining," Ella said, pointing again, this time to a green exit sign just before the accident. As they approached, a blue rectangle mounted below the exit sign showed a gas pump icon and an arrow pointing to the right.

"Could be a trap," Jakob said from the back.

"Probably," Anne said.

"Before the debate begins," Ella said, steering toward the approaching exit, "I would rather fight an army of people before giving up this tank of a truck and once again facing the prospect of crossing the country on foot. As long as we have wheels, our chances of surviving go way up. So, if they want a fight, I suggest we give it to them. Otherwise, it's going to be a long walk."

No one said a word as she steered the truck off the highway and onto the off-ramp. She slowed to ten miles per hour, inching up to the intersection, stopping completely when the first signs of the gas station came into view. The tall sign was just visible over the tree line.

Peter turned to Jakob.

"You up to handling the machine gun again?"

"Uh," Jakob said. "And shooting it at people?"

"If there are people that want to shoot us, yes."

Jakob thought on it for a moment but gave a nod.

"I'll do what I have to."

"Hop in the back. Stay down. Under the tarp. Out of sight. If things go south, I want a repeat of last night. Just remember to pick your targets and conserve your ammo."

"Right," Jakob said, "No pray and spray." The boy was trying to sound confident, but he hadn't fully hidden the quiver in his voice. Regardless of his fear, Jakob opened the back door, slid out, and climbed into the truck bed.

Peter turned to Anne. "Get between the seats and stay there until we're away, okay?"

She nodded and climbed down.

"We can't just pull in there like it's a normal gas station," Ella said, gripping the wheel hard enough to drain the blood from her fingers. "We'll be wide open for attack."

"That's why we're not going to. You are."

Ella's eyes opened wide. "And you'll be?"

"In the trees," Peter said. "If there's trouble, I'll handle it and meet you at the pumps. If you hear me shooting before you get there, turn around."

"And leave you?"

"If you have to, yes."

"I don't—

"You've got precious cargo," Peter said. "You *will.*" He opened his door slowly and slid out onto the pavement. "Give me ten minutes to check things out, and then come in slow." He took a step back, but Ella stopped him with a word.

"Peter." She reached out her hand.

He leaned back in, took her fingers in his, and squeezed. The stare between them said enough.

Peter withdrew his hand from hers. "I know." Then he closed the door and ran into the woods lining the off-ramp, armed with a pistol, a knife, and the desire to show whoever it was that was messing with them, that there were still more dangerous predators in the world than the ExoGens.

25

Ella waited five minutes before pulling onto the road and heading for the gas station. During that time, Anne remained silent and motionless. The girl had become skilled at stealth, knowing to remain still, body and soul, even while an enemy stood just feet away. The moment the illusion of nothingness was disturbed, the ruse was over, along with your life. Anne had remained hidden while their previous companions had been snatched away and eaten. Ella remembered the events with clarity, lying still under their camouflaged cloaks, listening to screams, and then the chewing. The memories disturbed her. Haunted her dreams. But she was an adult. How much more poignant would they be for Anne?

How different will she be from me when she grows up? Ella wondered. Endless questions without answers streamed through her mind. How would nurture affect the girl's nature? Her mind? Her resilience? She'd already proven herself strong, but would she crack?

Or will I crack first?

Ella thought back to what her life had been like as a girl. Normal. Quiet. And shared, with Peter. She tried to picture herself in Anne's shoes but failed.

At least she has Peter in her life now. We'll have that much in common, aside from our shared DNA.

Moving at a cautious 20 mph, Ella drove toward the gas station. As she neared the break in the treeline where the station resided, her apprehension increased. Heading into danger was not how they'd survived so far. Survival was only guaranteed by hiding or fleeing. But this...

On the surface, this felt wrong, like suicide, except she and Peter were putting their children at risk, too. She put a hand on the shotgun in the passenger's seat, ready to raise it at a moment's notice. With a sidelong glance at the woods to her right, she looked for any sign of Peter, but seeing further than the roadside was impossible. The newly resilient strain of RC-714-modified Zea saccharata—sweet corn—had filled all the gaps between the leafy trees. The corn looked like a wall, the trees like watchtowers, keeping intruders out. Finding Peter amid the fruits of her labor would be impossible.

He's not there anyway, she told herself. Peter was precise. He had said he would meet her at the gas station in ten minutes, so that was where he would be.

Except, he wasn't.

She slowed to a crawl as the gas station came into view. It was a small station with an attached, one-car garage. The building was painted white with red framing. A collection of never-repaired vehicles sat off to the side, rusting and framed by corn stalks. The logo on the shattered window was unreadable, but it had been mounted atop the two pumps also: 'Harrison's.'

With rising trepidation, she pulled up next to the pumps. Peter was nowhere to be seen, but fleeing wouldn't get them anywhere but stuck a few miles down the road when the truck ran out of gas.

No, she thought.

No running or hiding this time.

We'll fight if we need to.

"Stay still," she said through pursed lips. Not waiting for a reply from Anne, she shut off the truck, leaving the keys in the ignition. Then she opened the door and stepped into the warm, summer air. She hadn't even realized the truck's air conditioner had been running. The humid air now clinging to her dirt-caked body quickly saturated her, filling her with longing for a climate-controlled laboratory. She had become hardened. She knew that. Recognized the physical and emotional traits. But the real Ella was still in there, still pining for a soft bed, gourmet food, and the safety of a world without ExoGenetic predators.

Suck it up, she told herself. *That's not going to happen in your lifetime, so get over it. It's the future we're fighting for.*

Acting as casual as possible while clutching a shotgun, she scanned the area. They were surrounded by walls of corn and trees in every direction, except for where the crumbling pavement cut through. There could be a hundred Stalkers lurking all around them, and they'd never know.

I'd hear them, she thought, focusing on the lack of sound around her. With no trace of a breeze, the world was silent. Aside from the ticking of the truck's cooling engine, she heard nothing. No insects. No birds. No distant hum of humanity. The world had eaten itself. The only insects that remained were either pollen-consuming prey, or super predators that didn't announce their presence. The same was true for birds. The few she'd seen were massive things, Apex predators with twelve-foot wingspans, hunting each other into oblivion.

She opened the gas cap on the side of the truck, placing it on the flatbed's sidewall and mumbling. "I've never siphoned gas before."

Jakob looked up at her from below, whispering, "Where's my dad?"

"Haven't seen him," she replied, head down, scratching the back of her scalp.

Jakob pointed to a three-foot-long metal rod with a hook on the end. It lay next to a long coil of tubing and a hand pump. Jakob had been busy while hiding in the back. "Pumps won't work without power. Use this to open the gas reservoir covers."

Ella reached in, trying to emote an air of 'I do this shit all the time.' She plucked up the nameless tool and looked for the fuel reservoir covers. She found them fifteen feet behind the truck. While keeping watch on her surroundings, she headed for the nearest cover, looped the hook around a small receptacle, and lifted it free. The metal cover was heavy, but not prohibitively so. She moved it to the side, and then she repeated the process with the other three covers, assuming that air flow would help with the pumping.

The smell of gasoline stung her nose and erased all traces of the corn scented air. She stood suddenly tense. No longer being able to smell was nearly as unnerving as not being able to hear or see. In this world of hunter and prey, scent was often the first telltale sign of a predator.

Doubling her pace, she moved back to the truck, reached in, and took the pump and tubing.

Jakob's whispering stopped her before she could walk away. "Take the gas cans." He motioned to the back of the truck where three red gas cans sat. They'd long since emptied them into the dirty truck. "We need to treat the gas before putting it in the tank. Make sure it won't kill the engine."

"This is going to take too long," she grumbled.

"Is my dad back?"

She shook her head slightly.

"Then it's not too long, because we're not leaving without him."

Ella lifted the pump and walked away, setting it down by the open hatch. She went back for the gas cans, pausing for a moment to say, "He'll be back." Then she returned to the pump, moving fast, her sense of impending doom rising, a volcanic cloud blotting out her reasoning and discipline. Her hands shook as she unraveled the tube. The device looked like a bicycle pump, except for the long tube mounted to the side, just beneath the pump, and a second, shorter tube mounted to the side at the bottom. She didn't know exactly how the pump worked, but only the long tube could reach the gas hidden below, so she fed it into the open hatch until it disappeared inside and the line went taut. She placed the second tube into the nearest gas can and began pumping.

It was easy work at first, the pump moving up and down, but then the gas reached the pump, adding resistance. She was encouraged as air and fuel spattered out of the line and then flowed with each rise and fall of the pump, but her arm began to burn from the repetitive motion. She was also vulnerable; both hands occupied, her sense of smell shot, and her mind distracted by the task at hand. So, when she heard the crunch of approaching feet behind her, the sound didn't register until a hand wrapped around her shoulder and squeezed.

Reflex responded before her mind. She dropped the pump and swung a vicious backhand. Her fist was caught, slapping into the open palm of...Peter. He looked winded, soaked with sweat trailing clean lines down his soiled face.

"Peter!" she said. "Shit!"

"How much have you pumped?" Peter asked, eyes on the road.

"I just got start—" Before she could finish, Peter picked up the device and pumped hard, the fuel gushing into the gas can. "When this is full, prep it with the PRI in the truck and get it in the tank."

"What's going on?"

"We're about to have company," he said.

Ella scanned the area. Nothing seemed different. But that was part of the problem. They could be surrounded.

"How many?"

"Not sure, but we were right. This station is a trap."

"How do you know?" she asked, though she wasn't sure she wanted to know.

"Bodies in the woods."

"How many."

"Too many. And not all human." Peter yanked the tube out of the gas can and inserted it in the next, pumping hard again.

Not wanting to waste time, Ella hauled the heavy container back to the truck. When she arrived, Jakob sat up, looking relieved when he saw his father, and then nervous when he saw Ella's face. "What's happening?"

"You know how to get this ready?" she asked. "With the PRI?"

He nodded.

"Do it," she said, "and put it in the tank." She turned and walked away without waiting to see if Jakob followed her orders. She knew he would.

Peter was nearly done with the second of the three gas cans when she returned. He knew she had questions and answered without needing to be asked. "I went back to the highway. We got ahead of them, but they're hauling ass. They'll be here in a few minutes."

"They have vehicles?" she asked, surprised.

"Transportation, yes. Vehicles..." he shook his head. "Not exactly." He finished pumping and switched the hose to the third tank. "If we're lucky, we can stay ahead of them. But I don't think we can count on that."

"You think they're already coming from the other side?"

"Or permanently stationed there." He started pumping again. "Have you looked at the concrete? This gas station is a killing ground."

Ella glanced down, and then around the concrete rectangle that formed the floor of the gas station. Instead of a light gray color, it was stained dark brown. In response, Ella hurried the second gas can back to the truck. Jakob finished pouring gas from the first can into the truck and traded with Ella.

A distant horn blast sounded.

The pair froze.

"Was that a car horn?" Jakob asked.

"I don't think so," Ella said, and hurried back to Peter, who was somehow pumping even faster now.

"Only time for one more," he said, withdrawing the hose from the third gas can and pushing it toward Ella as she put the first back down. He was pumping even as he put the hose inside the spout. "Just cap that and strap it down in the back."

The horn blast repeated, louder this time, and no longer muffled by a forest of trees and corn. It sounded deep and throaty, less like a horn and more like a roar, organic and raw. Hungry.

"That's it! Let's go!" Peter said, standing and running back to the truck, his can half full, the pump clutched in hand, dragging the long hose behind, leaking fuel over the blood-stained concrete. "Keys?"

"In the ignition," Ella replied, loading the tank into the back.

Jakob finished pouring the second PRI treated gas can into the tank and practically threw himself back into the truck bed. He quickly took the gas cans and strapped them down with bungee cords. "I got this!"

"Strap in!" Peter shouted, climbing in behind the steering wheel. Ella started running around the truck, heading for the passenger's side door, when she was struck by a pang of guilt. She couldn't leave Jakob alone in the back.

And then she had no choice.

As an organ-quivering bellow swept over her, Ella jumped into the truck bed. The roar merged with the sound of screeching tires. Ella looked back as the truck pulled away, and her scream joined the chorus.

26

The shrill scream coming from Jakob's voice would have embarrassed him in most situations. But not that day, at that moment, when the inhuman emerged from the road, staring him down, hunger in its eyes...in *their* eyes. It helped that he wasn't the only person vocalizing a cocktail of surprise and terror. Ella, the scientist turned hardened survivor, let out a cry, as well.

The two large creatures were built like rhinos, but covered in matted, thick brown fur clumped into muddy dreadlocks. Emerging from the snout wasn't a horn, but what looked like a large antler with four prongs on either side, ending in razor-sharp, spoon-shaped tips. The creatures' large, black-pupiled eyes were peeled wide to reveal jaundiced, bloodshot orbs. Tendrils of frothy drool dangled from gaping, panting maws—and that was where things really got freaky. Inside each creature's mouth was a large wooden bit, attached to leather reins, the kinds Jakob was accustomed to seeing on horses. The reins rose up, clutched in the hands of a smaller creature sitting atop each beast. The riders had clearly once been human, but were now something else.

The one that caught his eye was, or had been, a woman. It was in those intelligent, feminine eyes that he saw more than hunger. He saw hate. Loathing. Abject and barely contained ferocity. And something familiar he couldn't quite place. Her face was stretched out, elongated to make room for teeth so long and curled that they pierced back through her mud-covered cheeks. The woman was naked, her body emaciated, but twitching with lean muscles. A mane of hair flowed from her head and down her back. She was a primal thing, hungry and hateful, but with still-human eyes...eyes that held his gaze a moment while the truck's tires spun over dirty concrete.

Did I know her before? he wondered, but he lost sight of the woman when the tires caught, and the truck lurched onto the road. Jakob was thrown down to the floor, caught by Ella, whose wide eyes reflected his own.

"You okay?" Ella shouted over the roar of the truck's acceleration.

Before Jakob could reply, the pair slid forward, crashing into the metal supply case. Tires squealed as the truck came to a sudden stop. The back window slid open, and Anne's face appeared. "Hold on! We're surrounded!"

Jakob moved to sit up and look, but Ella held him back. "Not yet!"

He wanted to argue, but her point was made a moment later, when the truck shot backwards, braked hard again, and spun 180 degrees, sending them back the way they'd come, back toward the pair of gargantuans filling the road. *Why would we go back?* he thought, and then he sat up, looking behind them. Six more of the creatures, each with a naked rider—flowing haired and big toothed—charged from behind.

Anne's face returned to the window. "Shoot the gas! Peter says shoot the gas!"

While Jakob wondered why they would shoot the gas strapped down to the truck bed, Ella jumped up behind the machine gun, spun it around so it was facing to the front, and opened fire. The rattling bullets drowned out the sound of the pursuing monsters, their broad feet pounding, their mouths breathing heavily. Jakob clung to the side of the truck bed and looked down the road toward the approaching gas station and the two rhino-things, holding their ground, welcoming them back to the slaughterhouse.

For a moment, he was surprised to see how poorly Ella was missing. The monsters were big targets, but her stream of bullets was nowhere near them. Instead, she was shooting at the gas station. At the concrete ground.

At the line of gasoline leading toward the reservoir.

Jakob's eyes widened as a white hot, orange tracer round struck the concrete, sparking and igniting the spilled fuel. The line of fire streaked across the blood stains and then descended into the still-open reservoir hatch. "Oh...my...oof!"

"Down!" Ella shouted, tackling Jakob to the truck bed's floor.

The shockwave and sound hit them just milliseconds apart. The front end of the truck was lifted off the ground, sending Ella and Jakob sliding toward the back. Jakob slammed into the rear hatch, while Ella became tangled in the mounted machine gun's tripod legs. Debris pinged off the armored sides of the truck, pocking tree bark and shredding corn stalks around them. Flames swirled around the truck, twisting in toward Jakob, the heat scalding, and then all at once, the blast contracted.

The truck fell back to earth, the rear vaulting up as the front end landed, throwing Jakob forward again. His head struck one of the tripod legs, the impact setting his vision spinning.

"Hang on!" his father shouted, his voice muffled and distant.

An impact like a second explosion struck the vehicle from the side. Ella was slammed into the side, her body falling limp, still tangled in the tripod. Jakob was flung upwards again, but this time when he fell, he didn't land on the hard metal truck bed; he fell several feet further and toppled onto pavement.

Onto the road.

With the wind knocked out of him, Jakob found moving difficult. He was sitting in the road, sucking air, his lungs desperate for more. The truck was in front of him, tearing away from the monster that had struck its side—one of the six that had been chasing them—its rider thrown by the impact.

The truck sped away, swerving around the ruined and burning body of the rhino-thing that had been nearest to the explosion—the one that had held the ExoGenetic woman with the familiar eyes. *They're going to make it,* he thought, feeling glad for them, while resigning himself to his fate.

I knew I would be first.

As the pavement beneath him shook, he looked back and saw the remaining mammoth creatures, and their riders, charging toward him.

Not toward me, he realized. *Past me. They're going after the truck.*

He didn't know if they saw the truck as larger prey or simply believed he couldn't escape on foot, but he wasn't going to ignore the opportunity.

Spurred like a hot brand was being held to his side, Jakob scurried to his feet and sprinted for the side of the road. Before entering the corn, he heard a grunt, looked back and wished he hadn't. The Rider, *with a capital R,* he decided, who had been thrown from his mount had recovered. The ExoGenetic man ran on all fours, like an ape, his arms long and muscular, the long hair on his head and back bouncing with each lunge forward. The man's mouth hung agape, the long, curved teeth jutting forward to impale.

Jakob lost sight of the Rider when he entered the wall of corn stalks. His pace slowed as the vegetation slapped against him, the oversized heads of corn striking like fists. He tried to move between the plants, but this wasn't a farm with neat rows, it was wild and aggressively growing corn, the distribution dense and random—impossible to find a clear path through. So, he took the beating, knowing that the man behind him, with broad shoulders, running in a crouch, would have to carve his own wide path...unless they'd already adapted for running through corn.

But he didn't think that was the case. The Riders had somehow formed a symbiotic relationship with the giant—*what would Anne call them? Woolies.* Hunters united. Sharing prey.

Sharing me if I don't get the hell out of here.

Unable to see more than a few feet, Jakob navigated by sound. He could hear the Rider behind him, huffing and snapping corn stalks with each lunge forward. Further away, he could hear the roar of an engine, so out of place in the world now, and the thunderous impacts of the Woolie herd giving chase. One of them bellowed, sounding frustrated. *Go, Dad,* he thought, *just go,* and Jakob angled to the left, on a path that he thought would take him behind the gas station and roughly in the direction of the highway. If he could reach that stretch of open road, there was a slight chance he could reconnect with his family, after they found another way around the roadblock.

"Utchaka!" a shrill voice screamed from behind.

Jakob couldn't tell if the man had shouted an actual word in another language, or if he was just spewing nonsense. Either way, the shout announced the man's arrival and his impending attack.

Jakob changed direction, cutting behind a tree.

The Rider emerged from the corn into the path hewn by Jakob's flight, swinging his thick-nailed hand out. Bark and tree flesh burst away from the impact.

Holy shit! Jakob thought, looking over his shoulder.

The Rider hissed in aggravation, slammed his thick fists on the ground twice and launched himself after Jakob again, moving at an angle to close the distance. Jakob zig-zagged through the corn forest, running in and out of as many trees as possible, while staying on a roughly northward trajectory. He glanced to the left and saw the gleaming white back of the gas station. A column of flame and smoke rose up from the ruined concrete out front.

His eyes lingered on the fire. He knew, in his heart, that he couldn't outrun the Rider chasing him down like a cheetah after a gazelle. This gazelle had been trapped inside a house for two years, and despite being skinny, he was already getting winded. Eventually, he'd have to stop and fight.

More like fight and die, he thought.

But the fire...mankind's oldest weapon... Maybe he could use it.

He cut hard left, making for the gas station.

"Cheepita!" the Rider shrieked, and Jakob felt sure the man was just shouting unintelligibly, once again announcing his assault. But this time, despite the warning, there was no avoiding the man. Four claws raked across Jakob's back. He felt hot streaks of blood running down his skin, followed by a burning pain that drew a scream from his lips.

But he didn't stop running, and the Rider, off balance from his strike, fell a few feet behind. As the cornstalks thinned at the edge of the parking lot, Jakob reached out and tore three stalks from the ground, carrying them as he cleared the forest and stumbled into the parking lot. He surveyed the area and found it empty, save for the dead Woolie burning in the road.

Super-heated air wicked the moisture from his skin and made him squint. His run became a jog, as acrid smoke swirled around him. He coughed and winced, but pushed forward, toward the flames he thought might give him a chance against his hairy and flammable adversary. When he noticed the front of the gas station was burning, too, he hurried to the smaller flames and held the corn out, roasting them. The lush plant sizzled, dried, and caught fire.

"Chuftack!"

Jakob whirled around, holding the burning corn toward the attacking Rider. The man flinched to a stop. He hissed and stretched his jaw, fully revealing the four-inch, needle-like, lower teeth and the shorter, but equally sharp, upper teeth. And then, the Rider almost looked bored, craning its head one way and then the other.

Jakob thrust the corn out like a spear, hoping the flames would set the thick, greasy mane of hair on fire. Instead, the Rider simply swiped one of his arms out and swatted the flames away, not frightened, intimidated or aflame. The man's muscles coiled. He lowered himself to the ground. *He's going to pounce,* Jakob thought, *and I'm going to die.*

"Rrrootacha!" the high-pitched scream from behind Jakob made him, and the Rider about to lunge at him, flinch in unison.

Jakob spun around to find the female Rider, her hair smoldering, her eyes locked on the male, teeth barred, a throaty growl reverberating from her chest. Jakob hadn't seen it before, but she was larger than the male, who was closer to Jakob's size. The male barked at her, hissing. And then she lunged. With a yelp of surprise, the male Rider bolted, plowing a new path into the corn, with no signs of stopping.

The female bounded once after the fleeing competitor, but her second leap spun her around. A small fraction of a shout escaped Jakob's lips before the Rider struck, slamming into Jakob's chest, knocking the air from his lungs, and then crushing him down on the parking lot, heaving out any air that remained. Jakob's vision quickly tunneled. He longed for unconsciousness, to not see what was about to happen, but that sweet bliss never came. Instead, he stared up into the eyes of the Rider woman.

Those familiar eyes.

She stared right back, hungry. Drool dripped from the long teeth, running down his cheeks. The woman tensed, about to bite, and then... she didn't. The fight went out of her like she'd been stabbed. Her jaws closed shut, the long, lower teeth sliding into deep, scarred pockets in her cheeks and nose.

Her blue eyes remained on his.

Her irises widened.

Then softened.

And then, all at once, they filled with a deep, welling sadness that Jakob knew.

She spoke slowly, testing the word. "Ja-kob?"

Jakob's heart nearly seized in his chest. His lungs burned for air. But he managed a single whispered word.

"M—Mom?"

27

Peter squinted as fire exploded up out of the gas station reservoir. "Get down!" he shouted to Ella and Jakob in the back, but he doubted they could hear him over the thunderous clap and the pressure wave that lifted the truck's front end off the ground. Shards of concrete assaulted the truck's armored shell, deflecting away or shattering. Had the truck not been lifted up, the windshield would have been torn apart, *and me with it.*

Flames expanded out, engulfing the truck's cab. The interior glowed orange, the heat seeping in through the vents. He let out a scream of anger, knowing his son was in the back of the truck, fully exposed to the heat, to the danger.

This God-damned world!

The flames dissipated, and the truck dropped. The frame rattled as the front shocks tried and failed to absorb the blow.

Peter caught a glimpse of the road ahead, burning and open.

One of the giant creatures had been torn apart by the blast, a massive chunk of concrete embedded in its burning side. Its rider was nowhere to be seen. The second creature and its rider were nowhere to be seen. Then the airbag deployed, erasing his view, and stalling his response.

The airbag fought against him as he reached for the knife on his belt. Before he could reach it, a rumbling caught his attention, and he glanced out the driver's side window, where one of the rhino-like creatures charged toward them, its massive head lowered, its split horn leading the way.

"Hang on!" he shouted, not knowing if anyone could even hear him.

The creature struck hard from an angle, knocking them sideways, but also propelling them forward. The creature's head struck the armored driver's side, impaling its face on one of the many savage spikes he'd welded to the exterior, and shearing a few prongs from its horn. The stunned creature bellowed in pain, flinching back for just a moment, but long enough for Peter to rein in control of the spinning vehicle and slam his foot down on the gas pedal. With a shriek of tires, the truck tore away from the monster.

Peter steered with one hand. With his free hand, he recovered the knife from his belt and stabbed at the airbag, which popped and blew white, dusty air into the cab. He dropped the blade into the passenger's seat and returned both hands to the wheel. Back in control, he directed the truck toward the gap between the stunned creature and the dead, burning one. *If we can just squeeze between—*

A third, even larger rhino-thing stepped in from behind, filling the gap. They were trapped. Again.

"Into the woods!" Anne shouted. She was seated behind him, strapped in tight.

"We'll hit a tree," he argued.

"Steer by looking up! You can see the trees over the corn!"

The girl was right. Looking straight ahead, he'd be blind, but he might be able to see the trees above them well enough to navigate. The angled, inverted V-shaped plow mounted to the front end of the truck would make short work of the corn. Without further discussion or thought, he yanked the wheel to the right. The truck burst through a column of smoke from the burning gasoline on his right and the roasting monster on his left.

"Shit!" he shouted when the smoke cleared, turning harder to the right to avoid a tall pine. They surged past the tree, scraping bark from its side and entering the corn forest. The riotous hiss of cornstalks slapping against the exterior sounded like a jet engine. The truck withstood the barrage, its armor and plow bending the ExoGenetic plants to the old-fashioned mechanical will of man. Peter found he could see better than he thought possible as the angled plow shredded corn stalks and shot them out to the sides, rather than up and over the windshield. He could also see the maze of trees, and steered back and forth, taking out saplings when unavoidable, but doing his best to dodge anything that might stop them in their tracks. The soft earth beneath the tires didn't help, but they were moving faster than he'd thought possible.

"Here they come!" Anne shouted, her little shaved head craned back.

Peter glanced in the rearview. A column of the monsters was gaining on them, having no trouble following the path carved by the truck.

Anne followed her warning with an even more frightened sounding, "I don't see Mom or Jakob!"

Peter turned around this time, seeing neither Ella nor Jakob in the back, but that made sense. They'd be on the floor, clinging to whatever they could find. He shouted as he turned forward and found a tree directly in their path. He turned hard to the left, the maize-slick tires slipping over the earth. The front end avoided the tree, but the rear bumper clipped it, sending a shudder through the vehicle and cracking Peter's head against the driver's side window. Blood trickled down the side of his face as he fought to regain control. Tires spun, hurling corn and mud, and then caught. The truck surged deeper into the woods, angling slowly back toward the road, where he was positive they could outrun the massive creatures, which would eventually tire and slow.

He glanced in the rearview again. A huge, ugly face with horrible eyes greeted him. It had a flaring, runny nose that sprayed like old faithful with each breath. The truck was seconds away from being struck from behind. The vehicle could take the hit, but it could knock them off course, sending them into a tree.

Peter searched for a solution and found it thirty feet ahead. He turned slightly without slowing, careful to keep the monster close behind him. A large tree emerged from the corn, directly ahead, its wide-spread roots fighting off the encroaching corn. But Peter was ready for it and gave the wheel just enough of a spin to narrowly avoid the obstacle. Thick roots sent the truck bouncing erratically, but they passed safely by.

The monster that had been following close behind dug its thick, stout legs into the soil, but it was too little too late. The long face careened into the immovable tree, crushed flat by the force of the collision. The rider, a hairy naked male, was flung forward, striking the tree head on, his legs and thick arms splaying out to the sides like one of those Halloween witch decorations. A second creature, following too close, rammed into the backside of the first, impaling it with the long, splayed horn. The rider was flung but held onto the reins and arced back to the ground, while the beast tried, and failed, to withdraw its horn from its now-dead companion's ass. Four more of the monsters rounded the scene and continued the pursuit.

Weaving back and forth, the speedometer showing a steady and reckless 40 mph, Peter carved a frantic path back toward the road. He could see a clearing ahead, stretching north and south—a band free of trees and corn. *Almost there...* He lined up a straight shot, ready to steer hard right and race away.

There was a slap on the back window, quickly followed by a muffled shout. He glanced back and saw Ella, her face bloodied. "We lost Jakob!"

"What!" Peter's mind rewound the past few minutes, since they left the gas station. He couldn't figure out when they had lost him.

"At the gas station!" Ella shouted, providing the answer.

Distracted by the news, Peter reacted to their return to the road a moment too late. The truck jounced up onto the road, spinning, shrieking, and stopping, its rear end halfway off the road on the opposite side.

Peter shook his head, trying to recover from the vicious spin and impact. The blood dripping down his face was hot and irritating, smearing his vision. *Gas station*, he thought, *need to get back—*

But it was too late. Corn and trees peeled away as the four creatures pursuing them calmly stepped out of the forest, surrounding the truck's front end. The riders on their backs looked smug and confident, chins lifted up. Noble savages.

Peter considered reversing into the forest, but the steering and seeing would be a nightmare. They'd be caught in seconds.

So, what then?

They're intelligent, he thought. *Maybe not like people, but smart enough to ambush prey. They could have attacked the church, but didn't. They chose to wait until they had the advantage.* He looked at their arrogant faces. He couldn't tell whether the long, exposed teeth were a grin, but he sensed pride in their gazes.

Peter picked up the knife from the passenger's seat and slid it back into the sheath. He yanked the door handle and shoved it open with his foot, sliding out of the truck.

"What are you doing?" Ella hissed.

"Just be ready with the shotgun if this doesn't work," he replied.

"If what doesn't work?"

"Domesticated animals require direction," he said. "I'm going to remove theirs." He stepped out around the door, leaving it open, the engine still running.

The four riders looked confused by his bold actions, their confidence floundering for a brief moment. Then Peter pointed at one of the ExoGenetic men, his eyes challenging. The four riders chuffed with what sounded like laughter, and the singled-out male leapt down from his mount with little effort. *Strong, intelligent, and agile,* Peter thought, watching the freed rhino-thing relax and sit on its haunches, *but not street-smart.*

Peter held his ground as the once-man charged, shouting, "Oufinarg!"

I'm coming Jakob.

Just stay alive.

I'll be with you soon.

All of Peter's CSO training came back as muscle memory, his body reacting without a need for thought. He side-stepped the attack, avoiding the outstretched claws that would fillet his flesh. He caught the creature's left hand bending it back, sharp and fast, cracking the wrist, but more importantly, stretching and exposing the skin underneath. With a quick swipe, he yanked the knife from his belt, pulled it across the wrist and followed the cut with a quick jab to the side of the neck.

The whole attack and counterattack took a single second.

Peter stepped back, unharmed.

The ExoGen man stumbled, looking confused.

He turned toward Peter, the fight in his eyes slowly draining, along with his blood. The man's brows furrowed low enough to be impaled by the long, sharp, lower teeth extending upward. He lifted a hand to his spurting neck, his slit wrist adding fluid to the bloody fountain. Then his eyes rolled back, and he fell to the road with a thud.

The dead man's mount didn't flinch. It stayed seated, looking dim-witted. *They might be predatory,* Peter thought, *but they're used to being fed, or led on a hunt. They no longer think for themselves.*

The other three riders reacted to their compatriot's death just as Peter had hoped they would. Rather than stomping him to a pulp with their mammoth rides, all three jumped down, hooting and hollering, ready to finish what the first had failed to accomplish. And this was where things got dicey. Taking on a physically superior fighter was simple one-on-one. In a group, not so much. One mistake and they could crush his skull or tear his arm off. They made it harder by running in a tight, single-file line. He couldn't see beyond the first, and even if he managed to kill the first, the other two would just bowl them all over.

Luckily, he wasn't alone.

"Ella!"

The shotgun boomed, drowning out Peter's shout and reshaping the lead man's head into something resembling a waning moon. As the first rider fell, Peter caught sight of the second, his eyes widening with surprise, too stunned to react. Peter lunged to meet him, thrusting the knife up under the creature's chin, through the roof of his mouth and into his brain. The man collapsed in a heap, as the shotgun roared again. Peter landed on his feet, bloody knife in hand. The third attacker slid to a stop at his feet, its neck sheared away, save for the spine. The body twitched madly, the legs still trying to run, and then it fell still.

Peter eyed the rider-less beasts. They returned his gaze, more curious than incensed. One by one, they sat, waiting for their dead riders to return and direct them. No longer fearing the giants, Peter ran to the car, jumped behind the wheel, and hit the gas, passing the stationary steeds. The door flung closed on its own, and with a screech of tires, Peter headed back toward the gas station, and he hoped, his son.

Smoke clouded his vision as they neared the station.

He pushed through, believing his son wise enough to avoid the smoke. As the last of the ash rose up over the windshield, the view became clear. For a moment, Peter's voice caught in his throat, and then it exploded out, "Jakob!"

Jakob lay on the gas station parking lot, pinned by the female rider, who was larger than the males he'd just fought. Her hair smoked. Her body was singed and naked. Her face hovered inches from Jakob's, the mouth working up and down, large enough to cleave his face away in one bite.

He hammered the brakes, announcing his arrival. He threw the truck into park before it had come to a stop and launched himself into the parking lot. To his surprise and relief, the female had already abandoned Jakob and was fleeing on all fours, into the corn. He fell by his son's side. "Jakob!"

The boy was conscious but dazed. "Are you okay? Are you hurt?"

Jakob just shook his head.

He's in shock, Peter decided, and scooped him up. He hurried back to the truck, as loud cries bellowed out around them. Some from the forest, some from the road leading back toward the highway. Ella opened the back door as he arrived, and he slid Jakob into the back seat. Anne moved over, gripped Jakob's shirt, and helped haul him inside.

"He's okay," Peter said to Ella, noting her concern, and then he motioned to the passenger's side door as the sounds of reinforcements closed in. "Get in." Peter ran to the driver's side, dove behind the wheel, and said, "We're getting the fuck out of here." Gas pedal to the floor, he steered the truck onto the road, away from the highway and sped off, hoping it wasn't true, but somehow knowing they now had an army hunting them.

28

The worst part about flying was the God-damned birds. There weren't many left, because competition for the air, where rivals could be spotted many miles away and confrontation was always guaranteed, was fierce. But those that remained... Kenyon called them 'Sky Tyrants,' because of how they ruled the sky, plucking prey from the ground with ease. When all was said and done, and the planet's evolving species ate themselves into oblivion, it would be a bird, he believed, one giant freaking bird, that would dominate the planet. Then it would eventually succumb to starvation, its skeleton confusing the hell out of some future or perhaps alien archeologist.

So when a bird was spotted, either by eye or by radar, the trio of helicopters tracking Ella Masse's slow progress across the country hit dirt, stopped their engines and sat still, hoping the predator hadn't ever eaten a giant wingless dragonfly, which the choppers resembled from above.

The helicopters weren't defenseless. They were armed with machine guns and rocket pods still capable of dropping most living things, but birds of prey posed a serious threat. They were super-evolved for aerial speed, maneuverability, and lethality—not to mention a hunger that blinded them to danger.

"Anything on the radar?" Kenyon asked. He sat in the back of the Black Hawk helicopter, trying to ignore the searing heat of the Midwestern summer day being absorbed by the vehicle's dark blue shell.

"Nothing for ten minutes," Mackenzie said. He was seated in the cockpit with the pilot. After landing, Kenyon had reorganized the team, putting the grunts, who generally smelled horrible, together in the other choppers, while he, Hutchins, and Mackenzie stretched out in the spacious Black Hawk with one lucky pilot, to 'strategize,' which really meant partaking in one of the wild crops still consumable. Between the four of them, they shared a single joint, enough to relax without completely compromising their combat efficiency—an age-old trick of soldiers around the world. Not that there was anyone to judge them. Those who had seniority over Kenyon were thousands of miles away. This was his rodeo, and if a bird forced them to the grass, they might as well smoke it.

Kenyon wiped his arm across his forehead, smearing his blond hair. He'd let it get too long. Preferred the high-and-tight look. But he wasn't about to let one of the men with him touch his hair. He wasn't even sure who to see about his hair back at ExoGen. Ella had done the job for a long time, sloppy at first, but before they left, she'd become a regular pro, trimming him up once a week. Now he felt like a shaggy dog.

Smoke swirled in the sealed chopper as Kenyon sat up and opened the side door. The cloud was caught by a breeze and swept up into the sky.

"All good things must come to an end," Hutchins mused. The man had an almost impish look about his face, looking cheerful even when he wasn't. He took one last drag on the withered blunt and flicked the tiny stub of paper out the open door. He blew out the smoke, asking, "What's the plan?"

"Where'd that bird go?" Kenyon asked.

"Last seen headed north, sir," the pilot said. His last name was Ford, and his first name was a mystery. Of the six pilots among them, he was the best and the most trusted, which was why he got to take part in the fishbowl, though he wasn't actually permitted to smoke. He had to fly after all, and the man needed his wits about him even more than the rest.

"Get us back in the air. We still have daylight to burn. Due east."

"Still chasing your hard on?" Mackenzie said.

Kenyon craned his head toward the younger military man, an eyebrow raised. "I'm going to let that go because you're baked."

"I'm being serious," Mackenzie said. "We all know this isn't just about ExoGen. The odds of her surviving out here are slim to none. We could just let her go and be done with it."

"She made it this far," Kenyon said, his buzz burning away like a forest fire, crackling with horrible energy.

The two men stared at each other for a moment. Mackenzie cracked, smiling and waving his hand. "I'm just yanking your chain."

Kenyon didn't believe that for a second.

He knew the men.

They were risking their lives every second they were out in the wilderness, facing the freakish terrors the company they served had unleashed. They all wanted to go home. If Kenyon was honest, so did he. But not without her. And God help anyone who stood in his way. He didn't have to say it. They all knew it. Mutiny was prevented by one simple fact. The gates of the ExoGen biodome wouldn't open to them without a code known only to Kenyon and Hutchins, whose loyalties were unquestionable. The code would allow them inside the quarantine zone, after which a series of blood samples would prove they had not consumed any of ExoGen's handiwork. And though all the men on the team could pass that test, none would get the chance without Kenyon or Hutchins opening the outer door. And if they tried, they'd be treated like hostiles. And that was assuming they survived the mutiny.

"You won't have to yank it for much longer," Kenyon said. "We're close."

"I hope so," Mackenzie said, facing forward and buckling up. He plucked up the radio receiver and toggled the transmit button. "Wake up, ladies. Wheels up in two minutes. Resume previous course, due east. We'll take point, so just follow the leader."

"Copy that," a pilot replied.

"Affimatory," said the second, in a faux, very exaggerated southern accent.

Kenyon grinned. *At least some of them still have a sense of humor.* His thoughts were drowned out by the whine of the helicopter's engine, slowly spinning the rotor blades. The sound grew louder, becoming a roar, and two minutes later they were airborne and cruising over the treeline, staying low to avoid any eagle-eyed predators.

It was only a minute into the rhythmic, choppy flight that the pilot, now speaking into a headset, said, "Sir, we have smoke in the distance. Single column."

The already-fading effects of their recreational respite dissolved. Smoke could mean many things, many of which were natural, but a single column of smoke meant a human source. Kenyon sat forward and looked through the cockpit window. It wasn't just a single column of smoke, it was a towering, black behemoth, the kind generated by burning fuel. "Get us there. Now."

The chopper leaned forward, the rotor blades hacking at the air, beating a drum that everything for miles around would hear. But that was always a risk.

And worthwhile.

I'm almost there, Ella.

As the helicopters ate up the distance, Kenyon grew more nervous. The smoke was a beacon, but an ominous one. Where there was smoke, there was death. Parties didn't limp away from fights anymore. Life or death was the rule of the land, and sometimes everyone died.

"Here we go," Ford said, maneuvering the chopper around in a tight circle so they could see out the side window.

Kenyon closed his eyes, seeing Ella's body, feeling that loss. He feared the moment that everyone but him believed was inevitable. It wasn't until Hutchins said, "Fucking hell. What a mess," that he opened his eyes to the destruction below.

Smoke and fire billowed from what looked like a crater in the ground, identifiable as a gasoline reservoir only because the small service station and its pumps had not yet burned to the ground. Not far from the station, also on fire, was a large creature. Some kind of ExoGen predator with a slab of concrete in its side.

"Bodies to the north," came the voice of a man from one of the other choppers, circling further away. "ExoGen, but the closest thing to still human I've seen."

Kenyon squinted at the scene below. Finding a variety of dead ExoGens in one area wasn't uncommon. They slaughtered each other regularly, but from what he could see, the creature below hadn't been eaten. "How did they die?" he asked.

There was a pause, and then the man's voice returned. "Uh, looks like they were shot, sir. Blast pattern suggests a shotgun. Close range. It's a real mess."

"I want boots on the ground. Three minutes tops. Find out what you can and get airborne." Kenyon turned to Mackenzie. "Have two of your men rendezvous with us at the station." Then to Ford: "Take us down and keep the engine hot."

This was the second time they'd be setting down on a still fresh scene, danger lurking behind the walls of corn and trees now shuddering under the chopper's rotor wash.

No one liked it, and he wouldn't get away with taking these kinds of risks much longer. Access to ExoGen or not, once the men were sure he was going to get them killed, they'd probably decide to take their chances, maybe cordon off a town. Eke out a living like some of the other poor human souls holding out in the wilderness.

Like Ella.

Kenyon jumped from the open chopper door before the landing struts even touched down. As usual, his only weapons were a long knife sheathed on one hip, and a .50 caliber Magnum on the other. He drew neither weapon, showing confidence in his own ability to defend himself, and his men's ability to do their job. He was tempted to draw the gun as he strode down the road, toward the fallen beast. But he resisted, and focused on his surroundings, which showed signs of a recent battle.

He pieced together the confrontation, or a rough approximation of it, and he felt confident that Ella had not only been here, but was still alive. There were no human bodies that he could see, and the road—he knelt down—told how the fight had come to an end. A trail of black tires, peeling away at speed, headed south. They'd fallen into a trap, but had managed to escape, most likely thanks to the reservoir's explosion.

Her companions are adept at blowing things up. Perhaps I'll recruit them.

His hand hovered over the revolver when he heard scraping footfalls on the pavement. Then two soldiers, weapons up, rounded the smoldering behemoth that looked part rhino, part something else... *Was this thing a beaver?*

"Just the three dead back there, sir," one of the men said. "Big fucking mess. Two with a shotgun, but the other was cut up. A professional job."

That caught Kenyon's attention.

"What do you mean, professional?"

"Better than any of us could do," the man said. "Special Ops for sure."

Great.

As Kenyon turned to leave, something about the creature caught his attention. He stepped closer, looking at the object clutched in the thing's mouth, attached to a...

Is that...? Holy shit.

Before Kenyon could voice his discovery, someone—Mackenzie he thought—shouted, "Incoming!"

He heard them before he saw them, the loud rattling sound barely audible over the helicopter. The helicopter above must have seen them moving between the trees.

"Let's move!" Kenyon shouted, running toward the chopper. The two men followed close behind. But not close enough.

Kenyon spun at the loud warbling sound, but never stopped running. It saved his life. The two men behind him knew what the cry meant and turned around to open fire. They never got the chance. A phalanx of Rattletails, nine in total, swept out of the forest, where they had been concealed by the corn. The gray-skinned creatures' plated backs carved through the air like shark fins in those old horror movies. They were led by the large female that they'd seen only once before, her twenty-foot length dwarfing the others. The Rattletails were annoyingly persistent, still tracking Ella after all this time.

Kenyon considered stopping. His magnum could take down a few, but he'd be sacrificing the chopper and the men inside.

And Ella. And that wasn't acceptable.

The two soldiers opened fire, but it was too little, too late. Without breaking stride, the female leapt up, caught both men in her hind claws, landed atop them, breaking ribs, and then ran while clinging to them like they were floppy slippers, staining the ground with their blood with each step.

The helicopter rose up even as Kenyon leapt in. In seconds, they were a hundred feet up and out of reach. He took one last look down as the horde of predators descended on the men still on the ground. Then he closed the door, turned to Ford, and said, "South."

29

After the hellish stress of the past days, the dichotomy of the endless and eventless road they had traversed during the past six hours left Jakob feeling anxious. It wasn't that he disliked the quiet, or the rapid progress being made, it was that every passing moment built the anticipation. They were headed toward disaster. No matter what direction they headed in, it would be there to greet them, arms open wide for a sharp-toothed embrace.

With every passing mile, conversation fell away, replaced by monotonous scenery and stress. Crops walled in the road, alternating every few miles, but Jakob avoided looking at them. Part of him thought he might spot hungry eyes staring back as they passed, or the long twitching tails of Stalkers rising up, but mostly the crops just made him hungry. They still had enough to eat—MREs and protein bars made before the ExoGen crops started being used by the food industries—but the scent of apples, oranges, and countless berries twisted his stomach up in a way he'd never experienced.

Worse than the crops and the constant threat of danger from ExoGenetic predators was the inexorable progress of the sun across the sky. It was behind them now, casting the truck's shadow out ahead of them. And he knew what that meant.

Night was coming.

And with it, nocturnal hunters. They'd only made it this far because most of the world's horrors still preferred to stalk their prey—each other—under the cover of darkness. His mind filled with images of predators stalking each other. With no real prey animals left, acquiring a meal demanded more than simply hunting and killing, because prey could fight back now, and it wanted, just as badly, to eat the predator. The world was a nightly battleground, slowly filtering out the weak and leaving only the most adapted and horrendous monsters behind. He'd asked Ella if the predators would eventually eat through their populations, and she thought they would, but their numbers were still high enough that it wouldn't happen for a long time. They'd probably become omnivores before fully dying out. If humanity couldn't somehow reclaim the planet, the future belonged to an ExoGenetic species.

Staring down, he flexed and clenched his fists, watching the blood moving in and out of his hand change the color from pink to pale white. The color shift was hard to see past the layer of dirt covering his skin, blocking his natural scent, and filling the truck cab with the smell of earth. *Better than blood,* he thought, surprised that he was still alive, still in shock at who had spared his life.

It was her, he thought.

She's alive.

But it didn't make sense. He remembered the night his father had dragged his mother outside, her hands bound, her teeth stained with both of their blood. The gunshot had been a defining moment in Jakob's life, the sound of it slamming the door on his childhood. He'd hated his father for doing it, but that wound had healed in time with the physical wounds inflicted upon him by his mother.

His eyes shifted from his soiled hands to his forearm, where a crescent moon of scars revealed where his mother had bitten him, just for a moment, before his father had intervened.

She tried to eat me.

But not this time.

She remembered me. Spoke my name.

He hadn't told his father about the encounter. It was ridiculous. Insane. His dead mother, now a monster, had pinned him to the ground and spoken to him? Even he knew it wasn't possible. *It was a hallucination,* he decided. Evidence of his fracturing mind. He'd been chased through the forest. He'd nearly been killed. Eaten. Again. How could he be sane after the past few days?

How was Anne?

He looked at the girl who might be his sister. She sat quietly, looking out the window, unfazed by the delicious scenery. How could she not be? She'd already walked through the endless fields of food without eating any of it.

Seeing it now, as a blur, was probably easy.

Anne slowly turned toward him, somehow feeling his gaze on the back of her head. She leaned forward, cracking a slight grin. "Are we there yet?"

Jakob was surprised when both Ella and Peter, who had been silent for the past hour, burst out laughing. Anne had cut through the tension with four words, and the look she'd given him prior to speaking said she'd done it on purpose.

Neither parent answered her question, but their conversation resumed, discussing what awaited them at George's Island.

Anne sat back in her seat, looking pleased. "A sense of humor helps."

"I have a sense of humor," Jakob said.

"You didn't laugh."

She was right. He knew what she'd done was funny, but the laughter they'd shared just a day previous was no longer a part of him.

"I thought you knew that already," she said.

"Knew what?"

"About laughing."

"What made you think that?" he asked.

She looked out the window for a moment. "Because you made me laugh."

"I hadn't been out here yet. I hadn't seen what you saw. Lived like this."

She frowned. "But we are still alive."

For how long? he thought but couldn't bring himself to say it. Not to a little girl who clearly needed hope. Or was she trying to give it to him?

"Why did the toilet paper roll down the hill?" he asked.

She laughed.

Well, that was easy.

"Why?" she asked.

"To get to the bottom."

She snorted and said, "That is the dumbest joke I've ever heard. Wait. *Wait.* Why did the toilet paper roll down the hill?"

Jakob squinted at her, wondering where she was going with this. "Why?"

"Because the Giant Pink Asshole wanted to use it!"

It was the kind of lame punchline that only a kid could conjure, but the image of that long-limbed, beaked pig flashed into his mind, chasing a roll of toilet paper down a hill.

"GPA strikes again," she said, and this time got a laugh out of Jakob.

"There you go," she said, and then shifted suddenly, growing serious. "Let's make a deal. No matter what. If you make me laugh, I'll make you laugh."

He grinned. "Sounds like I'm getting a raw deal."

"Bite me," she said, making him laugh again.

"Good enough," he said, and they shook hands.

After crossing two bridges, in and out of Illinois, a flash of bright blue color pulled Jakob's eyes to the window. The brightness of it, caught in the sun, made him squint, but the words resolved and opened his eyes wider, despite the brightness. He whispered the words, 'Welcome to Kentucky,' and then louder as they flashed past the sign, he said, "We're in Kentucky?"

"Told you he could read," Peter said to Ella.

Jakob leaned forward, head over the seat. "Are we going to Alia's? To the biodome?"

His father nodded. "It's on the way, and we could use some supplies. Brant is a good man. He'll help us out."

Brant was Alia's father. He and Peter had spoken on several occasions, sharing tips and tricks about the matching biodomes. They hadn't met, but like Alia and Jakob, they had become friends. Alia's mother, Misha, was still alive, too. Jakob had only spoken to her once, when calling for Alia, but she seemed nice enough. They were good people. Farmers, like his father, but also not like his father, because none of them had ever been an elite Marine CSO. They probably had some weapons, but he doubted they knew how to use them like his father. They probably didn't have an armored truck. Or an escape tunnel. Or a basement rigged with explosives. They were getting by, but could they survive outside the dome?

"We can't," Jakob said. "If we bring our trouble to them..."

"We've been driving all day without any sign of trouble," his father said.

"They could track us," Jakob argued.

Peter deferred to Ella, glancing at her. She turned back and said, "We've been tracked over greater distances, but were on foot at the time. We've been driving all day, at an average speed of fifty miles per hour."

"The Stalkers hold a grudge," he said.

"We haven't seen them since leaving home," his father said.

"And we have no reason to believe there are many of them alive," Ella added.

"What about the Riders?" he asked. The name, along with 'Woolies' had been endorsed by Anne and accepted by the others. "They were intelligent."

"They were," Ella said. "And it was a surprising adaptation. I didn't expect it to—"

"You expected predators to become intelligent?" Peter asked.

"It's a logical step in the evolution of most species...assuming it's a beneficial adaptation. That the Riders had once been human makes it less of a leap forward and more of a leap back. When their predatory instincts kicked in, human intellect took a back seat. Now that time has passed, hyper evolution has found intelligence and community to be beneficial attributes. But they didn't need to grow brains. They were already there. The Riders just needed to access them again, though they're clearly doing so in a limited, almost Cro-Magnon kind of way."

"Cro-Magnon men didn't ride domesticated animals," Peter pointed out.

"Regardless," Ella said. "They pose no threat to us now. Only one of the hunting party we encountered survived, and for all we know, she was the last of them."

Jakob's stomach soured. *She.*

"And while her evolution might be shaped by the encounter, she was also intelligent enough to realize a second encounter would not be in her best interest. Unlike the Stalkers, who've had many victories, and meals, along the way, the Riders will see no benefit to chasing after what they'll see as a superior predator."

Peter replied, making a joke, but Jakob tuned it out. He closed his eyes and remembered the female Rider's face. Heard her voice, familiar yet modified. Her body was large. Muscular and hair covered. Hardly human. Unashamedly naked.

But her eyes...

Jakob shook his head. It wasn't her. It was a monster. Ella was right. The Rider woman would have no more desire to follow him than he had to go back and face her again. *It's not my mother,* he told himself, doing his best to ignore the fact that he didn't really believe it, and to scour clean the memory of her speaking his name.

30

"This is far enough," Ella said, dropping the folded tarp on a bed of cushiony, densely packed soybean plants.

Anne put a backpack down and stretched. "This actually looks like it will be comfortable."

"Comfortable?" Jakob said. "Looks like the world's lumpiest mattress."

Anne crossed her arms. "Have you ever slept inside a raspberry bush?"

"Touché," Jakob said.

Anne knelt and pushed down on the nearest plant. "What I thought."

Jakob knelt beside her, testing the bed of plants with his hands. "Are we sure it wouldn't be better to stay in the truck? I'd feel a lot safer with metal walls around me."

"Metal and *glass*," Anne said. Jakob was smart, but sometimes she wondered how he'd survived this long. *Because of his father*, she decided. Jakob might have the survival instincts of a golden retriever, but his father... The man had gone to scout the area thirty minutes ago. Had presumably been tailing them, watching for signs of danger. And all the while, she hadn't detected even the faintest trace of his presence. There wasn't a single ExoGenetic predator she'd encountered capable of that.

"We can hide our scent," Ella explained, "but not the truck. It's too big, and everything about it smells different, especially since it's been running. The truck will attract attention. Empty, it will just be a curiosity, helping to pull attention away from us. But if we were in it..."

"Sardines," Anne said.

Jakob gave a slow nod, absently scratching at his dirt-covered arms, the dry dirt sifting up into the sunlight stretching down through the trees that broke up the crop. "Right."

She decided to not be hard on Jakob, though. He was nice. Made her laugh, and she him, which was a blessing in its own way. He also had proved he could fight when it mattered. He might not be stealthy or well versed in how to survive the new wild, but he'd also been cooped up in a house, learning how to farm small crops in boxes. He was older, but he was the more innocent of the two.

Ella began spreading the tarp over the soy plants. She looked up at the sky. The sun was nearing the horizon. "Anne, I think we have time to forage. See what you can find."

Anne swatted Jakob's arm. "C'mon. Time for Anne's survival school."

"We're going...alone?" Jakob asked.

Anne squinted at the boy. He seemed more skittish now, outside of the truck, but certainly more than the previous night in the church. She supposed it was because he'd nearly been killed. *He'll get used to that,* she decided, and waved him to follow her. "Your dad's out here, right? Probably keeping an eye on things."

"I suppose," Jakob said, rooted in place until Anne moved into a stand of trees. Then he hurried to catch up.

Not afraid enough to leave me on my own, Anne noted, feeling glad that she now had a foraging companion. She never let her mother see, but these little foraging trips, alone in the wilderness, terrified her. It wasn't the predators. She could outwit most anything in the wild, hiding her small body with ease. She simply feared that she'd find a bloodied and emptied camp when she returned. At least now, with Jakob, if she found her mother dead or missing, she wouldn't be alone. It was a horrible way to think, she knew, but not unrealistic. She'd seen friends eaten. Had listened as they were plucked from their hiding spots and torn apart. The wild tended to take people away from her. Before finding Jakob and Peter, their group had been whittled down to just her and her mother—who she thought survived by the strength of her convictions, to right the wrong she'd helped perpetrate.

So, Anne took Jakob along, knowing that if her mother died, she'd still have him, and if she died...it wouldn't be alone. Jakob didn't need to know that, and she hoped it wouldn't happen, but she couldn't deny the comfort his presence would provide if death finally claimed her.

"Yes!" Anne scurried over a patch of soy, heading for the base of a tree. She began plucking small green plants growing in the moss that covered the lower bark.

Jakob crouched beside her. "What is it?"

She held up one of the small, three leafed plants. "Clovers. Duh."

"Clovers... Are they for luck?"

"First, four leaf clovers are for luck," Anne said. "Second, all clovers, three or four leaf, are edible and non-ExoGenetic." She scooted to the side. "Help me collect them."

They worked in silence, plucking the small plants at the roots, stuffing them into a cloth bag that Anne pulled from her pocket. When there wasn't a single clover left, Anne moved on, checking the bases of all the trees. Where there was moss, there was often other edible things. Jakob split away from her, searching on his own.

He was only ten feet away, but Anne kept an eye on him, making sure they didn't get too far apart.

"What about this?" Jakob plucked something from the ground. He turned around, holding it up victoriously as Anne came to see what he'd found. "Mushrooms are—"

She swatted the long stemmed, white topped mushroom from his hands, shattering it like it was made of glass.

"The hell!" Jakob grumbled. "We used to have mushrooms like that all the time."

"Did you also have diarrhea, nausea, and stomach pain resulting in a coma? Wait, no, you didn't, because you're still alive." She pointed at the mushroom's remains. "That's a Destroying Angel. It would kill you."

Jakob deflated. "Oh."

"Just...only pick what I tell you to, okay?" Before he could reply, a bright patch of yellow caught her attention. She gasped and hurried toward the glow. When Jakob caught up to her, he was breathless, but more from panic than running, she thought.

"What is it?" he asked.

"Dandelions." She pulled one from the ground, carefully pushing her hands down, freeing the roots from the moss in which it grew. She held the plant up for Jakob to see, then popped the whole thing in her mouth and chewed. "They're good. You can eat the whole thing."

Noting his disgusted face, she searched the area and was pleased to find a few more edible bits of vegetation clinging to life at the fringe of the world's genetically aggressive crops. She pulled a small sampling of the plants from nearby trees, combined them in her hand and held it out for Jakob to see.

He looked dubious. "What is it?"

"Clovers, dandelion, chive, and a Chanterelles mushroom. None of it will kill you. Or even make you sick." She carefully placed bits of chive atop the flat, golden mushroom head, placed a few cloves on top and then wrapped it all up in a dandelion stem, the bright flower looking like an ornate bow on top of a present, which in Anne's mind, wasn't far from the truth.

She placed the small package in Jakob's hand. "Eat it."

He looked down at the slowly unraveling vegetation. "It won't kill me?"

"It's one of the last things on Earth that won't," she said.

He let out a long breath, then put the whole thing in his mouth. His nose scrunched up as he chewed through the dandelion stem, but then he looked surprised, and pleased. "Not bad."

"Right?" She pulled another dandelion and put it in her bag. "Now we just need to gather enough for four people."

Jakob frowned. Looked at the sky. Dusk and all its heinous possibilities was nearly upon them. "We better get to it then."

The two worked in near silence, gathering small plants under Anne's direction. Jakob paid attention to everything she said, which made her happy, and he willingly tried everything she pointed out, even the stuff that tasted gross. Within twenty minutes, they had enough for a decent-sized salad. It wouldn't be filling anyone's belly, but would provide some nutrition, and the pleasure of eating something real.

As they snuck back to camp, Anne told Jakob how to hide, how to detect predators—with his ears, with his nose, with his eyes. "If you're going to survive," she told him. "You're going to have to learn from the best."

He laughed at that, but the very fact that she was still alive made him listen. They approached the camp in silence, practicing stealth, which Anne thought Jakob needed the most help with. He even breathed loudly. But with some pointers, he became silent enough that they crept to within thirty feet of her mother and Peter. They were standing close; the way her mother used to with Eddie. They were speaking quietly, but their voices carried in the abject silence.

Anne flinched at what she heard, but when she looked at Jakob for confirmation that he had heard the same, he just looked confused.

"What?" he whispered.

Anne held a finger to her lips, but it was too late.

"C'mon out," Ella said, sounding casual. "What did you find?"

Anne pushed herself up and walked out like she hadn't been spying. She held up the bag of foraged plants.

Ella took it and looked inside. "Wow. You guys found a lot."

Her praise was out of character. She'd normally just take the plants, comb through them, and then divvy them up, eating in silence. Peter seemed to bring out a different side of her. A kinder side. Anne liked it but didn't trust it. If her mother got soft, it would be dangerous for both of them. Then again... Anne looked at Jakob and he smiled at her, munching on a dandelion. *I'm getting soft, too.* And if what she had heard was true, she understood why, and why remaining strong was more important than ever.

After a quiet meal of foraged salad and protein bars, the foursome crawled beneath the shelter Ella had created. The tarp, which had been rubbed with tree sap collected from some nearby pines, was laid out over the soybean crop. She'd covered the sticky surface with soil and a collection of strong-smelling plants. They'd be invisible to the eyes and noses of any predators that happened past them, as long as nothing stepped on them, and no one snored.

Under the tarp, the air got humid and hot, but Anne was accustomed to these conditions. She preferred it to the wide-open space or the hard surface of the church. Felt safer despite the lack of walls.

But sleep wouldn't come. The words she'd heard, spoken by Peter, kept repeating through her head, fueling her insomnia. "Are you going to tell her I'm her father?"

Her mother hadn't replied to the question before Jakob gave away their position, but the question itself implied her mother believed him to be her father, too. And that made no sense.

None at all.

But she hoped it was true. Because it meant she had a family.

A brother.

A chill ran through her body, and she was gripped by a sudden anxiety. If she had a family, it also meant she could lose a family, and if life had taught her anything, she knew in her heart that she would lose them.

She slowly reached out her hand, finding Jakob. He flinched, but then took her hand in his. They squeezed each other, providing comfort in the dark, eventually falling asleep.

Anne woke in the early morning hours. She couldn't see the sky beneath the tarp, but her internal clock knew that the sun was still an hour off. She also knew her fears from the night before were well founded. Something was moving around the outside of the tarp, near her feet. She held her breath, fighting the urge to pull her legs higher. She nearly screamed when Jakob squeezed her hand. She hadn't realized they were still holding on to each other.

Don't react, she thought, *don't move.*

But then he did.

Downward.

Dragged out of the tarp.

31

Sunlight glistened through Spring's thin green leaves, which were shifting about in the wind like they were nothing more than a layer of algae-colored water. The emerald light they cast, mixed with diamonds of orange, created a magical kaleidoscope. In the light was warmth.

Safety.

Familiarity.

Peter recognized the view. He'd stood here before, in the street, in front of his childhood home. He felt young again, seeing the world in more vivid colors than he remembered. But this is what it looked like, wasn't it? This is what the world had felt like back then. The magic of it had faded with age, but he remembered it now.

Missed it.

He wept, looking up, the tears streaming down his cheeks.

"Thank you," he said to no one. Maybe the trees. Maybe his subconscious.

Motion tugged him from the view. He resisted, but the trees vanished in a blink, replaced by darkness. The crunch of vegetation and the swish of a plastic tarp replaced the quiet of the memory made dream. The calm he had felt fled in the face of terror and rage, the latter of the two controlling his motions.

He rolled out from under the tarp, slipping out of the intolerably humid blanket and into the clear night. He moved instinctually, having no memory of what set him off, but somehow knowing it had been Jakob's scream that pulled him from the dream and set him moving. The boy's voice still echoed in his ears. The shotgun in his hand came up as a shadow descended over him.

Too late.

His arm was pinned beneath a boney limb.

The weight hit his chest next, driving the air from his lungs.

He froze when the cold edge of a blade—not a claw—pressed against the skin of his throat. He waited for the attacker to drag the knife across his neck, sever the artery, drain his life. But the assault stalled. The knife pulled back.

"You're dead," Ella said, as she leaned back.

"Ella?" Peter's body tensed, and he fought the urge to backhand her off of him. "What the hell?"

"A lesson better learned before it's real." She stood up over him. "You're dead because you came out."

"I heard Jakob—"

"And now you're dead."

"God-damn it, Ella. Where is Jakob?"

"Here," Jakob said.

With his night adjusted eyes, Peter found Jakob sitting at the foot of the tarp looking confused. "Are you hurt?"

"Just confused." The boy rubbed his head. "Maybe a bump on the head. Something pulled me out of the tarp."

Peter sat up, glaring at Ella. "Why? What's the point?"

"If you had stayed hidden, you'd be alive."

"I *am* alive."

"Only because I'm not an ExoGen."

"And you expect me to just cower under a tarp while my son is taken?"

"Anne and I are alive because of this rule. Once hidden, stay hidden. No matter what. People were taken during the night, and we survived by not moving."

"Maybe some of those people would still be alive if you had."

Even in the dull blue moonlight, Peter could see the disappointment in Ella's eyes. Had she really thought he'd buy into this? That he'd agree to not chase after his son, if he was taken during the night? Hell, he'd already faced down a hunting party of Riders to get him back. *That's why she's doing this,* he thought. *She would have left him there.*

"We didn't come up with this night one," she said. "A lot of people were killed, more from chasing after those who had been taken, than had actually been taken. When a rabbit is caught, the rest don't come out of hiding to face the pack of wolves. We're the prey now. Sometimes we need to act like it."

"If the choice is to hide or die beside my son, I'll die with my son."

Again, she looked wounded, and it took him a moment to figure out why. *Anne...* He hadn't really started thinking of her as his daughter. He barely knew her. But if she really was his flesh and blood, should he die beside his son, or survive to protect the daughter he just met?

I couldn't do it, he thought. *I couldn't abandon Jakob. No matter what.*

No one was more important to him. He suspected Ella felt the same for Anne, which was why this little object lesson was skewed. "You'd lay still while Anne was taken?"

"She'd never be found," Ella said.

"That's a dangerous opinion," Peter countered. "But the question is still valid. Would you let a Stalker make away with Anne while you hid beneath a tarp?"

"It's not the same," Ella said.

Peter climbed to his feet. "It's exactly the same."

Ella stepped back, the soybean plant crunching beneath her foot. She crossed her arms. "I'm not going to talk about this now." She started moving away, retreating into the shadows.

Peter followed her, grabbing her arm and spinning her around. "You don't have a choice."

Ella glanced down at his hand clutching her arm. "Really?"

He didn't remove his hand. "Tell me, Ella. Explain to me how your daughter is more important than my son."

Ella stood rigid, her normally full lips pinched together in a tight white line.

"We've been a lot of things to each other over the years," he said, "but we've never lied to each other."

Still nothing.

His grip tightened. Her eyes darted back down to her arm.

"You made me think my son was dead," he said, giving voice to the energy that was being expressed through his vice grip. He loosened his grip. "Tell me, or we're done."

"What do you mean, 'done?'" she asked.

"We'll go our separate ways," he said. "I can either trust you implicitly with the life of my son, or...I can't. In which case, you're on your own."

"You would leave us?"

"It's your choice."

She stared at him, her eyes wavering between doubt and resolve. Finally, her shoulders sagged. "Fine. But you're not going to like it."

He let go of her arm. "Didn't think I would."

Head lowered toward the bed of tightly packed soy plants, Ella said, "She's the best of us both."

"Anne," he said.

She nodded.

"You can't possibly expect me to favor one child over the other simply because Jakob was born from Kristin and not you. I knew you didn't like her. God knows, she hated you. But what you're suggesting, some kind of eugenics parental preference—"

"What?" Ella objected. "I'm not saying anything like that. Peter, you know me."

"I'm not sure how well this time," Peter said. They'd spent large portions of their life apart, but every time they came together, the relationship seemed to zipper right back together. He'd thought that was how things were playing out once again, but now he wasn't so sure. The world had changed, and Ella with it, neither for the better.

A deep sadness filled Ella's eyes, and for a moment, he saw Ella the way he remembered her on the day he had told her he was staying with Kristin.

And then, she was gone.

Long black fingers tipped with rounded, black talons slipped out of the darkness behind Ella, snapped closed around her waist and then yanked her back. The motion was fluid and unnatural, snatching Ella away in a blink. As she slipped back into the darkness, she managed to say, "Let me go, Pete," before falling silent.

Like a clubbed animal, Peter went rigid, stunned dumb.

It was Jakob who snapped him out of his surprise. "Dad!"

Peter looked back to find his shotgun in the air, tossed by Jakob. He caught the weapon, shouted, "Stay here! Hide!" and then charged into the woods after Ella, hoping that the exchange they'd just had wouldn't be their last. The way he'd left things with his wife was burden enough. He didn't think he could handle losing Ella this way. Not after the things he'd said. The way he'd treated her. Like she wasn't her. Wasn't Ella. His Ella. If she was different now, it was because she'd been hurt—was *being* hurt—and that was unacceptable.

She might be different.

She might be wrong.

But she was still...what?

Her. With a capital H.

The girl who helped form the boy into a man.

And he wasn't going to let her go, whether or not she was wrong. Not without a fight.

32

Running through the dark acted like a time machine, propelling Peter to some other place, charging down an enemy position to rescue a captured comrade. It had been equally hot then, but the kind of dry that scratches your throat with each breath. And the land beneath his booted feet had been hard-packed sand, not...this. Not crunchy plants that were impossible to run over silently. Each step brought the rubbery crunch of firm, water-laden leaves. His approach would not be stealthy, even if he cut his speed in half, so he poured everything he had into speed, while listening for a direction. The thing that took Ella had slipped away into the dark without a trace.

He tried not to think about that long-ago mission, though he could still feel its weight on him, threatening to spill over from memory to déjà vu. The conclusion of that now-ancient assault had ended with many dead enemies, but at a price. The lesson for him then was, 'sometimes there's nothing you can do.'

He heard the hard chop of blades—claws—striking bark.

It's moving through the trees, he thought, turning his gaze upward in time to see something like a bright apparition slipping through the sky. Was it a bird? *No,* he decided, birds didn't need to leap off trees. *Unless...* He remembered his earlier thoughts of those massive, flightless birds that had once roamed South America. But they were fast, like killer ostriches. Something like that wouldn't move through the trees. This was just another who-knows-what conjured by the vast trough of available DNA unlocked by ExoGen.

A flash of white ahead made him flinch. Instinct guided his hands as he raised the shotgun, taking aim at the broad, almost luminous surface. Part of him thought, *Don't shoot! You'll hit Ella!* but the rest of him knew that if he didn't shoot and slow this thing down, it would eventually escape. And at this range, even if a few pellets found Ella, they probably wouldn't be fatal. He had to risk it.

The gunshot cut through the night like some ancient cannon announcing the battle's start. It was followed by a high-pitched shriek, the target struck. But was it stopped? Or even slowed?

Peter kept the shotgun against his shoulder, ready to fire. His pace slowed as his ears fought to hear over the shotgun's echo.

A gunshot blasted to his left. Peter ducked, recognizing the sound for a breaking branch only after he hit the vegetation. The creature was getting sloppy. *Injured,* he decided, climbing back to his feet, and stalking toward the sound of crunching soy plants.

He slowed when a smell struck him: fetid, rotting and rank. He winced, putting his hand to his nose. The air was thick with the scent of ammonia, sauerkraut, and sun-baked, bloated fish. This was the scent of a kill. The animal, upon its death, had vacated its bowels, mixing the fragrances with blood from its wounds.

He stopped when he saw the thing ahead. It was a large mound of gnarly white fur, the size of a horse. He took a step closer, wincing once more at the smell. The too-strong smell. He'd just shot the monster, but it smelled a week old. Unless this thing had evolved to rapidly decay, which made no sense, the stench wafting up from this thing was manufactured. *Like a skunk.*

Closer now, he could see the white fur was actually a mottled gray, like the thing had been rolling around in mud. Its physical appearance was nearly as horrible as its smell. And then he knew what it was—or what it had been before DNA had been flung about through nature like a genetic Pollock painting.

It's playing opossum.

It is *an opossum—or was, once upon a time.*

He willed his eyes to see better in the moonlight's glow, trying to confirm that Ella wasn't going to be hit when he put a cloud of 12 gauge into the creature's back. It would quickly go from playing dead to being dead, but he wanted to be sure Ella wouldn't join it, if she hadn't already.

Keeping the shotgun aimed at the swath of putrid fur, he slowly crept around the creature's head, or what he thought was the head. The opossum was bent in on itself, most of its features concealed. Then the back moved.

Peter froze.

Was it an involuntary muscle twitch?

Was it preparing to strike?

He held his breath, sure that he was going to cough from the ammonia scent, triggering an attack. The back twitched again, and then again, further down. It was like something was twitching inside the thing.

Then a pair of eyes, black orbs like twin eight balls, opened from the creature's back.

Holy sh—

A second pair opened, further down, staring at him.

Like some demon from the Biblical apocalypse, this opossum had evolved eyes all over its body. Ten sets in all, opened to stare at him, hunger in every orb. He wasn't sure if the revelation, in combination with the death scent, was meant to confuse an enemy, or to intimidate. It was doing both, but he wasn't another ExoGen predator. So, this must have been a hunting technique, luring prey in close to...what? The body remained still.

Then one of the sets of eyes lifted upward to reveal a head. The opossum's face was recognizable. Its ears were tipped black, as was its long snout. But the head was the size of a German shepherd's. The mouth opened wide, hissing and revealing two-inch canines. Normal opossums, the size of footballs, had impressive jaws and teeth. This thing was worse than any attack dog he'd seen.

And it wasn't part of the larger creature's mouth, it was *clinging* to its back. The giant opossum was laden with ten young, each nearly as big as Peter. Knowing the ruse was up, the larger mother began to stir, shedding its young like Allied soldiers from a landing craft on the beaches of Normandy.

Peter took a step back, unsure of what to shoot first, or whether or not he should. *Ten young and an enormous mother.* He'd already fired one shell and didn't have enough to take care of the others. And that was if they lined up, nice and orderly, and let him take his time to aim and shoot. He'd have to pump each shell into the chamber before firing, and if these things came at him in any way other than one at a time, he was screwed.

So, he took another step back, hoping the distance would equal time. But he didn't think so. While these things were identifiable as once-upon-time opossums, mostly thanks to the hair and their behavior, they were built for strength and speed, closer to that of a jaguar than their more recent genetic history.

He shifted his aim to the mother. The smaller ones were each big enough to take him down, but they were still animals. Still young. Without the mother's living presence, the young might become confused, or even despondent. That would give him time for...what? He still didn't have enough shells, and there still wasn't any sign of Ella.

Had she been dumped in a tree? Killed and left behind? Whatever the case, he didn't see her, not even as the big mother stood on its hind legs and opened its mouth, which looked like it belonged more on a massive Nile crocodile. It hissed, pushing its death stink over him, causing him to gag. Its arms snapped open wide, the black, hairless limbs nearly invisible in the night. The tail, also black, snaked backward slowly, sliding up a tree trunk like a constrictor in the jungle, a mind of its own.

The mother was intimidating as hell, but a shotgun shell in the chest would change that. Peter stopped moving back and looked down the sights, placing the barrel directly on the creature's center mass. Impossible to miss. His finger slowly hooked around the trigger while he held his breath against the rank hissing flowing over him.

And then, with a twitch, he stopped.

The mother's gut moved.

Was it another young about to detach or...

Oh, God.

The form inside the mother's belly was human.

He could see the arms and legs moving. Straining. Ella was trapped inside the mother's belly, and if he took the shot, he'd hit her, too. But had the thing eaten her whole? Was she slowly being digested in its stomach? She'd surely be dead already if that was true.

But the truth was even more twisted. Pursued and perhaps wounded by his first shot, the mother opossum had played dead, but not before stuffing its catch into its pouch. The opossum was a marsupial, and while this creature had devolved in many ways, it had kept that ancient evolutionary trait shared by kangaroos and koalas. And it had adapted it for storing more than offspring. It was using the pouch to hold its prey. How many other meals had met their end in that pouch before being fed to its brood?

"Ella!" he shouted. "If you can hear me, I'm coming for you!"

The flailing movements inside the pouch froze for a moment and then really moved.

Ella was trapped, but she was still fighting.

Peter swung the shotgun toward the nearest opossum and pulled the trigger, erasing its head. The gore splattered into the face, and eyes, of the next creature, sending it into a mad shrieking spin, perhaps because it was disoriented, but he hoped a bone fragment had found its eye—or even better, its brain. He didn't wait to figure out which. He turned and fired again, putting a hole through another opossum's chest.

Only then, after two lay dead and one spun in confused circles, did the remaining seven, and the mother, take action—they scattered.

"Damn it!" Peter shouted.

If they scattered, he might never catch the mother. But the monsters weren't fleeing. They were doing what opossums did best—deceiving. All at once, like the maneuver had been rehearsed, the family of ExoGenetic marsupials altered course, coming at Peter from all sides.

He opened fire, pumping the shotgun after each trigger pull, dropping three more of the creatures. But as each young killer opossum fell, another took its place, leaping over its fallen brethren, along the ground, or climbing up the trees. Peter pulled the trigger as an airborne opossum fell from above. Guts blasted upwards, bloody Fourth-of-July streamers arcing outward, but the creature's momentum carried it downward, tackling Peter's back.

Air coughed from his lungs as the impact slammed him down on the firm bed of soy plants. Despite the dead creature laying over his torso and head, he still had a clear view of the now purple sky above, staring up through the portal of flesh carved by the shotgun. As the thing's guts slid toward his face, the view was blocked by another of the young opossums. It looked down at him, unflinching as it lowered its snout through the remains of its brethren, teeth bared to carve off Peter's face.

Peter felt for the shotgun, but he'd dropped it when he'd fallen, and he couldn't find it. Even if he could have, firing from the side would likely break his wrist. So, he gave up on the shotgun and reached down for his belt, freeing the knife, and swinging it up without looking. He felt a moment of resistance against the blade, and then it sank into something soft before striking something solid—meat and then bone.

His view cleared as the young killer opossum reared back. In that moment of clarity, Peter withdrew the blade from the thing's back and thrust again, this time putting all five inches of the blade through its temple, skewering its brain. The creature's long tongue lolled from the side of its toothy mouth. Then the black eyes became vacant, and the whole thing fell to the side, taking the blade with it.

Was that six down? Peter wondered, as he tried to squirm out from under the pair of dead opossums. *Or was it five?* He couldn't remember, but he knew that whatever the count was, he was dead if he couldn't get up and recover his weapons.

And then, that rare stench flowed down over him as the night sky was blotted out by a large body. The mother opossum stood over him, her awkwardly massive jaws open in a silent hiss. Her maw looked big enough to swallow him whole, and he thought that was exactly what she intended to do, as she reached down toward his head.

As the first trickle of drool struck Peter's cheek, dangling from a four-inch canine just a foot from his face, the opossum was cast in bright red light. Something roared and charged, striking the mother opossum in the side, its spiky horns piercing flesh. The mother was knocked aside, replaced by the rumbling body of his rescuer, which he recognized the moment it belched exhaust over his face and pulled forward.

Peter reached up and caught the spiked metal frame he'd welded to the bumper. Once he was pulled free of the dead, he rolled for his shotgun, snatched it up, pumped it and found a target. He pulled the trigger, knocking a young opossum back. A shriek spun him around, and he swung the weapon like a bat, catching a second youngster in the side of the head. It landed on all fours, stunned, but not dead. Peter rushed forward, put one hand on the back of the creature's coarse hair-covered neck, and the other beneath its long snout. He pushed down hard on the neck, while shoving the snout up. The sudden movement produced a loud crack, and the thing fell limp.

Peter spun, looking for another attack, but a sudden thunderous booming dropped him to the ground. Fire spat from the back of the truck as the machine gun unleashed its few and final rounds.

A voice cut through the silence that followed. "Dad! Get in!"

He turned and saw Jakob standing in the flat bed of the truck, which looked like it had seen some action during the night. It was covered in scratches, and the windshield was shattered, but maybe that had happened on the way, because if Jakob wasn't driving... He stood up and saw Anne behind the wheel, looking back. She waved.

Peter recovered his knife and stalked toward the mother. The creature was dead, one half of its head punched through with three clean holes, the other side missing completely. The thing's belly writhed as Ella fought. Her hand stretched out and then, with a sick tearing, a knife burst from within the opossum and slipped down through the skin. Ella emerged, eyes wide with horror, body covered in mucus. She saw Peter, blinked, and then fell, her eyes rolling back. He caught her slick body before she hit the ground, but she was out for the count. He carried her back to the truck, as Jakob opened the back door. Working together, they slid her inside.

"Buckle her down," Peter said to Jakob.

The boy nodded and climbed inside.

"I think they're all dead," Jakob said. "We don't have to ru—"

"We just made a hell of a lot of noise." Peter knocked on the passenger side door and waved Anne over. The girl understood and scooted out from behind the wheel. "I don't want to be around when every hungry thing within a few miles comes looking for a snack, do you?"

Jakob climbed into the truck without another word and set to work, buckling Ella's prone form.

When Peter climbed behind the wheel, Anne was smiling at him.

He paused, not comprehending what could have put a smile on the girl's face.

"I like your way better," she said.

Understanding, he grinned back. "Me too."

He shoved the gas pedal down, shredding soy plants as the tires spun and caught, propelling them back toward the road and the rising sun.

33

The sun rose, a beacon guiding them east. The roads were congested with vehicles, abandoned at the end of civilization. Some had been fleeing the Change, only to discover that there was nowhere to run, and then, that they didn't want to run at all.

They wanted to feast.

Jakob looked at a pair of SUVs stopped on either side of the road, their doors still open. In the middle of the road, between the two vehicles, were a pair of skeletons dressed in tatters, still locked in mortal combat as they attempted to devour each other, neither combatant having lived long enough to evolve into super-predators.

Jakob had seen a few people during the Change. Long black nails. Extended canines. He thought they had looked a lot like basic vampires, with appetites to match, though people weren't only eating people back then. They were eating anything they could catch—squirrels, livestock, pets. But people weren't the only creatures on the planet changing. Sometimes the pets ate their masters. Sometimes the herds turned on the farmer, before turning on each other.

He'd been protected from most of it, thanks to the forewarning and the biodome supplied by Ella. His father had tried to warn people, but no one believed him. Not even their family. Why would they? Food was plentiful, and nearly free. World hunger had been cured. To see a devil in those details took a level of paranoia that modern culture had mocked. Jakob didn't blame them. He understood the benefits of hacking genomes, and he understood the desire to feed the world had been *mostly* noble with a trace of greed. GMOs could have saved the world. He knew that. It was the rush, and hubris, that had turned the tools of modern humanity bad. But wasn't that always the way? Isn't that what history taught, back to the very beginning? The ExoGen crops were just the latest example of 'corrupted human ingenuity.' His father's words, though he didn't think Peter had ever said them to Ella.

She lay in a fetal position across the back seat, held in place by two seat belts, her legs across Jakob's lap. She was still unconscious but breathing. Anne worried her mother had fallen into a coma. Peter said she hadn't, but Jakob recognized the false confidence in his father's voice.

Looking at the woman sprawled across the back seat, it was hard to imagine his father having feelings for her. She was dirty, ragged, and hard. She had a scar above one lip, and another revealed by her shaved head. She was also decisive and confident. If he was honest, she was a lot like his father. His mother had been...soft. Fragile. Sensitive. She hadn't been cut out for the hard life of a farmer, let alone for the end of civilization. And in her weakness, or perhaps just to spite Ella's warning, she had eaten. In secret. Not a lot. Not as much as everyone else. But enough to instigate the Change. It just took longer. Had she been more like Ella...

Jakob shook his head. Images of his mother that he'd wanted to forget were coming to the forefront of his mind, not just of his mother launching herself at him, giving in to the hunger, trying to tear out his throat, but also of the woman-thing who had straddled him in the gas station parking lot. The woman he believed was his mother, but also wasn't. His mother was dead. What he saw had been something... stronger. Confident. And savage. Perfectly adapted to the new world. But he also knew that wasn't possible. His mother was dead. Shot. He looked up at the back of his father's shaved head. *Wasn't she?*

The skeletons in the road crunched beneath the truck's tires. Jakob winced at the sound.

"Sorry," his father said. "Couldn't avoid them."

"Crunch," Anne said. "They weren't people anymore anyway."

Jakob's brow furrowed. "They used to be. Isn't that enough?"

"They were monsters," Anne said. "Same kind we'd kill now without thinking about it."

"It's not that easy," Jakob said. "Is it, Dad?"

Peter kept his eyes locked forward, steering around an overturned 18-wheeler.

Finally, with a quiet voice, he said, "No. It's not that easy." He glanced back. "I'll try to avoid them next time."

Anne shrank down in her seat. "Going to have to be tougher than that to survive out here."

Jakob could hear Ella in Anne's voice, and he thought the girl was overcompensating for her mother's silence. "She's going to be okay."

"Shut up," Anne snapped. "You don't know that. Don't tell me something you don't know." She spun around and climbed to her knees. "You can't do that."

"Do what?" Jakob said, leaning back from Anne's angry eyes. "Geez."

"It's false hope," she said. "Just because your mom is—"

"Shut up, you little jerk," Jakob said, working hard not to show surprise at what he said.

"Asshole!" Anne said, lunging back, her fingers hooked. The look on her face was ferocious, and for a moment, Jakob thought she must have eaten some ExoGenetic food along the way. Then the anger shifted to surprise, as she was stopped in midair and yanked back.

"Hey," Peter shouted, the bark was so loud that Jakob and Anne were both stunned into silence. "Knock it off! Both of you!" He let go of Anne's belt, where he'd pulled her back into the front seat. He pointed at the seat and waited for her to sit. She complied with a huff, crossing her arms.

"Your mother is going to be fine," Peter said. "What she went through, it was hard on her body. She's unconscious, but her breathing is regular, and her pulse is strong. Her body and mind just need time to heal. She's a strong woman. You know that better than anyone. Just give her time, okay?"

Anne's arms tightened as her frown deepened. But then she offered a begrudging, "Fine."

Jakob was certain Peter would then make her apologize for her behavior. It's what his father would have made him do, but the man just continued staring ahead, stoic, a statue behind the wheel. Jakob watched him, seeing the concentration in his eyes. He glanced at the speedometer. They were going 40 mph, which wasn't fast by old-world standards, but it could be dangerous on a road as congested as this one. There were cars everywhere. Fallen trees. Predators hiding in wait, ready to pounce. At least, Jakob imagined there were. Since the previous night, they hadn't seen another living thing.

But that didn't mean they weren't out there.

And his father was thinking the same thing. He could see it in the man's eyes. And then, in the way his vision flicked back and forth to the rearview mirror. Jakob's eyes widened with the idea that something might be chasing them already, that his father was driving fast, with no regard for the dead, because they were being pursued.

He swiveled his body and cut a sidelong glance out the back window. He watched the road streak past, framed by trees, and pocked with the remnants of civilization. They crested a hill, and his vision turned upward. The sky above was bright blue, lacking even a trace of clouds, which seemed impossible given the humidity outside. *The clouds will come this afternoon,* he thought, *along with a storm.* Western Kentucky was on the fringes of the infamous Tornado Alley, where storms could roll in without warning, tearing entire cities to shreds. The sky above might be blue, but storm clouds could be rolling in behind them, or waiting to greet them over the horizon.

As they reached the bottom of the long hill and started up the far side, Jakob caught a glimpse of movement at the top of the hill. He strained to see what it was, but his view shifted to the pavement as they rose up a second hill.

"Jakob, buddy," his father said, sounding calm, but strained.

Jakob looked forward, meeting his father's eyes. He understood the look, which could be translated to something like, "Not a word." He was trying to spare Anne the stress of knowing they were being pursued. Jakob played along.

"Yeah, Dad?"

"You have the map back there?"

Jakob looked for their thick map book. Found it tucked into the back of the driver's side seat. Leaned over Ella to pluck it out. "Got it."

"We're about ten miles out—"

Jakob's heart hammered from the news. "From Alia?"

Peter gave a nod.

"But I don't think the direct route is going to work out for us. We need to find an alternative. Something more..."

"Winding," Jakob said, understanding the request.

"Probably a good idea," Anne said. "Since we're being followed."

Peter slowly turned toward the girl. Busted.

"But you knew that," she added, glancing up at the man who might be her father, too. "Two words. Situational awareness."

"How long have you known?" Peter asked.

"About five seconds after you saw them in the rearview," she said. "And a whole thirty minutes before Super Genius in the backseat knew." She motioned to Jakob with her head.

"Hey," Jakob said, but his offense lasted only a moment, mostly because she was right, and once again she had proved he had a lot to learn before he could survive on his own. He wasn't too proud to accept that. "So, who's back there?"

"*What's* back there," Anne corrected. "And the answer is always, 'nothing good.' So, find us a good route or hand me the map."

Geez, Jakob thought, wanting nothing more than to argue and put the girl in her place. But he remained silent, partly because he thought she'd win the argument, but also because they were just ten miles from Alia's biodome.

They'd be safe there. And with company.

He'd never seen Alia, but his mind's eye had painted a pretty picture based on how she had described herself. He assumed she might have embellished a little. He certainly had. But as the only other teenage girl... maybe anywhere, she'd be pretty much perfect, no matter what she looked like. He knew these were stupid thoughts to have, given the circumstances, but he was still a guy, and a teenager. As a non-ExoGenetic person, his teenage hormones were firing exactly as nature had created them to do. So, he turned to the map, found a circuitous, confusing route to the bio-dome, which had already been marked, and said, "Next exit. Turn right."

As they turned off the highway, Jakob looked back, watching the horizon. He saw nothing as they moved past the trees, invisible to whatever was chasing them. The side road was half the size of the highway, and curved like a snake, but it was mostly free of vehicles. Peter pushed the gas pedal down, bringing them to fifty-five, explaining, "We need to put some distance between us, so they can't hear the engine."

"If it's a bat-thing," Anne said, "that might not be possible."

"The trees will help," Jakob said.

Peter nodded, pushing five more miles per hour out of the engine and taking a sharp turn. The weight of the truck kept them on the road, but the tires chewed through gravel on the side.

"Next left," Jakob said, as they rapidly approached the turn.

Peter braked hard without screeching the tires and accelerated again. The rollercoaster continued this way for miles, leaving Jakob as car sick as he was desperate to reach their destination.

And then they did, parking at the edge of a treeline mixed with wheat. The field before them was covered in endless, almost luminous, carrot greens, poking out of the soil, flickering in the breeze. Jakob felt ill as he looked out across the field. All his hopes shriveled up and died as he saw compelling evidence that while the world had changed, Tornado Alley had still lived up to its name.

34

The farmhouse was in shambles. Branches had collected around the first floor, piled haphazardly by whatever great wind had swept through. Leaves shook in the breeze, rattling against the side of the house and the windows. The white home with green shutters had sustained the most damage to the second floor, which was caved in at the front. A soiled white sheet, clinging to the debris, rolled like a flag, signifying defeat. The biodome was equally covered in debris, but Peter couldn't see any breaks in the glass. But that didn't matter. If the house had been breached by the wind, predators could have easily followed.

And there was no denying that the place looked...

Dead.

"We should keep going," Anne said. "It's still morning, and this place doesn't look safe."

Peter was inclined to agree. They had a lot of daylight left to burn, and they could cover a few hundred miles if nothing happened on the way. The girl's instincts were honed for survival. Like her mother's. Like his had once been. Before he'd had a son, who he knew was about to insist they check.

"Dad," was all the boy said.

It was enough.

"We have to check," Peter said.

"It's a mistake." Anne turned back to Jakob. "You're going to get us killed."

"Since when did you become such a—"

"*Jakob,*" Peter said, silencing his son. He understood the boy's frustration. Anne had become antagonistic. But he also understood why, and he hoped Jakob would, too. With her mother unconscious, Anne had slipped into a kind of hyper-aggressive survival mode. She might trust Peter and Jakob in the simplest sense, but she didn't fully trust their ability to keep her alive. And safe. That deep trust was reserved for the woman sprawled across the back seat. Anne might be acting combative, but she was really just terrified.

"They're good people," Peter said to Anne. "Friends. We don't leave friends behind, just like we didn't leave your mother behind." He watched the girl's expression slowly shift. Her mother had taught her survival at all costs, but he still lived by a different code. No man left behind. And if the previous night's events had revealed anything, it was that Anne preferred the credo 'No man left behind,' over, 'Every man for himself.' He leaned toward the girl. "Right?"

"Ugh." Anne doubled her effort at crossing her arms so tightly she couldn't breathe. "Fine. But if there's a predator waiting in that house, I'm out of here."

Jakob leaned forward between the seats. "If there is anything not nice in that house, we'll face it together."

Atta'boy, Peter thought. Jakob had seen past the girl's walls and figured out what was really bothering her.

"As long as we're alive, you won't be alone," Jakob added, and the words acted like the sun on an ice cream cone, melting away Anne's anger.

She deflated, but recovered quickly, saying, "Laying it on a little thick, don't you think?"

"Had to make sure you'd understand," Jakob said. "You *are* a little slow."

Anne shook her head but was smiling now. "Going to kick you in the nuts when we get out of this truck."

Peter laughed despite what he feared they were about to find inside the house. "Okay now, let's get this over with. No nut-kicking." He put the truck in gear and idled forward. The mood shifted back to tense as they rolled over the carrot-shrouded pavement. Their view of the house was clear, but nothing had changed. The place was deserted and lifeless.

Or was it?

As he pulled closer, he noticed that there wasn't much debris on the ground around the home, just up against it. He also couldn't find any sign of destruction in the distant woods around the house. Either the tornado had touched down to smite the home, leaving everything else unscathed, or, "It's all fake."

"Is that like an existential comment?" Anne asked, leaning forward to look up at the house, as they stopped in the paved drive, fifty feet from the front of the building.

"Do you even know what that means?" Jakob asked.

"Do you?"

"Quiet," Peter said, and both listened.

The truck windows broke the silence, whirring as they lowered, letting in the wind and the hot, humid air. The vehicle's interior quickly became stifling, though not nearly as bad as the previous night, beneath the tarp. With the windows down, Peter turned the truck off. They listened for a full minute and heard nothing louder than the ticking of the cooling engine.

Peter picked up the reloaded shotgun from between the seats and opened his door.

"What are you doing?" Anne blurted.

"Can't take a look inside the house from inside the truck," he said, and then added, "can I?" so the kids would know he wanted them to stay put.

He normally would have wanted them as close to him as possible. But he wasn't about to leave Ella alone and unconscious in the back seat.

Peter leaned back in and tossed the keys to Jakob. "Anything happens to me—"

"Yeah, yeah," Jakob said, climbing from the back seat to the front and sliding behind the wheel. "I get it."

"I can probably drive better than him, you know," Anne said.

"Probably." Peter smiled, hoping to put the pair at ease.

They didn't like being left behind, especially unarmed. An hour after the sun had risen, he'd thought to look for the Beretta, but the weapon had been lost.

He'd realized that Ella had been carrying it the night before. Since she hadn't used it, and it wasn't on her person, he'd assumed the weapon dropped. With the machine gun drained, they were down to just the shotgun and a collection of knives. "But I have to make him feel important somehow, right?"

Anne just rolled her eyes and sat back.

"You see something, you honk." Peter said, and when Jakob nodded, he closed the door and turned toward the house. He was hoping to spot movement, perhaps someone ducking back as he turned, but the place was just as motionless. Even if the destruction was a façade, that didn't mean the inhabitants hadn't met with a dire fate.

He walked toward the house, shotgun held casually at his side, but ready to aim and fire. His eyes flicked back and forth, searching for signs of life, finding only the subtle shift of things caught in the wind, which rolled freely over the short carrot stalks. He took a moment to turn 360 degrees, searching the field and woods beyond for signs of life. But the world around the house was as dead as the inside.

He slowed as he got within ten feet of the front porch, sensing danger within the shadowy interior. Anne was right. Anything could be lurking in the dark. Going inside might be a mistake, but before he could turn around and explain that to Jakob, a voice, sudden and loud, startled him.

"That's close enough," a man's gravelly voice said.

He raised the shotgun toward the sound but held his fire. He recognized the voice, though it was deeper than he remembered. He lowered the weapon. "That any way to talk to a man whose best bowling score is ten points higher than yours?"

There was a moment of silence, followed by a confused, "Peter? Peter Crane? That you?"

During their radio conversations, they had discussed bowling more times than Peter cared to remember. Brant Rossi, Alia's father and the owner of this farm, had been something of a bowling enthusiast. Peter had only bowled a handful of times, but like most things of a physical nature, he'd taken to it easily. When he'd told Brant his top score, the man sounded like he'd had a heart attack. When he'd recovered, he'd revealed that Peter's near perfect score was in fact ten points higher than his personal best, after twenty years hurling balls. Since no one bowled anymore, they'd gotten a good laugh out of it, but Peter had heard the competitive tone in Brant's voice, hoping they'd one day get a chance to go one-on-one.

"It's me, Brant." Peter looked over the destruction. It looked just as real up close, especially that caved-in second floor. "Everything okay here?"

Brant stood from behind a tipped over table on the second floor. A metal table. Peter could have put all nine shotgun rounds into the table, and not one would have gotten through. The man was older, maybe late fifties with a full head of gray hair. On his own, he wouldn't be very intimidating, but the M16A1 assault rifle in his hands more than made up for his lack of physical prowess. "Don't mind the look of the place. Keeps out the curious. We did it a month ago, after some trouble with a hungry fellow." He motioned to the side of the house, and Peter saw the crumpled remains of something large.

"Oh, my God," came a younger female voice from inside the house. "Did you say Crane? Is that Mr. Crane out there?"

Brant chuckled but remained in place. "You think living with just your son is rough, try living with two women."

"We can hear you," said the younger voice, whom Peter assumed belonged to Alia, hidden somewhere back inside, probably being held back by her mother until Brant gave the all clear, which he had yet to do.

"So...what brings you this way? We haven't heard from you in a long time. You haven't been out there—" He motioned toward the horizon. "—this whole time?"

Peter understood the man's apprehension. If they'd been out in the wild all this time, there was a good chance they'd eaten ExoGen food. "Ran out of fuel for the generator. Was waiting for winter to risk finding more. We've only been off the farm for a few days."

"Why?"

"Company fell into our lap. Brought trouble with them."

The older man scanned the horizon. "A little bit like this?"

"Let's hope not."

"But no promises?"

"I wouldn't disrespect you by making a promise I might not be able to keep."

Brant's lips twitched back and forth. "S'pose any trouble you've led in this direction is going to find us whether you're here or not."

Peter didn't agree outwardly, but the man was right. If they were still being followed, Brant's family was in danger whether they stayed or were sent on their way. "Sorry to impose," was the best he could offer.

"Bring that beast round the side," Brant said, motioning to the truck. "Hide her in the garage.

Peter gave Jakob a wave, and the truck started with a roar, rolling slowly up behind him.

"That your boy driving?" Brant asked.

"It is."

"And is that your company in the passenger seat? Looks like a dainty thing."

Peter smiled. "Not in personality. Her mother is in the back seat."

"What kind of woman would bring a girl through this hellish world to see you?"

Brant meant it as a joke, but Peter answered. The Rossis were one of a select group of people who had biodomes supplied by Ella. They'd know who she was as soon as they saw her. "The kind who plans ahead for hellish worlds."

Brant looked confused, but only for a moment. Then his eyes went wide. "Don't tell me you've got Ella Masse?"

"I do."

"Well shit, I've got an earful for her."

He started toward the upstairs door, which upon closer inspection, appeared to be solid steel. Certainly not the original.

"I'm afraid you'll have to wait for her to wake up first," Peter said.

Brant paused, and a genuine look of concern crossed his face. "How bad is it?"

"Bad enough," Peter said. "But she'll pull through."

"She's a tough one." Brant sounded absent minded, lost in a memory.

"You knew her?" Peter asked.

"Knew her father better," Brant said, opening the silent, well-oiled metal door. "I'm her godfather."

Peter stood there, feeling a little dumb-founded. He thought he'd known Ella longer than any other living person. He now knew that wasn't the case. Ella had chosen her biodome recipients carefully. Apparently, they were occupied by people who wouldn't turn her away, regardless of her being accused of crimes against humanity. *How many other ex-boyfriends are waiting for her?* he wondered, and then he waved Jakob toward the garage. They needed to get out of sight before whatever was following them tracked them here. They'd done a good job evading whatever was pursuing them, but he wasn't about to believe they were safe here. Not for a second.

35

The inside of the home was Spartan, clear of any kind of normal household detritus. Metal tables, like the one he'd seen on the second floor, were positioned below all the windows. Nothing short of an RPG would reach anyone hiding on the floor, which begged the question, "You planning on being shot at?" Peter motioned to the nearest metal table leaning against the wall.

"Better safe than sorry," Brant said. "I think you told me that once, when I mentioned we were pacifists and had no weapons."

Peter looked around the living room where they stood.

There were two lounge chairs, a long couch upon which Ella laid, and guns. A lot of guns. Most were shotguns and assault rifles—Brant had an eye for the big stuff—but there were handguns, too. The weapons were arranged in lines, leaning against the metal tables, ready to be snatched up and fired at a moment's notice. "Looks like you took care of the weapon problem. Did you give up on the pacifism?"

Brant shook his head. "Ain't much left out there that's human, and I've never had a problem putting an animal down."

"Like your friend in the front yard?"

"He came around just a week after I visited the gun shop and found all this. Your advice was fortuitous. Don't think we'd have survived without it. Was a big sonuvabitch. Nasty. Did a real number to the second floor."

"So not all of it is a façade?" Peter asked.

"Losing the second floor inspired our new look." He led Peter into the downstairs hallway, where a lone china cabinet sat. "And it seems to be working. I've seen a few of them ExoGenetic bastards walk past at night without giving the house a second glance."

"How do you see them at night?" Peter asked, but then saw the answer to his question in the china cabinet. It was full of random military supplies, including ear buds, throat mics, night vision goggles and grenades—frag and flashbang—along with boxes of ammunition for a variety of weapons. "Hello, Santa Claus."

Brant opened the glass doors. "I kind of cleaned the place out. Figured no one else would need it."

Peter reached out but paused. "You mind?"

"Help yourself," Brant said. "I imagine you know how to use it all better than me."

Peter took an M67 fragmentation grenade from a box of four, each round, olive-drab explosive encased in perfectly fitted foam. "What kind of gun store carries frag grenades?"

"We're in Kentucky farm country," Brant said with a grin. "Plenty of varmints around need blowing up."

"Well, thank God for varmints then." Peter put the grenade back, mentally cataloging the contents of the cabinet. Before closing it, he took a cylindrical sound suppressor for an M16, slipping it into his pocket. "Though all the varmints I've seen since leaving the farm have tried to eat me."

"That rough out there?" Brant closed the cabinet and stepped toward the hall closet.

"You know where I served?" Peter asked.

"I remember."

"The last few days have been worse." Peter shook his head, replaying some of the things he'd seen and survived. "When I came back from Afghanistan, I struggled with PTSD. Nightmares. Mood swings. I got past it...but I was a trained soldier. I hate to think what this is doing to the kids. It's a hard world out there."

Brant gave a slow, thoughtful nod. "Kids are more resilient. More flexible. They'll adapt better than you or me." Then he opened the closet, revealing a stack of Kevlar tactical vests with an array of pockets and straps for ammo, grenades, knives, and anything else a soldier might want to carry.

"You're a saint," Peter said, taking a vest and slipping into it. Once it was secure, he handed a vest to Brant. The man held out his hands and shook his head. "Makes the missus uncomfortable."

"And the guns don't?"

"She's a peculiar woman."

"Where *is* Misha?" Peter asked. He'd heard all about Brant's wife, an Iraqi immigrant, which was both exotic and controversial in these parts, but he had yet to meet her. Alia, who had nearly tackled Jakob when they entered the home, seemed to get most of her genes from her mother. Jakob had been immediately smitten. Misha had yet to make an appearance.

Brant glanced up. "Keeps to herself mostly. Since the attack. Minds the bedroom, keeping watch over the fields. I'm sure she'll be down when she's feeling ready." Brant handed the vest back to Peter. "Give this one to your son."

"Appreciate it," Peter said, taking the vest. He would come back for supplies once everyone was settled. Speaking of which: "You know where the kids got off to?"

"I think they're kissing," Anne said, making both men flinch. She stood behind them, hands on the cabinet's glass door, looking inside like it contained boxes of candy.

Peter gently lifted Anne's hands away from the glass. "Don't even think about it. We'll get you sorted out later."

"Not much later, I hope," she said. "'Cause..."

"Not much later. But let me help you find what works best for you, okay?"

"Something that won't rip my shoulder off?"

"Exactly," he said.

"She can handle a gun?" Brant sounded surprised.

"We do what we have to," Anne said, looking into Brant's eyes.

The old man gave a slow nod. "S'pose you're right. But don't tell Alia that. She's liable to shoot her foot off."

Anne huffed a laugh. "Well then, she and Jakob are made for each other."

"Speaking of which, where is your—" Peter flinched to a stop, nearly saying, 'brother,' but managed to force out: "Jakob."

Anne scrunched her nose. "Where is *my* Jakob?"

Peter rubbed his temples. "Just...where is he?"

"Biodome," she said. "Making with the kissy."

Peter glanced at Brant, looking for a reaction at the news that his teenage daughter was currently unaccounted for and in the arms of a slightly older teenage boy. He hadn't said anything the first time Anne mentioned it, and he showed no reaction now.

"Where's the biodome?" Peter asked. He knew the way. Had seen the familiar entrance at the back of the kitchen when they first entered the house.

Brant pointed to the kitchen. "Through there." He took a step toward the stairs to the second floor. "Been away from my post too long. Never can be too careful, right? Better safe than sorry."

"Too true," Peter said, offering a smile that he hoped looked genuine. He was glad to see Brant alive, but the man wasn't well, perhaps suffering from his own PTSD. "Let's catch up later on."

Brant paused on the stairs. Turned to Peter.

"I'd like that. In the meantime, if you hear me give a stomp on the floor, it means we have company, so keep an ear out and your voices down."

"Will do," Peter said, and the man continued on his way and unlocked the heavy metal door at the top of the stairs, stepping through and relocking it from the other side.

Peter looked down at Anne. She was swirling an index finger around her ear.

"He's a good man," Peter said.

"He's off his rocker."

"Be nice."

"I'm serious," she said. "His wife isn't upstairs."

Peter froze in place. "What do you mean?"

"She's buried in the biodome, feeding the plants."

He turned toward the kitchen but didn't move. "Alia told you?"

"If she knows, she might be a little cuckoo, too, since she's kissing a boy just a few feet from her mother's corpse."

"It might not be her," Peter said, his voice dropping to a conspiratorial whisper.

"If it's not her," Anne whispered. "Then we might really be in trouble here."

Peter and Anne stared at each other.

The kid, as usual, made a good point. He opened the closet and motioned to the vests stacked on the floor. "See if you can find one that fits. Then stay with your mother." He stepped toward the kitchen and stopped in the doorway. "No matter what's going on, we're spending the night here. Try not to ruffle any feathers. It would be nice to avoid trouble for at least one night."

"Good luck with that," Anne said. She started rummaging through the vests.

Peter still wasn't sure if he was irked by Anne's straightforward nature, or appreciative of it. In many ways, she reminded him of some of the men he had served with, but they were hardened CSO soldiers, not twelve-year-old girls.

Not his daughter.

He shook the debate from his head and made his way through the spotless kitchen, eyeing the weapons lined up beneath the window, making a mental list of what was available. He'd left his shotgun in the living room, partly because he now associated the weapon with a slew of bad memories, but mostly because no matter where he went in this house, he was only a few feet away from enough weapons to hold the Alamo indefinitely.

Peter opened the biodome door and was greeted by the hiss of pressurization. He hadn't heard a generator running or seen any lights. Things like that would ruin the illusion that the home was dilapidated. But the decontamination chamber was still getting power from something. And that was a good thing. With the front of the second floor wide open, there would be ExoGenetic contamination throughout the house. He wouldn't be surprised if there were already small plants growing in the second-floor carpets. But with the fans whipping the air around him, sucking every fiber, pollen granule, and seed from his body, the biodome was safe...ish. The system wasn't perfect. Seeds could cling inside clothing. Pollen could hide in the treads of boots. Peter shook his body, helping the system do its work, but they'd all entered the home after days of rolling around in the ExoGenetic world. *He should have made us ditch the clothes*, Peter thought. *I should have*. But he'd been distracted. And it was too late now. Jakob and Anne had already been inside the biodome.

The fans cut off, and the second door unlatched. Peter pushed his way into the biodome and quickly said, "Stop!"

Jakob, who was sitting in an old wooden chair beside a raised garden bed, froze in place, a cherry tomato hovering over his open mouth. Alia was seated on the side of the raised bed, looking surprised and nervous. But was she acting like a teenage girl caught with a boy, or was it something more...like the long mound of dirt framed by potato plants in the next bed?

"What's wrong?" Jakob asked.

Peter thought for a moment, trying to figure out how to communicate his fears to the boy without panicking Alia, who had been eating this food during the months since the front of the home was compromised.

"You haven't washed your hands. Don't want to contaminate anything, do we?"

Jakob slowly lowered his hand away from his mouth, the silly teenage grin falling in time. He understood, but asked, "Are you for real?"

"Being cautious," Peter said.

Alia plucked the tomato from Jakob's hand and popped it in her mouth. Jakob started to object, but she stopped him with, "Dad checked for five miles in every direction. If it's growing out there, we don't grow it in here. So, if something new shows up, we'll know the food is contaminated. And yes, before you say anything, I know my mother is buried behind me."

Jakob looked like he'd been slapped. "Wait, what?" He flinched away when he saw the mound of dirt and understood what it meant.

"I'm sixteen," Alia said. "Not stupid. Dad says she's still alive, upstairs. I argued with him once. It's not a good idea, so don't try it. Whether he believes it, or is pretending, I think it's the only thing keeping him sane."

Peter locked eyes with the girl, evaluating her. Her almost orange-brown eyes remained calm and unflinching. "Were you two kissing?" he asked, trying to throw her off balance.

"Dad!" Jakob protested.

Alia just grinned and countered with, "Have you kissed your lady friend out there yet?"

"Can you fire those weapons out there?" Peter asked.

He knew this was the strangest parent-to-potential-girlfriend interview, but times and priorities had changed.

"I've only fired a gun once. I don't know what it was, but it was big. And loud. But it got the job done." Her eyes remained locked on Peter's, like she was the one interrogating him. "I'm not like my parents. Not like my father."

Peter read between the lines. It wasn't Brant who'd shot and killed the ExoGen creature outside. It was Alia. Kids in the new world were having to do horrible things to survive. Granted, even in the old world, kids in developing countries often had to kill to survive, but not so much in the heartland of the United States. Still, she was a survivor, and right now, that was the best anyone could ask for.

Peter smiled, turned, and hitched his thumb at her for Jakob to see. "She's a keeper, son. Don't screw it up."

"*Dad*," Jakob said again, horror reducing his vocabulary to a single word.

Peter turned back to Alia, intent on getting as much information about their current situation as he could. Their lives might depend on what the girl knew. "So, Alia..." His voice trailed off. Had he heard something?

"What was that?" Jakob asked, confirming Peter hadn't imagined the sound.

They fell silent, listening. The dull thud repeated three times.

Alia reacted first, just as Peter identified the sound as Brant's foot, banging on the floor of the home's second floor. "That's Dad!" she said, rushing for the door. "Something's here!"

36

Jakob followed close behind Alia, who ran up the stairs to the second floor. His father had headed through the kitchen without a word. They stopped at the metal door at the top of the stairs, surrounded by a collection of framed family photos hanging on horribly ugly patterned wallpaper—ducks and stripes.

"Dad gets...tense when he sees anything," Alia warned. "Best if you stay quiet, 'kay?"

"No problem," Jakob said, and he started to rethink the wisdom of following Alia rather than his father.

Alia knocked gently, three raps followed by a pause, then two.

Some kind of secret knock, Jakob thought.

Then with the gentlest of clicks, the door unlocked.

Alia crouched, hand on the doorknob. "Stay down, and we won't be seen."

Jakob squatted down and waited.

The door inched open so slowly that anyone watching wouldn't see the movement unless their attention was focused on it. With just enough room to slide through, Alia stopped pushing the door and slid in the upstairs hall, which appeared to be blocked by another metal table. She crawled behind the table and waved for Jakob to follow.

What he found on the other side of the door was a maze of tables, dressers, nightstands, and other large objects, all positioned so that someone could navigate the entire upstairs without being seen. Though he knew Brant had unlocked the door, the man was nowhere to be seen. He could apparently navigate the second floor like a mole in a tunnel.

Feeling like a World War I soldier crawling through a trench, Jakob followed Alia past several stations where weapons had been positioned. He wondered if they should stop and grab something, but Alia crawled right on past everything without pausing, so he followed, knowing he'd make a racket trying to move while holding one of the rifles.

They found Brant in what looked like Alia's bedroom. The walls were pink and hosted more than a few posters of teen heartthrobs, all better looking and more chiseled than Jakob. He felt a pang of jealousy, but it was quickly squelched by the knowledge that all the airbrushed faces smiling down at them were either dead or monsters.

"What is it?" Alia whispered to her father.

He was crouching by the front window, which had been mostly boarded up with planks of wood painted black. He lowered a pair of binoculars and turned to his daughter. He saw Jakob and looked surprised for a moment, then disappointed, then resigned. "I don't know. Something in the woods."

"Did you see them?" Alia asked. There was a trace of doubt in her voice, like maybe her father sometimes saw things that weren't there. Maybe this kind of alarm was a daily occurrence? Shifting winds moving shadows in the woods could be convincing illusions.

Brant's response was to hand her the binoculars. He moved aside to let her peek through the opening. As she did, Jakob thought about the sun's position in the sky. They were facing west, and it was still morning, so the sun was still behind them. But in an hour or two, they wouldn't be able to use the binoculars without risking a reflection.

"Yeah," Alia said, binoculars raised, voice tense, "something's out there."

She silently offered the binoculars to Jakob and moved aside. Brant didn't look happy about it, like Jakob's presence was disrupting the normal flow of things, but he didn't say anything. The brightness of the outside world, amplified through the lens, made Jakob squint. When his pupils adjusted to the light, he found himself looking at a blurry close-up of carrot stalks. He moved the binoculars up, watching the view become more distant, and more in focus. He stopped at the treeline, which was at least two miles off.

The only motion he saw was the gentle sway of the branches. Shadows moved in time with the branches, painting the wheat below with streaks of light and dark. Then, in one of the momentary beams of light, he saw something. It was pale, almost luminous in the flickering sunbeam.

And then, it was gone.

Moved, he thought.

He focused on the gap between the top of the four-foot-tall wheat stalks and the lowest tree branches, a good six feet of open space. In that emptiness, the shadows resolved, separating into subtly different hues and shapes.

Shapes that he recognized.

"Woolies," he whispered.

"Excuse me?" Brant said, his voice a little too loud.

Jakob looked back at the man.

Brant's face was screwed up in something between shock and revulsion. "You have a *name* for them?"

"We name everything we come across," Jakob said. "Well, mostly Anne does, but I—"

"You brought them here," he said.

"Not on purpose." Jakob could see the man's line of reasoning. If the Woolies followed them here, then they were responsible for whatever happened next. Jakob didn't necessarily disagree, but the look in Brant's eyes said the man wanted to dole out punishment. The rifle in his hands began to shift toward Jakob.

"We don't know if they've spotted us yet," Jakob said, making a case for why Brant shouldn't shoot him without coming right out and saying it. Alia looked oblivious to her father's intentions, and Jakob wasn't sure how she'd react. At the same time, Jakob shifted his left hand toward a handgun leaning against the metal table beneath the window. He wasn't sure if he could shoot lefty, or raise the weapon up in time to defend himself, or even if he could pull the trigger on another human being. But he didn't want to die.

So, he reached. And never made it.

"They know we're here," Peter said, causing everyone to flinch.

Jakob turned around, a pleading look in his eyes, hoping his father would understand the situation.

Peter gave Brant a nod. "We'll stand with you." He handed Jakob a Kevlar vest, its pockets loaded with weapon magazines, shotgun shells, a knife, a handgun, and other gear, some of which Jakob recognized, some he didn't. As Jakob took the vest, he noticed his father was wearing identical gear, similarly laden with supplies. He also had several heavy hitting weapons slung over his shoulder. After Jakob slid into the vest, Peter motioned to an automatic rifle leaning nearby. "The magazines I gave you are for the M16. You remember how to switch them out?"

"Yes, sir," Jakob said, feeling very serious, mentally running through the steps his father had taught him. *Magazine out, magazine in, chamber the first round, and shoot. And switch from the safe setting to fire, or auto if things get crazy.*

Peter turned to Brant. "Don't suppose you have a sniper rifle? We could stop this before it starts."

Brant just shook his head.

"You comfortable with holding the second floor?" Peter asked.

"Here for a reason, aren't I?" Brant's tone had lost all its friendliness. Even Alia seemed surprised by it. Then he added, "Can't leave Misha up here alone."

"Jakob," Peter said, placing a hand on his son's shoulder. "Hold the living room with Anne. Listen for my—"

"Something's coming out," Alia said, looking through a crack in the boards.

Still next to the window, holding the binoculars, Jakob looked across the field. Rows of wheat parted as something walked through them, carving a path.

Too small to be a Woolie, he thought, *which means,* "It's a Rider."

And then he saw the Rider's face.

It was her.

The hair was wrong, flowing like a mane from her head and down her back. The teeth were hideous, rising up like a fence to pierce the cheeks. But the eyes, even from this distance, looked familiar. As did the shape of her face.

His mother had followed them.

But it couldn't really be her.

He turned slowly back toward his father. "You killed her, didn't you?"

"Killed *who?*" Peter asked.

"Mom."

"You killed your wife?" Brant said, his voice far too loud and filled with revulsion. His weapon shifted toward Peter.

"She ate the ExoGen crops," Peter said quickly, making no move for his own weapon. "She *changed.*"

"But you killed her?" Brant said. "Killed your own wife?"

Peter looked torn, but then said. "No."

"What?" Jakob asked. His father had let him live with the idea that his monster-mother was dead and buried. "You shot her. I heard it."

"I let her go," Peter said. "She was still intelligent enough to know I could kill her if I had to. The shot you heard got her moving."

Jakob deflated. "Then she's alive."

"Maybe."

Jakob handed the binoculars to Peter and moved away from the windows. Peter took the lens and looked out the window. After just a moment, he frowned and said, "Yes." He turned to Jakob. "I didn't want you to be afraid of her."

Jakob said nothing. The idea that his mother, the monster, still existed and had all this time, filled him with nausea. Not because he loved her and wanted her back, or because he held out some kind of hope that their family could be reunited, though. She'd tried to *eat* him. And worse, when she'd pinned him to the gas station parking lot, she had *recognized* him.

She was here for him. He knew it.

"You should have shot her," Jakob said.

Peter just stared at his son for a moment, and then gave a carefully considered nod.

"She's coming," Alia said, looking out the window. "By herself."

Peter took a quick look and then gave Jakob's shoulder a tap. "To the living room. Same as before. Stay with Anne. Guard Ella." He turned to Brant and Alia. "You comfortable being overwatch from here?"

"It's why I'm here," Brant said again. He moved Alia behind him. "She'll stay with me."

"What are you going to do?" Jakob asked.

Peter turned and looked out the window again. After a moment, he said, "I'm going to go talk to your mom."

37

Shell-shock was a term coined in the wake of World War I to describe what was now known as Post Traumatic Stress Disorder, something with which Peter was familiar. But *shell-shocked* had become part of the general vernacular, applicable to everyday people in the grip of sudden and jarring surprise. After a car accident, an earthquake, a fire. Any traumatic event could leave a person shell-shocked, despite the utter lack of artillery shelling. Out of respect for the warriors who had given their lives during that horrible war, and those who, like him, knew what being shelled felt like, he had never used the term. But now, stepping out the front door of Brant's house to face his wife-turned-ExoGen-monster, he understood how a person, outside of battle, could feel the full and deeply profound horror of surviving an artillery or mortar bombardment.

His legs grew weak as he took the steps down to the brick walkway, which cut through the carrot greens and led to the long driveway. He stepped past the debris that made the house look dilapidated and abandoned, heading down the driveway, and stopping thirty feet from the house. If ExoGen Kristen wanted to talk, she'd have to come to him.

And she did. Confidently. He looked her over, seeing the face he remembered—if he ignored the long teeth poking up into her face and the elongated jaw accommodating them. But the rest of her... The once curvaceous body was slender, wiry, and twitching with muscles. Her hips jutted out like an emaciated runway model, but she didn't appear frail. She looked powerful. Long claws on the tips of her fingers matched the teeth. The last time he'd seen her, the claws had been an inch long. They were now at least four inches. A strong wind swept past her from behind, billowing her mane of hair in every direction, doubling her size, and making her look even more wild and dangerous. When the wind reached Peter, he caught a whiff of her scent, earthy and pungent.

In nearly all respects, the woman he once loved was now an animal. A monster. And yet, she was walking out to meet him like two parlaying generals before a battle. Parlay was usually agreed upon with the intention of finding a way to avoid bloodshed, but it was rarely successful. He didn't hold out hope that this would work out any differently, but if there was a chance, he had to see it through.

She slowed as she neared, eyeing the M16 in his hands. He lowered the weapon and slung it over his shoulder. A sign of good faith.

She stopped ten feet away, still standing in the field of carrots. Though she was completely unclothed, Peter felt naked under her gaze. She looked at him with predatory eyes, evaluating him. He was doing the same to her but found no weakness. She'd been reformed into an efficient killer, every part of her lithe form hardened for constant life and death struggle. She was still human in appearance, standing straight like a modern biped. She might have been a few inches taller, but unlike the Stalkers, she was still, beneath all the sinews and hair, human.

A Rider, he reminded himself.

What the Riders lacked in size, they made up for by forming a predatory symbiotic relationship with the Woolies. He glanced past her, looking for any sign of the lumbering beasts, but they were still hidden within the shadows of the distant forest. The question was, how many were there? And how many Riders? Until he knew that, Kristin had the advantage.

"Want son," she said, her voice deeper, but still familiar.

"Not a chance," Peter replied, matching her resolve. He also noticed her stilted language. While she was still clearly more intelligent than the average ExoGen predator, she had lost some of her previous sharpness.

But not her memory, he thought. *She knows who I am. Who Jakob is.*

He decided to appeal to her motherly instincts, if she had any left. "He wouldn't be safe with you."

She crouched down, shoved her fingers into the dirt and lifted a single carrot free. It was covered in soil, but looked thick and orange and delicious. She took a bite, dirt and all, her long, sharp teeth snapping the vegetable with a pop. She worked her jaw open and closed, crunching the carrot. Her teeth slipped in and out of the holes in her face. She swallowed loudly. "Will make son strong."

He understood the message. Jakob would be fed ExoGenetic crops and turned into a monster, maybe a Rider, or something worse. Or maybe her pals would just eat the boy. In all the infinite parallel universes that might exist, he didn't think there was a version of himself that would ever let that happen.

"You tried to eat him," Peter pointed out, though he doubted she would care.

To his surprise, she managed a slight frown that exposed the swollen gums holding her long teeth in place. "Hunger is...strong. But makes us strong. Too."

She stood up again, stretching out her lean body. "Stronger than soldiers. Stronger than you."

Peter held up his hands. "That might be true, but stronger is not always better."

She squinted at him, trying to make sense of his words.

"If I were stronger," he said, "I would have killed you."

All her twitching and agitation ceased.

"I would have shot you outside the house. Stopped you from..." He decided not to insult what she had become. "But I didn't. I showed you mercy. And kindness. Because I love you."

Her whole face seemed to relax. She dropped the carrot and took a deep, shaky breath. "Pe-ter..."

One slow step at a time, she exited the field and stepped onto the pavement, just five feet away. She stopped, just out of arm's reach. "Still... love?"

"Never stopped," he said, and it was the truth. He still regretted the decision to let her live, but only because he did love her. He could have spared her from this horrible life. Instead, he'd condemned her to endless savagery and painful adaptations.

"You come, too," she said, reaching for him.

He stepped back.

"I can't."

She looked wounded. "You said 'love.' You said—" Kristen sucked in a sudden and deep breath like she'd just been sucker punched in the gut. She doubled over, holding herself, stumbling back—and looking past him, toward the house.

Time seemed to slow as Peter turned around, turned his back on his enemy, and looked at the home. The front door was open, framing the small body of a woman whose head had been shaved, but was still easily recognizable to anyone who had met her.

Ella looked groggy and confused for a moment as she looked at Peter, and then beyond him. Then her eyes slowly opened, growing large with recognition. Despite the physical alterations, she still recognized Kristen, just as Kristen recognized her.

Jakob and Anne appeared in the doorway, reaching and grabbing, pulling Ella back and closing the door. But the damage had been done.

The wife he had loved, and spared, and wished he had killed, had seen his former lover, the woman who nearly destroyed them, who Kristen loathed with every fiber of her being. He had little doubt, that given the opportunity to kill Ella with no repercussions, Kristen would have done so long ago. And now, with him having just claimed to love her, she had seen Ella again, with her son.

A long string of curses flowed through Peter's mind as he swung back around, leaping away from Kristen as he did so. The move saved his life. Long claws sliced through the air where his neck had been a moment before. Had he not anticipated the attack, he'd be on his knees, clutching his neck and bleeding out in clear view of his son.

"We can leave in peace," he blurted, still hoping to avoid killing her in front of Jakob. He might regret letting her live again, but he still wanted to protect his son. "No one needs to get—"

Kristen unleashed a high-pitched scream and threw herself at Peter. As he blocked her first swing, a deep, bellowing roar replied. It was followed by the sound of thunder as massive feet charged over the carrot field.

The Riders were coming.

Kristen struck again, diving in a roll, and swiping at the inside of his leg. Kristen hadn't been a violent person. She'd never been trained in how to fight, yet here she was, trying to sever his femoral artery.

He leaped back and swatted down, pushing her hands away. When her legs bent to spring, he knew she was about to tackle him, and once they hit the ground, there would be no avoiding all her pointy parts. So, he kicked. Hard. A tooth broke in half as his boot connected with the side of her face and sent her sprawling.

His instincts said to go for the kill. Finish her off. But the man in him, who'd said, 'in sickness and in health,' who had held her hand while she gave birth, couldn't bring himself to shoot her where she knelt, like some captive POW.

He stumbled back. "Please. Kristen. Call them off. I'm giving you the chance to live again."

"Is not chance I want you to have," she growled, and then she dived to the side, moving on all fours. As soon as she landed, she leapt the other direction, closing the gap between them while keeping him off balance.

"Kristen!" he shouted. "No!"

Then she was upon him, arms and claws outstretched, jaws hung wide open, ready to cleave his face away. There was no avoiding what happened next. In the face of certain death, Peter simply reacted, instinct and training guiding his every move, while things like mercy and love took a back seat. He ducked down while reaching up to his chest. He drew the Glock 17 handgun from its holster, twisted his hand up, and pulled the trigger. The 9mm round sliced upward through the air before striking the soft skin beneath Kristen's chin and continuing on through her tongue, skull, and brain. As momentum pulled her up and over his body, the bullet carved a groove through the bone of her skull, following the curve and then ricocheting through the gray matter, shredding the brain, and erasing everything that was once Peter's wife, without ever exiting the body. Once upon a time, Peter would have called it a clean kill. As Kristen fell to the brick walkway behind him, blood dripping from the small hole in her chin, he thought it was tragic.

His wife was dead, by his hand, and their son had seen it happen.

And then, suddenly, Jakob was by his side, shouting, "Dad!"

But the boy didn't sound angry. He sounded worried. Like his now-dead mother was still alive and trying to eat him once more.

"Dad!" Jakob yanked on Peter's arm. Then the boy punched him. "Snap out of it!"

Peter glanced from his dead wife to his son.

"They're coming!" Jakob shouted, pointing to the field where Kristen had stood moments before. He looked and saw six Riders sitting upon their Woolie mounts, charging across the field, and moving so fast, Peter wasn't sure he and Jakob would make it to the door before the attack party arrived.

He shoved Jakob toward the door, shouting, "Go!" fully intending to follow his son, but then his sensitive ears picked up something over the rumble of the approaching Woolies. The rhythmic thud was easily recognizable to any soldier: helicopters.

38

Ella awoke kicking and punching, drenched in confusion and sweat, surrounded by an unfamiliar living room and the smell of tension. Hands reached out, grasping her arms. Whispered voices told her to calm down, that she was okay, that she was safe, but her last memory, of being *inside* the gullet of some monster, overwhelmed her common sense and told her to fight.

To flee.

To get out.

The hands on her shoulders, fingers hooked around her muscles, like tendrils or claws, slipped away. She lunged to her feet, vision spinning for a moment. The wall caught her as she stumbled forward, mumbling incoherent threats to what held her.

"You're out," someone said. "You're safe."

The words were like a fingertip of balm on a third-degree burn, wholly ineffective and not nearly enough. She slid across the wall and fell through a doorway, bumbling across a hardwood floor and catching herself on a small table that jabbed her ribs. The pain sharpened her senses but fueled her flight. When something grasped her shoulders from behind, pulling her back, she swung out a backhand, striking hard and being freed. Light drew her forward, toward a large wooden door. She fell against it, hands moving over the locks, snapping them open without looking. Blinding sunlight struck her a moment later, burning the green of the world outside into her retina. She squinted and stepped back, as the sight of endless crops helped her understand where she was.

In a house. A farm.

Not inside the belly of a predator.

Not consumed.

Safe.

Hands wrapped around her arms once more, two on each side, pulling her back. Voices urged with desperation, but she held her ground. There were fields outside, endless green, but there was also Peter. And he wasn't alone. An ExoGenetic creature...one of the Riders...stood just a few feet away from him.

She opened her mouth to shout at him, to tell him to shoot it, but then Peter turned around. His eyes locked on hers and then twisted in a kind of fear-fueled shock she'd never before seen on his face. That was when she shifted her gaze left, past Peter, seeing the ExoGen's face.

And recognizing it.

Despite the twisted nature of the Rider's body and the protruding teeth and feral hair, Ella had felt the loathing fire of those eyes before.

Her heart skipped in time with her faltering limbs.

But Kristen was dead. Peter killed—

No. He didn't. Of course, he didn't. The Peter she knew could never do that, especially to Kristen. She should have realized the truth before, but it wouldn't have changed anything. The odds of Kristen still being alive, or even still partly herself, were slim. But this was Kristen, with her memory and her hatred for Ella, still intact. The woman's eyes registered shock upon seeing Ella.

For a moment, Kristen looked wounded.

And then—with the suddenness of a crashing wave—rage.

Before Ella could react, she was pulled from behind, and this time she found herself powerless against the hands dragging her back. Seeing Kristen alive, standing before Peter, her still devoted husband, had sucked her will away. In that moment, she realized just how much she still cared about Peter. Her rock. Despite him staying with Kristen all those years ago, Ella had never doubted, that should some kind of desperate need arise, he would be there for her. It was why she had gone to his biodome first, when there had been others to choose from. She hadn't known Kristen was out of the picture then, but she had believed Peter would help her.

She had hated herself for thinking it, but Kristen's death, while tragic, had been a Godsend. She'd had Peter back. All of him.

But now...

She fell back onto the hardwood floor as the thing that was once Kristen let out a savage howl. Ella strained to see what was happening, but the heavy door slammed shut. Jakob was there, looking out the window, flinching at whatever was happening outside.

A sharp pain in her arm brought her attention over to Anne, who stood beside her and had just landed a kick. "Are you crazy!" the girl shouted. "Do you know who that is?"

"Oh no," Jakob said, hands snapping up to his mouth. "Oh shit! No!"

A single gunshot tore through the air.

Jakob's arms fell. His shoulders sagged. An invisible weight pulled his forehead against the window. He banged it against the glass once, and Ella thought the boy was about to crack. Whatever had happened outside was clearly devastating. One of his parents was dead. Given the gunshot, she assumed it was Kristen. While the boy had already believed his mother to be dead at his father's hands, this time he had watched it happen. Kristen had become a monster, thanks in part to Ella, but had still been his mother.

But then all signs of the boy's fragility disappeared. He perked up suddenly, brow furrowed. He turned to Anne. "You hear that?"

The hallway fell silent for a moment. The sound reached them through the floorboards, first as a faint vibration. Then a rumble.

Jakob stood on his toes, looking out the window, and then, without a word, he sprang into action. He flung open the door, revealing Peter standing over his wife's body, gun in hand, consumed by shock and grief. Jakob leapt from the porch steps and reached his father in three long strides.

The boy pulled on Peter's arm. "Dad! Snap out of it!" When Peter looked at him, he added. "They're coming!"

"Go!" Peter shouted, shoving Jakob back toward the door. He took one step to follow him and stopped, turning back, and then looking up.

What is he...

She heard it then. A familiar sound she'd come to know well during her time in San Francisco. But who would have helicopters all the way out here? Had ExoGen sent people looking for them? Were they really that valuable, or that much of a threat? She didn't think it was possible, so what could motivate these people to track them down?

She considered the possibility that the approaching helicopters were not from ExoGen, but she knew it was unlikely. If there had been other large pockets of survivors—people who had completely avoided eating the ExoGen crops—she would have known about it. No, this was ExoGen, and that meant they'd be ready for war.

Adrenaline spiking, Ella climbed to her feet and shouted, "Peter! It's ExoGen! Get inside, *now!*"

Her loud, '*now!* did the trick. He turned and ran for the house, pursued by several Woolies and their Riders, like Indiana Jones running from an Amazon tribe. She flinched when gunfire erupted from the second floor, peppering the field in front of the approaching horde. They weren't alone in the house, but whoever had opened fire was a horrible shot.

The door slammed shut behind Peter as he entered the front hall. Jakob started working the many locks, but Peter said, "Don't bother. They're not going to knock."

Peter rushed forward, and for a moment, Ella thought he was going to strike her. But he took her arm in his hand and pulled her up.

"Sorry," she said.

"Later. Get a weapon."

"Where?" she asked.

He let go of her arm and stepped into the living room where she'd awoken, slinging an M16 off his shoulder. "Anywhere." He pointed at Jakob. "Kitchen window!"

As the two Crane men separated, her eyes followed Peter, and then she really saw the living room's decor. In addition to a few pieces of furniture and old paintings hanging on the walls, there were weapons positioned under every window. With wide eyes, she turned and looked down the hallway, spotting the cabinet full of ammo and supplies.

"Here," Anne said, tossing a combat vest at her mother.

Ella caught the armor and slipped into it, quickly cinching it tight. It had already been loaded with what looked like AK-47 magazines, a Sig Sauer P229 handgun, and shotgun shells.

Gunshots rang out from the living room. Three-round bursts. *Definitely Peter.*

"Back him up," Anne said in a take-charge way that the girl hadn't displayed before. "I'll be with Jake."

Before Ella could agree with the plan, Anne, an M16 looking oversized in her small arms, headed for the kitchen. *What happened while I was unconscious?* Ella wondered, but she knew the answer to that question would have to wait. They had monsters to repel.

And then an army. She ran into the living room, and slid like she was stealing second base, stopping beneath one of the three windows where an AK-47 leaned against the wall. Before the Change, it had been the most common assault rifle on the planet, used by modern militaries and terrorists alike. The US military had no use for the gun, but it was popular with gun enthusiasts, and it wasn't surprising to find in a home that seemed to be overflowing with weapons.

Peter fired two more three-round bursts. She watched a Rider's head snap back, pulling up off his mount. The giant beast continued forward, oblivious to its passenger's dismount, and it wasn't alone. There were five more woolies, two of them now lacking Riders. But there was nothing that could be done to stop all of them before they reached the house.

Automatic gunfire erupted from above. *Two shooters,* she thought. And then from the kitchen. And then from Peter.

Ella popped out the magazine and checked that it was loaded. Seeing it was full to the top, she slapped the magazine back in and yanked back the rifle's operating rod handle, chambering the first cartridge. She flicked the safety off and thrust the weapon through a wide crack in the boards nailed over the window, shattering the glass on the other side.

She squeezed the trigger, unleashing a fusillade of 7.62mm rounds. But her efforts, like those of the other five people in the house, were too little, too late. The entire home shook as a Woolie slammed into the front porch stairs, careened through them, and then the porch, and then the front door. The wall to her right bulged as the large beast smashed through the front of the house, lodging itself in the hallway.

The enemy had breached the castle walls, making the fight more up-close-and-personal, which Ella didn't mind, but it also separated her from her daughter, which ignited a fire in her gut and unleashed a kind of human rage that had yet to be weeded out by millions of years of evolution.

39

Jakob held his fire. The shotgun he held would have little effect on the approaching creatures. Not until they were closer, at least. Anne arrived beside him with an M16 clutched in her arms. The gun looked massive in her hands. But like everything she did, Anne wielded the weapon without hesitation or fear, pushing the muzzle through the wooden planks and opening fire. Five rounds spat from the gun, the first three shattering glass and buzzing out into the open air. The last two struck the wooden barricade blocking the window as recoil punched her shoulder, sending her flying backward to the kitchen floor, sprawling atop a red-and-blue braided rug. Jakob dove to the side to avoid the spray of rounds but didn't make it more than a few feet before slamming into the wall.

"Did I hit anything?" Anne asked, pushing herself up and reaching for the weapon that now laid beside her.

"You mean besides the window?" Jakob moved back behind the overturned metal table and peeked outside.

"Don't be an ass—"

Jakob flinched as a flash of brown fur filled his vision. "Holy shit!" Off balance and moving fast, Jakob shoved the shotgun barrel through the window and fired a single blast, just as the house shook from an explosive impact. The kickback knocked him back onto the floor beside Anne just as the front hallway exploded. The walls cracked. Plaster shattered. Pots and pans burst from shelves with an unholy racket.

Anne shouted in surprise, and though she'd probably never admit it, fright. Jakob did, too. His father had once described what it was like to be on the receiving end of a mortar round. As the boom receded and the house groaned, the kitchen shelves still disgorging their contents, he felt this might qualify as a similar experience. Except it wasn't an explosive mortar round, it was a massive Woolie, its clumpy-haired body lodged firmly in the hallway, just to their left, blocking the living room door.

Jakob climbed to his feet and took a deep breath, willing the numb shaking of his limbs to stop. The Woolie, trapped partly in the floor, writhed and shook, trying to pull free of its self-imposed prison. It stopped, turning its jaundiced, bloodshot eye toward Jakob as he stepped toward it and pumped the shotgun. If it knew what was coming, it was incapable of showing it, even as Jakob raised the weapon.

He flinched when Anne opened fire behind him. His finger twitched and the shotgun punched his shoulder, sending a cloud of close-range pellets into the side of the beast's head, folding it inward and stopping the monster's gyrations.

Anne fired again, standing at the window, leaning into the weapon. It still nearly knocked her over, but the short burst and her stance kept her on her feet. But when she turned around, running toward the back of the kitchen, it appeared her effort had borne little fruit.

"Get back!" she shouted, sprinting around the table.

Jakob followed her without question. If she was running, there was a reason. Had he hesitated even a moment, the following impact would have knocked him to the floor and left him crushed beneath the body of a behemoth Woolie. The corner of the house bent inward and shattered. Wood and plaster flew, smacking Jakob's back and shoving him to the ground. He had a fleeting image of what the impact would have done if he wasn't wearing the tactical vest. The image wasn't pretty, nor was it long lasting.

He turned around onto his back while Anne took hold of his vest, trying to drag him back like some wounded soldier on the battlefield.

"C'mon!" she shouted.

But Jakob's attention remained fixated on the snorting and bloodied Woolie, which was pulling back out of the house. He could see the bit in its frothing mouth, the reins, and the mount, but the Rider was nowhere to be seen. *It got off before the impact,* he thought. And as the Woolie inched back out of the house, he realized they were about to get company.

As the bulk of the monster slipped backward, the corner of the home's second floor dipped down with a groan. The building couldn't take much more abuse before caving in on itself. As daylight squeezed past the Woolie, Jakob scrambled to his feet and ran with Anne, heading toward the back of the house. They stopped at an intersection. Straight ahead was the biodome with its glass walls and vegetables for cover, not to mention Misha's corpse. To the right was the back end of the home's main hallway, giving them access to the second-floor stairs. *Brant and Alia are up there,* Jakob thought, *and a lot more weapons.* He shoved Anne into the hall and shouted, "Up!"

There was a moment of annoyance at being pushed around, but Anne charged up the stairs, taking them one at a time in rapid fire, while Jakob took two at a time. They reached the metal door at the top together, pounding on its cool surface, neglecting the secret knock.

When Jakob shouted, "It's us! Let us up!" his words had the same effect as the knock. Locks snapped open and the metal door swung away.

Anne ran through, followed by Jakob. Alia stood next to the door, somehow looking both mortified and determined. She moved to shut the door, but then froze.

And screamed.

Jakob spun around.

A single, male Rider surged up the staircase. His arms were coiled back, fingers open and hooked, jaw wide, brows furrowed, wild hair flailing. Here was a demon, straight from the pits of hell, charging up to consume them whole. Jakob shouted and pulled the shotgun's trigger. The shotgun echoed strangely in the stairwell, stabbing Jakob's ears. The pain sharpened the pitch of his shout, but it was pain replacing fear, which had diminished when the Rider's body lifted up off the stairs and flew backward.

The airborne Rider slammed into the back wall, knocking down framed photos and leaving a splotch of blood where the hole in his torso struck the wallpaper. He crumpled into a heap at the bottom of the stairs. Jakob stood, looking at the man, remembering the similar scene of his mother being gunned down in the front yard. The event had shaken him to his core, but he also understood it, and he knew that his father had no choice. Not when he let her live the first time, when he'd been doing what he thought was right. And not when he shot her today, when he was doing what was necessary. Jakob didn't think he'd ever have the fortitude to shoot someone he knew, but these horrible Riders? He could live with that.

Alia shouted again and slammed the door shut. Jakob caught a glimpse of three Riders rounding the corner below and scrambling up the stairs. She managed to get a single deadbolt in place before the door was struck from the far side. Jakob helped her lock the remaining three and turned around to find Anne, hands raised, staring down the barrel of an assault rifle.

"They don't belong up here," Brant said, a wild look in his eyes, sweat oozing from every pore on his face.

"Dad!" Alia shouted over the pounding on the door behind her. "Stop it!"

"Your mother doesn't like company," he said. "They'll wake her."

Wake her? The noise booming throughout the house, from the door, and from a continued assault on the structure from outside, was enough to wake the dead. Jakob almost said so until he remembered that Misha was actually dead.

"They're our friends," Alia said. "They're here to help. To protect Mom!"

Anne stepped forward, lifting her M16 without pointing it at Brant. "We'll keep her safe."

Brant looked unconvinced. The pounding on the door got louder, each boom twisting tension into Brant's expression. When the door was struck loudly enough for a hinge to rattle loose, Brant looked down the sights of his weapon, aiming it at Jakob's head. "No! They have to go! Your mom says they have to go!"

The way Brant's voice cracked as he shouted told Jakob that the man had finally lost his mind. Between Misha's death and the chaos of battle, the man had cracked. And that meant he might very well shoot Jakob and Anne. But there was nowhere Jakob could go. Opening the door meant certain death, not just for him, but for Anne, Alia, *and* Brant.

"Sir," Jakob said, but stopped short when Brant's index finger slipped around the weapon's trigger and started to squeeze.

"Dad!" Alia shouted. "No!"

The explosion that came next made everyone shout, and Jakob wondered why he'd heard it at all. He should have been missing his head, but instead, he felt the floor beneath him shift. He opened his eyes and looked through the open front of the house. A cloud of dust and smoke rose up from the left side of the downstairs floor, where the living room was. The second floor to his left hung at an angle, just like it did above the kitchen, and he knew another portion of the home's support had been destroyed. He felt concerned for his father, but moved past it when Alia shouted, "Dad!"

Remembering the man with the gun to his head, Jakob turned and found empty space where Brant had stood. He was now sprawled on the floor, where he'd fallen when the floor shifted. But he looked startled, as though he'd seen a ghost. His weapon lay on the floor beside him.

Jakob knelt beside Alia and saw a shard of glass protruding through the tactical vest covering the man's chest. "What?" he said. "How?"

"Shrapnel from the explosion," Anne said, matter of fact. "Kevlar stops blunt impacts from bullets, but doesn't work against things like knives, or flying glass." She put her hand briefly on Alia's shoulder, said, "I'm sorry," and then stood, aiming her M16 at the door behind them, which was slowly rattling loose from the continued assault.

Jakob nearly shouted when Brant grabbed his arm with the speed and power of a striking anaconda. But the man's strength was fleeting. With each word spoken, his grip fell more slack. "Take...care of my... girls."

"I will," Jakob said.

"Both...of them," Brant said, tears running down his cheeks.

When Brant's hand fell away, Jakob took hold of it. "I'll make you a deal. I'll watch over Alia, if you take care of your wife."

Brant smiled, his teeth stained red with blood. "Deal." He turned to Alia, whispered, "Love you, girl," and then fell limp.

Alia let out a single, gut-wrenching sob, but then she seemed to suck her emotion inside her. As the door shook and screws fell to the floor, she gripped Jakob's arm and pulled. "We can get out the back!"

Jakob tapped Anne's shoulder, shouting, "C'mon!" and following Alia. They ran to the back of the hall and entered her parents' empty and perfectly kept bedroom. As Alia ran to the back of the room and unlocked the window, Anne slammed the door shut and shouted, "Help me!"

Working together, Jakob and Anne slid a full dresser in front of the door. Jakob then used the push button lock on the door and fastened a small hook and eye lock near the top of the door. He didn't think the barricade would hold for more than a few moments, but they had no other choice. He took a step back, raising his shotgun, ready to shoot through the wooden door.

"Let's go," Alia shouted.

Jakob looked back to see a rope, tied to the bed, dangling out the back window. Alia climbed out the window and started lowering herself down, out of view. Anne hurried after her. Jakob paused for a moment, unsure about the plan, because while there were three Riders inside the house, there were five Woolies outside.

Then he heard gunfire, distant and outside the house.

Two different kinds. His father and Ella had made it outside, too, and the realization jolted him into action, just as he heard the metal door at the top of the stairs slam open. Jakob reached the rope as Anne slipped out of view. He looked out and found the pair just eight feet below him, standing on the roof of the transitional hallway that led to the biodome. He heard the trumpeting call of the Woolies growing closer, perhaps tracking them by scent or sound, and he paused. But when the wooden door behind him shook and splintered, the dresser groaning as it shifted over the wood, Jakob slipped out the window, hung by his fingers and dropped down.

40

The impact at the front of the house created a pressure wave in the living room, hitting Peter like a stiff wind. Walls cracked. Swirling dust, mostly crushed and burst drywall, billowed into the room. Peter glanced toward the now bulging wall and found the bowed door frame blocked by an enormous, shaggy body. They were trapped, and the Woolie was still alive. The wall's supports cracked and splintered, threatening to cave in. Peter raised his weapon, intending to end the monster's life, and its struggle against the home's foundation, but a blur of motion in his periphery caught his attention.

He turned and looked out the front window.

A blur of dark brown nearly forced him back, but he held his ground when he realized the Woolie was simply rounding the corner of the house. A second followed, glancing at the window as it passed. If it saw him, it showed no reaction.

They have a plan, Peter thought.

Only a few seconds had passed since the impact, and in those moments, Peter had lost track of Ella. That changed when she stood up from the floor, muttering curses and looking a little wild.

Muted gunfire vibrated through the house, coming from the kitchen. The sound froze Ella in place but added an injection of intensity into her eyes. He felt his own pulse quicken when he heard voices: Anne's and Jakob's. Then with the suddenness of the front door's destruction, the house shook violently, as though a wrecking ball had just struck.

And the sound had come from the kitchen.

A loud wrenching wailed through the house, nails pulling from wood, beams bending to the breaking point. For a moment, it sounded like the whole structure would collapse, but then it got quiet again.

Peter glanced out the window again. He'd lost track of the running beasts, but he could still hear voices.

And then footsteps. The kids were running upstairs.

"Ella, let's—" Peter froze when he saw her. She stood at the front corner of the room, a fragmentation grenade in her hand, a finger looped through the pin. "What are you doing?"

The windows were too boarded up to throw the grenade outside, and he couldn't conceive of any good reason why she might detonate the device in a closed room—with them inside it. But then he could see in her eyes that she was reacting more out of emotion than logic. And in that moment, he understood her intentions. With no way out, she was going to make a way.

She glanced back at him as though to ask, "You ready?"

He grabbed a metal table from the side of the room where it was positioned beneath a window and spun it around, the legs against the back wall, a makeshift foxhole. Before he could shout, 'Ready,' and duck down, she pulled the pin, dropped the grenade into the corner, and ran. The grenade's handle sprang away, igniting the fuse.

Ella ran toward him, no fear in her eyes. Just anger. She had four seconds from the moment the handle shot free until detonation. She leapt into the air at three, slammed into the wall and fell behind the metal table at four, hands already over her ears. Peter ducked down, hands covering his head, eyes closed, mouth open. He trusted that the new, militant Ella knew to open her mouth, too. The pressure from the grenade in such a cramped and enclosed space could be enough to rupture their lungs.

The ordnance exploded with the sound of twenty rifles firing in unison. The pressure built around them for a brief moment and then vented out the front of the house, as first windows, and then walls, ruptured outward.

When Peter opened his eyes, the table legs had been shoved into the wall behind them, cramping the space. He unblocked his ears and found them ringing.

"You alright?" he asked.

Ella looked up but said nothing. She took her hands away from her head and closed her mouth. The sounds of pounding, harder than their kids could manage, came from somewhere in the house.

They're inside, Peter thought, but he didn't bother saying it.

Ella knew. And she reacted faster, standing up to leap over the table. But she stopped short, flinching back slightly.

Peter looked over the table and understood why. The old farmhouse hadn't stood a chance against the grenade. The corner of the structure, two windows, drywall and the wood siding had been vomited outward, strewn over what remained of the farmer's porch and the driveway beyond. Twisted coils of singed, pink insulation hung from the open walls, the home's guts exposed. The five exposed support studs were shattered, all but the corner beam with gaps between top and bottom. The ruined corner support was cracked at an angle, slowly shifting downward with a groan. The ceiling bent, splitting and releasing clouds of debris.

"The corner's coming down!" Peter shouted, shoving Ella from bhind. She dove out from behind the overturned table, snatched up her AK-47, and made for the slowly crumbling hole in the wall. Peter, still clutching his M16, followed close behind her, watching the top half of the wall descend, its exposed beams looking like giant shattered teeth, closing to swallow them whole.

Ella reached the corner first and slipped through the 16-inch space between studs. Peter knew he'd never fit, so he aimed his weapon at the base of a stud, unleashed six rounds into it and then kicked. The ruined wood bent outward, but not enough for him to fit past. The house shook and the wall dropped a few inches. Peter slung the rifle over his shoulder, took a few steps back and then charged like a linebacker. He struck the bent beam hard, finishing the job a grenade, an assault rifle, and his foot had started.

He sprawled across the porch, rolled off the side and hit the pavement hard.

With a loud crack, the gaping jaws of the open corner of the house slammed shut. Windows on the second floor shattered, raining down glass. Peter rolled onto his stomach and closed his eyes, waiting for the shards to finish pelting his back and the pavement around him.

"Peter!" Ella shouted, just as he detected vibrations in the pavement beneath his hands.

He looked up and saw two Woolies charging through the faux debris and over carrots, pounding past the side of the house toward their position. Unlike the masterless Woolies they'd encountered before, who stood still without direction, these seemed to have been worked into some kind of kill-everything frenzy.

Staying prone, Peter brought his M16 to bear, shouted, "Aim for the knees!" and then opened fire, unleashing a merciless torrent of lead toward the nearest beast's legs. Tufts of fur burst off the limbs. Blood followed. And then bone. The beast wailed but continued forward—until its chipped and cracked femur gave out, spilling the monster to the side and onto its face. Its twisted horn scraped pavement for a moment before catching and shattering.

Ella opened fire beside him, missing the legs and growing quickly frustrated. Then she just fired on full-auto into the giant's head until it suddenly slowed its assault, stumbled and fell over sideways, its massive tongue lolling out the side of its shattered mouth.

Peter ejected his spent magazine, reached under his chest for a fresh one, and slapped it in. He aimed at the still struggling Woolie he'd taken down, zeroing in on its eye. He pulled the trigger once. The bullet punched through the soft spot and silenced the monster.

He got to his feet and looked back at the house. The front porch was nearly non-existent. The front door was split wide and bent outward, a dead Woolie crammed into the space. Peter and Ella ran together, heading for the far corner, where a jagged hole gave entry to the kitchen. Like the damage to the living room, the support beams at the corner no longer existed, and the floor above had folded downward, but had yet to collapse. Banging echoed out of the hole, fists on the second floor's metal door.

Ella took a step toward the hole, but Peter stopped her and said, "Look."

At the back of the house were the three remaining Woolies. They stomped back and forth—looking up.

"They must have gone out the back," Peter said.

Ella watched the Woolies' behavior for just a moment before nodding in agreement.

"But someone could still be inside."

Her words were punctuated by the sound of a door slamming open, feet pounding on the floor above and then the sound of flesh striking a second locked door, one that sounded like wood.

"I'll go inside," Peter said. "You take the back."

Without waiting to see if she agreed, Peter ducked into the house. He moved through the kitchen, weapon on his shoulder, sweeping the space like he would have if his old CSO team had been moving in behind him. He nearly said, 'Clear,' as he pushed through the kitchen toward the back hall, but he held his tongue to maintain the element of surprise. He stopped at the entryway to the biodome and glanced through the window. The decon space and the greenhouse beyond looked untouched. He moved into the back hall and started up the steps, moving steady and silent. At the top, he inched past the metal door, which hung at an angle. Then he scanned the open-faced hall above.

He noted Brant's still body and saw the shard of glass protruding from his chest. Peter knew he'd been lucky to not be injured by the glass that fell on him. Brant's death proved it. "Sorry, buddy," Peter said, and he pushed past the ruined door.

He was about to turn left, but the sound of wood scratching over wood turned him around. He opened fire without thought, his subconscious identifying the mane of hair as belonging to the enemy. Three rounds punched into the Rider's back. It dropped in a heap without a sound.

The falling Rider revealed a second, starting out the window.

In normal battle, most soldiers felt a pang of regret or mercy for enemy combatants they were about to kill. In a blazing firefight, such things never crossed the mind, but when a target was in sight and the outcome was predetermined, it could be hard to pull the trigger. Not so with the Rider.

It's not even human, Peter thought, thinking of the thing and the window, and Kristen.

He pulled the trigger again, striking the thing in the head. It toppled forward out the opening, its heels flailing up and shattering the window. The body hung there for a moment, impaled on glass that gave way and dropped the corpse outside.

A scream from the open window revealed that the kids had fled in that direction. Peter started in, but only made it two steps before a blur emerged from a bright pink room and struck him in the side. He was lifted off the ground by the impact and slammed to the floor beside Brant.

Gasping for air, Peter tried to sit up, but a sudden heavy weight slammed onto his chest, pinning him back and shoving the rest of the air from his lungs. Pain lanced from his shoulders as the Rider atop him jabbed its long nails in Peter's flesh.

He stifled a shout and tried to shove the man away, but he was impossibly heavy despite his emaciated appearance. It was like the man's muscles and bones had shrunk but grown tighter and more dense.

No matter how much he struggled, Peter wouldn't be able to free himself from the Rider, and the man's body blocked all access to his weapon.

Loops of drool dangled from the man's mouth as he opened it wide, lowering the jaws toward Peter's neck. Peter shouted in frustration as he fought. But the Rider was too powerful, and Peter had no leverage. He turned away from the monster, looking into Brant's vacant eyes, which were looking down, as though directing Peter.

While Peter couldn't reach up, he could reach out. He bent his arm at an angle, pushing it a little farther than it was meant to go, but he found what he was looking for. He popped the button open, wrapped his hand around the handle and pulled. Moving in silence, Peter slammed his hand against the Rider's back, plunging the blade into its flesh, all the way to the hilt.

The Rider, whose face was just inches from Peter, looked surprised and then confused. Peter pulled the knife out and jabbed again. Then again. And again, until the surprise melted away from the Rider's face and its body fell backwards. The ExoGen man's long fingernails slurped out of Peter's shoulders. Warm blood dripped over his arms, but he paid no attention to it.

He climbed to his feet and ran for the back window, jumping over the king-sized bed and sticking his head out. Ella and the three kids were below, pinned down beside the biodome, the three remaining Woolies charging from three different directions. Ella shouted orders Peter couldn't hear, but Jakob and Anne responded quickly, aiming at different beasts. But before any of them could fire, the thudding rumble that had been constantly growing louder over the past few moments, turned into a raging thunder.

An Apache attack helicopter, flying dangerously low, flew past overhead. The Woolies skidded to a stop, looking at the flying beast, no doubt trained to spot airborne predators. They roared up at the chopper, their primal voices muted by the rotor chop. And then by a chain gun.

A beam of tracer rounds showed the path of the stream of bullets from the Apache to each of the Woolies, turning the monsters into bloody pulp, one at a time. When the sudden and ferocious attack finished and the chopper began making a tight turn around them, Peter shouted, "Inside! Now!"

The group gathered below turned toward him, but clearly hadn't heard him over the Apache. He shouted, "Inside!" again, this time pointing back to the house. "Get inside!"

At once, the group ran along the side of the house.

Peter bolted back to the stairs, descending three at a time. He slammed into the wall at the bottom but didn't slow as he entered the kitchen in time to see the others climb in through the hole. Just as Ella entered, a voice boomed from the helicopter above, impossibly loud. "We're here for Doctor Ella Masse. Send her out, or we're coming in." The Apache's thunderous chop was suddenly joined by the sound of two more helicopters, circling above, watching the home from every angle.

A moment later, a second voice cut through the racket, stating only, "Come on out, Ella. It's time to come home."

41

"That's Eddie," Anne said. "He's alive."

Peter's stomach soured, and not just because there was an attack helicopter outside capable of reducing the house to splinters. He looked at Ella for confirmation. She looked surprised and nervous, but wiped both expressions from her face, masking her emotions. She gave him a nod, answering his unspoken question. The man outside was Eddie Kenyon.

Her boyfriend and lover.

But not anymore. First of all, he was supposed to be dead, not hunting her from the comfort of a helicopter. Second of all, she'd moved on. He hoped. From what he knew of Kenyon, he was a good man, if not very bright, and he'd been kind to Ella. He'd helped her launch her expedition but had supposedly died in the wild. In that version of the story, Peter was thankful for the man who helped keep Ella alive. But now... The apparent truth was that he had survived, returned to San Francisco, and picked up crew to track Ella down.

And he wasn't here to rejoin Ella. He was taking her home.

Ella's hand on his arm brought him out of his growing anger. "This is a fight you can't win."

His body relaxed, and he realized he'd raised the M16 to his shoulder. "I'm not letting you go."

"I'm not worth getting all of you killed," she said.

Peter almost argued, but she was right. He looked behind him at Jakob, Alia...and Anne. Kenyon wasn't asking for Anne. He leaned in close to Ella and whispered. "You're leaving her?"

Ella leaned away and said, "She can hear this, too."

"It's okay," Anne said, striking out her chin, a brave little soldier trying to show no emotion, just like her mother. "You can go. I know Peter is my father."

"Sort of," Ella said.

Peter, Jakob, and Anne all repeated the words in unison. "*Sort of?*"

A voice boomed from outside. "I'm coming in, Ella. If anyone opens fire... Well, don't." The shifting pitch of a single helicopter lowering toward the ground pulsed through the house. They had just minutes before company arrived.

Kenyon was stopping himself short of making blatant threats. *If he still cares about Ella,* Peter thought, *he's not going to rush toward violence.* It was their only advantage, but to what end? There was no scenario he could imagine where he didn't lose Ella again.

And her main concern was clear. She stepped to Anne and brushed her hand against the girl's dirty cheek. "Are you strong enough?"

The girl stiffened. "You know I am."

Ella turned to Peter.

Whatever bomb she was about to drop, not even Ella Masse had the strength to say it to her daughter's face. "You weren't born. You were grown."

Every shock and surprise Peter had come across since Ella and Anne arrived at his doorstep felt small in comparison to this revelation.

"Holy shit," Jakob whispered.

Alia, who looked confused more than anything, whispered, "I don't get it. Who is she—"

Jakob shushed the girl, and Ella continued, looking at Anne, who hadn't moved, but whose eyes were getting wet. "Honey, Peter...is your father." She turned to him. "I used your DNA, to make her strong." She turned back to Anne. "And I used mine to make you smart."

"Where did you get my DNA?" Peter asked, having trouble believing what was turning out to be yet another tale of genetic tinkering gone awry. But had it gone awry? Anne was a wonderful kid. His growing affection for her was real. She even looked a little like him.

"The brush," she said.

"My hair brush?" He couldn't remember the last time he'd needed a brush or a comb for his close-cut hair.

"Eighth grade," Ella said. "The paint brush."

Peter's memory snapped back through time. He'd had longer hair as a kid, hair that Ella had been jealous of. So, he'd taken some of it, first pulling it out and then just cutting off a shock. He'd taped it tightly around the end of a pencil, making a crude paintbrush as she'd also liked watercolor painting at the time. "You *kept* that?"

"I kept everything you gave me," Ella said. "If my house is still standing, it's all still there, in a shoebox in my closet."

"I don't know if that's romantic or creepy," Alia said.

"Kinda both," Jakob said.

The lowering pitch of the rotor blades, along with a breeze now flowing through the open end of the kitchen, told Peter the helicopter was nearly on the ground. They were running out of time.

"But why?" he asked. "Why would you do that?"

"Anne," she said, waving the girl over.

After a moment's hesitation, Anne approached her mother.

"Turn around," Ella said, and the girl obeyed. "Stand still."

Ella drew a knife from her vest, but Peter caught her wrist. She looked at him, a wounded expression on her face, but then she wiped that away, too. "You're going to have to trust me. I've only done what I had to do so I could undo the mistakes I've already made."

He let go of her, and she lowered the blade tip toward a large freckle on the back of Anne's shorn head. "Stand still," she said again. "This won't hurt at all."

Ever dutiful, Anne stayed still. The blade pushed through her skin, creating a small incision. The girl didn't flinch, and before Peter could ask, Ella explained. "There are no pain sensors in the skin here."

Anne had apparently been very carefully designed.

Ella sheathed the knife and put her thumbs on either side of the dime-sized freckle, now sliced down the middle. She pulled the skin apart, revealing something shiny.

Peter leaned in close. "Is that..."

"A mini-USB port," Ella said.

"A *what?*" Anne stepped away, spinning on her mother and holding the back of her head. "What is in my head?"

"I gave you my mind," Ella said. "Exactly. Like a twin. All you're lacking is the knowledge I have, but all of that is in there, too, stored in flash memory, ready to be unlocked..."

"In case you die," Anne guessed.

That's why she's so important to Ella, Peter thought. *She's her backup. Literally.*

Ella spoke to Peter. "All you have to do is plug her in, and everything I know about all of this—" She waved her arms around her, indicating she was speaking about the whole world, "—will be available to her." She turned to Anne. "You can undo all the horrible things I did to this world. In your mind. In your blood."

"What do you mean?" Anne asked.

"Everything outside. All the food. It's safe for you." Ella took Anne's shoulders. "And you'll be able to give that gift to everyone else. If you reach George's Island."

Peter motioned to the back of Anne's head, where a small line of blood was busy sealing up the small wound. "*You* did this?" He was having trouble wrapping his mind about this further twisting of nature. His DNA had been used to create a girl, whose mind held computer parts that could unlock Ella's stored knowledge about genetics and who knew what else.

"I had help," Ella said, "but I'm all that's left of the team."

"*Am* I her father?" Peter asked.

"We didn't conceive her. Nor did I have your permission, and for that, I'm sorry. But genetically? Yes. She is the best of both of us. And if I could have done this naturally... Given birth? Yes. There is no better father for her than you."

Despite being moved by Ella's words, Peter's ears picked up the sound of a sliding door. The helicopter had landed, and they were about to have company. "We're out of time."

Ella took Anne's cheeks in her hands. "Baby, I love you. More than anything. No matter how you were born—"

"Created," Anne corrected.

"You are still my daughter. My flesh and blood and soul."

Tears sprang free from Anne's eyes, though she was still hiding her pain from her face.

"I need you to hide," Ella said. "Now. If Ed sees you, he'll take us both. It's better if he thinks you're dead." When Anne didn't budge, Ella added, "Please, baby. Peter and Jakob are your family. They'll take care of you."

Jakob stepped up next to Anne and took her hand. The girl's emotions overwhelmed her self-control. She turned to Jakob, hiccupping tears into his chest.

"You gotta hide," Jakob said. Anne nodded against him. He turned to Alia. "Find her someplace?"

Alia reached her hand out to Anne.

The girl turned to Ella, said a quick "Love you, too," and then disappeared with Alia, moving into the back hall.

Ella quickly wiped her eyes and turned toward the opening in the corner of the kitchen, where the crunch of boots on debris announced the arrival of company. Peter held his M16, but kept the barrel pointed toward the floor. Ella and Jakob did the same, armed, but non-threatening.

Three men ducked into the kitchen, the first two leading with raised MP5s. Peter evaluated both men, seeing the telltale signs of military training in the first, and the less disciplined, but no less deadly, air of private security in the second. When the military man offered a sharp, "Clear!" while training the barrel of his weapon on Peter, the third man entered. He had a gun on his hip but held no weapon in his hands. The cocksure attitude of his walk, and the way he surveyed the kitchen, like a king looking over his domain, identified him as private security as well, but it was the wide eyes and smile directed at Ella that revealed his identity as Ed Kenyon.

While the two armed men kept their weapons trained on Peter and Jakob, Kenyon strode through the kitchen, opened his arms, enveloped Ella, and planted a passionate kiss on her lips...which she returned in kind.

42

It took all of Peter's rigid military training and discipline to remain still and free of external jealousy while he watched what turned out to be a ten-second kiss. The desperation with which Kenyon clung to Ella revealed the man's affection for her was genuine. The real problem was that Peter couldn't tell if Ella's reciprocation was real. He decided it was somewhere in the middle. She once had feelings for the man, finding comfort in his embrace, but she could never kiss a man like this, in front of him, without feeling uncomfortable...and there wasn't a trace of discomfort in her body language.

She's protecting us, he decided. If Kenyon suspected she'd been with Peter, things might end badly. Even good men could turn bad from jealousy. The fire currently burning in Peter's chest, telling him to wipe Kenyon's existence from the face of the planet, was proof enough of that. Their only hope of leaving the house alive was Kenyon bearing Peter and his son no ill will.

To sell the act, Peter looked at the second private soldier and smiled, hitching a thumb toward Kenyon and Ella, raising his eyebrows. The man cracked a smile and gave a shrug, clearly embarrassed by his superior's behavior.

"Get a room," Jakob said, trying to joke through his discomfort.

The comment ended the kiss, and while Peter wanted to thank Jakob for that, the boy should have stayed quiet.

Kenyon slowly separated from Ella, leaning up to look over her head, staring at Jakob. For a moment, Peter tensed. If the man went for a weapon, Peter wouldn't hesitate to kill all three men. But Kenyon grinned. And then laughed. "We will, kid."

It was then that Kenyon seemed to remember there were other people in the room. He stood up straight, adjusting his combat vest. He turned to Peter, gave a nod, and cleared his throat. "Who are you?" He didn't offer his hand.

"Name's Brant," Peter said. He didn't want to risk the possibility that Ella had told the man about him. He hoped the soldiers wouldn't decide to search the house and find the real Brant lying in the hallway upstairs beside a dead Rider. He could lie about the body's identity, but a thorough search would no doubt turn up a wallet. "This is...was...my farm." He motioned to Jakob. "That's my boy, John."

Jakob gave a nod. "Sir."

Kenyon looked back and forth between the two, then turned his eyes toward the back of the house, at the entrance to the biodome. "Nice setup."

"We were lucky to have the greenhouse before the Change happened," Peter said, adding a thicker accent to his voice and once again hoping the man would be content to remain in the kitchen. If he inspected the biodome he would discover it was far more than the average greenhouse. He wasn't sure how familiar the man was with Ella's design. "Managed to avoid those GMO crops."

"You *never* ate them?" Kenyon said, squinting at Peter.

Peter frowned. "Truth be told, I wanted to. But the missus was paranoid about GMOs. Everything we grew, back when things were normal, were organic crops. A lot of it in the greenhouse."

"And where is the missus now?" Kenyon asked.

"In the greenhouse," Peter said. "Buried beneath the broccoli."

"When did that happen?" Kenyon asked.

"Ed," Ella said, hanging on his arm. "Give the man a break. He's been through hell. And they saved my life."

"That so?" Kenyon turned to her slowly. "Am I to understand you *want* to come back?"

A pained expression twisted Ella's face. "I've been out here on my own for too long."

Kenyon looked like he'd been slapped. He stepped back from Ella searching the kitchen. "Where..." He turned to Ella. "Is she?"

Ella shook her head. "Two months ago. The Stalkers caught up to us again."

"I'm sorry, El," Kenyon said. "Really. That kid was something special. Had a fierce heart. But...how did you..."

"Sometimes we have to let go of something we love so we can live," Ella said, her voice frigid. She spoke directly at Kenyon, but Peter knew the words were for him. "I survived. It's what I do. We all make sacrifices."

"Some more than others," Kenyon said, his voice softening. He turned his attention back to Peter. "You on the other hand, are full of shit."

"Ed!" Ella said, but he gripped her arm tightly, yanking her in front of him, when Peter let just a trace of menace filter into his gaze.

"There it is," Kenyon said. "The look of a jealous man. And a resourceful man. Army Ranger?"

Peter knew that at least part of his cover story was blown.

But that didn't mean Kenyon really knew who he was.

"Captain Brant Rossi. U.S. Marine Corps, Critical Skills Operator."

The military man said, "Sir, we could use a—"

"Quiet, Mackenzie," Kenyon said, reaching down and plucking his handgun from his waist with impressive speed, aiming the Sig Sauer pistol at Peter's head. "I know you've been with her since the farmhouse in Kansas. Real piece of work, by the way. You really blew the shit out of that place. And you've been leaving a trail of destruction in your wake ever since." He motioned at the house around them. "You've already left your calling card on this shithole. You know what? I don't even care if you confirm or deny any of this. What I want to know is, in all this time, have you been *with* her. I know you want to. Can't hide that from me. But *have* you?"

Peter wanted to punch the man's throat inside out. Instead, he said, "No."

"Eddie," Ella said, her voice tense. "Why would I be with a man I just met days ago?"

"Payment," Kenyon guessed, glaring at Peter with accusation.

But it was Ella who replied.

"Do you think that little of me, that I would sell my body? And for what? Protection? I can take care of myself. He was a means to an end, nothing more. But they're good people, and they don't deserve this treatment."

"How do you know him?" Kenyon asked. "I saw the remains of the biodome at the ruined farmhouse. Same as the one out back here. That means he's someone to you. One of your predetermined safe houses."

"She was roommates with my wife," Peter said. "At Berkeley."

Kenyon looked unconvinced. "Your wife that's buried in the greenhouse?"

"No," Peter said, letting the real emotion he felt about the subject infuse his expression. Tears welled in his eyes. "My wife that is lying dead in the driveway."

"There's nothing out there but an ExoGen—" A slight smirk slipped on to his face, revealing that deep down in his core, he was an asshole after all. "Are you saying the fugly thing lying in front of the house was your *wife?*"

"Her name was Kristen," Peter said. "Respect her in front of my son."

Kenyon pointed the handgun toward Jakob. "He telling the truth, son? That your mom lying out front?"

Jakob started to nod but was interrupted by Peter. "You better point that thing back at my head, or you and the men in this room are going to regret it."

The smirk on Kenyon's face turned into a full-fledged smile.

He turned the weapon back on Peter.

"Got some balls on you."

"Ed," Ella said, her tone a warning. "Don't."

Peter stayed silent and still.

The silence seemed to sap the man's spirit, but then Peter noticed he was actually listening to the earbud in his ear. He was receiving a report from the men outside. So were the other two men in the room, their less guarded expressions revealing trouble.

"Here's what I'm going to do," Kenyon said. "Ella's going to leave with me, and you and your son are free to go, nothing to fear from us."

Peter said nothing. He knew there was a catch. If a report hadn't just come in, he would have assumed the helicopters would blast the home apart before leaving. But Kenyon clearly believed their fates were sealed, and he was happy to leave them to it.

Kenyon headed for the opening, pulling Ella behind him. She glanced back, locking eyes with Peter for just a moment, apologetic and sad. Then she was shoved outside and gone from view.

"Stay inside the house until we're gone," Hutchins said, backing away.

There was no threat in his words, just a warning, and Peter understood. If he left the house, armed for battle, he'd be a threat, and they would respond.

"Understood," Peter said, as the man exited the kitchen.

The last of them, the man named Mackenzie, paused. "I was a Marine, sir. Looked up to the CSOs. We all did. You guys gave us something to aspire to."

"Get to the point," Peter said.

The man nodded. "You have incoming, sir. Rattletails."

"Rattletails?"

"Kenyon's lady...Ella... She calls them Stalkers. Not sure how many, but one is too many in my opinion. If you have a way to leave this place fast, you better go."

Peter began strategizing their escape, even as he said, "Thanks for the heads up."

The man snapped a quick but sloppy salute, the kind that would have gotten him fifty push-ups during Boot Camp, and exited, leaving Peter and Jakob alone in the kitchen.

"Find the girls," Peter said. "I'll gather what I can. We're leaving the second they're out of sight."

43

Peter didn't watch the helicopters leave. He could hear them well enough. Looking meant stopping, and he didn't think they had time for even a moment's pause. When Jakob returned to the kitchen with Anne, who looked dejected and lost, and with Alia, who was in a far worse state, he set them to work.

"Alia," he said, "I know you're hurting, and confused, and scared, but for the next ten minutes, I need you to be strong, okay?"

She nodded despite her quivering lip.

"I need backpacks. Bags. Pillowcases. Anything you have that can carry this." He motioned to the weapons he'd gathered and laid out on the kitchen table.

Alia hurried from the room without a word or any indication that she was agreeing to the task.

He turned to Anne.

"You're on hall cabinet duty."

Alia returned faster than Peter expected.

She held two pink backpacks, which had clearly once been hers, a long duffle bag and a crushed handful of grocery store plastic bags.

"Take the backpacks," he told Anne, "and get everything you can from the hall cabinet."

"I know what to look for," she said, her resilience springing her back to her old self, past the knowledge that she had a computer chip in her head, and that she'd never really been born.

"Jakob. Two bags. Hit the green house. Everything you can carry but try to get the denser foods that take longer to spoil. Root vegetables."

"Right," Jakob said. "No corn. No leafy stuff."

When he ran to the back of the kitchen and opened the decontamination room door, Alia looked after him.

"Go ahead," Peter said, taking the duffle bag. "As much as you both can carry."

As the kitchen emptied, Peter set himself to the task of filling the duffle bag with rifles, shotguns, and handguns, careful to select only those in the best conditions. Packing the bag so full that it was impossible to carry, or the handles ripped off, wouldn't do.

The pitch of the helicopters' rotors was building and growing more distant. The choppers were moving away, to the west as they rose higher. *They're bugging out fast,* Peter thought, *and it's not because of me.* While they'd had success against the Stalkers in the past, that was on his home turf, or in the truck with a fully loaded machine gun. They still had the big gun on the truck in the garage, but without ammunition the weapon was just for show. Intimidating to a person perhaps, but nothing to a Stalker.

The weight of the bag felt borderline too heavy as Peter lifted it up. He placed it back down, removed the M16 he'd been using, slung it over his shoulder and zipped up the bag. *Good enough,* he thought.

The sound of the choppers faded quickly. They would be out of sight in a few seconds, but he thought it would probably be safe to leave now. "Wrap it up!"

He shouted as loud as he could, but only Anne replied. "Five seconds!" Her small voice was tight and controlled. Peter felt a pang of emotion he couldn't quite place. Pride mixed with sorrow. The girl in the hallway was, genetically, his daughter. His DNA had been used without consent, which was an offense to which only Ella could answer. But would the end justify the means? Could Ella really start making amends for the genetic catastrophe she'd helped begin, by further mucking with the human genome—*his* human genome? The problem, he knew, was that given the chance, he'd forgive Ella. And she knew it.

I'm weak, he thought, but then he crushed the emotion down and headed for the rear kitchen door. He pushed through it.

The decontamination room fans didn't kick on, and he was able to open the second door without pause.

He banged on it twice with his fist.

"Wheels up. We're leaving. Now."

He heard Alia ask, "Wheels up?" but he knew his son understood the message and left before they replied.

Anne waited in the kitchen holding two very heavy-looking pink backpacks. He could see she was near some kind of emotional breaking point. They all were, but she had just lost her mother, who had kept her alive in the wild. He crouched down in front of her, put his hands on her shoulders and said, "I am your father. Doesn't matter if you were grown or born. You've got my genes, and that means you can kick ass and take names." She didn't look convinced. "It also means that I will protect you. And fight for you. And love you."

A tear fell, but she quickly rubbed it away. The fighter in her knew this was no time for crying. Peter didn't fare much better. Blinking away tears, he kissed her forehead. "Now, let's kick some ass."

A slight smile flickered across her face. The biodome door swung open as Jakob and Alia returned. They each held four plastic grocery bags laden with fresh, soil covered vegetables. Peter strode to the table and hefted the duffle bag over his shoulder. He stepped toward the open kitchen wall and listened. The helicopters were barely audible. "Straight to the garage. Eyes open." He looked at Alia. "I'm going to be depending on you for the fastest route out of here."

"Which way?" she asked.

"East," he said, and when she looked unsure, he pointed to the back of the kitchen and said, "That way."

"'Kay," Alia said.

"Move," Peter said, and he led the way out through the hole, step-ping carefully over what was left of the front porch while keeping his eyes on the distant woods. On the plus side, the carrot field was still empty. On the downside, he couldn't see anything beyond the treeline, and the wheat filling every available space was the perfect hunting ground for Stalkers.

Four sets of feet crunched over the pavement as they headed around the front of the house toward the detached garage, which was undamaged by the battle. Peter glanced at his fallen wife as he passed, saying a silent goodbye and an apology for leaving her body to the scavengers. He glan-ced back at Jakob, but the boy hadn't given his mother a second look.

Peter grasped the handle of the door on the side of the garage. He gave it a quick jiggle to confirm that it had been locked, stepped back and then kicked hard, planting his boot just beneath the doorknob. The wooden door was solid, but the rotted frame gave out. The door slam-med inward and Peter followed. Dust swirled in the sunlight that cut through the two windows, revealing an old pickup truck, and Peter's armored Dodge Ram beside it. Looking at the big truck with fresh eyes, he saw the beating it had taken. The front and sides were caked with chunky gray mud and dark brown gore. Stalks of vegetation were wedg-ed between every crevice. The paint job was scratched in several places, revealing long claw marks, some of which dug into the metal beyond the black enamel.

It had only been days since the big truck had started carrying them to safety, but it already looked like it had served a tour of duty in Afghan-istan. But, like all good soldiers, it wouldn't waver before heading into danger's path once more.

"Keep everything with you," Peter said as he opened the back door. He didn't trust that their new found supplies would stay in the truck bed if things got bumpy. He opened the driver's side door, confirmed that the keys were still in the ignition and turned to Jakob. "Start her up while I get the door."

"Am I driving?" Jakob asked.

"Not this time." Peter bent down to lift the large door. "Just get her ready."

Peter winced as the door shrieked, the old metal wheels grinding through their slots. Then the truck roared to life. If there was anything within earshot, they just became targets. The door banged into place. Sunlight blazed into the garage, lighting up the kids in the truck.

Peter looked at them through the windshield. He now had a seventeen-year-old son, the boy's sixteen-year-old girlfriend—or whatever she was—and a twelve-year-old, but not really, daughter. Had he been living comfortably at home, this arrangement would have frightened him. Now it terrified him, not because he didn't know how to act around teenagers, but because he was responsible for keeping all three of them alive in a world that wanted to eat them whole.

I'm going to have to train them, he thought, and he headed for the open driver's door. *I'm going to have to make them killers.* The real trick would be transforming them into predators while keeping their souls intact. He'd seen strong men break from training before ever seeing combat. But the kids' survival depended on them being strong.

He slipped behind the wheel and put the truck in drive but kept his foot on the brake. He looked at the three kids, meeting each of their eyes, glad to see determination. "No matter what happens, we're not going to stop. Everyone pick a weapon you can handle. If we're engaged, put down the windows before firing. Ready?"

"Let's move," Jakob said.

"Sure," Alia said, though she didn't sound sure.

"Fuckin' A," Anne said.

All eyes turned on her. "What?" she said. "I thought we agreed that a non-existent society couldn't—"

"Yeah," Peter said, his fatherly adoration for the girl growing a bit. "Fuckin' A." He hit the gas, launching out of the garage, and peeling down the driveway. He barely slowed when he reached the road and made a sharp right. The truck sped away from the farm, heading east at 60 mph, unscathed by whatever hunted in the woods, but headed into uncharted territory, where ungodly predators lurked, and an uncertain future awaited.

44

Ella looked down as the chopper rose in the sky. The ruined farm shrank beneath them and then disappeared as the helicopter turned west, speeding away even as they climbed. She turned to Kenyon, who was seated beside her in the blue Black Hawk. He smiled at her and squeezed her hand, which was now sweating, as he hadn't let go of her since they had left the kitchen.

"What are we running from?" she asked.

"Just want to put a little distance between us and your G.I. Joe friend." Kenyon turned away from her, feigning interest in the shifting view. "Seemed like a loose cannon to me."

She knew it was bullshit.

Kenyon was a horrible liar. She'd seen him lose at poker enough to know his whole face was a tell. He knew it, too. It was why he looked away, which in itself was a tell.

Kenyon wasn't about to give her any answers, so she turned back to the window, looking down. She had to stifle a gasp when she saw a clearing below. Several large bodies dashed out of the woods and into the clearing, tromping through the short, leafy crop and making a beeline for the trees on the opposite side, and beyond them the carrot field and Brant's farm.

She counted seven Stalkers, including one that looked to be the size of a T-Rex. *That's her,* she thought, *the queen of them that has been driving the rest, spurring their ruthless pursuit.* The creatures looked different now, their chests doubled in size. *They've adapted. Grown massive lungs for long distance running.* The plates on their backs were also bigger, like those of a stegosaurus, a creature that was not part of the human race's DNA history. *The larger surface area is cooling them off,* she thought, *like an elephant's ears.* But were they adapting in new ways not available in their unlocked junk DNA, or were they accessing creatures unknown to paleontology?

The scientist in her, visually dissecting the creatures' adaptations, was squelched when the pack of predators stopped and looked up at the helicopters.

I'm right here, she thought at the pack leader. *Follow us.*

The Stalkers seemed to be squawking and snapping at each other. Then the big one thrashed about for a moment and turned back to the forest.

No! Follow me! I'm right here, you bitch!

The pack leader glanced up one last time. With a wide-mouthed screech that Ella thought she might have actually heard over the loud rotors and through the headphones covering her ears, the alpha continued on its previous path toward the farm. The pack followed. When they disappeared into the trees, it took all of Ella's strength to not throw herself in the cockpit and force the Black Hawk back to the ground.

Before she could decide on any course of action, whether it be attack or resigned silence, she heard Kenyon talking. He was speaking—shouting really—into a satellite phone. She slipped the headphones off her ears and heard the crackling reply of a man's voice through the speaker phone.

"Say again. Is this Viper Squad?"

Ella rolled her eyes. Only Kenyon could have come up with that name.

"Affirmative," Kenyon said.

"We thought you all were dead," the man said.

"Some of us are," Kenyon replied. "Now put Lawrence on the line."

"I'm not sure he's—"

"Put him on, or I will personally come to say hello when we get back."

"Get back?" The man sounded mildly nervous.

"We're on our way to you now." Kenyon glanced at Ella and noticed she was listening. He offered her a half smile that disappeared when he spoke again. "We'll be home in a week, give or take a few days."

There was a moment of silence. Then, "Hold on."

A few clicks later, a familiar voice came over the line. "Kenyon?"

"Lawrence," Kenyon said. "Good to hear you again."

"My god. You're alive!"

"Very."

"And the package?"

"Ella is sitting next to me."

There was a moment's pause, during which the tension inside the chopper doubled. Hutchins, who was seated across from Kenyon, shifted in his seat. "And the girl?"

Ella knew in that moment, that while Kenyon had been there for her, she wasn't really the mission. Anne was. And that meant that they had discovered what she really was, and the threat she posed to their plans.

"Deceased," Kenyon said, his eyes flicking toward Ella for just a moment.

"You have the body?"

Kenyon's forehead wrinkled. The gears of his mind slowly turning, grinding, understanding. "No, sir." He turned to Ella. "Where is she?"

"I—I don't know," Ella said.

Kenyon's wrinkled brow shifted direction, burrowing down between his eyes. "I know what she meant to you. I know how much you loved her. If she were dead, you'd know exactly where it happened. Now, where *is* she?"

"Ed, I don't—"

He slapped her so hard and fast that she was thrown against the Black Hawk's door. When she turned to face him, all the forced affection she'd been putting into her loving gaze was missing. "If you hit me again, I'll kill you."

He squinted at her. "Anne's alive, isn't she?"

"Kenyon," Lawrence said from the phone. "If you return without the girl, I will not open these doors to you. Do you understand?"

"Yes, sir," he said, glaring at Ella. He hung up the phone and repositioned his headset. "All units, back to the farm. Double time." The chopper began a wide turn, tilting to the side. "Target is female. Age twelve. Dark hair. She is to be taken alive. Anyone who harms her will receive the same treatment." He paused a moment, then spoke while holding Ella's gaze. "Everyone else? Shoot to kill."

45

While 'the calm before the storm,' had become a cliché, fewer people talked about the calm *after* the storm. But people who had seen active duty in war zones understood it. There was a moment in every battle, whether it be when the enemy was dead, or you were being carried home on a Black Hawk, when reality snapped back in place. Some men wept. Some told jokes. Peter usually fell asleep, whether he was in a foxhole or riding in a chopper. Once safe, his body forced a recharge. Sometimes he fought it. Stayed awake because danger could rear up again. But he always felt the Sandman tugging him toward slumber.

But now, twenty minutes after leaving a second farmhouse in shambles, he was still on high alert. There had been no sign of pursuit and no danger on the road ahead, that he could see. He wasn't sure if it was just the nature of what they'd just faced, or that he'd killed his wife, or that Ella had been taken from him, but his nerves weren't settling.

And neither were the kids'. He glanced over at Jakob, whose wide eyes scanned back and forth. The boy gripped a shotgun the way little kids do their teddy bears. An M16 sat between the seats and two spare magazines lay in the center console. The girls in the back both had handguns and spare magazines, all of it resting on the seat between them. Anne hadn't spoken a word since leaving, and Alia only offered the occasional direction, keeping them off the main roads.

Peter felt a strange parental need to start up a conversation, to help the kids normalize after seeing their parents killed or kidnapped. But the only words that came to mind were things like, 'Give me a sitrep,' or, 'Everyone report in.' He was in full military mode, his mind reverted back to his CSO training—except the three people sharing the homemade technical with him were children, not warriors.

Calm down, he told himself, realizing that what he was feeling might be his old PTSD rearing back up.

But the danger he felt was real. It was constant.

The 'P' no longer stood for 'Post.' The danger was Present. And the stress was necessary.

It sharpened the senses.

Made him more aware.

And that was how he knew they were coming. He felt the slight pulsing in pressure before the sound actually reached his ears. The helicopters were coming back. *Coming for Anne,* he thought, glancing back at the girl who still hadn't heard the approaching choppers.

"Alia," he said, trying to sound calm. "Is there a town around here?" They needed to get off the road. The trees lining the winding road would provide some cover, but not for long if the choppers were flying high. With nothing else moving on the roads, they would be easy to spot.

Alia leaned forward, looking out the windshield. "Take your next right. Not far after that. Maybe a mile." She leaned back in her seat, back to watching the passing trees and strips of different crops growing between them.

Anne showed no reaction at all.

But Jakob knew something was up. Peter looked at his son, and feigned a cheek scratch, then he tapped his ear. Jakob didn't move but sucked in a quick breath. He heard it, too.

Peter took the right turn and accelerated, pushing the needle past what he thought was a safe limit, but he did it slow enough that it went unnoticed. He was hoping to find a place to hide before the girls knew they were in danger.

But that wasn't going to be possible.

He glanced in the rearview and saw three dark specks in the distance. The pilots would have already seen them.

Should have stayed straight, he thought, but there was no way to know where the choppers were.

"What's that?" Anne sat up straight, looking both ways.

"Company," Peter said, trying to sound nonchalant.

Anne turned around in her seat and looked out the rear window. "It's Mom."

"And the men with her," Peter said. "We're going to hide."

"Wait," Alia said. "The town is to *hide* in?"

"Yeah," Peter said, but then he didn't need to ask why. The trees cleared, and the small town came into view. The word 'small' didn't do it justice. There was a brick town hall, a combined convenience store and gas station, a few storefronts converted from houses lining the street and a small brick church. Corn grew from the flat roofs of the gas station and the city hall. The wooden structures looked ready to crumble, and probably were before the Change. There was only one option: town hall. The building would most likely have a fallout shelter, so it was more of a last-stand location than a place to hide, but it was better than facing them out in the open. And they had enough guns to make it one hell of a last stand.

"Listen up," he said. "Girls, take the pink backpacks and plastic bags. Jakob, you take the duffle bag. I'm going to—" Peter glanced in the rear-view, expecting to see the three helicopters rushing toward him. Instead, he found an open pair of long-toothed jaws reaching out for the back of the truck.

"Whoa!" he shouted and crushed his foot down on the gas pedal. The big truck lurched forward as the teeth snapped together behind them. He put them on a course straight through town and accelerated while weaving in and out of abandoned vehicles. A second look back revealed three Stalkers, giving chase, leaping obstacles, their chests expanded and armored plates waving back and forth. But the creatures maintained a safe distance.

When they cruised through the town's only intersection, where a now-dead yellow light hung, he looked left and right. To the left, a large, lone Stalker kept pace. On the right were two more.

We're being herded.

But toward what?

Then he saw it. The inevitable structure residing in or near the center of every town. The red brick church with a white steeple looked like the most well-maintained building in town...until the walls crumbled out into the road, shoved by a thirty-foot-long Stalker with a broad, powerful chest, wicked teeth, and ten foot, rigid sails down its back. It stepped into the road while the steeple crashed down behind it.

Their path had been blocked, with Stalkers on all sides. These things were human once, and it still showed.

The big Stalker stared the truck down and let out a bellow that shook Peter's insides. He considered ramming the thing's leg, and probably would have if he were alone, but the moment the truck stopped, he and the kids were screwed.

He slowed the vehicle as the smaller Stalkers closed in. "Windows down!"

Wind blasted into the cab as all four windows descended. "Pick a target!"

Driving while aiming an M-16 across his lap at the Stalker on his left wasn't easy. It would be even harder once he pulled the trigger. But he didn't think Alia, who was sitting behind him, would get the job done with her handgun. And he needed the Stalker on their left to be gone in about five seconds, so he could veer away from the big one.

He opened his mouth, then shouted, "Now!" but the word was drowned out by the sudden arrival of the three helicopters and the rattle of their machine guns. The Stalker on the left burst in a cloud of red, cut down from above. He heard bullets rake the ground to the truck's right, but he didn't see whether the Stalkers had been hit.

He cut the wheel hard to the left and hit the brakes. Tires squealed as they started to pull off the road into a field of corn that might have once been a park. But a fresh barrage of gunfire pinged against the truck's bed and struck one of the rear tires. There was a loud hiss, and then a grinding of the rim on pavement. He braked hard, hoping to spare the axle from permanent damage. If the spare was still in one piece, they could have working wheels inside of ten minutes, assuming they survived that long.

The big Stalker charged from the side, head lowered, jaws opened wide enough to engulf a portion of the cab. It would peel back the ceiling like a pistachio and find the meat inside.

Bullets traced a line across its snout, making it wince and pull up short. A helicopter roared past, and the monster leapt at it, snapping at the air. But then it turned and fled as a second barrage of gunfire opened up. Four Stalkers took off running, cutting through the fields that they were now too big to hide in, heading toward the distant woods. Two of the choppers peeled away in pursuit, firing at the creatures, driving them away. The third, the blue Black Hawk holding Kenyon and Ella, was landing behind them.

"What are they doing?" Alia asked. "Are they saving us?"

"They're here because of me," Anne said, coming to the same conclusion Peter had.

"We can rush them," Jakob said, pumping the shotgun. "Hit them before they land."

It was a simple plan, and it would work. But Ella was in the helicopter, and the moment they opened fire, the other two would swing back around. And there would be no hiding from them.

"You have to give me to them," Anne said.

"No way," Jakob said.

"Not going to happen," Peter added.

"Then what?" Anne asked, indignant. "We're just going to sit here and see what they do? You know how this is going to end. The only way of avoiding it is to let me go."

So much like her mother...

When he didn't reply, she grumbled something, grabbed hold of the ceiling-mounted handle, and lifted herself up. She swung out the window, feet first, landed on the pavement and headed for the settling chopper before Peter could reply.

He and Jakob exited the truck in unison, Peter with the M16, Jakob with the shotgun. Both took aim at the chopper, one protecting his daughter, the other his sister. They'd both lost and gained a family member today. Peter was determined not to lose another, and he could see the same determination in his son. Jakob had changed a lot. Was becoming a survivor. But unlike Ella's breed of survivor, neither of them wanted to let go of the things they loved.

The side of the chopper slid open. Ella climbed out first, followed by Kenyon, who had a knife to her throat. Mackenzie, the Marine, was the last out, looking uncomfortable, but aiming his weapon just the same.

"Same rules as before," Kenyon said. "I take what I want. You and your boy get to live." He glanced at the corn fields where the choppers were still chasing the Stalkers.

Chasing, but not killing.

They're letting the Stalkers live so they can kill us.

It was a cruel fate. A bullet would be merciful in comparison to being eaten alive.

"Deal," Anne said, hands raised.

"Stop," Peter said to her.

"Sometimes, to survive, you have to—"

"Bullshit," Jakob said.

"Boys," Kenyon said. "If you don't play along, everyone dies. Well, maybe not me, but everyone you care about, including yourselves. So, they can come with me, live cushy lives back in San Francisco, and you two can live for however long you manage, or you can all become juicy Rattletail snacks."

"I said, '*deal*.'" Anne continued forward. "I can speak for myself."

Ella said nothing. She just watched her daughter, their eye-contact never wavering.

Damn it. Peter couldn't think of a solution beyond the options Kenyon had laid out. With Anne along for the ride willingly, there was nothing he could do to stop them. If he fired at Kenyon, he might hit Ella. If he fired on Mackenzie, Kenyon still had Ella as a human shield. But if he let them leave, the Stalkers would likely return before he finished changing the truck's ruined tire. In both scenarios, he, Jakob, and Alia died. But in one of them, Ella and Anne lived.

Jakob lowered the shotgun. Even he knew they had no choice.

Anne walked behind Kenyon, stood beside Mackenzie, and stood like an at-ease soldier, hands behind her back.

Ella's eyes met Peter's. She looked grim, but not without hope. Then she mouthed the words, 'Get ready.'

Peter fought against his widening eyes when Anne's right hand came back out from behind her back, clutching a handgun. Jakob must have reacted, though, because Kenyon started to turn around. But he wasn't fast enough. Anne pulled the trigger twice, both rounds striking Kenyon's back. He flailed, arms open wide, releasing Ella, who dived away. Peter adjusted his aim, firing a single round near Mackenzie, the Marine diving for the ground, and then turned his weapon on the pilots through the Black Hawk's glass windshield. Both pairs of hands went up.

Anne stepped away from Kenyon, joining her mother. They retreated together, heading back toward the truck.

Kenyon gasped and pushed himself up, the two rounds stopped by a bulletproof vest.

"Start changing the tire," Peter said to Jakob, and then to Ella, "Help him."

While they headed for the truck, Peter approached Kenyon and kicked his arms out, knocking him back down to the pavement. "Stay down, asshole."

He looked back at Mackenzie, who still had a weapon, but hadn't tried aiming it again. "Will they follow your orders?"

Mackenzie nodded. "If he's dead."

"He's dead," Peter said, keeping his weapon trained on the back of Kenyon's head. "He's still breathing, but he's dead."

Mackenzie pushed himself up with a grunt. He understood the situation. It was a truce. Mackenzie and the pilots would live, and in return, they'd leave with the other choppers. But Kenyon wasn't going anywhere. The choppers could swing back and finish them, but Mackenzie had proven himself to be an honorable soldier. Peter didn't exactly trust him to keep his word, but he had no choice. Even if he could hijack the Black Hawk, the other two helicopters would shoot it down.

"Done," Mackenzie said. "We'll give you a few minutes to get sorted. But...you know they'll come back for you." Peter thought he was talking about the Stalkers until he added, "It might even be me."

ExoGen would come for them. For Ella and Anne.

"It's a big country to get lost in," Peter said.

"Yes, sir," Mackenzie said.

"Asshole traitor." Kenyon spat at Mackenzie's feet. The action drew everyone's eyes to the fresh wad on the black boot, and it gave Kenyon a fraction of a second to move.

And he did.

One moment, Peter was standing over the man, the next he was flat on his back, coughing, his weapon fallen several feet away. He heard a scuffle and sat up in time to see Kenyon knock Mackenzie down with a solid punch.

Peter climbed to his feet just as Kenyon whirled around toward him, extending his leg for a vicious spinning kick. Peter leaned away from the kick, but Kenyon wasn't done. The missed kick propelled Kenyon around, and he put the speed into a back kick that Peter managed to avoid, but not without stumbling. The barrage continued, Kenyon throwing kicks and punches with the fluidity of a man who could take on a gang of men and never stop moving. The rounds that had struck his back definitely hurt him, but he was good at ignoring the pain. Peter had been through days of similar punishment.

Physically, Kenyon had the advantage, and he delivered several hard punches, driving Peter back, further out of reach of his weapon.

And then Peter got pissed.

He stepped into a kick, letting Kenyon's shin snap his rib. Then he locked down the man's leg with this arm. Kenyon threw a punch, connecting with Peter's cheek, but the blow left his arm extended long enough for Peter to take hold of it also. As his head pulled back up, recovering from the punch, he put the motion into his neck, while pulling Kenyon with both hands. When his forehead connected with Kenyon's face, there was a crunch and a whimper. Then Kenyon's body fell slack, and Peter dropped him on the pavement.

Sometimes all the finesse in the world couldn't stand up against a good headbutt.

Peter stumbled back as both he and Mackenzie reached for their weapons. But when they stood again, neither took aim.

"Five minutes," Peter asked.

"We need them alive," Mackenzie replied. "Right now, letting you go is the only way to make sure that happens."

Peter took a step back. "You won't find them."

Mackenzie climbed into the chopper. "For both our sakes, I hope you're right." Then the door slid shut and the rotors spun faster.

Peter hobbled back to the truck. "Jakob!"

"Almost done!" Jakob shouted. He was crouched down by the tire, Ella by his side, spinning the nuts back onto the wheel. The shredded tire was on the road next to him. Peter rounded to the driver's side and got behind the wheel. He turned the key, and the engine bellowed. He felt the back end lower and then heard the clang of the tire kit landing in the truck bed. Both passenger-side doors opened. Ella climbed in the front. Jakob in the back beside Anne and Alia.

"Next stop Boston," Peter said, "Or wherever we end up before that."

"Fuckin' A," Anne said.

"*Anne,*" Ella said, sounding surprised.

Peter shrugged and grinned. "It's a thing we do now."

"End of the world lingo," Jakob added.

"Fuckin' A," Alia said, trying it on for size, but sounding fragile and small.

Ella sighed. "Fuckin' A. Now let's go."

As the sound of the helicopters faded, Peter sped away in the opposite direction, leaving the open small town behind them, and heading into a maze of roads through a thickly forested area. They'd come close to dying, again, and he hurt even more than he had just ten minutes ago, but they were back together. A family again. And the man who tried to pull them apart... He was in for a rude awakening.

Boston or bust, Peter thought. *Fuckin' A.*

Epilogue

Danger, like the odor of a rotting body, can be sensed before its source is seen by the eyes. Kenyon knew that. So, when he awoke, his face tacky with congealed blood, he lay still, keeping his breathing shallow and even. He didn't move his eyes. Even movement below the lids would give him away.

He smelled blood. His own.

But there was something beyond it. Something tangy.

An animal musk.

He heard the flow of air, moving in and out of oversized lungs. Felt the tickle of it sliding through his arm hair. Smelled the breath of a predator. Pictured the old meat caught between teeth.

He could feel the pressure of the bodies surrounding him. Felt the shifting sun on his skin as they swayed back and forth.

Without opening his eyes, he knew he was surrounded by Rattletails.

That there was no escape.

To open his eyes was to die.

So, he remained motionless, hoping that like some predators, the Rattletails would only consume meals they killed. If they believed he was already dead, they might leave him be. But if they were scavengers... The first bite would let them know he was still alive.

He tried to think of ways to fend off the attack, but he was unarmed, and he doubted the CSO or that bastard Mackenzie had left him anything. They wouldn't risk banishing him. This was a death sentence, pure and simple.

They knew it.

He knew it.

And the Rattletails looking down at him knew it.

So why weren't they attacking?

Without an answer, his thoughts turned to Ella.

Like Mackenzie, she had betrayed him. But it was *her* treachery that really stung. It burned him to the core. Filled him with a rage that was beyond description. He had loved her. Had protected her. Had endured hell and crossed two thirds of the country to bring her back to safety. But she had used him. Maybe from the very beginning. She had taken advantage of his affection, manipulated him to her ends, and left with a man who was a stranger to him, but clearly not to her.

How did she know him? Who was he?

Kenyon ran the man's face through his mind, inspecting it for some sort of familiarity. Something about him... The eyes. It was his eyes. He knew those eyes.

They were Anne's eyes.

The realization cut through his fear and sent his mind spiraling toward mania. Lacking any concern for his own safety or future, he shouted, "What the hell are you waiting for?"

When there was no sudden bite, or surprised roar, or any response at all, he slowly opened his eyes. The sun burned his retinas, forcing his eyes nearly shut. Then a silhouette slid into the light.

This is it...

Burn in hell, Ella.

The silhouette resolved slowly, shifting from a large mass, to a distinct shape.

Not a Rattletail. A humanoid shape.

"Alive," said a gruff, feminine voice.

Kenyon tried to push himself up, but a spear tip poked his chest, holding him in place.

"Truck man enemy," the woman said. There was no inflection, but he thought she was asking a question.

He leaned to the side and viewed his interrogator, free of the sun's glare. The face was long and feminine, sporting long, curled teeth that rose from the mouth and punctured holes in the cheeks. Her lean body was framed by a mane of wild hair that hung from her head and grew from her back.

She crouched over him, pushing the spear tip into his armor, snarling as she spoke again. "Truck man enemy."

Kenyon grinned. "Yes. Truck man enemy. *Hate* truck man."

The woman stood and withdrew the spear. "Kill truck man?"

Another question.

Kenyon sat up and wasn't stopped this time. He rose to find himself at the center of a battlefield. Three large, hairy beasts lay dead and dying. Two male versions of the humanoid monster beside him were dead as well. And all four Rattletails, including the thirty-foot specimen. These ExoGen creatures had fought a life-and-death battle around his unconscious form, one side eager to consume him, the other something else. He saw that same primal hunger in the woman's eyes, but something else. She hadn't lost all her humanity, or perhaps had simply regained some of it to survive. The result was an ExoGen with real emotions and complex thoughts, all leading to a desire he recognized as a mirror of his own heart.

"Revenge?" he asked.

The woman grinned, stabbing her face with her teeth. "Revenge. Kill truck man."

"Kill them all," he added.

The woman offered her long-fingered, talon-tipped hand.

Kenyon accepted.

BOOK TWO:

FEAST

1

"Mmm, wow," Anne said between wet, crunching chews. "Oh, now this... this is good." She took a second bite of the plump, uncooked corn cob and leaned back against a tree. Juice oozed from the sides of her mouth, as she chomped again and again, moving the food along her lips like a typewriter. She made no effort to wipe her face as she chewed, mouth open, corn sticking to her chin.

When she spoke again, this time to her mother, the twelve-year-old girl's words were garbled by the food. "I mean, I've had corn before, but this is amazing. And it's not even cooked. You guys didn't just make it grow like crazy, you made it *taste* better, too."

"You left out the part about how that vegetable turns people into monsters," Jakob said, staring at his younger sister. They'd only met a few weeks ago, but they already bickered, teased, and fiercely protected each other like lifelong siblings.

"*Zea mays L. var. rugosa Bonaf*," Ella Masse said, rubbing a hand over her shaved head. She spoke the words whimsically, like recited lines from a play in which she was the star. She watched her daughter take another bite, the juices making clean streaks through the dirt that covered the girl's chin, and the rest of her exposed skin. The dirt wasn't out of place. They were all covered in soil. It was camouflage for their white skin and human scents. "Sweet corn. And it's not a vegetable. It has vegetable features, and fruit, but it's actually a grain."

Ella looked at the corn for a moment, as though lost in thought. Then she stood up and walked away. The world around them, lush with her mankind-destroying creations, was a constant reminder of the biggest blunder in the history of the world. Ella's blunder, at least, in part.

"Really big grass," Jakob said, still watching Anne eat. A bowl of food sat in front of him, composed of foraged leaves, mushrooms, weeds, and mosses. All of it grew in the wild and had no ExoGenetic traits, which meant it lacked RC-714, the gene that had turned the rest of the world into monsters by unlocking dormant adaptations going back to the beginning of life on Earth. The gene had also unleashed an unspeakable hunger in all who had consumed it. Those who had eaten the crops unleashed by ExoGen, the biogenetic corporation for whom Ella had developed RC-714, became ravenous predators. Their bodies rapidly adapted to new environments, which included being surrounded by other rapidly adapting predators. Those who adapted faster, killed, and ate those who hadn't. Over a period of two years, the world's population had eaten itself nearly to extinction, until only apex predators remained. They still hunted each other, and still looked to devour the small pockets of humanity who had not yet consumed ExoGenetic crops. At the moment, that included Jakob.

Anne was torturing him on purpose, he knew. It was part of her job description as a sister, a role she took seriously. He picked up a mushroom in defiance and forced a smile, as he popped it in his mouth. It tasted earthy and sour, but it wouldn't make him sick, make him trip, or kill him. Still, it was hard to enjoy while he could smell the sweetness oozing from Anne's corn.

"Oh my God," Alia said, eyes closed, nose raised and sniffing. "It smells like a candy bar."

"Normal sweet corn has twice the sucrose of field corn and ten times more water-soluble polysaccharide." Anne took another bite, juices rolling down her chin.

"Sucrose?" Alia asked. "Polysaca-what?"

"Sucrose is sugar," Anne said between bites. "Polysaccharides are a bunch of other things you won't understand, either, so best to move on."

"I'm not stupid," Alia said, glaring at the younger girl.

"That has yet to be determined."

Anne took three more bites and smiled at Alia, the gleam in her eye revealing that she hoped the older girl would take the bait. But Alia had quickly learned to not match wits with Anne. She wasn't just smart, she was also ruthless—a habit picked up while traversing an ExoGen-populated countryside with just her mother. That was, until a few weeks ago, when they had showed up at Peter and Jakob's doorstep with a horde of monsters following in their wake.

"ExoGen corn is a super-sweet strain that has seven times the sucrose," Anne said, staying on topic, oblivious to the brewing teenage tension. She looked away from her food, like she was seeing something not there. "That's why it tastes good. Why *all* the crops taste so good. Why people couldn't stop eating them. Why the Change happened so fast."

"But not to you," Jakob said.

"That's great for her." Alia pushed her bowl of foliage away. "But she could at least try not to rub it in."

Uh boy, Jakob thought, *here we go.*

He sometimes wondered if Alia remembered her twelve-year-old self. It had only been four years ago, after all. He'd been through seventh and eighth grades, and had learned to avoid unnecessary clashes with his female classmates, especially those who were smarter, or bigger, than him. They might not get violent—though that wasn't always true with Anne—but they dragged them out. What could be resolved with a few punches between boys might last months or years with the girls. They weren't fights. They were feuds, and he really hoped that wouldn't happen between Anne and Alia—his sister and his girlfriend. There weren't any daytime talk shows left to help them resolve it.

"First of all," Anne said, "I can only eat this corn because I was *grown*, in a lab, from DNA that Mom..." She pointed at Ella. "...*stole* from Dad." She motioned to the forest surrounding them, where Peter was on guard. "I'm a genetically engineered freak, who, yeah, can eat corn. But I've also got a USB port in the back of my head." She stabbed a finger at Alia. "Do *you* have a USB port in the back of your head? No? Too bad for you. It's sooo fun. If you want, I can drill a hole and shove a—"

"Keep it down."

The deep, serious voice made them all flinch, but everyone relaxed when Peter stepped into the small clearing where they were enjoying—or trying to enjoy—their foraged lunch.

"Did you see something?" Alia asked, nervous. Of the five of them, she was still the most shell-shocked. They had become adept at avoiding trouble over the past few weeks, but the events that had brought them together and taken her father's life, had left her in a constant state of nervousness.

"We're clear," Peter said, and then he focused on Anne. "But *you* are being too loud."

Anne said nothing but took another bite of corn.

Jakob picked up a still-full bowl of greenery and handed it to his father. In the past few weeks, his father had gone from looking like a tough-looking Dad to a chiseled warrior. Caked in mud, head shaved, and carrying weapons that included a high-powered bow and arrows and a suppressed M4 rifle, Peter looked more like Arnold Schwarzenegger in *Predator* now, but a little less bulky and half a foot taller.

Alia said Jakob looked like his father, and to an extent, he agreed. They had the same facial features, dark eyes, and shaved brown hair, but that was where the comparison ended. Seventeen-year-old Jakob lacked his father's mass. He wasn't sure if he would ever be as strong as Peter, but he hoped he'd put on some muscle soon, if only to not disappoint Alia before she realized he was scrawny. He wasn't exactly the pinnacle of masculinity yet. But Alia...she was everything Jakob could have asked for. Kind, funny, and beautiful, with her mother's tan Arabian skin, dark eyes, and black hair. In this post-apocalyptic nightmare world, she was a flower blooming in the desert. Jakob felt more like a misshapen cactus.

Peter took handfuls of vegetation, shoving them in his mouth and chewing with efficiency. He was done in under a minute, and like Jakob, he was clearly not satiated by the meal. But he wasn't going to complain about it. Never did. Instead, he'd keep them moving, focused on their destination: George's Island, off the coast of Boston, where a laboratory had been set up before civilization had come to a screeching halt. Ella claimed she could rework the human genome so that ExoGenetic food wouldn't transform people into monsters. She couldn't reset the world, but she *could* increase their chances of survival and ensure the human race's continuation.

If they made it that far.

Apex predators hunted day and night.

And ExoGen, whose executives had known what the RC-714 would do to the world, and had prepared for it, were likely still searching for them. Still trying to stop Ella from freeing the human race. They didn't know why. Only that the corporation had a large, well defended facility in what was once San Francisco, and that they had sent their own private army in search of Ella. And in search of Anne, who held the key to mankind's future in her head...or rather, in the USB drive in her head.

Peter tensed. His eyes flicked up. They were surrounded by trees—maple, birch, and oak—and they were sitting on a carpet of potato plants. "Finish eating."

No one asked why. They just shoved what was left of their food into their mouths and consumed it quickly. Food was sometimes sparse, and they were loath to waste any of it. Unless danger was charging straight for them, jaws agape, they finished all their meals.

Jakob had just finished swallowing when he noticed what his father had already picked up on. The canopy above was still thick green with summertime foliage. But that didn't stop the sun from filtering through the myriad cracks in the armor of thick luminous leaves. Nor did it stop him from detecting the enormous shadow flitting past above them.

A bird, he thought, holding his breath.

Birds were among the most dangerous apex predators, mostly because they could spot you from miles away and strike from above, without warning. So, he was told. He hadn't actually seen an ExoGen bird yet. He had seen a few species of normal birds, which fed exclusively on non-ExoGen plants, like hummingbirds, but he'd seen none of the man-eating super-birds of prey said to be circling high in the atmosphere.

But now...was the shadow so large because it was low in the sky? Or was it just enormous? Experience told him it was the latter, and that it was close because it was hunting them. But they were concealed in the trees. How long would the ExoGen bird wait before giving up?

Fifty feet away, the canopy exploded downward, as something large pierced through the trees and struck the ground.

About that long, Jakob thought, getting his first look at an ExoGen bird and quickly wishing he hadn't—not just because it was a hideous sight, but because it wasn't alone.

There were two of them.

2

Peter nocked an arrow and took aim before the first massive creature struck the ground. One good shot from the powerful bow could drop most anything alive—before the Change and after it. But when the creature reared up after landing, Peter held his fire. The two creatures were focused on each other. And that was a good thing.

A small voice in Peter's mind shouted at him to run, to sneak away with the others and never look back. But this was the first time he had ever seen two ExoGen creatures locked in combat. And from the looks of them, they were both top predators, whose recent rapid evolutions had taken them in divergent directions. He crouched with the others, peering out from behind a thick oak trunk, watching the two behemoths tear at each other.

Peter guessed that the creature on the bottom, which might have once been a crow, was what he'd detected flying above them. Perhaps it had been zeroing in on their scent, despite their best efforts to mask it. Its ten-foot-long wings were covered in black feathers, but the rest of its dark body was cloaked in what looked like long black hair. A line of long spines jutted from its back, flaring up as the bird-like thing snapped at the second creature's exposed neck. The biting jaws, filled with sharp teeth, fell short, but one bite would be enough. Its long legs, ending at massive, talon-tipped, three-toed feet, kicked and scrambled, but to no avail. It was pinned by its larger adversary.

The second creature, which had no doubt dived down on the giant crow-thing from above, might have once been a falcon, but Peter had a hard time spotting any features resembling a pre-Change bird. This featherless beast, with an elongated beak, twitching, sinewy muscles and taut brown skin, looked prehistoric. More like a pterodactyl, but with long powerful legs for running and a long tail tipped with a tuft of feathers. A blood-red crest rose up behind its yellow eyes, which were focused on its equally hungry prey.

The crow-thing gave up trying to bite the larger creature's neck and opted for a less deadly attack. It twisted its own long neck to the side, clamped its jaws around its enemy's lower leg, and sank those long teeth deep into the flesh.

The Exodactyl's eyes just widened, but Peter didn't think it was from the pain. The creature looked excited, like this was the moment it had been waiting for. With startling speed that made Peter flinch, the creature jabbed its long sharp beak downward. The strike began and ended in less than a second.

The crow didn't even notice the gaping hole in its neck.

But it slowed its biting and thrashing, as blood pulsed from its throat.

When its flailing limbs finally fell still, the victorious creature leaned down close to the bloody hole.

Peter expected it to start tearing the dead bird apart, rending it with beak and talons, but that was not what happened. A long tube-like tongue extended from the beak's tip, sliding into the open wound. It then began to twitch, as a slurping sound filled the air.

It's drinking blood, using its tubular tongue like a straw.

Despite having seen combat violent enough to cause a bout of PTSD, not to mention the past few weeks of ExoGenetic horrors, Peter found himself getting queasy. As a former U.S. Marine Critical Skills Operator—part of the most elite fighting force within the Marine Corps—he had been trained to keep his emotions, and his stomach in check.

But the others...

A gurgling sound followed by a wet smack made him freeze in place. He glanced over his shoulder and saw a glob of partially chewed, now regurgitated corn kernels laying atop a flattened potato plant stalk. Anne. As tough as she wanted to be, or wanted everyone to think she was, she was still a twelve-year-old girl. And yeah, she had seen some shit that would leave most adults damaged for life, but she still processed trauma like a kid. Sometimes, that meant puking at something gross.

Without moving his head, Peter swept his gaze back to the Exodactyl. Its body hadn't shifted position, but the slurping sound had stopped, and its tongue no longer twitched. Peter nearly shouted in surprise when he spotted the baseball-sized yellow eye turned straight toward him.

Man and beast locked eyes and froze.

Would it attack with a fresh kill underfoot?

Did it think of them as prey? As competition?

Was it even thinking at all?

No, Peter decided. *And it's not going to let us leave.*

That was one of the defining attributes of ExoGenetic creatures—ravenous hunger. Unceasing. Despite having a meal underfoot, it would hunt them all down, kill and consume them, and then return to the mutated crow. Or some variation of that.

"Everyone get ready to run on my mark," he whispered. He didn't expect to hear confirmation or see any nods. They would follow his lead, knowing full well that to stray from the plan, even an evolving plan, would likely lead to a horrible death for one of them, if not all of them.

"Now," Peter hissed. "Run."

As he heard the others turn and run, he stood up, in clear view, arrow already nocked and drawn back. Their movement freed the large bird-like creature from its predator rigor mortis. It turned to face Peter, leaning toward him. It then opened its beak wide and let out an ear-piercing squawk.

Peter's fingers withdrew from the string. It snapped forward, propelling the arrow at three hundred and seventy feet per second, meaning the arrow left his fingers and entered the creature's open maw before the creature could react to the sound. The Exodactyl's beak snapped shut, and its head twitched back in surprise. Its wide eyes had an almost humorous 'what the fuck' look about them. But the arrow hadn't lodged in the bird's throat. Instead, it pierced the layers of flesh and skin, emerging on the far side and striking a tree, twenty-five feet away. It was the one free shot Peter would get, so while the creature was distracted by the confusing pain, he turned tail and chased after the others.

Ten steps into his run, he began to second guess his flight.

I should have taken a second shot, he thought. *Should have put it down for good.* He'd killed other ExoGenetic monsters before. Why not this one?

There's no way to know if more arrows would have done it, he told himself. *The first arrow only confused it. How many more would it take to kill it? I'm not even sure where its vital organs are. It could have two hearts, for all I know.*

They were all logical arguments. To a point. But none of them was the truth.

The truth was that he was afraid. The moment he saw those sinister eyes and the blood-sucking tongue, the mental switch in his psyche that was normally switched to 'fight' got flicked over to 'flight.' In a world of predators, no matter how well prepared or armed a person was, true humans were still prey, and those instincts couldn't always be overcome.

But there was no sense in second guessing his decision to run. He was committed to it. He knew if he reached the road, just a few hundred feet ahead, he would reach the truck. The kids had nicknamed it *Beastmaster*, on account of its many spikes and metal shields. Peter had argued that *Mad Max* was a more appropriate nickname for the post-apocalyptic death machine, but Anne's ceaseless arguing had won the day. Peter tried to explain the *Beastmaster* movie to them, but they didn't make it past the thongs before bursting into laughter. It had been a lively debate, and a good day.

But not all days were good. Most were defined by fear and violence.

Like today, Peter thought, glancing back, as the Exodactyl let out a shriek.

The massive creature tilted its body forward, its tail rising up as a counterbalance. Then, with eyes locked on Peter, it lunged forward and ran.

The dead crow-thing's jaws, locked in a death grip, still clung to the Exodactyl's leg. But the larger predator didn't slow or try to pry itself free. It just charged forward, dragging the corpse along for the ride, leaving a trail of blood in its wake.

With the chase in progress, there was no reason to be quiet anymore. "How close are you?" he shouted.

"Nearly there!" Ella replied.

Peter couldn't see the others through the maze of trees, both standing and fallen, but he knew they weren't too far ahead. They'd have just a few seconds before he, and then the hellish Big Bird, entered the clearing ahead.

He angled his course, aiming for the road behind the armored, black Dodge Ram, and guesstimated his ETA. "Seven seconds! Behind the truck!"

"I'll be ready," Jakob replied. "Don't stick around."

Peter understood the message and poured on the steam. The forest floor began to shake with each of the Exodactyl's footfalls, but more so when it stepped with its left limb, slamming the still-attached, giant, dead crow into the ground.

Rounding a tall pine to confuse the predator on his heels, Peter looked back and shouted in surprise, as the massive beak snapped shut just inches from his face. It sounded like two wooden planks clapping together, the noise loud enough to hurt his ears.

As the Exodactyl rounded the tree behind him, momentum carried the crow out in a wide arc. Its limp body wrapped around the trunk of a sturdy maple, bones cracking. The snagged corpse pulled the larger creature's limb back, keeping it from lunging one more time and clamping on to Peter's skull. The frustrated creature shrieked after Peter and then tore its leg from the dead crow-thing's mouth, leaving deep and bloody slashes in its own flesh. But it was oblivious to the pain, as it flung itself back into the chase.

Peter threw his forearms up over his face as he crashed through a wall of crisscrossing dead branches that blocked his path. He felt his exposed skin tear, but when his feet hit the pavement beyond, he didn't slow to inspect his wounds, he just charged right out.

Moving across the open road, he looked left, seeing Jakob standing in the flatbed, aiming the big M249 light machine gun toward the woods, where Peter had exited. As Peter dove into the woods on the far side of the road, he expected to hear the cacophonous roar of the big weapon, followed by the groaning impact of a slain ExoGen, but neither of those things happened.

Peter climbed to his feet and stepped back into the road, eyeing the forest, where Jakob kept the weapon trained.

Where the hell did it go?

"Where the hell did it go?" Jakob shouted, channeling his father's thoughts.

Then Peter saw it.

The long beak slid out of the forest, looking almost like just another branch, slowly positioning itself to strike, fifteen feet above Jakob.

3

Ella Masse had experienced moments of heightened awareness. When the blood is pumping double-time and oxygen saturates the mind, the world seems to slow down. Things become clearer. Colors appear more vivid. Smells develop more layers. And sounds become crisper. In her old life, she had experienced this phenomenon on the cusp of discovery. Most people picture science as a dull, laborious job of endless repetition. To a degree, it was true. But after months, or even years, of hard work, that moment of breakthrough, of Earth-changing discovery... There are few other rushes that compare. She'd felt it when she first laid eyes on the initial results for RC-714. The test corn not only grew in the harshest of environments, it had also spread aggressively.

They were going to feed the world.

Instead, they'd made the world hungrier than ever before. They gave humanity an endless food supply that had made everyone, and everything, that ate it, ravenous for flesh. Any flesh. The smallest animals were affected first. Species of rats, squirrels, rabbits, and mice had turned on each other in great bloody wars. Then they had attacked other species, including people, and then each other. And it wasn't long before larger mammals, including people, joined the fray. As the Pandora's box of ancient genes became available, evolution, spurred by ceaseless hunger, mutated nearly every living thing into something monstrous.

Only those who managed to not consume the ExoGenetic crops had remained unchanged, and of them, only those prepared for the violence to come, had survived.

Since leaving the safety of the ExoGen facility in San Francisco, Ella had experienced several more moments of heightened awareness. At first, they had left her feeling shaken and disturbed. Adrenaline did strange things to the body and left most people shaking as its positive, life-saving effects wore off. But she had come to embrace the feeling, knowing it made the difference between life and death, for herself and her family, which now included Peter...and Jakob.

The boy wasn't exactly keen on her yet. She understood why. She was his father's former mistress. Loyalty to his mother made her the antagonist, and she wouldn't argue against it. Had Peter chosen her over his wife all those years ago, Ella wouldn't have tried to change his mind. But Jakob's mother had also tried to eat the boy. Ella, at least, hadn't done that.

And now, as the oxygen pumped into her brain by adrenaline-fueled blood sharpened her sense of the world around her, she saw a chance to win the boy over, by saving his life.

She twisted her shotgun up, aiming into the tree branches above the truck, where a triangular spear was aimed at Jakob's chest. The Apex bird had given up chasing Peter and was now poised to strike his son.

Unless she could stop it.

But she couldn't.

With the shotgun still in motion, she shouted, "Jakob!"

She couldn't see how the boy responded to her warning, because she didn't take her eyes off the creature above them. When its head exploded from the trees and stabbed its spear-like beak toward the truck, she had no idea whether the strike found Jakob's body. She didn't hear a scream, but then, the strike was so fast and powerful she didn't think the boy would have time to scream.

The bird's head came up for a second strike at the same time Ella's shotgun finished swiveling upward.

God, that thing is fast, she thought, and then she pulled the trigger.

The shotgun roared, firing a storm of 12-gauge pellets into the large target, just ten feet above her. The blast would have shredded most living things on the planet a few years ago, but now, the pellets simply embedded themselves in the monster's thick skin.

Closer, she thought. *Point blank will—*

Her thoughts locked up when the bird turned its head and killer beak toward her. Instead of killing the creature, she'd managed to seal her own fate.

An arrow whistled through the air, striking the beak, and bouncing away. The massive, featherless bird paid it no heed.

Ella heard Peter shout her name, but she didn't turn. If this was her end, she would face it head on. She pumped the shotgun and saw the bird's eyes flicker slightly wider. It was going to strike faster than she could pull the trigger.

A loud boom hiccupped a shout from her mouth, but her fright was as short-lived as the bird's predatory confidence. A small implosion punched a red hole into the creature's chest. It was quickly followed by a much larger explosion from the bird's back. She heard the burst flesh slap against the trees and leaves behind the creature, and then a series of booming reports erased all other sounds. A line of bullet holes stitched its way up the creature's writhing body. The final round punching into one eye and out the other, came from a different direction. The bird fell in a heap, crumpling in a bloody mass of chewed-up avian meat.

Ella turned right, from where the final shot had come, and found Anne clutching a handgun in her small hands, the barrel smoking.

The girl looked Ella up and down, her forehead twisted in worry.

"I'm okay," Ella told her daughter, and she knew who she had to thank for that. Jakob stood in the back of the armored pick-up truck, still holding the M249 machine gun mounted in the bed. Blood trickled down his right arm, revealing just how close he had come to being impaled...before saving her life.

So much for scoring brownie points, she thought.

She was about to thank him when he beat her to it. "Thanks, Ella. If you hadn't shouted..."

She smiled and replied with a genuine, "Thank *you*."

"Everyone okay?" Peter charged around the back of the truck, nocked arrow aimed at the very dead ExoGen. Upon seeing the creature, he slowly removed tension from the bow string and removed the arrow. He scanned the group, eyes lingering on Jakob's arm for a moment before moving on. "Where's Alia?"

Fear flickered into Jakob's eyes for a moment, but then Alia slid out from beneath the truck, a pistol gripped in her hands. Despite being four years older than Anne, Alia lacked the younger girl's experience and defiant bravery. They had been training Alia while on the move, but she was a slow study. Jakob had struggled at first, too, but a few weeks in the wild had done a lot to boost his confidence and quell his fears. Ella saw more and more of Peter in the boy with every passing day. But Alia...she was still a liability. So, when things got crazy, her job was to get out of the way, and this time she'd chosen to hide under the truck.

"FYI," Alia said, a quiver in her voice, "under the truck isn't the best place to hide."

Jakob glanced down at the truck bed, his eyes widening. "Holy shit."

A six-inch wide hole had been punched in the floor—one of the few outer surfaces that didn't have extra layers of armor plating welded to it. Luckily, the strike that had sliced Jakob's arm and hammered through the floor had missed anything important, above and below the truck bed's surface. The look in Alia's eyes as she squirmed out from beneath the truck, said it had been a close call though.

"Everyone in," Peter said, climbing into the driver's seat.

No one complained or argued. This wasn't a family vacation. All the sound would have attracted the attention of any Apex ExoGens within earshot, and once they were close enough to smell the massive amount of blood from the two dead birds, they'd be whipped into a frenzy. Ella had little doubt that the scene would be littered with more dead bodies before the sun set.

The faster they left the area, the better. There was still a chance they would run into an ExoGen while fleeing the scene, but better to deal with problems head on than linger around and face three hundred and sixty degrees of trouble.

As the kids slipped into the back seat, Ella climbed into the front, feeding a fresh shell into the shotgun. They had found and raided a National Guard Depot, pilfering guns and ammo, just a week ago. Ella had claimed an M4 assault rifle, which she used most often, but in the close confines of a thick forest or a building, she preferred the shotgun. They'd also managed to find a good amount of 5.56×45 mm NATO rounds for the machine gun. If they hadn't, she would have become an ExoGen shish kabob.

Peter pointed at the first aid kit beneath Ella's legs and snapped his fingers twice. The first aid kit had been heavily customized over the past few weeks, containing supplies that made it closer to a mobile surgical suite than something you could pick up at a grocery store.

She handed the box to him, and he held it back over the seat.

"Anne, patch him up."

"Seriously?" Jakob said. "She can't sew a straight line."

"You'd rather Little Miss Barfs-A-Lot puke in the wound before stitching it?" Anne asked, taking the kit, and popping it open.

Alia raised her hands. "I'm not touching it."

"See?" Anne said, removing a hooked needle from its sterile packaging and handling it with her grimy fingers.

"Anne," Peter said. "Your dirty fingers are nearly as bad as Alia's fictional puke. Keep it clean. Do it right."

Anne frowned and sighed, but her attitude quickly shifted to something resembling professional discipline. She had come to respect Peter over the past few weeks. When he spoke in that deep, serious tone, she listened. And learned. She had become quite deadly during her time in the wild, with just Ella. But they had survived mostly through an almost cruel cunning. Now she was disciplined. Learning to keep her cool and react with her brain as much as with her instincts.

Jakob calmed when he saw the shift in Anne's attitude. He lifted his short sleeve up over his shoulder and stayed quiet as Anne began to clean the arm with alcohol.

With everyone settled, Peter started the truck. The engine roared to life, making Ella flinch. The truck always felt too loud, but once it was moving, the sound was minimal. Anything able to hear them, would likely see them anyway. They had talked about ditching the truck, but it got them where they needed to go faster, could outrun some enemies, and provided hard-hitting protection in the form of armor and a light machine gun. Their route east had become circuitous thanks to broken bridges, blocked roads, and dangerous territories, but they were still making better time than they would have on foot.

Instead of heading directly northeast for Boston, as intended, they had been forced southeast, all the way down through Charlotte, North Carolina, and into South Carolina. The plan was to hit I-95 and follow it north, all the way to Boston. If the road was clear, they would make the trip in a day. If it wasn't, and they were forced to follow more winding back roads, they might have a few more weeks on the road. But before that happened, they had one last stop to make—at Little Hellhole Bay. It didn't sound like a nice place to visit, before or after the Change, but it was one of many locations Ella had helped build a biodome farmstead. She felt the occupants might be able to help her work at George's Island... if they were still alive, and if she could convince them to leave.

As dangerous as life in a biodome could be, it was still a lot safer than trekking through the wilderness in a truck.

Jakob hissed as Anne slipped the needle into his skin and pulled the two-inch-long slice together. The wound would heal, and Jakob would live, but Ella was under no illusions. They were hunted by nearly everything left alive in the world, including her former employers, who wanted them for far worse reasons than satiating their primal, unceasing hunger.

4

"What do we think?" Peter asked, looking out the windshield at what looked like a busy supermarket.

There were cars still in the lot. The day was clear and warm. The corn growing on the large flat roof looked like a neat haircut, but there was so much growth covering absolutely everything that Alia Rossi filtered it out. If not for the stench of their odor-masked bodies, she might have been able to convince herself that the nightmare had come to an end…that the Change had never occurred…that her father had never gone mad, and her mother was still alive.

But she couldn't even pretend, because if she felt just a hint of her previous life, she would cling to it like an addict.

Except that it's gone, she told herself.

This is the world now.

She tried to be strong for Jakob. Modeled herself after Ella, and Anne, and Peter. But she was no good at it, really. And when push came to shove, and then teeth and claws and twisted freaks of nature, she cracked. Hiding became her specialty. No one judged her for it or complained. Better that she was out of the way, rather than in it. But that didn't stop her from feeling useless.

So, when Peter posed the simple question about what looked like an untouched oasis from the past, she thought, *I can check expiration dates on food,* and said, "Let's do it."

"Well, if Princess Pouty-Pants is in, I'm in." Anne smiled at Alia.

Alia couldn't tell if the younger girl was really mocking her or engaging in some kind of playful banter. Anne was a mystery to her. Funny, but jaded. Young, but somehow older than her and Jakob. Their relationship was rocky at best. Anne took every sarcastic potshot that presented itself. Alia came to the conclusion that the girl was trying to thicken her emotional skin.

Maybe because she cared about Alia. Maybe because she cared about Jakob and didn't want to see him hurt. He was doubly at risk because of Alia. He took risks protecting her, and if he ever failed to protect her, the fallout might be enough to break him, too.

Jakob was adapting. Learning. Growing stronger, tougher, and more resilient. He was a far cry from Peter, Ella, and Anne still, but he was cruising ahead, while Alia was standing still.

But I can read labels, she thought, and opened her door first.

After a brief and cautious walk, they stood in front of the grocery store entrance. The doors were shut, and the interior was dark, far more ominous than Alia expected. "So...we can't break a window, right? That would be too loud."

Peter's response was to step up to the automatic door, grasp the metal handle and pull. It resisted for a moment, but then the gears that hadn't moved in a long time, gave way, whirring as the door opened.

Before entering, Peter said, "Lights on. We'll do a sweep of each aisle and then break into two groups."

After turning on their headlamps and chambering rounds in their silenced weapons—Alia had a handgun, but she couldn't remember what kind—they crept into the store. Peter took the lead, followed by Jakob, Alia, Anne, and Ella. This was their usual formation, and Alia understood the point of her position. There were two layers of people who could fight on either side of her.

Protecting her.

They moved across the front of the store, which faintly smelled of rotted food, but more like dust. They paused for a moment at the cereal aisle, where a heap of dead bodies lay between the Cocoa Puffs and Cinnamon Toast Crunch.

"There was either a really good sale, or these guys got a hankering for fresh meat all at the same time." Anne seemed unfazed by the mound of death, but Alia thought...hoped...it was just an act.

When the Change started affecting humanity, people resisted their growing urges. At first, they ate more meat. And then only meat. And then raw meat. Eventually, someone would succumb and take a bite out of a neighbor, family member, or total stranger at the grocery store. And once the smell of fresh blood filled the air, it triggered a response in everyone nearby. Alia had no trouble picturing that here. One of these people, probably someone buried beneath the rest, had snapped, and attacked. Then everyone in the store on the fringe of changing had lost the battle against it and had joined in.

She shivered as her imagination took over, replaying scenes of spraying blood, gnashing teeth, and tearing fingernails. It would have been like some kind of zombie apocalypse, but worse. Because people weren't just killing each other, they were changing as they did, growing more efficient and deadly and hungry with each kill. Whoever walked away from this feeding frenzy probably didn't even look human anymore.

"Okay," Jakob said. "Cereal was never on the list anyway." As one of the most genetically modified and processed foods available before the Change, cereal was generally off limits. But it had remained popular even after ExoGenetic crops sprang up everywhere. Everyone was fed during those days, but that didn't stop people from wanting their microwave meals, instant puddings, and chocolate-dipped donut bites. Fresh produce was no longer sold in stores, but processed food never went out of style.

"Looks like this store is a mixer," Jakob said. He'd coined the term at the last grocery store they had visited. Mixers didn't separate organic food from regular food, but shelved them together, making their best bet at finding safe food a little bit harder.

After finishing the sweep, they split into two groups—adults and kids—but Anne wandered off within thirty seconds of the split. "You guys need some smoochy time," she said as she wandered away, scanning lines of boxes. "Just like Mom and Dad."

Alia didn't think that was true about Ella and Peter. They hid their affection for each other during the day, but Alia wasn't deaf. She heard them on occasion during a sleepless night. She never got up the nerve to peek, but it didn't sound like they were having thumb wars.

But for her and Jakob...time alone was at a premium, so Alia didn't complain when Anne walked away.

And neither did Jakob.

They didn't speak for a few minutes as they scanned the shelves, but they grew steadily closer. When they stood shoulder to shoulder, Jakob leaned closer and said, "You smell horrible."

She laughed and said, "And together, we're like a bouquet of shit."

He put his arm around her and squeezed her close.

As she turned to kiss him, her eyes locked onto a jar on the far side of the aisle. She stopped mid-pucker and said, "Whoa."

It was peanut butter.

Organic peanut butter. *Chunky* organic peanut butter. The holy grail of post-apocalyptic treats. Peanut butter had a long shelf life. Back when there was still an Internet, she'd watched a video of a man eating sixty-year-old peanut butter rations from the Korean War. If the expiration date, which was more of a suggestion to keep food moving off the shelf, was early enough, there would be no fear of ExoGenetic contamination. They could eat it. *All* of it. And there were at least thirty jars.

Jakob picked up a jar, twisted it in his hand and smiled wide. "Jackpot." He lifted the jar and looked inside. "It's separated—"

"Organic peanut butter is always separated."

"Well then, it's perfect." Jakob looked up and down the aisle. "Now we just need to find some coconut oil and dark chocolate and we'll be in business."

Both items, when organic, were on Ella's safe list. Coconut was not an ExoGenetic crop, and organic, free-trade chocolate was one of the last crops to be overrun. They also had very long shelf lives. If the dates were right, they could have the makings of an epic snack, unlike anything she'd had in two years. Her mouth watered, but the food took a sudden back seat when Jakob, in his excitement, wrapped her in his arms and kissed her.

They had kissed before. A lot. Their awkward first kiss had been back at her farmhouse, in the biodome, just a few feet from where her mother had been buried. They had never met, but shared a kiss that expressed their elation at finally meeting. There had been many more kisses, snuck in during brief private moments. In the darkness of night. When Anne fell asleep in the truck and the parents were looking out the front. But this...this was different. This was passionate.

When they separated, Jakob looked bewildered. "I guess peanut butter is an aphrodisiac."

Alia said nothing. She just took him by the hand and led him away.

"Where are we going?"

"Bathroom," she said. "I saw them in the corner of the store."

"Why?"

"I have to pee." That was the truth, and she never passed up a toilet, whether or not they flushed. But that wasn't the whole truth, and as Jakob's hand grew sweaty in hers, he knew it, too.

When they reached the door to the women's room, she put her hand on his chest and said, "Wait here."

He looked a little surprised, but said, "You really do have to pee. I thought that was like code or something."

"Real and code," she said.

"Hold on." Jakob pushed the bright blue door open slowly, aiming his rifle inside the room, scanning it from side to side. With no signs of danger or even a bad smell, he stepped aside and held the door open for her. "Your throne awaits."

"Be just a minute." Alia said and stepped inside. When the door was closed, she tried to let herself feel normal. *It's just a bathroom.*

She opened the first stall. The toilet was pristine and empty. There were few things more disappointing than a post-apocalyptic toilet that hadn't been flushed.

Just pretend the power is out, she told herself, dropping her pants and sitting on the cool seat. When she was done peeing, she reached for toilet paper and smiled. It was a simple thing, but she'd gone without it too many times. Once was too many times. It was a stupid thing, but it brought her joy, and as she wadded it up, wiped, and then stood to pull up her pants. She was lost in the moment. Her hands moved on muscle memory, first buckling her belt, and then reaching back and pushing the small metal lever.

Her mind woke up as the lever shifted downward. She flinched her hand away, but it was too late. Water pressure that had been contained for years exploded into the toilet with uproarious urgency.

The bathroom door burst open.

"Alia!"

She stepped out of the stall, face twisted in concern. "I flushed. I didn't mean to. It just—"

The wall between them shook. A long, hooked talon punched through, separating them. Alia screamed and reeled back. The hard shell was green, and its bottom side was serrated like a massive knife.

Jakob fell back out of the bathroom, raising his rifle to fire. A second exoskeletal appendage slammed through the wall and struck the door, slamming it shut.

Alia scrambled away, slipping on the smooth tile floor, grasping for the silenced handgun she had holstered before sitting on the toilet.

The massive limbs moved in and out, sawing through the wall with frantic jerking motions. Alia's screams were drowned out by a loud chirping that tore through the air like an alarm. It was the most noise she had heard since the battle at her parents' farmhouse, and if anything else was around, it would already be on its way.

The wall gave way, coughing a cloud of drywall into the room. Support beams bent and broke. And then a head slid into the room, insect like, but unidentifiable. It had massive oval eyes that shimmered under the glare of Alia's headlamp. Three sets of mandibles opened and closed, while smaller grinding mouths twitched. The thing lacked any kind of expression, but exuded menace, and hunger.

Alia drew her weapon and pulled the trigger. The first three rounds missed, despite the creature's size. But the rest struck the oversized insect's head and forelimbs, ricocheting into the ceiling and walls.

The 9mm weapon, about all she could handle, was ineffective.

Through the frenzied chirping, she thought she heard voices. The bathroom door shook from the far side. It opened an inch, but when it struck the creature's leg, it was pushed back, sealing predator and prey in a fifteen-foot-long space with no other exit.

Not even a window.

A claw snapped out and cracked the tile floor, just missing her legs. She pushed back farther, but stopped when her back struck the wall.

The insect pushed deeper into the room, incensed by its failure.

Alia tried to reload her weapon, but she managed only to drop it and the spare magazine.

When the creature struck again, so fast that the limb looked like it had teleported from one spot to the next, Alia pushed herself up onto her feet. She screamed, again and again, but the sound was lost in the insect's chirping, a symphony of life and death.

With nowhere else to run, Alia dove into the stall, yanked the door shut and twisted the lock. She huddled atop the toilet, clutching herself, sobbing.

The metal walls vibrated. The tip of a claw stabbed through. It pulled free with a shriek of carapace on metal. The next strike would be hard enough and deep enough to find her.

A cacophonous boom shook the air.

The floor trembled.

A second boom rang out.

The chirping fluttered and stopped.

In the silence that followed, Alia wept. Then something moved.

It's coming back!

Walls crumbled. Tiles crunched. It was right outside the stall.

The door shook.

She heard voices shouting her name, but she couldn't hear who, over the sound of her own ragged screams.

The door was torn open.

It was Peter, shotgun in hand, face covered in white gore.

She fell into his arms, vision fading. She remembered being carried. She saw a large number of empty shells lying on the hallway floor as she was rushed out of the bathroom. Peter had resorted to using the loud shotgun when normal bullets had failed. The rest of the retreat from the grocery store, and then the area was a blur. Somewhere along the line, she fell asleep.

When she woke up again, everyone was quiet. She said nothing, but started crying when she found a jar of peanut butter in her lap. She could have gotten them all killed, but they were still showing her kindness. Alia wondered how long that would last. Sooner or later, she was going to get someone killed.

Sooner or later, she was going to have to leave.

5

"Are we there yet?" Anne asked. It had become a running gag and was usually good for a chuckle, harkening back to a time of normalcy, when driving across the country with siblings was considered mind-numbingly boring. But now, with the possibility of every turn revealing a new horror, crossing the country was far from dull. They rode mostly in silence, each of them keeping watch in a different direction.

Jakob had told Anne about how, when he was younger, he used to imagine a man running in time with the truck, leaping from building to building, or trees, or whatever else they passed. She thought it was strange at first, but sometimes caught herself imagining a giant sword extending from the side of the truck, cutting down all the trees and endless fields they passed.

Instead of laughing, Ella replied, "Almost," which killed the joke and put her fellow backseat riders on edge. So far, the two biodomes Anne and her mother had visited had been left in ruins. Lives had been lost or uprooted. Jakob and Peter had nearly died on multiple occasions, and Alia had lost her father. The man had already been out of his mind, but he was still her father. Anne was still getting to know her father, but already she couldn't picture a future without him in it. He was brave, and strong and disciplined. While the world had fallen into chaos, he brought order and balance, even to her mother, who had become somewhat savage to survive. Anne didn't hold that against her mother. They'd both survived only because they were willing to do horrible things, and Peter was equally willing, but his strategic mind was better at avoiding trouble, or getting out of it without losing a piece of his soul in the process.

Or maybe he just lost less of it. He'd seen combat before, and not the kind where people were killing ravenous monsters. He had fought and killed other people. Normal people. And it had left scars on his body and psyche. He had told her about it one day while foraging. At first, it seemed like he was just shooting the breeze, telling stories to his daughter. But then she understood that it was a morality lesson about the horrors of war. A warning to not get lost in the killing and death and non-stop adrenaline. "It can change the way you see the world," he had said. "When you become numb to death, you become numb to life, and it's a lot easier to lose something you can't feel."

"Like I might cut off a finger if I can't feel it," she had said.

"Mmm," he had agreed, "except that losing your finger only affects you. If you were to die..."

She had thought his concern was about how Anne dying might affect Ella. But when he turned away from her, hiding his face and whatever emotion was going on there, she understood that he was becoming as fond of her as she was of him.

Since then, she had fully embraced the idea that she now had a complete family unit. Maybe the only one left on Earth. And for that, despite all the death and violence and horrible monsters trying to eat them, not to mention a good deal of the numbing he had warned her about, she felt blessed.

And now, as they approached another biodome, she couldn't help but feel a growing sense of impending doom. Would they be welcomed? Would they face yet more monsters? Would a member of her family—even Alia, who sometimes irked Anne—be in mortal danger? And how could Anne's parents not see these risks? Why not just drive around and keep on going? Could the people holed up there be that helpful? They probably weren't even alive.

"You've got to be kidding me," Jakob said, looking out the side window opposite Anne. She blinked out of her thoughts and understood her brother's disheartened tone. The roadside for miles had been flanked by unending fields of what looked like miniature trees with green, orb covered stalks topped with lettuce heads. Her mother said they were Brussels sprouts. Actually, she had said, "Brassica oleracea var. gemmifera," but Anne knew what that meant...somehow.

But now the Brussels sprout plants were giving way to lush, swampy land. It wasn't the terrain itself that was frightening, but the kinds of creatures that once might have populated the area, and what they might have become since the Change.

"Aww, geez," Alia said, leaning over Jakob, her body nearly lying on top of his. Was she really afraid or just copping a feel? *Teenagers*, Anne thought with a roll of her eyes. She hoped she'd never be one. Not that she wanted to die, she just hoped she could skip past that stage of life. From what she could tell from Jakob and Alia, not to mention her own mother's monthly cycle, hormones were hell.

"Did you see the name of the street?" Jakob asked.

While street names weren't very important to Anne's day-to-day life, she often read the signs anyway. She made a game out of guessing why the name had been chosen. Was it random? Did it describe the terrain? A person who lived there?

The funniest she'd seen was French Hussy Road.

She had been tuned out for the past few minutes and missed this sign.

"Alligator Road," Jakob said. "*Alligator*. They were bad enough before. What could—"

"Hey Jake," Peter said, sounding calm. "Do me a favor?"

"Uh," Jakob said. "Yeah?"

Peter glanced in the rearview, making eye contact with his son. "I think you know."

"Right," Jakob said. "Sorry. I'll try not to point out what a bad idea this is."

Anne cracked a smile. Jakob had been picking up some of her biting sarcasm. She liked it.

A wooden sign on the side of the road read, 'Alligator Creek Ahead.'

"So, am *I* allowed to say what a bad idea this is?" Anne asked. Peter just smiled. He wasn't stupid. He knew they were entering dangerous territory. But really, everywhere was dangerous territory.

This just *sounded* worse.

The small two-lane road was framed by lush trees and wet ground, full of ferns and moss and surprisingly few ExoGen crops. The already aggressive swamplands had maintained some of their territorial grip. But not all of it. A mixture of crops grew in patches. Anne whispered their names as she spotted them. "Beta vulgaris. Brassica oleracea var. botrytis. Brassica oleracea var. capitate. Oryza sativa." Otherwise known as sugar beets, broccoli, cabbage, and rice, which grew right out of the water.

She wondered again how she knew all these strange scientific details, but her line of questioning was cut short by yet another sign, this one for "Little Hellhole Bay."

"Okay, seriously," Jakob said. "Little Hellhole Bay? Did you search the map for the most ominous sounding stretch of road on purpose?"

Ella looked back over the seat, a slight grin on her face. "Actually, that's where we're headed. That's where the biodome is. Just because it doesn't sound safe, doesn't mean it's actually unsafe."

"Pretty much does these days," Jakob said. "If things like lemon trees can dissolve people from the inside out, and suck them dry for nutrients, then a place like Little Hellhole Bay can live up to its name."

"Only one way to find out," Ella said.

"Are the people there really worth the risk?" Alia asked.

"One's a geneticist. The other is a computer scientist. So, together, they're like a replacement me."

"I thought *I* was the replacement you?" Anne asked, a spark of anger creeping into her voice. She still hadn't really come to grips with the idea that she'd been grown, in a lab, as some kind of better version of her mother, with all her mother's knowledge stored on a USB drive embedded in her skull. How numb did her mother have to become to make decisions like that? What kind of person steals DNA from a long-lost boyfriend, engineers a daughter, and implants tech into her head? Anne had no memory of the surgery, so they must have done it when she was young. Anne had wondered how old she really was but didn't ask. Her oldest memories were hazy, and *felt* really old, but that didn't mean they weren't manufactured or implanted. Maybe she was ten years old, or three. Either way, she didn't want to know. It made her feel less human. Less alive. Less...loved.

Sadness swept over Ella's face.

"Anne, you're—"

"Better," Anne said. "You've said. The best of you both. I know. That doesn't mean...forget it. Also, people with guns at two o'clock."

Peter hit the brakes and brought the truck to a jarring stop, angling the vehicle, so that if bullets started flying, they'd hit him first. Three men dressed head-to-toe in black military uniforms stepped onto the road, assault rifles aimed at the truck.

"Three more in the trees," Ella said.

Anne saw them a moment later, perched on hunting hides mounted to trees, partially concealed by the lush, green foliage. All weapons were trained on the vehicle. If these people wanted to, they could riddle the windshield with holes and kill them all far more efficiently than a lone ExoGen. Even in a world full of rapidly evolving death machines, the human race could still get the job done when they banded together.

Peter rolled down his window and extended both hands, showing that he wasn't armed. His assault rifle was just below his hands, easily within reach, but the message was clear: We aren't looking for a fight.

The three armed men strode toward the car, but only one of them kept his weapon turned on Peter. The other two started scanning the surrounding swamplands.

The nearest of them, leaned in and peered through the windows, his eyes hidden behind a mirror-lensed facemask. "Well, gol-dang. Y'all out for a Sunday drive?"

Is it Sunday? Anne wondered. She'd stopped keeping track of days a long time ago.

"We're here to visit some friends," Peter replied, his voice calm and neutral.

"That so?" the man said. "What're their names. Might know 'em, seeing as how these are my stompin' grounds."

Ella leaned toward the window. "Bob and Lyn Askew."

"Bob and Lyn..." The man cocked his head to the side. "Oh, right. Yeah, I know 'em. They're back inside the compound."

"Compound?" Peter asked.

"Up the road a ways," the man said, motioning back behind him. "Safe place, if y'all want to kick up your feet for a spell."

Anne squinted at the man's reflective face and saw Peter's skeptical reflection.

"You know," Peter said. "I think we'll just—"

The man pulled his facemask up to reveal a gaunt face covered in random patches of hair. He grinned, revealing a gap where his front teeth had once been. "Well now, I'm going to have to insist. Folks round here don't take too kindly to people refusing our hospitality. Best you all step out of the vehicle, slow and steady, like that turtle that beat Bugs Bunny in the race."

Peter glanced at Ella. She shook her head slowly, almost imperceptibly. Anne couldn't discern if she was telling him to not act, or to not listen to the man. Then Peter raised his empty hands a little higher. "We don't want any trouble."

"Listen to what I'm tellin' you and you won't find none," the man said. "Name's Boone."

Peter offered his hand, and the man shook it. "Peter."

"Why ya'll shave your heads?" Boone asked.

Really? Anne thought. *That's the first question he has to ask?*

"Lice," Peter said, and Boone quickly withdrew his hand.

Anne nearly laughed, but held it in.

"Fair warning," Peter said. "There is an M4 between me and the door. I'm going to have to catch it, so it doesn't fall out."

Boone took a step back and aimed his weapon at Peter's head. "Like a turtle."

"Ayuh," Peter said, apparently imitating the cartoon turtle. He got a laugh out of Boone and then opened the door slowly, lifting the M4 by its handle in the most non-threatening way possible. He then placed the weapon in the truck's flatbed.

When he lifted his empty hands again, Boone lowered his rifle. "You all seen some shit."

"Shit's seen us," Anne said, and got a laugh out of the man.

"Well, all right then. If ya'll wouldn't mind stepping out, one at a time, I'll take you to Bob and Lyn. Can't say whether or not they'll be happy to see you, but I'll take you to 'em, just the same."

Ten minutes later, they were completely unarmed and headed down the road on foot, while a few of the men stayed behind and rummaged through *Beastmaster*.

Anne glanced back at the men, taking stock of them, wondering which of them they might have to kill first. She wasn't sure if her parents were buying into Boone's Southern charms, but she doubted it. Boone, on the other hand, exuded confidence and an air of cockiness that made Anne want to kick him square in the nuts. But she'd hold back until the time was right. Until *Peter* said the time was right. And then she would kick, scratch, bite, and stab her way to freedom. She hoped Boone wasn't stupid enough to try to prevent them from leaving, but she had a strong hunch he was far stupider than that.

6

"Open up," Boone shouted at the twenty-foot-tall gates that looked like something out of King Kong. The two massive doors had been constructed from tall tree trunks, sharpened at the top. The poles were bound by a mishmash of ropes, nailed planks, and screws. Not the work of a master builder, but sturdy nonetheless.

Peter took note of the dark brown stains marring some of the sharpened tips. The wall had stood up to attacks from something large enough to impale itself atop the twenty-foot-tall spikes.

Several dull clunks sounded out as the doors were unlocked from the inside. They opened slowly, revealing two men and one woman. They were dressed in dirty shorts and T-shirts, lacking all the military garb worn by the men outside. The only obvious feature they shared with Boone was a lack of hygiene and the weapons they carried. The woman held a hunting rifle and the two men carried AK-47s, the preferred weapon of terrorists, back when there was such a thing. The weapons had been legal in the United States when converted to semi-automatic. A quick glance at the weapons revealed a third pin hole, meaning these had either been purchased illegally, or converted after the world went to hell. Laws didn't matter anymore, but the first option—illegal arms dealing—spoke to these people's character, which was called into question the moment they threatened his family. He didn't care how subtle or polite Boone was acting. The man wasn't fooling anyone. They were in mortal danger, and walking deeper into a shit-storm with every step. The problem was that Peter hadn't seen a way out of it without getting his family killed.

So, he waited, and watched, taking in every sight, sound, and smell that might provide him with the key to their salvation.

While Boone and the other good ol' boys outside the gates were dressed like military, their swagger, grungy appearance, and lack of discipline marked them as weekend warriors who got the chance to go full time when civilization came to an end. Peter suspected they might have even enjoyed the end of the world and the new status it brought them in this small community of survivors. It was impressive, to be sure, but Peter wasn't sure if the horrors inside the fence would be any better than those outside it.

"Marcus, Stevie," Boone said, pointing at the two men with the muzzle of his AR-15 assault rifle.

Definitely not military, Peter thought.

"Lock up behind us, and quit gawking. These people are my guests."

Marcus and Stevie both turned their eyes down to the ground. They hadn't really been gawking, just taking in the newcomers with interest, maybe even a hint of hope.

Boone was either the leader here, or at least someone of authority. Perhaps they operated on some kind of caste system. Peter had a strong suspicion that life inside the gates was only slightly more tolerable for Marcus and Stevie, than life on the outside.

"Hey, baby," Boone said to the woman, who was dressed in a dirty flannel shirt and short shorts. Peter guessed she was of Cuban descent.

She looked like a too-tan Daisy Duke: a little too short, a little too chubby, and sporting a smile so phony it broke Peter's heart. While some of the people here were having the time of their lives, it seemed that just as many lived in fear, despite the weapons in their hands.

"Hey there, Boone," the woman said. Even her Southern accent sounded forced. "You make some friends while you were out?"

"Well," Boone said, "that has yet to be determined, but they seem like nice folk. Don't want no trouble."

"No, sir," Peter said with a nod and a fake grin that was far more convincing than the girl's. He held his hand out to her and said, "Name's Peter."

There was momentary light in faux Daisy's eyes. She started to lift her hand, saying, "Isabe—"

Boone cut her short by placing the rifle muzzle atop her hand and slowly easing it back down.

"Now, girl, don't forget yourself." Boone, a foot taller, stood over the girl, still acting casual, but exuding menace. Marcus and Stevie paid the scene no attention, closing the gates and sliding several long metal beams back in place across the seam. Peter gave them a second look, trying to find common ground between them and the girl, whose full name he guessed was Isabel. While her skin was deeply tanned, the two young men were almost pale white. Marcus had freckles and red hair. The other had flat brown hair.

Upon seeing Isabel, Peter thought the caste system might be racial, but the two gate guards were as white as white got.

"Sorry, Boone," the girl said, deflating, eyes on the ground.

Boone hauled back and slapped Isabel's backside. On the surface, it looked almost playful, but the impact drew a pained cry from the girl's lips. Her smile became even more forced, as tears began to well.

Ella took a step forward, but Peter gripped her forearm, holding her back. If Boone attacked the girl with deadly force, they would act, but not until then. And hopefully not before fully understanding what they were up against.

"Go tell Mason we got visitors," Boone said, not noticing Ella. "I'm gonna take 'em to see Bob and Lyn. Then we'll be up."

Isabel looked confused by this last bit, but scurried away with a nod. "Will do, Boone."

Boone cupped a hand around his mouth and called after the girl. "And I reckon I'll be callin' on ya this evening. Finish what we started here, aight."

The girl's quick walk turned into a jog.

Boone flashed a smile at Peter and winked, clucking his tongue. "Girl is dumber than a sack of rocks, but rides my..." His eyes turned to Anne, then moved back to Peter. "Well, you know what I mean."

"I think I do," Peter said.

"Well, all right then." Boone started walking backward deeper into the camp, extending his arms out to either side, "Welcome to Hellhole Bay, bastion outpost of humanity's only surviving population. Well, until you all showed up. Been a while since anyone came a-callin'."

Peter ignored Boone's theatrics and scanned the area. The massive fence was really a wall stretched out in either direction as far as he could see. Just inside the fence was a twenty-foot stretch of water, like a moat on the wrong side. The waterway narrowed as it cut across the path ahead, where a log bridge, just wide enough for a vehicle, but maybe not strong enough for one, allowed them passage. Peter looked down into the water as they crossed, half expecting to see alligators writhing about, ready to devour intruders. But the water was clear and fresh. A slight current moved toward the far end of the site.

"Water flows in on one side, from a crick," Boone said, noting Peter's attention. "Out the other side. Metal grates keep the critters out. Gives us fresh water for the crops."

The word crops turned Peter's attention forward. The outer fringe of the strange complex ahead of them was basically scorched earth. There were nubs of things that had grown and been burned. "You burn the crops that grow?"

"Yep," Boone said. "Anything green outside the domes is toast."

Domes, Peter thought, looking beyond the scorched earth, confirming Boone's use of the plural as accurate. Like all the biodomes Peter had seen, there was a farmhouse providing access. But extending from the backside of the glass biodome was a second, and a third. There were five biodomes in all, and what looked like a sixth under construction. These people had taken Ella's design and duplicated it. With the Southern climate, sunny weather, and a plentiful—and filtered—water source, they could grow enough food to support a village, which was precisely what they were doing.

A small town of ramshackle homes, constructed from sheets of stainless steel, PVC pipes, and plastic siding, filled the space between them and the farmhouse. Each single-story structure looked just big enough for one or two people, and Peter suspected they were really just for sleeping. Most didn't even have doors. Privacy would be hard to come by in a place like this.

There were a few ragtag people milling about. An older woman swept trash from the grid of dirt paths between the homes. A few men carried supplies here and there. But most of the village's residents were somewhere else.

"Where is everyone?" Jakob asked.

Peter flinched when his son spoke, but it was a harmless question.

"Either outside the wall doing what needs to be done, working on the new dome, or serving inside with the others. Most people think tending the crops is the sweetest gig. Fresh air, fresh food. And yeah, they're not supposed t' eat that food. S'posed to get rations like the rest of us. But we all know they're skimming. Who in their right mind wouldn't? I mean, me and the boys maintain our musculatures by foraging what we can out in the swamp. We don't share none, either. If yer lucky, and don't fuck around, you two—" He pointed at Peter and Jakob. "—might find yerselves back outside the fence. Reunite you with that sweet ride. Goin' on supply runs. Shootin' up critters. Shit is a good time. I'm tellin' you. I'm *tellin'* you."

When Boone faced forward again, Peter felt a tug on his shirt. Anne walked behind him, swirling an index finger around her ear, and rolling her eyes in the universal symbol for: 'He's nuts.'

Peter gave a subtle nod and faced forward again, taking in every nook and cranny of the strange amalgam of medieval and futuristic worlds. Is this what the future of humanity would look like, even if they could eat ExoGen crops? *Probably*, he decided, but hopefully without the kind of abuse he suspected was the norm at Hellhole Bay.

Boone led them through the maze of small shacks and then toward what looked like short lean-to stables. Maybe for goats. Unlike the small homes now behind him, the six units stretched out in a row, all had doors. Chain link doors. And concrete floors. As he got closer, he could see that some of the cells were occupied—by people.

"Now," Boone said, turning around again, walking backward. Peter noticed the man's index finger had slipped around his weapon's trigger. Whatever they were about to see, Boone expected it would get a negative reaction out of them. "Ya'll keep in mind that there are reasons for everything here. It's like what Einstein said, equal and opposite reactions for every action. Aight?"

Peter slowly took Ella's hand. She was trembling with rage, close to unleashing that savage fury that had kept her and Anne alive in the wild. But this was not the right place. If they were going to stay alive, they also needed to stay calm. To play along.

He gave her a squeeze, and she responded with two of her own. She got it.

And she proved it by saying, "Not a problem." She hadn't spoken much at all, and she let a slight Southern drawl trickle from her lips. "We all like Einstein."

Boone looked like he'd tasted something sour for just a moment. Peter thought he was trying to figure out if Ella was really on board or mocking him. But he apparently couldn't figure out which was the truth. He shrugged his eyebrows and twisted his lips, turning back to the cages. Then he thrust his arms out like a conductor. "Welcome to the coop. It's where all the Questionables go."

"For how long?" Jakob asked.

Boone grinned. "'Til there ain't no doubt about their loyalty. To Hellhole. Our way of life. And Mason. Really, it's up to him."

"This is where Bob and Lyn are?" Ella asked, working a little too hard to sound casual.

Boone stepped to the side, motioning to the next chain link gate. "In there."

Ella took a step closer, and Boone stopped her with a raised hand. "Remember..."

"I remember," Ella said with a nod. Then she and Peter looked through the chain link fence together. When Peter saw what was inside, he took Ella's hand again. She squeezed hard, digging her nails into his palm, channeling her rage. He accepted the pain without flinching.

He barely noticed it.

Inside the cage was an emaciated woman. She looked eighty years old, but Ella had said Lyn was forty-five. The woman's blue eyes glanced in their direction, but she remained in place. Beside her lay her husband, Bob, whose white, withered eyes were motionless.

Bob was a corpse.

7

"Ya'll have had your curiosity satiated, yeah?" Boone had taken a few steps back, rifle raised. Peter couldn't tell if the man was expecting trouble, or hoping for it. Either way, they weren't going to give him an excuse to pull the trigger.

"What did they do?" Peter asked.

"Insurrection," Boone said, and then spat on the ground by his feet. "Tried to change the natural order of things."

"This was their land," Ella said, showing some of their cards. "Their home."

"No such thing as land ownership anymore. World went and changed. Only the fittest can survive. Some of the weak, too, I s'pose, if they don't question things. Plenty of unfit people still living inside these walls on account of what the strongest of us provide."

"Makes sense," Peter said. The words were hard to say, but sounded believable. "Like having kids." He motioned to Jakob, Anne, and Alia, who had yet to see what remained of Bob and Lyn.

"Hey," Anne complained. She fell silent when Jakob gripped her shoulder.

But she didn't go unnoticed.

"I reckon you're right about that," Boone said, leaning down to Anne's height. "You're a feisty one, yeah?"

"You have no idea," Anne said, the words nearly a growl.

Boone chuckled. "Looks like you're made of good stock. White, but not like them two Cat-lickers." He looked the group over. "Naw. Not a Fire Crotch among ya."

It took Peter a moment to decipher what Boone was saying, but he came to the conclusion that Marcus and Stevie were Catholic, and that 'Fire Crotch' was a reference to Marcus's red hair and Irish ancestry. *The caste system isn't just racial,* Peter thought, *it's also religious and ancestral, focusing on old prejudices.*

Boone clucked his tongue and gave Anne a wink. "Too young yet, but time's still moving forward, ain't it?"

That last comment shocked a strange kind of stillness into the group. Boone had just revealed the stakes. If they didn't get out of here—or got killed in the attempt—life would become a nightmare, especially for the girls.

"So, Mason did all this, then?" Peter asked, redirecting the man the way a parent would a child in the throes of a tantrum.

Boone stood up, looking a little more relaxed after his revelation of Bob and Lyn, not to mention his not so veiled sexual threat to a twelve-year-old girl, didn't incite violence. "Yes, sir. Well, he organized it. Was a contractor before things went crazy. Built the first of these here domes." He raised his chin toward Lyn and Bob's corpse. "For them. Found out what it was for and took matters into his own hands. Had three of 'em built before the world turned to shit. Most of us working on the outside have been here since the beginning, though we sometimes bring in new blood." He nodded at Peter. "Something you might cotton to, if you're still around tomorrow."

Peter heard the threat. If they weren't around tomorrow, it wouldn't be because they were set free. "Imagine I would," Peter said. "We've been living in the wild for so long, I'm not sure I could stand more than a few days inside these walls without getting blood on my hands."

Boone gave a gap-toothed smile, clearly hearing Peter's threat as comradery. "We are speaking the same language, my friend." He pointed to the cell at the end of the row. "Now, yer rag head's gonna have to sit things out for a bit. Kids, too, though I don't think them two will be there long." Boone raised a hand when he looked at Ella. Her anger was bubbling to the surface. "I know they're your kids an' all, but we got rules, and kids can't go inside the house. And since yer new, I can't let 'em have the run of the place, neither. Soon as Mason says ya'll aren't Questionables, we'll assign shelters and jobs. Till then, you best do as I say."

"I have a name," Alia said, her voice jolting tension through Peter's body.

Why couldn't she have just stayed quiet?

Boone squinted at her. "That so?"

"Alia," she said with a raised chin.

Peter half-expected Boone to backhand her, which would set off Jakob and then their chances of escape would evaporate. But Boone's reaction wasn't violent.

It was worse.

He looked the girl up and down. "Well now, Alia, I reckon you're of age."

"Of age...for what?"

Alia had led a sheltered life before the Change, and a hermit's life after it. Her only relationship with a boy was with Jakob, and the pair hadn't been alone since their first kiss in Alia's father's biodome. Her innocence was on full display now.

"Marriage," Boone said. "I ain't never been with a rag head before. Course, I ain't sure I want to marry one neither. Course, I ain't got to marry you to pork—"

"Hey, Boone," Peter cut in, sensing things were about to go downhill. Jakob's fists had clenched, and his eyes followed Boone like a bird of prey preparing to strike. And since Peter had been training his son for the past few weeks, Jakob might even be capable of...what? Killing a man? An Exo-Gen creature was one thing. Killing a human being left a mark on a man's soul. He didn't want that for his son. He motioned to Anne. "Young ears."

The fiendish look in Boone's eyes melted into a lop-sided grin. "Right you are." He sniffed and rubbed his nose with a dirty finger. "Follow me, then."

He led them to the last cell in line. Peter counted three people already inside, barefoot and hidden by the slanted roof's shadow. He could see them shifting about, though. *At least they're not corpses.*

Boone twisted a key in a padlock and popped it free. The chain link gate creaked open. The people inside withdrew deeper into the shadows.

Boone motioned inside the cell. "Welcome to Casa de Questionable."

Anne looked inside but didn't step closer. "Why are *they* in there?"

"Stealing. Lying. General disregard for the status quo. Don't you worry none. Not a one of them is prone to violence." He gave her a wink. "Not like you, anyhow."

Anne sighed and stepped inside without any further protest. Alia hurried after, the prospects of staying free with Boone worse than being locked up with strangers. Jakob paused by the gate, looking back at his father. Peter just gave the boy a silent nod, and Jakob returned it. That nod, simple as it was, said a lot. Promises were made. Trust sought and given. One way or another, Peter was going to return for the kids, and leave this place.

Jakob stepped inside the cell and pulled the gate shut behind him. He even put the latch back in place.

"Much obliged," Boone said, slipping the padlock into the latch and locking it once more. "Ya'll ready?"

Ella crouched by the gate, fingers hooked around the chain link. She whispered to Anne, who nodded a few times and then said, "Love you, too," loud enough for Boone to hear. Peter doubted the pair were sharing typical parting words between mother and daughter. But there was no way for Boone to know that. In part, because they'd spoken softly, but also because he was a few bricks short of the world's smallest chimney.

"Ready," Ella said when she stood back up.

Boone led them back toward the farmhouse. It was three stories tall, white, and in a very simple sense, it reminded Peter of his own home, before he blew it up. But there were a few obvious differences that stood out. The windows were barred on the lower floors. Peter wasn't sure if that was to keep monsters out, or to keep people in. Maybe both. But with the twenty-foot wall and armed guards, keeping monsters out was a solved problem.

Maybe the bars came before the walls? Peter wondered, but he knew he was just being hopeful, and that could be a fatal mistake. He chided himself for trying to find the best in the people who lived here. He should be on the lookout for the worst.

Presently, that was Boone.

"Be polite," Boone said, as he led them up the farmer's porch stairs toward the front door. Peter imagined the door had once been solid wood, but it was now a slab of steel. "Tell the truth. He can always tell when someone is fibbin', and there ain't no faster way to wind up in the Questionables. If he offers something, accept it. And if he asks you to do something for him, only appropriate answer is a 'Yes, sir,' and a nod."

Peter was surprised by Boone's aid. The man had grown more friendly since taking them from the truck. He'd made some threats, sure, but most of them, aside from the sexual allusions directed at the girls, also included ways to avoid unsavory outcomes. Peter had gone out of his way to be agreeable, and it seemed to be winning Boone over. He doubted the man who'd organized this outpost of humanity would be as unperceptive, but maybe there was a way to avoid violence?

There I go hoping again, Peter thought.

Boone thumped his fist against the steel door three times. "It's Boone. Here to see Mason."

The sound of locks snapping open came from the other side.

Boone motioned to the door with his head. "Takes 'em a while. Not sure why, but Mason keeps the place locked up tighter than a nun's poontang."

The opening door kept Peter from having to come up with a reply. A black woman dressed in a traditional maid's uniform bowed as she opened the door. "Mistuh Boone," she said in an old-fashioned, Southern accent, stilted and unnatural. "Massa Mason is expecting you. He's in the study."

Massa? Peter thought. *Did I hear that right?* Peter went rigid as his eyes shifted from the uncomfortable maid, to the foyer wall where a large Confederate flag hung. A hint of music wafted through the air. It sounded pleasant enough on the surface, but in the current environment it felt more like acid in his ears. He heard the lyrics, 'With a holy host of others standing 'round me, still I'm on the dark side of the moon,' and he recognized the song as James Taylor's *Carolina in My Mind*.

Mason, whoever that was, had a deep love affair with all things Southern: good, bad, the ugly, and probably even worse. The poor woman at the door was the last straw for Peter. He no longer wanted to just escape this place alive, he wanted to stage a coup in the process. There were good people here, people who deserved better lives, free of subjugation to racist assholes. Leaving them like this...

He just couldn't.

As Peter followed Boone down the hallway, old wooden floorboards creaking underfoot, he came to the conclusion that he was, without a doubt, a Questionable. But the real question was, could he keep that from Mason long enough to kill the man?

8

Eddie Kenyon had gone native. With the exception of eating ExoGen crops, he had completely abandoned civility and decorum. He rode bareback upon a massive wooly steed, like something out of the last ice age. The brutes could travel for days without food or water, though both were plentiful. Their powerful bodies and rhino-like horns that split at the ends into an array of sharp, scooped blades, fended off all manner of creatures. Alone, the creatures might fall to an Apex predator, but their strength was in numbers, like the tribe's.

They called themselves Chunta, and they had a kind of language. Most was grunts and shouts, but there were words and phrases spoken by the males. Still, this was a matriarchal tribe. The three women stood a foot taller than Kenyon, who was just as much taller than the other males. The males were mostly covered in hair, ran with a sideways galumph, and attended to the females' every need.

Kenyon, while male, held a position of prestige. The matriarch, Feesa, who spoke stilted English, understood that Kenyon was smarter than the rest of them. And *he* understood that she could rend his arms from his body as easily as he could petals from a flower. He had become an advisor, helping them defeat enemies, find sufficient food and shelter, and most importantly, track their prey.

While Kenyon was still fully human, and he managed to remain so by foraging non-ExoGen foods, his thirst for vengeance matched the feral woman's. The Chunta were fiercely loyal to each other. Kenyon suspected that the Change had happened late in these people, when most everything else had already turned into ravenous killing machines. They'd banded together in the early days, forging a bond that remained, even after the Change. Instead of evolving into individual monsters, they had evolved as a group. As did their steeds, which Kenyon thought might have been bison from a farm. Copulation was frequent and polyamorous, often devolving into sweaty, hairy orgies that Kenyon had trouble stomaching.

But he did his part, using his knowledge of female anatomy to help maintain his high stature.

Over the weeks, he had shed his clothing, and thrown himself into tribal living. There were times he even enjoyed the primal comradery. But he never forgot the reason for his devolution and long sojourn across the country: Ella Masse. She had used him, betrayed him, broken his heart, and left him for dead. She could have returned to ExoGen with him and Anne. Could have been safe. Could have made things right. Instead, she chose a life on the run, in the wild, with the fucker who had nearly killed him. Peter Crane.

When Kenyon caught up with them, he was going to kill Jakob, Peter's son. Make his father and Ella watch. Then he'd do Ella. Make the bitch pay. He'd kill her, but not Anne. That was Ella's deepest fear, that her precious Anne would have to live in this screwed-up world without a mother. And then it would be Peter's turn. But Kenyon wouldn't get the pleasure of taking that asshole's life. That fell to Feesa, the matriarch, who had been close to the previous matriarch, known as Kristen in her life before the Change. She had been Peter's wife, whom he killed in front of his son, and the tribe. It was an offense that Feesa would not forgive, and the others followed her lead.

Kenyon appreciated that about Feesa, and even believed that should he be slain, she would seek vengeance for his life. He wasn't sure he would do the same, but he had grown fond of her, as much as a man could for a woman like her...if she could really be considered a woman still.

Calling her ugly was an understatement.

Her bottom teeth, like all Chunta, were long, curved and pointed. They jutted out from her pouty lower lip, curling upward several inches before punching back into the skin of her face. The wounds were really just deep, hard scars now, but it was still disturbing to look at. Her nose had evolved to deal with the teeth, pulling back into the face, so that there was barely a nose at all. The only bearable trait about her was that unlike the men, and to an extent, her female companions, the hair on Feesa's body was fine and soft, and her breasts were ample. Kenyon liked her, more because of her powerful spirit than any kind of physical attraction, but the parts of her that remained feminine helped make his more visceral duties bearable—and if he was honest with himself, sometimes fun. The Chunta lived without inhibition. He'd never felt such freedom, but he would risk it all for revenge. As would Feesa.

He stood in a tree, looking down at the men below, all of whom were oblivious to his presence. Feesa was perched on a branch beside him, cocking her head to the side, while the men escorted a familiar armored truck down a long dirt road.

He sensed Feesa coiling to strike. Seeing the vehicle enraged her, and her simple mind no doubt linked these strangers to Peter. But now was not the time to strike. These men had clearly encountered Peter and Ella, and would know their fates. There was intelligence to be gathered. Plans to make. But these concepts were beyond Feesa, who was guided primarily by instinct.

But not completely.

Kenyon reached out slowly and tapped her forearm. When she looked at him, he shook his head. Then he raised his hand and made a gun shape with his fingers. She shook her head at this, frowning so deeply that the teeth embedded in her cheeks strained against the skin. Kenyon tapped his head in a gesture that she understood was him telling her to think, that this was a matter of strategy, that she needed to trust him.

And she did.

Her face scrunched, but her muscles relaxed.

When the men were a hundred feet beyond them, Kenyon and Feesa climbed down the tree into the foot-deep swamp water. Kenyon's instinct told him to be wary for snakes, turtles, and gators, but in the new world, most of those things had already eaten each other nearly to extinction. Those left alive wouldn't be hard to see coming. Not in shallow water, anyway.

But when Feesa raised her flat snout and sniffed the air, he remained still and vigilant. She hooked her fingers and raked them through the air—the Chunta sign for an Apex. Then she shook her head and pointed in the direction from which the men had come. Whatever it was, it was far enough away to not concern Feesa much. But Kenyon didn't share her confidence. If there was an Apex hunting in these swamps, it might already be tracking these men. If that was true, it wouldn't be long before it was tracking him and Feesa, too. And that was a problem.

While the Chunta were ExoGenetic creatures, they weren't Apex. As a group, sure, but individually, they didn't stand a chance against a super-evolved predator.

Kenyon pointed to Feesa's eyes, ears, and nose, and then back down the dirt road. She nodded and said, "Careful. Yes." Her voice rumbled out of her throat, sounding more like Barry White than a woman—or even a monster who used to be a woman.

Then they started off through the swamp, following the oblivious men. If the men didn't lead him to Ella or to one of her group, he could interrogate them. If that didn't work, he'd let Feesa interrogate them. Either way, he was going to find out where Ella and Peter had hidden themselves. If they were dead, these men would pay for stealing his vengeance. If they were alive...the swamp was going to run red.

9

Mason was a soft man—not at all what Ella had been expecting. The palpable fear emanating from Hellhole Bay made her think the man in charge would be tyrannical in action *and* appearance. But the man sitting behind the mahogany desk, peering over the top of a pair of thin reading glasses, looked more like a turtle without a shell. He was dressed in white slacks and a short-sleeve, white, button-down shirt, both of which matched the wispy hair poking out from the sides of a gray Ascot cap. He flinched at their entrance, pale blue eyes squinting at Peter. But when he looked at Ella, those eyes widened. He reached out to a CD player, turning down the music, stood from his seat, and tipped his hat like a true Southern gentleman.

"Ma'am," Mason said, looking her up and down. "It's an unusual pleasure to welcome someone such as yourself into my humble abode."

"It's equally unusual to have my children locked up in a glorified chicken coop," Ella said, flashing a smile as phony as Mason's, though she thought he did a much better job.

Or maybe he really is happy to see us?

So far, the man had no real reason to dislike them, other than the fact that they were traveling with a 'rag head,' but maybe that prejudice was Boone's alone? *No,* she thought, remembering the maid at the door. Her ridiculous outfit and forced accent harkened back to darker times for anyone not wealthy and white, a role Mason seemed to be enjoying.

The office was lined with bookshelves. Most of the tomes were popular novels. The dog-eared book resting on his desk was titled *The Dirge of Briarsnare Marsh.* They weren't exactly the books of a thinking man... but they were literature nevertheless. Memories of Bob and Lyn Askew flitted to the forefront of Ella's mind. Bob with his action and horror novels. Lyn teasing him about it. These were Bob's books. Bob's office.

Bob the corpse.

Mason cleared his throat and widened his smile.

"I am sorry about that, truly. But I assure you, there is method to the madness. With the future of mankind at stake, and our food source at constant risk, we've been forced to take drastic...sometimes cruel, measures to ensure our survival." He motioned to the two antique chairs opposite the desk. "Please, sit."

Ella didn't feel like sitting, but when Boone gave Peter a nudge in the back, she realized it wasn't a request. When Peter motioned to her chair and said, "Go on," she realized he was still playing along. Still thinking with his head instead of his heart, and right now, that's what would keep them alive. So, she smiled and took a seat, knowing the other two men, gentlemen both, wouldn't sit until she had. Peter sat down next, followed by Mason, who looked pleased by the way the ritual had progressed.

"Now then," Mason said, leaning back in Bob's office chair. "You all have been living out there for how long now?"

"A few weeks," Peter said before Ella could even think to answer. And it was just as well. Peter was the better liar. If Mason really was good at detecting untruths, it was better if Ella kept her mouth shut.

"And I hear tell that you arrived in what, some kind of tank?"

"A technical," Peter said.

"Technical," Mason repeated. "Can't say as I'm familiar with the term."

"Military jargon," Peter said. "Just means it's a truck with a big gun mounted to it. In this case, a Dodge Ram with an M249 light machine gun."

"Uh-huh..." Mason twiddled his fingers together. "Sounds like you know your way around guns."

"Served in the U.S Marine Corps," Peter said.

He's being honest, Ella realized, *but leaving out details.* Telling the man he was a Marine would explain Peter's knowledge of weaponry, and help validate the story of their survival. But leaving out the fact that he'd been a Critical Skills Operator would make him seem less dangerous. Peter wanted the man to see him as a potential ally—another gun-toting grunt—but not a threat.

"You look a might too long in the tooth for active duty," Mason observed. "What was your rank when you left the corps?"

"Sergeant Major," Peter replied. It was a demotion from Captain, but high enough and said with conviction. "Served two tours. Afghanistan."

"And you left because..."

"PTSD," Peter said, still being honest. "That's Post Traumatic—"

"I know what it is," Mason said. He leaned forward, elbows on the desk, hands clasped. "So how does a man with PTSD survive the wilds of the new world?"

"I worked through it, sir. A long time ago." He reached out and took Ella's hand, his affection catching her off guard. "I had help."

"You're a whole man again, then?"

Peter nodded. "Yes, sir."

Mason looked them both over for a moment. "Since neither of you are wearing wedding bands, am I to assume you're living in sin? Had the boy and girl out of wedlock?"

Ella glanced at the window behind Mason. She could see the Questionable cells in the background. *He was watching.*

"No, sir," Peter said, pulling Ella's attention back to the polite interrogation. "Wearing rings in the field is a bad idea. Might end up with a ring avulsion—what happens when your ring gets caught on something and yanks the finger out of joint, or clean off." He reached into his shirt and pulled out a silver chain with two rings dangling from it.

Ella tried to show no reaction that Peter kept his and Kristen's wedding bands around his neck. She wasn't surprised. Peter was an honorable guy like that, and he had loved his wife. Why not remember the time they had by keeping a memento of their marriage? What she was, was jealous. But that was ridiculous. Kristen was dead, killed by Peter's own hand.

"And I don't think we've been properly introduced. I'm Peter Crane, and this is my wife—"

"I think it's time I heard from the lovely lady herself." Mason turned to Ella, his gaze friendly, but discerning. Peter had apparently passed the man's truth test, but Mason wasn't fully convinced. So, it was Ella's turn to endure his scrutiny. "Your name, ma'am?"

"Kristen," Ella said. "Kristen Crane."

"Doesn't exactly roll off the tongue, does it?" Mason chuckled at himself.

"My father always said it sounded like a Marvel Comics superhero name," Ella said. In truth, it's what she had thought about Kristen, when she heard about Peter's wedding plans. "You know, Peter Parker. Jessica Jones. Kristen Crane."

"Mmm," Mason said, his smile wavering. She was failing his test. Forcing her words. "An unfortunate amalgamation of names, then."

"Yes...sir," she said, and nearly said more, layering on phony quips about something as insignificant as their names. She stopped herself, clearing her throat and then waiting for Mason to continue.

The man sat in silence for a good ten seconds and then asked, "How did you survive the Change?"

Peter opened his mouth to reply, but Mason held his palm up, "Let the lady answer."

"Well, we had the truck," Ella said. "And a lot of—"

"I don't mean the past few weeks in the wild," Mason said. "I have boys that can do the same. What I'm wondering is how, when the rest of the world started eating itself into oblivion, you all remained..." He swept his hands out toward Ella and Peter. "...as you are. Human. I know how my people survived, but you are the first outsiders we have encountered that are not..."

"Evolved," Ella said.

Mason grinned. "That's a word for it, I suppose, if you believe in such things."

Ella smiled and followed Peter's lead of near complete honesty. "We had a biodome. Like yours. But just one of them."

"I see," Mason said. "And how did you acquire said biodome?"

Ella let her discomfort over the subject show. "From Ella Masse."

"The very same woman who provided the former residents of this home with their biodome. How fortuitous for you. The very same woman, if I recall, who created the crops that led to the unhinged *evolution* of all life on Earth."

"She tried to warn—"

Peter was silenced once again, this time with a harshly raised index finger.

"Tell me, Kristen," Mason said. "What made you worth saving, while the rest of the world went to hell?"

For a moment, she was worried that he recognized her.

Before the Change really took effect, she had been on TV several times, warning people about the dangers of ExoGen crops.

That was before the company caught up with her, kidnapped her, and threw her in a cell until she agreed to stay quiet and continue her work for them. At first, she had wondered why they hadn't simply killed her, but later she had realized it was her mind they wanted. The genetic tinkering they had done, for reasons that still evaded her, was just the beginning. Despite having been a somewhat public figure for a few weeks, she was now far skinnier, had a clean-shaven head and was covered in grime.

Her own parents might not recognize her.

Ella looked at the floor, and then glanced at Peter. "He did." She met Mason's eyes. "She wasn't interested in saving me. Just him."

Mason waited for more.

"They had an affair. Had been childhood friends, and then more than that for a while. We ended up back in the same town with that bitch, and he..." She shook her head at the very real memories. "He couldn't say no to her. Never could."

"And yet here you are," Mason pointed out. "Together, and by all accounts, in love."

"He...made the right choice in the end. Chose his wife and children over something...shallow. She was nostalgia. A reminder of younger days. I have struggled to forgive the choices he made. I've hated him for it. God knows, I have. But in the end, he chose his family, and that...that is a man worth loving, despite his faults."

Mason gave a nod and leaned back in his chair. "Takes a strong woman to forgive such grave misgivings."

"Wasn't easy," Ella said.

Mason gave another nod. "Now then, near as I can tell, the Askews were friends of Dr. Ella Masse. Like-minded science-types, whom you asked for by name, yes? Given your husband's adulterous past, I'm surprised you accepted such a generous gift."

"There isn't anything I wouldn't do to protect my children," Ella said. "That woman...she was a lot of things I didn't like, but she was also brilliant. When someone like that tells you your world is coming to an end, you listen, even if it means accepting help from someone who hurt you the most."

"And the Askews?"

"There was a list of names and locations," Ella said. "Of biodomes around the country. Eighty-seven of them. Bob and Lyn were on the list. It's why we came here."

"And where is this list now?"

Ella shrugged. She'd thrown the list away long ago, and really didn't know where it was. "I memorized it."

"Uh-huh. And how did you come upon it? The list."

Ella took in a deep breath and let it out as a sigh. "She came to our house."

"When?"

"Five weeks ago."

"Where is she now?"

"Dead," Peter said. "I put a bullet in her."

Mason's eyebrows crested high on his forehead. He appeared to be enjoying the story now.

"She came to us seeking shelter," Ella said. "It's why she paid for the domes. So, she'd have places to hide. But when she came to us, she brought trouble in her wake. Stalkers. Horrible creatures with tails that look like wheat stalks. Hard to see in the tall crops. They hunted in a pack. And we...Peter, had to destroy the house to escape."

"And Dr. Masse? She died at the house?"

Ella nodded, and then spoke to Peter. "But it didn't need to be done in front of the kids."

"Couldn't have been avoided," Peter replied, anger creeping into his voice.

"Now, now," Mason said. "I am not a fan of lover's quarrels."

"Sorry," Peter said. "It's all still...raw."

"What about the girl with you?" Mason asked, shifting subjects.

"Sir," Boone said, speaking for the first time since entering. "I was wondering if I might—"

"Let them answer, Boone," Mason said. "Be polite."

"Her name is Alia," Peter said, and when Mason didn't shush him again, he continued. "Daughter of Brant and Misha Rossi, owners of the first biodome we reached. I promised I'd look out for her."

"What happened to the parents?"

"We were attacked."

"More of those Stalkers?"

"ExoGen," Peter said. "They were looking for Ella. They had a Black Hawk and two Apache helicopters."

"And yet you survived," Mason said.

"Not all of us," Peter replied.

"And have you seen these helicopters since?"

Peter shook his head. "I told them she was dead. I think they believed me, but they tried to kill us anyway. The leader, a man named Kenyon, I think he had feelings for her."

"Sounds like Dr. Ella Masse was a knockout." He held a hand out to Ella. "No offense to you, Mrs. Crane. A woman with that much control over the opposite sex tends to bring trouble wherever she goes."

Ella grinned. "I couldn't agree more."

A knock at the door turned everyone around. Boone opened it, revealing a nervous looking Stevie.

"Better be important," Boone said.

"Gunshots," Stevie said. "Three of them. Distant. Perimeter guards haven't seen anything, but Roy and the others aren't checking in. We've tried calling them a bunch of—"

Boone unclipped a handheld radio from his waist, flicked it on, and spoke into it. "Roy, this is Boone, come back?" He lifted his finger and waited, listening to static. Then he pushed the call button again. "Roy, quit fuckin' around. If you're hearing me, you best answer. Over."

When no reply came, Boone just looked to Mason.

"Go ahead," Mason said. "But take Mr. Crane with you."

Peter grew tense but didn't complain.

"Sir, I don't think taking this—"

"Nonsense," Mason said. "I believe Mr. and Mrs. Crane have been forthright in their answers to me, and while I still have questions that need answers, I don't see any reason to refuse this man's help...if he's willing to provide it."

There was no mention of the children, but everyone in the room knew Mason had them as collateral.

Peter stood. "I'll do my best."

"Very good," Mason said, standing and offering Peter his hand. When Peter shook it, the older man added, "And don't worry about your wife none. I'll entertain her in your absence."

Peter smiled and withdrew his hand. "Thank you." He turned to Ella and said, "Be back soon." Then to Boone, "Lead the way."

When the two men had left, Ella turned back to Mason, whose smile had widened enough to reveal teeth as white as his clothes. "Well then, Kristen, what am I going to do with you?"

10

"Don't look at them," Jakob whispered to Anne, who was staring at the people sitting on the far side of the cell. He didn't fully understand what made someone a Questionable, but he guessed they'd done something wrong to end up here. Sure, the people who ran the place had an obviously skewed sense of right and wrong, but that didn't mean they only locked up nice people. Murder and theft were probably still jailable offenses, even to the morally ambiguous.

"They're not going anywhere fast," Anne said, not averting her eyes. "*Look* at them."

Against his own advice, Jakob followed Anne's instructions. She was a lot younger than him, but when it came to the wild world, she was far more experienced. That included dealing with people. While Jakob had spent two years holed up in a farmhouse with his father, Anne had lived in a large community, and then fled across the country with a group of people, including Eddie Kenyon, a man who turned out to be a little psycho. So, he trusted her judgment. Not of their cellmates' character, but of their ability to cause him harm.

The three people sharing the concrete floor with them—two men and one woman—were in various states of living decay. The oldest of them, a skinny man with wispy gray hair, looked the worst off. He stared back at Anne with defiant eyes, as though he resented her assessment, but was still unable to prove her wrong. The second man and the woman, were huddled up together in the back corner, clutching each other, more afraid of Jakob than he was of them. They had the wide-eyed look of people who expected the worst to happen at any moment, probably because it often did.

Jakob's fear turned to pity. What had these people endured? None of them looked dangerous, not even the defiant old man. They looked... normal. Emaciated and hungry, but normal.

"I'm Jakob," he said to the group.

When no one replied, he motioned to Anne and said, "This is my sister, Anne. And my..." he glanced at Alia. They had been romantically involved, to be sure, but they'd never had a discussion about official titles. What were they? Friends with kissing benefits? Girlfriend and boyfriend? Would they become more? Were they already? Maybe romance was accelerated at the end of the world, when there was no one else left? He decided to jump to the logical conclusion. "...my girlfriend, Alia."

Relief flowed through his muscles when she smiled and gave a slight wave. It was corny, he knew, to be concerned about his relationship with Alia while they were being held prisoner inside a hostile compound, separated from his father and Ella, but... Well, hormones paid the apocalypse no attention. And with the whole world out to eat him, a little bit of teenage affection—Anne called it 'obsession'—kept him sane. And that was a good thing. One of the few left in the world from his point-of-view.

No one replied. Blank eyes stared back. For a moment, he thought the three of them might actually be dead. Then the woman blinked.

Jakob focused on her. She had ratty-looking blonde hair that hung in clumps over her dirt-covered face. He'd seen the look before. Hell, he emulated it. "Were you living on the outside?" he asked. "In the wild?"

The woman's eyes twitched.

"We were, too," Jakob said. "At least, for the past few weeks. Our farm was attacked." He hitched his thumb toward Alia. "Hers, too. Now we're here."

"And here you will stay," the old man said, his voice rattling like he'd enjoyed a few too many packs a day. Jakob reassessed the man. Was he starving or just miserable from nicotine withdrawal?

"H-how long have you been here?" Alia asked.

The old man turned toward the couple. "Two years in the camp. About a week in the cell?"

"For what?" Jakob asked.

"Well," the old man said. "I took too long with the lemonade. These two were caught...well, doing what men and women sometimes do. And if that sounds ridiculous to any of you, the only men and women allowed to engage in such activities are those approved by Mason, and that is generally relegated to Mason himself and a handful of his most trusted hands. Mason's got himself a real harem inside that house. Most of them want no part in it, but they don't really have a say anymore."

Anne clenched her fists.

"Why doesn't anyone help them?"

The old man grunted like a cantankerous horse. "Most people living outside the house never see them, let alone communicate with them. I only know them because I worked inside, too. I'm a handy kind of guy, and I know my way around a kitchen. Was a line cook in Philly, for a while. Aside from his motley gang of enforcers and guards, I was one of the few men let inside the house. Mason believed I was too old to fraternize with his wives." The man tapped the side of his nose with his forefinger. "More than a few of them know that's not true. I might have twenty years on Mason, but the plumbing is still good, and I've spent more than a few nights tending to wounds inflicted by that man."

He took a deep breath, and as he let it out, the fight that had been building in his voice seemed to melt right out of him. "This place could have been a blessing. There's food enough for everyone in those domes. The walls provide safety. The human race could have begun again, right here. Instead, he took Hellhole Bay's name to heart. Brought his own kind of hell to Earth."

Anne seemed unfazed by the man's doom and gloom.

She nodded her head at the woman.

"Why aren't you, you know, in the house? Looks like you might be pretty under all that dirt."

The woman's eyes flicked to the man beside her, with whom she'd apparently had an unsanctioned relationship.

"You don't need permission to speak," Anne said. "From him or anyone else. At least, not while you're already locked up. What more can they do?"

The old man guffawed. "I'm going to walk out of this cage. So will she, despite the scarlet letter Mason's branded on her chest. His boys can still have their fun with her. But him..." He pointed at the younger man. "He's either going to wither and die in this cell, be thrown out against the next monster that comes looking for trouble, or be used for target practice. Whatever the case, his end won't be—"

"Shut up," the woman said.

"Carrie," the young man chided.

"No reason to keep quiet," she said, her Southern accent far thicker than the old man's. "He's right. They won't do anything more to me, and there ain't nothing I can say that will make things any better or worse for you." She turned to Jakob. "John, here, thinks old Willie in the corner there, is a spy for Mason, on account of his life in the house. But he's just as hungry and dirty as the both of us."

"Why would Mason want to spy on you?" Anne asked.

"On account of him fearing a rebellion. Mason and his men make up roughly thirty percent of the compound's population. The rest of us are kept hungry, weak, and separate. Took me a while to figure out why, but it's because he's a paranoid man. A little food and respect would have made loyal servants out of us all, but he chose the alternate route, and now he fears us. Maybe even more than we fear him. So, every now and again, he conjures up a reason to deem some of us Questionables. Throws us in here. Less frequently, he puts someone to death, and I reckon ol' Willie is right about John's fate."

John, a twenty-something year old man who looked like he'd stepped into a hurricane and walked out the other side with a story too horrible to tell, let out an anguished sigh, but said nothing.

"They caught us screwing, dead to rights, but we're just friends."

Ouch, Jakob thought. *Post-apocalypse friend-zoned. Harsh.*

"Was just letting off some steam," she continued. "And it's not like anyone else was having a go. One case of the creeping crawlers and those boys had no interest in dipping their wicks. Good for me they didn't know the difference between crabs and them little red spiders. Sprinkled 'em on and presto, I was a free woman. For a time, anyway. Now I'm here, still not planning an insurrection."

"Maybe you should," Anne said.

The three captives on the far side of the cell tensed.

Jakob almost shushed Anne.

For all they knew, their cellmates could be there to determine whether or not newcomers were a threat. If they spoke of rising up against Mason, maybe these three would tell him? Even if they weren't spies, they might tell him with the hopes of gaining his favor. Of course, Willie and Carrie had already confessed to several other infractions that Jakob could trade for favor.

When he saw fear creep into Willie's and Carrie's eyes, he realized that they were thinking the same thing. The duo had let their guard down, probably because they were speaking to three kids they'd never seen before, but now they had that terrified look of children caught looking at pornography.

Jakob held up his hands. "We're not here to spy on you, either, I swear."

"Why's she talking about rebellion?" Carrie asked.

"Because I don't like being caged like an animal," Anne said, "and if there were a few more people willing to help, our Dad would—"

"Ignore her," Jakob said. "She has an inflated opinion about what our father can do. You know how kids are."

Anne kicked him but didn't say any more.

"Your father the big fella Boone was talking to?" Willie asked. "And that tough looking lady with him...that your mother?"

"Yeah," Jakob said. It was far more complicated than that, but Jakob didn't want to explain.

"Certainly looked as capable as the girl claims," the old man said. "But if he's a smart man, he'll join up and do Mason's bidding. Only real way to get the lot of you out of this cage." He pointed a shaky finger at Alia. "Except maybe her. Racism runs deep in these parts. Only a few people with skin darker than a sun given tan are here, and that's because they're useful. Used to be more at the beginning, but these Questionable cells have seen a lot of use over the years. So, my advice to you, young miss, is to make yourself useful."

"B-but, I'm just a kid," Alia said. "I don't know how to do anything."

"Better learn quick," Willie said, "or lie and then learn quick."

"It won't come to that," Jakob said to Willie, and then turned to Alia. "My father won't let it happen."

"Sounds like you have a little more faith in your old man than you wanted us to know, eh?" Willie tapped his nose again and gave a nod. "You have nothing to worry about from any of us. We're already up shit's creek. Might as well be in cahoots, too." Willie leaned forward, elbows on knees. He moved faster than Jakob would have thought, more aged than emaciated. "Your daddy trust you?"

"Yeah," Jakob said.

"How much?"

"As much as anyone can," Jakob said.

"And he's a good man?"

"The best," Anne said.

"Says his daughter."

"I only met him five weeks ago," Anne said.

Willie grunted and met Jakob's eyes. "She telling the truth?"

Jakob returned Willie's gaze, trying to get a read on him. Was he crazy? Was he a spy? Was he exactly what he seemed to be—an old man sick of living in a literal hell hole without much left to lose? "Yeah. He's honorable, if that's what you're asking. Nothing like that Mason guy."

"That's exactly what I was asking," Willie said. "Now then, let's talk insurrection."

"Thought you said there wasn't one," Anne said.

Willie grinned and looked to John, then Carrie, who returned his smile and nodded. "Well, there is now."

11

To Peter's surprise, the search-and-rescue party sent after the missing group of men was composed solely of Boone and himself. That told him a few things. First, Boone had no fear of what might be hunting him on the outside, which meant he was supremely stupid, or genuinely good at surviving—but still stupid in most regards. Second, it meant that the majority of Mason's most skilled and loyal men were currently outside the gates. Sure, there might be armed guards watching the walls, and some of them were probably hardliners like Boone, but Peter guessed most of them were more like Stevie and Marcus.

He couldn't be sure, though, and until he was, playing along was the safest option—until the kids were set free.

Or was it? Boone had the keys. Peter had no doubt he could take them by force. But would the gates be opened to him if he returned alone? And if they were, would he be greeted with a bullet? Even if he could take the keys, re-enter the camp, free the kids, retrieve Ella and leave again, without waging a one-man war, something still nagged at him. Hellhole Bay, perhaps the last bastion of humanity outside a scattering of biodomes and ExoGen themselves, was a corrupt, evil place.

Could he just leave? Even if they reached George's Island and altered the human genome so that ExoGen food didn't turn people into rapidly evolving eating machines, what good would that do if their fellow survivors were still monsters at heart?

"Sure you don't want to wear something a little more protective?" Boone asked. He was dressed in black military clothing and body armor. It would stop a bullet, but wouldn't do a whole lot of good against an Apex predator, or a knife for that matter. It looked cool but had limited mobility. If they were walking into a conventional battle, he'd have taken Boone up on the offer, but out here in the wild, he was happy with the dirt-covered tan cargo pants and equally soiled black t-shirt. Not only were they a natural-looking camouflage, but they also smelled like the outdoors.

"I'm good," Peter said. "Thanks for the offer, though."

Boone stepped over a log, gripping his AR-15, back to Peter. It was the thirteenth time the man had left himself completely open to attack. Peter couldn't decide if it was an intentional test, or if the man simply had no combat awareness.

Neither, Peter decided. *He trusts that I care about Ella and the kids, and won't endanger them by doing something stupid.*

"Your funeral," Boone said.

The swamp around them was still, lacking the non-stop sound of birds and insects normally present in such locations. Peter eyed the water, half expecting something to burst out and snatch one of them. But Boone moved with more confidence, following a worn path through clumps of moss-covered islets. ExoGenetic crops grew around them, protruding from the water and from the mounds of land scattered around them. They mixed in with hearty plants and ferns that hadn't retreated from the Exo-Genetic advance. But the path ahead was clear. Maintained. This wasn't just a jaunt through the wilds in search of missing men.

"Where are we headed?" Peter asked.

Boone waggled his hand forward, indicating the winding path that disappeared behind a stand of short, twisting trees. "The lot. Where we keep vehicles."

"Why don't you keep them at Hellhole?"

"Firstly, the bridge at the entrance ain't big enough for a vehicle."

"That's the only way in?"

"Yep. And secondly, it keeps the degenerates and unknown Question-ables from stealing them."

"They'd have to be pretty desperate to leave the safety of Hellhole, don't you think?"

Boone shrugged. "People do stupid things. A few have tried leaving on foot. Sure you can imagine how that ended."

Peter could, but his mind's eye didn't conjure images of ExoGenetic creatures hunting down those poor people. He saw Boone looking down the sights of that AR-15 in his hands, pulling the trigger with a smile on his face. "Sure can."

"None of them was like you and me, though."

"How's that?"

Boone looked back with a lopsided grin. "Killers. Men who do what it takes to survive, eternal soul be damned."

Peter gave a nod. "I suppose you're right."

"Glad t' hear it."

You shouldn't be, Peter thought. Then he asked, "And the men we're searching for?"

"More of the same," Boone said, trudging through foot-deep black water separating one islet from the next. "Dangerous men. Survivors."

"You all have a name?" Peter asked.

Boone looked confused. "We all have names."

"I mean as a group," Peter said.

"Like a nickname? Naw. Seems kinda cheesy if you ask me."

"More like a callsign," Peter said. "All the most elite units in the military have them. Have for thousands of years. The Persians had The Immortals. King Arthur had the Knights of the Round Table. The Paladins fought for Charlemagne. In the Marine Corps, I was a member of the Raiders. Groups of fighting men deserve a name. Helps form bonds in battle. Unity." He was pouring it on a little heavy, but he wanted Boone to start feeling that sense of comradery with him. Naming this group of men would be a step in the right direction.

"Huh," Boone said. "S'pose there is something to it."

"Something like Mason's Devils," Peter offered.

"Not bad, I guess," Boone said, pondering the issue he'd never before considered. "How 'bout Redneck Rampagers?"

It was a horrible name. Not even grammatically correct. But it *was* accurate and revealed that Boone was not only aware of his backwoods nature, but proud of it.

"Perfect," Peter said.

"Redneck Rampagers it is, then." Boone froze in his tracks, eyes focused straight ahead, like a cat who'd just spotted prey.

Peter looked past him, searching for what had the man spooked, but he saw nothing. The idea that Boone's attention to detail or ability to detect danger was beyond Peter's irked him. *The man had no formal training,* Peter thought, *but he did grow up here. He knows the smells, sights, and sounds. If something is off, he'll know about it long before me.*

The realization made their prospects of a simple escape less likely. Boone would be able to hunt them down, which meant he would have to be dealt with first. But that was the brewing plan anyway. Peter, in good conscience, couldn't abandon the large number of people living under Mason's oppressive rule. It had been a while since Peter had assisted in a regime change, and he didn't always agree with it, but in this case, with the future of humanity at risk, he wasn't going to look the other way.

"What is it?" Peter whispered.

"Should be a guard up ahead." Boone pointed to a tree, where a perfectly camouflaged hunter's tree stand was mounted, twenty feet off the ground. Boone let out a bird call, which sounded convincing, but in this lifeless swamp, it would attract the same kind of attention as shouting. Peter kept that to himself, though. If the guard was missing, or dead, they could be in trouble. But what kind of trouble?

"The stand looks intact," Peter said. "No claw marks. No blood."

"Uh-huh," Boone said. "Wasn't one of them mutates, that's for sure."

"Maybe he heard the men at the Lot were missing and went to check?" Peter asked.

"If he did, he's gonna get throttled." Boone crept forward, heading for the stand. When he reached the tree, he slung the AR-15 over his shoulder and gripped the coarse bark on either side. Then he shimmed up, scaling the fifteen feet in seconds. He slid over the camouflaged wall and into the hide.

"Sombitch," he muttered.

"He dead?" Peter asked.

"Surely is." Boone emerged from the hide and slid down the tree. Peter had never seen someone move through a tree with such ease. Boone hadn't just been raised in the swamp, he'd become one with it. "Dumb shit's neck is broke."

Peter eyed the tree stand. "You know what that means, right?"

Boone nodded. "Some*one* killed him. For sure weren't no mutate."

How had someone scaled the tree, entered the stand and broken the man's neck?

"Was he armed?" Peter asked.

"Sheeit." Boone spat at the tree, and Peter wasn't sure if he was cursing the dead man or whoever it was that killed him. "Yeah, he was. Hunting rifle with a scope. Sidearm, too. Can't remember what kind."

"So, the men at the Lot have gone silent and your lookout is dead. Weapons missing. You're under attack."

"Sounds 'bout right."

"Should we get reinforcements?" Peter asked.

Boone sniffed and shook his head. "Redneck Rampagers don't need no reinforcements. Whatever this is, I can handle it."

Peter suspected Boone's decision had more to do with a lack of reinforcements rather than an absolute faith in his abilities. If someone had come through here and killed his men, they might have done Peter a favor. Then again, he might just be trading one Devil for another. Until he knew, Boone was the closest thing to an ally he had.

"Can I have a weapon?"

"You shittin' me?" Boone said. "This all started not too long after y'all showed up. For all I know, you're in cahoots with whoever is out here."

Peter frowned. "Good point." And it was a good point. Had they been followed? And if so, by whom?

"Thank ye," Boone said, starting down the path once more. "Lot's a quarter mile ahead. Follow close, but not too close, and keep your trap shut."

"You got it," Peter said, eyeing Boone's sidearm. It was a Heckler & Koch P30 with .40 caliber rounds. Not heavy enough to do serious damage to an Apex, but heavy hitting enough to drop a human target with one shot to the right spot. He resisted the urge to take the weapon, fell in line behind Boone, and followed him down the path.

He wasn't sure what they would find, but he suspected there would be bodies. The question was, would Peter and Boone join them?

12

"Sweet tea?" Mason asked, leaning against the side of the wooden desk. He'd been polite since Peter left with Boone, but he had a gleam in his eye that made Ella uneasy. He had the cocky arrogance of a high school football star, but if he had trophies, she suspected they'd be something closer to heads mounted on stakes.

She wanted to dive over the desk and bury her nails in the sides of his neck. She could do it. As deadly as he might be, it wasn't because of his own prowess, but rather the men who followed him—and at the moment, none of them were present. But neither was Peter, or the kids. So, she stifled her urge to channel the primal instincts she'd discovered in herself over the past few months, and tried her hand at charming the man in return.

"Sweet tea?" she said, smiling. "God, yes. Don't tell me you have ice, too."

"In cubes. Yes, ma'am." He picked up a small bell from the desktop and gave it a shake.

The door opened and the black woman wearing the maid outfit took a single step inside before bowing her head. Her eyes flicked toward Ella, making eye contact for just a moment before returning to the floor. Her face was hard to see, but Ella felt the woman's embarrassment. Or was it shame? "Massa Mason. What can I do for you?"

"Sweet tea for two," he said.

"Yes'ah." With another quick bow, she turned around and scurried away.

"Won't be a long wait," Mason said, "but how about a tour in the meantime?"

"Absolutely," Ella said, standing. Despite her willingness to play along, her body still burned with tense energy, looking for an outlet. "I'd love to see the biodomes."

"Sure you would," Mason said, "but as a former biodome resident, you know that can't happen in your..." He looked her up and down. "...current state."

Shit, Ella thought. She'd set herself up for what was coming next, and with enough enthusiasm to ensure that backing out would look suspicious.

Still, she had to try. "Another time, then."

"Nonsense." Mason stepped around her and entered the hallway. She noted the lump on his back where a gun was hidden, tucked into his gleaming white pants. "Once you're cleaned up, I will personally escort you through the biodomes. We've managed to accomplish a lot. I think you will be duly impressed."

Ella smiled and said, "I'm sure."

Mason stopped at the end of the hall, resting a hand on the polished banister and calling through the formal dining room, into the kitchen. "We'll take that tea upstairs, Charlotte."

"Upstairs?" She sounded nervous.

"That's what I said, indeed."

"Yes, massa."

He grinned at Ella and motioned to the hardwood staircase. "Now then, ladies first."

"A true, Southern gentleman," she said.

"One of the few left on Earth, I'd guess."

"Perhaps even the last," she said, stepping by him and heading up the creaky stairs. She could feel his eyes on her, watching her shifting backside as she took each step. She was covered in dirt and dressed in unflattering cargo pants, a black tank top and a green, plaid flannel shirt, but men sometimes saw reality and fantasy at the same time. To Mason, she was a world of new possibilities. *More than he knows,* she thought, and she continued up the stairs, putting a little extra thrust into her hips.

The second floor felt much like the first: old wood, white walls, and the gentile décor of a middle-aged Southern woman. Still life paintings hung on the wall. A small table cloaked in a doily held a vase of wildflowers—freshly picked by the look of them.

Ella flinched as a door to her left swung open. A woman dressed in a maid uniform, similar to Charlotte's, but far too tight, stepped into the hall. "Something I can get for you, Mister—" Her eyes registered surprise at seeing Ella, then a flicker of something else, like pity, before turning toward Mason as he crested the staircase. "Something I can get for you, Mister Mason?"

"Not right now, Shawna," Mason said, taking her hand and kissing the back of it. "Perhaps later. In the meantime, heat up a towel for our guest."

Shawna feigned an 'aww shucks' kind of smile. It was a noble effort, but her jaw was clenched tight. She was pale white, like she hadn't seen the sun in a long time, with straight black hair and a curvaceous, almost plump body. *Locked inside, but well fed,* Ella thought, *like cattle.* But there was something about her, in that clenched jaw, that said she wasn't quite as docile as a cow. *That's what Mason likes,* Ella thought. *What gets him off. Breaking defiant women.* She didn't look like Shawna or Charlotte, but she had defiance in spades, and he had no doubt taken note.

Ella took a small measure of comfort in the fact that Mason had requested only one towel, and that he seemed interested in Shawna's...services...later on. He might be interested in Ella, but he wasn't ready to be overt about it. Ella thought he was still evaluating whether or not she was his type, and no doubt trying to conjure a way to get Peter out of the picture—or perhaps just hoping that would happen while he was out with Boone. Had the two men shared a signal that she missed? Was there really an emergency, or was Boone taking Peter into the swamps to execute him? If that turned out to be the case, Mason would find out that Peter wasn't the only member of their ragtag, post-apocalyptic family worth fearing.

"Of course, sir," Shawna said with a strained giggle. "Anything for you."

They're living out his fantasies, Ella thought. *Role playing.* The vivacious, slutty maid. The old-world, Southern, black maid. She wouldn't be surprised if the next maid she met wore a short skirt, held a feather duster, and spoke with a French accent.

Maybe that's what he has in mind for me?

And if not, maybe that's where I can get his mind.

When Shawna headed downstairs, Mason snuck around Ella and opened the next door on the left. Inside was a large bathroom with a claw-foot porcelain tub, a white tile floor and marble countertops. Mason flipped the light switch turning on a row of large bulbs mounted over a massive, wall-sized mirror that reflected the bathroom. *And everything that happens in it,* Ella thought.

"Bathroom is one of the rooms I upgraded after resettling Hellhole. It's a far shade more luxurious than it was before. Hot water, soap, shampoo, and conditioner are at your disposal—not that you'll have much use for the latter two, but your hair will grow back in time." Mason grinned. "Shawna will stop in with a warm towel and some fresh clothes. I'll come to collect you in what, twenty minutes?"

"Sounds divine," Ella said. "The bath, clothes, and towel, I mean."

"Not the company?" Mason said with a faux pout.

"That has yet to be determined," she said. "But you're off to a good start."

He flashed a sly grin and tipped his Ascot hat. "Best I can ask for. I'll leave you to it."

Ella stepped inside and offered Mason a parting smile as he closed the door behind her. Her smile dropped into a grimace. She rolled her neck, hearing her vertebrae pop from the tension. Then she looked at herself in the mirror and froze. It wasn't that her reflection was almost unrecognizable—she was too skinny, covered in dirt, and had a few fresh scars—it was how the mirror itself was constructed. She looked it over quickly, inspecting the side closest to her, and then the top and bottom. It was five feet tall, rising up from the bottom of the sink, all the way up to the ceiling, and it stretched the twenty-foot length of the bathroom. She looked for clips holding it in place, but there weren't any. The mirror wasn't mounted to the wall, it was part of it.

Her eyes widened for a brief moment, but then she forced a casual smile back onto her lips, the kind of smile a woman thinking about a man might have. The kind a man hoping for something more might want to see. Then she leaned in close to the mirror like she was inspecting her face and placed her fingertips against the glass like she was holding herself up.

She turned her face side to side, looking it over, glancing at her hand against the glass just once. But it was enough. Ella had worked in enough labs, in her long years of schooling and outside it, to have been on both sides of an observation mirror. There were two dead giveaways that a mirror was two-way, designed for spying. First, the mirror was part of the wall, not hung on it. The second was called the 'finger test.' A finger placed up against a normal mirror can touch its own reflection. A finger placed up against a two-way mirror was separated from its reflection by the thickness of the glass, in this case, a quarter inch.

Mason was on the other side of this mirror, watching. Observing. Waiting for a show. And if she didn't give him one...

She stared into her own eyes for a moment, picturing Mason on the far side of the mirror, looking back.

If it's a show he wants...

She lifted her shirt slowly, bunching the fabric beneath her breasts. She'd lost a lot of weight and dropped a cup size while living in the wild, eating a diet of foraged food. If she wore a bra, it was a sports bra, but the tank top had enough support built in, so she'd opted to go braless. And today, that worked in her favor. She let her breasts fall out of the shirt together, smiling beneath the fabric as she lifted it away. If Mason was watching, he was already entranced.

She walked to the tub and turned on the hot water. As steam wafted into the air, her smile turned genuine. She could, at least, enjoy this. Before they went back into the wild, she'd have to wallow in mud again like a pig. But for now, she'd enjoy the bath, and the notion that it would completely disarm the man behind the glass. Thinking of her hands around his throat, she pulled down her pants.

13

"So, let me get this straight," Anne said. "No one has tried to break out of these cells?"

"I think it's generally assumed that escape would be worse than being caged," Carrie said in dismay. "Besides, the gate is chain link."

"And the floor is concrete." Anne rolled her eyes. "I can see. I have eyes. But I'm starting to wonder if you guys need glasses. Or maybe new brains."

She looked at old Willie, then Carrie and finally John. The first two seemed befuddled. John seemed almost uninterested, resigned to his fate at the end of the hangman's noose, or whatever these people did to execute people.

A groan rose from Anne's throat when Jakob seemed equally baffled.

"Seriously?" she said to her half-brother. "Have you learned nothing?"

"What?" he said. "No one knows what you're talking about."

And no one is taking me seriously, because I'm twelve. "Ask a question. Observation. Hypothesis. Test. Repeat—if necessary. And when that's all done, take action."

Jakob sighed. He'd heard her modified version of the Scientific Method, which she called the Survival Method, more than once. She tried to teach him. Tried to make him memorize it and use it the same way Eddie Kenyon had taught her. He turned out to be a bad guy, but the method still made sense. Still worked. But Jakob resisted learning from his little sister. In the safety of *Beastmaster*, with her mother and father, it hadn't bothered her much. But here and now, with their lives on the line, she wished he'd taken the lesson more seriously. Especially now that she had to convince a bunch of adults that she wasn't a foolish child.

"Question," she said, "Can we escape? Observation. One, the floor is concrete. We're not digging out. Two, the gate is chain link, padlocked shut and screwed into a sturdy wooden beam. It's not going anywhere. Three, the ceiling is made of corrugated metal held together by bolts."

All eyes turned upward. The waves of metal siding, used for a slanted ceiling, were indeed held together by bolts.

"Holy..." Jakob reached up and tried to twist one.

"Observation," Anne said. "They're rusted. It's humid as a fat man's ass crack here."

Jakob grunted, trying to twist the bolt. He hissed in pain, withdrawing his hand and shaking it.

"Hypothesis." Anne raised a finger. "Humidity affects wood, too. Rots it. Especially when the lumber isn't pressure treated." She patted the wall behind her. "Like this wood. So, the cell's weakest point is the exterior wooden walls." She pointed to the front gate, the side wall behind Carrie and John, and the back wall behind Willie. "There, there and there."

"How do you *know* all this?" Carrie asked.

Anne shrugged. "I read a lot." It was true. Before her life in the wild began, she didn't do much more than read and cause mischief in the ExoGen facility, pulling pranks and spying. But there were a lot of subjects Anne knew a lot about that she couldn't remember learning. Like with pressure treated wood. Everything back in San Francisco was metal and glass, built to survive the end of the world.

"Continuing hypothesis," Anne said, but was interrupted by Alia.

"The roof overhangs in the front and back, so those walls probably stayed drier during rainstorms." Alia crawled across the cell, stopping short when she noticed the five-gallon bucket. She winced and reeled back.

"Found the shitter," Willie said, leaning up. He took hold of the bucket's handle and dragged the concentrated filth to the back of the small cell. "Might seem gross now, but sure beats soiling yourself."

Alia just scrunched her nose and continued on her way, a little bit slower now, carefully picking the spots she put down her hands. "Hypothesis," she said, upon reaching the side wall beside Carrie and John. "Of the three outside walls, this one will be the weakest."

She reached out and pushed on one of the vertical planks. It bowed, but held strong. She moved down the line toward Willie, testing each plank.

"Not that way," Anne said. "The other way. Specifically, behind him." She pointed at John, who looked more annoyed than surprised.

Carrie shifted away and swatted John's shoulder. "Move out of the way."

John obeyed, but didn't move far. Alia had to partially lean over his cross-legged knee to reach the wall. She probed the middle and then moved down. "This feels wet, still. I think—" Alia let out a yelp as the wooden plank folded outward at the bottom. Without the wall's support, she fell forward, face-planting. "Oww!"

Alia reeled back from the impact, sliding back across the floor, hand to her face, into Jakob's arms as he rushed to meet her.

"You all right?" Jakob asked, trying to look past the girl's hand.

She took her hand away from her face to reveal a bloodied nose. "How bad is it?"

Anne leaned over the girl, reached out and squeezed her nose between her thumb and index finger.

"Oww!" Alia said, flinching back.

"What the hell was that for?" Jakob asked, glaring at Anne.

"She's fine," Anne said. "Just pinch it."

Jakob motioned to Alia's face. "Her nose could be broken."

"If it were broken, she would have screamed instead of saying 'oww.'" She took hold of Jakob's arm and squeezed it hard. "And we have bigger problems."

The intense pressure on his arm and Anne's deep, threatening voice, which he had learned to never ignore, freed him from his mind-numbing concern for Alia. Jakob had overcome a lot of his weaknesses over the past few weeks, but his girlfriend had replaced them all. She distracted him. Put him in danger, and by extension, put the rest of them in danger.

"The hole in the wall?" Jakob asked.

Anne shook her head and sang, "One of these things is not like the others."

Jakob looked confused. "Sesame Street?"

Anne shared his expression. "What?"

"That song is from Sesame Street," he said.

"People on a street sing that song?"

"It was a TV show. For little kids."

"I spent my 'little kids' days in a tube," Anne said. "I've never seen—" But then she remembered it. The people. The strange fuzzy creatures.

What the hell?

"Tell me how to get to Sesame Street."

"Exactly," Jakob said.

"Brought to you by the letter H," Anne said, her mind drifting, and then snapping back to reality. "H for hypothesis. One of these things is not like the others." She left out the sing-song tune and looked at Carrie and John. Then turned to Willie. "How badly do you want your freedom? And I don't mean just from this cage."

The old man squinted at her. "What exactly are you asking me, kid?"

"Before we talk about getting out of here, and about who will help us once we're free, and about how Mason and his pals can be...usurped, we need to make sure that only the right people hear the plan."

"No one here but us," Willie said. "And they only check on us twice a day with food and water."

"What I'm asking you, Willie..." Anne said, leveling her most intense gaze into the man's eyes. He was old enough to be her great grandfather, but was listening carefully. "...is this. To regain your freedom, for however few years you have left, are you willing to listen to me?"

"I'm listening now, aren't I?"

"Are you willing to fight?" she asked.

"Much as an old man can."

"Are you willing to kill?"

"Anne," Jakob said.

"Same question goes for you, Jakey boy." She turned to Carrie. "And you."

Silence settled into the cell, squeezing her eardrums until John leaned forward and spoke. "And what about me?"

"I already know about you," Anne said. She pointed at the ring on his finger. "School ring, top of the class, worn proud. Don't recognize the school name, but you're not stupid." Her finger rose to his hair. "That haircut makes you look handsome to the ladies, but it was also done with a sharp pair of scissors, by someone else."

Carrie leaned away from John, looking at his hair. It wasn't exactly styled, but the cut was even, bordering on professional. Carrie's scrunched up forehead said she hadn't noticed the hair before, but she did find it odd now that it had been pointed out.

"Seriously?" John said. "You don't like my hair?"

"I don't like your face," Anne said, "but that's not really the problem."

"Then what is?" John asked.

"The knife strapped to your right leg."

All eyes shifted to John's right leg, which was covered by dirty jeans. The fabric was wrinkled, but among the folds was the slight outline of a thin blade, easy to miss when someone was sitting cross-legged.

John leaned forward quickly, hiking up the pant leg and reaching for the now exposed blade. It was flat and black, the handle and blade all one piece of forged metal. It looked like a throwing knife to Anne, but that didn't mean it had to be thrown to be deadly. In the tight confines of the cell, the young man, easily stronger than all his cellmates, could probably kill every one of them. But Anne had planned ahead for this moment.

Just as John slipped the knife from its sheath, a large, booted foot collided with the side of his head. John flopped to the side, unconscious, the knife clattering to the concrete floor. Anne winced at the sound. If anyone was within earshot, it would undoubtedly attract attention. She scurried across the floor and snatched up the blade.

John groaned, dazed, but still conscious.

"Still dangerous," she said, closing on the man, knife in hand.

"Anne," Jakob said. "Don't!"

"We can't risk him living," Anne said. "Even if we knock him unconscious, he'll give us up the moment he wakes up."

"It's murder," Jakob said.

"It's a revolution," Anne said.

"We just got here," Jakob argued. "They might even agree to let us go!"

Anne held the knife above John's heart, but kept her eyes on Jakob. "You know our parents. You've seen enough of this place. Do you really think they're going to just sit back and do nothing? How long do you think it will be before someone comes for us? Before someone uses us for leverage?"

Jakob said nothing, but she could see he agreed.

Part of her wished he didn't, that he'd talk her out of what she was about to do. But he couldn't, and he wasn't hard enough to do it himself, so...

She pulled her hand back, ready to thrust the blade into John's chest. But before she could, John was lifted up by two gnarly hands, one under his chin, one supporting the back. With a quick jerk, John's head snapped too far in one direction, the sound of snapping vertebrae opening his mouth in a silent scream. Then his head twisted in the opposite direction, again too far. The second crack made John's body fall limp, leaning back into Willie's arms.

"No way I'm going to sit back and watch a little kid kill a man for me," the old man said, dragging John into the cell's back corner and positioning his corpse so it looked like he was sleeping. When he turned back around, he grinned and said, "Viva la revolución. Let's get the hell out of here."

14

"That's the Lot," Boone whispered, lying in foot-deep muddy water, peering out between the ExoGenetic rice stalks that had claimed this portion of the swamp. A hundred feet ahead, on the far side of a paved road, was a combination gas and service station with a large, fenced-in parking lot for cars being worked on.

Peter took a deep breath through his nose, smelling earthy decay and something sweet that he thought must be the rice—most likely engineered to smell and taste like it had been dipped in maple syrup. He remembered hearing about this strain on the news when people first started eating the out-of-control crops. Boiling it and eating it plain was supposed to taste something like rice pudding, without the cinnamon and raisins. The thought made his stomach rumble loud enough for Boone to hear.

"When was the last time you ate something?" Boone asked. "Sounds like you got an angry coon in your gullet."

"Early this morning. Bunch of leaves and mushrooms." The displeasure in Peter's voice was genuine. Eating vegetarian was hard enough. Eating foraged foods...

It just wasn't enough, especially split between four people.

At least Anne could eat the ExoGenetic crops, but the rest of them were getting skinnier and weaker by the day.

Boone lifted himself part way out of the muck, unzipped a pouch on his chest and pulled out a Slim Jim. "We got a shit load of 'em. Old enough to eat. Enough preservatives to keep a zombie fresh."

Peter accepted the dried meat snack with a nod.

He peeled the wrapper open and devoured the food in three bites. It wasn't much, but the simple act of kindness gave Peter a flicker of hope that Boone wasn't as sinister as he appeared.

Of course, he thought, *he could just be trying to keep my stomach from giving away our position.*

"Why is there a gas station way out here?" Peter asked, looking at the place, which was surrounded on all sides by swamp. The sign by the road read: 'Gas and Gears.'

"Nearest town is a few miles down that way," Boone said, nodding his head to the right. "Next nearest town is a few more miles that-a-way. Fastest way 'tween here and there is this stretch of road. It's a little out of the way, but most people pass by it eventually. Plus, Austin, the previous proprietor, kept his prices low. Course, he sometimes put saw dust in the gears, too, but that don't matter none now. His corpse is rotting away in the swamp out behind the garage."

"What's his body doing out there?" Peter asked.

"It's where I dropped him, after putting a bullet in his head."

"He changed?"

"If that makes you feel better, sure." Boone pushed the rice stalks further apart. "Ain't nobody here."

"Wait," Peter said, but it was too late. Boone stepped out into the road, weapon ready, but totally exposed. If someone had been out there, or some*thing*, he'd be a dead man. But nothing happened. They were alone. And once again, Peter couldn't tell if Boone was lucky or had an exceptional knack for being in tune with this environment.

Feeling vulnerable without a gun, Peter stepped from the water, dripping wet. He hurried up behind Boone.

Halfway across the road, Boone's foot fell just short of the yellow line, and he stopped. He looked like a runner, taking his mark. Then the rest of his body went rigid. "You smell that?"

The same mixture of sweet rice and decaying swamp filled Peter's nose as he breathed deep. Then something else. He winced. "Smells like shit."

"And a lot of it," Boone added, starting across the road again, angling for the service station's entrance.

The glass door, stenciled with the same Gas and Gears logo as the sign out front, opened without a sound. *Boone and the boys have been keeping the place up,* Peter thought, *probably treating the Lot like a home away from home, free from the authoritative gaze of Mason.* A piece of paper taped to the inside of the glass held a chicken-scratched message.

No shirt, no shoes, you better have tits.

Peter smiled at the sign, but only because Boone was watching him.

"Me and the boys like to hang here on occasion. Not nearly as safe as Hellhole, but a good place to blow off steam." Boone stopped Peter just outside the door. "You ain't gonna be tellin' Mason, are you?"

Peter could see that the countertop had been converted into a bar, complete with stools. The shelves behind it were covered in bottles of various liquors and wines, probably old enough to be safe. Maybe old enough to be spectacular. "You have bourbon?"

"Blanton's," Boone said, a grin creeping up one side of his face.

"Then your secret is safe with me."

"Well, all right then." Boone stepped inside, and Peter followed, letting the door close behind them.

The fecal smell disappeared. *Whatever it is,* Peter thought, *it's not coming from in here.* The smell had him on edge, but the prospect of tasting Blanton's bourbon again... "Mind if I get a glass now? You know, in case we die?"

"Now that's a good toast if there ever was one." Boone took two shot glasses from the shelf. They were smudged with fingerprints on the outside, no doubt used and reused multiple times without a wash. But the alcohol would kill whatever germs the previous users had left behind. Boone snatched a round Blanton's bottle from the shelf, gripped the small horse and rider mounted atop the cap, and pulled the cork. Peter caught sight of the date written on the label. It was twelve years old and very safe to drink.

Boone poured two shots, right to the rim and slid one to Peter. They downed the alcohol in unison, neither man showing a reaction to the burn. Peter put his glass down and relaxed.

"One more for the road?" Boone asked, about to pour another shot. He stopped short when Peter put his hand over the glass.

"While there isn't much more in the world I would like to have at this very moment, than a second shot of that liquid gold, it's been a while since I had a drink. I can already feel it."

Boone scoffed. "Wouldn'a figured you for a lightweight." He refilled his own glass and downed it before Peter could remind him that something outside smelled like sundried shit.

"Gal dang," Boone said. "At least you have good taste in drinks." He put the bottle back on the shelf, carefully, almost reverently. To Boone and his good ol' boy buddies, this was a sacred place: like ten-year-old boys with a fort in the woods with nudie mags hidden in a buried safe. "Now," Boone said, "let's ferret out the source of that smell. And let me tell you this, if it's something my boys did, you're going to see exactly how this fella—" He tapped an index finger against his own chest. "—keeps his men in line. I ain't no stranger to the fine arts of corporal punishment."

Peter gave a fervent nod but stayed quiet. Boone was more of a lightweight than he thought or wanted Peter to think. The alcohol had loosened him up, and fast. And while that might help Peter subdue the man, if necessary, if things went sideways as they often did, he'd prefer the man fighting by his side to not be three sheets to the wind.

Boone led him through the office-turned-bar and into the garage, which had been converted into a real man-cave. There was a pool table, several dart boards, and a collection of antique chairs. It actually looked like a place Peter would enjoy kicking back in for a few drinks with his friends. If his friends were still alive. And though Boone seemed a little more human now, it was unlikely. *When pigs fly,* Peter thought, and then he shook his head. It was fairly likely that a flying pig existed someplace in the world.

"Get the door, would'ja?" Boone lifted his AR-15 to his shoulder, ready to fire.

Peter unlatched the door and then yanked it up, the clank of metal wheels sliding through the guide bars making him wince. *Too loud,* he thought, wondering how this place had yet to be overrun by an Apex predator.

Boone paid the loud door no attention and stepped out into the paved lot, scanning back and forth with the weapon. There was an assortment of vehicles, mostly trucks and SUVs. There were also a few cargo vans, and at the back, a large moving truck. Between the vans and truck was *Beastmaster*, parked in line with the rest, but not in the same condition he'd last seen it in. The armored pickup truck had been shot up, beaten, and abused over the past few months, but it had never been... violated.

This is personal.

Boone saw it, too, and he made his way toward the truck, aiming between the other parked vehicles as they passed. But they were alone. Whoever had defaced the car was long gone.

Boone stopped in front of *Beastmaster*, cocked his head to the side and read the message, written in shit, smeared on the windshield. He added his own inflections to the message, written in perfect English. "'Peter, Peter, Kristen beater, gonna find yer girl and eat 'er.' Am I reading this right? Kristen is yer wife. And yer girl is Anne? If my boys—"

"Your boys didn't know our names."

"Well then, ain't this something." Boone swiveled around, leveling the assault rifle at Peter's chest. "Seems you haven't been completely honest with me, have ye? Who's with you?"

Peter ignored the weapon, focusing on the message instead. "Why would anyone with me threaten my family? Why would they expose themselves like this?"

"Then who is it?"

Peter's mind raced for an answer, but before he could find one, a *thunk* from the back of the nearby moving truck made both men flinch.

"Someone's in there," Boone said, adjusting his aim toward the back of the truck.

Peter placed a finger to his lips and crept toward the large sliding door. He put one hand on the latch and counted down from three on the other, dropping one finger at a time. At zero, he unlatched the door and threw it up.

The sight inside the truck stumbled Peter back, as a wall of old-penny smell rolled over him. The inside of the truck was floor to ceiling gore. Bodies lay mangled and torn apart. It was hard to tell where one man ended and another began. But there was no blood outside the truck, meaning the men had been herded inside and then slaughtered. But who could do that? Or what? These men had been armed. But here in their secret fort, their guard might have been down. They might have been drinking. And whoever did this...they were good. And ruthless. And apparently, they had a grudge against Peter.

A man near the door shifted as the late day sun bathed him in light. He was missing both legs at the knees and pretty cut up.

It's a miracle he's still alive, Peter thought. *Must have just regained consciousness.*

Boone rushed over to the man. "Who did this, Ty? Tell me!"

The man named Ty, covered in blood and chunks of human meat that did not come from his own body, struggled to speak. "T-t-tweren't h-human. Cept for one f-fella. Big b-big...hairy..." His eyes rolled back and he fell limp.

"Ty!" Boone shook the man. "Ty!" Then he dropped his friend back, and without checking for a pulse, declared, "He's gone."

All of Boone's confident bravado drained from his body. His limbs went slack. He stumbled back until he bumped into the hood of a BMW and sat. Tears welled in his eyes. Boone, like everyone still living on Earth, had no doubt seen his fair share of death, gore and inhumanity, but these men—his men—might have been the last thing in the world that brought him any kind of joy. And he lost all of them at once.

He's breaking, Peter thought. *He's no good to me broken.*

"Ty was murdered." Peter wasn't sure if Ty was really dead or just unconscious, but it didn't matter. He'd be dead soon, no matter what they did for him. And since the man was already unconscious, he'd pass in relative peace. What did matter was the description. A man among big, hairy non-human creatures. "Someone did this to him."

Peter saw a flicker of light in Boone's eyes.

"You mean some*thing*," Boone said.

"ExoGentic creatures don't simply slaughter men," Peter said. "They eat them. And they damn well don't herd victims into a moving truck first. Ty said one of them was human." He gripped Boone's arm, squeezing his own sense of urgency into the man. "Your men were murdered, and their killer is still out there."

The spark ignited. Boone's jaw clenched. He stood, ready for action, but still unsure about what to do or where to go. But Peter had ideas about both.

"How many good men are defending Hellhole?" Peter asked.

"Most of them were here," Boone said, his voice shifting from quiet to grave anger. "Maybe a handful. Fifteen, if you count the bunch who will turn tail, first sign of danger."

"Won't be enough." Peter said.

That got Boone's attention. He turned to Peter, eyes wide. "Enough for what?"

"I need a weapon," Peter said. "And this time, I'm not asking. Because if I'm right, Hellhole is about to live up to its name like never before."

15

The strange lopsided grin stretched across one half of Mason's face left no doubt that he had been entertaining himself by watching her bathe. *How many women has he watched through that one-way mirror? How many of them have ended up in maid's uniforms as a result?* It occurred to her that the whole, 'take a bath' routine might be a tried and true vetting system Mason used to select which women worked on his staff—pun intended. She smiled back, but only because she pictured the kids' reaction to her mental pun. The way Anne and Jakob had bonded, like lifelong brother and sister, gave her hope. It also gave her more than enough reason to plunge her thumbs into Mason's eye sockets. But not yet.

She wanted to learn more about Hellhole and the people in it first.

"That was the second most pleasurable experience of my life." Ella stood from the King size bed where she had been sitting, and stretched, letting the clean white blouse hug her chest a little tighter. The bedroom was clean and fresh, with white walls, curtains, and a canopy over the bed. The furniture was solid cherry, gleaming with a fresh polish. A faint lemon scent hung in the air. None of it had any effect on her, but she did her best to look as comfortable as the bedroom was designed to make women feel. When she relaxed again, she took note that Mason's eyes, like the Grinch's heart, had grown two sizes. The man's libido was in full swing, despite his age.

She glanced down and saw more evidence of the man's still raging hormones. "Your zipper's down," she said.

Mason looked caught off guard for the first time since they'd met. He staggered back a few steps, smoothing his shirt for a better look at his crotch. He fumbled with his fly and zipped it up. "So it is," he said, fixing his shirt. "How embarrassing."

Ella shrugged. "Nothing I haven't seen before."

"I'm sure," he said, the smile returning. "Do your clothes fit?"

She looked down at the white blouse and flowing white skirt fringed with what looked like a doily at the bottom. A real Southern belle's outfit, so clean and gleaming that out in the wild, she'd stick out like a fluorescent fishing lure in a pond, attracting ExoGenetic monsters with every shift of her body. Like albino animals born outside of captivity, she wouldn't survive long. And perhaps that was part of the message: you're only safe inside the walls. But Ella thought that Mason just liked it. In fact, the only major difference between her outfit and the maids' was the color. White and black.

Oh God... Ella fought to keep the disgust from showing on her face. *He's treating the dress like a wedding dress. White, because he hasn't had me yet.*

It was just a guess, but it made a sick kind of sense. Mason had managed to lead all these people through the Change, had built multiple biodomes and had a true Southern gentleman charm about him. But he was also, quite clearly, a sexual predator. And perhaps always had been.

She smiled wide and ran her hands over her hips. "Everything fits perfectly." *And you're never going to see me in black,* she thought.

"Good," he replied. "Very good. Now, if you'd still like a tour—"

"Love one," she said, and there was nothing phony about her earnest desire to see how this man—a contractor in the world before—had taken her design for a self-sustaining biodome and turned it into a series of interconnected domes.

"Then I would be delighted to provide one." Mason tipped his Ascot cap and motioned to the door. "Ladies first."

She stepped into the hall, headed for the stairs, and descended slowly, searching the first floor for any signs of trouble. The house décor was a mix of old and new. Antique furniture, also perfectly polished, filled the living and dining rooms. But the paintings on the walls...while some were older, boring examples of Southern landscapes, others looked more modern. Then she saw a painting she recognized and paused in front of it. The style was modern, but the painting was at least seventy years old.

"You have good taste," Mason said, stopping in front of the Picasso painting. "It's titled 'Head of a Woman.' The palette is rather subdued, don't you think? But I feel it is a good representation of mankind's dual nature. She looks frightened, but not of something external."

"Of what she is becoming," Ella said. The broad strokes cleaving the woman's face into odd shapes was distinctly Picasso, but the inhuman visage it created really did resemble some of the half-human monsters roaming the world now.

"He painted this in France. 1943."

"During the German occupation?"

Mason grinned. "A woman who knows her history... You are better educated than I would have guessed."

She waved off the compliment and hoped to hide her intelligence. "Discovery channel."

"Mmm." Mason reached out and traced the black line curving down through the woman's face with his finger. "Dora Maar. That was her name. Picasso didn't get along with her. I sometimes wonder if all these lines represented some inner desire to...cleave his subjects with a different kind of utensil. Of course, the brush is the gentleman's preferred tool."

"You know a lot about Picasso," Ella noted.

Mason shrugged. "The boys were smart enough to steal the placards with the art."

"These aren't prints?"

"Procured them a few months back. From the Ackland Art Museum in North Carolina. Not too far. Four hours by truck."

"Not too far? A lot can happen in four hours. Your boys are lucky to be alive."

"You survived a *much* longer journey."

"I had Peter."

Mason scrunched his lips, twisting them side to side. "You have that much faith in his abilities?"

Ella paused before answering.

Would intimidating Mason with Peter's prowess make the man afraid to overstep, or would it solidify his resolve to have Peter killed? *He's going to kill him either way,* she thought, and decided to put the fear of God into him.

"He's seen and done things that most people can't even imagine."

"I'm not so sure about that." The grin on Mason's face was more convincing than his words. This was a brutal man. But what he didn't know was that surviving in the wild had turned her into a brutal woman. He wore his savagery very close to the surface, but he still had no idea who she was, or of what she was capable.

"The world has made us all do...unsavory things," Ella said. "But my husband's long list of violence started long before the Change. Killing monsters is one thing, killing people..." She shook her head in faux disgust. "That takes a different sort of man."

"That it does." Mason started down the hall toward the kitchen, a spring in his step. "Peter sounds like the sort of man I need. Think he would be interested in staying on? All of you could stay, of course. Even the...girl traveling with you. Unless you have someplace you'd rather be?"

Mason paused by the kitchen door, motioning for Ella to once again take the lead. "I know the Askews were your friends, and I regret the condition in which you found them, but I think you'll agree that this oasis is worth saving, no matter the cost."

Ella couldn't hide her anger over Bob's passing and Lyn's deplorable condition, but she also couldn't blatantly disagree with him. While Bob and Lyn's fates were horrible, and something Mason would pay for, she couldn't deny that this last colony of humanity outside of ExoGen needed to be protected. "I do. Agree. But I don't like it."

"No one does," he said. "Not at first. But a few nights without fear of being consumed tends to alter perspectives."

Ella stepped into the kitchen.

Three women turned to greet her. She recognized Charlotte, who was rolling out what looked like a pie crust. Shawna was there, too, chopping apples.

Apples? Ella peered at the bright red fruit. *There must be an old, non-ExoGenetic orchard nearby.* Her mouth watered at the prospect of eating an apple again.

The third woman was blonde and aquiline, her features sharp and defined. Where Shawna was curvy, this woman was thin, almost frail. "Salut," the woman said in French, confirming Ella's fears about maid choice. But if this was the French maid, what did Mason have in mind for her?

She determined to never find out.

"Hello," Ella replied, and then to the other women. "Hello again."

Forced smiles were the only replies before the women returned to work, their eyes evading Mason's. They were terrified of him.

"Sabine," Mason said. "This is Ella. Could you prepare her something to eat?" He paused, thinking for a moment. "And have the same brought to the children with the Questionables."

Sabine gave a curtsy, her movements fluid, almost poetic. "Oui, Monsieur Mason."

She was a dancer, Ella thought. *Before the Change. A ballerina.* But was she even French? Ella didn't think so. She spoke French, that was clear, but the accent didn't sound authentic.

"Thank you, kindly," Mason said, as he breezed through the kitchen and into the back room. Once upon a time, the space might have been a mud room, where tired farmers, or a family's children, would have kicked off dirty shoes and boots. Now it would lead to a very modern door, offering passage to a biodome.

As Ella followed Mason toward the back of the kitchen, Sabine's hand snapped out. The woman's movement was so fast that Ella nearly punched her, but when she saw the look in the woman's eyes, and felt the steady grip on her hand... It was a warning.

She's telling me to get out, or maybe to make myself undesirable somehow.

Ella returned the squeeze, offered a grin, and gave her a knowing nod. The woman let her go, but took no solace in the message being received.

Are they really just concerned about my wellbeing? Or is there something else? Something I'm missing?

The hiss and pop of a decontamination room coiled Ella's insides. She'd heard the familiar sound all too often in her life, and during her time with ExoGen, after the Change, it served only to remind her that she was a prisoner. That was, until she had escaped. And here she was, about to walk through another decontamination chamber. *One that I designed,* she reminded herself, *but a prisoner once more.*

For now.

She stepped into the chamber and waited as Mason closed and sealed the door behind them.

"Removes any and all particulates from bodies and clothing. So if—" He waved his hand dismissively. "What am I saying? You already know all this. You recognize the design, of course?"

Ella nodded slowly. "It looks the same as ours."

"The one provided by your husband's mistress..." He shook his head like he still couldn't believe Peter's betrayal, like he was stung by it himself.

"I hated the bitch," Ella said. "But she also saved my family's life."

"Interesting perspective." The decon fans kicked on, filling the chamber with a tumultuous, roaring wind that shifted direction every few seconds, nearly tearing the skirt from her body. There was nothing she could do to keep it from lifting up, revealing the lacy white panties she'd been provided. But Mason had already seen a lot more. It didn't keep him from leering, though. He was so intent on looking, that he didn't see her own gaze, leveled at the thick vein on the side of his neck, or her hooked fingers, a twitch away from tearing into him.

Then the fans fell silent, the pressure equalized, and the door on the opposite side of the chamber unlocked. Mason opened the door, flooding the small space with the fragrant smell of growing things. The odor nearly brought tears to her eyes, and Mason did notice that.

"It's moving," he said, "for everyone. The first time they come here. And smell this. See it for themselves. *Taste* it. But to truly appreciate it all, you need to see the macro view. Lead the way."

The layout of the biodome hadn't changed from her original design.

There were twenty raised rectangular garden beds. Each fifteen feet long and seven wide. A central aisle divided the space into even sides with walkways between the beds and along the walls. A network of water pipes crisscrossed overhead, with three nozzles positioned over each garden, providing an even spread for the plants growing below.

And they were growing.

Whoever was in charge of the dome had a green thumb. But right now, she and Mason were alone. She'd expected to find people—more women—tending the gardens. *It can't be just Mason and the maids. Not with five functioning domes.*

He sent everyone away, she thought. *Wanted the place to himself. Away from prying eyes or judgmental glares.* He might have already visited the self-service station while she was in the bath, but he apparently had vigor to spare. In fact, now that she could see him up and about, he looked bigger and fitter than she would have guessed. But was he a threat —aside from the gun tucked into the back of his pants? That would be determined the moment he tried anything.

"What do you think?" Mason said, walking the long way around the room, admiring the crops. "Take a closer look."

Ella obeyed, crouching down beside a row of carrots. The stems were lush and green. Fragrant, too. Her stomach growled.

With a chuckle, Mason said, "I heard that from here. Take one. Try it."

That was an invitation Ella couldn't pass up, and doing so would be supremely suspicious. She uprooted a carrot, surprised and delighted to find its bright orange body a full foot long. She stood, wielding the carrot the way an actor might an Oscar award, and she carried it to the sink mounted to the side wall. She looked at the root vegetable, almost glowing in the bright sunlight beaming through the glass dome above, protecting this oasis from the deadly crops outside.

"Daucus carota ssp. Sativa. It's perfect," she whispered, and then took a bite.

Flavor exploded with each chew.

It was distinctly carrot, but almost like carrot concentrate, enough to make her pucker, salivate and crave more. She took a second bite without swallowing, chewing vigorously as the sweetness hit her.

The flavor, on par with the best cake she'd ever eaten, was followed by a realization.

She'd gotten the carrot's identification wrong.

This is Daucus carota ssp. Sativa variant RC-714.

This is an ExoGenetic *carrot!*

Her jaw stopped moving, the toxic food frozen in her mouth and stuck between her teeth. *Did I swallow it? Oh god, I swallowed it!*

"Too good to be true," Mason said, slowly moving toward her. "Right?"

She pushed the carrot chunks out of her mouth, letting the food fall to the concrete floor. She spat a few times and then used the sink to rinse out her mouth.

Mason stopped ten feet way. "Didn't your parents teach you not to waste food, Ella?"

Her mouth was full of water, ready to spit into the sink, when the last word of his sentence sank in.

'Ella.'

He knows.

He knows who I am!

Ella turned toward Mason, fists clenched, but he'd already closed the distance.

16

"I can't do that," Boone said, taking a step back from Peter. "Not until I get Mason's say so."

"Your men are dead." Peter motioned to the back of the still-open moving truck. The gesture was unnecessary. Boone knew what Peter was talking about. But it got the man to take another sobering look. The absolute carnage filling the inside of the truck—and only the inside—revealed an attacker, or attackers, who were incredibly strong and smart. And if Peter was right about who that was...

"We're running out of time."

Boone stared at him, no doubt weighing the dangers of trusting Peter and betraying Mason's orders. And while he was doing that, Peter was gauging the likelihood that he could subdue Boone and take the weapons he needed. He hoped he wouldn't need to do that. Weapons weren't any good without people to aim and fire them.

"Don't try it," Boone said, taking another step back and bringing his AR-15 up a little. It wasn't quite aimed at Peter, but the threat was clear.

"Damnit, Boone." Peter gripped the sides of his head, trying to contain his building anger. "You don't know what—"

A loud *thunk* against the outside of the moving truck interrupted and pulled Peter's eyes toward it. A spear protruded from the metal side. The tip was stone, but it had been thrown with the incredible force of someone no longer human.

When Peter turned back to Boone, the man held a hand up to his cheek, where it had been sliced open. Blood flowed into his beard. The spear throw had been meant for his head, a realization that slowly crept into Boone's eyes. Too slowly.

"Down!" Peter yelled, diving into Boone. He shoved the muzzle of the AR-15 down and tackled the man to the ground as a second spear sailed past, puncturing the truck's large tire.

Peter scrambled back to his feet, yanking Boone up with him and searching their surroundings for attackers. The fenced-in lot was clear, but they were surrounded by swamplands. The spears gave him a direction, though—across the street, in the trees through which they had come. *They're blocking the path back to Hellhole.* Peter glanced at his truck... *If we go on foot.*

"Where are my keys?" Peter shouted.

"In the garage," Boone replied, stumbling forward as Peter shoved him toward the garage door. Movement atop the chain link fence surrounding the lot caught Peter's attention and confirmed his fears. It was a hair-covered Rider. The creature, who had previously been a man, was a foot shorter than Peter, but it would be far stronger. And the long, curved teeth protruding from his lower jaw and curving up into the skin of his cheeks, were a formidable weapon, not to mention the long, black fingernails turned into claws.

Peter yanked the spear from the truck's tire, triggering a loud hiss of escaping air. He lobbed the spear at the Rider about to leap into the lot. The spear missed its target, but it forced the man-beast to lean out of the way. He lost his grip and fell away. It was a momentary reprieve, but it gave Boone time to reach the garage.

Boone turned in the doorway, dropped to one knee and brought his weapon up. Peter flinched when he looked down the weapon's barrel. The rifle coughed. Bullets buzzed through the air. There was a shout of pain and then a thud of flesh hitting pavement.

Peter spun around to find a dead Rider laying behind him, three rounds stitched up its chest. Even as blood pooled around it, the creature still reached for him, black claws flexing. Peter had saved Boone's life and Boone had returned the favor.

"Move it!" Boone said, his shock giving way to the confident actions of a man who had seen action in the past and come out on top. But how many men had Boone had by his side during those encounters? And how many monsters were out there now?

Only one way to find out, Peter thought, as he charged for the open door. *The hard way.*

Boone closed and locked the door behind Peter, watching through the glass. "The hell are they? You know, don't you?"

"We call them Riders."

"Riders? What do they ride?"

"Woolies, but I didn't see any out there, and that's a good thing."

"But..." Boone looked stymied. "They're working together? Like people?"

"Most ExoGenetic creatures became solo predators, hunting each other toward the mass extinction of all life on Earth," Peter explained. "But the last creatures to turn during the Change—some people and some herd animals—adapted into packs. And in this case, they evolved as cooperative species. Almost symbiotic."

"Symby-whatic?"

"Means they need each other to survive."

"Seem to know a lot about this stuff," Boone said, suspicion creeping back into his voice.

Peter moved to the front office, ducking low as he looked out the window. "Also means the Woolies won't be far." He snuck back into the garage. "Now would be a great time for those weapons we spoke about."

Boone hesitated for just a moment and then kicked open a chest against the wall. Inside was a collection of weapons that looked like they might have been taken from previous captives. Atop the haphazard mass of metal was Peter's own rifle. He picked up the weapon and ejected the magazine. It was full, but he didn't see any spares in the chest, or ammunition. He looked out at the lot again. *Beastmaster's* back hatch was down. His cases of supplies and ammo still surrounded the mounted machine gun. Boone's men had been interrupted before they could fully pillage the vehicle. "We need to get to my truck."

"These walls are concrete," Boone said. "Safer in here."

"Against spears maybe," Peter said, and then as though to prove his unfinished point, the garage's side wall folded inward, vomiting concrete blocks as something massive plowed through.

Peter and Boone both dove for the pool table, sliding beneath the solid sheet of slate. The table shook as chunks of wall toppled into the room, but it withstood the assault. Before the last blocks hit the floor, Peter poked his head out and saw the ugly face of a Woolie pulling out of the newly formed gap. The creature looked like a cross between a hairy rhino and a buffalo. The single horn on the tip of its nose split like an antler, ending in razor sharp scoops. Tendrils of brown hair hung in clumps, matching the drool dangling from its mouth, sweeping back and forth across the floor, like a lazy janitor's mop. Its jaundiced eyes twitched toward Peter, but it made no move to attack. It just lumbered back.

Making way, Peter thought. "We're about to have company!" He pulled himself out from under the table, climbed to his feet and chambered the first round. Before he could aim the weapon at the massive hole in the side wall, the window beside him shattered inward. He twisted toward the sound and caught sight of a male Rider curled up in a ball, unfurling his body as he catapulted through the air.

Peter tried to fire his weapon, but it wasn't designed for close quarters combat. The Rider struck him in the side. Man and beast went down together, sprawling across the concrete-littered floor.

A spear tip stabbed toward Peter's throat before he could get back to his feet. He caught the shaft, stopping the blade just an inch from his throat, but he only managed to delay his death. The male Riders, while smaller than Peter, and the females of their ExoGenetic species, had powerful muscles. Like apes, who could out-muscle a man more than twice their size.

When the tip of the spear met Peter's skin and began slipping through it, he nearly lost his grip. And as a shout of pain and emotional agony at failing his family rose up in his throat, the blade sank deeper.

And then, with a blast of noise, the blade slipped out.

Peter's chest heaved as he watched the Rider fall to the side, an arc of blood flowing out behind its head, while a plume of gore sprayed out in front of it. He stared at the creature, as its body struck the floor, kicking up a cloud of powdered concrete. Its lifeless eyes looked back at him.

Then a voice cut through the shock. "Get the fuck up, man!"

Peter gasped a deep breath and adrenaline carried the oxygen straight to his brain, sharpening his senses and speeding up his reaction time. The effect, which he'd felt before, was that time had suddenly slowed. In reality, he was simply processing the world around him much faster.

A shadow moved in the open wall. He gripped the spear lying next to him and hurled it toward the opening without fully registering what was there. By the time he saw the Rider, it was already falling back, the spear planted firmly in its sternum, its long-toothed lower jaw slack in surprise.

Thumps echoed down from the ceiling. Shadows shifted in the swamp outside the ruined wall. A Woolie bellowed from the street, its call like a foghorn. *That's going to attract a lot of attention,* Peter thought, but maybe that was the idea. If the man accompanying these creatures was who Peter feared it was, they might be calling reinforcements.

Peter hauled himself up and shouted at Boone. "Keys!"

Boone gave a nod and made for the front office.

Movement outside the garage door spun Peter around. A Rider had leaped down from the roof and was coiled to spring. As the creature dove into the garage, Peter pulled the trigger and held it, putting six rounds into the Rider's head. The first shot killed it. The force of the remaining five stopped its forward momentum and deposited the body at Peter's feet.

Boone stumbled back into the garage, stepping over debris and jingling the keys. "This them?"

Peter snatched the keys from Boone's hand and turned for the ruined door. "The moment we're out in the open, they'll be on us."

"Ayuh."

"Don't stand your ground. Don't even slow down. Just get in *Beastmaster* and—"

"Beastmaster?"

"The truck."

Boone flashed a grin. "Well, all right then. Let's kick this in the nuts and get 'er done."

"I'll take point, you cover our six," Peter said. "Steady pace. Stay close."

"Copy that."

Peter stepped through the ruined door, leading with the assault rifle, sweeping back and forth, looking for targets. The lot appeared empty, but he could hear movement just beyond the fence.

Riders hiding behind the cars, he guessed.

Boone shuffled out behind him, walking backwards, aiming up at the garage roof at first, and then in all directions.

"Don't see nothing," Boone said.

Peter ignored him and kept moving.

They were fully exposed now. It wouldn't be long before they proved too irresistible a target.

The attack came just three steps later, but the Riders were done throwing spears and attacking one at a time. A fog-horn blast bellowed from the swamp across the street. It was followed by the rumble of heavy bodies charging across the pavement. Six Woolies, three with Riders, three without, burst from the trees, headed straight for the lot.

"Run!" Peter shouted, tugging on Boone's shoulder. He pressed the 'unlock' button on the key fob and was happy to see the taillights flash on twice. The doors were unlocked.

As they reached the truck, the first of the Woolies reached the lot, plowed through the chain link fence, and slammed into the truck parked there. The smashed vehicle shot across the lot and crashed into a second with tremendous force.

The second Woolie did the same. They were turning the parked vehicles into massive projectiles, while simultaneously blocking off any chance of retreat back to the garage.

Peter put the key in the ignition.

A third truck careened across the lot, followed quickly by another.

The gear shift clunked down into Drive.

A pickup truck whooshed past, directly behind them, clipping one of the spikes welded to the back of *Beastmaster*. The flung pickup sprang into the air, slamming down on the open moving truck, further violating the corpses.

Peter shoved the gas pedal down. The big Dodge Ram roared forward, striking the chain link fence with a clang, and peeling it away from the metal support poles. The fence stretched out, trying to hold them in place like a spider web clinging to a bird. The truck pushed forward until the fence slipped up and over the roof and sprang back toward the lot, just as the last Woolie struck, closing the gap where they had been just moments before.

Peter peeled hard to the left, flinging mud as he avoided a drop off into the swamp. Tires squealed as they reached the road.

"That way!" Boone shouted, pointing to the right.

As its windshield wipers and cleaning fluid attacked the excrement-soiled windshield, the truck roared away from the scene. But it wasn't alone. The powerful Woolies and their Riders were unfazed by the impacts with the vehicles. Peter and Boone weren't more than fifty feet away by the time the creatures turned to follow them.

Peter glanced in the rearview, expecting to see the Woolies fading in the distance. *No way those big things can keep up*, he thought, as the truck moved past fifty miles per hour. But what he saw in the mirror reminded him that making assumptions about creatures who could rapidly evolve and adapt was often a fatal mistake. It had been weeks since he'd seen these things, and while fast and powerful then, they'd obviously evolved some speed since. The Woolies weren't just keeping up—they were gaining.

"Get back there," Peter said, hitching his thumb toward the truck bed and the machine gun mounted there.

Boone turned to climb over the seat, but stopped short, head turned out the passenger side window. "What in the—aww shit!"

Peter glanced out the window in time to see a massive pair of jaws, filled with foot-long conical teeth, explode from the swamp, reaching out for the side of the truck. Before he could take action or even shout in surprise, the open maw snapped closed.

17

Ella saw the incoming attack too late to do much about it. The punch was aimed at her temple. If she tried to lean back, the fist would connect with, and most likely break, her jaw. Dodging Mason's broad-knuckled fist was impossible. But she could make him regret it.

She turned to face the blow and tilted her head down, shifting the impact from her temple—which would have knocked her out cold, if not killed her—to her forehead.

His fist full of old phalanges struck hard, colliding with the thickest part of her skull.

Two shouts of pain echoed off the curved glass ceiling.

Ella's was cut short by a flicker of unconsciousness. The solid strike had snapped her head back, mashing her brain into her skull. She toppled backward into a raised garden of potatoes, regaining consciousness on impact.

Mason's yelp of pain became a hiss. He shook his right hand, and then held his index finger in his left hand. He squeezed hard, unleashing a muffled pop that was followed by another yelp. She didn't know if he was trying to set a broken bone, or fix a dislocated joint, but when he was done, he didn't try bending the finger.

Ella blinked and tried to get back to her feet, but she felt like she'd just woken up from a long sleep after a night of binge drinking.

Her limbs were not fully obeying her commands yet.

Mason looked down at her but didn't take a step closer. "You're a crafty bitch, aren't you?"

"At least I'm not a geriatric rapist," Ella said. Each word sent a pulse of pain through her head. She tried to hide it. To look strong. But she knew her squinting eyes and downturned lips were projecting her vulnerability.

"You are far worse than that," Mason said. "The Bhagavad-Gita and Oppenheimer both got it wrong. The world wasn't brought to its knees by a multi-armed Vishnu, or the atomic bomb. Civilization was destroyed by *you*, Dr. Ella Masse. Seems only fitting that someone bring you to your knees."

Despite the pain in Mason's hand, a hungry look returned to his eyes. It lingered on her face for just a moment longer, before traveling down to her skirt, which had been flung up, exposing her legs.

"You were a mess when you first entered the camp. And to be honest, the shaved head still isn't working for me. But it's different. And different is fun. Despite the grime and old blood and whatever else you'd been rolling through out there—" He waved his hand toward the wall, indicating the world outside. "—I saw your potential. I've been with all manner of women, but they were all...soft. In body, mind, and spirit. But not you. You are a hard woman." He raised his injured hand. "And you have not disappointed."

He took a step closer, but not too close.

"The problem is, we're under something of a schedule. Your friends are on their way."

"Peter will—"

"I'm not speaking about your counterfeit husband." Mason leaned his head to the side, eyes traveling up Ella's exposed thigh.

She pulled the skirt down and shuffled back. Her head throbbed, stopping her short. It hurt like hell, but not quite as bad as she made it seem. She groaned and held her head, rolling her eyes for a moment before gripping the potato bed's plastic edging.

"I'm talking about your employers."

Ella held her breath, the shock on her face genuine.

"Yes," Mason said. "ExoGen is on their way here. Just for you. And your daughter."

"W-what? How?"

"We installed a HAM radio just a week ago. I'm not sure why, but we never thought to try it before. S'pose we just assumed there was no one else out there to talk to. Imagine my surprise when I heard a message broadcast by the harbingers of doom themselves. They were looking for the one and only Dr. Ella Masse, and her daughter—both of whom were hiding the secrets to preventing the Change from taking place. Tsk, tsk, Ella. I don't know what your motivation for destroying civilization was, and I can't even say I don't appreciate this new world you've created, but if turning you over to the company you duped means a future beyond these walls, I have to do my civic duty."

"They're trying to *stop* me from fixing the problem," Ella argued.

"Says the architect of hell."

"I tried to warn people," she said. "I built these domes to save people. And you've done that like no one else."

"My vanity cannot be fluffed, but other things... Well, perhaps we can arrange your escape."

Ella glared at the man. Was he offering her a chance to escape in exchange for a sexual favor? Was he really that preoccupied by the exploits of his manhood? As the first repulsive notion of considering Mason's offer entered her thoughts, Ella's hand felt a large lump just beneath the soil's surface. She dug her fingers down and lifted a dirty, football-sized potato from the soil. "These are Solamum tuberosum, variant RC-714. They're ExoGenetic. Is this what you're eating?"

Mason grinned. "It's what we're all eating."

"For how long?"

Mason took a deep breath and let it out slowly, counting on his fingers and wincing when he moved the injured index digit. "Thirteen months. Are you impressed?"

Ella *was* impressed, but not with Mason. "The Askews. They did this."

Mason nodded. "The crops, as you noted, are still ExoGenetic, but the RC-714 gene that unlocks millennia of dormant adaptations, has been blocked. The crop's adaptations remain intact, but they no longer modify the DNA of those who consume it. Lyn said they had rusted the revolving door shut. The problem, of course, is that these crops can only co-exist with the crops outside. They can't replace them. Which means that these biodomes are still required. We have more than enough food but remain prisoners of Hellhole."

"The Askews fed you, and you repaid them by locking them up? By starving Bob to death?"

"They questioned my authority."

"Because this was *their* home."

He shrugged. "There are no governments. No laws. No land rights. Who is to say what is right and what is wrong? *I'm* writing history now. Whoever comes next will remember me as humanity's savior."

"Did you tell ExoGen?"

"They're on their way. Were surprisingly close. Tracking you, I suppose."

"Not about me," Ella said, shaking the potato at Mason. "About this?"

The trace of doubt on Mason's face came and went like a Formula 1 race car zipping past, but it was enough to confirm Ella's fears.

"Mason, listen to me." She held the potato up. "This is a gift. Not just to you. But to the world. It's not a solution, but it's big. You can feed people. Really *feed* people."

"I've heard similar words come from your mouth before," Mason said. "That was on TV, and you had nicer hair then, but you were a snake oil salesman then, and you're a snake oil salesman now."

"I didn't know," she said between clenched teeth.

"Mmm." Mason took a step closer, leering again.

"Mason, they are going to kill you and everyone here. They told you the truth about my work. I am working on a cure. On a way to alter the human genome, so we can eat any ExoGentic crop without fear of mutation. The human race can have a future. But that's not what they want. That's not their design."

"Why would they want to stop the human race from being able to eat?"

Ella sat up a little straighter, her head clearing. "For the same reason you hold back this bounty from most of the people in this camp."

That seemed to sink in.

"Control," he said. "To what purpose?"

She wanted to grill him about *his* purpose. About his sick preoccupation with having a house full of fantasy maids. His motivations were as base as they come, without unlocking a single prehistoric gene. But that would only incite him and cloud the rational thought slowly pushing against his aging, but raging, libido.

"I don't know yet," she said, and it was true. She'd never been part of ExoGen's inner circle. She knew some of them. Even liked some of them. But the reason why they released the ExoGenetic crops, even after they understood what would happen, or perhaps because of it, was still a mystery. She had always assumed it was a more complex version of Hellhole Bay. Mason had remade this small part of the world to suit his every desire. And it was only possible because the old world had died. ExoGen was no doubt doing the same, but on a much larger scale. A worldwide scale. With a longer endgame. And whatever that was, it still required that the remnants of humanity, including Mason and every living soul in his Hellhole, to be changed into monsters or slaughtered. "But they have control. Absolute control."

She pushed herself up a little higher. "You're right. There are no governments. No laws. No right and wrong. Society is being rewritten, but by whom? Not you. Have you considered how ExoGen survived the end? How they have helicopters en route? They're located in San Francisco. You know that, right? And yet, here they are, on the East Coast, looking for me. How many people are living here? A hundred? Do you know how many people, loyal to ExoGen's future, are alive and well on the far side of the country?"

He just stared back at her. He didn't know. Hadn't thought to answer any of these questions.

"Thousands," she said. "The cradle of humanity's future isn't here in Hellhole, it's in San Francisco. With ExoGen. *Unless*...unless I can set the rest of us free. They're coming here for me. And for Anne. That's true. But once they have us? You and your harem are dead. These domes will be reduced to rubble. You will not be remembered in anyone's history books."

Mason grinned. "A riveting speech."

"It's the truth."

"Perhaps," Mason said. "Perhaps not. Either way, my earlier offer still stands."

"Oh my God, are you serious?" Ella gripped the potato tightly, lowering it back toward the soil. "Don't you get it? Whether or not I degrade myself for you, they *know* where you are. You are going to die."

He sighed, but it sounded more like a growl—exasperation mixed with primal desire. "And what are you suggesting we do?"

"Fight!" she shouted, and lobbed the massive potato at him.

18

Peter swerved hard to the left, tires squealing as he nearly drove head-long into the swamp on the left side of the road. He cut the wheel back before plunging into the inky black waters, and since they were still on the road, and not being crushed by monstrous jaws, he assumed his last-ditch maneuver had worked, pulling them just out of the creature's reach.

He looked in the rearview and saw the last of it careen over the far side of the road. The massive beast was a blur one moment, and then concealed by an enormous splash that hid its dark body from view the next. Peter didn't see much of it, but what he did see urged his foot to push on the gas pedal a little harder. Not that it did much good. He already had the pedal pushed against the floor.

"What in the name of St. Peter's shit was that?" Boone shouted, eyes wide with surprise, a hint of a grin on his lips. Peter understood that the smile wasn't some kind of mania or psychotic thrill-seeking rush, but a genuine delight at still being alive.

Peter was smiling, too.

A brush with death, and the adrenaline that brings, can leave survivors feeling elated for a bit. The numbing shock, body shakes, and sleepless nights of fear-induced sweat would come later.

"Apex."

"That worse than those hairy things?" Boone looked up over the seat through the rear window. "Which, by the way, are still on our tail."

Peter looked in the rearview again. Four of the six Woolies and two of the Riders had already passed the creature in the swamp, cloaked in shadow. If the Riders were operating under the normal guiding force that drove most ExoGenetic species—insatiable hunger—they would have turned on the newcomer. Instead, they'd continued pursuing Peter and Boone, which meant they had objectives. They were coordinated. Thinking. Evolving intelligence that could guide their hunger. But more than all of that, it meant the attack was something else. Something that confirmed Peter's fears.

It was personal.

This wasn't random.

Wasn't hunger-driven.

This was revenge. Against him. Against his family.

He pushed the pedal even harder, but it still did nothing to help. The Dodge Ram was a powerful vehicle, but weighed down with armor, weapons, and ammunition, it was closer to a tank than a dragster. Acceleration was a slog, but once it got going, there wasn't much that could stand in its way. Unfortunately, both a Woolie and whatever had lunged across the road, were big enough to stand up to the truck. Fortunately, they were all still in the rearview. But Peter suspected there would be more between them and the camp.

That's where Ella is, he thought, *that's where Kenyon will be.*

"There it is!" Boone shouted. "I see it in the swamp! Keeping pace with the stragglers!"

Peter glanced from the rearview to the side-view mirror. He flinched when a massive shape exploded from the swamp, clutched the last Woolie and Rider in its jaws and plunged back into the water on the far side of the road. The fifty-foot-long creature was easy to identify this time. The long body and ridged tail were familiar to anyone who had spent time in the swamps of the South.

"Gall dang, that's a croc!" Boone's smile had faded. He'd spent enough time in the swamps to have a healthy fear of the average American alligator, which grew to a maximum length of fifteen feet and weighed five hundred pounds. They were man-eaters capable of dismembering, consuming, and crapping out even the largest and strongest human male. But this thing...it was worse. And not just because it was larger.

"It's coming back!" Boone shouted.

Peter watched the action in the mirror. Trees burst and toppled over, giving way to the largest ExoGen Apex he had ever seen, larger and more intimidating than even the matriarch Stalker. It didn't have a pack to add to its strength, but it didn't need one. The jaws were large enough and powerful enough to snatch up a Woolie the size of *Beastmaster* and kill it with a quick squeeze. Alligators can bite down with the force of 2,125 pounds per square inch, strong enough to flatten a human skull or shatter the intensely strong shell of a snapping turtle. The Nile Crocodile can take down even tougher prey with its 5,000 PSI bite, but even that monster, at 20 feet long was dwarfed by the Apex surging back onto the road. It probably could crush down with 30,000 PSI—more than enough to mash the armored truck, but that, at least, would be a merciful end. Anything human caught in those jaws would be instantly reduced to paste. There would be no pain, just an immediate lack of existence.

The ExoGator hit the pavement running.

Not running, Peter thought, *galloping.*

Alligators were one of the most perfectly evolved species on the planet. They'd been around for a hundred and fifty million years without needing to evolve. While other species came and went, alligators and crocodiles, dominated their habitats. They were already Apex predators when the Change began, and even with RC-714 unlocking their genetic potential, they didn't have much need to evolve. That was, until food became scarce, and they had to move over land. So, this alligator reached back into its past, found an ancestor with long limbs, and evolved to run. Fast.

The second Woolie was snatched up from behind, mewling briefly as its backside was flattened inside the mighty jaws. When the hairy beast fell limp, the alligator gave two shakes of its head, severing its prey in two. While still running, the creature tipped its head back and swallowed the Woolie's ass-end whole. Then it set its sights on the rest of them.

"Here!" Boone shouted. "Here, here, here! Turn left!"

Peter slammed the brakes and turned the wheels. Tires squealed out a high-pitched staccato rhythm as they bounced over the pavement. A lighter vehicle would have flipped. Facing the wide dirt road, Peter accelerated, kicking up a cloud of dust that would let their pursuers know exactly where they'd fled.

The cabin filled with the grinding rumble of loose rocks beneath the tires. Peter's hands tingled as the steering wheel shook in his iron grip. He twitched the wheel back and forth, eyes glued to the winding dirt road, delicately balancing between speed and control. One wrong move and they'd slam into a tree or plunge into the swampy waters. Whether or not they perished on impact, stopping would be a death sentence.

When Boone climbed into the back seat, Peter tried his hardest to not look at the man. "What are you doing?"

"Manning the big gun, right?"

Peter's instinct was to argue. To call it what it was: too dangerous. But Boone wasn't his family. The man was a fighter and, if Peter was honest, expendable. They had bonded as warriors in the heat of battle, but family still came first, and a hail of 5.56 X 44mm bullets spraying from the backside of *Beastmaster* would increase his odds of reaching them. "Do it."

The rear window slid open just in time to allow a pain-wracked bellow to fully permeate the cabin. They'd just rounded a bend and couldn't see the ExoGator or the Woolies, but it sounded like the alligator was continuing its mobile smorgasbord. On one hand, Peter was glad for the help, on the other, he knew the line of entrées ended with him and Boone.

Peter focused on the wheel, slowing a bit as they approached a sharp turn. Boone was halfway through the small opening in the back window, worming his way into the truck bed. If the truck turned too hard, the man might fly off the side. Peter wished he'd had time to explain the rubber band system he'd repaired with Jakob. Once strapped in, the machine-gunner could be jounced around without fear of falling away. But there wasn't time.

Peter heard Boone chamber the first round. A few seconds after rounding the bend, the machine gun beat a rhythm in the air, keeping time with a frenetic metronome. Fifteen rounds later, the weapon went quiet, replaced by a string of curses.

"What's happening?" Peter asked. The side-view mirror revealed three Woolies still in pursuit, two with riders. They were a hundred feet back and gaining with each thunderous foot fall.

"I can't hit shit while we're moving around," Boone called, his voice nearly inaudible as wind whipped the words away.

"You want me to stop?" Peter asked with a grin.

"You shitt'n me? Fuck no!"

Soldiers joked. In the quiet times. In the face of bullets. Even in the face of death. Humor kept them human. Kept them sane. At least until they went home. Humor tended to stay behind, on the battlefield.

A second blast of machine gun fire ripped through the air. The lead Woolie twitched, stumbled, and then kept on coming. But its rider, flailed back in a burst of red, toppled through the air, and rolled to a ragdoll stop in the dirt road. The man-thing lay still for just a moment before the last thunderous shaggy beast crushed him beneath its feet, leaving a trail of gooey red in its wake.

Peter shouted in surprise as the alligator catapulted out of the swamp beside the road and snapped at the Woolie, which leaned to the side, evading the bite. Then, instead of continuing the pursuit, the Woolie turned to face its adversary and charged, its deadly, scooped horn leading the way. The horn was no doubt sharp enough to pierce the gator's thick flesh, and the Woolie powerful enough to drive it deep, but would it be enough to kill the monster?

Not even close.

The ExoGator twisted its head around toward the Woolie. Instead of plunging the horn into the gator's side, it ran headlong into those gaping jaws. Teeth impaled flesh. Blood sprayed. And with a quick upward snap, the Woolie was sent cartwheeling through the air, dropping back down far out of sight.

Boone adjusted his aim.

Puffs of dirt raced up the road, making a line toward the gator and then striking it. The struck flesh rippled like water, but there were no holes. No spurts of red. No explosions of gore from the far side. The gator flinched but was not injured. It clamped its empty jaws together, the clomp loud enough to hurt Peter's ears. Then it was up, resuming its horrible gallop.

As Peter followed the bending road to the left, he saw the ExoGator run straight, plunging back into the swamp. While *Beastmaster* and the short-legged, hairy Woolies were confined to the road, the gator moved freely through the swamp, instinct guiding it to follow the old adage: the fastest route between two points is a straight line.

"Hang on!" Peter said, pushing the truck toward unsafe speeds and then beyond. The curving road took them directly into the gator's path, and he didn't want to be there when it arrived.

The roadside crumbled as the truck skirted the edge.

The rear tire slipped over the side for a moment before jouncing back up, nearly knocking Boone from his post. He shouted a string of Southern obscenities, most of which Peter didn't understand, but he held on. When the road straightened out, they picked up speed, and just in time.

"Here it comes!" Boone shouted. His voice was followed by the machine gun's roar. Peter looked out the side window. The gator was lunging toward them, mouth open, loping through the four-foot water like it was a road. Small red spots pocked its pink tongue, the bullets punching through, but doing nothing to slow the behemoth.

Movement in the side-view got Peter's attention. Two Woolies and a single Rider were right behind them. The Rider was on his feet, legs bent, clutching handfuls of clumpy hair.

He's going to jump, Peter thought.

But then the view became a mass of tangled and tumbling limbs. The croc missed the truck and slammed into the two Woolies. All three beasts went down in a writhing mass of angry limbs. The impact and subsequent battle would give Peter and Boone time to escape, or at least increase their lead. Peter focused once more on the road ahead, until he heard thumping in the back.

"You okay?" Peter shouted back over his shoulder.

There was a thump and a gasped shout. "H-help!"

The rearview showed Boone in the clutches of a Rider, its arms wrapped around his back, squeezing him tight. The hairy man-thing had its mouth open so wide that it looked dislocated, the hooked four-inch-long spears it had for lower teeth just inches from Boone's neck. The only reason it hadn't taken a bite was because Boone had both hands on the creature's face, holding it back, but inch by inch, he was losing ground with each beat of his heart. The man had just seconds to live, and then Peter would be next.

19

Eddie Kenyon was impressed. After seeing the number of still-human men at the gas station, he suspected one of Ella's biodomes would be nearby. Sure, the swamps could be scavenged for food, but the men had looked well fed. And he'd seen some of their stomach contents spilled out on the floor of the moving truck. The men were eating vegetables, and not the kind that could be foraged. His suspicions were soon confirmed when the men spilled their guts, literally and figuratively. He learned the location of the camp, known as Hellhole, and that Peter, Ella, and the kids had been taken there as captives. Easy pickings.

After leaving a contingent of male Chunta and their steeds behind to watch the gas station, Kenyon, Feesa, and the other female warriors had trudged through the swamps, moving slowly and quietly, until they spotted the twenty-foot-tall wall that looked like it could take a beating. They wouldn't be forcing their way inside, though he suspected the large gates might eventually give way to a persistent assault from their steeds.

But the wall wasn't what had him on edge. From his perch in a tall tree, he looked out at what might be the last vestige of civilization outside San Francisco.

The camp was vast. More like a small town. There were five biodomes. He could see the lush plant life growing within them. Enough to feed dozens of people. The shanty town surrounding the farmhouse at the camp's core looked like it could house a hundred people. And there were signs of activity everywhere he looked. Everything was maintained. Footprints were scattered about the barren earth. And the land itself was completely clear of ExoGenetic crops, a feat that could only be accomplished through persistent and daily labor, the evidence of which could be seen in the form of ash. There was a layer of it mixing with the brown soil beneath. The place looked like it should be a beehive of activity.

But there was no one in sight.

No workers. No guards.

No Ella.

Were we spotted at the gas station? Kenyon wondered. *Did they evacuate? Are they hiding inside?*

He could tell Feesa wanted to leap the wall and find out for herself, but she didn't fully understand the strength of mankind. The men they'd attacked earlier were unsuspecting, caught out in the open. It had hardly been a fight. But here, with a wall separating them, if the occupants of Hellhole were ready for a fight, the Chunta could be mowed down in a hail of gunfire before reaching the shanty town. For all he knew, there was a minefield between them and the house.

He placed his hand on her hairy arm and felt the muscles beneath quivering with anticipation. Her mind was primitive, but she understood that this was the place they'd been told Peter Crane had been taken. "Patience."

Her hand squeezed and crushed the branch to which she clung. They were in the trees again, just high enough to spy inside the camp, but not close enough to leap over the wall. The trees had been cleared away, thirty feet back. The space between the tree line and the wall had been filled in by densely packed cauliflower plants. The bulbous white heads would provide firm enough footing, but each step would let out a rubbery crunch. They wouldn't be able to approach without announcing it. And leaping over would be impossible from this distance, even for Feesa. Whoever built this place had planned its defenses well.

They're in there, he thought. *Waiting. And with those biodomes, starving them out isn't an option. Damn.*

"We go," Feesa said, pointing at the farmhouse. "Revenge inside."

"We wait," Kenyon replied, then repeated the mantra that had carried the Chunta this far and helped them overcome a myriad of deadly encounters. "Watch. Listen. Think. Plan. Attack."

"Just attack," Feesa said.

"Then Chunta die."

Feesa looked about ready to tackle him out of the tree and rip out his throat. The female warrior had bonded with him in more ways than one, but the Chunta, like all ExoGenetic creatures, were guided by instinct first and intellect only on rare occasions. Luckily for Kenyon, Feesa was one of the most rare ExoGenetic creatures, capable of rational thought, and at times, restraint. She opened her mouth, sliding the long, hooked teeth from their cheek pockets, and hissed at him. But she didn't attack.

Kenyon wasn't sure if Feesa had simply retained a portion of her human intelligence, or if she'd lost it and then evolved a new primitive intelligence. That she could still speak limited English suggested the former, but if she had any memory of her life before the Change, she never spoke of it, nor seemed disturbed by what she had become. *Smart enough to understand revenge*, Kenyon believed, *but not emotionally complex enough to experience regret.*

Kenyon on the other hand... Regret fueled his need for revenge. He'd put his trust—his love—in a woman who betrayed him. Who might have planned to betray him from the very start. He'd been a tool. Nothing more. And even after several weeks, his chest still burned with a new-found fury. Not because he'd never really had her, or lost her to another man, but because despite all of that, he still loved her. And he hated her all the more for it.

Sloshing water revealed the return of their scouts. They'd sent two of the females around the wall's perimeter, searching for weak points or signs of life. Feesa exchanged words in the Chunta's ape-like language, which was composed of grunts, a few actual words, and a good number of hand gestures. The returning females scaled the trees as the conversation came to a close, joining the fifteen other warriors waiting to attack. Their steeds were positioned deeper in the swamp, tended to by a handful of smaller males, all waiting to be called to action.

"Wall all around," Feesa told Kenyon, tracing a circle in the air with her black, claw-tipped finger. "No people." She snarled, her embedded teeth stretching the skin of her face. It was a horrifying sight, but one he'd grown accustomed to. "No revenge."

“They’re here,” he assured her, pointing at the biodomes. “Inside. Hiding.”

Had the residents of Hellhole fled, the two scouts would have picked up their scent.

“Think,” Feesa said.

Kenyon nodded.

“Plan.” Before Kenyon could agree, she added. “My plan.” Then she turned to one of the females perched in a nearby tree and let out a deep huff, a few barks, and a finger pointed at the house.

The female Chunta obeyed immediately, leaping down from the tree. She landed in the cauliflower with a crunch that was far from stealthy. Then she charged across the gap toward the wall, leaving a mangled path of vegetation in her wake that anyone would spot.

He wanted to chide Feesa, to tell her she didn’t think hard enough, but he knew better. Not only did she have the patience of a ball-clamped bull at a rodeo, but he understood the Chunta. They weren’t the disciplined surgical strike team Viper Squad had been. They were a brute force instrument of destruction that was made more effective when they were guided. Right now, Feesa was at the helm. If the female’s fact-finding mission bore fruit, he had no doubt that Feesa would consult him before taking action. They’d built up that trust, though he was aware seeing Peter, her hated enemy, might send her into a primal rage. And that could undo his own plans for a protracted revenge, but he could live with that. As long as Peter Crane and his brood didn’t.

He watched the female leap to the top of the wall. She clung to the carved spikes that had been hardened by fire. When she hoisted herself up into clear view of anyone on the other side, Kenyon expected a bullet to tear into her. But nothing happened. The female looked back to Feesa, who urged her onward with a bark and waved hand. The female jumped down and loped toward the house. When she reached several feet in without being blown to bits, Kenyon was convinced there was no mine field. When she strolled through the shanty town without incident, he felt positive the residents were holed up inside the house. But when she stepped onto the steps of the farmer’s porch without being gunned down, he began to doubt every scenario he’d imagined so far.

The distant female took one step at a time, her body language shifting as she did. *What the hell?* Kenyon thought. The female normally stood hunched over, but by the time she reached the top step, she was standing tall again. Like a human. *Is she trying to trick the people inside?* Kenyon nearly laughed at the ridiculousness of it. And when the female rapped her knuckles against the door, all casual, like a neighbor just stopping by to say 'hello,' Kenyon did laugh.

Feesa grunted at him. Was this all part of her plan? Had all this been transmitted during the grunting exchange? If so, the Chunta might be more intelligent than he gave them credit for. That meant they'd been holding back, hiding their true selves from him all along.

Not trusting him.

And for the first time in weeks, Kenyon wondered if he should so fully trust these...monsters.

He shook his head, unable to consider the idea of being betrayed by another woman, especially one as devolved as Feesa. She might be able to come up with a plan that involved knocking on a door, like people used to, but she lacked the subtlety to string him along for weeks.

He glanced at her, watching her yellow eyes track the movement of her scout.

How smart are you? he wondered.

Her eyes shifted toward him, meeting his gaze. She squinted.

Too smart, he decided.

Then Feesa beat her chest twice and coughed a series of low chuffs. In response, the Chunta warriors shook branches, getting geared up like ancient soldiers about to charge the field of battle. "Go," Feesa commanded, and the horde descended from the trees as one, charging the wall.

Feesa reached a hand out for Kenyon, and he understood the unspoken request. At times like this, when the tribe was on the move, Feesa would carry him. It was degrading, but he couldn't move as fast as the Chunta, and he certainly couldn't scale a twenty-foot wall without help. He hesitated for just a moment and then moved toward her arms.

But before they could leap down together, a male Chunta sprang into the tree. His sudden arrival startled Feesa, and she nearly bit his face off. The male reeled back, but then barked a few words, one of which

Kenyon recognized. "Petah." The male pointed behind them, toward the dirt road approaching the camp's gate. "Petah."

Feesa gave a nod and chuffed a few commands.

She then turned to Kenyon and said, "Peter."

She pointed toward the road. Then she said, "Ella," and pointed at the farmhouse.

Before Kenyon could respond, the large leader of the Chunta sprang from the tree and headed for the road, leaping between trunks, and calling out to the nearby males gathered with the steeds. Then Kenyon was scooped up in the male's arms. He was smaller than Kenyon, but far stronger. The male dropped down to the ground and followed the other warriors' path to the wall, which he scaled with ease, even while carrying Kenyon. Just seconds after Feesa's departure, Kenyon found himself deposited inside the compound. Ducking low, he brought his assault rifle around from his back and scanned the house, looking over the barrel. He'd taken the AR-15 from one of the dead men at the gas station. It wasn't a long-range weapon, but in his practiced hands, it would do the trick. Seeing no immediate threat, and knowing this would be his one and only chance to breech Hellhole's defenses, he joined the charge.

20

The hurled potato missed its mark—Mason's nose—but struck his forehead and sent the Ascot hat fluttering away. The blow did daze him, though, and as he stumbled back wiping at his eyes, Ella realized some of the soil clinging to the root vegetable had sprayed into his eyes.

A growl escaped her lips as she got her feet underneath her and sprang toward the man. She drove her fist into his gut. He doubled over, clutching his stomach with one hand while still pawing at his eyes with the other.

"Bitch," he hissed.

Ella hooked her fingers and swiped at his face.

She was aiming for his eyes, hoping to make his temporary vision problems permanent. Instead, she struck his cheek, digging three troughs through his skin. He screamed in pain, reeling back.

I've got him, she thought, eyeing the bulging jugular vein on his neck.

Her stomach churned. Survival in a post ExoGenetic world meant sometimes devolving into something like the beasts that now populated it. Occasionally, savagery was the only way to survive. And if it meant saving her family and ridding the world of one of its worst monsters, she would go down that path and deal with the ramifications to her soul another time.

Hooked fingers reached out, ready to latch on.

She opened her mouth, teeth bared. She lacked the sharp canines of a true predator, but the human jaw was strong enough to bite through raw human skin, muscles, and veins. One bite. *One bite and he's done.*

Ella dove for his neck.

And missed.

Mason's heel slapped into a raised garden bed, and he toppled backward. Ella sailed over his body, and when her shin struck the same bed, she sprawled onto the concrete floor, tumbling into a collection of hard metal gardening shovels, which collapsed atop her with a loud clanging.

Wounded, but not defeated, Ella shrugged off the shovels with an angry shout and leapt to her feet. She turned to continue her assault, but Mason was already up and facing her, standing in the garden bed. He had one eye squeezed shut, his left hand on his gut, and rivulets of blood running down his cheek, but his right hand clutched a handgun. He leveled the weapon at her chest. Then he moved it lower.

"How long will it take you to die, if I shoot you in the stomach?" he asked. "Hours, I imagine. Of course, shock will set in long before that. You won't struggle much then, will you? No, you'll be as docile as a bunny." His face lit up with a grin. "Oh, that's good. Bunny. That's going to be your name. I'll even get you ears and a little fluffy tail to wear." He frowned. "Or not. You won't be any fun when you're dead. My tastes aren't that aberrant."

"You need me alive," Ella said, trying hard to hide her anger. "Exo-Gen—"

"Will believe whatever I tell them. You tried to escape. I had no choice." He motioned to his bloody cheek. "I've got the wounds to prove it. And it's your daughter they really want."

He stepped out of the raised garden bed. "I wonder why that is. Why are they more interested in a little girl than in the great Ella Masse, architect of the apocalypse? Of course, maybe I'll say she escaped. Let them head off into the wilderness in search of your precious daughter. She could be my Bunny. She'd look precious in a set of ears."

Ella took a step toward him, fingers hooked once more.

He stepped back and raised the gun at her head. "Not another inch."

"They're going to kill you," she said. "You know that, right?"

"Words of a desperate woman."

"Hellhole is a direct threat to their plans."

"And what plans might that be?"

Ella wasn't entirely sure. She'd never been let in on that secret. But she had her suspicions, and she decided to share them with Mason. "They're rebooting the human race. On their terms. With the creation of RC-714, ExoGen stopped mucking with the genomes of plants and turned their attention toward other forms of life, including humanity. They're building better people. Better animals. And when the ExoGenetic world eats itself into oblivion, ExoGen would repopulate the world. Humanity as we know it is nearly extinct. It's ExoGen's creations that will inherit the Earth."

Mason stood silent for a moment, and then said, "Why would they doom themselves by creating a replacement species?"

"They're changing themselves, too," Ella said. "You've seen what RC-714 can do. Imagine if you could select the adaptations. What kind of person could you build? What kind of person could you become? And for their plan to work, humanity—all of it—needs to perish."

She motioned to the dome around them. "This place wasn't supposed to exist. You and everyone else here should be dead. The only reason you're not, is because of me. Because of the good people you locked up in a cage."

She pointed at the vegetation growing all around them.

"People who could have helped undo the damage ExoGen did... with my help. And now...you naïve, pitiful man, you're going to die."

Mason grinned. "Perhaps. But I still have something they want. I still have you. And Anne." He squinted. "She's one of them, isn't she? A new kind of person. What's different about her?"

Ella didn't move. Didn't talk.

"Tell me!" Mason stepped closer, leveling the gun at her head, finger on the trigger.

The decontamination chamber hissed and opened.

Mason didn't flinch. Didn't take his eyes off her. He'd learned how dangerous she could be.

"If this is not a matter of life and death, I will cut out your tongue and have it cooked in a pot pie." Mason didn't know to whom he was speaking. Ella didn't think it mattered. But when a man replied, Mason looked thrown.

"Uh, sir. I'm sorry, but—"

Mason gave a quick glance toward the door. Too fast for Ella to attack, but she had no intention of attacking. While Mason felt afraid to take his eyes off Ella, she was free to look at the newcomer. He looked like one of the good ol' boys from the swamps outside the compound, but she didn't recognize him. What she did recognize was the terrified expression on his face.

"What the fuck are you doing in here!" Mason shouted, and he squeezed off a round toward the door. The bullet ricocheted off the wall just below the glass dome and punched a hole into a raised garden. The man ducked back behind the door, but he didn't fully retreat. Just as fast as he'd taken the shot, Mason pointed the gun back at Ella.

"They're gone, sir!" the man shouted.

"Who is gone?"

"E-everyone."

The coiled muscles wrinkling Mason's face flattened a bit. "What do you mean, everyone?"

"The captives. The wall guards. The workers. Even your girls. They're not in the house."

"Shawna, Charlotte, and *Sabine* are missing?"

"They're not here. I checked. They're all, just...gone."

"You're the *lookout*, Chad. You can see the whole compound from the third floor. How can they just be *gone* without *you* seeing?"

"I-I..."

Even Ella could guess that the man had fallen asleep on the job. Probably had many times before. Life in Hellhole had gotten too safe. Too comfortable.

Mason fired off two more shots toward the door, shouting in anger. Ella took a step toward him but stopped when the gun swiveled back in her direction.

"There's just me and Dave left. He's watching the front door."

A hissing filled the air behind Chad. It was followed by a buzz and a flashing red light. The airlock had been overridden and the system was flashing a warning. Whoever was coming in might be contaminating all this food. And whoever it was likely knew that. Something was seriously wrong in Hellhole.

Chad ducked back inside the decontamination chamber and partly closed the door behind him. She could hear two men whispering in a rapid-fire verbal sparring match that ended with, "Shit...shit!"

The door reopened and Chad's head poked out. "Sir...someone is at the door."

"One of the missing people?" Mason asked.

"Uh...no. A big, hairy lady. She's knocking on the door."

Ella snapped her head toward Chad and took a few steps in his direction.

"Hey!" Mason said, stepping in front of her, gun raised.

She looked around him. "Describe her face."

After a few hushed words with the second man, who could only be Dave, Chad leaned back out. "Long teeth coming out of her lower jaw, poking into her cheeks. Real gnarly looking."

"Do you have any weapons in the house?" Ella asked Mason. "Bigger than that?" She motioned to the gun in his hand.

His face twitched with confusion.

"You're going to need them," she said.

He said nothing. Just stared at her.

"If you stay here, you're fucked. We're all fucked."

"What's out there?" he asked. "Who is the hairy woman?"

"Friends of Peter's wife." She looked Mason in the eyes. "Who he killed five weeks ago...in front of them."

21

During his life, formerly as a Marine, and recently as a survivor of the ExoGenetic apocalypse, Peter had made a good number of tough calls. Sometimes people died as a result. Sometimes at his hands. Most often the dead were his enemies, occasionally an ally, and once...his wife. And now he was faced with another tough call.

Option one: he could keep driving and give the wheel a quick twist, flinging both Boone and the Rider from the back of the truck. It was the safest and fastest option. The Rider probably wouldn't be killed, but Boone certainly would be, by the impact, or the Rider.

Option two: he could stop the truck and join the fight, helping Boone defeat the Rider. Boone had a better chance of survival, but would risk the Woolies, or the gator catching up. And if that happened, they were all going to die.

Option three: he could try something reckless without stopping and maybe save Boone's life in the process, or maybe screw up and crash, which would bring the outcome back to option two.

The crux of this internal struggle was Boone.

Was the man an ally? Was he an enemy?

They had fought side by side. Had saved each other's lives. That meant something among warriors. But was there a difference between trained soldiers and weekend warriors? Could he trust Boone, who had revealed himself to have a questionable moral compass? But maybe the man just needed redirection. If too much time under Mason's influence had brought out Boone's baser instincts, perhaps some solid redirection could bring out his best? Like Luke did with Vader, Peter sensed some good left in the man.

Convinced there was a chance, even if just a small one, that Boone could be redeemed, Peter's mind was made up for him.

It was time to get reckless.

With one hand on the wheel, his foot on the gas and his eyes on the road, Peter leaned forward and reached under the driver's side seat. He felt nothing at first, and he worried that Boone's men had already discovered the hidden weapon. Then his fingers grazed something solid. It had been jostled deeper under the seat. Had one of the kids been in the truck, they probably would have had an easier time retrieving it from the back.

He leaned a bit further and found himself stopped by the steering wheel. His shoulder felt about ready to pop from his socket as he stretched out. The bumpy rubber grip tickled his fingertips, but it clung to the carpeted floor, pressed down by the weapon's four and a half pounds. He needed a few more inches.

A shout of pain twisted him around. The Rider's long, hooked teeth had punctured Boone's neck. Without thought, Peter twitched the wheel to the left, kicking the truck's back end out just a bit. The sudden movement nearly toppled the two combatants in the truck bed, but the Rider adjusted its body and remained upright, slipping its teeth out of Boone's flesh.

With a shout of rage, Boone took advantage of the distraction and slipped his thumbs into the Rider's eyes. The creature howled in pain, but what might drop a man to the ground had the opposite effect on the Rider. Instead of reeling away from the thumbs about to burst its eyeballs, the Rider leaned into it, mouth open, ready to exchange its eyesight for blood.

Peter wasn't sure if the creature was just in a mindless rage, or if it understood that its body could evolve the ability to regrow eyes or develop another sense to replace its eyes. It didn't really matter. Either way, Boone was outclassed. And soon, he'd be dead.

"Shit," Peter said, twisting the wheel hard to the left, doing his best to not throw his passengers, while keeping them on the road around a bend. Back on a straightaway that continued as far as he could see, Peter stretched for the weapon again and came up short. Knowing time was short, he toggled the adjustable tilt switch on the side of the wheel, which sprang up.

It still wouldn't allow him to lean straight down, but that wasn't the plan.

Leaning to the side, Peter slipped down beneath the steering wheel. He kept one hand on the wheel with the hopes of maintaining a straight course, but when the back of his neck struck the leather wheel-grip, he was pretty sure they were careening toward the swamp at a slight angle.

Peter's hand slipped beneath the seat, easily reaching the hidden weapon. He gripped the handle, pulled it out, and sat back up. The road came back into view. So did the swamp. Peter turned hard to the right, narrowly avoiding the drop-off into several feet of water and even more muck. The sudden move kept the truck on the road but pulled Boone's feet out from underneath him. The man toppled backward, and the Rider followed him down.

The Rider lifted its head up, howling in victory. Its prey was pinned and defenseless. The creature's eyes had been compressed. One of them was a mess of blood and viscous white fluid. But the injuries only fueled its mania.

Peter lifted the Smith & Wesson Model 500 revolver and aimed it over the back seat. He had discovered the weapon behind the counter of a convenience store they had pillaged for water and any food old enough to safely consume. They hadn't found much, but the gun was a rare gift. It was a .50 caliber hand cannon. Not quite as long barreled as Dirty Harry's, but equally as powerful. And that meant a few things. First, anything roughly the size of a human hit by a single round would find itself with a basketball-sized hole in the bullet's wake. Something like a Woolie might take two or three rounds, but a single shot in the right spot would still do the trick. As for the gator, Peter had no idea. But the Rider? One shot was all he needed, if he didn't miss...or hit Boone.

And one shot was all he might get. Firing a weapon like the Model 500 generally required two hands. The kickback would be substantial, and if the weapon didn't buck from his hand, it might very well break his wrist. On top of that, he was firing one of the world's most powerful handguns inside the enclosed truck cabin. The padded floor and ceiling would absorb some of the sound, but every hard surface inside the vehicle would reflect the cacophonous boom right back into Peter's ears.

This is going to hurt, he thought, leveling the sight through the back window. As soon as he drew a bead on the monster, its lower jaw opening wide enough to envelop Boone's head and whatever limb he tried to defend himself with, Peter pulled the trigger.

The explosion slammed into Peter's ears and forced his eyes shut.

He didn't see the weapon tear free from his hand, but he felt it leave his fingers and then strike his forehead. As though the impact of a spiraling four-pound revolver wasn't bad enough, it was the scorching hot barrel that struck him, hissing briefly as it burned a red line above his brow.

When he opened his eyes again, the first thing he saw was a clean hole in the rear window. The bullet had punched through so suddenly that the rest of the glass remained intact. And beyond the window... nothing.

Did the Rider bite down?

Did he miss?

When the Rider hunched its back and rose into view, Peter knew he had failed, and that Boone was dead.

Then the rest of the hairy body rose up, and he relaxed. Red blood chugged from a gaping wound where its head had been.

Boone sat up, hands on the headless Rider's chest. He pushed the creature up and then shoved it hard, sending the ragdoll body toppling into the road.

When the scent of smoke tickled his nose, Peter faced forward. He shouted but could only feel the air bursting from his lungs. Aside from a buzzing, he heard nothing else. Peter turned hard, following a fresh bend in the road. When the big truck was back under control, he lowered the steering wheel and pulled the revolver off his pants, which had begun to burn. He placed the cooling weapon in the passenger's seat and focused on the road.

A moment later, he jumped when something tapped his shoulder. He spun to find Boone leaning in through the back window, shouting something.

Peter tapped his ear. Shouted, "Can't hear! Gun was loud!"

Boone shouted something else. Peter still couldn't hear him, but the man's smile and obvious relief hinted that Boone was thanking him. And then everything changed. Boone's face morphed back into fear. His eyes wide. His forehead a mountain range of wrinkles. Peter could even hear a little bit of Boone's screamed warning. All of that and Boone's pointed finger turned Peter's gaze forward. To the road. And what stood in its center.

A Rider.

Female.

She was large. Taller than Peter. In one hand she held a spear. Her free hand was pointed at the truck. *No,* Peter thought. *At me.*

On the surface, this Rider looked a lot like Kristen had. For a moment, he wondered if she had somehow survived their last encounter and was back to haunt him. But the eyes were wrong. Where he saw a hint of the wife he'd once had in Kristen's eyes, here he saw only a monster.

A monster out for revenge.

The idea that this creature might have followed him all this way simply because he killed the tribe's ExoGenetic leader surprised him. Then again, Ella and Anne had been pursued halfway across the country by the even less intelligent Stalker pack.

Peter eased up on the gas.

He heard Boone shout. His voice sounded like he was speaking through a tin can. "What are you doing? Run it down!"

Peter's instincts were the same as Boone's.

"Kill it and grill it!" Boone shouted, his voice clearer.

Well, not exactly the same, Peter thought, slowing even more.

At first, he wasn't exactly sure why he was slowing down, rather than speeding up. But then he figured it out. The soldier's worst enemy.

Empathy.

For the enemy.

Peter stopped thirty feet short of the lone female. It wasn't until he opened the door and stepped out that he noticed she wasn't actually alone. Hidden just inside the swamp on either side of the road were seven Woolies and four male Riders. *Where are the other females?* he wondered, scanning the area, but then he refocused on the living blockade hidden in the swamp. Had he sped through the female's position, he would have been met head on by a living wall.

And the confused and somewhat disappointed look on the female's face told him that might have been their plan. She and Boone were equally confused by his actions.

"Hey," Boone whispered, as Peter stepped down onto the dirt road. He was back inside the truck cab, leaning between the front seats. He handed the Model 500 handgun to Peter, keeping it below the window. "If yer fixin' on going out there, best take some protection. Also, you know, there's a good chance we might have trouble crawl'n up our backside any moment now."

Peter took the weapon and slipped it behind his back, tucking it into his pants. Then he stepped out from behind the door, hands raised. He walked toward the lone female, who was now even more confused, but had yet to take on an aggressive stance.

All that changed when Boone slipped back into the pickup's bed and swiveled the machine gun forward. The female raised the spear, cocking it back, ready to throw.

But she didn't.

Instead, she waited, and with every step Peter took, her arm lowered a little further. She might want vengeance on Peter for what he did—he couldn't think of any other reason she'd be here—but she was also smart enough to be curious about his strange response to her aggression.

She's still an ExoGen, Peter thought. If she moved to throw that spear, he wouldn't hesitate to draw the handgun and fire. He was no Billy the Kid, but he could draw a gun and fire accurately, faster than most, especially at such close range.

Twenty feet from the ExoGenetic woman, Peter stopped. They stood in silence for a good ten seconds, and then Peter spoke first, offering the only words he could think of that might carry his true feelings about what had happened to his wife. "I'm sorry."

22

Ella sat on the first-floor staircase, hands linked behind her head as instructed. She kept the grip light, her head still recovering from the blow that knocked her unconscious. Mason stood at the bottom of the stairs, revolver leveled at Ella, but his eyes on the front door. The hairy woman standing on the far side of the door, visible through the side windows, was swaying back and forth impatiently, waiting to sell Girl Scout cookies, or Mormon Jesus, or Jehovah's Witness Jesus. She was a Rider. There was no doubt about that. The hooked teeth were impossible to mistake, and that adaptation, combined with the hair-covered body, was an unlikely combination to be repeated.

But why was it knocking on the door?

To call it strange behavior was an understatement. ExoGenetic creatures were driven by instinct. By *hunger*. They didn't knock on doors. Then again, they weren't supposed to talk, either, but Peter had communicated with Kristen before he shot her. Perhaps the other Riders could speak as well?

It didn't matter. None of it.

What mattered was that the creature outside wasn't just her enemy, but the enemy of every living thing that wasn't also a Rider or a Woolie. It was a predator. They were its prey.

"You need to give me a weapon," Ella said.

Mason waved her off, keeping his attention on the door, but his weapon trained on her. Dave stood by the door, clutching an assault rifle that he didn't look very comfortable holding.

Ella guessed he'd never fired the weapon, at least not at anything living. The men outside the compound, the ones who had taken them captive, were the real fighters. Dave and Chad guarded the house, and manned the third-floor lookout, but they weren't even good at that.

"Mason," Ella said. "The creatures outside are killers. Savages. And my kids are missing."

"They're not all your kids," he said, turning toward her. "Are they?"

"They are now."

"How noble of you."

"Let me save them. Let me help you fight."

"What good are hair and teeth and claws against bullets?" Mason asked.

Ella laughed. "When was the last time you stepped outside these gates?"

He said nothing, which was answer enough. He hadn't been in the wild since before the Change. He'd heard stories but filtered through the bravado of his men.

"I should have known," Ella said. "Rape and subjugation are the tactics of a coward."

Mason's left eye twitched, but he said nothing. Just stared.

Then the Rider knocked again, louder this time, hard enough to rattle the thick wood.

"Shit," Dave said, taking a step back from the door.

Chad entered the foyer, arms clutching an array of weapons. Rifles and assault rifles. All of them presumably loaded, but there wasn't a spare magazine or even loose ammunition in sight. He stumbled, fell to his knees, and let the weapons clatter on the hard wood floor. "Sorry, sorry."

The barrel of each and every weapon was pointed in Dave's direction, and when he saw them hit the floor, he reversed course, back toward the door. His fear of a misfire wasn't unfounded, but in that moment of confusion, he mistook the falling weapons as the greater danger.

Ella slowly backed up a step.

Dave's back pushed against the side window beside the door. The solid glass panel was ten inches wide and four feet tall. It shattered inward as a large, hair-cloaked fist punched through. The thick fingers opened like a fisherman's net, wrapping around Dave's face. The man's muffled scream rose to a high pitch as he was lifted off the floor, and then was silenced as he was yanked through the window.

The ten-inch-wide space was far too narrow for Dave's body. As his chest shot through the space, the jagged edge peeled away his shirt, and his skin from both his chest and his back. His sudden motion came to a jarring halt as his buttocks and hips became jammed in the narrow space. Past the thudding of his twitching legs, there was a pop and a slurp.

Then the body, half inside, half outside, hung limp and still.

Even Ella was immobilized by shock.

She, Mason, and Chad stood motionless, eyes on Dave's savaged remains.

Five quiet seconds ticked by.

The spell was broken when Dave's head and torn-free spine arced back through the window like one of those 'The More You Know' stars. And there was a lesson here: never underestimate the ExoGens. It was a lesson Ella found herself learning over and over. Making any kind of assumption about any ExoGenetic life—in this case that the Riders lacked the intelligence, mental and emotional, to track down their slain leader's killer—was deadly.

Ella backed away another step, preparing to flee upstairs. The windows on the second floor were barred, but the third floor might not be. And if it was, maybe she could hide?

She stopped when a wide-eyed Mason turned to her. His face was slick with sweat and his lips were quivering. His first real up close and personal experience with an ExoGen wasn't quite as glorious as his men had likely described it. "Okay."

"Okay, what?"

"A weapon. Take your pick."

"You aren't afraid I'll shoot you?"

He frowned but then said, "I'd rather be shot than end up like that." He waggled his revolver at Dave's *The More You Know* head and spine.

Ella moved down a step, not fully convinced. But a second look at Dave's head, torn free from his body, twisting coils of nerves still attached to the spine, helped cover up her animosity for Mason. She would fight beside her enemy, for now, and if they survived, she'd put a bullet in his dick. And then his head.

She stood and made it two steps down before a voice called through the broken window. "Hello, in there."

The voice wasn't just human. It was familiar. It was unmistakable. Eddie Kenyon had survived, and he'd tracked her down. She closed her eyes and shook her head. They should have killed him. Instead, they'd allowed this very dangerous man to befriend and join forces with inhuman savages, all of whom wanted her and Peter dead.

"Don't answer him," Ella warned, but Mason's body language had already shifted. While the old man was no good in a fight against monsters, he could verbally spar with the best of them.

Mason swiveled his handgun back around toward Ella's chest. "Sit."

Ella sneered but obeyed. She wasn't far from the weapons but couldn't risk diving for one until Mason's eyes shifted away from her.

"I said hello in there," Kenyon repeated, louder. Closer.

From her perch on the stairs Ella saw more hairy bodies climb up onto the porch. They spread out to either side. Waiting. Strategizing. When the time came, they could each plunge through a window and bring the fight inside. Mason and Chad might get off a few shots, but the brute force and speed of the Riders would quickly overwhelm them.

"Sorry for the messy introduction," Kenyon said, "but these ladies aren't really known for their subtlety. Let's call it a show of force. A taste of things to come, if you do not reply right this *God-damned second.*"

"We're here," Mason said. "We're listening."

"Excellent," Kenyon said. "So, let's get right to it. We have come a long way and my patience is like paper."

"Yes, sir," Mason said. "What can we do for you?"

Ella enjoyed hearing the terror in Mason's voice but would have preferred it be in response to her, not Kenyon and a bunch of female Riders.

"We are looking for a group of people and have reason to believe you are sheltering them here."

Mason's gaze became incredulous. Ella could nearly hear his thoughts, 'You brought this upon us?' If bending his index finger didn't cause him so much pain after cracking against her skull, he might have even pulled the trigger, but he refrained and said, "Anybody that's here, that you want, you can have."

"Appreciate that," Kenyon said. "Let's start with Crane. Peter Crane."

Incredulity turned to anger. "He's not here."

"Don't fuck with me." Kenyon's voice shifted into rage so fast that Ella wondered if he'd resorted to eating ExoGenetic food.

Maybe he's not fully human anymore, Ella thought. *Maybe he's one of them.*

"He left 'bout two hours ago. But he'll be back. We have his kids."

"They inside the house?" Kenyon asked. "Because there's nobody out here."

"That wasn't you?" Mason asked.

"What wasn't me?"

"The missing people."

"You are the first person I've spoken to since I had a sit-down chat with your men at the gas station. What's your name?"

"M-Mason."

"Mason. My name is Edward Kenyon. You can call me Eddie. You sound like a reasonable man. Like a real Southern gentleman. How about we stop talking through a closed door and you tell me where everyone is. If this is an ambush, I—"

"Ella is here," Mason blurted out. "I don't know about the kids, I swear. But Ella is here. Right behind me. You want her, too, right?"

After a beat of silence, Kenyon spoke.

"You have no idea."

"I'll bring her out." Mason shoved the gun at Ella's face and motioned for her to stand up. "Just...Just get down from the porch, okay? Give us some breathing room."

Heavy feet stomped over the front porch as the shadows hovering by the windows faded back.

"Come on out," Kenyon called.

Mason hissed at Chad and then motioned to the door with his chin. "Open it."

Chad looked horrified, but part of him was still equally afraid of Mason. He flitted to the door like a nervous mouse, starting and stopping, until his hand wrapped around the knob and twisted. The door swung open, smooth on its hinges. He pushed open the storm door next, cringing as the glass pushed up against Dave's headless and gored body. Dave's wet flesh squeaked against the glass, leaving deep red smears.

Kenyon stood ten feet back with a group of female Riders. He stood partly behind two of them.

Living shields, Ella thought, wondering if the two creatures understood why he had positioned them that way. They might not fully understand the danger posed by the weapons Mason and Chad carried, but Kenyon certainly did. And he was armed with an assault rifle of his own, though he kept the barrel low and unthreatening.

Mason waved Ella out and she complied.

As she passed Mason, she met his eyes and offered him a fiendish grin. "Your funeral."

A flash of doubt and horror flickered over his face, doubly so when he noticed she'd ripped her shirt, revealing the bra he'd supplied her. Then she was outside, on the porch, limping, crying, and holding one hand to her head. "Eddie, thank God."

Kenyon's face was a frozen mask. He didn't look angry or confused, but Ella knew that it was his poker face. Just because he wasn't showing emotion didn't mean he wasn't feeling it. The question was, what was he feeling? Anger? Hate? Concern? The emotion she was hoping for, the one that would get her the result she sought, was love. If he loved her still, despite her betrayal, he wouldn't be able to ignore what she said next.

Stumbling toward the steps, she said, "He sent Peter away to be killed. He's probably already dead." That didn't get a reaction, but it wasn't really supposed to. That information was only offered to lend credence to what came next. "He kept me here. Dressed me like this." She motioned to her Southern belle outfit and let her hand stop over her chest, pulling Kenyon's attention to the lacy bra he knew she would have never worn by choice. "Eddie..." She fell to her knees, eyes on the ground and the large hairy feet at the bottom of the steps. "He *raped* me."

23

Peter gauged the distance between him and the Rider, then took a step closer. If the creature attacked, it would be close, but he thought he could manage it. They'd have to then survive the horde of male Riders and Woolies positioned on either side of the road, and whatever might still be following them, but facing problems one at a time was the only way to ensure things got done right. It had been drilled into his head during Marine training, and it made a lot of real-world, logical sense. In the same way as finishing folding laundry before starting the dishes, you didn't aim at a new target until the first was down. Getting ahead of yourself was a good way to get dead, he'd been taught. Just one of many lessons learned during his time as a CSO that kept him alive.

So, he ignored the future problems presented by the monsters closing in from all directions and focused on the one standing right in front of him, spear aimed to kill, but still in hand.

The creature was showing restraint.

And the look in its eyes—confusion—suggested it had understood his apology.

"I'm sorry," he said again.

No reply.

"For Kristen."

No reply. No reaction.

"For killing your leader."

The female snarled. That resonated.

"Family," she said, her voice deeper than his. "Kill family."

The words stung. Peter hadn't just killed his wife and his son's mother, but this Rider's surrogate family member as well. *No wonder they tracked us down.* But what was Kristen to this Rider? A sister? A mother figure? Something more...intimate? Kristen was as heterosexual as someone could be, but she'd changed in nearly every other way, so it wasn't impossible.

"Leader," Peter said, and then patted his chest with both hands. "She was my wife. *My* family."

The female growled again, and then stabbed her spear into the dirt road. She let go of the weapon that she really wouldn't need if she decided to kill him and pointed at his chest. "You killed family."

"*Protected* family," Peter said. "Kristen—your leader—tried to eat my son. Her son. She tried to *eat* him."

The female showed no reaction, including anger, which Peter took as a good sign.

"Do you understand?" Peter asked.

A nod.

"Do you have a son? A child?"

The Rider's face contorted. "Not...anymore."

Peter didn't have to ask. He knew the child's likely fate. But the Rider seemed to be in a sharing mood.

"Daughter." The female linked her arms like she was holding a baby. She rocked them back and forth, looking at the memory of a bundle. For a moment, her eyes looked nearly human. Then her natural ferocity returned. "Killed by...monsters." She opened her arms, looking at the gnarly hair dangling from them. "Like me."

"You would kill to protect your daughter," Peter said. It wasn't a question. With parents, it never was.

"I did kill," came the quiet answer.

"I did the same," Peter said. "I killed my wife, your leader. I killed her to protect my son. I am sorry for that, but...I would do it again."

The female grunted, and Peter had trouble hiding his shock. Was he getting through to her? Could this creature reason? He'd been surprised when Kristen was able to recognize him and Jakob, and to think clearly enough to demand her son back. But this...this was a step beyond. The Riders were evolving, becoming more intelligent. And with intelligence, they were gaining understanding. And empathy.

But all the empathy in the world couldn't change the fact that he and Boone had killed even more Riders, though most of the dead could be chalked up to the ExoGator. Then again, the Rider caste system seemed to value the much larger and stronger females. So far, he'd only killed males.

He needed a way to remove himself from the hit list, and the only way he could think to do that was nearly as disturbing as ending this confrontation in battle.

Peter put a hand on his chest. "My name is—"

"Peter," the female said. "Peter Crane, enemy of the Chunta—" She opened her arms to indicate the Riders and Woolies. "—of Feesa—" She placed a hand on her hair-cloaked breast. "—and of Eddie Kenyon."

Peter tensed at Kenyon's name. He'd suspected the man's involvement but hadn't yet confirmed it. If Kenyon was working with the Riders ...the *Chunta*...then working through whatever lies, or truths, he'd told them could prove impossible. Just because they'd found some common ground didn't mean the Rider was planning to let him walk away. But this creature valued family and understood the pain of losing it so deeply that she had pursued him across a large portion of the country. He wasn't sure if Feesa's bond with Kristen had really been that deep, or if his wife's death had picked free the scab sealing in the pain wrought from her daughter's death. But there might be a way to make things right, or at least salve the wound.

He risked a step closer, hands outstretched. "Kristen. Your leader. She was like a mother to you?"

"Sister," Feesa said. "She was sister."

"She was my wife." Peter took a few steps closer. They were just ten feet apart. He looked for signs of aggression but saw none. So, he stepped even closer. Within arm's reach, he stopped. He pointed at Feesa. "Your sister." Pointed at himself. "My wife."

A nod and grunt were confirmation that she heard him, but it was the sudden blink and widening of her eyes that told him she understood. He waited for her to say it. She looked up, eyes meeting his. "Brother."

In-law, he thought, *but close enough.* He smiled, reached out slowly and placed a hand on her hairy arm. "Sister."

And then he sweetened the deal. "My son. My daughter."

Feesa inhaled loudly, a smile on her lips. Her shifting teeth tugged at the skin of her face where the tips were hidden. "Nephew," she said. "Niece!"

Peter nodded.

In a screwed up, post-Change world, none of this was far from reality. There were no laws to govern such things, and family could be determined however anyone chose, especially if that someone was strong enough to tear a man in half.

Peter stayed silent. Feesa's twitching eyebrows reminded him of the Golden Retriever he'd had growing up. Named Mr. Miggins, the dog's eyebrows spoke a language of their own. Young Peter had tried to find meaning in the dancing brows, but came to the conclusion that Mr. Miggins's eyebrows revealed he was pondering something—usually food or tennis balls. But Feesa had a bit more going on upstairs than Mr. Miggins.

Her deep thinking about new familial connections ended with a look of grave concern. One that Peter shared.

"Kenyon?" he asked.

"Will kill family," she said, and then added the magic words that gave Peter an inkling of hope. "Our family."

"We can stop him," Peter said. "Together."

Feesa grunted with something that sounded like agreement, but then she cocked her head to the side and looked beyond Peter. "But first, that."

She said it so casually, that Peter thought she must be referring to *Beastmaster* or Boone, who was still manning the gun. But then Peter felt a rumbling underfoot. As he turned to look, he knew what he was going to see, but still felt a measure of shock upon seeing it.

The ExoGenetic alligator, bits of flesh and clumpy brown hair dangling from its jaws, galloped toward them. A cloud of dust billowed in its wake, giving it the appearance of some kind of hellish beast. But this was no denizen of a supernatural underworld. It was a flesh and blood creature, modified by science gone awry, but still mortal.

Still killable.

"Boone!" Peter shouted, pointing at the gator. He turned back to Feesa. "Let it pass. Then attack from behind."

When Feesa began barking at the surrounding Riders in a language that was far from the English language, Peter assumed she understood, and he ran for the truck. He leapt into the driver's seat and shouted out through the open rear window. "Hang on and aim for the eyes!"

"Just go, man!" Boone shouted, and then he yelped in surprise as the whole truck rocked to the side.

Peter glanced back. Feesa had leaped into the truck bed beside Boone, spear in hand. She crouched and looked through the window. "Go!"

Well, all right then, Peter thought, and crushed his foot against the gas pedal. *Beastmaster* surged through the first twenty miles per hour of acceleration and then started to crawl slowly faster. Peter looked in the rearview. The gator was going to reach them long before they matched its top speed. If his new friends didn't help balance the scales, they were all dead. Given the ease with which the gator had dispatched both Riders and Woolies during the earlier pursuit, he didn't have high hopes.

24

Starting an insurrection was far easier than Jakob imagined it would be. Granted, he didn't have a lot of experience in such things, but he thought there would be some pushback. A fight. Maybe even a few dead people as a result. But Mason was a hated man. The guards patrolling the wall, the two guys who had been manning the gate—Marcus and Stevie—and every other hard working person inside the compound, were all but giddy about the idea.

Word spread fast, and people gathered inside the unfinished shell of the biodome still under construction. Most of it was complete, except for the glass, which had to be collected from a warehouse hundreds of miles away. The walls and the distance from the house were enough to hide them from view, though Marcus had assured him that the lookouts were notorious nappers. Still, Jakob, Anne, Alia, Carrie, and Willie had snaked through the compound using water tanks, solar panel arrays, storage sheds, and shanty villages for cover, spreading the word as they went. "Meet in the unfinished dome. We're taking Hellhole."

Jakob felt a little like Paul Revere, riding through towns, warning of the Red Coats. It was a fun fantasy and helped him cope with the reality of what was going to happen. Blood would be spilled. People would die. Maybe even him. Or Anne. Or Alia.

And now, here they were, a small army of nearly seventy-five people. It was more people than Jakob had expected to ever see in one place again—including three babies, all of them Mason's.

Despite the large number of people gathered, clumped into nervous, whispering groups, the majority of them weren't in any condition to fight. Mason kept them hungry. They were just strong enough to do their work, and desperate enough to follow his commands. Of the seventy-five souls happy to see their oppressor overthrown, only nineteen of them were in any shape to fight. And of them, only fifteen had weapons, and that included Carrie, Willie, Anne, and Alia. The guards had access to spare weapons and ammo, but not nearly enough to arm everyone. Hell, half the people weren't strong enough to hold up a rifle for more than a few seconds anyway, let alone aim and fire, and deal with the recoil.

After hiding the weak, hungry, young, and old behind the wall of the dome, the small group of fighters gathered in a tight circle. Jakob waited for someone to speak, half expecting the aged, but feisty Willie to lead the charge. But when he looked around the circle, he noticed all these people had one thing in common: they were looking at him.

Jakob's pulse quickened. Apex ExoGenetic monsters he could deal with. Public speaking, not to mention leading men and women into battle... His stomach clenched and he nearly vomited in front of them all. He focused on his father. Imagined him in this same situation. How would he handle it? How would he speak to these people?

Jakob met Anne's eyes first, her gaze so intense and confident that it bolstered him. Alia smiled at him and gave a nod. Her belief in him helped, too. But it was the desperate hunger in the eyes of the rest of them that gave him the strength to push past his anxiety. Empathy became anger, which he used to fuel his bravery. He met the eyes of the men and women around him one by one. Willie and Carrie. Marcus, Stevie, and Isabel, who'd greeted them at the gate. Three women in maid uniforms, who'd fled the house of their own accord after noticing the gathering throng headed for the unfinished dome. Out of all the people ready to fight, those three seemed the most eager. Clutching hunting and semi-automatic rifles, they looked like something out of a Grindhouse movie.

"Thanks for coming," Jakob said to the group, and he closed his eyes at how dumb it sounded.

"Ain't an AA meeting, kid," Willie said.

The joke got a nervous chuckle from everyone but the maids.

Funny or not, it helped Jakob relax. "What kind of fight can we expect?"

"Right now?" the maid named Sabine said, "Not much."

"Two guards in the lookout," said a second maid, Charlotte, "but Chad's a pushover. He'll avoid a fight if he can. Probably will root for us, though he's probably not brave enough to turn on Mason, or Dave, who *is* loyal."

The third maid, Shawna, spoke next.

"The trouble is that they have a house full of weapons and a defensive position."

"If they hold out until Boone and the boys get back..." This came from Isabel, who Boone had seemed interested in, even if he showed it in an inappropriate way.

"They're the real problem," Stevie said. "If we can't take the house before they get back, we're fucked."

"Is Boone that bad?" Jakob asked.

For a moment, no one answered. They seemed to be considering the answer. It was Isabel, the object of his rude affection, who replied. "He's a Southern prick and occasional testosterone-fueled asshole...but he also sneaks the pregnant women food. Helps maintain things when others are too tired or hungry. When Mason tells him what to do, he falls in line without complaint, but on his own... He's not all that bad. And as much as he is loyal to the old man, the boys are loyal to him. They're like frat brothers or something. With guns."

"So, if Mason is dead," Jakob said. "Is he going to be set free like the rest of us, or is he going to seek revenge?"

Isabel just shrugged. "I'll try to talk him down. He might listen to me. And if that doesn't work—"

"We'll kill him," Sabine said. "All of them."

"If we don't have to—"

Sabine cut Jakob short with a pointed finger. "You don't know what it's like inside that house. Not all the 'boys' are like Boone. Some are worse than Mason."

Half the people in the circle were nodding in agreement. This wasn't just about freedom for them, it was about vengeance. And he couldn't blame them. They had freed Lyn Askew from her Questionable cage and had given her what meager food and water the group had, but she was severely malnourished. And she sported scars and bruises from numerous beatings, some at the hands of Mason, some from Boone's men.

Knowing there was nothing he could say to undo years of abuse, Jakob nodded. "Do what you have to."

Anne's small hand gripped his wrist. She mouthed the word 'Mom' at him.

Jakob flinched back from the word. With all the excitement of mounting an insurrection, he'd forgotten about Ella. He turned to the maids. "There is a woman inside. A prisoner."

"He'll have her in one of these," Charlotte said, motioning to her uniform, "before the day is out. Probably trying to have his way with her right now. It's the same initiation we all got."

Jakob's mind froze up a bit, his thoughts stuttering as he tried to comprehend and deny the horrible words he'd just heard. "You mean... like..."

"He's going to rape her," Shawna said. "If he hasn't already. And if we don't take this place from him today, he'll keep on raping her, right along with the rest of us."

"Fuck this shit." It was Anne. Despite being the youngest and smallest member of the group, she was armed with a handgun. Three of the unarmed people were adults, but Anne had far more experience with weapons than anyone else, including Jakob. She racked the slide, chambering the first round in the 9mm handgun, and stormed toward the exit.

"Anne," Jakob said, chasing after her. "We need to do this right."

She wheeled around on him. "We need to do this *now*."

"We won't be much use to anyone if we're shot before reaching the house."

"Mom is in there. She's...she's..." Anne bared her teeth and slapped Jakob's cheek. "You just pretend to care about her. To care about both of us. But you've never really seen us as family, have you?"

"Anne," Jakob reached for her.

She swatted his hand away. "Go have your little scrum." Her forehead scrunched up, confused for a moment, like she'd said something strange. Then she refocused her glare on Jakob. "I'm going to save my mother."

Anne ran.

Despite being younger and smaller than Jakob, Anne could match his fastest sprint. He had no hope of catching her, but he wasn't about to let her charge into a fight alone. She was wrong, and stupid, and impulsive, but she *was* his sister, and he loved her, even if she didn't believe it.

"We're doing this," he said to the others as he ran backward after Anne. "Now!"

There was just a moment of hesitation, but then Alia followed. Then the maids. And then the rest of them. They had no real plan, but at least surprise would be on their side.

Anne followed the biodome walls toward the house, staying close and low, so anyone looking out from the third floor wouldn't see her. *Stupid,* Jakob thought, *but not dumb.* Jakob followed her lead and motioned for the rest to do the same. They moved in a single file line, snaking toward an uncertain fate.

Anne slowed when she reached the back of the house. She peeked into one of the quarter-sized basement windows and then scooted past. Jakob caught up with her when she stopped at the second. He put his hand on her shoulder, turning her around. "We're with you," he whispered, motioning to the line of people paused behind him. "*I'm* with you. Always will be. But you can't go out there first."

"Why not?"

"You know why," he said. Of all of them, Anne was the least expendable. She had the secrets to ending the Change locked away in her head. She needed to survive. More than him. More than Ella. More than any of the rest of them, and she knew it.

"Fine." She leaned against the wall and let him step past, but snagged his belt as he moved toward the front of the house. "Check the window, dumbass."

Jakob sighed and peeked through the basement window. Nobody home. She let go of his belt and he crept toward the front corner of the house, stopping a foot short. He turned around, eyes wide, and tapped his ear. "Listen," he mouthed to the others.

There were voices. More than one. He couldn't make out what they were saying, but he recognized Ella's voice. And then a second voice. His body tensed. The AK-47 in his hands grew slick from his sweating hands.

Eddie Kenyon...

How is he here? How is he alive?

Jakob held an open palm to the group leaning against the side of the house. Then he pointed at Willie and waved him forward. The old man hobble-jogged to the front of the line. Jakob leaned in close to the man's ear and whispered. "Keep Anne hidden and quiet."

He knew his sister might hate him for it, but if Kenyon was here, she was in more danger than ever.

"Ain't going to be easy," Willie replied. "I've seen what kind of fuss she can kick up."

"Do what you have to do," Jakob said, glancing at Anne who looked irate at being left out of the hushed conversation.

"Aight," Willie said, leaning back. Then he thrust the butt of his rifle into Anne's head. She dropped, but Willie caught her in one arm.

Jakob was enraged. If Kenyon wasn't around the corner, he would have attacked the man. Then Willie hoisted Anne up over his shoulder and mouthed, "Safe and quiet."

Despite his anger at Willie's method, Jakob couldn't deny its effectiveness. Anne would survive, and she wouldn't be around to get herself in trouble. He gave Willie a nod and watched him head back toward the biodomes. Then he heard Ella's voice loud and clear.

"He raped me."

Had Anne been conscious a few seconds longer, and heard that, she would have charged out firing. Jakob was tempted to do the same but restrained himself. Instead, he slid up to the corner, peeked one eye around the edge and snapped back. He'd seen just a snapshot of what awaited them, but it was enough.

We are so screwed, he thought, and he turned to face the group of insurgents. Killing Mason and a few men might be possible, even for this untrained group of half-starved people. But taking down Riders? His mind flashed back to his previous encounters with the savage creatures. They were stronger, faster, and far more brutal than a human being could be without consuming ExoGenetic food. But they weren't impervious to bullets. His father proved that when he put a round in his mother.

What would Dad do? he asked himself. *Would he wait? Would he fight?* Jakob's thoughts turned to Ella, the only person around the corner who was not his enemy. She was important and had become a mother-figure in his life. He wasn't sure if he loved her like he did Anne, but he cared about her. And she cared about Anne. Would die for her. Would want to be left to this fate to protect the girl. But this wasn't her call. It was his. And he knew what his father would do. Aside from Jakob, and maybe Anne, Ella was the most important person in the world to his father. And had been for far longer. He loved her. Had loved her even while he loved Jakob's mother. He might have chosen to stay with Kristen over Ella, but Jakob thought that was more for him, than his mother.

Dad would fight for her, he thought. *He would risk everything for her. Everything except for me.*

But Peter wasn't there. Jakob knew his father might sacrifice Ella to save him—he had done as much when Kenyon caught up to them at Alia's house—but that wasn't a decision Jakob could make for him. Dad loved her and would risk his life to save her. Jakob wanted to do the same. But unlike Anne, or even his father, he wasn't going to rush into a fight he didn't think he could win. Hoping he was making the right call, he turned to face the group and motioned for them to retreat.

25

"What?" Mason said. "I-I did no such thing!"

Kenyon stood his ground, eyes moving from Ella to Mason and then back again.

"We are civilized here," Mason said. "Good people. Surviving. She and her upstart family have been trying to undo all that since they arrived."

"This morning," Ella added. "We've been here just a few hours. How could we disrupt civilization that quickly?"

"The same way you ended it for the rest of the world." It wasn't a logical argument. Mason was trying to appeal to Kenyon's sense of justice. She was the woman who ended the world, after all. Or, at least, that's what the few people surviving outside of ExoGen's San Francisco facility believed. The truth was much more complex. It involved a cabal of people working with her, and then when she had tried to warn people, working against her. Since then, she'd been forced into their employ once more, against her will. Much of it was inexcusable, and in simpler times, worthy of a death sentence.

But Eddie Kenyon didn't give a shit. He drank Exo-Gen's Kool-Aid long ago. He might not know the finer details of their long-term plan—even Ella didn't know that—but whatever it was, he was on board.

Or was he?

He wasn't here with helicopters and guns a-blazin'. Instead, he kept the company of monsters. Of Riders. He looked comfortable with them, and they had apparently fully accepted him as one of the pack. This wasn't the ExoGen pickup summoned by Mason, which meant more trouble was on the way.

"Look at me." Ella pointed at her forehead. She didn't know what it looked like, but you didn't take a punch to the forehead without something to show for it. She placed her fingers against her head. It was hot and swollen and conjured a very honest hiss of pain. "I didn't do this to myself, Eddie."

From his position behind the living wall of Riders, Kenyon said, "You'll say anything to survive, Ella."

"That's right," Mason said. "She's a liar. She's—"

"Shut. Your. Mouth." Kenyon pushed his way through the two females, showing no revulsion at the coils of dirty hair rubbing up against him. Even across the twenty-foot distance, Ella could smell their stench. Kenyon seemed not to notice.

He's gone native, Ella thought, looking him over from head to toe. Kenyon was still human as far as she could see, which meant that he'd avoided eating ExoGenetic food for the past five weeks. It also meant she had a slim chance of reasoning with him. Or at the very least, manipulating his still very human emotions and desires. Betrayal or not, Kenyon was obsessed with her. He might make her life a living hell, but he'd also keep her alive, and if she was alive, there was hope. Of escape. Of survival. Of fixing the world.

Kenyon stopped ten feet away and crouched. "Tell me the truth."

There was no threat tacked on. Didn't need to be. Ella understood the situation. If Kenyon even suspected she wasn't being forthright, this would end the way he had probably been imagining it for the past five weeks. Part of it anyway. She had no idea what had befallen Peter or the children.

"Fine," Ella said, sitting up a bit straighter, letting an angry fire burn behind her eyes. Kenyon knew the look. He liked the look. Had said so on a number of occasions. "He *tried* to rape me. Was *still* trying when your hairy friend knocked on the door. It wasn't going so well for him until he drew that gun." She motioned to the revolver, which shifted toward her head. "He calls this place civilized, but—"

"Enough!" Mason lunged forward, caught a handful of Ella's shirt, hauled her up, and placed the revolver's barrel against her head.

Ella let out a yelp of surprise, despite Mason's actions being exactly what she'd been hoping for. While she was still in mortal danger, Mason had simultaneously made himself Kenyon's enemy and rekindled her ex-boyfriend's protective feelings for her. The pair had been potential allies, but now...now one would kill the other. And given the number of Riders now spreading out, poised to attack, it was pretty clear that the remainder of Mason's time on Earth could be counted down in minutes, if not seconds.

Ella tried not to smile as Mason's arm wrapped around her throat. He dragged her back toward the front door. "One move from you or your ugly bitches, and I'll put a bullet in her head."

"They can understand you." Kenyon looked at the Rider beside him. "Can't you, ugly bitches?"

"Understand," the nearest Rider said. "Kill old man now?"

Mason doubled his pace, but Ella let her body become a dead weight. He could just shoot her, but she was the only thing keeping him alive at the moment. She didn't think the house would help his situation much, but walls were walls. They provided a sense of security, even if it was unjustified.

"Chad!" Mason barked. "The door!"

But Chad had begun backing away, moving down the farmer's porch. He held one hand up and the other out to his side, clutching the assault weapon by the handle in as non-threatening a posture as possible. "If it's all the same to you..." He was speaking to Kenyon, not Mason. "I'll just walk away."

"You traitorous son-of-a-bitch! I knew I shouldn't have trusted a Yankee like you!"

"I'm from Idaho," Chad said, still backing off.

Ella could feel Mason's hand shaking, drilling the revolver's barrel into the side of her head. He wanted to shoot Chad, to vent his anger into the man's skull, but he'd leave himself wide open to attack, and not just from Kenyon or the Riders. The moment that barrel came away from her head, she would strike.

Kenyon watched Chad take a few more steps. "Wait."

Chad stopped, petrified. "Sir?"

Kenyon pointed his assault rifle at Ella. "Was she telling the truth?"

Ella understood the situation instantly. If Chad denied her story of attempted rape, Kenyon would likely shoot her and Mason. But if he confirmed it...the stalemate would continue.

Luckily for her, she had told the truth, and Chad had seen enough to at least confirm a part of it. Even better, confirming the story would keep his attention on Mason. The moment she and Mason died, all attention would shift to Chad.

"Uh, yes, sir. He had her locked up in the dome. When I found them, he had her on the ground, pistol aimed at her head. Looked like she had put up a fight, though."

"She would," Kenyon said.

"And she wasn't the first one. He dresses them up. Watches them bathe. Has a two-way mirror in the bathroom. Sometimes he—"

That was all Mason could take. He shifted the barrel of his gun away from her head and toward Chad. Ella tilted her head forward the moment the barrel cleared her skull, and then with all her strength, threw her head back.

The gun went off.

Chad screamed and dropped to the porch.

Ella's head struck the weapon, and then Mason's face, which she felt fold inward under the force of her strike. His grip loosened. She tore herself away and ducked, knowing what would happen next.

But it didn't play out exactly the way she pictured. Instead of a bullet shot by Kenyon, Mason's end came at the tip of a spear. The weapon was thrown with such force that the blade punched through his face, exited his skull, shattered the storm door's window, and embedded in the solid wood door beyond. The storm door shook from the impact, its screws tearing loose from rotted wood. The door came loose, slipped over Mason's twitching form, and toppled to the porch. Mason hung like a puppet in storage, waiting for someone to bring him to life. Then he went suddenly still. His bowels let loose, drizzling stench onto the porch.

Ella moved away from the widening puddle and caught sight of Chad, lying on the porch. He was clutching his arm, still very much alive. She gave him a glare that said, 'stay down,' and turned to face Kenyon, who seemed amused by what had just taken place.

He turned to the Rider beside him. "What was that?"

The furry female shrugged. "He said ugly."

"And not very bright," Kenyon said, eliciting a sneer from the creature, but nothing more. "He had information I could have used."

The female motioned to Mason's lifeless body.

"Ask him questions now."

Kenyon's confusion shifted toward annoyance when the female barked a laugh and the others joined in, hooting and slapping themselves.

Kenyon focused on Ella. "I keep on trying to tell them they have poor senses of humor—the punchline usually involves a corpse—but they seem to think they're ready for prime time."

Ella forced herself to stand up straight, despite the fresh pain pulsing through her head. She felt dazed, near passing out again, but through strength of will alone, she managed to stay upright, and step toward Eddie. Each step down the farmer's porch threatened to send her sprawling, but she didn't use the railing. Didn't want to appear weak. She needed Eddie's affection, but also his respect. Without both, he wouldn't be malleable.

But her body had other plans.

Upon reaching the bottom step, a wave of nausea swept through her. The world spun. She reached for the railing and missed. Knees buckled. She toppled forward, but instead of landing on the ash-covered, scorched earth, she was cradled in a pair of strong arms.

When she opened her eyes again, she saw blue sky and the outline of the farmhouse cutting into it. Kenyon's face slid into view.

He looked concerned.

"That's good," she said.

"What's good?" he asked.

She blinked, trying to think clearly, but felt drugged. "The view."

Kenyon looked up at the farmhouse. The sky. The cumulus clouds, promising an afternoon rain.

"This isn't impossible, you know," Kenyon said.

"I don't know."

He looked at her again, amusement mingling with concern. "Once this business with you and your biodomes is wrapped up, we're going to start again. First in San Francisco. Then in other locations around the world. Anywhere you want, Ella. Where do you want to go?"

Kenyon's face blurred, and his words drifted in and out of focus.

Where do I want to go?

"Boston," she said, then cringed as she realized the word had been spoken aloud.

"Boston?" Kenyon sounded surprised. "You know it snows there like six months out of the year, right?"

Ella's pulse quickened. Adrenaline spiked.

She'd nearly ruined everything. Her thoughts began to focus. "Kidding," she said. "San Diego. Better yet. Baja. There aren't any borders anymore, right?"

"Right," he said. "And I can make that happen. I can."

As Ella's mind cleared, she began to recall some of what he'd said. None of it made sense to her, but Kenyon clearly knew more than she did about what ExoGen was planning. "How? When?"

"How about this?" he said. "I'll tell you. And I mean everything. No secrets. But first you tell me what's in Boston." While she tried to come up with something believable, he shook his head. "Is that where you've been headed all this time? Kind of a roundabout route, don't you think?"

"You're not with ExoGen," Ella said, looking at one of the Riders. "They left you to die. You don't need to—"

"I've never not been with ExoGen." The words came out like a growl. Kenyon rolled his neck, tempering his anger. "You can either be with them, or dead. Eventually, anyway. And I'm a survivor. Like you. I might have been left for dead by that asshole, Mackenzie, but that wasn't a corporate move. You and your boy toy might have made things personal for me, and believe me, I have dreamed up scenarios for all your deaths that would make you sick, but my loyalty is unflappable."

Ella knew that was true. It was why she was still breathing and not slain in one of the horrible manners he had dreamed up.

"So, you, me, and the girls here can pay a visit to Boston, see the sights and head back to San Fran before the first leaves of Fall start to change color. I hear it's beautiful, but I'd rather be on the West Coast when the snow starts falling, wouldn't you? And with the Chunta—" He leaned in close to whisper. "That's what these nasty ladies call themselves." He reverted back to his natural speaking voice. "—we won't have to worry about surviving the journey. Not as much anyway. Though I think our relationship needs to stay platonic. Feesa, their leader since Peter offed his wife, has kind of a thing for me."

Ella couldn't hide her revulsion.

"We're survivors," he said. "We do what we have to. And honestly, it wasn't that bad. Mostly I just pictured you."

Ella wanted to vomit, slit his throat, and laugh all at the same time. She'd traded a loveless pervert for a lovesick psychopath. But at least she understood this psychopath. The problem was that he also knew her, and now he knew that Boston was her ultimate destination. Boston wasn't a small city, though, and George's Island was just one of many dotting the coast. *He'll never find it,* she told herself, but the thought lacked conviction. Kenyon was a smart man. And determined. That he'd survived the wild on his own and befriended a tribe of ExoGens revealed as much.

But as long as Peter and the kids were free, there was a chance they could reach the island first. Once they plugged Anne in, Ella's presence shouldn't be needed. She wasn't certain about that. Anne's...design had never been tested. Any number of things could go wrong. But there was still a chance.

Ella closed her eyes and pushed her will toward the children. *Run. Wherever you are. Run.*

It was the closest she'd come to praying in a long time, and apparently just as useless.

"Put up your hands and step back!" The voice was angry and full of faux authority. It was also young and very familiar. Ella opened her eyes to see Jakob, standing in the farmhouse's doorway, an AK-47 raised at Kenyon's head. "Get away from her. Now."

26

Jakob had looked death in the eyes more times in the last few weeks than he thought anyone should throughout their lifetime. Nearly every living thing in the world wanted to kill and eat him, and not necessarily in that order. But in all those instances, he hadn't tried to hide his fear. Wouldn't have been able to, even if he had tried.

But now, Ella's life was on the line.

The woman his father loved.

His sister's mother.

So, when he aimed the AK-47 at Eddie Kenyon, half his mind was focused on the target. The other half was trying to hide his shaking, keep the contents of his stomach locked down, and keep the wetness in his eyes from spilling over. If Kenyon saw any of these signs of weakness, he might act. And if he did that, Jakob was dead.

Kenyon would outshoot him. And not because Jakob was a bad shot, or even afraid of taking a human life. What he was afraid of, aside from his own painful demise, was that his bullet would take the wrong human life. In the time it took him to pull the trigger, Kenyon could slip behind Ella.

Jakob was there to save Ella, not kill her.

What made it all worse was that Kenyon showed no fear at all.

"I don't recall the prodigal son returning with an AK-47," Kenyon said.

Jakob said nothing. He'd put everything he had into his first words. Speaking now would reveal the quiver in his voice. Instead, he adjusted his aim slightly, putting the crosshairs between Kenyon's eyes.

"I can wait," Kenyon said. "Kid like you can't hold that weapon up forever. Better off just taking the shot now."

Jakob blinked.

He was right. But the moment he pulled the trigger, several things would happen at once. Ella might be shot, either by Jakob or Kenyon, though he doubted Kenyon would kill her. After what he'd seen and heard, he was pretty sure that Ella's ex still clung to the idea that they had some kind of future. Then there were the Riders. As dangerous as Kenyon was, they were worse. And Jakob's rag-tag militia, who were taking up positions throughout the house, wouldn't be much safer behind walls and bars that the ExoGenetic women could tear through like paper.

It would be a blood bath. For both sides. But Kenyon had the advantage. He had Ella, and he was right; he could wait. The assault rifle already felt heavy in Jakob's arms. He'd gained a good amount of strength and stamina on the road, not to mention survival skills. But five weeks of toughening couldn't really compensate for years of sitting behind a computer screen, shooting up digital bad guys and taunting human opponents with variations of 'noob,' 'newbie,' and his personal favorite, 'umad bro?'

In the multiplayer gaming realm, his style had been bold, reckless, and effective. He'd charge into a room, praying and spraying, draining his rapid-fire weapon of choice, and more often than not, it worked. But only because there was no fear associated with what was essentially a suicidal tactic. His life was expendable because if he died, he would respawn a few seconds later and be right back at it. He understood that. But most players still reacted with fear, as if their digital life still meant something, and that's why it worked.

In games.

This was real life. If he died here, there would be no second chance. And praying and spraying...that would get Ella killed for sure.

He lacked his father's skill, strength, and patience. He couldn't take a masterful shot and know, without a doubt, that he could hit Kenyon and not Ella. He couldn't come up with a plan that would then deal with the primitive Rider rage that would follow and still likely lead to his and Ella's demise.

Umad bro? he thought at himself. As much as he liked using the obnoxious taunt, he hated being on the receiving end of it even more. He squinted, adjusting his aim once more, as a new kind of rage tamped down his fear and he considered, really considered, trying something crazy.

But he couldn't do it alone. Luckily, he didn't have to.

Glass shattered behind him. Windows belched glass from the first and second floors of the house. It clattered against the porch floor and slid down the porch roof like rainwater. A dozen weapons slid through the gaping holes, aiming at Kenyon and the Riders, who were growing agitated.

Kenyon smiled. "Well, now. Looks like a genuine stand-off."

"A stand-off is when both sides are evenly matched," Jakob said, surprising even himself. His rising anger had soothed his churning stomach, bolstered the strength in his arms and removed the fear from his voice. "This isn't a case of mutually assured destruction."

Kenyon scanned the area, looking at the weapons pointed in his direction. "But I have her." Faster than Jakob could react, Kenyon slipped fully behind Ella. To put a bullet in Kenyon would mean putting it through Ella first.

Jakob's aim wavered for a moment, but then zeroed in on Ella. If Kenyon attacked, he'd have no choice. *Please God,* Jakob thought, *don't make me have to kill her.*

Ella's eyes met Jakob's. Once she had his attention, she gave a subtle nod. Permission to shoot. Then she glanced at her shoulder and followed it with a wide eyed glare. She wasn't just giving him permission to shoot her, she was telling him to. If he put the bullet through her arm, it would hit Kenyon's as well. If they were lucky, it would make him drop his weapon, or at least give Ella the chance to break free or attack. If they were unlucky, and his aim was off by a few inches, Ella could die.

Do something suicidal, Jakob thought. *He'll never see it coming.* But this wasn't his life he was putting at risk.

"I can see it in your eyes, kid," Kenyon said. "You have the look of a man about to do something stupid."

Jakob felt a measure of despair return. Kenyon saw it coming, saw it broadcast on Jakob's face.

"Aww, don't look so sad." Kenyon chuckled. "You're not your dad. Probably never will be. Some people are born strong. Some people go through the forge and come out strong on the other side. Like Ella. But most people...most people just melt. You're melting, kid."

"Umad bro?" Jakob said.

"What?"

"You mad?"

Kenyon's voice took on the familiar tone Jakob had heard in many a team deathmatch game. "*What?*"

"You think you've got the win. You think you're walking out of here alive? That any of you are? Ella would rather die than go with you. I know that, because she told us all about you. About your whiny voice. About how you fawn over her like a little schoolboy. About how she played you. A bat of the eyelashes, and you did exactly what she wanted. Even now, even after knowing the truth about what you mean to her, you're still willing to risk everything just to get her back? One of us never left high school, and it isn't me."

Kenyon said nothing but looked furious.

Jakob finished with the coup de grâce that lowered the IQ of most guys. "She also told about your little dick."

Kenyon's eyes twitched, but he didn't move. Didn't talk, either, which meant he was getting angry. Really angry.

The real icing on his rage cake was when the dick comment elicited chuckling from the Rider females.

"So, bro," Jakob said. "Umad?"

"Little shit!" Kenyon shouted, stepping back from Ella, and raising his weapon.

Jakob cringed at the realization that Kenyon was reversing the tactic Ella had requested. He was going to put a bullet through her—maybe a bunch of them. The resulting spray of shattered lead would burst out the front of her body and strike Jakob.

But Kenyon never got the chance.

A single round was fired from the second-floor window, striking Kenyon's shoulder. He spun, dropped his weapon, and fell to the ground. Someone from the second floor had saved Ella's life.

Momentarily.

The Riders twisted to watch Kenyon fall, and then coiled to spring. Ella would die first. Then Jakob. Then the people holed up in the house, and maybe even the rest of Hellhole's residents hiding in the unfinished biodome, including Anne.

But the next sound to cut through the air wasn't a gunshot, a scream, or an ExoGen battle cry. It was the thunderous *whup, whup, whup,* of a helicopter.

27

"You're late. Get up."

Anne opened her eyes. The sprawl of her bedroom surrounded her. Clothes covered the floor, posters hung on the walls, and her dog, Jasper, stood by the bedside, wagging his tail.

"C'mon," her mother said, rapping the locked door with her knuckles.

"I'm up," Anne said, but something about her voice sounded off. When she sat up, Jasper couldn't hold himself back anymore. He jumped onto the bed, stepped into her personal space, and started licking. Anne fended him off, shaking his cheeks and ears. Then she squished up his loose fur, transforming his Labrador face into something closer to a pug. "Who's a squishy boy? You are."

There was that voice again. *I need a drink,* she thought, but instead of heading for the bathroom, she climbed out of bed and moved to her desk. While the rest of the room looked like it had survived a nuclear war, the desk was a gleaming bastion of organization. It wasn't empty. Not even close. But the textbooks, note pads, pens, and pencils all had their place.

She pulled a sketchbook out from beneath the stack of biology books and gently sifted through the pages, finding the most recent entry. There were notes scrawled in pencil, sketches of wildflowers and a folded-up piece of paper towel.

She opened the towel to find a pressed flower. "Hell-o, little daisy."

It looked perfect. Better than the last one, which had lost petals on one side, and looked like a balding man with a bushy beard.

Three knocks filled the room, and she nearly shouted at her mother. But then she realized where the knocks had come from and clamped her mouth shut. Anne moved to the window, tugged the shade down, and let it snap up. The boy on the other side nearly fell away in surprise, but he managed to cling to the overhang.

Jasper leapt up, front paws on the sill, and barked.

"He needs to go out," her mother shouted from somewhere in the house.

"I know!" Anne replied and opened the window.

Jasper assaulted the boy with licks. The boy laughed, pushed the dog aside, and slid into the room. It wasn't a graceful entrance, but it was silent.

He'd had practice.

Had been visiting her for years.

But...who is he? Anne wondered, and then she realized there was a third person in the room. A girl with brown hair, like hers, but straighter and longer. A lot longer.

The girl petted Jasper and said, "I'll let you out in a minute." Then to the boy, "You're early."

"You're late." He smiled and Anne saw something familiar about him. "Overslept again? You know, just because you get 'A's on all your tests doesn't mean that Mrs. Heintz won't dock you for missing classes."

"Won't miss any if you leave and let me change." The girl gave the boy a playful shove.

"I'll just turn around." The boy faced the window. "Won't peek, I swear."

"Pete!" The girl said, kicking the boy.

Pete? Anne tried to speak, but she couldn't. This was *her* room. *She* was late for school. Who were these kids, and what were they doing in her room?

It's a dream, she thought. But that wasn't right. It was more than that. *It's a memory. Mom's memory. And the boy. He's...Dad.*

"If my parents find you up here, you're a dead man."

He nodded and smiled. "Even deader if you're changing. But it'd be worth it."

The girl...Ella...smiled. "Thought you weren't going to look?"

God, Anne thought, *they flirted like that when they were kids, too. How old are they anyway?*

She looked at the pair. Fourteen at least. Maybe fifteen. Teenagers in full bloom.

Peter shrugged and headed back to the window.

"Perv," Ella said, but she didn't look at all upset.

"Meet me out front?" Peter said.

"You should go ahead. My grades aren't really a concern, but yours..."

Peter shook his head. "Not going to leave you."

"My hero."

Peter hung outside the window, poised to climb back down the pipe he had used to scale the wall hundreds of times during their childhood. Anne remembered it all. Remembered what happened next, too. "Heroes get rewarded, you know."

Without thinking it through, Ella lifted her shirt and flashed Peter. She'd done it twice before, but never after having just woken up...braless.

Peter was so stunned that he lost his grip and fell.

Anne felt herself slip into her father's perspective. She saw the blue sky above, and then coughed in pain as she struck the ground. Peter had sprained his ankle that day. Hopped to the front stairs, threw himself on them and pretended he'd tripped. Instead of school, he and Ella spent the morning at the hospital. No one found out about the pipe. Her father was a crafty man, in more ways than one, and he really did love her mother. And she loved him. She'd understood this on the surface level but had never really felt that kind of romantic love, or even affection for a member of the opposite sex. And now, she'd lived her mother's feelings for her father, which was eye-opening, and kind of gross.

But it helped her understand them.

The vision turned hazy and speckled as a tingling sensation rolled from her fingers and toes to her torso.

Then darkness, followed by a face.

When she saw Willie standing over her, looking concerned, she knew the dream-like memory had come to an end. "Sheeit, kid, you had me scared."

"Says the old asshole who knocked me unconscious."

"Did what had to be done."

Anne sat up and found herself back in the unfinished biodome. She was lying on the concrete foundation, surrounded by the feeble and hungry residents of Hellhole Bay. She winced and held the back of her head. "You throw me down like a sack of rocks? Geez."

"You had a seizure or something," Willie said. "Bucked yourself free."

"Maybe that's what happens when you clock a twelve-year-old girl with the butt of a rifle?"

"Like I said—"

"Did what you had to do. I heard. How long was I out?"

"Just got back." Willie shrugged. "Not much more than a minute."

"What's happening?"

"Don't know. Your brother got spooked by something. Said to bring you here. Seemed like he thought you were in a specific kind of danger."

ExoGen, Anne thought.

Has to be.

Anne looked back and forth, scanning the group of people hiding along the back wall. Not one of them had a weapon. But Willie did.

The old man noted her attention and took a step back. "You got some sass to you, but ain't no way you're disarming me."

She considered the idea, but quickly dismissed it. Willie was old, but he had already proven himself tough. He'd probably knock her unconscious again.

"You're Ella's girl?" a tired voice asked. It was the woman they'd come here to find, Lyn Askew. "You look a lot like her. Like your father, too."

"You knew my father?" Anne asked. She'd woken with a large chunk of her mother's childhood memories dumped into her mind, like they were her own, but this woman wasn't in any of them.

"Knew of him. She kept a photo of him in her office. Spoke highly of him when I asked. I think losing him was one of the toughest experiences of her life."

"Probably harder for the wife he was cheating on."

Lyn smiled. Her dry lips cracked. Beads of blood formed and smeared like lipstick. The woman didn't notice. "Imagine so. But it was good to see them together. Is she happy?"

Happy? "Lady, the world has gone to hell, largely because of my mother's work. She's one of the most hated people on the planet, by the few people who are still alive and capable of feeling anything beyond abject fear."

"But not him," Lyn pointed out.

Anne sighed, her thoughts drifting back through the past few weeks. Her memory recalling window visits made by young Peter. She felt the joy he brought her. "Yeah," she finally said. "She's happy."

"And you?"

"Me? What about me?"

"I noticed you're a little more...fleshed out than your family. You've been enjoying the fruits of our labor, haven't you?"

"What's she talking about?" Willie asked.

"Nothing."

Lyn waived her off. "I helped work on you, you know. Tell me, how does it taste? As good as I've imagined? Better, I'm guessing. I put some of that same work into the food here." She motioned to the completed domes behind her. "Made it safe to eat, but it lost some of the flavor. Not all of it, mind you. Still the best vegetables I've ever had...when I was allowed to eat them...but not the same as the good stuff. Not what you've been eating."

"Shut up, lady," Anne growled, but it was too late.

"Now, hold on a minute." Willie gripped her shoulder. "You've been eating the ExoGenetic crops? On the outside?"

A few of the people around them heard his question and perked up. A few more looked terrified and shuffled away.

"It's okay." Lyn dismissed Willie with her hand but could only keep it up for a second before her strength wavered. She'd been fed and given water, but it would take days of the same before she really started to recover from the mistreatment she'd suffered as one of Mason's Questionables. "The girl is immune to the effects of RC-714."

"Bullshit," Willie said. "How?"

"She was made that way. Designed. And when you're building a person, it's not impossible to remove all those genes that RC-714 wakes up. Through millennia of evolution, all living things adapt to new environments and evolve, sometimes becoming something stunningly different from where it started. When this happens, the old, now useless adaptations are locked away as junk DNA, never to be accessed again. It's like partitioning a hard drive and separating old data into an encrypted file. RC-714 removed the encryption. But with Anne..."

"You wiped the hard drive clean," Anne said. "But not completely."

Lyn looked confused. "How do you mean?"

"I mean I've got my mother's memories. Some of them anyway. And I know things she knows, but I shouldn't. And, you all put a thumb drive in the *Back. Of. My. Head.*" Anne tapped her head with each of the last four words.

Lyn looked mortified. "I—I had no idea. It doesn't sound possible."

Anne turned the back of her head toward the woman. Pointed to the mole that covered the USB port. Her mother had cut it open five weeks ago, to show Peter, but when it healed, it didn't heal shut. It was more like a tab of skin that could be opened and closed. So, she dug a nail in and lifted the skin flap.

Willie leaned back, repulsed. "Who does this to their kid?"

Lyn leaned closer. "But...why?"

"All of her research is in there," Anne said. "But I think it's more than that. I think she made a digital copy of herself. Of her knowledge. Even her memories. And some of them are leaking out."

Willie turned away, rubbing his hands through his hair, clearly disturbed by what he'd seen and heard. Lyn turned her eyes down, deep in thought, no doubt pondering the thumb drive's purpose. While the pair were lost in thought, Anne stood. Without making a sound, she weaved her way past the people now staring at her. She gave them fake smiles and kept on going, heading for the one way out of the dome where Willie couldn't follow.

The door connecting the unfinished dome to the finished one led to a functional airlock and decontamination chamber. It was no doubt locked from the inside, the outer access panel turned off, but Anne knew her way around the system as well as anyone. She knelt at the controls and pushed against what looked like a solid metal wall. It shifted in with a clunk.

Anne glanced back. Lyn was still on another planet. Willie had started to look for her but was searching in the wrong direction.

She pulled the panel away, revealing coils of wires and circuitry.

Where did Mason get all of this? He might have been able to put it all together, but he certainly couldn't duplicate this technology. There were supposed to be ten biodomes up and down the East Coast. Her mother had marked them on a map at Peter's request. But Anne guessed at least six of those, maybe more, never got built. Mason had stolen these domes, from the people they'd been intended for. People who could have helped her mother. Without knowing it, he had helped ExoGen's cause.

"Hey!" Willie had spotted her and was charging toward her. The old man's scowl said he meant business.

Anne flipped a switch that activated the outer door. She left the panel off and punched in a five-digit sequence into the keypad.

"The hell are you doing?" Willie said. And when the door whooshed open, he broke into a jog. "Hey! Kid! I told your brother I'd—"

Willie's voice was silenced by the closing door. He thumped his fists against the outer glass, shouting something, but his voice was muffled beyond the point of discernment. And without the five-digit override code, he wouldn't be following her.

Standing in the first chamber, Anne began shedding clothes. She'd been in the wild far too long for the system to reliably suck up every bit of ExoGenetic material from all the folds of her clothes. She discarded her shoes, pants, and shirt, until all she had on was matching white underwear and a tank top. "I look like Ripley," she muttered, wondered who Ripley was, and then she recalled a movie her mother had seen as a child. The film had terrified young Ella but didn't seem all that dissimilar from the world her mother had helped create.

Anne stepped into the decontamination room, closed the door behind her, and stood still as the turbines did their thing, whipping her body with a tornado of wind, stripping every loose fiber and seed from her body, clothes, and hair. When it was done, she stepped inside the familiar confines of a biodome. It smelled lush and delicious. Her mouth watered. But she didn't linger or even take a snack for the road. She ran barefoot, across the greenhouse, where it attached to the next biodome via a second decontamination chamber.

Mason hadn't taken any chances. Even if one dome became contaminated, the others wouldn't be. Had he been a good man, Hellhole compound would have been an oasis. She repeated the process, over and over until she reached the final decontamination chamber leading to the farmhouse. She entered the chamber, waiting somewhat impatiently for it to run its course, and then stepped out into the farmhouse. To her right was a laundry room, stacked with folded clothing. She ducked into the room and tore through the clothing until she found a pair of blue sweatpants that weren't obscenely too large. She cinched the drawstring tight and slipped back into the hall. She could hear people moving around on the first and second floors. Hushed voices. *The house was supposed to be mostly empty,* she thought, glancing into the kitchen for a knife or a frying pan. Then Charlotte walked across the hall, ducking low, a rifle in her hands.

They already took the house?

Commands were hissed across the first floor and repeated upstairs. A moment later, several windows shattered. It sounded like every window at the front of the house. She stepped into the hallway and froze. The front door was open. Jakob was framed by it, standing on the porch, aiming an AK-47 at her mother. No, not at her mother...at the man hiding behind her like a coward.

Eddie.

She couldn't hear what was being said, but she understood the situation. She ducked into the kitchen, found a knife, and then tiptoed to the staircase. There were eight people on the first floor, all aiming their weapons outside. *That's a lot of firepower for one man,* she thought, then she sprang up the stairs. An unarmed woman standing at the top of the stairs, no doubt positioned to help coordinate, looked surprised by her arrival, but said nothing. Anne had been knocked out and carried away, but they were still on the same team. That, and Anne gave the woman her best, 'get the fuck out of my way,' glare, while doing nothing to hide the blade in her hands.

"How many are out there?" Anne asked.

The woman shrugged. "Not sure it matters. They're huge. Starting to think this was a bad idea."

Anne ignored the woman's fear and headed for the bedroom at the front of the house. She stepped inside the room and found Carrie and Shawna, each armed with a rifle, pointed out the window. Both women turned when she entered but said nothing. Anne quickly assessed the pair, moved to Carrie, and whispered. "You even shot a rifle before?"

"Not really."

"Not really? That's pretty much a yes or no question." Anne wrapped her small hand around the weapon's barrel. Carrie resisted. Wanted to be part of the fight. Good for her, but bad for the people she was supposed to be covering, which included her brother and mother. "You can give it to me, or I can give you this knife."

Carrie glanced at the menacing steak knife. Anne hadn't directly threatened her, but Carrie read between the lines and lifted her hands away. Anne hefted the big rifle up, leaned her shoulder into it and looked out the window.

She nearly gasped, but held it in. Kenyon's companions were just about the last thing Anne expected to see. Riders. Each of them as ugly as Jakob's mother had become before Peter killed her. And they seemed to be following Kenyon's lead, waiting for a command.

She focused on what was being said and nearly laughed when she heard Jakob say, "She also told us about your little dick."

Kenyon didn't like that, but he stayed hidden behind Ella. *Hidden from Jakob*, she thought, adjusting her aim. *But not from me.*

When the hairy beasts beside him revealed they had a sense of humor, laughing at Jakob's jab, laughing at Kenyon, the man's face turned red.

"So, bro," Jakob said. "Umad?"

"Little shit!" Kenyon took a step back and raised his weapon toward her mother's back.

Anne exhaled.

Slipped her finger around the trigger.

Prayed that Carrie had chambered a round. And squeezed.

The rifle bucked hard, punching her shoulder back with the same force Willie had used to knock her unconscious. The boom echoed and faded, giving way to Kenyon's scream of pain, and then the thunderous roar of modern killing machines. Anne adjusted her rifle's aim, as the first Apache attack helicopter swung past overhead. It made a tight circle over the compound and then hovered. Then a familiar, blue Black Hawk helicopter flew into view and descended. A soldier clad in black stood in the open side door, manning a machine gun.

Kenyon leapt to his feet waving his good arm.

The soldier leaned forward a little, looked surprised, then offered a wave. After speaking to the pilot for a moment, the chopper began to descend, its rotor wash blasting the house, kicking up a cloud of ash and flattening the weaker buildings in the nearby shanty town.

It took all of Anne's willpower to not shoot Eddie in the head. But if she did that, then these choppers might open fire, killing everyone in the house and the family she hoped to save.

Then she realized it wasn't her family she should be worried about.

They're here for me, she thought. And while she wasn't a coward, and would happily face these odds in a fight, she was beginning to understand that the fate of the human race might just reside in her head. If ExoGen found her...the human race would be replaced by whatever ExoGen was cooking up.

She ducked back out of the window and turned to the two women. "I need to hide. Now."

28

Eddie Kenyon felt like he'd been dipped in the Jordan River by John the Baptist himself, remade and reborn. But this transformative moment wouldn't be followed by miracles, parables, or his martyrdom. His remaining time on Earth *would* change mankind's outcome for the next two thousand years, though. Probably longer. Time would be measured in three epochs: B.C., A.D. and A.C.—*After Change*.

Ella refused to see it, covering her vision with moral scruples. And people like the now dead Mason were incapable of seeing it.

But he could see it, just as clearly as he could see the familiar Apache helicopter swinging into position. The war machine had enough firepower to wipe out every living soul in the Hellhole compound, human or otherwise. And it wasn't alone. He could hear the second Apache, not far away, and the Black Hawk, which roared into view above the farmhouse. The side door was open. His man, Hutchins, stood behind the machine gun.

The open door and prepped weapon told him they hadn't just stumbled on Hellhole. They came here knowing they would find people, and if they came here at all, it meant they knew exactly who they would find. Hutchins was here for Ella and Anne, still trying to complete their mission, so they could return to the safety of ExoGen's San Francisco facility.

Kenyon glanced at the limp form of Mason, hanging from the open front door. He offered the dead man his silent thanks for summoning ExoGen to the site, and then waved at the chopper. He smiled when Hutchins responded with a smile and wave. Despite being left for dead, these were still his men.

And that meant the brazen little shit Peter had spawned would soon meet his maker, along with everyone else in hiding in the farmhouse, including the asshole who put a bullet through his arm. As the chopper descended, sending a whirlwind of ash and debris into the air, Kenyon looked at the wound. It was more than a graze, but the bullet had punched clean through. He'd had worse. Much worse. But the bullet had hit a nerve or tendon, limiting the functionality of his right hand.

He knelt to pick up his weapon, hoping that no one in the house was stupid enough risk a confrontation with the Apache. When no one fired on him, he grasped the weapon with his left hand. He'd still be able to fire it, but his speed and aim would be diminished until his right arm healed. With two Apaches and a Black Hawk, though, not to mention the hardened men inside them, he could order the deaths of everyone here without pulling a trigger.

And he wasn't the only one who knew it.

"Eddie," Ella said. "You can let these people live."

"I could," he said, and let that linger.

"I'll come with you."

"We already played that game once," he said, recalling the last time they had captured Ella and flown away, only to be sent back after her daughter. Eddie's priority had been Ella, and he'd allowed himself to be duped by her affections, which part of him still believed were genuine. But ExoGen had different priorities. They wanted Anne, and he wouldn't be allowed to return home without her. "Where's Anne?"

"I don't know," Ella said, and he actually believed her. If Mason had her locked up inside the house, then she might not really know where the girl was. But the kid would know.

He turned to Jakob. "Back to square one, Jake."

"Go fuck a duck," Jakob said, but he kept his weapon aimed at the ground.

"You've been around Anne too long," Kenyon said. "Picked up some of her potty mouth."

"You've been screwing ExoGens too long," the kid replied, but he was only pretending to have a set of balls. Kenyon saw right through his bravado. But he did raise a valid point.

Kenyon observed the Chunta for a moment. They were nervous and confused by the arrival of the choppers. They probably viewed them as ExoGenetic predators, but they might also remember seeing them before. With the arrival of his men, and their modern weapons, the creatures became a liability, and he'd have no problem leaving them, or worse.

But for now, he needed their unpredictable nature contained.

"Chunta," he said, addressing them all. The hairy females gave him their attention. He pointed at the helicopters. "Friends." He patted his chest, wincing as he moved his right arm. "My friends. *Your* friends."

They didn't look convinced, but they didn't attempt to argue, either.

"Trust Eddie," he said, and he nearly backhanded Ella when she laughed. But he controlled himself and gave the nearest female a pat on the arm. She looked him in the eyes, her true thoughts unreadable, or perhaps nonexistent. "Trust Eddie."

When the female grunted her agreement, he said. "Stay here." He pointed at the farmhouse, indicating the people hiding within. "Watch them. If they move, kill them."

A louder grunt meant she understood. Killing was second nature to the monsters he'd lived among for more than a month. But that dark time in his life would soon be a memory he could let go.

The chopper landed a safe distance away. Hutchins stepped out from the side door, a second man now manning the gun. But Hutchins didn't approach. Wasn't about to put himself at risk. He could see the weapons still sticking out of the windows. Could see the Chunta bobbing and anxious, and was probably confounded by the fact that the monsters weren't simply tearing into every human being around.

Kenyon pointed his rifle at Ella and motioned toward the Black Hawk with it. "Let's go have a chat with our old friends, eh?" He smiled at Jakob. "And you, enjoy the last few minutes of your life. Too bad, dad's not here to share in the fun."

"Eddie," Ella said. "Don't be a dick."

Eddie chuckled. He missed Ella's straight forward nature. And even if she didn't love him, she was going to be with him. They would ring in the A.C. together. And if they could find Anne, who was undoubtedly nearby, Ella would do whatever he asked. No one was more precious to her than her daughter.

"Hey, I'm just having a good time. If I were being a dick, the kid would be dead already." And he really did want to kill the kid. The problem was that if Ella didn't know where Anne was, and Peter was M.I.A., or perhaps already dead in the swamps, then Jakob might be the only person who knew where Anne was hiding. And if they didn't find her soon, the girl was bold enough, and probably skilled enough, to head out into the wild on her own, never to be found. "Now move it."

He followed Ella toward the chopper, appreciating the sway of her hips in the flowing white skirt. She'd cleaned up well under Mason's brief care. Eddie still didn't appreciate the shaved head look, but it would grow out. And really, any look Ella tried would be better than the Chunta punta he'd experienced.

Granted, not all of it had been bad.

He'd gotten to know a more primal side of himself, but it was comparable to finding the virtues in a fruitcake. A starving man might be able to find them palatable, but if an apple pie came along, well, the fruitcake is seen for what it is: an ugly, nasty-tasting brick that people were willing to buy once a year, but not eat.

With Ella back, he was done with metaphorical fruitcakes.

Hutchins looked slimmer than Kenyon remembered. Had kind of a haunted look in his pale eyes, too. Viper Squad had seen some tough times without his leadership. But they were still alive. Still fighting.

And very present.

When he and Ella got within fifty feet of the chopper, Hutchins came forward to meet them. The rotor was still slowing, but talking over the engine's whine would be tough. He moved with caution at first but broke into a faster walk when Kenyon stepped out from behind Ella and smiled. When the two met, Kenyon shook the other man's hand and winced from the pain. Hutchins drew back. "Shit. Sorry, sir. Didn't see that you were wounded."

Kenyon looked at the bloodied arm. "The least of our concerns."

Hutchins looked past him at the gathered forces of people and Chunta. "We didn't think you were alive. Some guy radioed from this location. Said he had Ella and the girl."

Kenyon nodded but said nothing. He had a lot of questions, and a good number of requests, but there was one pressing issue that needed to be resolved. "Where's Mackenzie?"

"We went back for you," Hutchins said. "But by the time we got there, your body... You, were gone."

"Where is he?"

"Dead," Hutchins flexed his hands. "Should be, by now. We were going to shoot him. For what he did. But he got away. Pretty sure he had a bullet in him, though. Even if he didn't, there's no way he'd make it alone."

"*I* did," Kenyon said, looking back at the Chunta. "Though I wasn't exactly alone."

"Mackenzie isn't you, sir."

That was true. Mackenzie was a soldier. A good soldier.

But he played by the rules, and Peter being a Marine—and a CSO to boot—had shifted the man's allegiance. Despite there being no U.S. government, and no more Marine Corps, the man couldn't betray a fellow jarhead. And that kind of straight forward thinking didn't work in the new world. If you weren't willing to break any and every rule or notion of right and wrong and didn't have men and helicopters to back you up, you were as good as dead.

"Good enough," Kenyon said, though he regretted not being able to crush Mackenzie's head beneath his boot. He'd thought of nothing but revenge for the past month, and so far, the objects of his wrath were all still alive.

Someone had to die today, but first he would reclaim his future.

"How many are left?"

It was a vague question, but Hutchins understood it. "Manke, Kissock, and Drummond...obviously."

They were the pilots. Kenyon had already deduced as much. But he didn't need pilots now, he needed boots on the ground.

"Then there's Mendez and Crawford."

Kenyon had already seen Mendez take Hutchins's position behind the machine gun, where he should stay. But Crawford was a good fighter. Loyal, too. "Who else?"

"Uhh, that's it, sir."

"What the hell happened?"

"We were on the ground. Refueling. Thought we were safe, but this... I think it might have been a spider. It-it..."

"I get it," Kenyon said. He was disappointed in Viper Squad, but a team is only as good as its leadership, and while Hutchins was a solid warrior, he wasn't exactly Alexander the Great when it came to strategy. "I want Crawford with us. Tell the choppers to kill anything that moves..." He pointed to the Chunta. "Except for them. For now."

"What about her?" Hutchins motioned to Ella.

"She's going to call Anne for us."

"I'll do no such—ahh!"

Ella's voice was cut short by a shout of pain, as Eddie snatched her pinky finger and snapped it quickly back. He didn't want to hurt her, but he knew how to draw pain without permanently disfiguring. And when Anne heard her mother crying out, the girl would come running.

29

Hiding was for cowards. Anne believed it with all her heart, but she also *knew* better. Hiding meant surviving, and survival was the name of the game. Sometimes an enemy could be defeated simply by staying alive long enough for something else to kill it for you. In this case, hiding meant the human race, as it had evolved over millions of years, still had a chance to reclaim the planet from what ExoGen had done to it.

She believed that even more than she believed hiding equaled cowardice. But was that really how she felt, or were those her mother's emotions leaching into her, along with her memories and knowledge? Or maybe she was having a similar emotional response to those memories? She was her mother's daughter, after all, even more than the average daughter.

Shawna the maid, who wasn't really a maid, but had been dressed up like one, led her to a large bedroom at the back of the house. It had a king size bed, perfectly made with the fluffiest, most inviting comforter set that Anne had ever seen. As she walked past the bed, part of her longed to climb into it, fall asleep and forget the world and her part in it. Then she smelled the room. It was distinctly masculine. Like something she'd smelled as a child. Her father's scent.

That's Mom's memory, Anne thought, identifying the scent as Old Spice, and recalling the cologne's beige bottle with a sailboat. Her mother had liked the smell. But it was tinged with something else Anne couldn't identify. Something that made her wince. Shawna too, though she suspected the woman knew what she was smelling, and it twisted her face up with discomfort. Bad things happened in this room.

Shawna rounded an old dresser that looked hand-carved, like some kind of ancient antique. Above it was a fancy gilded mirror, like something out of a fairy tale. *Probably taken from a museum,* Anne thought, and she paid the furniture and décor no more attention. Shawna opened a door, revealing a walk-in closet stocked with the clothes of a Southern gentleman.

"We're going to hide in a closet?" she protested. "Isn't that like a cliché or something? Won't this be the first place someone will look?"

Shawna ignored her and began separating the shirts hanging on the left side of the closet. "I found this by accident. I didn't go inside, but I think I know what it is."

"I don't see anything," Anne said. "It's just—"

Shawna pressed on the wall. The small amount of pressure revealed a thin rectangular seam. When she removed her hands, a door popped open. It was just three feet tall and two feet wide, but big enough to fit through. Big enough for an adult to fit through. "I don't think this was part of the original house. But Mason was a contractor. I think he added this space, or at least converted a large closet into two separate spaces."

"Why would he need a secret room inside a house he controlled?" Anne asked. "Is it like a safe room?"

Shawna frowned. "I don't think so. Let me go in first."'

"Whatever is in there, I can handle it." Anne pushed the woman aside. "I have seen things that would make you puke. Hell, I've done things that would make you puke. Nothing in here could be worse. And we don't really have a choice."

"Suit yourself," Shawna said. As kind as the woman was being by hiding her, Anne sensed that the woman had paper-thin patience. And who could blame her? She'd been a prisoner and slave for how long? And now a kid she didn't know was bossing her around.

But Anne didn't think there was time for being nice. Not now. Not until Kenyon was dead or gone. Because if he found her... She didn't want to think about it, but images of ExoGen came unbidden to her thoughts. Her earliest memories were just a few years old. At first, they weren't that bad. People were kind. In retrospect, they were too kind—the sort of nice that people put on like a mask to hide what they were really thinking. Then came the tests: mental, physical, and emotional. Her mother took part in some, at first, but was later pulled from the project. The project of her.

These memories had been vague up until now. Or perhaps repressed. But her mother's leaching memories were bringing out details.

While her mother grew fonder of Anne, treating her like an actual daughter, rather than a creation, Anne began to feel more and more like a lab rat. She didn't know what they were looking for, or testing for, but they were relentless, until one day, they weren't. She had, apparently, failed their tests. It was then that she had been allowed to live with her mother full time.

A memory slipped into her mind. Her mother's. And unlike most, it was more recent.

She was in an office. Someplace fancy. The air was pure. Smelled like a thunderstorm. A bald man sat behind a desk, back to her. He was looking out a window, large enough to squeeze an elephant through. It looked out upon an empty city with a massive red bridge and a fog shrouded ocean beyond. The view was both disconcerting, and inspiring.

"Lawrence," Ella said. "You don't need to terminate this one."

"I heard you grew attached," the man said, his voice echoing off the sharp angles in the sparsely decorated space. "You know better."

"None of them need to be terminated," Ella countered.

"You know we don't have the resources to feed them yet." The man's fingers tapped on the armrest. Bored. "Nor do we have the time or personnel to raise them. Teach them. If bleeding hearts ran this place, rather than logical minds, we would have hundreds of malnourished, undereducated, potentially rebellious people to look after, all of whom would keep us from continuing our work on schedule and without distraction. But you've known that all along. It's why you haven't raised this issue before, despite your resistance to our—"

"You murdered humanity," Ella said. She was trying hard to stay cordial, to not ruffle the feathers of the man whose word was law.

"And you gave us the knife," the man said, "which is why you are still alive. Your skills and knowledge will help what's left of the world, something you have at least attempted to make peace with. Your work *is* progressing. But this...obsession with the girl? It needs to stop."

"I won't continue my work without her."

The man's fingers stopped tapping.

"An ultimatum? You've made them before. We both know you prefer life over death. You have never done well with pain."

"People change," Ella said. "You of all people know that better than most."

"The question is why?" Lawrence said. "We changed the world. Not quite overnight, but in evolutionary terms, RC-714 did what took billions of years for evolution to achieve, in the blink of an eye. But what could change a woman like you, who even while she is repulsed by her own work, and toils against it in vain—we know about your biodomes, by the way—always returns to it? Drawn by insatiable curiosity. Pushed by threats of violence. Of starvation. Of being set loose in the wilds of the new. You always return to work."

Lawrence swiveled around in his chair, facing Ella for the first time. He had a kind face and a genuine smile. His head sparkled in the sunlight filtering in through the window. His eyes matched the water in the bay behind him. And his loose clothing looked like something out of a kung-fu movie. This was a man who should be stretching on a yoga mat, not overseeing the end of life on Earth. "So, what about this girl, subject 229—"

"Anne."

"—would spur you to make such a threat? And why do you think that after all your failed attempts at resistance, things will be different this time?" He leaned forward, elbows on the desk, his smile unwavering.

"Because this time I mean—"

"Why?"

Ella froze up, not wanting to answer.

"Let me help loosen your lips," Lawrence said. "ExoGen specializes in genetics. It's right there in the name. Half of the people working in this facility, and thus half the people alive on this planet, are, like you, geneticists. Now, you might be one of our more gifted minds, but even some of the people in the sanitation department know how to run basic DNA tests."

When Ella said nothing, Lawrence laughed. "So strong willed, and yet so easy to disarm." He leaned back in the chair. "I had the girl tested the moment you allowed her to share your quarters. I knew what the results would be when I learned that you had named the girl but was still surprised when my suspicions were confirmed. But you have always been one to try the unconventional. It's what makes your genius so potent. So valuable. And it's why I would rather not have to threaten you, or even worse, follow through on those threats. But I still need to hear it from your lips. Tell me, who is the girl to you?"

"My daughter," Ella said. "And if you let her live...if you let me have her...you never need threaten me again."

"And if I don't?"

"I will be all out of reasons to live."

Lawrence squinted at her. "You didn't make her for the experiment, did you?" His smile slowly returned. "You made her...for yourself. Like a pet." The smile became a laugh. "Ella, you would never admit it, but your mind is as twisted as you claim mine to be. And when you see that for yourself, I will let you into the fold. But for now...I will let you keep the girl."

Anne stumbled out of the memory and into the small room hidden inside the walk-in closet. When she looked up and saw the room's contents, she wished she could retreat back into that horrible memory.

30

Ella looked Jakob in the eyes as she was led past him. She said nothing but tried to communicate a simple message with her facial expression alone: *I'm sorry.*

He just glared back at her. Angry at Mason. At Kenyon. At the Riders. Probably at her, too. He'd risked his freedom, his life, in an attempt to rescue her, but had really just delivered himself as a second bargaining chip. Kenyon hadn't even disarmed the boy, or the rest of the people in the house. Didn't have to. No one wanted to commit suicide by Apache helicopter. Though as suicide went, it would be one of the faster ways to die. The attack helicopter's rockets and chain gun didn't just kill people, they erased them. Turned them to sludge. They were brutal weapons.

Overkill, really. But they were also merciful in their swiftness. Death would come faster than the nervous system could register it.

Despite the graveness of their situation, she wasn't without hope. First, she trusted that once Jakob knew Kenyon was involved, he would have hidden Anne away before revealing himself. If he'd done a good job, Anne was far from here, maybe not even in the compound anymore. Maybe even with Peter. And that was her second hope. Had been for most of her life. Peter was alive. Of that, she had no doubt. But was he fighting for his life somewhere else? Against Boone and his boys? Was he lost in the swamps? Or had he already returned, maybe even waiting inside the house? Whatever the case, if he showed up, she'd be ready. And if he didn't...she'd do what she did best—survive.

But what she wouldn't do is let these men have Anne. She'd die before letting that happen.

So, as she took the steps onto the farmer's porch, she steeled herself for the pain to come, and determined that she would not scream.

She paused in the doorway where Mason's corpse still hung. Blood tapped out a rhythm on the hard wood floor. She heard movement in the house as people scurried about, hiding, retreating, or simply trying to get a better view. She ignored them and turned her attention to Mason. His death had been too sudden. Too merciful. But that didn't mean she couldn't vent her rage on him. She punched his torso three times, twice with her freshly broken finger. Then she grasped his arms and drove her knee into his groin, again and again. On the fourth strike, the spear tip slipped free of the door. His body crumpled at her feet.

She kicked the body twice and then stopped. Sweat coated her forehead. Her muscles twitched. The man's violent sexual advances had affected her more than she thought.

"He really did what you said," Kenyon said. He actually looked concerned.

"Tried to," she replied, and hoped he might learn a lesson from her brutalization of a dead man. She stepped over the corpse and into the house. There were two women and one man in the living room to the right of the foyer in which she stood. One of them was Alia. The girl looked at her with a newfound fear. Ella regretted it, but Alia needed to grow a thicker skin. The days of Millennial coddling came to an end right along with the rest of civilization. She wanted to tell her as much but didn't even let her eyes linger on the girl. If they were lucky, Kenyon wouldn't recognize her. When Kenyon stepped into the foyer behind her, the girl wisely looked away, letting her hair cover her face. Hutchins and Crawford stepped in after them, scanning the hallway and the surrounding rooms with their weapons.

"Ella," Kenyon said, glancing at the armed residents of Hellhole Bay positioned in the living and dining rooms on either side of them. He didn't even show a flicker of concern. "I'd rather not do this. You've been through enough."

"Much of it at your hands," she said. "And we both know how this is going to go, so why don't we get to it?"

"You've changed," he said.

"We're all evolving." Ella held out her left hand, offering him another finger. "Some of us slower than others."

"I came here to kill you, you know." He sniffed, feigning sincerity. "I dreamed of it. Your death. And Peter's. Even the kids'. That's what kept me alive. Tracking you. Hunting you. You made it hard. I couldn't have done it without the Chunta. But even with their help, the only reason I'm here at all is because I hated you so much.

"And now that we're here, and your life is in my hands... I know that what I thought was hate, was jealousy. Because I love you. And I want what's best for you. That's not a life on the run. Or in a shithole like this. You and Anne can live long, safe lives."

"While ExoGen remakes the world?"

"That can't be stopped. It's far too late for that."

Ella didn't like the sound of that. "What have they done?"

"You'll find out when you come back with me," he said. "You can enjoy the fruits of your labor. You can live out your life...again and again. With Anne. With me. Regain ExoGen's trust and they might even let you help shape the future. Your morality is questionable, but your abilities will always be valuable to them.

"Tell you what. I'll even throw in the kid. Peter is a no-go, for obvious reasons. Just saying his name makes me want to slit my own throat for being kind to you. But I will spare his son. I'll take him to San Francisco with us, and I will let him live out his life. Just once, though."

That was the second time Kenyon alluded to being able to live more than once. Had ExoGen discovered some sort of immortality gene, buried in the junk DNA that she had helped unlock?

It was a tempting offer. Being human came with a mystery expiration date. Erasing that fateful moment...if really possible...would be seductive to most anyone on the planet. But giving up her daughter, not to mention the human race she'd already done enough to destroy, wasn't worth a thousand lifetimes.

In response to his offer, she reached up, took hold of her own finger, and with a quick jerk, snapped the digit. A roar of pain built in her chest, but abject defiance kept it in. "You won't make me scream. I will die first."

"Mmm," Kenyon said. "What about you?"

The question confused Ella until she saw where he was looking: in the living room, at Alia. She was glad Jakob was still outside. If he saw this, she had no doubt he'd try something stupid.

Kenyon snapped his fingers. "What's your name? Alex? Anna? Starts with an A, right?"

Alia peeked at him through her overhanging hair.

"Yes, you," Kenyon said. "Come over here, now, or I'll order my men to shoot your boyfriend outside. And please do leave your weapon on the floor."

Alia lowered her rifle. Placed it on the floor. Her hands quivered, electrified. She stood slowly on wobbly legs, and stepped toward the foyer. The man and woman she left behind just watched, despite the weapons in their hands. They might have been brave enough to make a stand against Mason. But against Kenyon, a gaggle of Riders, and three military helicopters? Whatever strength they had mustered had faltered. Though at least one of them had the gumption to take a shot at Kenyon. Whoever it was, she hoped he'd never find out.

When Alia stopped in front of him, he put his fingers under her chin and lifted it. She was covered in grime, but her quivering lower lip and tear-filled innocent eyes betrayed her weakness. Jakob was still adapting to the world and would one day be able to fill his father's shoes. But Alia...

Her days were numbered. This might even be her last.

"Where is she?" Kenyon asked.

"W-who?"

"The only 'she' in your group not currently present."

"I d-don't know."

"You're a very bad liar."

Alia said nothing but looked close to breaking down.

Kenyon turned to Crawford. The man had a block-shaped face and a square nose, like a pugilist who had taken too many hits to the face. "Knife."

Crawford drew a long blade from the sheath on his hip, spun it around in his hand, and handed it, hilt first, to Kenyon. The blade came up under Alia's throat so fast that the girl yelped.

"That's good," Kenyon said. "But try it a little louder for me."

The girl's resistance broke at the same moment her skin did. She screamed like only a teenage girl can, as piercing as a siren.

"Alia?" It was Jakob from outside.

"Stay outside, Jakob," Ella called. "She's okay."

"If he—"

"Stay outside!" Ella shouted.

Something on the second floor thumped. All eyes turned upward.

"Sweep the first floor," Kenyon told Crawford. Then he gave Alia a shove. "Up."

Alia started up the stairs, clutching the railing as she went. When Ella moved to follow, Kenyon pointed the knife at her. "You stay here." He looked to Hutchins. "If she tries anything stupid...shoot her legs."

Kenyon headed to the second floor, prodding Alia with the barrel of his rifle. When they reached the second floor, Hutchins adjusted his aim toward Ella's thigh.

"I used to think you were a nice guy, Paul," Ella said, using Hutchins's first name.

"Never really liked you much," he replied.

"Don't let Eddie hear you say—"

The scream that tore from the second floor was full of genuine pain. As hardened as Ella was, the sound worked its way through a chink in her emotional armor and brought a tear to her eye. Whatever innocence the girl had managed to cling on to was being ripped straight out of her heart. And everyone who heard it reacted in a different way, but all at once.

31

Beastmaster was a heavy truck with an amazing suspension that absorbed bumps and potholes with ease. Most of the cross-country trek, on road and off, was fairly smooth. But now, the truck bucked like a sugar-high kid in a bounce house. Peter struggled to maintain a straight course down the middle of the dirt road, which was smooth as far as dirt roads went. There was the occasional string of divots carved out by the rain, and large rocks spread out like road pimples, but none of that accounted for the rough ride. That came from the monster charging up behind them, its massive weight sending shockwaves through the earth with each heaving step.

The machine gun roared to life in spurts. In between the gunfire, Peter heard Feesa hooting loudly. He wasn't sure if the she-beast was frightened by the gun, pumped for battle, or communicating with the Riders. But she hadn't attacked Boone, so he figured it was one of the latter two options.

Behind them, the ExoGator gained. It could outpace them with ease. The only hope they had of outrunning it were the Riders, who surged out of the swamp in pursuit of the beast as it passed. The gator, locked on target, paid them no attention.

Woolies bounded onto the road, their shaggy hair undulating as they quickly matched the gator's speed.

Peter punched the steering wheel. "C'mon you slow son-of-a-bitch!"

Hundreds of tons of ExoGenetic horrors were careening toward them and *Beastmaster*, whose name Peter might have to rethink, was accelerating like a pot-smoking quadriplegic turtle.

"Faster!" Boone shouted from the back.

For the first time in his life, Peter felt Scotty's pain, and he nearly added the Star Trek engineer's Scottish brogue when he replied, "Going as fast as I can!"

When Boone squeezed off another fusillade of bullets, Peter watched in the rearview. If any of the rounds struck the gator, it showed no sign. But Peter did notice one of the Riders twitch and fall back off its steed. He held his breath, waiting for Feesa to exact her revenge on Boone, but she had either not noticed her brethren go down, or didn't understand that Boone's bad aim was the culprit.

Peter tore around a bend in the road, focusing all his attention on not driving the truck into the swamp. After turning hard in one direction, and then the other, the road straightened out again.

The gator didn't bother taking the turns. It plowed straight ahead, shattering trees and displacing thousands of gallons of water. Its crazed efforts pulled it ahead of the tribal ExoGens and closer to the truck.

Before Boone could open fire again, wasting even more ammunition, Peter called out. "Boone!"

The man ducked down and looked through the open window.

"Get in here and take the wheel," Peter shouted.

Boone gave a quick nod and slipped through the window. After falling into the back seat, he popped up behind Peter. "Can't shoot that thing for shit." Then he vaulted into the front passenger's seat beside Peter.

"Take the wheel," Peter said, and when Boone took hold with one hand, he added, "Foot on the gas. Ready?"

Boone slid into position, his foot hovering over Peter's.

"Now!" Peter yanked his foot away and Boone shoved his down. There was a brief jolt of deceleration—something *Beastmaster* had no trouble with—but then they were hauling forward again. Peter pushed up out of his seat and then slipped over Boone's head to the back seat.

"How much further to the gate?" Peter asked.

"We're only 'bout a mile out as the crow flies, but it's a winding road, so roughly two miles, give or take."

Which translated to just over two minutes at their current speed. Not a lot of time, but more than enough for the gator to make a meal of them. "Just keep us on the road," Peter said and started pushing himself through the tight back window. His ribs scraped against the frame, popping through one at a time, but he fell into the truck bed beside Feesa's large, hairy, and odorous feet.

Before standing, Peter scooped up the two large rubber bands attached to either side of the bed. He looped the carabiners at the ends to his belt and then stood up. The truck tore around a bend a moment later and he had no trouble staying upright. He clutched the machine gun, leaned his shoulder into the stock and looked down the metal sights. His finger looped around the trigger, but he didn't squeeze.

In the time it took him to clip himself in, stand, and aim the weapon, the Riders had made their move.

Two of the Woolies now flanked the gator on either side, their Riders coiled and ready to leap.

What the hell are they trying to do?

Before he could surmise the plan, Feesa raised her arms and bellowed a call, like some kind of Neanderthal orchestral composer. The Woolies reacted as one, turning in and thrusting their splayed horns. They struck with enormous force, bending and then punching through the gator's thick hide. Upon impact, the Riders, each a foot shorter than Peter, sprang into the air, spears in hand.

The two Riders arced through the air and landed atop the gator's back, just as it started reacting to the pain in its sides. The faster of the two males thrust his spear into the gator's back. He had something to hold on to when the monster bucked. The slower of the two was launched away, catapulted into the swamps, where he struck a tree, his body impaled on a branch, hanging limp.

The gator reared up its head and thrashed from side to side, losing momentum as it tore free from the horns. Rainbows of blood sprayed from the many puncture wounds, but it didn't look like enough to make a creature that size bleed out. The wounds would coagulate long before that happened.

But if the man on top can—

Peter's thoughts were cut short when the gator leaped into the air, performing what could only be described as an airborne death roll. The self-propelled ExoGator's spiral failed to fling free the strong male Rider, but it didn't have to. The man-thing was smeared beneath the massive reptilian body as it came back down to the dirt road, sliding as it continued to roll.

And then as suddenly as it leaped up, it sprang back to its feet, stopped on a dime, and wheeled around. It caught one of the two closest Woolies in its jaws, crushing it with untold PSI of force. The second Woolie was struck by the massive tail, which snapped out and slapped the Woolie into the swamp. Its body careened through trees and water with equal ease, coming to a stop far out of sight.

What followed was a crunching, slurping mess as the remaining Riders and Woolies slammed into the gator's side. The massive reptile let out a low, guttural growl that sent pressure waves pulsing through the air, but Peter suspected it was more an expression of frustration than pain. It reacted by thrashing back and forth, its massive jaws opening wide and snapping back down, over and over.

Riders screamed in pain.

Woolies groaned pitifully.

After a few bites, the gator's snout came up red. Blood and flesh sprayed with each bite. It was a gory fireworks display. And with each pop of flesh, each muffled scream and each flung and severed corpse, Feesa deflated a little more. Her bravado melted away.

Peter watched her, and to his surprise, he felt pity for her. She had been a woman once. Fully human with a life of her own. With a daughter, and maybe a husband. She hadn't asked to have that life stripped away. She still mourned the loss of her daughter. And now, this tribe of ExoGen monsters turned family, who he had wounded by killing Kristen, was being torn apart.

Feesa had suffered a lot.

They all had.

He leaned up from the weapon, which, as they increased the distance between them and the gator, became useless. "Feesa." When she didn't respond, he put his hand on her hairy arm. "Feesa."

She reeled around on him and roared. The stench of her breath made him wince, just as much as the four-inch fangs about to bite off his face. But she didn't bite. Instead, she sank back down into a hunched position, eyes on the truck bed.

Peter paused for a moment. The gator wasn't entirely finished mauling and consuming the Riders, but it had heard Feesa's cry. And like most ExoGens did, it responded by turning its attention to whatever living thing remained. He lost sight of it as they rounded a bend but had no doubt it would resume the chase. And when that happened, he needed Feesa to be more than a hairy mass of mourning.

He nearly told her that it would be all right. That she would get through it. But that was the kind of comfort people liked to hear. Then he remembered who he was speaking to. Despite the loss of her people and the very real anguish she was experiencing, she was still an ExoGen. At heart, she was guided by hunger, but for the Riders—the 'Chunta,' Feesa had called them—that unquenchable desire to hunt, kill and consume had been replaced by something else: revenge.

"Feesa!" he shouted. She started and looked about ready to attack, but the display was short-lived. Peter didn't want it to be, so he shouted again. "You are Chunta! You are strong!" He pointed behind them, where he expected the gator to emerge at any moment. "Alligator killed Chunta. We—" He thumped his chest, "—will kill alligator." Then he pointed over the roof off the truck. "We will kill Kenyon. We will protect our family."

That perked her up a little.

"Chunta sacrificed themselves to save our family." He was laying it on a little thick, but he didn't think her emotional states were very complex. She understood the big bold strokes of his stilted proclamations. She understood what family was. And for now, through some primitive familial loyalty, Peter and his own, were part of her brood. He thumped his chest, bringing the message home. "My family is your family. Your family is Chunta. *I* am Chunta, and we can still save them."

Feesa stood up so suddenly that Peter flinched back. Had he not been strapped in, he might have toppled over the side. But he sprang back into place as Feesa lowered her face to his. Her baritone voice rumbled out from between her long bottom teeth. "I...trust you."

He didn't hear a question mark but took it as such. "Yes. Family... family is everything. And ours is still alive."

The truck skidded to a stop. Peter looked forward and saw the closed gates of Hellhole Bay just ahead. "Gates are closed!" Boone shouted. "And ain't no one manning the post." Peter scanned the top of the gate. There had been a lookout position just to the side, before.

Now, it was empty.

They were locked outside.

He pointed to the gate and spoke to Feesa. "Family is inside."

"Kenyon too," she said.

"Can you open the gate?"

She responded by bounding onto the truck's cab and then launching off it. Her weight shook the vehicle and dented the roof, but Peter barely noticed. She landed near the top of the gate and started scaling it to the top.

But Peter didn't see her reach the top or drop down to the far side. All his attention snapped back to the road behind them, as an explosion of trees, blood, and water gave way to the gator, a quarter mile behind them. It skidded across the road, dug down with its long claws and then pounded toward the back of the truck. It was bringing all its millions of years of evolution, coupled with a few years of rapid-fire adaptations, to bear on a lone man, standing his ground. Not because Peter was brave, but because there was no other choice.

And then, something in his mind clicked. Beyond the pounding of primeval feet, the chug of *Beastmaster*'s engine and the rushing of his own blood, Peter heard something familiar, and close. Behind him. Inside the compound.

Helicopters.

They found us, he thought, and he removed his finger from the trigger. As much as he wanted to drill a hole through the ExoGator's eye socket, he didn't want the people on the far side of the wall to know he was coming, though once the gate opened, it would be impossible to hide.

32

"What has been seen, can never be unseen." Those words had been spoken by Jakob two weeks previous, when he'd stepped around a tree against which Anne was leaning, pants down, going to the bathroom. She'd thrown a turnip at him and chased him back to their parents, but the embarrassing–for both of them–event became a funny story. And 'What has been seen, can never be unseen,' became a catchphrase for a few days. When they saw an ugly creature. When Mom delivered a meal. When Dad woke up in the morning. The phrase went through her mind now as she looked up at the small room into which she'd fallen, but the phrase lacked all trace of its former humor.

"Shh," Shawna said, crawling in after her. "Are you trying to announce where we're hi–oly shit." The woman paused halfway through the door, her eyes angled up toward the walls.

For a moment, the two of them stared in silence, frozen by revulsion. Then Shawna seemed to remember that she was an adult, and as such, the moral guardian of anyone whose age still began with the prefix, 'pre.' "Don't look at it. Just stare at the floor."

Anne heard her but didn't listen. As much as she wanted to, she couldn't look away.

Shawna crawled the rest of the way into the room and then leaned back out, pulling the separated clothing back together. Then she pulled the door shut, yanking on the small handle, until the seam disappeared once more.

"Seriously," Shawna said. "This stuff isn't good for your brain." She then began plucking the 8x10 photos off the wall.

Despite the woman's verbal concern for Anne's psychological well-being, Anne knew better. Shawna was embarrassed. She might eventually take all the photos off the wall, but she was starting with the photos of herself. In some, she was alone. Changing. Bathing. Standing in front of a mirror. But in others, she had company. The man Anne assumed was Mason. His old raisin-like body was a stark contrast to Shawna's plump, grape-like curves. But what was he doing, pressing his gross self, up against her, his face warped with what? Pleasure? And her face... She didn't look happy. Or sad. Or angry. She looked dead. She looked...

Unconscious.

Then Anne saw it. *Really* saw it. What his body was doing to hers. To the other maids—Charlotte and Sabine. To women she didn't recognize. And a few she did, including Carrie.

Anne nearly threw up but contained her revolting stomach.

She looked away from the walls and found herself looking through a window that revealed the bedroom. She ducked down, afraid of being seen. "Get down!"

Shawna ducked with her, clutching the lewd photos of herself. "What is it?"

"A window," Anne said, keeping her voice quiet. She pointed up at the window, but even now she was starting to realize the truth. She'd walked right past the gilded mirror and hadn't thought anything of it. But it wasn't just a simple mirror. You couldn't see in, but you could see out.

"I should have guessed." Shawna stood back up and resumed pulling down photos. "I don't care if there really are just a hundred people left in the world. Mason didn't deserve to be one of them."

"He's not the only one," Anne said, but didn't elaborate. Instead, she inspected the rest of the room's contents, careful to avoid looking at the walls. There was a video camera mounted on a tripod. It was positioned off to the side, but it could be set up in front of the two-way mirror. The cord dangling from the camera led to a computer sitting atop a desk in the corner of the room. There were two flat-screen monitors, speakers, and a very nice, high-end printer. Stacks of photo paper and ink cartridges lined the floor of one wall.

What looked like a thick notebook sat next to the computer keyboard and mouse. Anne opened it to find page after page of DVDs, carefully labeled with names and dates, and slotted into protective sleeves. Anne noted that the dates on the first ten pages went back to well before the Change. She turned dozens of pages at a time, counting more than thirty different names. Then she reached a page with just three DVDs, and stopped, not because it was the last page—though it was—but because she recognized the name on the final DVD: Ella Masse.

Anne's eyes flicked to the printer. A single page lay face down in the tray.

She reached out for it slowly. Her fingers fumbled with the page edge until she lost her patience and crushed the whole page in her hand. She nearly fell over when she turned the image around and saw her mother's naked form. She had seen her mother with no clothes on several times. And she was expecting to see a candid shot of her. But the look on her mother's face… It was seductive.

"Your mother was a smart lady," Shawna said.

"She doesn't look very smart," Anne replied, wondering for a moment if this is how her mother seemed to get her way with men. "She looks like a slut."

"A smart slut, then." Shawna shrugged. "She was giving him the show he wanted. Disarming him. Distracting him. Men like Mason think with their...never mind."

Anne was about to say that she wasn't as young as she looked, but the truth, she was beginning to realize, was that she was far younger than she had been led to believe. She might look twelve, and act twelve, but her formative years had been rushed past. "I don't need to know."

Shawna looked relieved. "The point is, this photo of her doesn't reveal a weakness. It reveals a strength. Probably why she's still alive and Mason is a piñata."

Anne nodded. She knew it was true. *Mom would do just about anything to stay alive. For me,* Anne thought. *She stayed alive for me.*

No, that's not right. She stayed alive for everyone.

As much as Anne liked to think Ella's dedication to her was all about the bond between mother and daughter, she knew a large portion of it had more to do with what Anne meant to all of humanity. Lawrence might have thought to check Anne's DNA, but it had never occurred to him to search for a USB device hidden in her head. Why would he? It was ludicrous.

And Ella had clearly used these same...skills to enamor Eddie. Did she ever care about him? Or was he always a pawn? Would she be able to reignite his feelings for her? It seemed likely since he didn't kill her on sight. Or was he now playing her to find Anne? Adults were confusing.

But what really befuddled Anne now was the sneaking suspicion, and concern, that Ella was also using Peter. Her father.

What if he's not *my father? What if we look alike only because he and Mom look alike?*

The memories Anne had of young Mom and Dad didn't support this theory. She'd felt what her mother felt for him. But she also had a large chunk of her mother's memories missing, including the time period when Peter chose another woman over her mother.

That couldn't have gone over well.

But would she betray him? Would she manipulate him?

Yes, Anne decided. If it meant keeping Anne safe and undoing the wrong she had inflicted on the world. Ella would do anything.

Anything.

So, the question was, in the case of Peter, did Ella need to lie, or was the truth enough?

"What are you going to do with those?" Anne pointed at the growing stack of photos.

"Burn them."

Anne handed the photo of her mother to Shawna. "The computer and DVDs, too."

The woman sneered at the disc collection. Confirmation enough. When Shawna looked back up, her eyes went wide with surprise and fear. She was looking at the two-way mirror.

Anne turned around and looked into Mason's bedroom. What she saw made her whole body go rigid.

Eddie stood in the bedroom, looking right at them.

He can see us! Anne thought, and then she realized the truth. Eddie was looking at his reflection and forcing Alia to look at hers. The girl, who annoyed Anne most of the time, but had started growing on her, was wet with tears.

Her whole face trembled.

Kenyon had a long knife, the tip of it pressed against Alia's cheek.

He shouted something at her, making a demand.

Despite her fear, Alia shook her head, denying the man's request and gaining a boatload of respect from Anne. Alia might be a burden in the wild, but she was braver than Anne would have guessed. Defying a man with a knife to your face took a lot of guts. But in the case of Eddie Kenyon, it was also stupid.

Eddie relaxed a little. Let out a sigh.

"No," Anne said. "Stop."

Eddie showed no sign of hearing her.

Shawna wrapped a hand around Anne's mouth. "Shut up!"

Eddie loosened his grip but kept the knife in place. He spoke to her again. Anne imagined his soothing voice, reassuring her that everything was going to be okay, if she just did what he was asking.

Right when Alia started to buy into it, relaxing her body, staring right into Anne's eyes without knowing it, Eddie shoved the knife blade through her cheek and yanked it out just as quickly. There was a wide-eyed beat as Alia tried to comprehend was had just happened, then blood began to gush over her face, and from her mouth.

Alia screamed.

It had to have been loud, but Mason's secret room had apparently been soundproofed. Anne couldn't hear a thing, but her tough heart broke for the girl on the other side of the mirror.

Alia was suffering for Anne.

"What the hell is he doing?" Shawna asked. "Why is he torturing her?"

"To get to me," Anne said. "To get me to come out."

Anne started rummaging through drawers, disgusted as more photos, DVDs, and other more tangible evidence of Mason's perversions spilled onto the floor.

"What are you doing?" Shawna asked.

Anne pulled a sharpened pencil from the drawer. It wasn't much, but it was better than nothing. "He's good at his job."

Shawna said nothing, but had a distinct, 'what's that supposed to mean?' look on her face.

"You're welcome to help me," Anne said. "But don't get in my way." Then she stepped to the small hidden door and yanked it open.

33

Kenyon winced. The girl's scream was far louder than he'd anticipated. It blasted into his left ear with the kind of high-pitched decibels that went out of musical style when the 1980s came to a neon-clad closure. Despite the horrendous sound, and the pain it brought, Kenyon was pleased. Anne was a tough girl, but Kenyon knew part of her bravado was to hide her bleeding heart. She cared about people. All people. Even ones she didn't like. He didn't know if Anne and Alia were close, but he did know they'd been together for the past five weeks. That meant, if Anne was hiding in the house, she'd probably expose herself to save the girl. And if she wasn't, Alia would scream until she died.

Kenyon yanked the girl by the back of her shirt, positioning her between him and the open door. From here, Anne would be able to hear the screaming from anywhere in the house and out the front door. And if Ella or Jakob got any suicidal ideas, she'd make a good human shield.

When Alia began to cry, Kenyon leaned down next to her bleeding face. "You're going to scream for me now, aren't you?"

Tears mingled with blood as she nodded.

"If you make me ask again, I'm going to carve holes in your cheeks. Understand?"

She nodded once more and tried to groan an 'Mmm hmm,' but an uncontrolled sob bubbled up from her chest. She tried to hold it in, but the sound popped from the side of her ruined cheek, spraying blood onto Kenyon's face.

His smile gleamed white. He didn't mind the blood. And the girl was already screaming again, even louder than before.

Over the shrill anguish ripping through the air, Kenyon heard something new and disconcerting: the Apache's chain gun.

It's the kid, he thought. Ella wasn't foolish enough to risk her life, and everyone else's because of a scream. But Jakob, he'd also spent the past five weeks with Alia, and she was a looker. Probably head over heels. How could he not be? She might be the only teenage girl left alive on the planet.

Eddie chastised himself for not realizing it sooner, but it didn't matter. If the Apache was shooting at him, the kid was stew.

His smile returned.

Jakob's demise would definitely bring Anne running. Her friends were dying, and that was something he knew she couldn't abide. He'd seen her face every time they lost a member of their original party. Ella was cold and indifferent, the way a survivor had to be. Like Eddie. But Anne? Every life lost chewed her up inside. She eventually got good at hiding it, cloaking herself in a shell of indifference, but that didn't mean she was invulnerable to loss.

When the string of chain gun rounds echoed to a stop, Eddie prodded Alia in the back and said, "Again!"

As the scream bubbled up the girl's throat, something about the light in the room changed. A shadow. Moving fast. Kenyon's first thought was that one of the helicopters had flown past, blocking the sun for a moment, but he hadn't heard a change in the rotors' pitch. *Someone's in the room,* he thought, but he dismissed the idea. He'd checked under the bed and in the closet. The room was empty.

But his neck prickled when he detected just a hint of a pulsing vibration in the floorboards beneath his feet.

Someone's running. Charging.

Move!

Kenyon shifted to the side, while twisting to face his stealthy attacker. The movement saved his life. Instead of puncturing his jugular, the pencil punched a hole in his already wounded arm. It hurt like hell but wouldn't make him less capable than the bullet already had.

But the attacker wasn't done. The pencil came out with a slurp, reeled back, and stabbed again before Eddie could counter. This time, the writing utensil struck a nerve in his elbow, sending an electric shock up his brutalized arm. He stumbled back, thrown by the pain.

Sensing she was free, Alia scrambled from the room, clutching her cheek, lost in terror. But as Kenyon turned to face his attacker, knife in hand, he forgot all about Alia. She'd fulfilled her role.

Anne had come out of hiding.

The girl stood before him, pencil wielded like a blade.

She looked mostly how he remembered her, but with a shaved head. There was something different about her eyes though. He recognized the ferocity, but there was something else in the mix.

Confidence, he realized.

Anne charged, targeting his wounded arm. It wasn't a bad attack. The more holes she put in him, the more he'd bleed. And with loss of blood came loss of energy, and eventually death. And she nearly tagged him with the pencil again, but the rest of him was still operating at 100%, and eager for a fight. He sidestepped and kicked out his left leg, slamming his shin into hers.

A shout of pain burst from Anne's throat. She tumbled forward and nearly drove her face into the corner of a nightstand, which would have been unfortunate. She reached out and caught herself before colliding, dropping the pencil.

"You don't need to fight me," Kenyon said. "You and your mother can come back to ExoGen. You can live long, happy lives."

Anne grunted, pushing herself up, favoring her right leg. "We were happy."

"Out here? In this miserable world?"

Anne's eyes flicked around the room, no doubt searching for a weapon, but other than the pencil that had rolled through the open door and into the hallway, there was nothing. Kenyon held his knife out, letting her see the long blade. He also had the assault rifle on his back, but it would be impossible to quickly retrieve with one arm. She'd be out the door or trying to gouge his eyes out before his hand found the grip. "There are a hundred ways I can make you hurt, without killing you."

"And there's a hundred ways that I don't give a shit."

Kenyon remembered he was arguing with a twelve-year-old. Logic and threats weren't going to get him anywhere, especially with Anne.

"And what about your mother?" he asked.

"She's taking care of herself," the girl said.

Kenyon was about to reply when Anne's words sank in.

She hadn't said Ella could take care of herself.

She said Ella *was* taking care of herself. Present tense. It was then that Kenyon heard the sounds of a struggle rumbling up from the first floor. Hutchins and Crawford had been engaged, and so far, not a single shot had been fired.

Then a voice rolled up the staircase. "Alia!" The kid. Not dead. So, who had the Apache shot?

Anne charged with a scream, fingers hooked like claws, something she'd learned from her mother. Kenyon aimed for her arm and swung the knife. The cut would be deep, and take the fight out of her, but it wouldn't kill her. The blade slid through the air and struck nothing. Anne dove beneath it, rolling onto her back and then kicking up hard.

Kenyon felt his balls compress. The sensation was followed by pain and nausea that threatened to drop him to the floor. But that wasn't what happened. There were few things more painful, but most men struck in the nuts fell to the ground, not out of pain, but for attention. He did pitch forward though, and that's when Anne drove the same foot up into his chin.

He staggered back but caught hold of Anne's extended leg. With a surge of anger, he lifted the light girl and flung her across the room. She bounced off the bed, struck the far wall and fell over the side.

Kenyon stumbled back into the wall, shattering a framed painting of a farm, the kind the world used to subsidize. He fought against the urge to puke, and kept his eyes on the bed, waiting for Anne to reappear. And when she did, the gloves would be off. He would try not to kill her still. She was his golden ticket, though he didn't really understand what made her so valuable. But he had every intention of beating her to within an inch of her life. No more kid gloves.

Anne vaulted around the back of the bed, charging him head on. "Asshole!"

He swung with the knife and realized too late that Anne was also armed and swinging. At first glance, he thought it was a baseball bat. When it struck his knife hand, lancing pain up his arm, he recognized the weapon as an oversized rubber phallus, which she wielded like a cudgel. The knife clattered to the floor, but Kenyon wasn't holding back now.

She might have caught him off guard—again—but she couldn't stop him.

Not with a dildo.

With his hand free of the knife, he grasped onto her wrist and squeezed hard enough to elicit a scream of pain. Then he flung her like a trebuchet. She slammed into a dresser, above which was an ugly gold mirror.

Anne groaned and started pushing herself up.

"Stay down, Anne," Kenyon said, stalking toward her.

"You can stick that big—"

Kenyon kicked her in the gut. She buckled forward, gasping for air. Didn't even fight back when he leaned down and wrapped his fingers around her throat. She kicked when her feet came off the ground, but she lacked the energy to hurt him. She raked her nails over his arm, drawing blood, but as the oxygen to her brain dwindled, so did her efforts.

Not too hard, he told himself. He wanted her unconscious, not dead.

"Just go to sleep," Kenyon cooed. "Close your eyes. That's a good girl."

Despite the pain she'd caused him, he really did like Anne. When they'd trekked through the wild after first leaving ExoGen, he'd even let himself see her as something like family. A Goddaughter. Maybe even a stepchild someday. It was a fantasy, and one that would likely never be realized now, but things like anger and hate can fade over time, especially when you're safe and well fed.

Anne's eyelids flickered as consciousness drifted. *Just another second.*

Kenyon blinked. His view of the room shifted. Made no sense.

What the hell?

Instead of looking at Anne, and his own reflection in the mirror behind her, he saw a sideways view of the floor. Anne was still there, no longer in his grasp, but the world had gone from horizontal to vertical.

How did I end up on the floor?

Pain was his answer, throbbing at the back of his head along with a spreading liquid warmth.

A foot stepped into view, barefoot and feminine. A decorative butter churn dropped to the floor beside it. A woman dressed as a maid crouched down between him and Anne. She shook the girl gently, whispering before turning to the door and yelling, "Help! Someone help!"

Eddie could hear movement in the house.

People shouting.

People screaming.

Gunshots rang out, inside and outside. Something bigger than his bedroom scuffle was going on.

Get up, he told himself. *Get up and get out.*

While the maid was focused on Anne, he slid across the floor, reached beneath the bed, and took hold of the dropped knife. His body ached with every movement, but he fought against the pain. *Save it for later, Eddie. Just fucking move!*

Eddie swung the knife.

Metal slipped through skin, muscle, and tendon. The maid shrieked and dropped like Achilles, but without the legendary build up. He wanted to kill her, but he sensed there wasn't time. While the woman writhed in agony, Kenyon got his feet beneath him and stood.

Footsteps approached the doorway, rapid fire, coming to help.

He threw the knife.

A woman walked into it, taking the blade in her chest. She toppled over beside the maid, still alive, but not even close to putting up a fight. Kenyon pulled the assault rifle over his head and laid it on the bed. He then hoisted Anne off the floor and slung her over his shoulder, balancing her limp form. Next, he retrieved the weapon and turned to the window, prepared to kick it out. But there were bars on the far side of the glass.

Mason had turned the place into a prison.

Kenyon stepped over the women on the floor and into the hallway.

Ahead of him was the staircase to the first floor, which sounded like a battle zone, and the staircase to the third floor. Would the windows up there be barred as well? Kenyon replayed his memory of the home's outside. The windows were barred, but he had also seen a small deck with a door. People fleeing Mason's prison might not be able to get past the door, and if they did, they probably wouldn't throw themselves from a third-floor balcony. But Kenyon had a keychain made of bullets, and he wouldn't have to jump.

He took a step toward the stairs and stopped when his name tore through the air. "Eddie!"

He glanced down toward the first floor. Ella was there, covered in blood, rifle in hand.

"You'll come with me now," he said. "You have no choice."

"There's always a choice, Eddie," she said, and she raised the weapon to fire.

Eyes wide, Eddie dodged to the side as a fusillade of bullets chewed up the banister. He ran up the stairs for the third floor, propelled by the sound of Ella Masse, charging up after him, out for blood.

34

Jakob acted without thinking. He realized it two steps into his sprint, but there was no going back. And he was pretty sure that meant he was toast.

The Riders stood close enough to pounce on him, though they seemed a bit overwhelmed by the number of people, the three helicopters, and Kenyon's disappearance inside the house.

Then there were the choppers. One had stayed a safe distance back, slowly circling the house, high above. They'd no doubt spotted Hellhole Bay's residents hiding in the unfinished dome but hadn't opened fire on them. The Black Hawk was on the ground, its rotors churning slowly, ready to speed back up, but it wasn't defenseless. A man stood behind the large machine gun, moving it back and forth at the house, looking for targets, of which there were many. And then there was the Apache. Its ominous insect-like cockpit was turned directly toward him. He wasn't an expert on attack helicopters, but he knew this one had a machine gun, or two, and a crap-ton of rockets hidden inside the tubes mounted on either side.

He heard the whine of a chain gun spinning up. He recognized it from video games, though the real thing was far more metallic and grating. His eyes crushed shut while his legs kept pumping.

A Rider roared. He heard it charging.

Bullets scorched the air.

Hot wetness splashed against him. He was struck hard, all at once, the pain everywhere, just as he'd imagined.

Except, he kept on feeling the pain.

He'd been struck, but not by chain gun bullets.

He tried to move but found himself locked in place.

Couldn't see anything.

Am I paralyzed?

Am I dead?

He decided he wasn't. Because despite the darkness and immobility, he could hear. Everything was muffled, but he could hear the thrumming machine gun beating out a steady rhythm. He could hear shouts and screams and small arms fire. All of it mixed with the hooting of angry Riders.

He could also smell. Noxious and visceral. Meat and blood. Then he tasted it, slipping through his lips and along the side of his tongue.

His thoughts returned to death. The scent of his own gore. The fading audio. The darkness.

But through it all, the pain continued. If his soul was slipping into the hereafter, wouldn't the pain fade, too? Or was that hell?

I'm alive, he told himself, focusing on his limbs. *Now get up and deal.*

Jakob pushed with his arms. His body shifted upward, but only moved an inch off the ground before falling back down beneath a massive weight that stole his breath away and sent stars dancing in his vision. He might not be dead yet, but he soon would be.

During that second of momentum, a sliver of light illuminated the fleshy prison pinning him to the ground. Marbleized gore and bones wrapped around him. A corpse. He could feel the hot organs slipping over the back of his legs. He kicked and found his feet free to move.

Fighting back his emotional percolation, Jakob bent his knees and shimmied them up toward his chest, creating a gap. Fresh air billowed in, but it served only to coil more of the stench deeper into his nose. His stomach lurched and dry heaved. He used the motion to slide out of the slick weight. His progress slowed as something sharp, like a set of claws, raked his back, lifting his shirt. The fabric peeled off over his head as he spilled back into the light of day and saw three Riders, or what used to be Riders, piled up where he'd been lying. Then he saw what had been clawing at his back and dry heaved once more. They weren't claws. They were jagged, exposed ribs. His shirt, removed from his body, hung from the longest of them.

The creatures had launched an attack only to be mowed down by the Apache, who had also been firing at him. Their bodies were shredded and turned inside out, inadvertently protecting him from the bullets.

Riders weren't stupid, but they weren't exactly smart.

Or lucky.

Jakob's intelligence was debatable. Anne reminded him of that every day. But his luck...his luck was undeniable.

The Apache peeled off around the side of the house as gunfire from the second floor pinged off its body. The helicopter could tear the home apart, but with three men inside, they were holding their fire.

The Black Hawk was spinning up again, prepping to leave the ground and its dangers behind.

The Riders that hadn't been cut down had thrown themselves into action. Two were chasing after the Apache. One was headed for the Black Hawk, and three were assaulting the second floor of the farmhouse, shaking the bars mounted over the windows and trying to reach the people inside, peppering them with bullets and screams.

The path to the first floor was open, right up to the door. That's where the last of the Riders was, pounding its fists into the porch and shrieking like a deranged chimpanzee.

Jakob took only his third step toward what was supposed to be an impulsive rescue attempt, but was stopped again, this time by the realization that he was now unarmed. He looked at the leaking mass of ExoGenetic flesh and saw the butt of his AK-47 sticking out. He crouched down and grasped the wood stock, eyes up, hoping no one would spot him.

If not for the massive amount of blood lubing the bodies, he wouldn't have been able to move the weapon, but it slowly came free until the rifle was birthed, covered in blood, mucus, and who knew what else. Jakob quickly tried wiping the weapon clean, but he realized his entire body was equally covered in gore.

That didn't mean the weapon wouldn't work. His father had taught him about common weapons over the past few weeks, and one of the best things about AK-47s was that they were virtually weatherproof, functioning despite sand, dust, and water. So, the rifle might still fire.

Might.

He found out a moment later when a battle cry turned his eyes up. One of the Riders had spotted him, covered in the blood of its tribe, standing over their bodies. It flung itself off the farmer's porch roof and dropped down toward him, fists raised.

Jakob raised the rifle, tripped back over a Rider's severed limb, and pulled the trigger. The weapon barked like a faithful dog, cutting a line of red splotches up the Rider's body. The creature looked undeterred until the line reached its head. All its coiled rage disappeared, and the beast fell at his feet.

Pushing himself up, Jakob ran for the door this time, his legs shaky, but his determination surging. "Hey!" he yelled at the Rider blocking the door. It spun around and lunged, claws reaching. The thing had been waiting for a target and found one in Jakob, but he had already fired. Four rounds struck the diving monster head on.

It fell to the porch and tumbled down the stairs next to Mason's corpse, as Jakob vaulted up them.

He raised the weapon, clutching hard against the slippery film coating it. But he didn't fire.

Couldn't fire.

Like the Rider before him, there was too much going on to attack one side or the other without killing friend and foe alike. The man named Hutchins had Ella around the waist, his back against the hallway wall, his face red with the effort of trying to control her.

"Ella," the man shouted. "It doesn't need to go down like this."

But Ella had other ideas. She had one leg extended up against Crawford's throat, pressing him back against the opposite hallway wall. With her free arm, she swatted at his hand, which held a pistol he was attempting to point in her direction. Beyond the brawl, he could see people rushing about, some keeping track of the choppers, some fleeing, but no one helping Ella.

They don't know who to help, he realized. Ella was as much a stranger to most of them as Hutchins and Crawford.

But Jakob knew who was who, and what he had to do.

He shifted the AK-47's dripping barrel toward Crawford, who was close to turning that gun on Ella, and who posed the greatest threat to Jakob as well.

When he heard a fight further up in the house, and what he thought was Anne's voice, he nearly pulled the trigger. Not wanting to shoot Ella's foot off, he shouted, "Drop it!"

Three sets of eyes turned toward him and simultaneously widened. Even Ella looked horrified by his appearance. Then she snapped back to the struggle and used the distraction to her advantage, slamming Crawford's gun hand against the far wall, pinning it in place.

"Jake," Ella said. "You don't need to—"

"They need us," Jakob said, and Ella knew exactly who 'they' were: Alia and Anne.

Ella looked confused for a moment, but then Anne's voice filtered down from the second floor. "Asshole!"

"Do it!" Ella shouted, all her concern for what taking a human life might do to Jakob evaporated by a single word from her daughter. Anne was upstairs. Alia was upstairs. And so was Eddie Kenyon.

Jakob pulled the trigger, firing a single round that punched through Crawford's head and into the wall behind him. His head left a red streak as his body slid to the floor.

Covered in the remains of things that once were human and having borne witness to countless horrible deaths, including his own mother's, Jakob felt very little over taking the man's life. *It was justified,* he thought, when doubt started creeping into his thoughts.

Ella wasted no time debating right and wrong. No longer contending with Crawford, she twisted and drove an elbow into the side of Hutchins's head. Once, twice, three times. The third strike hit his temple and his grip wavered.

Ella tore free and raised an open hand to Jakob. "Weapon!"

Without thinking, Jakob tossed her the AK-47. She caught it and turned toward the stairs, just as Eddie Kenyon stepped into view. Anne hung limp over his shoulder.

"Eddie!" Ella shouted, and aimed up at the man.

He stopped and looked down at her, something like a smile on his face. "You'll come with me now. You have no choice."

"There's always a choice, Eddie." Ella raised the weapon and fired as Eddie ducked to the side. When Ella took her finger off the trigger, Eddie's footfalls could be heard pounding up a flight of steps. Ella raced after him, taking the steps two at a time.

Before Jakob could follow, he was struck in the leg. Off balance, he had no defense against Hutchins, who got back to his feet and flung Jakob into the staircase. The man shouted, "You crazy bitch!" after Ella and then he retreated out the front door.

Jakob groaned and rolled back to his hands and knees. Moving slowly at first, he started up the stairs after Ella.

At the second-floor landing, he turned to head up the next flight when he heard crying. He turned toward a closed bedroom door. "Alia?"

He pushed the door open. Alia was on the floor, clutching her face, covered in blood. She shrieked and winced back.

"Alia!" He rushed in and fell by her side. She yelped in fright but fell into his arms.

"I'm sorry." She quivered against him, broken. "I'm sorry."

"It's okay," he told her. "You're okay."

She wasn't, not really. She'd been injured, maybe not mortally, but it wasn't something that would heal fast, or that she'd ever forget. And they were nowhere near out of danger yet. But he couldn't think of anything else to say. So, while she continued to repeat, "I'm sorry," again and again, he countered each apology with, "It's okay."

As they fell into the tennis match chant, Jakob heard a familiar deep and rumbling machine gun, coupled with a roaring engine.

Beastmaster! Jakob thought, a trace of hope returning.

But then there was something else.

Something bigger.

Its arrival shook the house.

Something *much* bigger.

35

In every conflict, there was a point of no return. When a soldier had to take action, damn the consequences, or things would get FUBAR faster than could be corrected. That moment was rapidly approaching Peter, about fifty feet per second, as the galloping horror closed in on the immobile truck.

But what could he do, really? Shooting the creature wouldn't have that much effect unless his aim was impeccable. And that would be nearly impossible. Despite the long legs, the gator's long body and snout made it run in a kind of awkward vertical slither, like a reptilian ferret.

He could run, but there was no way that would extend his life beyond a second or two, and it would mean abandoning Boone. They could attempt to scale the gate, like Feesa had, but that would likely end with them being plucked off the wall and gobbled up.

If we survive this, I'm picking up some grenades, Peter thought.

He'd passed on the explosive devices before, because unlike most projectile weapons, they couldn't be sound suppressed. The best way to kill ExoGenetic creatures was to not invite more to the party. The machine gun mounted in the back of *Beastmaster* was the one exception to that rule.

It was a weapon of last resort and was generally used on the move.

Peter looked down the machine gun's sights, shifting his aim up and down, attempting to match the rhythm of the gator's gait. But its head moved in jerky circular motions, so he held his aim steady. He timed his trigger finger with the moment his small target slipped back into the kill zone, or in this case, the wound zone. He had no illusions about killing the beast. He just wanted to slow it down.

Fire, he thought as the gator's black eyes slipped in and out of view.

Fire.

Fire.

He let his finger twitch with each pass.

Fire.

Fire.

He pulled the trigger, letting loose a burst of bullets that started low and traced a line upward. He saw the gator's skin bend and ripple as the large rounds punched against it. The eye snapped shut for a moment, but it was just a flinch. The thing didn't even slow down.

As he looked down the sights again, Peter's ears perked up. He could hear the gate's locks sliding away, one by one. Feesa was doing her job, but maybe not fast enough. Then, over the din of helicopter blades, he heard gunshots. And shouting. He felt a moment of confusion, as his mind backtracked. The battle inside the compound had begun, while he was aiming at the gator, but he'd filtered it out.

The hell is going on in there? he wondered, but he already knew. Choppers meant ExoGen, and if they were here, and Kenyon was here, Anne and Ella were in grave danger. They might not be killed, but they would certainly be taken. For Peter and the rest of humanity eking a living outside San Francisco, that was a very bad thing.

He pushed all his worries aside and focused once more on the gator. He had just seconds before its arrival.

Fire.

Fire.

He pulled the trigger again, this time holding it down and following the gator's circular motion, peppering its face and snout with three rounds every second. Four seconds in, and just four more from being bitten in half, the gator convulsed.

Mid gallop, the monster pawed at its face. With the limb raised up, the body crashed down to the road, grinding to a stop just forty feet away from Peter. It scratched at its face, trying to dislodge what had caused it such sudden pain. But the bullet was too deep and too small to retrieve. The gator just ended up smearing the gooey remains of its ruptured eyeball.

The creature opened its jaws wide and let loose a guttural growl of frustration, plastering Peter with a wave of fleshy breath. Tufts of Woolie fur dangled from its traffic cone-sized teeth. The mouth snapped closed, the sound clapping against Peter's ears. Then the beast death-rolled with nothing in its mouth. It flailed across the road, churning into the swamp, where loosely rooted trees toppled beneath its girth.

Then it stopped.

The waters settled.

The creature's belly heaved with each breath, but it seemed to be calming, regaining its monstrous composure.

C'mon, Peter thought, but he dared not say anything. The gator's simple reptilian mind had forgotten them for the moment.

And that was when Boone revved *Beastmaster*'s engine. The rumbling exhaust sounded angry and alive.

The gator twitched its head to the side, looking directly at Peter with its one good eye.

Damnit, Boone, he thought, and then he noticed the truck was moving. He glanced forward and saw the gates opening. They were through, but too late. The ExoGator exploded from the swamp, slipping in the muck for a few steps before launching back onto the road.

The truck heaved forward in time with the creature. Peter fired at the healthy eye, but missed as the truck shook from an impact. Feesa had leaped onto the cab's roof. She was crouched and ready to leap, spear in hand. But she wasn't looking at the gator. She stared straight ahead.

Peter risked a quick look and saw the farmhouse, the familiar blue Black Hawk on the ground, an Apache in the air with its back to *Beastmaster,* a collection of Chunta on the ground and—

"Jakob!"

The boy broke into a run.

Several Chunta dove for him, hackles raised.

The Apache opened fire. Blood and carnage ruptured like a fireworks display, fanning red in all directions, much of which splattered across the farmhouse's white exterior.

Peter screamed in time with Feesa, as their families were mowed down.

Small arms fire responded from the home's windows.

Peter tried to swivel the machine gun around to blow the Apache from the sky, but he was still locked in place by the rubber bands. And that was a good thing. Had he not been, the truck's rapid acceleration would have thrown him into the gator's open maw, just twenty feet back.

Filled with anguish and desperation, Peter screamed and held the trigger down, punching bullets into the Apex predator's throat. The massive tongue twitched and flailed, rising up over the throat like a meaty shield. But Peter kept on firing, digging a crater into its flesh.

The truck bucked as they rocketed over the bound logs bridging the wide stream. Peter's aim went high, and he stopped firing.

The gator stepped down on the logs, shattering them. Its leg dropped into the stream, slamming its chin into the scorched earth. Ash billowed up around it, and in *Beastmaster*'s wake, but it was quickly swept away by the Apache's rotor wash. As the creature scrabbled in the stream bed, trying to pull itself up, the truck pulled away.

Peter unclipped himself from the rubber bands and ducked to the window. "Stay on that chopper!"

"But the gator!" Boone protested.

"Do it!" Peter said, burning with rage that dwarfed the gator's.

Boone didn't look happy about it, but as the Apache canted to the side and fled the gunfire coming from the house, the truck turned hard to follow it.

Peter clung to the machine gun as the truck's motion threatened to spill him over the side. When the truck straightened course again, Peter had the weapon turned forward, ready to fire over the cab and take down the Apache. The attack helicopter was tough. Built for war. They weren't easy to take down without a missile, but the M249 could do the job, especially if you knew where to aim. But the view between Peter and the chopper was brown and hairy.

He nearly fired through Feesa to take out the Apache. If the chopper hadn't killed his son, the Chunta clearly would have. And the females still left alive were assaulting the house, and the people within it. Feesa might have made peace with Peter, but her sisters hadn't. They were still aligned with Eddie.

"Get out of the way," he shouted at Feesa's back.

She reared around and roared at him, her face twisted with a fury that matched his own. She'd seen most of her tribe get decimated today, most recently by the chopper, but what could she do against a killing machine like that?

The Apache stopped and turned, its body now ninety degrees to the truck, its weapons aimed at the house, but not firing.

They have people on the inside, Peter thought.

The pilot must have seen them coming, because the chopper suddenly swiveled in their direction. But the angle was wrong. It wasn't aiming at the truck; it was aiming behind it. Peter glanced over his shoulder. The gator had not only freed itself from the stream but had also closed the distance.

Vengeance or survival? He had just a second to debate the matter. But it was Feesa who made the call.

Vengeance.

The warrior tribeswoman leapt off the truck's roof, denting it inward and soaring thirty feet in the air, bringing her face to face with the Apache and the shocked pilot behind the windshield.

Machine guns whirled, prepping to fire.

Feesa cocked the spear back.

Peter opened fire, punching a string of holes through the empty passenger's seat, distracting the pilot long enough for Feesa to lob the spear.

The idea of a spear taking down an Apache was ludicrous. But when it was thrown by a hulk of a woman, with a force greater than Peter could get out of his compound bow, it wasn't impossible. That was the lesson learned by the pilot when the spear punched through the windshield, and then his chest, just inside his left shoulder. Pinned back against his seat, and in mind numbing pain, the pilot lost control.

As Feesa landed on barren earth, the chopper twisted, tilted, and descended straight for the truck.

Boone turned a hard left, plowing in the shanty village, sending sheets of metal flying like giant throwing stars. Peter ducked as a corrugated metal square spun over his head and struck the gator's side, digging in deep. But Peter barely noticed the fresh wound as he saw the gator's attention had shifted from truck to chopper, which plunged on a collision course with the massive reptile.

The gator lunged into the air, its jaws open wide.

The Apache spun in tight circles as it descended.

As the cockpit turned to face the attacking super-predator, the behemoth bit down. There was a crunch as the armored vehicle momentarily repulsed the immense crushing power. The spinning rotor blades struck the snout, cutting deep, but shearing away, one at a time. Angered by the fresh wounds, the gator bit down hard, and the cockpit began to fold inward as the locked pair dropped back down to the ground, but never made it.

Peter could only guess what went through the pilot's mind. He had been speared and then locked in the crushing embrace of an alligator as large as the Apache he thought would keep him safe. But the man's response, whether it be a calculated risk, or sheer panic, was deadly—to both man and gator.

The Apache's rocket pods flared to life, spewing a cascade of explosives that struck the predator head on and burst. Flesh and metal rained down in a tangled mess of monster and modern marvel. As the two killing machines burst into flames, Peter looked over the truck's cab and saw the farmhouse dead ahead. A moment later, the man named Hutchins barreled out of the front door and sprinted for the Black Hawk, which was spinning up for takeoff.

Peter was tempted to engage the second chopper, but there was still a second Apache around. He was also almost out of ammo, and he couldn't stop thinking about his son's fate.

As they neared the house, where a pitched battle between man and beast was taking place, Peter slapped the roof and shouted. "Stop here!"

The truck skidded to a stop. Kicked-up ash flowed over Peter as he jumped from the truck bed, and he ran toward where he saw his son fall.

One of the Chunta charged him, beating its chest, mouth open, teeth primed to sever meat and bones. Peter drew his revolver and leveled it at the monster's head but didn't fire. "Feesa, friend!"

The creature slowed but didn't stop. Peter pointed toward Feesa, who had just cleared the shanty town. "Feesa, family!"

He lowered the weapon and the Chunta turned and saw Feesa, who was now calling out in a booming voice. The fight went out of the Rider, and she rushed toward her incoming leader.

Peter dove down by the heaped up dead Chunta, looking for his son's body, but all he found was an empty shirt hanging from exposed ribs.

He yanked the shirt free, opening it wide. He didn't see a single hole.

He's not here. He's alive!

And then he heard his son's voice from inside the house, quickly followed by Ella's and a series of gunshots. Peter vaulted over the dead, took note of Mason's mauled corpse, and sprinted for the open front door. The inside of the house was a mass of confusion, but no one in the rag-tag group looked like a threat. He heard loud feminine crying from the second floor and took the steps three at a time. At the top of the stairs, he turned toward the sound and nearly collapsed with relief when he saw Jakob clutching a sobbing Alia in his arms. They were both covered in blood, but sitting upright, the way people do when they're not about to die.

Jakob whirled toward him, afraid at first and then desperate. "Dad! Upstairs! He has Anne!"

The sounds of a scuffle from the third floor, along with Jakob's declaration, propelled Peter around the banister and up the next flight of steps, where he suspected he would find Ella, Anne, and the man he should have killed with his own hands. It was a mistake he intended to correct.

36

Ella's scientific mind sat in the backseat, buckled up, and watched with familiar trepidation as her feral side took over.

Gunshots pounded her ears in the tight hallway. Wood splinted. A door was kicked in. Eddie had reached the third floor. And she wasn't too far behind him, rounding the stairway's corner. The door, its ruined knob and lock hanging limply, swung slowly closed. On the other side was Eddie, with her daughter, about to escape via the balcony.

And she wasn't going to let that happen. As valuable as Anne was to the world, as much as she loved the girl, she would be damned before letting ExoGen have her. Even if it meant risking her daughter's life.

The AK-47 in her hands was slick with the red sludge and would be hard to aim reliably for more than a single round, but as long as she could see a quarter of Eddie's body, she thought she could make the shot. *Aim for the legs,* she thought. *Take him down and then finish him off.*

She struck the door with her shoulder, slamming it open.

The AK-47 came up, her finger started squeezing, but never finished.

The hallway was empty.

And then, the door pushed back.

The hard wood smashed into Ella's side. Coupled with her speed, the impact sent her sprawling. She struck the frame of the open door, spun from the second blow, and fell to the floor, losing her grip on the assault rifle. As the weapon slid across the unfinished wooden floor and struck the leg of a folding table covered in someone's solitaire game, Ella spun around to the sound of footsteps.

Anne lay on the floor across the hall, unmoving, unconscious, and maybe worse. Ella watched for a moment until she saw the girl's chest rise and fall. It was a moment too long. Eddie descended on her.

He jabbed the rifle butt toward her forehead, going for the knockout blow. Ella rolled her head to the side. Rifle struck wood, and she struck back. Ella kicked up hard with her left leg, aiming for Kenyon's crotch. He flinched back more than she was expecting, but the diversion still worked. While he was protecting his boys, Ella grasped hold of the assault rifle, slipped her finger around the trigger, and pulled.

A spray of bullets buzzed past Kenyon's face, chewing up the ceiling and knocking free a cloud of dust. She tried to angle the barrel toward him as the weapon continued to fire, and she nearly succeeded as he held it at bay with just one hand. She mashed the trigger down until the magazine went empty. Kenyon looked aghast for a moment—she'd nearly shot his head off—and then he just looked pissed. Really pissed.

Ella tried to roll out of the way of his foot, but her body was too big a target. He caught her in the side, slamming the air from her lungs. She tried to kick back, but she wasn't fast enough. His body dropped atop hers, straddling her.

She punched his wounded arm, eliciting a shout of pain, but he struck back, twice as hard, directly in the sternum. The blow compressed her chest, expelling the air from her lungs and flexing her ribs inward. There were two sharp cracks as ribs gave way, followed by a silent scream that had no air to give it voice.

All of Ella's fight faded away in the wake of that one punch, perfectly placed with devastating force.

"You know I love you, right?" he asked, a hand around her neck.

Ella wheezed in a breath that was cut short by a sharp pain in her fractured chest.

"Always have. Well, not always, but since we met. Do you remember that day? It was Lawrence who introduced us. Me, the head of security. You, the prized geneticist who didn't really want to be there, despite your role in fucking over the human race. Not that I mind, of course. I'm on board. My job was to watch you. To make sure you played nice. So, I got you in bed. Gave me a reason to see you so much. Of course, it wasn't just a ruse. Lawrence thought so. Commended me on it. But it was real, for me. Just like it was for you."

Ella tried to speak, but she could only manage something that sounded like a whale call, as she attempted to suck in another breath. The pain in her chest kept her from breathing deeply enough to counteract the lack of oxygen in her lungs. She saw flecks of red and white, twisting in her vision. They'd have been pretty if not for the ominous message they brought: if she didn't get enough oxygen soon, she was going to pass out. And then she *and* Anne would be at Kenyon's mercy.

"Don't worry about speaking. I know you'd deny it. You can pretend all you want. You can tell Peter that you never cared, that all the sex was fake, that you were thinking of him the whole time. But you and I will always know the truth, and it can be our truth again."

He smiled and then punched her head. "You just need to sleep on it."

Despite the pain, Ella couldn't groan. Still couldn't breathe. The weight of his body and the pain in her chest kept her from even considering taking action, even blocking his second punch, which he delivered to her forehead.

Her vision faded in and out, teetering on the fringe of unconsciousness.

She watched through blurry vision as his fist raised up again, then dropped like a hammer. But when it came down, something was attached to it.

"Get off her!"

Anne.

Awake and on the attack.

The weight on Ella's body lifted away. Kenyon screamed in pain. She heard bodies tumbling. A moment later, Anne spit something on the floor. Kenyon stood above her, clutching his ear. Blood flowed between his fingers.

Beaten and breathless, Ella managed a chuckle.

The sound distracted Kenyon for just a second, but Anne took advantage of it, throwing herself at the man. But she wasn't fast enough or strong enough. Eddie hopped out of the way and shoved, using Anne's momentum against her. She slammed into the wall and fell to the floor. Not quite unconscious, but definitely out of the fight once more.

"You two are a real pair," Kenyon growled. "You know what? Fuck it, Ella. I'm done trying to save you. If you want to live? And I mean really live? With your daughter? You know where to find us."

He took hold of Anne's shirt, lifted her off the floor, and dragged her to the door. Her little feet thumped over the cracks in the floor, each bump taking her daughter further away. And as the girl's limp feet bounced down the hall in time with the chop of the helicopter above, she knew she'd never see the girl again.

Ella wept as she dragged herself toward the hall. She lacked the strength to stand, and all the willpower in the world couldn't overcome her injuries. She sagged to the floor when she reached the doorway, head turned toward the far end, where Eddie stood with Anne. He dropped her by the door at the end of the hallway and started working the lock. There was a deadbolt, two sliding locks, and a padlock.

When he reached the padlock and failed to yank it free, Eddie started back down the hall. When something large outside exploded, he stepped over Ella without a second look or a taunt. He returned to the hallway with the AK-47 in hand. Then he walked to the end, shot the padlock off and discarded the weapon.

Eddie opened the door, grabbed hold of Anne once more, and stepped out into the light of day. He looked back at Ella, shaking his head as she raked her fingers against the wall, pulling herself up in a last, desperate attempt to save Anne. "You know where we'll be. And you'll always be welcome."

He looked up and started waving.

Ella took one slow step after another, moving down the hallway, toward Eddie. Toward the rifle. She tried to speak, to delay him, but she still had no voice.

That she was mobile at all was miraculous.

The pounding pulse of a helicopter rotor roared down the hall. A tornado of air struck Ella head on, and it took all she had just to remain upright. If she went down again, she wouldn't get back up.

Eddie reached up and caught a metal wire with a carabiner and a harness at the end. He looped the harness around his waist and legs, wincing as he used both arms. Locked in place, he picked up Anne again, holding her to his waist with one arm. Ella wanted to scream at him. To tell him to lock Anne in, too. But Anne's safety wasn't his primary concern. He was just trying to escape. To survive. Just like everyone else, but in his own screwed up way.

Ella reached out a hand as she took one step after another, resisting the rotor wash, fighting against her pain, and closing the distance. Anne's name squeaked out of her throat, but nothing could be heard over the thunderous chopper.

Eddie turned his back on her, eyes on the chopper above.

I'm going to lose her, Ella thought.

And then the view changed. At first she thought her vision had gone screwy again, but then she focused and saw the body of a man charging down the hallway.

And not just any man—

Peter.

"Kenyon!" Peter shouted, his voice cutting through the din.

Eddie spun around and dropped Anne, his reflexes guiding him to defend himself. But there was nothing he could do to stop the two hundred pounds of solid Marine barreling toward him. Peter struck Kenyon head on. The pair crashed through the wooden railing, sailed off the balcony and struck the greenhouse's glass dome.

The impact knocked both men unconscious, and while Peter slid down the glass and out of view, Kenyon was lifted skyward like bait on the end of a fishing line. Ella bumbled to the end of the hall. Tried to pick up the AK-47 but lacked the strength to lift its slick body. When Anne groaned, she fell by the girl's side and checked her over. Aside from a number of superficial wounds, she found nothing life-threatening.

"Was that Dad?" Anne asked, wincing as she sat up.

Ella crawled to the edge of the balcony and looked over the side. She expected to see Peter's twisted body three stories down, but she found him lying just ten feet below, sprawled on top of the decontamination unit linking the house to the biodome.

He blinked and opened his eyes.

When he saw her looking down at him, he smiled. "You have terrible taste in men."

"No shit," she said.

Gunfire from around the farmhouse filled the air. It was joined by the rumbling thud of *Beastmaster*'s machine gun. The second Apache cruised past overhead, following the Black Hawk, as Eddie was reeled up by a winch. Bullets pinged off the fuselage until it was out of range. The two choppers rumbled away, headed north, and slowly faded from view.

"Do you think they'll come back?" Anne asked, pushing herself up.

"No." It was Jakob, standing in the doorway, covered in coagulation. Alia stood beside him, a blood-soaked towel held against her cheek. "They don't need to."

"Why not?" Ella asked.

"Because," Jakob said. "They know where we're going."

37

Kenyon woke to the familiar white noise and vibration of a helicopter. Over the past year, he'd woken up under similar circumstances, and for a moment, his memories of the more recent past remained distant. But they returned with the pain. His body ached, just about everywhere. His left arm burned at a constant rate. It was the scorch of an open wound. And then it flared white hot.

He saw the Black Hawk's ceiling above. Then Hutchins leaning over him, concerned and annoyed. "Stop moving, God-damnit."

The man had a hooked needle pinched between his fingers, a taut thread leading back down to Kenyon's arm. Kenyon relaxed. The pain was a good thing. If Hutchins was sewing him back together, it meant he would survive.

"Where is she?" Kenyon asked. As far as he could see, they were the only two in the chopper.

"Who?"

"Anne."

Hutchins slipped the hook through two folds of skin, pulled them tight, and then said, "You don't remember?"

Kenyon closed his eyes. His memory was splotchy, still trying to catch up to the here and now. But he couldn't get past the pounding in his head, the nausea and the ringing in his ears. He recognized the symptoms. Had suffered from them, and others, on multiple occasions during the past year, and during his former life as a high school and college football running back. "I have a concussion."

"Makes sense," Hutchins said.

"Why?"

"You got tackled off a third-floor balcony, fell nearly a story and crashed into a wall of solid glass strong enough to stand up to four hundred pounds of falling man meat."

"I was tackled?"

"Hard," Hutchins said. "After that, it was limp city. Honestly, I thought you were dead when I pulled you in."

A memory of falling flickered through his thoughts. Of pain. And disappointment. "I lost her."

"Yeah, you dropped Anne before–"

"Not Anne."

Hutchins frowned. "Right. Ella. I didn't see her."

Kenyon turned his face away from Hutchins, who might mistake his sadness for weakness. He remembered the fight with Ella. Remembered her nearly killing him, and what that felt like, to know she didn't love him. To consider the possibility that she never really had. Who had duped who? But after that...after opening the balcony door, Anne in hand, his memory was reduced to a twisting coil of emotions.

Desperation. Surprise. Rage.

The deep welling anger filled in one of the blanks. "It was Peter."

"Hit you like a missile," Hutchins confirmed. "For what it's worth, while you were pulled up, he fell. He's either dead or very broken. No way he could fall three stories without getting fucked up."

Kenyon turned back to Hutchins, his despair replaced by a growing anger. "You didn't stop to check?"

"We were under fire," Hutchins said. "You were completely exposed."

Kenyon grumbled his understanding, but he still wasn't happy about it.

"I can send the Apache back," Hutchins said. "Level the place."

"Apach*e?*"

"We lost Drummond to an ExoGen. An alligator, I think. Used to be, anyway."

None of this was acceptable, but he wasn't surprised. Viper Squad, without its leader, had lost its venom. And though their numbers had been drastically reduced, they still had firepower enough to kill their enemies and capture Anne *and* Ella. She might not love him now. Maybe hadn't before. But she would learn to. And if she didn't, maybe Mason had the right idea.

"Should I send Manke back?" Hutchins asked.

Kenyon shook his head. "He might kill our targets."

Hutchins nodded. He already knew that, but wanted Kenyon to make the call, and Kenyon respected him for it. He might not be a good leader, but he was loyal, and nowadays, that counted for something. Counted for a lot.

"We don't need to go back." Kenyon hissed in pain as Hutchins tugged on the stitch, cinching it tight and tying it off. "I know where they're going."

Not only that, but he was in no condition to fight. Not against Ella, or even Anne, and certainly not Peter—*if* he survived. But there was time to heal. Time to prepare. Instead of chasing their prey across the country, they could lay in wait. He always did appreciate ambush predators. The shock and panic of prey caught off guard was comical. And he longed to see that look on Peter's face.

Hutchins placed a bandage over the sealed wound. "Couple weeks and you'll be good to go."

Kenyon disagreed with the prognosis. As tough as Hutchins remembered him to be, Kenyon knew he was stronger than that now. Life with the Chunta had thickened his skin. Pushing past pain and injuries were part of life, and his body had already begun to adapt to it. He thought of Feesa for a moment, wondering what would become of the beast and if she was still alive. Part of him would miss her companionship. In the most basic sense, they were two of a kind, hunters both. But they would have clashed eventually, and Kenyon had no illusions about who would have won that fight. Parting ways with the Chunta was a good thing. And if they were all dead, even better.

Hutchins's hand went to his ear. He wasn't wearing the earphones that were customary in helicopters, blocking out the ambient noise, but he must have been wearing an earbud.

"Copy that, weapons free. Engage."

When he took his hand away, he said, "We have incoming."

Kenyon started to sit up, but his body protested.

"Sir," Hutchins said. "You shouldn't—"

Kenyon lifted his good arm up. "I want to see."

Hutchins shook his head but smiled. "Nothing can keep you down."

"Not for long. Not yet."

Hutchins pulled Kenyon up, helped him onto a bench, and quickly strapped him in. "Give us a view," Hutchins said into his comms.

The chopper banked and turned. Through the side window, they watched the Apache tear through the sky on a collision course with what looked like an inflated squid, pulsing and flapping through the sky. Kenyon had no idea if the thing had started out as a denizen of the sea or not, but he didn't care. All that really mattered was that it be killed.

While he had allied himself with the Chunta, their days had always been numbered. That was the point of RC-714 and the Change it kicked off. Why bother culling life on Earth through a virus, a nuclear war, or some other equally messy means, when you could let the planet eat itself into extinction? There was no radioactivity to deal with and no corpses to clean up. The Change had whittled life down to a few million Apex predators, and they would slowly but surely come into contact with each other. In the end, there might be a few hundred creatures separated by vast distances. When that happened, ExoGen would take care of the rest. The planet would be pristine once more, Eden reborn and awaiting its inheritors. Killing the ExoGenetic creatures they came across only hastened that eventuality, so he watched the event with a smile on his face.

When the flying creature turned to face the pair of helicopters, its tendrils open, ready to grasp, a series of bright flashes flared on either side of the Apache. Smoke trails snaked through the sky, chasing a swarm of rockets. Fire and flesh ruptured into the blue sky.

Beautiful, Kenyon thought, as the liquefied creature rained down toward the land below. When they flew through the pink mist lingering in the sky, Kenyon sat back, feeling hopeful.

"Where to?" Hutchins asked. "We need to stop for supplies and fuel, but we can map out a route once we have a destination."

Kenyon looked out the window, watching the blur of trees and empty homes passing by below them. The world was nearly empty, but not quite empty enough, and it wouldn't be until Peter Crane and his son, were dead. Lost and feral among the Chunta, he had desired Ella and Anne's lives too, but that was when he thought his dreams of the future were dead. But now...now everything could be his. Everything.

"Beantown," he said, smiling at his blood-caked reflection. He turned to Hutchins, who looked as confused as Kenyon expected him to. "Boston. Take me to Boston."

38

When it came to war, people generally focused on the fighting. It's dramatic, and violent, painful, and exciting. Adrenaline pumps. Bullets fly. Hoorahs fill the air as the enemy falls. Fewer people think about what follows a war, which for a soldier, is sometimes physically agonizing, sometimes emotionally taxing, and always—always—long winded.

Everyday noises become explosions.

Kids playing sound like kids burning.

Life transforms into a confusing world of chaotic illusion, and soldiers lie awake at night with the realization that the enemy they killed were human beings.

And no one liked to talk about that. Better to pretend it's not a problem. They're soldiers, after all. They can deal, right?

Peter had dealt, but not on his own. PTSD had left him shaken and exhausted, but he had pushed through it with the help of family, friends, and three good therapists. It was a longer, harder battle than the war itself, and now, in the wake of the fight for Hellhole Bay, he felt the familiar emotional and physical twitches creeping up on him.

The war's not over, he told himself, trying to stuff the emotions back down. *Deal with this shit when we're done.*

Done with what? he wondered, and then answered, *Saving the human race.* But it was simpler than that. He never really focused on the big picture, just on what was in front of him. His family. His son. They were reason enough to fight a war. As determination took root, the PTSD symptoms retreated, biding their time.

But Peter was not alone in his struggles. All around Hellhole Bay were the faces of men and women who had fought for their lives. And their battle began long before Peter or Kenyon set foot in the compound. Mason had seen to that.

And he had received his just reward, but that didn't change what he had done. Nor did it help those who dutifully obeyed him.

Boone was alive, but in the new status quo, he was the lowest of the low. The man looked relieved when he saw Mason's dead body, but it would be a long time before the people of Hellhole Bay trusted him.

Although they didn't have much of a choice. With all of Boone's men killed, and most of the still living residents of Hellhole lacking any kind of fighting ability, he was their best chance of survival. In the days following the attack, people had rallied against Boone, demanding his weapons, but Peter had stood beside the man. Technically, he'd sat beside the man. Three days passed before he could stand without much pain. A week before he could walk.

It had now been two weeks.

Boone wasn't their leader. Hellhole Bay was now a democracy of sorts, split into mini-sections of government that covered food, energy, sanitation, and defense. Given their knowledge of most of the camp's functionality, the three former maids, Shawna, Charlotte, and Sabine wound up in charge of the first three. They had begrudgingly allowed Boone to oversee the camp's defense, along with some unlikely allies.

The Chunta were staying. Five females, including Feesa, along with two Woolies, had survived the battle. There had been some tension at first. The citizens of Hellhole had killed a few of the Chunta, but Feesa explained Kenyon's deception and that Peter and his kin were family, a title never bestowed on Eddie. The creatures, who were already predisposed to symbiotic living, now resided in the swamps surrounding the compound, watching over the people within. And Boone was busy training those who were willing and able to carry weapons. Willie was his second-in-command and would be more than willing to put a bullet in his boss, if Boone ever got out of control. Said as much, right to his face, which Boone accepted with a grateful nod. He knew it was more than he deserved.

The girl who had helped Anne and Jakob's insurrection, Carrie, survived the knife in her chest. Barely. She was laid up in one of the beds and would likely stay there for another few weeks. The wound had been deep, but missed her heart, lungs, and major arteries. Shawna and Charlotte had experience patching up Boone's men in the past, and Sabine had been a nurse. Without them, Carrie would have died. The three women had been busy since the two choppers flew away, patching up the wounded and getting food and water to everyone.

They had tended to Peter and his family, and had even sewn up Alia's cheek, inside and out. The girl would have scars, emotional and physical, for the rest of her life, but she had survived. It didn't change the haunted look in her eyes, though. Kenyon had broken her.

Kenyon...

As far as they knew, he was alive. And Peter now knew better than to assume the opposite. Peter wouldn't believe the man was dead until he saw him bleeding out at his feet. Until he saw the life leave Kenyon's eyes. War was generally not a personal affair. But Kenyon had made it one. At the same time, Peter would do his best to avoid the man. Better to win the war without fighting. A soldier who could do that was the very best.

At the same time, Kenyon knew they were headed to Boston. He didn't know where, which was good for the people already on George's Island, but he'd be there, waiting for them.

Hope for the best, Peter thought, *prepare for the worst.*

He dropped *Beastmaster*'s hood and pronounced the vehicle fit for duty. It had a lot of cosmetic damage, but it had survived the battle in one piece.

"Good to go?" Jakob asked. He stood in the bed, cleaning the machine gun. During the day, he seemed like his old self. At night...not so much. Nightmares were common, especially when they walked the Earth, but Jakob's fears got the best of him. He was plagued by doubt, and by guilt over what had happened to Alia. Blamed himself for letting her be part of that fight. For not reaching her sooner. According to Ella, it was chivalrous bullshit, but Peter understood. He blamed himself for everything that happened after running into Boone on the road. He could have backtracked. Could have run and found another way around. Could'a, would'a, should'a. It *was* all bullshit. Hindsight and all that. What happened wasn't Jakob's fault any more than it was Peter's. They'd done their best, and their family was alive and present because of it.

"Good as it's going to get," Peter said, patting his hand against the armored siding. "Are you ready?"

Anne leaned out of the truck's open side window. "To live without big walls, and beds, and electricity, and running water? Ooh, can't wait."

Peter grinned at the girl's sarcasm, which had slowly returned with each passing day. She had taken her lumps along with the rest of them, but she seemed to recover more resiliently. Then again, she, like Ella, had fought her way through the wild for far longer than Peter and Jakob. For her, living out there might feel more normal. And what was normal for Anne? Before trekking through the ExoGenetic landscape, she'd lived in a protected facility. Until she and Ella fled with a group of scientists, the girl hadn't set foot outside. Weird was her normal.

"I'm good," Jakob said, but he didn't sound very convincing. Then his face lit up a little. Alia was headed toward them.

Jakob hopped down from the side of the truck and wiped his greasy hands off on his pants. "Where's your stuff?"

As reward for aiding in the liberation of Hellhole Bay, the residents had made sure they were leaving fully stocked. They had fresh clothes and plenty of food and water. Of course, they would cover the clothing and their clean bodies with mud after leaving the compound, but they didn't tell *them* that.

Alia's eyes flicked from Jakob to Peter and back again. Peter knew what was coming before the girl spoke. Had suspected it for more than a week now. "I-I'm not coming."

Jakob deflated, but he didn't seem surprised.

"It's for the best," Anne said. "She'd just get you killed."

"Screw off, Anne," Jakob said.

Anne was about to launch a verbal counterstrike when Peter gave her a look that mirrored Jakob's message and defused the girl's bravado. She rolled her eyes and sat back in the truck.

"She's right," Alia said. "You're distracted when I'm around. Everyone is. I can't track, or forage, or fight, or even stay out of the way. I can't even get canned food from an empty grocery store without freaking out. What you're doing... I can't do it."

"I know," Jakob said.

Alia's eyebrows raised. "You know? And you still wanted me to come?"

"You got kitchen duty, right?" Jakob asked.

"Charlotte asked me today...just twenty minutes ago. How—"

"I told her you were a good cook," Jakob said with a grin and a shrug.

"I'm a *horrible* cook."

"Then you'll learn fast."

"She's a slow learner, too," Anne said from the backseat, and when everyone present glared at her, the window slid up, shielding her from rebuke.

"That doesn't mean I didn't want you to come," Jakob said, "But I understand why you'd stay. And we'll come back for you." He looked to Peter. "Right?"

"Without a doubt," Peter said, trying to hide his doubt. If they survived, he had every intention of returning to Hellhole. If humanity had a chance of rebuilding, it was here. Not necessarily inside these walls, but with these people. He'd also warned Boone that if he returned to find Hellhole devolved into another monarchy, there would be actual hell to pay.

Peter gave Alia a gentle touch on her head. "I'll take care of him." Then he left the pair to say their goodbyes, make their promises, and share a farewell kiss. Ella was walking toward him, accompanied by the newest member of their small crew: Lyn Askew. She'd slowly returned to health over the past few weeks, and despite her treatment at the hands of Mason and the death of her husband, she was eager to help set things right. Her work at Hellhole, modifying the ExoGenetic crops so they could be eaten, was a good step, but it was the human genome that needed a tweak, and she could help get that done in Boston. If she survived the trip. She wasn't a fighter, and she was still quite skinny and frail looking, but she had the right kind of determination—the kind that pushes a person to see things through to the end, even if the end is death.

Boone was with them, carrying bags.

"Meet you in the truck," Peter said to the ladies, who continued on past.

Boone stopped and held the bags out to Peter. "More food. Root veggies. Should keep for some time. We got more than enough."

Peter nodded his thanks and took the bags. One of them was a lot heavier than vegetables should be.

Boone pointed at it. "That one there is something special for you. Made a run last night."

"That wasn't smart," Peter said. With Hellhole Bay being self-sufficient, there wasn't any reason Boone or anyone else had to leave. Doing so could attract the wrong kind of attention.

"Them hairy Chunta ladies were with me," Boone said. "Can't say I like the way they been looking at me, all horny an' shit, but they're playing nice." When Peter put the bag on the ground, Boone flinched and said, "Be gentle with it."

Peter buzzed the zipper open to reveal a collection of grenades.

"Fragmentation, flashbangs, smokers, and offensive, if you need something with a little more kick. You're heading into a shit storm, right? Ain't nothing better in a shit storm than a bunch of grenades."

"A tank would be nice," Peter said. "But thanks."

Peter shook Boone's hand, parting with the words, "Keep them safe and the world might just have a future."

"I'll do what needs doing," Boone said. "S' long as you do the same."

Peter gave him a nod, recovered the bags, and headed for the truck. "So long, Redneck." Boone had adapted the Redneck Raiders term for his own personal use as a callsign.

"See you soon, Ricochet," Boone replied, using Peter's old callsign, which he had learned from Jakob, while regaling the boy with the story of how he and his father had faced off against the ExoGator.

Back at the truck, everyone was inside and waiting. Ella sat in front. Lyn sat in the back seat, between the kids, both of whom looked to be dealing with their own personal miseries. Alia was nowhere to be seen. Peter climbed into the truck, slid behind the wheel, and let out a sigh.

"You okay?" Ella asked.

"Will be, when this is over."

She gave his arm a rub and said, "We should go."

It was just seven in the morning, but they wanted to reach their first destination long before the sun set, giving them time to search for the kinds of weapons that would allow them to stand up to an Apache attack helicopter, not to mention the ever-evolving ExoGenetic creatures between Hellhole and Boston.

"We're waiting on one more," Peter said, and when the back of the truck sank down a bit, he knew she had arrived.

"Am here, family," Feesa said through the open back window.

Stunned eyes looked from the Chunta warrior to Peter.

"She insisted," Peter said.

"Protect family," Feesa said. "Kill Eddie."

"Good enough for me," Ella said.

"Her breath smells like a Woolie fart," Anne said, which got a hoot of laughter from their Rider compatriot and kept the girl from joking again.

"Family," Jakob said, and he held his fist out to Feesa. She pushed her larger fist against it, gave an approving nod. Then she leaned back out of the window, sitting in the truck bed, arm up on the side as though ready for a nice drive in the sun, which was probably as far from the truth as you could get.

Peter started the engine, shifted into drive, and left the safety and comfort of hell behind. "Next stop, Fort Bragg."

Epilogue

Anne leaned her head against the window, watching the endless streaks of crops pass by. Bored by the monotony, she started naming the vegetation, whispering to herself. "Asparagus. Beets. Corn. Peas."

And then at some point during the brain game, she didn't know when, she switched to the crops' formal identifications. "Chenopodium quinoa. Spinacia oleracea. Lycopersicon esculentum. Triticum aestivum."

The words were an audiobook narrator's worst nightmare come true, but she could rattle them off as quickly as the crops shifted from one to the next. She'd become fluent in her mother's botanical geek speak. She'd also decided to keep her growing knowledge, and the memories that came with it, from her family.

Because as the amount of information stored on the USB drive leached into her head increased, so did more recent memories. And with every new memory came the growing fear that she couldn't fully trust the woman who had grown her, dragged her across the country, and introduced her to her biological father.

Ella, she was beginning to realize, was a first-class manipulator. Anne knew it was a useful skill to have in the current state of the world. Anything to stay alive. But she didn't think that applied to her father. Sure, she'd only met him just over a month ago. And yeah, he hadn't willingly donated his DNA. But they *were* family. By blood, and now more.

Anne knew her feelings for Peter and Jakob were genuine. But her mother's feelings? She wasn't sure.

Memories peppered her like nearly forgotten dreams.

She remembered them the way that steam wisped above a boiling pot, clear for a moment and then dispersed into the air. She could feel its lingering humidity but could no longer see it or experience it directly.

And one of those memories left her worried.

She couldn't recall the events around it.

Couldn't tell you where she—where Ella—was, or what she was wearing, or what the room smelled like. But she could remember the emotion, raw and angry, close to how she imagined an ExoGen felt every time it saw another living thing.

But it wasn't hunger Ella felt, it was *hate*.

For Peter.

She looked away from the blur of crops and watched her parents. Peter was behind the wheel, keeping them at a steady forty miles per hour, eyes on the highway headed north. Ella sat beside him, scanning back and forth, always vigilant despite the relative quiet they'd experienced since leaving the swamps of South Carolina behind. Their shaved heads, now covered in a thin layer of scent-concealing dirt, matched. As far as the post-apocalypse went, they looked like a couple. More than Jakob and Alia ever had.

And they acted... Well, they acted married. Happy in an intense way. Trustworthy. A team. Everything she wanted them to be. But those were the best deceptions. The ones that were too good to be true. Eddie learned that the hard way.

Would Peter?

The question conflicted Anne, because as much as she loved Peter and Jakob, she felt the same for her mother. But on top of that love was the unshakable belief that her mother's every action since leaving ExoGen was solely for Anne's benefit. And ultimately the world's. So, she still trusted her mother.

For now.

Maybe Ella really did hate Peter. Maybe he wasn't even Anne's biological father. Maybe she had no father at all, and no brother. The questions put a deep ache in her chest and nearly brought tears to her eyes.

Grow up, she told herself. *Life is about surviving. There's no place in the world for tears.*

Ella had spoken those words to her a week after they first fled into the wild. They had resonated and become part of Anne's core belief system.

But no matter how hard she tried to ignore the questions, and the emotions they unraveled, she couldn't help but wonder about it all. If she was going to help save humanity, she wanted to know that it was worth saving. That they were on the right side. And that her mother wasn't also lying to her.

So, Anne rested her head against the window glass and tried to remember more.

Tried to remember everything.

BOOK THREE:

FAMINE

1

"Would you quit making out with yourself and hurry up," Anne said, bouncing from foot to foot.

Jakob's muffled voice replied from inside the men's room. "Go use the ladies' room. That's what you are, and that's what they're for."

Anne cracked open the men's room door and whisper-hissed through the crack. "*Feesa* is in the ladies room."

"Ugh," Jakob said. "Then...just come in here. There's, like, three stalls."

"No way, you're probably standing at one of those wall-sinks with your dangly bits hanging out."

"It's a 'urinal,' and no, I'm not using it."

Behind Anne, emanating from the women's room, was a long squeak followed by a sploosh of toilet water and a deep sigh. She took a deep breath, closed her eyes for a moment, and entered the dark men's room. "There are a lot of things I can stomach, in addition to all the food on the planet, but being trapped in a room with her rotten meat farts... I just can't."

"Don't blame you," Jakob said.

Anne bent down, aimed her flashlight along the floor, and found Jakob's feet in the last stall. "There you are. Took the biggest stall, huh? Aren't those for people with wheelchairs?"

"Master of my domain," he said. "You seen any people in wheelchairs lately?"

She thought on it. "Just one, but really it was just his bottom half, and he was mostly bones, so that probably doesn't count."

She entered the farthest stall from him and checked the toilet's contents. Clean and unused, which on its own was a rare treasure. Anne freed herself from her tangle of post-apocalyptic clothing and took a seat.

After a few uncomfortable moments, she said, "So...what do guys talk about when they poop?"

"Mostly they don't talk at all."

"Right," she said. "Pooping is serious business. But I'm not a guy, and you're not pooping, so let's have a little chit-chat so I can squeeze one out before it's time to go."

Jakob chuckled, but it was subtle. Repressed.

Anne sighed. "You're doing it again, aren't you?"

"Doing what?"

"Moping."

"I don't mope."

"'I miss Alia, waah, my girlfriend is so far away, boohoo.'"

He chuckled again. "How do you even know?"

"You're sitting on a toilet, in the bathroom of a Walmart, and your pants aren't down. Only times you want privacy are when you're pooping, and that's clearly not happening—because you told me I could come in—or when you're moping, and... Wait a second. If you're moping, why did you ask me to come in? Tricky move, Bro. Throwing me off the scent."

"*Saving* you from the scent," he said, trying to sound chipper. "Remember? Feesa stank? I was being merciful."

"Nah," she said. "You wanted company. But you miscalculated, I think. Because we both know I won't coddle you."

"Don't need coddling," he said, sounding grouchy now.

"Uh-huh." Anne knew her half-brother like he'd been her whole brother for most of her life, rather than just for the last few months. They were together all the time. Fought together. Hunted together. Hid together. And now, they pooped together. He was sensitive, caring, and easy to read. "Look, I'm sure Alia is fine. Hell of a lot safer back at Hellhole than out here, scavenging department stores, fighting Apexes, and traveling north toward Boston where, by the way, the bad guys are waiting for us. Kenyon's the one who put that hole in her cheek. You don't want her having to see him again, right?"

She waited.

"Right."

"Exactly," she said. "But listen up, bucko. You miss her. Fine. You spend more time touching yourself. That's your business. But you don't get to be a mopey downer when everything is kinda horrible already, got it?"

He let out a huff. "Yeah. Makes sense."

"Great. Now, did you know that when Feesa uses a toilet, she stands on the back and hovers over the bowl?"

Jakob snickered. "You're joking."

"I'm serious. It's like she's been crapping in the woods so long that she doesn't know how to sit and shit."

"Man, you are lucky no one gets on you about your language. Dad would have given me a hard time, even after the world ate itself to death."

"Yeah, lucky me. No one cares if I curse because the society that deemed certain words evil mutated into perpetually hungry killing machines. All the other kids on the planet must be sooo jealous. Oh wait, their parents *ate* them.

"You know, I don't even remember life from before," she said. "Even worse, I don't know if that's because I didn't have a life before, because I was grown in a lab. Even *worse, worse,* my earliest memories, and my *only* memories of what the world used to be like, are my mother's."

"How's that going, by the way? You haven't talked about it much lately."

"The seeping of my mother's memory and knowledge into my own? It's delightful. There are some things a girl shouldn't know about her mother. Or our father."

"Eww."

"Right. I don't talk about it because there're a lot of things I want to forget. But...I don't even know if I *can* forget."

"Because you're suuuper smart, I know."

"Okay, I know I say that a lot, but only because it's true. It's not like I'm bragging—okay, I *am* bragging, but I'm not smart because of anything *I* did. I was *made* this way. Mom gave me the best of her and Dad, and she put a hard drive *in my head.* The truth is, I envy stupid people like you. Faced with the daunting tasks ahead, in a world that wants to kill or eat us, your simple mind is fixated on the primal urge to copulate. You must sleep so soundly, dreaming of reuniting with your lost love. 'Oooh, Alia. Smooch smooch.'"

"Something like that," Jakob said.

"Thought so."

"You done yet?" he asked.

"Almost," she said. "Feel like I'm giving birth over here."

"That's...great. Nice visual. Thanks."

"Jake." His father's voice was whispering, but loud over the radio Jakob carried with him, the sound reflecting off the bathroom's tile floor and walls.

Anne listened in silence. Peter only whispered when something bad was about to happen.

"Here," Jakob whispered back. "What's up?"

"Company. Non-human. Parking lot. It's getting a nose full of Beastmaster."

Beastmaster was their armored truck. The plow on the front end cleared the road, the machine gun mounted on the back mowed down ExoGenetic creatures, and the new trailer attached to the back carried their supplies. They now had a lot of weapons and expired MREs—old enough to safely eat—picked up from Fort Bragg on their way north. Being separated from it by an Apex could be a problem.

"Is it tracking us?" Jakob asked.

"Best to assume so. Better get out here."

"Will do."

"ETA?"

"Anne?" he asked. "How's it going over there?"

Anne let out a grunt, which was followed by a sploosh. "Take that, Feesa. I'm good. Shouldn't take more than thirty seconds to wipe. All this fiber in my diet makes everything come out nice and clean."

"Sixty seconds," Jakob said, and exited his stall. "I'll wait for you outside."

"Let Feesa know, while you're out there."

Anne took care of business while she listened to Jakob exit, and a moment later, open the ladies' room door. "Hey, Fees—ugh, oh god... Feesa, Apex out front. Try to stay quiet."

A grunt replied.

The ladies room door thumped shut, followed by the men's room door opening again. Jakob entered as Anne exited the stall, business complete. She smiled at the look of abject horror on his face.

"Hey, I warned you."

"Yeah, but I didn't really know... Oh, my god."

Anne retrieved her pistol from where she left it beside Jakob's AK-47. Peter had tried convincing him to take an M4 while they were at Fort Bragg, but Jakob said he trusted the AK. Anne thought he liked it because it had a cooler post-apocalyptic vibe.

Not sure who he'd be trying to impress, but hey, teenagers.

Feesa exited the ladies room behind them. She was her normal hairy self, built like a female Sasquatch with a homelier face, including two bottom teeth that grew out of her mouth and curved up so far that they punctured her cheeks. Peter had offered to file them down, but the size of a Rider's teeth, and how far they penetrated the cheeks, seemed to be a source of pride. "No pain," Feesa had told them. "Just itch, sometimes."

She didn't carry a gun. Didn't need one. She stood a foot taller than Peter and was incredibly strong. Her only downfall was a lack of complex foresight, the ability to predict outcomes beyond 'me punch, you hurt.' That, and her rank-ass poop.

Jakob turned off his flashlight, and Anne did the same. Feesa didn't need help seeing in the dark. They moved through the aisles, guided by the daylight pouring through the storefront's large windows. Jakob pushed a silent cart, filled with pillaged survival gear. There were plenty of guns and ammo, but nothing that hit as hard as what they had already gathered. Jakob left the cart behind as they approached the front of the store. Peter and Ella waited for them behind a magazine stand.

Peter waved them over with one hand while holding an index finger to his mouth with the other.

Jakob slid down beside them, careful to stay out of sight. Feesa squat-walked. But Anne was guided by curiosity. Rather than ask, she just had a look for herself. "Huh," she said, eyes widening as she took in the writhing mass of furry gray creatures leaping and sniffing around Beastmaster. "That's different."

"Hey," Jakob whispered. "Ahh...where is Lyn?"

The group collectively gasped, cursed, and grunted as they all remembered that Lyn—their aged traveling companion—was taking a nap.

In the truck.

2

"Are they...are they mice?" Ella asked, peering through the Walmart window. They were small enough to be mice. Hopped and moved like them. But there were hundreds, and they were very interested in the truck.

"They're the smallest things I've seen," Jakob said. "Since before."

"Look like snacks," Feesa said.

Everything living, animal or plant, looked like a snack to Feesa. She, like Anne, could eat the ExoGenetic crops Ella had helped develop because she'd already been changed by them. She was a monster, one of millions of different mutations unlocked by RC-714, which gave every living thing on the planet that ate the modified crops the ability to access junk DNA going back to the beginning of life itself, and use those genes to adapt, in real time, to any environment.

Ella had nearly saved a starving world. Instead, she had killed it.

"Things like mice don't exist anymore," Peter said, ever cautious. "They're Exos. We just don't know how yet."

"It's a murmuration of mice," Anne said.

"Small words," Jakob grumbled. "Not all of us have super brains."

"Not all of us emerged into this world via a vagina," Anne shot back. The words stung Ella. Not because they were untrue, but because the frequency with which Anne casually mentioned the subject meant it genuinely bothered her. Genetically, she was Ella's and Peter's child. Only, she had not been conceived. Had not been carried for nine months inside the womb of an adoring mother-to-be. And she had not been given birth to. She had been removed from an artificial womb. The process of her creation had been impersonal and sterile. But Ella loved her just the same. So did Peter and Jakob.

The past months had been hell but had also forged the four of them into a family. Not the kind of nuclear family that had been admired so much by 21st century American culture, but the kind that could survive and maybe reverse the extinction of humankind.

"A murmuration is when a big flock of birds, like thousands of them, fly through the air like they're one big organism. They bend and twist and soar, all together, all at once. I know that and I've never even seen it." Anne threw her hands in the air. "I've never even seen a real bird!"

"She's right," Ella said.

"Of course, *they* agree," Jakob said, and the words hurt. Part of Anne's intelligence was her own—a mind inherited from her parents. But there was more to it than that. Some tinkering on the back end and what appeared to be a leaking of Ella's memory into her daughter's mind. That was not the plan. Anne was meant as a vessel to carry that information—to retain it for humanity, if Ella died. But she never imagined Anne's modified mind could absorb not only Ella's research, but the complete copy of her own memory and life.

"We *agree*," Anne said. "Because it's the truth, and we're not dolts."

"Voices. Down." Peter glared at them. The mice outside might be small, but the way they moved in concert—a murmuration—wasn't normal before or after the change. They'd come across a few examples of tribal behavior during their cross-country trek. The Stalkers. The Riders. But they were groups made up of individuals, who had somehow retained some vestige of humanity and intelligence. These mice...they were a collective.

And they'd be fools to assume that was the only adaptation.

"How do we kill them?" Ella asked.

Jakob shrugged. "Maybe they'll just carry on when they can't get into the truck?"

"They'll get in," Peter said. "Through the vents. The filters. A normal mouse could get through all of that with enough time. This many of them, adapted to this world... It won't take long."

"I go eat them?" Feesa asked.

Peter shook his head. "They'd probably eat you."

"Feesa does not taste good," she said, nibbling on her own hair for a moment before scrunching up her gnarly face in disgust.

"I don't think mice care about taste," Jakob said.

"They're getting in the engine," Anne said, drawing their collective attention back to the scene outside. Several mice were squeezing under the hood. Others were leaping up into it from the top of a tire. They had minutes at best.

Peter turned to Jakob. "Did you get everything I asked you to?"

Jakob nodded. "Backpacks, knives, propane, lighters, cooking—"

"Good." He turned to Anne. "You know what a propane regulator and hose is?"

Anne blinked a few times, which made Ella wonder if she could now access all the information locked away in her head just by thinking about it. "Sure do."

"Get two of them," Peter said. "Six foot. Quick as you can."

Anne would normally ask why or debate the validity of a plan, but not with Peter. She knew well enough that when it came time to fight, track, or kill, all the knowledge in the world couldn't replace Peter's experience. She took off running into the store's depths, swallowed up by the darkness.

Peter then turned to Jakob. "Backpacks." And then he turned to Feesa. "Propane tanks." He pointed to the grocery cart and elaborated before their brutish 'sister/aunt' could ask what he meant. "Big, white, round metal things."

Feesa grunted and headed for the cart with Jakob.

"You're not planning what I think you're planning?" Ella asked.

Peter just grinned.

Jakob returned with the backpacks, eyes wide. "You're not planning what I think you're planning?"

It was the same question, but instead of being laced with dread, Jakob sounded delighted.

Peter unzipped a pack and held it open for Feesa when she returned with both twenty-pound tanks. "Inside."

She placed one tank in Peter's pack, and the second in Jakob's after he opened it.

"You *are* planning what I think you're planning!" Jakob said.

Peter nodded. "And you're helping."

That smoothed out the happy grin on Jakob's face. It was one thing to watch his father MacGyver a flamethrower to use on a horde of Exo mice. It was another to take part in the family roast.

Before Peter could elaborate, or Jakob could express his concern, delight, apprehension, whatever, a series of footfalls rapidly approached. Anne's feet squeaked as she rounded a circular stand of bras, the sound making them cringe. Then she was standing before them, heaving for air, holding two long black hoses.

Peter took the hoses, snapped open his knife, and cut the regulators off the ends.

"Why did your feet squeak?" Jakob asked, while Peter took the hoses and began connecting them to the tanks.

Anne poked out a foot. There was a pristine new sneaker on it. "Picked these bad boys up on the way. Only added thirty seconds to my sprint. Cause I'm wicked fast. Is that something people say still? 'Wicked?'"

"Only in New England." Peter twisted the second hose into place.

"Well then, since we're in Connecticut, these are wicked awesome."

The sneakers looked well-made and were actually camouflaged. Had they been a bright color, or white, they'd have to be smeared with mud, like the rest of their clothing. The caked-on dirt helped conceal the group in the wild, and helped block their scent—which was, at the moment, overpowering. Though most of that could be attributed to Feesa.

"Okay," Peter said, standing up with a backpack laden with a propane tank. It was a tight fit, but he made it work. He helped slide it around Jakob's shoulders and cinched it tight. Then he attached the hose. Down on the floor, Anne attached the second hose to Peter's pack. Ella continued to marvel at how level-headed the girl was when things got dangerous.

Ella was a fighter. Could survive in this wild world. But Anne, like Peter, excelled at it. If she weren't still a kid, Ella suspected Peter would be strapping the backpack over Anne's shoulders instead of Jakob's. The boy was brave, and he was learning to hold his own in a fucked-up world, but he lacked the raw instinct of Anne and Peter.

"When the time comes, just twist this open a little, and light it. Then crank it all the way open and point it toward everything with fur."

"Light it with wha—"

Before Peter could finish, Anne's hand shot up, a lighter pinched between two fingers. Looked brand new. She probably had her pockets stuffed with them.

Jakob took the lighter. "Thanks."

"No problem, broseph."

Jakob grunted. "Never say that again."

"Sure, broseph."

"The *broseph* part," Jakob grumbled.

Peter finished sliding his backpack on and pulled the straps tight. "Stay close, slow and steady, sweep back and forth, low to the ground. Keep your left hand free."

"Free for what?"

"To pull them off of you," he said. "Or me."

"Pull them off," Jakob said, adjusting his pack. "Great. This is great."

"Buck up, Jakey-boy," Anne said. "This is going to be wicked fun."

"For you," he said, following Peter toward the front door. "For us..." They paused by the pair of sliding doors that had been manhandled closed during their shopping excursion. "...it's going to suck."

Father and son heaved the doors open in unison, metal shrieking against metal, and all at once, the murmuration of hopping Exo-mice forgot about the truck and the withering prize within. With a solitary mind, they shifted focus and swarmed toward Jakob and Peter.

3

This is crazy, Jakob thought.

This is stupid.

"Light it," Peter said, twisting the valve atop his propane tank just enough to let out a gentle hiss. He then flicked his lighter at the end of the propane tank's hose. A blue flame snapped to life.

Jakob followed his father's movements, something he'd gotten pretty good at over the past few months.

Valve open.

Flick the lighter.

Unleash the flame.

But Jakob had loosened the valve more than his father, and the flame that shot out caught him off guard. The hose fell from his hand, dangled by his leg, and doused his pants in blue-hot flames. If not for the crust of old mud covering them, his clothing might have caught fire. But the layer of old dirt blocked the heat long enough for Jakob to reach down and take back control of the hose.

"Crank it!" Peter shouted, as the tsunami of savage mice hopping in unison bounded toward them. When the creatures moved like this, all at once, it gave the illusion of being something much larger, which was probably why they never grew big like other species. And it would have advantages. Like fish swimming in a school, predators could never take them all out. Some would die, but the species, or in this case, the adaptation, would go on.

Unfortunately for them, Peter and Jakob weren't here for a snack, and didn't intend on becoming one, either.

Jakob twisted the valve on his propane tank all the way open. A jet of intense flame burst from the end of his hose. He angled it toward the ground in front of him, directly in the path of the swarming mice. But they continued toward him, lost to ravenous hunger, undeterred by the fire.

The miniature mob closed in, allowing Jakob to get a good look at their little faces, glowing orange in the blaze of fire light. Their teeth were no longer the twin buck teeth that were associated with rodents. Instead, they were razor sharp triangles of doom arranged around a mouth the size of a quarter. If Peter and Jakob lost this fight, their deaths would be slow and agonizing.

"Whoa!" Jakob shouted as the first of the pint-sized Exos leapt toward him. The creature entered the column of flame with a mindless bluster, its unblinking circular eyes surrounded by a poof of wild hair, looking manic. Mindless.

Lost to a flesh-craving lust.

Then, for a moment, the Exo was gone, consumed by the fire.

It emerged as a ball of flame, twitching and writhing, arcing through the air like some ancient projectile launched by a trebuchet, letting out the tiniest of shrieks.

"Move in an arc," Peter said, "so they don't hit you."

Jakob glanced at his father, who was being attacked by far more of the Exos. He wasn't sure if that was because they saw him as a bigger threat—which was true—or if the majority of them simply followed whichever of the creatures was in the lead.

Stepping to the side, Jakob kept his flame pointed forward and discovered his father's advice was accurate. As usual. The little savages continued their hopeless barrage, leaping into the flames and emerging as falling stars. It was a colonnade of death. *Maybe they're lemmings?* Jakob wondered. He'd played a game called 'Lemmings,' once upon a time, and he had always wondered if the little animals really would follow a leader over a cliff. *Suppose it's not unheard of,* he thought, *or maybe these things just haven't encountered fire before.*

He adjusted his aim, burning a few of the creatures circling around him. But the shift left an opening in front, and two Exos made it through the fiery gauntlet. They sprang back and forth and then bounded onto Jakob, clinging to his clothing, scrabbling higher, toward his face.

Jakob imagined he could take a bite in the leg, or his butt, or back, and not be bothered too much by it. The little assholes would have to bite through his tough clothing before reaching skin. But they seemed to sense that, and they were looking for his exposed flesh. His cheeks. His nose. His eyes.

"Dad," he said. "Little help?"

The moment he asked, he knew help wasn't coming. Not from his father. The swarm had shifted almost entirely in Peter's direction now. To compensate, he stepped backward, sweeping his torch in a steady back and forth motion, leaving behind a trail of smoldering bodies. Jakob doubted his father could even hear him over the hiss of fire and the chorus of horrified little voices being cut short as the flames consumed the creatures.

It was almost enough for Jakob to feel bad for them.

Almost.

"Hold still," Anne said from behind. "I got you."

He felt a thumb on his back and glanced over his shoulder to find Anne, one of the Exos impaled on the tip of her knife.

"You could have stabbed me!" he said.

"I would never do that," she replied, "on purpose."

Jakob flinched back as she swung the blade again, putting the knife through a second creature and declaring, "Exo-kabob!" She flicked the knife toward the ground, flinging the twin creatures onto the pavement and crushing both under her new sneakers.

Free of the distraction, Jakob went to his father's aid, scorching the horde from behind. The fire spread beyond them, moving out into the horde, one creature to the next. Because of their instinct to huddle together, there was no escaping the flames.

It wasn't until there were just a few of the creatures left that the horde's bravado faltered. With a final burst of motion, the last three of the small creatures broke rank and sprinted for the forest at the fringe of the parking lot. The trees weren't thick, but the space between them was filled by ExoGenetic corn stalks, each of them ten feet tall. The moment the three escapees entered, they were gone for good—or at least until they reproduced enough to form a new murmuration.

"Hey, dingleberries," Anne squatted on the pavement, poking one of the dead creatures with her knife. "I don't think these were mice. Or rats. Or whatever. You know, before. I think they were something else."

"They could have been anything," Ella said. "Some creatures have adapted so far, and so often, that little of their original selves remain."

"Yeah, I get that," Anne said. "I know what you know."

"Not *everything* I know."

"Getting there," Anne said, "and besides, even without your thoughts in my head, I know a *fish* when I see one."

"A fish?" Peter asked, lowering his backpack to the ground, and wiping sweat from his forehead.

"Yep." Anne scraped her knife along the dead creature's body, removing the last vestiges of singed hair, which grew in tufts, out from in between shiny scales. "The gills are gone. They grew arms and legs. Probably bigger brains. But they kept the one thing that worked for them."

She picked up the dead fish, turned its face to the group, and opened the creature's little jaws.

Seeing it as a fish now, Jakob had no trouble identifying the species it had been, once upon a time.

"A piranha?"

"A little far from the Amazon," Ella said.

"Probably a pet," Peter said, "once upon a time. Also: zoos."

His father had always made a point of avoiding zoos on maps. When it came to apex predators, the United States didn't have many left, before the change. But zoos...they had some of the biggest, scariest predators in the world, all caged up until they were big and strong enough to leave their enclosures. Peter didn't let his fear show very often, but when they'd discussed zoos, he looked horrified.

The idea of an Exo tiger, or polar bear, had been enough to give Jakob nightmares for a week. Though he didn't mind all that much. He hadn't been sleeping a lot anyway. When the sun went down and the world grew quiet, save for the occasional scream of something eating, and something else being eaten, he was alone with his thoughts.

And they always led to Alia. He worried about her constantly. About her safety. About her being around someone like Boone. About her finding someone else. It was a constant distraction, so much so that he felt angry at her for no reason at all, and at himself for supporting her staying behind.

There really was no avoiding it. She was safer back at Hellhole Bay, even with Boone, who his father believed would be a changed man with Mason out of the picture.

But Jakob didn't like it.

"Mmph." The sound was followed by the wet slurp of flesh being torn from bones and the sloppy chomp of a Rider consuming a partially cooked fish. "Is good."

Feesa stopped chewing when the others all stared at her. She slowly motioned to the smorgasbord of fricasseed fish. "What? No okay to eat?"

"Honestly," Peter said. "I'm just jealous."

Jakob licked his lips. He hadn't had meat in a long time. If he didn't know eating the four-legged fish would turn him into a killing-machine monster, he'd dig in alongside Feesa.

Which was exactly what Anne did.

Not only could she eat all the crops, Anne could also consume an Exo. Aside from the RC-714 gene, there was nothing about an Exo that made them bad to eat. They were still just animals.

Beastmaster's door *thunked* and swung open. Lyn slid out of the back seat, down to the pavement, her eyes half-closed, totally unaware of her surroundings. Jakob's father had pointed that problem out to her several times. She'd gotten accustomed to living inside protected walls. Out here, you could never let your guard down.

Lyn yawned and stretched. Casually closed the truck's door and then turned toward the store—seeing the group, and the scores of little dead monsters, smoldering and filling the air with the scent of burnt hair and flesh.

Her eyes snapped wider. "Well...what did I miss?"

4

"From now on," Peter said, "no napping in the truck."

"Pff." Lyn waved her hand. "I was perfectly safe. I've seen this big truck of yours drive straight through a building, not to mention a few living creatures, with hardly a dent. I'm not sure what a few fish-mice could have done."

"They were climbing inside," Jakob said. "They had piranha teeth."

"Son," Lyn said, "I got teeth of my own." Lyn chomped her teeth in Jakob's direction.

She was somewhat unflappable. Viewed life in a kind of casual sense. Ella said she hadn't always been like that. Peter guessed it stemmed from having to watch her husband slowly starve to death in Mason's outdoor jail for 'questionables.' Something like that—watching a slow agonizing death—has just as much effect, if not more, on the psyche than the sudden, violent death that was now so prevalent in the world.

"I'm afraid I'm going to have to insist," Peter said, which was his way of declaring the debate over. "You were lucky it wasn't something larger."

"Like a GPA?" Anne asked.

"What's a GPA?" Lyn asked.

"Anne," Ella said with a sigh. "Don't—"

"Giant pink asshole," Anne said. "It was a pig. Once upon a time. Then it was an asshole."

"And now?" Lyn asked, one eyebrow raised.

"Oh, it's dead," Anne said.

Lyn smiled. "I expected nothing less. Now, did anyone get me the new undergarments I asked for? My current apparel is starting to chafe." She shook her head. "I do miss the showers at Hellhole."

"Yeah, the showers where Mason was—"

Jakob leaned forward and gave Anne a sidelong 'shut-up' glance.

"What?" Anne said, making the subject impossible to avoid.

Jakob groaned.

They'd been instructed to leave out the lurid details of what had been uncovered in Hellhole. Mason's cameras, recording through mirrors in bathrooms. He'd documented the private moments of every woman in the camp, including Lyn, who wasn't young, or traditionally attractive.

"It's okay, dear," Lyn said, patting Jakob's back. "I know all about Mason's...indiscretions."

Peter didn't think that was entirely true, but it did keep Anne from divulging more. He suspected that Lyn knew enough to know she didn't want to learn more, and she was using psychology to discourage Anne from sharing.

Anne grunted, sat back, and crossed her arms. She frequently recounted their past events. Not really because she enjoyed them, as she wanted people to believe, but because she was still a kid, whose whole life had been traumatic, and she had a lot to process. "How much longer?"

"Well," Ella said, "Shouldn't be much more than three hours to Boston, unless we run into traffic." She paused for someone to laugh at her joke. No one did. "Hard part is going to be finding a way to George's Island."

"Lots of boats in Boston," Peter said. "If we don't find one still floating, I'm sure there will be plenty just sitting in storage, wrapped in plastic."

"Like big snack food containers," Jakob said.

Peter glanced back at his son. He'd been through a lot, too, and had really come into his own, but he tended to look on the downside of things first. Peter didn't blame him. There weren't many positives left in the world, but if you only saw the negative possibilities, that was all you would ever find.

"Speaking of," Anne said. "We've been driving up the East Coast for a while now, but I say the word 'coast' with heavy quotation marks. Because we haven't seen the ocean once this whole time, and as someone who was grown in a tube and has never seen the ocean, I was kind of looking forward to it."

"We're not sightseeing," Peter said.

"We're not taking the most efficient route either," Anne said. "You've been avoiding the ocean. Why?"

Peter shared a glance with Ella. She gave a subtle nod.

"We're taking the safest route," he said.

"Uh-huh." Anne nodded, like that was obvious. "That's what you always do. The point I'm making is that if we're taking the safest route, and avoiding the ocean, then that means the ocean is dangerous."

"It's..." Peter paused a moment to think of how best to word things. "It's— We don't know. Not really."

"But the ocean is full of the biggest and scariest creatures on Earth," Anne said. "And that was before the change. Now... Whales. Sharks. Jellyfish even. They're all going to be horrible, right?"

"It's a possibility," Peter said. "I haven't been to the ocean since the change, and I didn't hear anything about them before communications went dark."

"They were the last to change," Ella said.

"Maybe they didn't?" Jakob asked.

"Or maybe people didn't notice because by then they were all eating each other," Anne added.

"Oh," Lyn said. "You all have such worrisome and active imaginations. How about this? We worry about what lurks in the abyss if we live to see it. Until then, I suggest we keep our eyes on the road and our foot on the gas." She leaned forward and gave Peter's shoulder a grandmotherly pat.

Lyn wasn't in charge. Far from it, in fact.

But she sometimes used her age as a way to defuse conversations or arguments that could, on occasion, fill hours of what she'd prefer to be quiet time. Peter didn't know much about her life before, but he imagined her quietly working, quietly sipping tea, and quietly doing yoga.

In comparison, they were a rowdy bunch.

The only time Lyn seemed to fit in was when danger was afoot, and everyone was silent. Which was quite often because danger was always present.

Peter turned his attention to the road, as requested. There were cars all over the highway, but Interstate 95 was wide enough that they could maneuver their way around the abandoned vehicles. Even the multicar pileups left space on one side or another. And if there wasn't room, Beastmaster could make a way through. The downside of all that horsepower was noise. They made a lot. Beastmaster allowed them to cover a lot more ground than they could on foot, but a lot of Apexes had keen hearing. Roaring up an otherwise silent highway was akin to ringing a perpetual, traveling dinner bell.

However, they'd been prepared for everything the East had to offer thus far. Between the mounted machine gun, their sizeable armory, and a bag of grenades gifted to them by Boone, they'd made short, messy work of a T-Rex-looking porcupine, a six-armed bear the size of a tank, and a wasp large enough to decapitate a human, with a stinger powerful enough to punch through Beastmaster's armor.

But .50 cal bullets were still .50 cal bullets and, as far as Peter could tell, human beings were still the deadliest living things on the planet... when they were still fully human. And armed with things that shoot.

Thirty minutes into the silent drive, Peter found himself yawning. He was tired. Was always tired. But he tried not to let it show. They had just a few hours left to go, but the day was fading, and traveling at night was a really bad idea. Predators in the old world were mostly nocturnal, and that hadn't changed.

"Jakob," he said. "Map time. Find me a small town. The kind without a lot of people, but big enough to have a few defensible structures."

"I know, I know," Jakob said, rifling through their collection of maps. "Schools, churches, town halls, and National Guard. We in Massachusetts yet?"

"Crossed the border twenty minutes back," Ella said.

"Here we go," Jakob said, unfurling a map of the area. "Small towns..."

Anne let out a long, exasperated sigh. Jakob thought she had ADHD, but Ella believed Anne's mind was so different, that there was so much information bouncing around in there, that she needed near constant stimulation to keep from getting overwhelmed.

The post-apocalypse suited her, but there was still a lot of downtime—even though it hadn't been that long since they'd set a super-coordinated horde of pint-sized killer fish-mice on fire. While everyone else probably still felt overwhelmed by the encounter, she'd moved on and was looking for something else to occupy her mind.

She found it, as she often did, in her memories.

Sometimes her mother's memories.

"Anyone remember when I clocked Kenyon over the head with a giant dildo?" she asked.

"Oh my," Lyn said.

"Anne," Ella said, chastising.

Jakob chuckled while scanning the map. "I love that story."

"Bright pink," Anne said. "Size of a baseball bat. Heavy, too, but kind of floppy. That didn't matter because the veins—"

Peter cleared his throat.

Anne paused, looking to her father. They hadn't known each other long, but she respected Peter and wanted to please him. He gave a subtle shake of his head.

Anne deflated and blew air through her lips, sounding like a horse—before they had grown horns and claws and wings.

The sliding window at the back of the extended cab opened.

"Feesa!" Anne announced happily. The big hairy female Rider turned family member was always good for spicing up any conversation. She didn't ride inside with them—not because there wasn't room, and there wasn't—but because she preferred the outdoors. Tight confines like a vehicle irritated her. So, she sat in the truck bed, beside the machine gun, soaking up the sun and keeping an eye out. And an ear. And a nose.

Like other Exos, she had keen senses.

Unlike other Exos, she could think, reason, and control her urge to eat everything around her.

She was a social creature, and they, through a convoluted series of relationships, were the closest thing to a genuine family she had.

"What's up?" Ella asked. Feesa didn't normally poke her head inside unless there was a problem. Then again, she was usually hooting and pounding on the roof as well. This was different. She was quietly concerned.

Feesa extended her hairy arm out toward Ella. The car's cab quickly filled with the hairy female's body odor. They'd gotten accustomed to it, but those first few seconds of exposure were always rough. In between her black skinned fingers was a clump of hair. "Me hair fall out."

Ella took the clump and inspected it.

"You're probably just shedding. A lot of animals do that. Several times a year."

"Me never shed before."

"Mmm," Ella said, likely thinking the same thing they all were, but not wanting to say it aloud.

Feesa took care of it for her. "Me changing. Again. Me Apex…" She turned her head down. "Me dangerous to family?"

Ella took Feesa's hand in hers, offering comfort and trust. "No, Feesa. You are safe. How about this? When we stop, I'll check you out. Look for any obvious changes. If we don't find anything, you're shedding, and that's all. Okay?"

Feesa took a deep breath and let out a sigh. "Ok, Ella. When stop?"

"Aha," Jakob said, tapping the map. "In two exits. About ten minutes. I think there's a place that will work."

5

"Everyone knows the drill. Let's do this like clockwork. No noise. No jokes." Peter looked each one of them in the eyes. No matter how many times they did this, Anne never noticed him take it any less seriously.

"Hold on," Anne said, before leaning to the side and letting out a squeaker that made Jakob laugh and Lyn wave a hand in front of her nose.

"Heavens," Lyn said. "Child. I will never get used to that."

"Okay," Anne said, delighted by the responses she got. "I'm ready."

"You sure?" Peter asked. "Nothing else stored up in there?"

Anne moved her body back and forth while looking at the ceiling. Then she stopped. "Nope. I'm good."

"Right," Peter said. "You're with me."

"What?" Ella said.

"What?" Anne repeated, followed by a big grin and a, "Seriously?"

Her father always took backup. Mostly Jakob. Sometimes Ella. Feesa just once.

But never Anne. She was usually made to wait in the truck with whoever was manning the machine gun mounted in the bed.

"You can't be serious," Ella said.

"She's earned the chance," Peter said. "And things have been quiet for a while. We might be in a dead zone."

Dead zones were what they had come to call areas where life had burned itself out. Everything had eaten each other and the last Exo standing had moved on to new hunting grounds.

"There's no way to know, I—"

Peter put his hand on Ella's. "She'll be with me."

Ella had nothing to say to that. She knew, as well as the rest of them, that the safest place to be when an Exo-whatever attacked wasn't with the machine gun, hiding in Beastmaster, or riding piggy-back on Feesa. It was by Peter's side.

Anne's mother relented. The point couldn't be argued.

Peter nodded. "Jake, on the gun. Feesa—"

"Perimet—" she said, trying to say the full word, but falling short.

"Almost got it," Jakob said to her, which got a big smile. Then Feesa was off, slipping into the woods, where she would move silently from tree to tree, making sure nothing nefarious was stalking them.

"Ella," Peter said. "Lyn."

Lyn waved him off. "We know what to do—or what not to do in my case. We've done this enough times."

Peter smiled at her but remained resolute. "The moment we let our guard down is the moment we make a mistake."

Lyn rolled her eyes, leaned forward, reached behind her feet, and sat back up with a shotgun in her hands. "You're the boss."

"What should I bring?" Anne asked. She was bouncing in her seat. Hadn't been this excited in a long time. Not just because clearing a building sometimes led to a confrontation with something that needed to be shot, but because this was her chance to show her father she could handle it.

"Things have been quiet, so I'd like to keep it that way," Peter said.

"Got it. Time to bust out the Old Woman."

"Excuse me?" Lyn said.

Anne waved her off. "Not you. The Old Woman is an FNX-45 Tactical with an Osprey sound suppressor."

"Why...do you call it an old woman?" Lyn asked.

Anne sighed. "'There was an old woman, and what do you think? She lived upon nothing but victuals and drink: Victuals and drink were the chief of her diet; And yet this old woman could never be quiet.' Mother Goose. The gun is sound suppressed, but not silent. It tries to be quiet, but it's drunk...on bullets...or something. Point is, it's quiet, but not silent. Like the old woman."

"Seems like an awful lot of thought to put into a gun's name."

"The best weapons have names," Anne said, like it was a fact everyone should know. "Excalibur. Mjölnir. Whipsnap."

"I suppose that has a name, too?" Lyn hitched her thumb toward the M249 Light Machine Gun mounted behind her.

"Nah," Anne said, unlocking her door. "That's a part of Beastmaster." She gave the door an affectionate pat. "Like his penis or something." Then she opened the door, slid out, and closed it in Lyn's unamused face.

Anne took a moment to enjoy the early evening air. It smelled of new growth and decay. The crops growing everywhere were constantly rotting and regrowing in a never-ending cycle. The others were growing tired of the smell, but Anne enjoyed it. Probably because she could eat everything she was smelling. Cauliflower. Corn. And...beets? It had been a while since she chomped into a fresh beet. Maybe Peter would let her pick some after the building was clear.

"Hey," Jakob said. He was in the truck bed, unclipping the tarp that covered the machine gun. "Don't be nervous."

"I do stuff like this all the time," she said.

"About my father. About Dad." Jakob pulled the tarp away and folded it up. "You don't need to try impressing him. You just need to...be you. If he asked you to go with him, it means he thinks you're ready the way you are. He's not expecting you to become James Bond or something."

"I don't know who that is," Anne said. "You go to school with him or something?"

"Or something." Jakob offered his hand, and Anne took it. With a quick pull, she was up inside the truck bed with her brother.

"Whoa, muscle man," Anne said. "Have you been doing secret push-ups or something? You're getting stronger."

"Another 'or something,' I guess." Jakob looked away. He didn't handle compliments very well.

"Oooh, I get it..." She opened one of the many weapons cases. The one decorated with butterfly stickers. She'd only seen one butterfly in her life. It was the size of a house and tried to eat her. Her father had set it on fire. That—was a fun day.

She removed the handgun, pulled back the slide, and gave the weapon a once-over. Everything looked good and clean, just the way she'd left it. She plucked the sound suppressor free next. It screwed onto the FNX's threaded barrel with ease. Next came a magazine, which held fifteen bullets. She slapped it in place and chambered the first round. The weapon's recoil was a little annoying. She had to use both hands and keep a tight grip, but if a weapon didn't kick the user, it wouldn't hit the target hard enough to make much of a difference.

Her father said that once. She'd memorized it.

Repeated it to herself whenever she got to practice, and her hands grew sore from the kickback.

"Get what?" Jakob asked.

"Huh? Oh. I got sidetracked by my sweet, sweet Old Woman." She petted the gun and then holstered it on her hip. While she put on the small-sized Kevlar vest that took them ages to find, she said, "You're trying to get all buff so that after we save humanity, you can go back to Hellhole and be like, 'Yo, Alia, honey cheeks—'"

"Honey cheeks?"

"Or whatever you call her."

"Mostly Alia."

"Hey, sugar buns, check out my new ripped bod from saving the world. Run your hands over my barely hairy chest. You feel that? You *feel* that? Those are the muscles that saved humanity, baby. Drink 'em in, bebe. Now let's get busy!"

Jakob tried to contain his laughter. They weren't supposed to be making any sound at all, but Anne knew how to get him laughing.

"You don't even know what 'getting busy' means," Jakob said.

"Jakey-boy, you have no idea what is—" She tapped her head with each word. "In. My. Head."

"Right. Your mom's memories." He cringed. "*All* of them?"

"*Enough* of them," Anne said.

"Ugh. Is Dad in them?"

She just gave him a sour look.

"Keep it down back there," Peter said, his voice low. He stood by the truck's cab, sound suppressed M4 in hand—another gift from Fort Bragg.

"Sorry," Jakob said, taking hold of the machine gun and giving it a test swivel back and forth. He wouldn't chamber a round until he knew the weapon needed to be fired. "I'm ready."

"We're both ready," Anne said, and then she leapt over the truck bed's sidewall. Peter reached up and caught her, placing her on the ground like they'd rehearsed it. Anne, unlike Jakob, was a natural at all this post-apocalyptic stuff.

"Channel five," Peter said, and Jakob confirmed his hand-held radio was on the right channel.

"Channel five," Jakob said. "El checko."

Peter gave a nod. "Show me the codes."

"We need to do this every time?" Jakob asked.

Peter just waited, eyebrows raised.

Jakob quickly squeezed the call button on his radio twice. Two faint clicks emerged from Peter's radio. "Two clicks, all clear." He pressed the button again, three times, more slowly. "Three clicks, danger near."

"Good," Peter said. "I know you think I'm taking your sister on the part of this that is more fun and more responsibility, but I'm trusting you to protect precious cargo." He glanced at Ella and Lyn, whose combined knowledge was enough to undo the damage done by RC-714 and allow humanity to eat again.

Jakob nodded. "I'm on it."

"Good," Peter said and turned to Anne. "Ready to rock n' roll?"

"Affirmative, big daddy." She gave a salute and, as Peter led the way through the cracking parking lot toward the gothic church made creepier by the orange sky, she stuck her tongue out at Jakob.

He rolled his eyes and got to work.

She turned around, drew her pistol, and leaned against the building's wall beside the front entrance—a set of thick, wooden doors—opposite Peter.

"I'll breach. You clear. Close and silent."

She nodded. "What if we see people?"

"No one has lived here in a very long time. If it's breathing, shoot it."

"Copy that," she said, licking her lips.

Peter grasped the door's handle and gave it a slow turn. Unlocked. They were in luck.

When it was turned all the way, Peter mouthed, "Three...two..."

"One," Peter said, and swung the door inward. He allowed Anne to go in first, watching her move. She slid inside, weapon raised, sweeping the foyer right to left and then back again. Her timing, form, and instincts were all on point.

Just as he'd expected. And not because he had trained her.

He had been training all of them, even Feesa, every time an opportunity presented itself. Jakob had been with him the longest, but while he was competent, he wasn't tactical like Anne. Probably never would be. Some people just didn't have the ability to switch everything off and go into hunter-killer mode.

But Anne was so natural, maybe even *unnatural*, at it.

Because she didn't just move like a well-trained operator. She moved like him. Like she'd gone through the same boot camp, fought in the same battles, and killed the same people.

She'd been inheriting her mother's mind and the memories that came with it. Peter believed something similar was happening with her skillset. She was either absorbing memory and skills through Peter's DNA—something he'd have thought impossible before—or she was able to replicate his abilities by observing them once.

That didn't feel right. Because he'd never cleared a building with her before, but she was a natural.

"Clear," she whispered.

Peter followed her in, weapon held high, careful to avoid pointing it in Anne's direction.

The foyer was dark, lit only by the setting sun, which burned through the orange and red stained glass on either side of the sanctuary. The dulled light left an uncomfortable amount of deep shadows around the room. They'd have to check every single one of them.

"Flashlights," Anne said, taking the lead and the words from Peter's mouth. She clicked on a small handheld one mounted on the side of her pistol. He did the same with the larger flashlight on the underside of his M4. "I'll take the left aisle. You take the right. Slow and steady."

She paused like she'd been caught stealing dentures from an old blind lady. "I mean, that's what you'd say, right?"

"It is." He forced a smile at her, and thought, *exactly what I'd say*.

She gave a nod and stepped through the sanctuary's left entrance. Peter took the right, focusing less on Anne now and more on the shadows, which could hide any number of hungry beasts.

But he doubted it.

ExoGenetic creatures weren't known for patience or stealth. Hunger drove them to madness and savagery. Anything in these shadows would likely have attacked the moment they stepped through the door. But there were always exceptions. That was the problem with infinite adaptations. There was no way to know what you were up against until it was standing over you, ready to feast.

Especially now that there was so little to eat.

Nearly everything left alive was an Apex, and the more they ate each other, the fewer there were.

Most creatures weren't breeding any more—aside from the occasional social species, but they were even more rare than the Apexes themselves. In an overfed world made even hungrier, there was now a famine.

Peter and his family were some of the last food items on the menu.

He lit up one pew after another. Each of them empty. On the far side of the sanctuary, Anne did the same. Step, scan, clear, move on. They shifted from their sides to the middle, alternating who checked the center without having to coordinate. They glided through the room, performing a series of movements like they'd been rehearsing it for years. He hadn't felt this kind of simpatico tactical partnership since his time in the service.

Definitely not normal.

But welcome. If something happened to him or Ella, Anne would need to carry on without them. He was more confident than ever that she could.

"I don't think anything is in here," Anne said.

Peter turned to face her and agree when a look of shock snapped onto her face, and her weapon came up, aimed toward the pulpit. She squeezed off three rapid shots, while Peter took aim, found her target, and added another two to the monster's chest.

The thing didn't flinch. Didn't move.

Because it wasn't alive, and never had been.

"Holy shit," Anne said, "that...that's not normal for a church, right?"

Peter pointed his light up at the statue they'd killed. It stood eight feet tall and twelve wide thanks to its unfurled bat-wings. From the waist down, the statue's body was that of a goat's, ending in cloven hooves. The creature's torso was feminine, sporting two prodigious breasts. Its hands were held out, one pointed up, the other down, two fingers extended on each. On the statue's stomach was a crisscrossing snake symbol that Peter normally associated with medicine. The head was also a goat's, twisting horns rising up, framing a pentagram.

All of that was strange, but what really stood out was the pair of innocent looking children standing on either side of the figure, staring up longingly at the beast.

"Ten bucks says everyone who worshiped this Baphomet thing got eaten by something that looked just like it. I heard the Exo-goats were pretty horrific."

"Haven't seen one yet," Peter said. "How do you know its name?"

"Because...it's Baphomet?" She shrugged. "Is that not a normal thing to know?"

"Not remotely," he said, reaching into a pew and pulling out a black book. The gold foil title on the black cover read, 'The Satanic Bible.' "Wonderful," Peter said, placing the book back.

"Hey," Anne said. "I mean, the big guy upstairs hasn't exactly been helping out. Maybe we should invoke the name of Baph—"

"Not funny."

"Mmm. I guess we have enough demons to deal with already."

"More than enough," Peter said, taking one last look at the statue. "By the way. Nice shots."

Baphomet had three chips taken out of his forehead, one from Peter, two from Anne. Another three were dead center in its chest, two from Peter, one from Anne. Six rounds total, each one of them a kill shot.

"Know anything else about this...church?"

Anne shrugged. "Well, this is Baphomet, so that probably means this is a Satanic Temple, *not* the Church of Satan. That's old school. This is new school, and even though this guy looks scary, they don't actually believe in him, or Satan, or anything supernatural at all. All this stuff—" She waved a hand at the statue. "—is about getting attention. A PR stunt. They're basically using Satan's name in an effort to disregard God, and anything else metaphysical, paranormal, or transcendental, which is kind of boring if you ask me."

"Huh," Peter said. "Interesting tactic."

"Deception. Sleight of hand. It's pretty blatant, I think."

"Go a level deeper," he said. "Psychological warfare. What's the best way to surprise an enemy?"

She thought on it, for just a moment. Then her eyes widened. "Make them believe you're not there." Her brow furrowed. "So...you're saying, that if *you* were Satan, you would start a church that disproved you existed?"

Peter nodded. "The most powerful enemy is one that is never seen."

"Like a sniper."

He shook his head. "Like the kind that never actually needs to fight."

"Huh," she said. "That's kind of boring, though, isn't it?"

"Sometimes boring gets the job done."

"But it's still boring," she said. "And boring is dumb."

"Good thing there are no debate teams left on the planet," Peter said, "because wow."

For a moment, Anne beamed. Then...she squinted. "You're mocking me."

"Big time." He waved for her to follow him, and they moved to a door at the back of the sanctuary.

"You know, I could use my superior intellect to win the debate, right? I'm using simple layman's terms for your benefit."

"Okay, mini Khan," Peter said, leaning against the wall beside the door.

"Khan? Genghis or Kublai?"

"Noonien Singh."

"Never heard of him."

"Never did get your mother to watch the movie."

"I'll watch it with you."

Peter smiled. "It's a date. Ready?"

Anne nodded. Peter opened the door. They swept in together, repeating their quick scan of the room on the other side.

"Clear," Anne said. "Sort of."

She shined her flashlight on the long dead corpse of a man who'd taken his own life with a shotgun. His head wasn't so much missing as it was spattered, coagulated, and later *cemented* to the wall by long-since dried liquified gray matter.

"You okay?" Peter asked.

"If he'd held on just another thousand days, we might have reached him in time..." She sniffed back fake tears and turned to Peter. "Fine. In fact—"

Click, click, click.

They both froze, listening. The sound repeated.

Click, click, click.

Anne looked up at Peter, fear in her eyes for the first time since they entered the building. "Three clicks, danger nea—"

Her voice was drowned out by a low moan loud enough to rattle the stained-glass windows and force their hands to their ears. Whatever was coming, it was big.

7

Ella pulled her hands away from her ears and leaned forward to look out the windshield. Whatever let out that cry sounded like it was right on top of them. But she couldn't see anything aside from the gothic church building, the surrounding woods, and the crops filling every available space of earth that wasn't still paved over.

"Lord above," Lyn said from the back seat. "What was that?"

"I'm not sure..."

"Have you ever heard something so loud in all your life?"

"Not even close."

Ella continued searching. The sky was still orange, but the sun's light no longer landed on the patch of land they occupied. The shadows were deep and dark—the time of day when getting indoors and staying quiet was a good idea.

A tap on the rear window made Lyn yelp. She clamped her hands over her mouth and mumbled sorry. Behind her, Jakob, who had attempted to not startle them, shook his head. When Ella made eye contact with the bewildered boy, he pointed.

Up.

Ella leaned forward and craned her gaze upward. Still nothing.

She looked back through the rear window again. Jakob was looking up, and back, hands by his sides. Not on the machine gun. He wasn't afraid.

Movement in her periphery caught her attention. Something was coming out of the woods! She was about to shout for Jakob when the creature stepped out into the parking lot.

It was Feesa, eyes on the sky, looking dumbfounded.

"What the hell..." Ella said and decided to see for herself. She carefully opened the passenger side door, slid out, and turned her eyes to the sky.

"What..." She whispered, staggering back a step. "...the hell?"

A shadow cut across, blotting out much of the orange sky.

The bulbous thing was a hundred and fifty feet long, half as wide, and stretched near to bursting. At first, Ella had no idea what she was looking at. Then the details started to make sense.

The expanded underside was ribbed. Lines of white and gray ran front to back. They were stretched out as the body expanded from a lighter-than-air gas, perhaps generated by internal fermentation. The powerful arms and legs dangling limply from the creature's sides confused her at first. Each limb ended in a thick, stubby mass of flesh, like an elephant's foot—only large enough to step on an elephant. But right now, they had no purpose, because the thing was airborne, being propelled by a massive tail of translucent membrane stretched between two sets of bone.

"Ella," Jakob whispered from the truck bed. "Is that a whale?"

"*Was* a whale," Ella said. "Blue whale, once upon a time. But now..."

"Exo-whale," Jakob said.

"Apex-whale," Ella corrected.

"It seems peaceful, though. It's just floating up there. Minding its own business."

The creature let out another low moan loud enough to shake the ground.

Ella winced, clasping her hands on the sides of her head.

When it was done, Jakob said, "It sounds sad. Sounds lonely."

"You understand whale calls now?" Ella asked.

"Well, no. But—"

"You know what whale calls are for, right?"

"Uhh."

"Communication," she said. "With its pod."

"Oh... OH."

"Right." She lowered her voice. "As...majestic as it might seem, we need to treat it like any other Apex. Stay still. Stay quiet."

"Stay out of sight." Jakob ducked behind the cab.

Feesa, out in the parking lot, either came to the same conclusion or overheard their conversation with her keen hearing. She backtracked into the forest.

"So, you think there are more of them?" Jakob asked, crouched low in the truck's bed. "A whole pod?"

"That's the logical assumption," Ella said. She didn't like it but couldn't think of any other explanation. And it was just another sign of a growing trend—surviving Exos seemed to be species that had maintained, or developed, a community.

Power in numbers.

The same could be said for the remnants of humanity. Alone, they were doomed. Together, they were still mostly doomed, with a sliver of hope. But humanity was currently divided. ExoGen still wanted her—probably dead or alive—and they wanted Anne even more. And then there was Kenyon, who wanted her for himself. It was the kind of primal male dominant outlook on courtship that might have been prevalent when Neanderthals still roamed the Earth. 'Me Thug, you mine, we make boom boom.' While some men, like Peter, remained evolved, others like Kenyon and Mason devolved into primitive versions of their formal selves, no ExoGenetic tinkering required. For some people, all you needed to do was remove the restraints provided by modern society.

The whale bent its body and swished its tail through the air, sliding through the sky with effortless grace. It was as beautiful in the sky as it had been in the ocean. But also ominous.

Because it didn't get that big by eating sky plankton.

The church's front door opened. Peter and Anne exited with strategic ease. For a moment, Ella didn't recognize her daughter. The girl rarely took anything seriously, and when she did, Anne performed her duties with exaggerated flourish. By Peter's side, sound suppressed gun in hand, she looked...dangerous.

Professional. Like she knew what she was doing. Because she did.

Because Ella had tinkered with genetics a second time, to make herself a daughter using her own DNA and Peter's. The unexpected consequences of that, and the digital information Ella had stored in her brain, accessible by computer via a USB port in the back of her head, was that the girl had their memories and, it would seem, skills. There were times Ella felt guilty about it, but when she saw Anne like this, excelling in this world, she felt better about the choices she'd made. Anne had a real chance at survival and might be the key for the rest of humanity's evolution.

Ella made eye contact with Peter and pointed to the sky.

He and Anne carefully stepped out of the church's overhang and turned their eyes to the now purple sky.

Ella heard Anne whisper, "Holy whale shit," when she saw it. Peter said nothing. Just set his jaw and got to working on plans, contingencies, and last resorts.

Just as Anne finished her comment, the whale seemed to obey her command, unleashing a chunky torrent of white effluent from its backside. The bus-sized feces fell to the ground and landed with a distant thump. A moment later, a rumble slid through the pavement beneath Ella's feet.

Letting out an earsplitting call of what might be relief, the whale spun itself upside down, arced around, and swam through the air, headed further north. It hadn't seen them. Hadn't been hunting. But it would be soon.

"*Inside*," Ella said to Jakob and Lyn. "Now!"

Jakob hopped out of the truck, retrieved their night-packs from the trailer, and jogged ahead.

Ella made sure Lyn got out of the back okay and then walked beside her. Lyn was older but didn't really need constant attention or help getting around. Ella was just protective of her. Together, they might be able to do the work that was necessary to undo the damage caused by RC-714. Both of them had solved part of the puzzle. They just needed a lab in which to assemble the whole thing.

"That was...different," Peter said as they approached.

"Worse than I imagined," Ella admitted.

"That why we've been avoiding the ocean?" Anne asked.

"It is," Peter said.

"Well, *I* thought it was cool," Anne said. "And did you see that poop? I mean, I feel like I've dropped a few fibrous bombs in my day, but that... whew. That was something."

Jakob smiled. "We'll be able to smell it by morning."

Anne's eyes lit up. "You think?"

"What I think," Peter said, "is that something that big is probably hungry all the time, even when it's not ExoGenetic. We were lucky it was... preoccupied."

"Is it clear?" Ella asked, tilting her head up at the door.

"We didn't get through every room, but there's no sign of activity. We're good." Peter held the door open for them. "But I'm not sure everyone will want to stay here." He glanced at Lyn.

The old woman understood who he was talking about without seeing the glance. "Hush." She waved at him. "A roof and a locked door are all I need."

Ella gave him a quizzical glance, but he just motioned them inside and said, "See for yourself."

Ten seconds later, he had his hand wrapped around Lyn's mouth, muffling her scream. "Mmmf ahhh emmmmoom."

"That," Anne said, "is Baphomet. He might look scary, but he's not real. I mean, maybe demons are real and all that. I'm not here to debate theology. But that Baphomet is a statue. We shot him six times, so it's not even one of those Apexes that looks like a rock, but actually wants to eat you."

Peter slid his hand away from Lyn's mouth. "Okay?"

She let out a huff. "You could have said something."

"I could have," Peter said, "but this was more fun."

Lyn swatted his shoulder. "You're horrible."

Peter smiled and backtracked to the door, locking it behind him. "Let's eat, get some sleep, and head out at first light. Tomorrow's going to be a big day."

"Because of Boston?" Anne asked.

"Because we're heading north," Jakob said. "Same direction as that whale. And..." He frowned. "Because Boston is surrounded by ocean."

"It'll be worse than that," Ella said. "Without people managing the city? It will be *in* the ocean."

8

Peter enjoyed driving in the morning. Always had. The sun to the east. The flowers waking up. Dew left behind from the previous night's chill. It was invigorating.

It was also the safest time of day. Because most Apexes hunted at night and slept through the morning. Around noon, things would get sketchy. By sunset, they'd have to hunker down again. If they were lucky, they'd be on George's Island tonight, safe in an ExoGen lab that Ella said had been left empty since the change began.

They'd have company waiting for them, though. Kenyon and a few of his men. Maybe more, if they managed to get ahold of the main facility on the West Coast. Peter hoped not. If Kenyon had reinforcements, there'd be nothing they could do. They'd have to find another one of Ella's secret installations scattered around the country, and hope that, like Hellhole Bay, it hadn't been co-opted by sinister operators.

Even if Kenyon didn't have back-up, they'd still have a fight on their hands. They might outnumber the ExoGen security men at the lab, and Feesa was a force to be reckoned with, but Kenyon had time to prepare. Sometimes, that alone was enough to defeat a superior foe.

So, this morning, with everyone sleepy and quiet in the back after a long night of lying on pews, was the quiet before the storm. Peter leaned his head toward his open window, closed his eyes for the briefest moment, and breathed the morning air—

"What...the hell is that?" Anne asked, beating Peter to the question by a millisecond. Instead of vegetation and evaporating moisture, the air smelled deeply and profoundly of acrid shit.

"There!" Ella said, pointing to a field of broccoli off to the left. The plot was divided by the remnants of a crumbling road and dilapidated houses, many of which had tall stalks of wheat growing from their rooftops and gutters. But it was the massive lump of white, half crushing a house, that Ella was really focused on.

"Holy crap," Anne said. "It's shit." Her eyes widened. "Flying whale shit!"

Ella put her hand on Peter's arm. "We need to stop."

"No way," he said. "It's too—"

"She wants to see what's in it," Anne said. "What's in the shit."

"Can you stop saying 'shit,'" Ella said to Anne, and then turned back to Peter. "I want to see what it's been eating. A creature that size... Exo-Genetic creatures still burn calories. Still need to eat enough to support themselves or they starve to death. That whale...it was big."

"That sh—" Anne rolled her eyes. "That *poo* is big, too."

Peter twisted his lips and slowed the truck. Glanced back at Jakob. His son just shrugged. He looked to Lyn, who offered a forced grin. "They're not wrong. Understanding what is happening in the world of our enemy might give us the information we need to defeat them...or at least survive them."

The moment Lyn framed things from a strategic perspective, Peter understood two things. They were right. And Lyn knew how to manipulate him when she needed to.

She gave him a wink and a real smile.

"Me not agree," Feesa said, peeking in through the back window. "Air smell like butt. I no eat butt. No like shit smell."

"No one likes it," Ella said. "We'll be quick, I promise."

"She gets to say 'shit?'" Anne shakes her head. "I refuse to conform to this reformation of old-world linguistic standards where kids aren't allowed to use the same language as adults, as if words actually have the power to corrupt. So, 'shit.'" She nudged Jakob. "C'mon, man. Fight the power. Shit. Shit. Shitty, shit-shit."

Jakob chuckled. "Shit, yeah."

Ella sighed. "Fine. Whatever." To Peter, she said, "Can I go inspect the shit now?"

Peter didn't bother pulling over. There were no other cars on the road, and the broccoli grew right up to the edge. He considered driving into the neighborhood, but the road was all chewed up and pocked with bunches of vegetation. Last thing they needed was to get stuck in a broccoli patch.

"Ten minutes," he said. "Jakob, on the gun. Feesa, stay with him, but keep watch."

Anne raised her hand. "I'm going to the shit!"

Peter nodded. "We both are." He pointed at Ella and Lyn. "You two stay close. Work fast. And don't even think about bringing a sample."

"It's possible the scent alone could deter—"

Feesa thumped the truck's roof with her big fist. "Me. No. Like. Shit. Smell."

Ella raised both hands. "Okay, okay. We won't bring any with us."

"Less talking," Jakob said, shooing everyone out of the truck. "More getting this over with."

Peter exited the vehicle, shouldered his M4, and scanned the surrounding area. Like most highways in New England, there were a lot of trees where something could be hiding. At this time of day, it was less likely. But not impossible. So, he took the same time and care he always did, even if the smell made him want to hurry things along.

On the back of the truck, Jakob uncovered the machine gun and swiveled it back and forth. Above him, Anne climbed onto the cab, performing her own visual search, while Feesa sniffed the air. They were like a little mob of meerkats, scouring the savannah for danger.

"Clear," Anne said. "I think everybody's asleep."

"Or there're no Apexes left in this area," Jakob said. "Aside from the stank-ass flying whale."

Feesa grunted in agreement. "Clear. No smell, but…hard to smell anything but shit. Me also like that word. Shit."

"Right?" Anne said, holding her hand up for a high five, which Feesa followed through on, hooting with laughter over the moment of camaraderie. While Anne warmed up to Feesa right away, it took everyone else a while to relax around her. Feesa's species of Exo was primitive, and violent, and savage. She had been their enemy for a time and would have killed them all if not for her strong tribal instincts, and Peter's path of logic that made them family.

"Clear," he said, and he gave Ella and Lyn a nod.

Ella led the way, wielding a shotgun. Anne followed her mother with the silenced FNX.

Lyn scurried after them, and Peter brought up the rear, watching their flanks.

The closer they got to the feces, the stronger it smelled of spoiled bacon grease mixed with rotting fish left in the sun. While the others held their shirt collars over their noses, Peter kept both hands on his weapon, ready to open fire at a moment's notice, smell be damned.

When they moved from the crumbling road to the compact field of broccoli, Peter had to shift his gaze to the unsteady terrain beneath his feet. He didn't like it, but the broccoli, while tough, could break if you didn't step in the plant's center. Even then, the small mounds made for questionable footing.

"It looks like marshmallow that's been held over a campfire too long," Anne said.

She wasn't wrong, but Peter frowned. Anne had never eaten or even seen a marshmallow. Her knowledge of it wasn't her own. Peter hated thinking about what she knew about him, and his past with her mother. There wasn't really anything horrible, but there was a lot that was private.

He remembered being taught once that, during the end times when humanity would be judged, all our actions and impurities would be exposed for the world to see. The embarrassment he felt over just the idea of his inner demons being revealed horrified him. Anne's emerging memory felt a lot like that. Except he thought Anne might be a more merciful judge. She'd embarrass them for sure, but she'd never condemn them.

"I'm seeing some definition within the mass," Ella said. "Disparate parts of whatever was consumed are still intact."

"Corn does the same thing," Anne said. "I should know. I eat a lot of it."

Peter barely registered the comment as he refocused on the broccoli field around them. The house upon which the giant pile of shit had landed hid them from anything to the west, and Jakob, Feesa, and Beastmaster gave them some protection from the east, but they were exposed to the north and south. Anything within a few miles, with keen enough eyes, would spot them moving out in the open.

Ella snapped on a pair of rubber gloves. For a moment, Peter was confused about where they'd come from. Then he realized they were dish washing gloves that Ella must have picked up at the store. They'd become survivalists and warriors now, but first and foremost, Ella was a scientist. And she liked to be prepared for moments like this, when the appearance of a gigantic shit ignited her curiosity.

"I see it," Lyn said, leaning uncomfortably close to the sludgy surface. "It looks like... Is that..."

"I think so," Ella said.

The hush in their voices shifted their tone from curious excitement to horrific realization. Peter had heard it before. Never meant anything good. He took his eyes off their surroundings and looked up at the megalithic dung. "What am I looking for?"

"Bodies," Ella said.

"Something we've seen before?" Peter asked, finding shapes within the mass that he couldn't identify.

"You've seen them before," Anne said, seeing the same thing the two women could. "Every day."

That's all it took. That slight suggestion gave Peter the necessary perspective to see things for what they were. The bodies. The tangled, decomposing limbs. The eye sockets and open jaws.

It was people.

All of it.

"Back to Beastmaster," Peter said, and then he added a growl to his voice that said he was not to be questioned. "*Now.*"

9

"It was *people?*" Jakob asked. "*All* of it?"

Anne had announced their discovery as they hurried back to the truck. His father's clenched jaw was confirmation enough.

"We're leaving," Peter said.

Jakob locked the machine gun in place, pulled the tarp back over the top, and cinched it down. While part of him wanted to see the bodies for himself, the rest of him wanted to get as far away from the smell as fast as possible. So, he leapt to the pavement and climbed back in the truck.

"I don't get it," Jakob said, buckling his seatbelt. "How could it all be people? That would be a lot of people, right?"

"Hundreds," Anne said.

Jakob threw his hands up. "We haven't seen that many people since leaving the house. Not even at Hellhole."

Ella shook her head. "There must have been a…a community. Some place people managed to survive. But I don't see how that's possible. The only place on Earth with that many people is the ExoGen headquarters… in San Francisco…" Ella's brow furrowed. "Unless…"

"Unless what?" Peter asked, his hand on the key, ready to start the truck.

Ella looked him in the eyes. "Unless they came to Boston."

"All of them?" Lyn asked, sounding incredulous.

"If they didn't have a choice," Ella said. "If they lost control. Were overrun. George's Island would have been the only other facility capable of housing everyone."

"So, all this time we've been running and hiding from ExoGen, they've been on the run, crossing the country, headed toward the same destination as us?" Jakob said, wanting to punch something. It was all ridiculous. The enemy, all of them, had beat them to Boston. And now, instead of a safe haven in which they could save the world, they faced impossible odds.

"We don't know that they made it," Ella said.

"Some of them would have flown," Lyn points out, and turned toward the massive mound of shit. "That…was probably their families. Non-essential personnel."

"The kids," Ella said.

Peter blinked out of whatever plan he was working out. "Kids? There were children at ExoGen?"

"I never saw any," Ella said, then turned to Anne. "You were different."

Anne rolled her eyes. "No kidding. I think what you mean is that I was a pariah, unfit to play with the normies."

"Probably the opposite," Jakob said.

"Aww, look at you," Anne said, leaning over Lyn to pinch his cheek. "Trying to get in good with the little sis."

"What do we do?" Ella asked Peter.

Peter started the truck. The engine revved to life. "Plan doesn't change. We get to Boston, assess the situation, and do what needs doing."

"That how you did things in the Marines?"

"Marines take and follow orders," he said. "But I'm not a Marine this time around... I'm—"

"The general!" Anne said.

"I was going to say 'in charge,' but 'general' works, too." He gave Anne a wink and put the truck into drive. "I want all eyes on the sky today. If you see anything, and I mean anything, shout it out. I didn't come this far to play Pinocchio in a whale's stomach."

"Ugh," Jakob said. "I hated that movie."

"Right?" Anne said, followed by her and her mother both saying, "Such a fever dream."

An awkward moment followed, during which Jakob was sure they were all wondering the same thing. Would Ella's memories take over eventually? Would Anne lose her identity? Change her name? Become Ella 2.0? It was a horrible thought. Even with some of Ella's knowledge and memories seeping through, Anne was a great kid. Jakob wouldn't say that aloud because she'd use it against him every time they argued, but he really liked having a sister, and was glad it was her.

But if she became a child-sized Ella?

That would be...weird. And sad because it would mean that Anne, as a person, was erased.

With that happy thought in mind, Jakob turned his eyes to the right, watching the tree line shift up and down as they sped along the highway. Two hours passed like that. The sky always empty, the trees occasionally interrupted by an office park, neighborhood, or field, all of them overgrown with lush vegetables that none of them—aside from Feesa and Anne—could eat.

He began imagining an Exo chasing them. It had eight legs, an insect-like body, and could leap from tree to tree. When they hit a clearing, four translucent wings snapped out and carried it across the gap. Somewhere in his imaginings, he fell asleep, and his subconscious continued the narrative—much more convincingly.

Jakob woke with a gasp, just as he'd been tackled in the dream. He glanced over his shoulder. Everyone was focused on keeping watch. No one had noticed him fall asleep or wake up.

His father gave him a casual glance. *He'd* noticed. Which wasn't surprising. His father noticed everything. It was annoying sometimes, more so when he seemed to know Jakob's very thoughts. He'd tried teaching Jakob how to do it, how to read people, but Jakob saw only broad strokes. People's secrets, apparently, hid in the details. Anne was a natural at it, of course.

"Jake," his father said.

"Yeah. I'm good."

"Good," Anne said with a huff, followed by the sound of mock snoring. "Right."

Okay...they all knew he'd fallen asleep. Whatever.

"I'm good," Jakob repeated.

"Still have the binoculars with you?"

Jakob checked the floor between his feet. He bent further, looking beneath the passenger's seat. The brown leather case was tucked in there. "Got it. Why?"

"We're nearly there," Peter said.

"To Boston?" Jakob asked. "Really? Already?"

Anne started snoring again. "Short trip when you're unconscious."

Ella shot Anne a look. "Leave him be. Some of us didn't sleep well last night on account of someone else's snoring."

"Top of this hill..." Peter pointed ahead. They were heading up a steep road that looked clear at the summit. "I want you on the roof. See what you can see."

"Got it," Jakob said.

He knew he wasn't as good at all the survival stuff as Anne, but he appreciated his father still including him, and trusting him with things—like the machine gun. Jakob didn't mind being the less intelligent of the siblings, as long as he got to unleash the thunder on occasion.

"Here we go," Peter said as they crested the hill's top.

They all leaned forward to look through the windshield. Boston's skyscrapers were visible in the distance, but some trees blocked their clear line of sight.

"Get to it," his father said, "and—"

"Make sure the sun doesn't reflect off the binoculars," Jakob said, opening his door. "I know. Battlefield 3, remember? Video games were good for something." He closed the door behind him and was about to climb up into the truck bed when a shadow fell over him.

Feesa.

"Give boost?" she asked.

He gave her an odd look. It was a new request.

"Help up," she said, as though explaining the words to a newborn, motioning toward the roof with her hands.

"I know what it means," Jakob said. "Sure."

Jakob expected her to reach down and haul him up. Instead, she jumped out of the truck, grabbed him beneath the arms and tossed him into the air. Jakob managed to stay upright as he arched up over the truck. Even stuck the landing, which resulted in surprised, muffled shouts from beneath.

"Thanks," Jakob told Feesa. "Good throw."

The hairy woman was thrilled with herself. "Feesa strong. Feesa help Jakob. We good team."

She wasn't wrong. They often found themselves on watch together and had become something like friends. Not a lot of long, heartfelt conversations, but that didn't matter much to teenage boys or, apparently, to devolved adult ExoGenetic women.

"Yes, we are," he said, standing tall and putting the binoculars to his eyes with one hand while using his free hand to keep the sun's rays from reflecting off the lenses. Boston came into focus.

Wasn't as big as he'd imagined it, partially because there weren't nearly as many skyscrapers as the few cities he'd been to before the change—New York and Toronto. But also because anything shorter than five stories tall was totally submerged. He could see where the coastline had been. It was lined by a few tall hotels, apartment buildings, and a nearly submerged parking garage, but they'd need a boat long before they reached the city.

"What have you got?" Peter asked. Somehow his father had exited the truck and climbed into the truck bed behind him without making a sound.

Jakob offered the binoculars. "See for yourself."

"Feesa help!" Feesa grabbed Peter and flung him up onto the vehicle's roof with as little effort as she had Jakob. The main difference was that his father made it look cool, almost effortless, like nothing fazed him.

When his father looked through the binoculars, Jakob asked. "How do you do that? Make everything look easy. Like, you knew she was going to throw you. Like you expected it."

"Fake it," his father said, turning back and forth.

"Fake it?"

"And practice." Peter lowered the binoculars. "Takes a lot of time to perfect."

"But why fake it?"

"Makes the people with you feel more confident in their safety, which actually helps contribute to their safety. Few things worse than panicky people. And it intimidates the enemy. You can charge an overwhelming force on your own, and they'll think twice about engaging because your confidence will make them think they've missed something. Odds are, the first of them will run, and when they do, the rest will follow."

"Psychological warfare."

"Doesn't work on Exos, so never try that."

"But does it help you at all?" Jakob asked. "Like faking being calm keeps you calm?"

"Not really," his father told him. "Like right now, I probably seem calm and unruffled, right?"

"You're faking it?" Jakob asked.

"Feel my pulse." Peter guided Jakob's hand to his neck. His father's heart was pumping hard and fast. Really fast.

Jakob's eyes widened. "What's wrong?"

Peter handed the binoculars back and pointed out to sea, where a few large islands were surrounded by sparkling ocean water. It was a nice view. "Just past the islands."

Jakob lifted the binoculars to his eyes, shifted his view to the islands, and then beyond, where a large part of the ocean had gone flat and swirly.

"That's a footprint. Whales make them when they swim near the surface, creating a current that cancels out the waves. But that...that is about ten times larger."

"You think it's the flying whale?" Jakob asked, lowering the binoculars.

Peter shook his head, looking grim. "I think it's something else." He pointed to the footprint with his finger, and then traced a line to the left, to an island with a large modern facility built atop it. The white and glass structure glinted in the sun, just a half mile closer to shore than the footprint. "And that's where we need to go."

10

"Me is Feesa. Feesa is happy." When she was alone, Feesa worked on her song. She often had trouble remembering the lyrics, so she freestyled them and the tune during every practice session in the back of the truck, letting the sound of the road and rushing wind whisk her voice away so no one else would hear. It was why she enjoyed sitting in the back by herself. That and the sun. And the rain. There was little about the outdoors that didn't please her.

"Feesa sitting in the back. She love family." She frowned and grunted. The song was wrong. The tune. The sound of her voice. No matter how much she practiced, it just never sounded right to her ear.

"Why not sound right?" she asked herself.

She sensed the answer, just beyond reach. She wanted to roar. Wanted to tear something apart. Instead, she closed her eyes and took a deep breath, the way Peter did when he was containing his frustration.

Peter was a good man. Good protector of the family. She always listened to him because his brain was good. Everyone thought Ella had the best brain, but Feesa knew better. The best brains kept people alive. Peter did that the best and understood how to let Feesa help.

"Peter is good. Peter is great. Me take Peter on a date."

Feesa grunted. She didn't know what a 'date' was. But it *sounded* like 'great,' and that *did* please her ear.

Make words that sound same, she thought, and then she set her mind to the task. "Jakob is nephew. Jakob is..." She shook her head. It was too hard. But she didn't give up easily. "Me like Anne. She is small, but... follows plan!"

Feesa hooted in excitement.

She'd done it again.

Words that sounded the same were magical.

Words that sounded the same were... A *new* word popped into her head.

"Rhyme..." she said.

"Words rhyme. Sound the same. Look...*book.* Scoop...*poop!*" She hooted with laughter, slapping both of her knees.

When Jakob turned around and looked at her through the truck window, she reined herself in, controlling her physical reaction to the epiphany, but not her excitement.

It felt new. Exciting.

It had been a long time since she learned a new word.

But she hadn't learned the word rhyme.

She remembered it.

From the time before, she thought, *when I was...*

She shook her head. *No time before. Only Feesa. Time before is no real.*

"Feesa not pretty," she said, quickly souring. "Feesa not know how to sing. Feesa not have...not have husband. Not...not...no baby."

But her dreams disagreed. In them, she was human and the people in them, strangers at first, had begun to take a hold of her waking thoughts. She could hear them sometimes. Their voices. But not their words. They were like ghosts, haunting her.

"Stupid faces," she said, pulling at the hair on her forearms. "Stupid feelings. No like." The pain in her arms helped drown out the faces and voices, clearing her mind.

When she'd calmed, Feesa opened her eyes and looked at her hands. They were full of hair. Tufts of the stuff, pulled out of her arms.

Her forehead scrunched.

It hadn't hurt her that much.

She tossed the clumps of hair away and watched them swirl up into the sky, behind the moving truck. As the distraction faded into the distance, she inspected her right arm, using her left hand to brush back the thick coat of brown hair on her arm. Didn't take long to find a hairless patch. Her skin beneath the hair looked like nighttime.

"Skin," she said, touching the smooth patch on her arm. "Smooth skin."

The only other exposed parts of her body—palms, foot soles, nose, were all tough, calloused, and scratchy. But her arm beneath the hair...

It felt, "Soft..."

A memory crashed into her mind like another unbidden dream. It was a person she once knew. A woman looking at her. Her skin was dark, the hair on her head curly and big, her clothing bright and colorful. The woman offended Feesa. She was weak.

"No," Feesa grumbled. "No! Me no—" She froze, hands raised to pound the truck bed. Peter would be upset at her for the loud noise, and for scaring them, but that was not why she stopped.

She smelled something.

Something bad.

"Apex..."

She stood and scanned the road behind them. "Not behind."

She was sure of it, not because she hadn't seen something but because the wind was coming from the truck's front end. They were headed toward the Apex. With that realization came a plan. It just popped into her head. She couldn't articulate it, but she could see it.

She slid the rear window open and shouted, "Peter! Stop!"

By the time Feesa had pulled her head back out of the window, the truck's tires were screeching against the pavement. Feesa used the momentum to spring forward, up onto the roof, from which she launched herself into the trees beside the road.

The first tree she struck was too feeble to hold her. The top of the pine bent under the grasp of her feet, and it snapped when her weight bent it too far. But there were plenty of trees and branches. She had no trouble course correcting, swinging herself around a branch, onto a nearby tree, and then back out into the road, forty feet above the Apex that had just emerged from the roadside where it had lain in wait.

An ambush, Feesa thought.

The concept had been taught to her by Kenyon. She had believed him an ally for a time. Perhaps even a mate. He had done sex with her. Jakob had a funny word for it. 'Snu snu.' He said it was from a TV show. That she wouldn't understand the reference.

But she remembered TV. The glowing box.

Feesa focused her attention on the creature below. It was four times her size. Big, but she had killed bigger. It would be stronger than her, but she was smarter. Like Peter. She had a plan. Had a weapon, too. A...machete. Hard word to even think, but she liked it because it cut deep when she swung it. Cut anything deep and hard enough, it died. That was a fact of life, and she was an expert at it.

As she arced up over the creature, she drew the machete from its sheath, attached to a belt that Jakob had found for her in a store. He didn't buy it. Didn't earn it. But that he thought of her at all had made her happy for a week.

Her keen eyes scoured the Apex's body, looking for weaknesses.

When she didn't see any, she tried to identify it. What it had been before the change.

What was I? she wondered.

The distraction was momentary, but it was enough.

The creature's head, which bobbed forward and backward with each step, turned sideways. Its large eye locked onto her. For a moment, they looked into each other's eyes, one monster against another, then Feesa couldn't see. Her vision filled with sunlight reflected off the giant's shiny feathers.

She raised her hand, blocking the light just enough to see.

The giant...what was it called...*bird*...had turned its sharp beak toward Feesa. But it hadn't opened to eat, it was closed tight, the tip like a spear. Feesa understood the attack, thanks to Kenyon's and Peter's training.

She swung the machete, striking the beak hard with the flat side of the blade. Instead of being impaled by the beak, she knocked it to the side just enough to grab hold of it with her free hand. She swung down, colliding with the Apex's neck and clung on.

The machete blade, slid under the hard feathery armor, would take the creature's life. She was sure of it. But before she could stab, all the feathers flared out. Each one of them was like a sharpened metal panel, slicing into her arms, legs, and torso.

Pain loosened her grip, and she fell to the ground far below, landing on her back hard enough to take the air from her lungs and consciousness from her mind.

In the darkness that followed, she heard a voice.

"Get up, Val. Get up!"

Feesa's eyes opened to a reflection of herself. For a moment she was confused by the view. She saw a woman looking back at her. Dark skin. A beautiful face. Big hair. A voice that could sing. The same woman from her dreams.

It was...her.

It was Val.

She...was Valerie Wood. Before.

Her face twisted with raw emotion and became monstrous again, her tusks digging deeper into her own cheeks. "No!" she screamed. "Me no like! NO!"

She climbed to her feet and faced the Apex's backside. It was charging past her toward Beastmaster. Peter was climbing out with his loud weapon. Jakob was climbing into the back of the truck. Neither of them would be fast enough.

Fueled by a new kind of rage, Feesa leapt into the air and dropped down toward the giant bird's back. Its feathers reflected a hundred different images of Feesa's monstrous face, each one of them mocking her. For who she was. For what she had become.

"Me. No. *Like!*" Feesa said, stabbing downward, all her weight behind the blade.

There was a moment of resistance. Then a crack. The blade slipped through armor and found the flesh beneath.

The Apex bird let out a pitiful cry of something much smaller. Its wings flapped in a flurry as it tried to dislodge Feesa.

But she held onto the sharp, bladed feathers, indifferent to the wounds they caused her hand. She stabbed over and over as the thing spun around. "Me no like! Me no like!"

The machete struck something hard, bounced, and then punctured deep. It felt different than the other strikes. *Not like me. Softer.* The Apex spasmed and fell to the side, dislodging Feesa, who rolled to her feet.

Still filled with rage, she walked back to the beast, took hold of the machete, and yanked it out. She sheathed the weapon and looked at her reflection between the rivers of blood pouring from the gaping wound over the Apex's spine. She took one of the feathers, twisting and pulling until it came free.

"Feesa!" It was Peter, running around the dead Apex, weapon on his shoulder, but aimed at the ground. "Are you okay?"

Jakob was right behind him. "Feesa. Holy shit. You killed a giant chicken!"

The two men stopped beside her waiting for an answer.

"Feesa?" Jakob said.

She looked from her reflection to her nephew. "Me no like," she said and cracked the feather panel in half with her hands. She dropped the debris to the pavement and started back to the truck. "Me no like at all."

11

Ella sat in the back of the pickup truck with Feesa and a first aid kit. Jakob was with them, manning the machine gun, but he wasn't paying attention to them. His eyes were on the crops and buildings around them. They were passing through Dorchester, just south of Boston, following back roads through neighborhoods of apartment buildings, duplexes, and thick Exo-Genetic growth. It felt like a giant maze, the gaps filled in by tall stalks of corn, in which anything could be hiding. Jakob didn't lower his guard.

Despite what he thought about himself, Jakob had become a competent, trustworthy young man with a great deal of survival skills. He might not be as ruthless or violent as others, but those attributes weren't as important as the some he displayed—patience, loyalty, and determination.

Those were the things humanity would need to recover.

She was glad Anne had him for a brother.

"Let me see," Ella said again.

Feesa kept her hands turned away from Ella, clutched like she'd fall over a cliff if she let go.

Ella couldn't see the wounds, but she could see the blood. Could see the way Feesa flinched when she squeezed her hands.

Those Apex chicken feathers were like swords, and Feesa had handled them with the same caution she might give a ball of yarn.

Ella raised her eyebrows. "*Feesa*."

"You no tell Feesa what to do. You not mother."

Ella didn't know if Feesa remembered ever having a mother, but she didn't think now was the right time to ask.

As long as she'd known the hairy woman, she'd been fairly even keeled. Capable of extreme violence and savage hunger, but never directed at them. She was their stalwart protector and, like with Jakob, Ella was glad Anne had her around. It was a strange family to be sure, but it worked in the world that had resulted from Ella's mistakes.

"Sister," Ella said, using the role Feesa had bestowed upon her. "And sisters don't keep secrets. Plus, if you don't let me tend to your wounds, they could get infected. You could get sick."

Feesa huffed and rolled her eyes, something she'd picked up from Anne. "Feesa no get sick. No get infested."

"Infected," Ella said. "*Infes-s-sted* is different. Also bad, though."

"In-fect-ed. That what I said. Anyway. Me no get that. Me change before can happen."

"What?" Ella asked, stunned.

"Me change," Feesa said. "Ahh…you word…Ahhh dapt. Adapt. Change."

"You understand that you have changed?" Ella asked.

"Everyone changed. All things. Except you. Except family. No eat crops. No change. But I…I ate crops. I still eat crops. I…still change. *Am* changing."

Ella did her best to hide her concern.

If Feesa was changing, that could be bad for all of them.

Through the initial change, Feesa and those like her—the Riders—had managed to retain some of their human intelligence and form a symbiotic relationship with other Exo creatures, allowing them to survive the world as a community, some of which had remained behind to help protect Hell-hole Bay.

"How are you changing?" Ella asked.

Feesa shook her head.

"I can't help you if you don't show me," Ella said. "And that includes the cuts on your hands. How about we start there? With the cuts. Then we can talk about the change."

Feesa stuck out her lower lip while considering the deal. "Cuts, but no change."

Ella suspected that whatever was happening to Feesa was on her arms. She'd been hiding them along with her clutched hands.

"C'mon, let's get this over with before something else tries to eat us." That sunk in. Feesa grunted, unfurled her fingers, and held her palms out. Ella did her best not to gasp. Feesa's hands weren't just cut, they looked like they'd been used to deflect a dozen swords. The cuts were deep, down to the bone in some places. There were signs of accelerated healing, though, the wounds sealing, but Ella didn't think that was the change Feesa spoke about. It was just a natural side-effect of being an Exo.

Ella opened the first aid kit. They had several, and this was the largest. It would have enough to get the job done, but it was going to take some time. She plucked out a bottle of alcohol. "First thing we need to do is disinfect the wounds."

"Me no understand," Feesa said. "Just do."

"It's going to hurt," Ella said. "A lot. All of this is going to hurt."

"Me no mind pain. It okay."

"You're sure?"

Feesa leveled a comical 'You're kidding' look at Ella, holding out both hands.

"Have it your way," Ella said, pouring the alcohol over Feesa's hand.

She expected a yelp.

Maybe a growl. But Feesa just maintained her unflinching stare at Ella.

"See," Feesa said. "Me no mind pain. Me strong. Me tough. Me... I am..." She sighed and deflated.

Ella didn't know it was possible, but Feesa seemed to have something on her mind.

Maybe that's the change? Ella wondered. *Is she getting smarter?*

With the wound disinfected, Ella got to work sewing. She was a biologist and a geneticist. Spent most of her career working on plants, but that included sewing together species in an effort to create novel hybrids. Before genetics took over the field.

She'd also sewn up Kenyon more than a few times back in San Francisco, and she'd helped in the infirmary when needed. Enough time spent with a needle and thread left her confident in her ability, but Feesa's skin was thick and callused. Pushing the needle through took a lot of effort. Luckily, Feesa really didn't mind the pain. Maybe didn't even feel it.

Peter drove slowly, avoiding potholes and pile-ups, carefully making his way north past hundreds of buildings that had once been homes. They bore the scars of the horrors that followed. Blood stains. Shattered windows. The skeletal charred remains of burned-down homes now drowning in ExoGenetic growth.

All things considered, Feesa was the best patient Ella had ever treated. She was calm, unflinching, and didn't talk about her personal problems the entire time. Though Ella suspected their simple family member was thinking hard on something. Feesa's gaze remained distant, and her brow furrowed through each prick of the needle and tug of the string.

After finishing with the needle and thread, Ella gently applied antibiotic ointment to Feesa's hands and wrapped them in gauze. As she taped everything in place, she let her attention drift to the rest of Feesa's body. Nothing stood out as different or unusual. She was big and hairy. Her face was the same, too, tusks digging into her cheeks. There were no new horns. No vestigial tail growing. No scales or anything their genetic ancestors might have donated to their junk DNA stores before humanity emerged.

Ella was about to give up and chalk up Feesa's mood to fluctuating hormones, which must have been chaotic for all ExoGenetic creatures. Then something caught her eye. On the underside of Feesa's forearm. The hair was thinner.

That's right, Ella remembered, *Feesa was shedding.* Losing hair. But the patches on her arm looked almost devoid of follicles.

Ella slowly slid her hands from Feesa's along her arm, rubbing gently as she had while applying the bandages. The big female didn't notice the change. The matted hair didn't part easily, but Ella kept at it, teasing strands away until a patch of hairless black skin was revealed. It looked... human.

With a careful hand, Ella stretched out her fingers and touched the clear skin. It was soft.

Feesa grunted. Her eyes snapped to Ella. She'd noticed.

"It's okay," Ella said, as calm as she could manage under Feesa's disapproving gaze. "This..." She gave the hairless patch a gentle pat. "This is okay."

Feesa huffed, taking in a deep breath, and letting it out all at once. It was a strange burst of emotion. And were those tears in her eyes? Feesa was changing...but not in a way Ella could have predicted.

Ella put her hand beside Feesa's wet eye. "This is okay, too."

"Feesa is *not* okay." She turned her big head fully toward Ella, but glanced up at Jakob for a moment, making sure the boy wasn't paying attention to them. Then she tugged at the hair of her arms. "This is not okay. Feesa is hairy. Feesa is ugly."

Ella wasn't sure what to say. Feesa...wasn't wrong. To a human being, she was a monster. Even now, after all this time, her face evoked a lot of feelings, none of them positive—most commonly dread. Ella had still come to appreciate her, call her family, and even feel love for her. However, Feesa was...scary.

But Feesa had never known that. Had never considered it.

She was undergoing a slow physical change, but also a harder to notice mental change.

She was...evolving. Forward. Ella didn't think it was possible, but a thinking, talking Exo never should have been.

This was uncharted territory, and it couldn't have come at a worse time. The truck was slowing down.

"Feesa is good," Ella said. "Feesa is wonderful. But we'll need to talk about this another time, okay?"

"Ella," Feesa said, taking the smaller woman's hands in her giant bandaged oven mitts. "Feesa is *not* Feesa."

"What do you mean?" Ella asked, her heart pounding. Exos were unpredictable. Who was to say Feesa's hunger hadn't taken over again? *Not possible,* Ella told herself. If it had, she would already be dead. This was something else. Something that was wounding the beastly woman. "Tell me."

"Feesa isn't Feesa," she said. "Feesa...is Val. Is Valerie Wood."

12

"Here," Peter said, wading through knee deep water inside what once was a sporting goods mega-store. They'd visited several during their journey, replenishing their survival gear, but never in search of this particular item.

"Kayaks?" Ella said, sounding dubious. "Why not a canoe at least? They're bigger. Look at that one, we could probably all fit."

"Show of hands," Peter said. "Who here has paddled a canoe?"

Only Peter lifted his hand.

"They're not as easy as you think, and they're loud. Kayaks are easy to use, fast, and quiet. Ella, you can double up with Anne. I'll take Feesa. Jake, you can take Lyn."

"I...can?" He was nervous, and rightfully so. In all their time out in the wilds of this remade, horrible world, they'd never ventured out on the water.

"You'll be a natural," Peter said. "Give it a try now. Get used to it. If Lyn sits still, it will feel the same." He glanced up at Feesa, who was perched atop a nearby shelf, keeping watch, swaying back and forth like she was having a conversation with herself. "Here."

Peter pulled down a two-seat ocean kayak and rested it in the water between him and Jakob. "You just sit and—" He pulled a kayak paddle from a bin and mimicked how to use it, back and forth. "That's it."

"Ten bucks says he flops right out," Anne said. She was seated on a display case, legs crossed, holding the lantern that was illuminating their shopping trip.

"You've never even seen money," Jakob said.

"Have so. They used it at ExoGen. For playing poker. There was blue money. Orange money. Yellow—"

Jakob laughed. "That's Monopoly money."

"What's Monopoly?" Anne asked. "Aside from having exclusive control over an industry."

"A board game," Jakob said, hefting himself up onto the kayak. He swiveled himself around into the seat and took the paddle from his father. "I'll show you next time we're in a store with a game section. We can take all the money we want, and I'll teach you to play poker."

Anne squinted at him. "What makes you think I don't know how to play already?"

"Well," Peter said. "Your mother was horrible at it..."

"Dad," Anne said. "C'mon, man, I was trying to bluff."

"Can't bluff a Crane," Peter said and gave his son a wink before giving him a little push.

Jakob began paddling and quickly got the hang of it. He slid through the water, turning around and coming back with a smile on his face. "You were right. It's easy."

Peter turned to Ella, a questioning glance. She gave a nod and said, "Okay."

Ten minutes later, they glided out of the store's front entrance atop three kayaks. They worked their way around the small mall and back to the portion of parking lot that hadn't been submerged.

They headed toward the lot where they had left Beastmaster behind, a smiling Lyn waving from the back seat. She tired easily, and often sat out foraging tasks. After their last fiasco leaving Lyn alone in the truck, Peter had vowed to not repeat the mistake. But Lyn had been insistent, and the tired look in her eyes suggested she had good reason. Not only was she older than the rest of them, she'd also been imprisoned, starved, and forced to watch her husband die slowly beside her. He suspected there was more. Some kind of health issue she had yet to tell them about.

Something that could sap her strength. Without Beastmaster, the journey north would have been too much.

She stepped out of the truck to greet them. "Kayaks. Fantastic idea. Bob and I used to take them out on the lake. I was always afraid of them, but he insisted, and when Bob insisted, he didn't stop until you gave in. But...he was almost always right. Been a while, but I think it'll come back to me." She looked over the three kayaks and landed on Jakob. "Looks like it's you and me, Jake. Good. It'll give you a chance to put those young muscles to work. Not sure how much help I'll be."

Peter watched Lyn as he headed for the truck. They couldn't take much with them in the kayaks, but they'd need rations for a few days, and enough weapons to wage a small war. The only kayak carrying its max weight already was his and Feesa's, so they'd be traveling light, but the other two vessels could hold a few hundred pounds more.

Peter and Jakob set to work loading their gear while the others kept watch, binding everything to the kayaks in preparation for stage one of their journey.

"I don't get it," Jakob said. "Why can't we just paddle over to the island and get it over with?"

"First, it's a long journey. Binoculars have a funny way of making things look closer than they are, you know?"

"Ha. Ha." Jakob shook his head. "But we could make it in a few hours."

"You saw that footprint in the water."

"Yeah, but there's nothing we can really do about it, right? Whatever made that footprint is too big for us to kill. And if it's just waiting out there, that creature's going to eat us, now or later. Might as well get it over with."

Peter cinched a rope tight. "If it's all the same to you, I'd rather not get eaten. If we can learn the Exo's patterns, or even determine that it's gone, we can cross the water without getting eaten, or having panic attacks."

"C'mon," Jakob said. "You're not afraid of anything."

"I'm afraid of everything," Peter said. "I'm just ready for it."

"Cute." Jakob finished strapping down a weapons case and turned his eyes to the view of Boston. The city loomed nearby, rising out of the ocean, the rooftops coated in ExoGenetic crops. "You really think we can get to the top of one of those?"

"Not all of us," Peter said, and glanced at Feesa.

"You want her to recon for us?"

"Not exactly."

"You being vague is never good."

"Feesa is the transportation. I'll be staying on below to watch the others. But you, my brave son, you will be doing the recon."

Jakob's eyebrows lifted toward his forehead with the steady rise of the incoming tide. "You want *me*—" Jakob pointed to himself. "—to go up there—" He pointed to the tallest building. "—with her?"

"No." Peter said, waving him off like he was being silly. "Not *with* her. I want her to carry you."

"You've lost your mind," Jakob said. "I can't do that. Wait, this is why you wanted me to help you load the boats."

"Kayaks."

"Whatever! Dad, c'mon. That's..." He looked toward the building again. "That's insane."

"The world is insane right now and the only three people who might be able to set it right, are over there." He glanced at Ella, Anne, and Lyn, all in the back of Beastmaster. Ella and Lyn were keeping watch while Anne pretended to be gunning down enemies with the machine gun. "My job is to keep them alive. I need to stay with them."

"So, I'm expendable?" Jakob asked.

"Not to me," Peter said. "Never. But in the big picture...we're both expendable. Feesa, too. We need to take the risks, so that they don't need to. So that humanity doesn't go extinct. And there is no one else—no one—that I trust more to get the job done right. I know you don't see it, but you'll be better at all this than me someday. And today, you're the best man for this job. Think about it for a moment. See if you agree."

Jakob turned away, paced by the waterline, then looked back up at the skyscraper a few miles away.

It was an imposing sight. The water. The height of it. He'd never been fond of heights, but that was just the beginning of what his imagination could be conjuring. Peter would be surprised if there wasn't an Apex lurking in the city. Beneath the water. Perched on a skyscraper. Hell, there were millions of people here. There could still be multiple

Apexes roaming the area, not to mention the floating whale with the penchant for human flesh.

"Fine," Jakob said. "You're right. I don't like it. At all. And if I die, you'll hate yourself forever—"

"I'm aware."

"But yeah, I'm the best man for the job...because I'm literally the only man for the job. Thanks for the pep talk, though. It was convincing."

"Jake." Peter took hold of his son's shoulder. "I meant every word. You're ready for this."

Peter thought Jakob believed him. Maybe even believed in himself.

That perception changed an hour later when they glided to a stop, beside the towering building. The trip through the city had been non-eventful, but tense. The kayaks were silent, and no one spoke. But they could hear life all around them. Most of it could be chalked up to the wind rolling off the ocean and through the city, howling through holes in buildings, rattling debris. Didn't take much of an imagination to picture hordes of predators tracking them, waiting for them to leave the water—where maybe even worse things lurked.

The water was nearly level with the building's fourth story. After tying off outside a broken window, Peter helped everyone inside and began to unpack their essentials. "We'll be here. Try to be back by sunset. If you can't make it in time, find a safe place to spend the night. We'll move in the morning."

"Dad," Jakob said, following his father as he swept through the floor, M4 shouldered, ready for action. "I can watch everyone down here. Really, I—"

"I'm sorry, son, but you can't..."

"Don't trust me enough?"

"Wouldn't trust anyone enough," he said. "Now, take the binoculars. Watch out for—"

Jakob sighed. "If you're actually trusting me to do this, then trust me to do it right."

When they found a stairwell, Peter opened the door and cursed. Something horrible had gone down in this building, long ago. The walls were covered in old, dried gore. The staircase was blown to bits.

They wouldn't be climbing up.

"Well, there goes recon, I guess," Jakob said, relieved.

It faded the moment Peter looked at Feesa and said, "Plan B."

"Ohh," Feesa grunted, leaping back, and searching the hallway. "Plan B." She led the way, just twenty feet before stopping at a pair of flat, brushed metal doors. "Elevator."

"I don't think an elevator is going to work," Jakob said. "Not without electricity."

"No have elect—that. But we have power." Feesa forced her fingers between the doors and pried them open. She smiled, which was hard to look at, and flexed her hairy arms. "Me power." She looked up at the cable dangling from high above. "Me climb."

"No," Jakob said, looking at his father. "C'mon."

"You'll be just like a baby monkey," Peter said. "All you need to do is hold on."

"Feesa—" She looked confused for a moment. "Not Feesa… Wait. Yes, Feesa do, but Feesa no Feesa. Feesa is Val."

"That like a nickname?" Jakob asked his father.

Peter shrugged. "Question for another time." He turned to Feesa. "Okay, Val, climb up, listen to Jakob, have a look around, and come back down."

"Unless night," Feesa said. "Then we hide."

"Perfect," Peter said.

"Not perfect," Jakob said.

"Okay, Jake-y-boy," Feesa said, picking him up and holding him against her large chest. "You hold, I climb."

"Dad," Jakob said. "Seriously, do we have to—oooh!"

Feesa leapt out into the elevator shaft, grabbing hold of three cables, one in a hand, two with her feet. She held Jakob in place until he wrapped his legs around her waist and clung to her neck. She gave Peter a thumbs up and then climbed the elevator shaft like she'd been born for the task.

Peter was glad for Jakob, even if the boy didn't understand this moment. It was a big step. A dangerous step. Jakob had become an impressive young man, but now he was in charge of a mission, headed up into what would surely be another world. Peter wasn't just trusting him to complete the task, he was entrusting him to protect that which was most precious to Peter in all the world: himself.

13

"Holy shit," Jakob muttered. "Oh, my god. Holy shit."

"Why Jake is cursing?" Feesa asked, lunging up the elevator cable, rising another story higher all at once.

"Because I'm about to shit myself." He clung to her fur, as tight as he could, but his arms grew sore as a result. How long could he hang on? He was beginning to wonder.

"But shitting is normal. I do every day."

"I'm aware," Jakob said, cringing as she leapt up again. "But not from being afraid."

"Jake is afraid?" She shook her head. "Jake is brave."

"If Jake falls, Jake goes splat. Jake is dead."

She hooted a laugh. "Feesa not let Jake fall. Feesa is strong. Only way Jakob fall is if Feesa falls. Feesa not fall. Ooh!"

They dropped a few feet before jolting to a stop. It was enough to get a panicked shout out of Jakob.

He was about to say, "See?!" when Feesa began hooting with laughter.

She did that on purpose?

"You scared the shit out of me!" Jakob said.

"Now Jake lies," Feesa said. "I no smell shit."

"I need a break," he said. "Seriously. Open the next door. I need something solid under my feet for a minute."

"Break for Jake," she said, pausing outside a pair of closed elevator doors. "Piece of cake." Hooting again, she reached out for the door, pushed her fingers between them, and tugged. For a moment, they resisted. Then, with a screech one of the two doors slid open.

A breeze washed over them, carrying a smell they both recognized.

Death.

Feesa tensed, about to continue the climb.

"It's okay," Jakob said. "It's old. Smell it."

She paused, sniffing at the air.

"It happened years ago," he said. "It's just been trapped in here since."

She grunted the way she did when she was unsure about something.

"My dad put me in charge, right?" he asked. "This is my first mission. And I'm telling you, I need a break. We can go all the way to the top after. Okay? Just give me a few minutes, 'cause I really do need to use the bathroom or I might literally shit myself."

She took a deep breath, let out a long sigh, and then bounded the distance to the open door. Jakob slid out of her grasp, onto the solid floor. He wanted to kiss it, but it was dirty with stains of who knows what.

"Okay," Feesa said. "Jake find corner now. Go squat. Me keep watch."

"I'd prefer a toilet with a door," he said, climbing to his feet and looking down the hallway. It resembled a hotel. Opulent if you ignored the scars of ancient battles. Doors on either side. He didn't think the building was a hotel, though. It was tall. Dad said sixty stories. But he didn't see a sign anywhere. Could have fallen off, but this place felt solidly built. It would be standing for a long time to come, even with its base submerged in oceanwater.

Jakob slipped the submachine gun he had strapped over his back into his hands. It was an MP5. Sound suppressed, like everything they carried. Fully automatic military gear that his father seemed to know everything about. "Let's open a door. See what's on the other side. If there's a bathroom, awesome. If not... I'll find a cubicle or something."

He led the way toward the nearest door, twenty feet away.

"Jake feels shame about poop?" she asked, creeping along behind him.

"What? No."

"Jake feels shame about...body?"

"Not really," he said. "More like...I don't know. It's just a private thing."

"Poop is fun...in a group." She huffed a laugh.

"You working on rhyming?" He paused in front of a door, numbered 301.

"What is rhyming?"

"Words that sound the same. Poop. Group. Soup. Loop."

She laughed again. "Yes. Words sound the same. Rhyme. Make happy."

"Like in songs," he asked.

"Yes. Songs. Val love songs."

There was that name again. She'd reverted back to calling herself Feesa during the climb, but something about their conversation brought up this other name.

"Who is Val?" he asked.

"Val is me." She looked confused for a moment. "Old me. Old Val. She understand shame...even if I no do. That why I ask about you poop shame. She is shamed about me." She motions to her body. "About this. But she still there, look!"

Feesa turned the underside of her arm to Jakob, revealing the patch of smooth skin. "Ella say we talk about it another time, but me can tell she afraid. Of me change. Exo-me."

Jakob peered at the patch of smooth, dark skin.

"You're changing?"

"Hair fall out," Feesa said. "Me no like hair anyway. Me want...me want..." Her face scrunched up like the idea she was trying to express hurt too much to consider. "Me want you to poop."

He smiled. Tried the door. Locked.

"Can you open this? Quietly?"

She nodded and placed her hand against the wall beside the door. With a quick shove, her fist smashed through the wall, followed by her arm. In the abject silence, it felt loud, but it was mostly muffled, and far quieter than her ripping the door away, which was more her style. This was a unique solution that required some good thinking.

If Feesa was changing, Jakob thought it might be for the better. He understood why it would make Ella afraid. ExoGenetic changes were unpredictable and usually resulted in adaptations designed to make killing and consuming prey easier.

There was a clunk of a deadbolt unlocking. The knob twisted from the inside, and the door swung open. Feesa pulled her arm out of the wall. She was covered in drywall, wood splinters, and tufts of insulation, but she lost more of her own hair in the process.

Jakob stepped through the door, and despite his curiosity about what they'd find on the other side, he did his best to mimic his father's unflinching focus. MP5 shouldered, he led the way in, pushing open the door with his foot, sweeping the room on the other side, and then moving on until every space had been scanned for danger. Feesa was behind him the whole way, moving with him, fluid and practiced. She'd cleared many buildings with his father. Knew the drill. Knew her part in it, letting her heightened senses see, hear, and smell things normal people couldn't.

After a five-minute search, Jakob said, "Clear," and lowered his submachine gun. Only then did he fully comprehend where they were. "It's an apartment." He scanned the open concept space with fresh eyes. It wasn't just an apartment. It was a luxury apartment, and it hadn't been touched by the change. The only thing marring its perfect surfaces was a small amount of dust.

Even Feesa seemed enamored by the artistic décor, open spaces, and abundant light streaming through all the tall windows. "Is nice."

"Very nice," Jakob said. "Maybe we can live in a place like this, after we save the world."

She grunted her agreement. "Lots of corners to poop in."

And just like that, Jakob remembered the growing urgency with which he needed to find a bathroom. The apartment had three, including a large master suite. "Using the bathroom. There are two others if you need to!"

Jakob hustled through the master bedroom, running his hand over the perfectly made, impossibly soft bed. Then he was in the bathroom, on the toilet, finishing the job in record time. Nothing like being carried three hundred feet up to loosen the bowels. When he was done, he stood, did up his pants, and flushed the toilet.

"Shit," he said upon hearing the swirl of water. Alia had nearly died as a result of a single toilet flush. He knew better. They used toilets all the time, but *never* flushed them.

It was a reflex he'd struggled to grow out of, and not just because the sound gave away his position. Sometimes toilets still flushed, if they still had water in the tank. It was gross, but toilet tanks often contained drinkable water. When water flowed into the bowl, Jakob knew it was well made, the water inside unable to evaporate over the past five years.

But what happened next froze him in place, in the bathroom's doorway. He slowly turned around, looking at the hissing toilet.

He recognized the sound but hadn't heard it since they left Hellhole.

The toilet was refilling.

"No way," he said, pulling the tank cover off, watching it refill. "Holy shit..." He moved to the shower and turned it on. After a few sputters, a high-pressure stream of water sprayed.

"Yes!" he shouted.

His cry was followed by the thumping of heavy feet and the sudden appearance of Feesa in the doorway, ready to rip Exos to shreds. All she found was Jakob, smiling like a doofus. He motioned to the shower, wide-eyed and grinning. "Look!"

Feesa's face twisted with confusion, leading to a slow realization, or a distant memory. "Show...er?" She reached out her hand, feeling the water. She smiled in her awkward way. "Shower... How?"

"We're in a skyscraper," Jakob said. "They used to pump water up into big tanks on the roof." He pointed up. "So, it doesn't need electricity to work. Until the tank runs dry. But this is a big place. I bet that will take a long time."

He raised his hands. "Listen. Hear me out. Dad gave us all day to complete the recon mission, right? Until the morning, really. And how many hours of daylight are left? Like five. It didn't take long for us to get here, so taking thirty minutes here won't really matter."

"We...take shower?" she asked.

"Well, not *we* as in together. But yeah. There *are* three of them. Been a long time since I was clean."

"I do not remember clean," Feesa said.

"You'll love it," Jakob said. "I promise."

14

Stupid Jakob. Stupid Dad.

Anne's thoughts blazed with aggravation. Jakob was out having an adventure at the top of a skyscraper while she was stuck at the bottom. She'd never been in a building like this, and the apartments they'd found were interesting, but it wasn't six hundred feet in the air, or searching for bad guys. Instead, she was helping Dad clear a bunch of old living spaces that had been empty for a long time.

"Clear," Peter said, exiting a bedroom that looked like the inside of a blender that exploded. The walls were spattered brown. Chunks of old bodies had dried to the ceiling and walls.

Her father looked a little more disturbed than he normally would at such a sight.

"Hey, at least it looks like they probably died fast, right? And a long time ago."

"Mmm," Peter shut the bedroom door behind him, and walked to the fourth-floor window. Staying on the floor that was accessible from the water was a bad move, strategically—anything could let itself in without warning—but without Feesa as an elevator, or an unblocked stairwell, they were stuck at the bottom. "Two more apartments and then we're done. You still good to go?"

She rolled her eyes. "You know I am, and you know that stuff like that—" She motioned to the closed door. "Doesn't bother me."

"Good," he said. "On my six. Stay close. Stay quiet."

He was more serious than usual. Less conversational. Not that he was really ever casual and chatty. But there was often a glint in his eyes that revealed his secret—that he enjoyed this. The actiony bits. Not because he delighted in killing or the idea of being eaten, but because the more he stood up to his fears, the more distance he put between himself and the PTSD that had plagued him after his time in the military. He didn't say any of that, but she knew it. Or rather, her mother knew it once upon a time, and thanks to the memories embedded in Anne's head, the knowledge belonged to her as well.

It was a strange thing, to know a father she met just months ago, like they'd been close her whole life. However long that actually was. It felt confusing now, having her mother's childhood mixed up with her own lack of one. She remembered being younger, but not ever being a baby, or a toddler. One day, she'd just gotten out of bed, and the memories began.

Peter led the way back out into the hallway and down to another door that had been broken down long ago. He didn't have to go far this time to find the grisly scene. The small foyer looked like the inside of a person.

"What kind of an Exo does something like this?" he asked, looking up and around. The floor, walls, and ceiling were all covered in ancient, dried flesh, like the surfaces had been texture painted with the inside of a body.

"It's kind of cool," Anne said.

Peter gave her a disapproving glance.

"I don't mean the death part," she said. "I mean, the not knowing. After everything we've seen, we're still surprised by how things can change. It's like...yeah, their junk DNA is unlocked, but what kind of extinct animal could do this? It's like the Exos can use the old DNA *and* adapt it to be used in new ways. It's interesting."

"Fascinating," he said, not holding back the sarcasm. "What adaptation do you think could do this?"

"Well," she said, stepping past him to inspect the scene a little more closely. "The blood and viscera are evenly distributed, like whoever this was just...popped, but look—" She pointed to some small bits of hardened flesh on the ceiling. "That's the brain. And this—" She gestured toward a few crisp strings stretching between the small room's walls. "Intestines. I mean if you look closely..." Anne's brow furrowed. "If... Huh."

"What do you see?" he asked in a way that meant he'd already noticed something she'd missed.

"Well, first, whatever did this, it didn't eat this person. Everything is here. Doesn't look like much now, but this would have been a chunk-fest years ago. Problem is, there is one very large piece of the human puzzle that's missing." She looked back at Peter. "The bones are gone. All of them."

He nodded. "Been like this in every apartment. No bones."

She mentally kicked herself for having missed it. She was so upset about Jakob's adventure that she'd overlooked what made staying behind intriguing. Maybe she'd be the one having fun while he was just sitting around looking at the water.

"Can we check the last apartment now?" she asked.

Peter shook his head. "Still need to finish this one."

She twisted her lips. "Fine."

Peter led the way through the dried gore. It crunched beneath their feet. M4 and FNX pistol at the ready, they swept through the apartment. It went faster this time. The living spaces had different décor and aesthetics, but the layouts were identical. They moved from room to room, checking closets, bathrooms, and bedrooms. Peter must have been sure they were alone because with just two rooms left, he motioned for Anne to check a smaller bedroom, while he headed for the master bedroom.

She gave a nod, looked down the sights of her pistol, and approached the door. Her foot thumped against the wood, but the door didn't budge. She carefully turned the handle and shoved. The door swung open silently until it tapped against the wall. The mounted flashlight on her weapon illuminated the room. She swept the floor, first. Finding no sign of monster or death, she raised the light and scanned again. This time she found a splatter of death.

It wasn't as large as the others they'd found, occupying just the upper half of one corner.

Maybe it was a dog? she wondered, inching closer. The gore told no secrets, but the bed from which the splatter had emerged told her everything she needed to know and more.

It was a crib. The victim had been a baby.

She hoped it had been asleep at the time. That its death was fast.

In the end, it didn't really matter, she figured. Dead was dead. How you got there was irrelevant once you arrived at that final destination. The fear and pain that comes with life would be gone, no matter what awaited: afterlife or non-existence.

Having seen enough, she backed out of the room and found Peter doing the same thing to her left.

They'd both found something upsetting.

He turned to her. Cleared his throat. "What did you find?"

"Baby," she said. "What's left of it. You?"

"The bones," he said.

That tidbit was interesting enough to turn her attention away from the popped baby. She put it out of her mind and headed for Peter, stopping outside the master bedroom. "How many bones?"

"Enough to account for everyone on this floor," he said. "Maybe a few more. Hard to be sure without trying to put everyone back together again."

"Count the skulls," she said.

Peter blinked. "What?"

"Don't need to count whole bodies. Just skulls. That will give you a total number, though I don't see the point in having a number, other than just feeling depressed about it."

He nodded. "You're right."

"Usually am," she said, and started into the room.

He caught her shoulder. "What are you doing?"

"While I'm not interested in the number of dead, I *am* interested in what killed them, and Mom will be, too. So, unless you want to revisit this place in a little while, let me have a look. She'll trust what I tell her, and if whatever did this is still around, we'll have a better idea of what it can do, and a better chance of not painting more walls with our insides."

"You're really up for this, aren't you?" he asked.

"You could say I was born for this, but I wasn't really born, was I?" She gave him a smile and stepped into the room. It was more than she'd hoped for. The bones weren't heaped in a pile, they were neatly arranged and stuck to the walls by a crude mortar. *Their insides*, she thought. And the bed...it had been converted into a kind of throne.

Whatever had done this retained at least a piece of its human intelligence, seeing itself as some kind of king of the damned.

"This was early days," she said. "Probably a few days before the change swept across the world. That's why there's no sign of a struggle between Apexes. Whoever did this would have had a leg up from the beginning. Could still be alive now, but maybe less...sophisticated. More evolved. Devolved. Whatever you want to call it."

She picked up a bone. A femur. Looked it over, and then checked another, placing each one back where she'd found it.

"I think we're looking for something with a long..." she motioned like she was stretching out her nose.

"A long nose?" Peter said.

"No. That'd be silly. A stylet. A proboscis. Like a mosquito. Something that can be used to explode a person from the inside out, and..." She picked up another bone and held it up for Peter to see. The top had been broken off and the inside revealed. It was hollow.

"It wasn't eating their bodies," Anne said. "It was sucking the marrow out of their bones."

15

Feesa hooted as the shower's water sprayed against her body. It wasn't the temperature that surprised her, it was the pressure. The hiss of it. For a moment, it stung. Then it felt nice.

"There," Jakob said. "You see? That's how it works. Just turn the knob like a door handle. Left is on. Right is off. Though I don't really think we need to worry about wasting water."

"But sound?" Feesa said, concerned that the hiss was too loud.

Jakob thought on it for a moment. "Nothing and no one has been up here in a long time." He was trying to make himself sound confident, but she could hear his worry. "I think we're clear. We are. Definitely. I'm going to the other bathroom now, okay? Thirty minutes and we're gone."

"Uhng," she grunted, losing herself in the flood of water, letting it spray against her face.

"I'll take that as a yes," he said, and then left, closing the door behind him.

Jakob was funny. A good fighter, but also unsure of himself. Full of doubt, and discomfort, especially around Feesa when she was doing things he said were private. Like the shower.

He didn't want to show her how it worked.

When she climbed inside, he'd grown nervous, like he wasn't supposed to be there. She didn't understand why they couldn't use the same shower. On one stop, they had all washed in a river. Ella and Anne kept some clothes on, but Feesa was just Feesa, but wet.

Same as in the shower.

She didn't understand why he hurried away. Jakob was funny that way. Hard to understand. Not...what was the word...*primal*, like she was.

She shrugged and put her face back in the stream of water, blowing against it with her lips, gargling, making fun sounds. When she eventually bored of her games, she inspected the shower. The walls were a smooth stone. Shiny, too. Not like they were outside. And there were bottles. She understood bottles. That they held things like drinks and Ella's medical liquids.

She picked up a bottle. Sniffed the outside.

It smelled like apples. She liked apples. She popped the top, angled the small opening toward her mouth and squeezed. Viscous liquid glopped into her mouth. It was...bitter. It was horrible. She understood that food could spoil, but it never bothered her before. But this...

She held her mouth open to the water again, attempting to rinse the flavor away. Instead, it melted and then spread. Her eyes widened when a column of bubbles rose into her vision. The liquid was transforming.

A laugh coughed from her mouth, sending bubbles into the air. The nasty liquid was changed by the water. Became something else.

Like Feesa, she decided.

She rinsed the rest of the foul taste from her mouth, humming while slapping her lower lip. It made a funny noise and more bubbles. Jakob was right. Showering was fun.

With the flavor in her mouth mostly washed away, she took the bottle in hand once more and squinted at it. What secrets did it hold? This time, she squirted out a small amount on her hand. She leaned down and looked closer. There was nothing unusual about it, though it smelled so good she nearly tried eating it again.

Instead, she held her hand in the water. Bubbles appeared once more, but smaller. Mostly it just came apart and rinsed away. So, she squirted more and decided to encourage it. She leaned down close. "You can change. You know you can. So, do it."

She held the liquid to the water again, but now there were even fewer bubbles. Frustrated, she mashed her hands together and began wiping her failure away.

And that was when it transformed. Bubbles emerged from between her fingers. She rubbed her hands together faster until a bubble froth emerged. She hooted with joy, playing with the bubbles, replicating the experiment. Then she took it a step further, rubbing the liquid all over her body. Soon, she was covered in bubbles and cackling with laughter.

When her laughter faded, she began to relax. Muscle memory guided her hands over her body, scrubbing and untangling knots. She didn't remember how she knew these things. And she didn't remember the song she was humming while she did them. She wanted to sing. Had memories of it... In the shower. It was her favorite place to sing.

But her voice... It was even unpleasant to *her* ears. How could she have ever sung?

The song persisted, and she gave in to it, scrubbing and humming, eyes closed, feeling a kind of euphoria sliding through her, guiding her hips, knees, and head.

It was dancing. She'd seen Anne dance, but it didn't look like this felt. This moved with the song in her head. Anne just wriggled around to a tune she made up.

As the bubbles washed away, Feesa's hair became almost sticky.

Because it's clean, she realized, *not covered in filth and grease.* Those things hadn't bothered her before, but now...she knew...she *remembered* what it felt like to be clean.

Then her skin began to itch. She rubbed her body, erasing the feeling, tugging at her hair. This felt good, too. As the feeling spread and she chased it down with her fingers, the song in her head continued. The water beat against her, and the song echoed in the solid stone bathroom.

The more she washed, the smoother she became.

She turned her back to the shower. The feeling spread down her spine, scratched by the water pressure. She moved back and forth letting every inch of her body be scoured.

Cleansed.

Remade.

She didn't understand what was happening. What she was feeling. But tears came to her eyes. She hiccupped a sob but continued her song.

When the song ended, she took a steadying breath—and opened her eyes.

Below her, a gnarled brown creature lay dead on the bathtub floor.

For a moment, she feared the mound was her child, carried and born without her knowledge. It wasn't until she reached down and plucked up a handful of brown fur that she understood its origin was not from within her, but from outside.

She dropped the fur and looked at her arm.

It was smooth, like Ella's, but black. Both arms were the same. She leaned forward and looked down.

"Feesa hair fall out," she said, feeling afraid. "Feesa changing is bad... Feesa becoming...Apex?" She considered the possibility. Imagined charging into the other bathroom and consuming Jakob. The thought repulsed her.

She shook her head. "Not Apex. Not Rider." She clenched her jaw. "Never again."

Hands held up, she looked them over, noticing how the thickness had faded. She traced a line over her arm and watched as goosebump rose up behind the gentle, smooth touch. "Can change," she said.

Her voice was followed by the *thunk* of something solid landing on the shower's stone floor. It looked like bone.

A hooked bone.

She picked it up. Looked it over. Recognized it for what it was—a Rider's tusk.

Her...tusk.

She placed a hand to her mouth, feeling where the long, curved tusk had grown out of her jaw. It was missing. Fingers slid against her lip, finding the other tusk intact, but stinging. She pinched it between her fingers and pulled. The tusk popped free in her grasp. The constant pain caused by the sharp bones stabbing into her cheeks faded.

"Jakob?" she said, and then louder. "Jakob?"

He couldn't hear her. Two closed doors and two running showers made him deaf to her cries. And her song. Which was a shame, she thought, because she knew how to sing. Used to. And would again if she could just remember how...how to do it right.

With a quick twist, her shower went silent. She stepped out into the bathroom and looked toward the mirror. She understood how they worked. That she'd see her own face in it, but this time would be like seeing herself for the first time, again.

She walked toward the sink. Stood in front of it, head lowered, eyes cast down. "It okay. It still me." She opened her eyes and looked at her hands, squeezing them into fists. "I still in control. No Apex, even if I worse than before."

With one last sigh, she lifted her head, looking in the mirror—

—and screamed.

16

"Ideas?" Peter asked, lowering his weapon. Anne was just a kid. Felt strange to be asking for her opinion on life and death matters, but the more time he spent with her, the more the girl's knowledge base mirrored her mother's. With one difference—she processed all that information the way he did. Understood the real-world significance and projected future results. Ella theorized and tested. Anne predicted, often accurately. She didn't even know she was doing it most of the time.

"Seems pretty clear to me," Anne said. "A mosquito sucked the blood of a human being, absorbing their DNA and RC-714, allowing it to incorporate not only the human genome into its own, but also all that locked away junk DNA. Even though it started out small, it was able to quickly become an Apex, maybe one of the first, and started doing what mosquitos do best, only its proboscis was weaponized, and it had a craving, not just for blood, but for the part of a human where 95% of the body's red blood cells are created."

"I meant about what to do," he said, "though your theory sounds about right to me."

"The real question is, did the Apex move on?" She looked at the ceiling. "Did it move up? Or did it make this place its home? If the creature is still living in the building it would be inside now. Maybe."

"Why?"

"Mosquitoes don't like direct sunlight. They feed in the early morning and evening because the sun dries them out—unless you're in a shaded area—like the interior bedroom of a fancy apartment with no natural light. Then you're still fair game.

"Unless…it's adapted to negate that limitation. It *is* an ExoGenetic creature after all, with human DNA and ancestry combined with its own insect history. Who's to say how it's adapted?"

"Well, we've cleared the floor," Peter said. "Let's get back to your mom and make sure our position is defensible."

"Before we go back, can I ask you a question? Like a private question you won't tell Mom?" It wasn't really fair, asking him to keep secrets, but she wasn't sure she could talk to her mother about it.

Peter looked at her for a moment, and then, with a resolution that left no doubt that he'd respect her wishes, said, "Sure."

"Okay. Also, you can't freak out."

"I don't freak out."

She pursed her lips for a moment. "Good point. Okay. Well. You know how Mom's memories are kind of seeping into mine, right?"

He nodded.

"I remembered something a few weeks back, when we were leaving Hellhole, and I wasn't sure what to make of it, because it was weird and incomplete. Like the memory of a feeling without any context. I was hoping I'd get the rest of it, but so far, no luck."

"And you think I can fill in the blanks?"

"Not sure," she said. "But I also thought I should warn you. Just in case."

"Warn me?"

"About Mom."

He squinted at her. "Spill it."

Anne sighed. The subject made her uncomfortable. "She...hated you."

"Hated me?" Peter's eyebrows rose, and she thought the revelation had hurt his feelings.

But then he smiled. "I bet she did."

"You know about it?"

"I loved your mother, and she loved me, but life pulled us apart. We grew distant, and while she focused on her work...I got married. To someone else. Who I also loved. And that hurt your mother. A lot. In a sense, it was a betrayal of what we'd once had, but I also knew she wouldn't give up on her work for me. She replaced me with scientific curiosity, but I replaced her with another woman. She probably hated me for a while. Love is weird like that. In the right circumstances, it can quickly become hate."

"Huh," Anne said. "That's a lot sappier and a lot less nefarious than I worried it would be."

"Not everything has to be blood and guts and screaming," he said with a smile. "C'mon, let's get back before—"

"Hold on, buckaroo. We're not done yet," Anne said, and motioned to the bedroom's closet.

Peter eyed the door. "It's been opened."

Anne nodded, looking at the bones that had been slid to the side by the door's prior opening. There was no way to tell if it had been opened years ago, or minutes before their arrival. Apexes weren't known for hiding, though. If something had detected them, it would have come running for fresh marrow.

"Let's get the job done," Peter said, aiming his M4 toward the door.

Anne crept toward the closet, took hold of the knob, and gave it a slow twist. They'd done this for every closet on the floor—Anne opened, Peter aimed, nothing happened.

Peter hoped the same would happen now.

He gave a subtle nod and Anne pulled.

Let it be empty, Peter thought, but he quickly saw his wish, or prayer, or whatever it was, hadn't reached or registered with a higher power.

At the same time, he didn't see a need to pull his trigger.

"Wow," Anne said, stepping back.

"You know what this is?"

"Best guess, some kind of chrysalis." She crept closer.

"Careful."

"When am I not?"

Peter grinned.

He didn't need to tell her, 'All the time.'

She knew damn well.

She placed her hands against the papery material stretched out between thin ribs that spanned from one side of the closet to the other. "It's dry. Been here for a while."

"There something inside?" he asked.

"I have a hard drive in my head, not x-ray vision." She holstered her handgun and drew a knife.

"Stay to the side," he said.

"Clear line of sight. Got it."

Standing well to the side, she stabbed the blade into the papery material and slid it down. The sharp blade sliced downward with ease. She cut all the way to the floor, sheathed the knife, and drew her pistol again.

Peter inched closer. He poked the M4's sound suppresser through the opening, finger on the trigger, ready to unleash a point-blank barrage. But nothing moved, or attacked, or made a sound. He pushed the papery material to the side, lighting the closet beyond.

Only it wasn't a closet.

Not anymore.

The space was empty of clothing and bones. It looked organic on the inside. Wet, too, glistening with clear slime.

Anne grasped the edge and yanked, tearing open a large hole. The walls were like a well-made puff pastry: dry and flakey on the outside with hundreds of layers leading toward a denser and moister interior.

"Definitely hibernating," she said. "Recently, too."

The idea of hibernating Apexes didn't sit well with Peter. Meant there could still be a lot more of them out there, just waiting for a snack to show up.

"Any idea when this one woke up?"

Anne gave him an amused look. "You testing me?"

"Trusting you," he said.

She squinted. Didn't fully believe him, and he didn't blame her. She was, after all, still a kid. But he was being honest. When it came to the natural world recreated by RC-714, she was the most knowledgeable person in the room. "I'd say it woke up right around the same time we entered the building, and it exited over there."

She pointed, realized Peter couldn't see from his angle, and then ripped down the wall on the left side of the closet, revealing a hole on the opposite side, through the cocoon and the drywall. It might have entered through the closet, but it didn't leave through it.

"Shit," Peter said.

Anne finished the thought. "Mom... Do we fall back or track it?"

Peter considered the two options. Tracking the creature would lead to confrontation. Finding Ella and Lyn and hunkering down in a choke point might avoid it all together—or at least increase their odds of survival. There was also the possibility that the creature might have already found Ella and Lyn, though it certainly hadn't attacked. Lyn was prone to nodding off, but Ella was always on guard. She'd been surviving in the wild longer than the rest of them, and Ella understood Exos as only their creator could. The moment the Apex found them, it would meet a barrage of gunfire. Until that happened, they had time to track it, and maybe kill it, without a struggle.

"On my six," he said. "Nice and quiet."

"Stealth mode," she replied. "Got it."

He nodded and stepped through the papery wall. The closet's insides were covered by the hive-like walls, coated with viscous slime that smelled sweet.

Anne tugged on his shirt. Pulled him down closer and spoke quietly. "Hydrogen sulfide."

"That's what we're smelling?"

She nodded. "It's what makes a toot smell bad. But farts are just 1% hydrogen sulfide. To smell good, like this, it'd have to be at least 30%. And too much of it is going to give us headaches."

"Is there a point where it becomes deadly?" Peter asked.

"I mean, if the percentage of hydrogen sulfide gets too high, it's displacing the things we're used to, like nitrogen and carbon dioxide, and the thing we need: oxygen. Too much of that will make you sick. Fast. And if you get a single whiff at a hundred percent? Instant death. So don't do that."

"Got it," he said, and ducked down to climb through the hole made by whatever had been sleeping in the cocoon. He emerged in a narrow hallway framed by unfinished drywall. The floor and ceiling were both concrete. It was a space between apartments.

When he turned around, Anne was already squatting down, inspecting a set of footprints.

"Four toes," she whispered. "Claws too. Big enough to squish a person's head and make this...hallway a tight fit." She pointed to the wall beside Peter. It was dented and covered in gouges, as something a little too big for the hallway had squeezed through.

He crouched beside her but ignored the footprint. He was more interested in the opening. It bulged outward and was torn up, but there was very little debris on the floor. He shifted his light to the left and found what he was looking for. A panel of sheetrock precisely cut. This creature, once a man, had lived in the apartment before, and had traversed this hidden hallway before the change, for one reason or another. Likely nothing good.

Peter stood and motioned for Anne to follow. They worked their way around the corner, pausing at an intersection. It wasn't just one hallway; it was a network of them that could reach every apartment on the floor. He followed the damaged wall to the right.

A pinpoint of light confirmed Peter's suspicion. He leaned in close to the hole and had a clear view of a bedroom, its door open, light streaming in from the city view beyond. Twenty feet farther, another hole. A bathroom, cloaked in shadow.

"What a perv," Anne whispered.

"There have always been monsters," Peter said. "Most of them are just easier to spot now."

Peter quickened his pace, following the maze, worrying they'd be too disoriented to quickly find their way back to Ella once they emerged.

He rounded a corner and his worries about Ella quickly faded.

Something lurked in the shadows ahead, waiting, shifting about so subtly he almost missed it.

The hunt was over.

The fight for their lives was about to start.

Peter lifted his rifle, and the mounted flashlight, illuminating the hallway ahead.

17

"What's for supper?" Lyn asked, leaning back in the kitchen chair she'd claimed as her own. The apartment they'd found was mostly clean, and borderline opulent. She imagined an up-and-coming lawyer had lived here. Close to the peak of his career, but not quite there, and not yet married. The décor was particularly manly—meaning there wasn't much, and the solitary painting in the living room was a reclining nude woman in the style of some long dead painter but featuring a very modern—skinny—feminine aesthetic.

Some kind of confrontation had taken place here. There was a broken mirror. The huge TV screen was shattered. But there was no blood. No bodies. No monsters.

So, they'd made themselves at home, sitting at the kitchen table, and preparing for a proper meal that would only leave Anne feeling satiated.

"Well, let's see," Ella said, grinning. This had become a routine. Helped make the lack of food a little more bearable. "We have dandelions, assorted mushrooms, some edible leaves, chestnuts that we need to somehow roast to make them edible, and, wait for it. This one is a real treat..." She pulled out a Ziploc bag containing a rare treasure that made Lyn sit up a little straighter.

"Are those blueberries?"

"Elderberries," Ella said. "Tasty, nutritious, and an excellent immune booster."

"I know what elderberries are used for," Lyn said, fiddling with her things. "But they won't do any good."

The two women looked at each other. Lyn shook her head and sighed. "Should have known you'd see through my act. I was once given the smallest role in a play. I was cut after the first rehearsal. Replaced by a girl with special needs. Ugh. I'm a dreadful actor. That girl who replaced me? Brilliant. That was a real low point in eighth grade."

Ella laughed, but it was half-hearted.

"You going to tell me what it is?"

"Cancer."

"What kind?"

Lyn smiled. "All of them? It doesn't matter anymore. There's nothing to be done."

"How long?" Ella cringed asking the question. It was a cold way to discuss a terminal disease.

But Lyn understood the situation, and the value her life added to their quest. "Weeks, I'd guess. Maybe less before the pain isn't manageable with ibuprofen."

"We can raid a hospital for morphine," Ella said. "Boston has plenty of—"

Lyn waved her off. "Any work I managed to accomplish would likely be gobbledygook."

"That's not what I was thinking about," Ella said. "I don't want you to suffer—"

"Whole world is suffering," Lyn said. "No reason I should be exempt. Thanks to you, I never became one of those things."

Ella huffed. "Thanks to me? It's because of *me* that anyone changed. It's because of me that there are no hospitals, that there's no treatment for your condition, that we're sitting in a flooded city, waiting for my daughter to finish sweeping the floor for monsters—that I made."

"It's not all bad." Lyn snapped her fingers at the elderberries. "Your daughter has a father. You have a son."

"Because my actions killed Peter's wife. Jakob's mother."

Lyn opened the Ziploc bag, took a handful of elderberries, and tossed them all into her mouth. "Oh! Mm. Tart!" She chewed them down, her lips turning purple. She handed the bag back. "Don't tell anyone I helped myself before we rationed them."

"The stain on your lips will tell the story," Ella said. "But don't worry, I won't let you take all the blame." Ella took a handful and ate them.

Lyn started laughing, but not about the elderberries. "Oh, Lord, can you imagine, going through all of this, destroying all of humanity, just to get a man back?"

Ella choked on the berries in her mouth, laughing along.

"Don't even joke about that."

"Well, I mean, it worked, right? Kind of high on the collateral damage scale, but hey, you got the man in the end, right? Foolproof plan if you ask me. I might consider wiping out humanity if it meant getting Bob back. Then again, I suppose I'll be off to see him sooner than later." She smiled. "Life sure did take an interesting turn, didn't it?"

"That's the gentlest way to put it." Ella opened a paper bag of mushrooms. Handed it to Lyn. "These are starting to look wet. We should eat them all today. Divvy them up for me?"

"Ohh, yummy," Lyn said. "Soggy mushrooms." She began counting them out onto four small paper plates. "You know, I used to love mushrooms. Bob made these fantastic stuffed mushrooms. Really simple. Just mushroom caps and Stovetop Stuffing. The diced stems mixed in. Baked with a drizzle of butter, which was more of a waterfall when Bob was cooking, but oh my, those were—"

Something thumped.

Both women froze. Lyn turned toward the living room where the image of the large naked woman smiled back at her. "Was that..."

"Something inside the wall," Ella said, reaching for her sound suppressed B&T APC9K submachine gun that Anne had named, 'Mommy's Little Shit Kicker.' Peter had her use it in indoor situations because it was the ideal 'spray and pray' weapon. 'Accuracy and discipline weren't prerequisites for fucking shit up,' he'd said. Which seemed to work for Ella. She'd become adept with a variety of weapons. They all had. But it was nice to just let loose.

Ella held a finger to her lips and Lyn nodded, picking up her shotgun, but not pumping it. They could shred the wall, but there was no way to know what was beyond the wall. Could be an Exo. Could be Anne. Would be just like her to go bumping around in someone's closet.

The thump repeated and then again, along with a scratching sound. Something was moving. Pushing through a tight spot.

Then it turned the living room's corner and scurried toward them, inside the wall. Ella's aim snapped to a closet at the end of the living room. Lyn pumped her shotgun, and Ella didn't seem to mind.

Confrontation was inevitable.

It was then that Lyn heard a second set of footsteps. More solid. Wearing shoes. Human.

"Peter and Anne," Lyn whispered. "They're hunting it."

Ella nodded.

It made sense. If they found something, they'd chase it down and kill it if they could. No sense in letting it go only for it to come back. Only way to protect your life in this new world was usually to take something else's.

Peter's and Anne's voices came through the wall, muffled, but present. Definitely at the far end. It was impossible to discern what they were saying, but even Lyn could tell when Anne was afraid, and that wasn't very often. Whatever they had cornered scared her.

And Ella clearly couldn't abide that.

She motioned for Lyn to guard the closet door while she stepped into the living room, lifted Shit Kicker toward the wall, and held down the trigger. Forty-five rounds blazed from the gun in just over two seconds, tearing into a large portion of the wall.

A loud shriek tore out of the holes in the wall, quickly followed by a crash, a rumble, and the crack of wood.

The closet door split down the middle and birthed a monster. It was black, its back covered in spines. The creature had bulbous insect eyes that reflected hundreds of tiny, frightened Ellas and Lyns back at them. A long stylet protruded from its face, completing the insectoid look. But beneath the stylet was a very human mouth.

And it screamed at them. In rage, fear, pain? Lyn couldn't tell, but it was horrible enough to stun her into inaction.

"Lyn!" Ella shouted, snapping the woman out of her shock.

The shotgun fired but was a moment too late. The Exo leapt onto a wall and then toward the apartment's front door. It took the buckshot in the back, but the blast had little effect. The creature shouldered its way through the thick front door, removing the wood from its hinges. This thing was tough, and fast, but it fled their gaze. *Strange behavior for an Exo,* Lyn thought. It could have just as easily leapt toward them. If it had, she would likely be dead, and Ella not far behind.

"Ella!" Peter shouted, kicking his way out of the closet, sweeping right after the Exo, and then left, finding Ella and Lyn. "You're alright?"

"Fine," she said.

Anne emerged from the closet behind Peter, FNX pistol in hand. She beamed at Ella. "Mom, that was awesome!" Then to Peter, she said, "Hey! It's getting away!"

Peter motioned for the women to follow and then charged out the door.

"Left!" Ella shouted. "It went left!"

Peter broke left, following a trail of blood. They'd injured it, but Lyn doubted that would be enough.

"There!" Peter shouted, doubling his pace, and running toward the open elevator door that Jakob and Feesa had ascended.

He fired two shots, both of them sparking off metal when the Exo leapt inside. "Shit!"

"Time to wangle dangle!" Anne said.

"What is wangle dangling?" Ella called out but was ignored.

"You're sure?" Peter asked as the pair neared the elevator.

"Doing it with or without you, old man!"

Lyn could have sworn she saw Peter smile. *Peas in a god-damn pod.*

Peter arrived at the elevator first, bracing his feet against either side of the open doors while flinging his M4 over his back. He then leaned down and reached between his legs, just as Anne came up behind him and slid like she was stealing second. Their arms linked as she swooped beneath him. Then she twisted around and leaned out over the elevator shaft while Peter braced his body with one hand.

Without missing a beat, Anne pulled her trigger until the magazine ran dry. There were two yelps from the creature, but when Peter pulled her back into the hall, Anne stomped her foot and said, "It was all over the place. Couldn't stop it."

"You did good," Peter said.

"Good?" Ella said. "Good? She could have been killed."

Anne waved her off. "I might get my brains from you, but I think I get the rest from Dad. Also, we've been practicing cool stuff like that."

Lyn knew they had. She's seen them practicing all kinds of strange maneuvers, but she thought they'd just been having fun. Father-daughter bonding. She never expected to see them utilize that kind of...insanity in combat. Clearly, Ella hadn't expected it either.

"And it almost worked," Anne said.

Lyn realized she was breathing hard.

She noticed Ella giving her a concerned look, and then she realized a bigger problem. Ella put a hand on Peter's arm. "Call Jakob. Let them know they have—"

Peter already had the radio in his hand. "Jake, you copy?" He gave it a moment, and then said, "Jake, if you can hear me, heads up. You have incoming!"

18

Jakob hadn't sung in a long time, but the shower—and a triggered memory—inspired him to hum, and then belt out a song he hadn't heard in ages. The woman who had sung it had a voice like no other. The words just melted over the listener, encasing them in a warm embrace. He remembered lying in bed, listening to her voice, the sound of it easing his mind.

In the shower, surrounded by the hiss of water, he could have sworn he heard it again, flowing out of the past to comfort him. He found himself inspired. His childhood memories resurrected the lyrics. The song, titled *Darkness*, chronicled the singer's journey through a painful childhood, from which she emerged as a stronger woman.

He wasn't a girl, but he could identify. Childhood for him had been interrupted by the apocalypse. They had yet to escape it, to rise above it, but the song gave him hope. So, he belted it out, replacing forgotten lyrics with his own, or the occasional mumble.

He paused for a moment, thinking he'd heard his father's voice. But that wasn't uncommon. He often woke from dreams in which he'd heard his father's urgent voice, only to find the man sound asleep.

Jakob closed his eyes, leaned his head into the cool water, and let it rinse away weeks' worth of grime, starting the song fresh again. He was lost in the water and the song, allowing himself to pretend, for a short time, that life was normal.

That life was good.

Again.

Then an aberrant sound ruined the illusion.

He jolted out of the fantasy, standing still, eyes wide, listening.

Did he imagine it, or did he actually hear—

A scream, louder than any human could manage.

Feesa.

It had to be. But it didn't sound like her. It was a few octaves too high. Too human.

But nothing else made sense. There was no way for his father or Ella to reach the thirtieth floor.

Jakob turned the water off. Opened the shower door. "Feesa?"

Outside the bathroom door, Jakob heard what sounded like panicked mumbling. Definitely Feesa, but was she upset? Was she laughing? Was she crying? He'd never seen Feesa cry, but she laughed plenty and it didn't sound like this.

He raised his voice and picked up his MP5. "Feesa?"

Another scream.

Guided by instinct and post-apocalyptic reflex, Jakob whipped open the bathroom door, charged through the master bedroom, and stepped onto the hard marble floor of the open-concept living space looking down the sight of his submachinegun. He swept left to right, found no targets, and moved toward Feesa's bathroom, leaving a trail of water droplets behind him.

The floor ahead was wet, from the open bathroom door, into the kitchen and around the island. Was Feesa in trouble? Or having...fun? There was no blood on the floor.

"Feesa?" he called, almost positive the response would come in the form of a roar from some kind of abomination.

"Jake!" Feesa shouted, as a black blur emerged from the open door.

Jakob tracked the target, finger squeezing the trigger. But it was too fast for him. By the time the first round left the muzzle, the creature had reversed course and ducked back inside the bathroom. A line of bullet holes appeared on the wall, but he'd missed the creature entirely.

He adjusted his aim toward the door. "Feesa, are you okay?"

"Why Jake fire gun at Feesa?"

"What? At you? I didn't—" His mind slowly wrapped itself around the possibility that the creature he'd seen as a black blur was, in fact, Feesa. How could that be possible? Feesa was covered in brown fur. Maybe the coloration was from layers of dirt, but he didn't think so, and *whatever* he'd fired at didn't have hair.

"I change," she said.

"Change? Like Apex change?"

"I don't... I no think so. But also, yes."

"You don't feel hungry, though, right?"

"I no eat Jakey-boy."

"That's not what I asked," he said.

"No hungry," she said. "I...happy."

"Because you changed?"

"Change is good," she said. "Look, but no shoot."

Jakob lowered the weapon. "No shoot."

Feesa jumped out of the bathroom and raised her arms in a 'ta-dah' gesture. She looked so different that Jakob nearly raised the weapon again. But then she spoke.

"You see? Changed." She rubbed her arms. "Hair gone." She pointed to her mouth. "Dumb pokey teeth gone." She tapped her throat. "Voice changed. More like before, when human."

"That was you..." he said. "Were you singing?"

"I love to sing," she said.

"I think I heard you." Jakob's eyes began to wander. Feesa had been remade, and it was more than just hair removal and a new voice. The shape of her body was different. She was curvaceous...or maybe she always was, but there had been no way to know with all the fur. But now she was hairless. Jakob's eyes moved to Feesa's ample breasts, and then down.

Completely hairless.

His stomach twisted. He was locked in place, both mesmerized and terrified. His heart pounded. He'd never seen a naked woman before. He'd imagined it, had hoped for it with Alia, but this was unexpected and left him unnerved, unable to process what he was feeling because it was all physical, and had nothing to do with his mind, which had switched off.

Feesa stopped moving. Her brow, still thick, furrowed. She pointed at Jakob. "Why Jake ready for sex?"

"W-what?" Jakob staggered back a step, slapped from a trance.

Feesa laughed, clutching her belly. "Oooh. Jakey-boy like new Feesa, too!" She rubbed her hands up over her body, sensual, but mocking. Exaggerated. Didn't matter. Jakob's body responded with a rush of adrenaline and other chemicals that made thinking difficult.

He backed away a step.

When Feesa grasped her breasts and squeezed them together, he said, "Oh god," and turned away, retreating toward the master bathroom. Behind him, Feesa had a good laugh.

"Silly Jakob. I your aunty. No sex with aunties!"

Jakob entered the bedroom and closed the door behind him. He leaned against it, catching his breath. "What the hell? What the fuck?" He looked down at his erection. "Go away! You asshole!" Images of Feesa's body snapped back into his thoughts. She was still a monster. Still tall. Still muscular. She had claws and sharp teeth, but she was also feminine. Intensely feminine. Like She-Hulk from the comics.

Jakob took a deep breath, held it, purged his mind of thoughts that should not be there, and tried to focus. They were in a skyscraper that had been flooded by the ocean. Monsters were everywhere. The human race was on the brink. If he ever ate the wrong food, he'd become an Exo and maybe eat his family.

The list of horrible truths was long, but he struggled to defeat the images of Feesa...holding her breasts like that...

She's my aunt, he told himself, hoping to feel revulsion.

But she wasn't.

I love Alia, he thought, and it was true, but wow... The images didn't stop coming until—

A voice. The one voice that could snap him out of any distraction, including the vision of his first naked woman—his father.

"Jakob. Come in. Are you there?"

He sounded angry. Worried. Maybe even panicked. He also sounded faint. Jakob hurried back into the bathroom. Picked up the radio, which he must have accidentally turned down. He turned the volume back up. "Dad! I'm here! Sorry, the volume got turned down."

"Jakob, thank god." It was strange that his father sounded more relieved than angry. "You have incoming."

"What? From where?"

"The elevator shaft. Whatever the hell you're doing up there that's sending water down the drain, you need to knock it off, or it's not going to have any trouble finding you."

"You can hear it?" Jakob was stunned and embarrassed.

"It's a big building," Peter said, "but it's also silent. The sound of running water in the walls stands out."

"Already done," Jakob said, glancing at his shower, feeling pretty stupid. It was just the beginning of a long list of things he hoped no one would ever hear about but knew the shameless Feesa would likely discuss in detail with everyone.

"Are you someplace defensible?"

"An apartment," Jakob said. "There was running—"

"Later," Peter said. "Black. Spikes on the back. Tail. It's fast and strong. Comparable to Feesa, but you need to avoid its...nose. It's like a needle."

"It sucks blood?" Jakob asked.

"It...injects its victims with gas." There was a rustle over the radio and then Anne's voice. "It will explode you, Jake. Take the meat right off you and suck the marrow from your bones."

"Not funny, Anne," Jakob said, and there was another rustle.

"Not a joke," Peter said. "It's not big, but it's nasty, and it knows the building. Don't hold back. Take it down. But most of all, be quiet."

"Copy that," Jakob said, and then he cringed as a song filled the air, bellowed by a voice reborn, carrying the tune he'd been singing in the shower just minutes ago.

"Shit," Jakob said, and he charged back out of the bedroom, bare-assed, ready for a fight, and still a little distracted by what breasts looked like.

19

Feesa had found another mirror in one of the big rooms. It reflected her whole body. Feeling inspired, she sang a song she didn't remember hearing, but to which she knew all the words. And when she sang them, the words just flowed. Not like when she spoke, struggling to form sentences.

The new *her* was fantastic.

She delighted in it. And hoped the others would, too.

But not like Jakob. Silly boy.

All men were silly like that.

She smiled, remembering that she hadn't been that different just weeks prior. Her more primitive self, with Kenyon and the other Riders, had been interested in sex on a daily basis. She remembered that self, and how overwhelming the urge could be. If Jakob was going through the same thing, she felt bad for teasing him.

She had no compulsion for sexing with Jakob. He was young, and not strong enough. But she didn't mind his reaction to her changed body. It meant the reflection was real, and her assessment of her beauty was accurate.

When the door to the bedroom whipped open, she glanced toward it in the mirror. Jakob hurried back out, still not dressed. For a moment, she feared he was determined to have sexy-time, but then she noticed Jakob was no longer...prepared for it, and he was holding his weapon.

"Stop singing!" he shouted. "Apex!"

Feesa's voice cut short, mid-note.

She ducked low and leapt toward the front door, moving on all fours until she reached the wall that led to the hallway, at the far side of which was the apartment's door. "Where?"

Jakob stood on the opposite side of the hallway entrance, holding his weapon. "Coming up the elevator. If it heard you—"

He stopped talking when something sharp scraped down the outside of the apartment door.

Jakob aimed his weapon around the corner, toward the door. She'd seen Peter do the same on several occasions, using a gun to shoot something on the far side of a wall or door, but this wasn't the same.

"Gun too small," she whispered to him, shaking her head. "Door too thick."

Jakob lowered his weapon and sighed. "Damnit."

The scraping sound slid to the side, across the wall, tapped twice, and then stopped.

"The hell is going on?" he asked.

"It thinking," she said.

"Apexes don't—" Jakob's eyes turned to Feesa, his gaze no longer wandering over her body. "You might be right."

"Feesa always right," she said with a grin. She cocked her head to the side, listening. "You hear?"

Jakob shook his head. People's ears weren't as good as hers, even after her hair fell out. She looked more like one of them, but she wasn't.

"It moving." She motioned her hand in a circle. "Around."

"In the hallways," he said. "Through other apartments?"

She shook her head. "Inside walls."

"Inside the walls? How the hell could it—"

Even Jakob could hear the scraping that followed. He redirected his weapon toward the sound, and when the wall bulged outward, he pulled the trigger. It was a short, controlled burst. A test. Five holes punched into the wall, resulting in a shriek of pain followed by a flurry of motion that was hard to track, and suddenly the creature fell silent.

They waited, back to naked back, waiting for some sign of the creature.

"Can you hear anything?" Jakob asked.

Feesa shook her head. "Is quiet. Maybe not moving?"

"Maybe," he said. "Maybe being more careful."

Most Apexes were savage predators prone to headlong attacks with no sense of self-preservation. Hunger was all they could think about. But the most dangerous of them were patient. Stalkers who understood that the best way to catch and eat a meal was to also survive the encounter. Ambush had always been, and would always be, the best way to achieve that goal.

Feesa lifted her nose and sniffed the air. Nothing. It was invisible to her.

"What Jakob know about Apex?" she asked.

"Spikey back," he said. "About your size. Has a tail. All black. Oh, and watch out for its long nose. If it stabs you with it, you can explode."

"Boom nose..." she said, sounding doubtful.

"Big boom nose," he said. "To remove meat from bones. It likes the stuff inside our bones. The marrow."

"Mm," Feesa said. "Meaty goo inside bones tastes good."

"Great..." Jakob said. "Cool. Sooo cool. How long do you think it will wait?"

"As long as it need," she said. "Until we let guard down?"

"How could it possibly know that if it can't see us?" he asked.

She shrugged. "Maybe it can. Or sniff our pher...fur..."

"Pheromones?"

"That it. Stinky emotions. Ella call phero—whatever. Or it hear better than I do. Hear our heart thump. Hear when they slow down. I do that, too. Your heart slower now...than few minutes ago."

"About that," Jakob said.

"Me understand. New Feesa is beautiful."

"You really are," Jakob said, sounding more like himself now. "But can we, like, not tell anyone about, you know, my reaction?"

"Because they laugh at you?"

"That, yeah, but more because it would make Alia sad."

"Alia beautiful, too. And Alia has long hair."

"Both true, but Alia is also a teenage girl."

Feesa wasn't sure why, but that struck a chord and made her laugh.

"Okay, Jakey-boy. I no tell. Now we have secret. I feel like we are better friends."

"Yeah," Jakob said, "me too," then he yelped when she slapped his bare butt and laughed.

Feesa understood two things.

The conversation they'd just had served two purposes. It was genuine, but also a ruse. Somehow, she and Jakob had silently agreed to a plan that neither of them had voiced. They weren't just better friends, they were a better team. Maybe that was what being naked with people did? She didn't know, but she could hear a third heartbeat now, pounding hard, preparing to strike.

"Jakob," she whispered. "It above."

She gave him a little shove when it was time, and they dove apart just as the ceiling caved in.

Feesa rolled on the hard floor, and came up with claws and teeth bared, ready to disembowel anything that came through. But all she found was debris, and Jakob, flat on his back, weapon raised. He wasn't far from the hole in the ceiling. Probably meant to slide, but his clean, naked body had stuck to the smooth stone.

"What see?" she asked.

"Hole the size of a basketball," he said.

"Me not know bask-et..."

"Like this big." Jackob held his hands up in the shape of a large circle. "I think it just punched through."

"It separate us," Feesa said.

"Not sure what it accompli—"

The wall beside Jakob exploded outward, covering him with debris and filling his eyes with grit. He attempted to turn the gun toward the black Apex that had emerged, but it slapped the weapon away and carried him back into the wall.

Before Jakob's dropped MP5 hit the floor, Feesa was in motion. She dove into the darkness inside the wall, where she could see just as well. There was a narrow tunnel system that seemed to wrap around every room. The Apex was just twenty feet ahead, its spines scraping the walls as it fled. Jakob was dragged behind it, held by his head. He clutched the monster's arm as well, which was probably the only reason his neck had not yet snapped.

The Apex was quick, but it was too large to maneuver the tunnels like Feesa. She scrambled from wall to wall, lunging closer with each step. But the beast knew the tunnel network better. When she leapt for its neck, arching up over its spines, the creature took a sudden right turn.

Feesa missed her mark and crashed into a wall, which buckled from her weight. She grunted, got back to her feet, and continued the chase.

"Let go," she howled. "Of my nephew!"

She doubled her efforts, closing the distance again. This time, the creature slid, dragging Jakob behind it, and it slipped through a hole already torn out of the wall. She dove after it, emerged on the far side in a bedroom, and spun as she sprang upward, searching for a target that any one of her limbs could claw at.

What she found was a large femur, crashing into her face with enough force to flip her backward twice before she struck the floor.

Through blurry vision, she could only watch as Jakob was tossed to the side. Was he unconscious? Was he dead?

Rage demanded she get up and fight, but vertigo kept her rooted to the ground. She swiped at the creature twice but missed. It didn't even have to dodge.

It stood over her, rotating around her, over and over, licking its lips, two bulbous eyes looking her up and down. Then, with a gravelly voice, it said, "Big bones," and the creature sucked in a deep breath.

It's going to explode me, she thought. *And then Jakob.*

She cinched her eyes shut, tried to center herself, imagined where the Apex really was standing, and swiped her claws in as broad an arc as she could.

She missed and toppled onto her back.

Eyes open again, she watched, helpless now as the monster stood over her, its body expanding with pressurized air, its needle-like snout lowering toward her gut.

"No," she said, reaching up, trying to grasp hold of the needle—and missing.

The monster chuckled and stabbed downward.

Feesa closed her eyes, expecting her last moment to be a blaze of pain as her flesh burst away from her bones.

But it was just...warm, wet, and painless.

She opened her eyes to find the Apex above her, frozen in place, its needle nose just inches from her belly. It had grown a second appendage, this one white and extending from its mouth.

She blinked, focusing her vision, and she finally understood what had happened. A jagged bone protruded out of the creature's mouth. A small fountain of blood rolled over the bone, drizzling onto her waist. She leaned to the side and found Jakob standing over the beast, holding the bone piercing the Apex's neck and spine. He was covered in scrapes and blood, teeth grinding in anger, arms shaking.

Then he said, "Little help?"

Feesa put her hands on the Apex's shoulders and shoved it away. When she sat up, she found they were in a room filled with a variety of bones, human and not, all of them clean and hollow.

"Thank you," Jakob said.

She rolled backward, onto her feet. "You no tell about saving Feesa, Feesa no tell about excited penis."

Jakob let his shoulders sag and then shake as he laughed. "Don't use that word, please."

"Anne uses all the time."

"Just..." Jakob extended his hand. "Deal."

Feesa shook his hand and asked. "I hear Ella use other words for penis when talking to Peter late at night. They whisper, but I can hear."

"No. Please, God. No. Just... private parts. How about that? Now let's get back to our gear and cover ours—" Jakob paused, looking down at the ExoGenetic corpse. Everything about it was a nightmare, but there was one small part that stood out.

A chain. Around its neck. Jakob crouched down and pulled at the chain. At the end, was a card. He plucked it from the monster's neck, turned it over, and looked at the face on the other side. "This is an ExoGen keycard... This guy worked for them. And this..." He waggled the card. "...could let us access the lab."

Feesa thought she understood but was still curious about one thing.

"Who was he? What his name?"

Jakob looked at the card again and read the name aloud. "Doctor Jeffery Sexton."

20

Peter paced, radio in hand, waiting for his son's voice to come back over the radio. It had been twenty minutes since he delivered the warning about the approaching Apex. Twenty minutes.

It was too long.

Something must have gone wrong.

"C'mon, Jake," Peter said.

"I'm sure he's fine," Lyn said. "He and Feesa are a formidable pair."

She wasn't wrong. Jakob knew how to handle himself, and Feesa... well, she was practically an Apex herself. But the creature was intelligent. Knew the building's layout. And the way it killed? Peter squeezed his eyes shut, willing himself to stop seeing visions of Jakob's body bursting. Of the monster sucking the marrow from his son's bones.

"Have some elderberries," Lyn said. "They'll distract you."

"She's right," Ella said, seated across the kitchen table from Lyn. They both had small plates of foraged food. "You need to eat. Need your strength...no matter what has happened."

"Jake's fine," Anne said. She was in the living room, seated on the back of a couch, munching on a thick corn cob—her favorite ExoGenetic crop. She was mesmerized by a large painting of a naked woman. "If he'd died, I would have felt it. Because we're siblings. That's a thing right, feeling when a brother or sister has died?"

"You're thinking of twins," Lyn said.

Anne shrugged. "Still think I'd feel it."

"Dad?"

Peter nearly dropped the radio at the sound of Jakob's voice.

"Here. You okay?"

"A little scratched up, but we're both fine..."

In the background, he heard Feesa say, "Feesa better than fine."

He didn't know what that meant, but they both sounded relaxed, which meant the danger had passed.

Anne hopped off the couch and approached Peter.

"You see? They're fine." Then she pushed the radio's call button. "How did she do it?"

"Do what?" Jakob asked.

"Kill the Apex? How did Feesa kill it?" Seeing Peter's incredulous glance, she added, "What? You don't want to know? That thing was gnarly."

"Actually," Jakob said. "I killed it. With a sharp bone. In the back of the neck, out the head."

"Nice!" Anne said. "Our little man is growing up."

"Also," Jakob said, "I think he worked for ExoGen."

Peter noticed how quickly Jakob changed the subject from the story of the Apex's death. Anne and Jakob normally took their time detailing their exploits. They were both natural storytellers and were prone to big-fishing their retellings. Jakob brushing over the fact that he'd killed the Exo was out of character. There were details he wasn't sharing, but that could wait. He was alive. And safe. That was what mattered.

Ella perked up. "What did he just say?"

"The Apex was a man who might have worked for ExoGen." Anne said.

"How does he know that?"

Anne took the radio from Peter's hand and asked. "How do you know that?"

"It had a keycard around its neck," Jakob said.

Ella snapped her fingers at Anne, which was her way of asking for the radio. She held out her hand until Anne delivered the device.

"Jakob, is it a photo ID card, or just a keycard?"

"Photo ID."

"What was his name?" she asked.

"Doctor Jeffery Sexton."

Anne chuckled.

"*Sex Ton.* Good name for a pervy guy."

Ella's brow furrowed, shaking her head.

Anne plucked the radio from her mother's hand and walked away with it. "All right, Jakey-boy, spill. I want all the deets."

Peter focused on Ella. "That name mean something to you?"

She didn't hear him.

"Ella. You know who this Sexton guy is?"

"He was part of my original team," she said. "I lost track of him during the change. Assumed he was dead. But if he was here..."

"The Boston lab has been active all this time," Lyn said.

"We won't be entering an empty facility," Ella said. "They'll have security."

"If they haven't been overrun," Peter said. "For all we know, the bones in this building could be his coworkers."

Ella's expression soured. As did Lyn's. Most people working for ExoGen didn't know the company's true intentions. Not many people fully understood their endgame. Not even Ella. Sexton, on the other hand, clearly had a nefarious private life before the end of the world.

Peter had heard enough. He didn't need to know any more about Sexton or the Boston lab. It would all be memory and speculation. What he needed were facts, and the only people who could provide those were Feesa and Jakob. He looked for Anne, but she was gone.

He listened for a moment.

Her voice was hushed, but her half volume matched most people's full volume. She was in one of the bedrooms. Door closed.

Peter approached the door and slowed. Jakob had been cagey with the details. He'd obviously done something foolish and didn't want Peter to be upset with him. But he might tell his sister.

Mistake or not, Jakob had really proved himself today. Killed an Apex by hand that he and Anne had failed to kill with guns. That was what Peter would focus on. Victories mattered more than mistakes. And Jakob clearly knew what he'd done wrong. Life in the wild taught poignant lessons.

"Yeah," Anne said, her voice muffled. "I'm telling you, she's sick."

Peter paused by the door, listening.

"No, not like a cold or anything. Those aren't really a thing anymore. Not enough people. I mean like sick, sick. Cancer sick. All the signs are there."

There was a pause and then she said, "I know I'm not a doctor, dummy. But I just know these things. Just like Mom. I bet she knows, too."

Peter's stomach twisted.

Was she talking about Ella? Did Ella have cancer?

"How long?" Anne said. "Well, even a real doctor wouldn't know that without running tests. But she'll probably die in a few months. At the most. And there's no way she doesn't know it. She's tired all the time. Her skin is turning yellow. She's not stupid, you know. The question is...would she rather die or become an Apex. Because, you know, ExoGenetic-modified cells don't just adapt to external factors, they also adapt to internal factors."

A pause, and then, "Yes, factors is a real term. I don't just make things up. Anyway, that's what's on my mind. Now dish, what really happened up there?"

Peter leaned closer to the door, but Jakob's voice was impossible to hear.

All he could make out was Anne's responses to Jakob's story.

"A shower? Oh, you lucky asshole. Wait. Hold on. You were in the shower before this? Were you—" She laughed. "Were you naked? You were, weren't you?" Another laugh. "Oh, my god. You killed it...with no clothes on? Are you serious? Okay, that is impressive. Bonus points.

"What's Feesa talking about? Her hair or something?

"No, not later. I want to know now.

"Oh, come on." She sighed. "Fine."

Peter knocked on the door.

"Hold on," Anne said, disappointed in how the conversation was ending. "Dad found me. Shocker."

A moment later, the door opened, and Anne held the radio out to him. "Here. I'm lying down." She closed the door in his face.

"Jakob?" Peter said into the radio.

"Here."

"You still on task?"

"Starting back up the elevator the moment we're done talking. Should be topside in ten minutes. Then we'll spend a few hours checking things out and be back inside before dark. This place is great, though, right? Okay if we stay in up here tonight? These apartments are nice."

"If there is any sign of immediate danger, you—"

"I know," he said. "We'll come right back. Obviously. How about you guys stop the next Apex from coming up?"

Peter smiled.

Jakob didn't rib him often. That he *was,* meant that the victory over the Apex had boosted his self-esteem, which was good. Believing you're capable is usually the first step to being capable. Same with anything else. Glass half full people usually achieved more than glass half empty, simply because they believed challenges were surmountable, rather than doom. "Will do. Once you get topside, check in every thirty minutes."

"Copy that," Jakob said. "And Dad, thanks...for teaching me how to fight. Would have been dead without you, even if you weren't here."

"You got it," Peter said, feeling both proud of his son, and guilty for not training him more. He'd been putting most of his effort into Anne because she was a natural. But Jakob had proven himself a warrior.

"Out," Jakob said, and static followed.

Peter lowered the radio and joined the others at the table. He sat down for a meal of fungi and weeds while his son was carried up an elevator shaft, risking his life for the rest of them. Peter had never felt so proud, and he hoped he wouldn't have the chance to again for a very long time.

21

"This work?" Jakob asked, holding up a dark red T-shirt with a yellow Nirvana logo on the front.

Feesa took the shirt, scowling. "I do not wear clothes."

"You do now," Jakob said, opening another drawer, looking for something that would fit a shapely woman. The apartment had women's clothing, but it was all far too small. The man's clothing was larger, but—

"How this?" Feesa asked.

Jakob glanced back. Feesa had put the shirt on despite her protest. It was skintight and left little to the imagination. "Better."

He looked away quickly and was glad he'd already put his clothes back on. Last thing he needed was to broadcast how the tight shirt made him feel. It was actually a little more distracting than when she'd been wearing nothing. And...she had no clothing on from the waist down.

"But I no like clothes," Feesa said. "Clothes are stupid."

"Clothes keep you warm when you don't have fur."

"It already hot outside," she said.

She wasn't wrong. It was late in the summer, but the heat wasn't giving up the fight. If not for the skyscraper's windows being both tinted and mirrored on one side, they'd be roasting inside the building.

"Look, you just...you need to cover up." He waved his hand at her body. "Because, you know. It's distracting to see people with no clothes on."

"It's normal for Riders."

"It's not normal for people."

Feesa frowned. "That why Feesa wears clothes now? Is Feesa...people?"

Jakob didn't know how to respond. Feesa had been a monster. For a time, she'd been all monster. A tribal creature. Savage and raw. Then she became family. A monster still, but an ally. And now...she was more than that. But had she ever been less? Had he been wrong to ever think of her as a monster?

"Yes," Jakob said, holding up a pair of black cargo shorts. "You are people. And people, wear clothing."

"Because boobs are distracting?" she asked, pressing her chest together with her arms.

Jakob's teenage mind took a mental snapshot in the fraction of a second it took him to look away. "God. Yes." The T-shirt wasn't going to be enough. He moved to the closet, ignoring Feesa while she fought with shorts. She might not remember clothing, but her muscle memory knew how to get dressed. He rifled through hung pants and shirts, landing on a light orange, red, and yellow plaid shirt that looked unworn. He checked the size. Triple extra-large. That was why it hadn't been worn. It was far too big for the man that once lived here. He plucked it off the hanger and tossed it back to Feesa. "Here. Put that on, too."

"*Two* shirts?" she grumbled.

"Please," he said.

Jakob pretended to keep looking through the closet while she finished dressing. For a moment, life felt normal, like it had never changed. It was just him, in a closet, looking through clothing that could have been his father's once upon a time.

"Am ready," Feesa said. "How look?"

Jakob turned around and grinned. Feesa looked good. And not an in overwhelmingly sexual way. Anne would say it was a good 'ensem.' A little 90's grunge, but it worked on Feesa. The shorts and shirt were snug, and the plaid shirt hung loose and open.

Jakob smiled and motioned to the mirror mounted on the inside of the closet door. "See for yourself."

Feesa's face lit up. She turned side-to-side. "Feesa looks like…not Feesa."

Jakob was confused. "Is that a good thing or a bad thing?"

Her smile faded. "I not sure. I…confused."

"By what?" he asked. "I think you look great."

She sat on the bed. "Feesa looks like Valerie."

"Who is Valerie?"

"I is Valerie. Ella told me no worry about who was. Only worry about who am. She say I can be who I want to be. But I not know now." She pointed to the mirror. "*That* not Feesa."

Jakob looked at her reflection in the mirror. She still towered over him and was built like a wrestling champion, but she was right. Feesa was an Exo. The woman in the mirror was different, but…a woman. And very pretty, with prominent cheek bones and big brown eyes.

He wasn't sure when Ella and Feesa had talked about this, but it was definitely before all Feesa's hair fell out. "I think Ella was right. You can be who you want to be. But…do you remember who Valerie was?"

"Some… Valerie was singer." She closed her eyes. "I love sing but is hard now. Because voice. Because thoughts, and words, are hard."

"Your name was Valerie…" Jakob said. "And you were a singer?"

"Mmhm."

"Do you remember singing in front of people?"

She closed her eyes. A smile crept onto her face. "So many people."

"You were…Valerie Wood?" Jakob asked, stunned.

Feesa stood and spun around toward Jakob, nearly falling over. "How you know name?" She stomped right up to him, looking down. "You know Feesa from before?"

"Did *I* know you?" Jakob sat on the bed behind his knees. "The whole world knew you. Valerie Wood. Holy shit. I was just singing your song in the shower." Jakob cleared his throat and began singing the song.

Feesa's eyes widened. She sang along. Knew the words. Didn't sound bad either. Not like her old self. Not even close. But there weren't many people who could match her vocal range and sense of rhythm, even when there were eight billion people on the planet.

They stopped singing after the first verse. Feesa had tears in her eyes. "What song called?"

"Darkness," he said.

"What is about?"

"Your childhood. Overcoming challenges. Becoming..." Jakob huffed a laugh. "Becoming a new person."

Feesa smiled. "I like."

"Everyone did."

"I...Valerie, again," she said. "Now. But you call me Val."

Jakob stood. "Sounds good. Aunt Val."

"Aunt," she said, heading for the door. "Auunntt. No sexy time."

"I know, I know. God." He followed her. "Let's just get to the roof before it's time to check in with Dad."

Getting to the roof was easier said than done. Val, who was Feesa no more, had no hair to which Jakob could cling. He held onto the outer shirt, but it shifted around a lot. As a result, Val ended up doing most of the work, her arm around his waist, clutching him tight. She moved with the same confident grace as before. While it seemed her personal desire to be her old self was triggering her recent adaptations, no part of her wanted to give up on the physical benefits of being an Exo. It was the best way to survive in the new world.

Jakob had thought about what he'd like to change, if given the chance. A broader chest. Stronger legs. Probably wings because flying would be awesome. Nothing too drastic. No tail, or fur, or weird eyes. Mostly human. Just with a few tweaks. But he'd never really considered the possibility of being able to control which adaptations took root and which faded back into history.

"We at top," Val said, prying open one half of an elevator door and tossing him through before leaping in beside him.

They were in a hallway that seemed to separate two huge spaces. To the right, was a large living room area. To the left...a kitchen and dining area. He chose left, only because the massive windows provided a stellar view of the east, the islands, and the ocean beyond.

"Is not roof," Val said, following Jakob, inspecting and smelling what appeared to be ancient decorations. Swords. Shields. Spears. Many of them were in labeled cases. Others were mounted on walls. The construction was modern, the ceiling twenty feet high, but the kitchen was full of brushed metal appliances and old-looking tiles. It was an interesting mix of old and new. Like a museum that someone had lived in. Someone very rich and very powerful.

"This isn't the roof," Jakob said with a nod, "it's the penthouse."

"What is penthouse?"

"Where you would have lived in your previous life," Jakob said.

"This is my house?"

"No, no, no," Jakob said. "Not *this* penthouse. But somewhere, I'm sure there is a place like this that belonged to you. Or some sprawling ranch, or like a—" Jakob stopped at the windows looking out over Boston Harbor. "Wow."

"Oohf," Val said, looking unsteady as she looked down. "We are very high."

"Weird, right?"

"We jump in water from here?" she asked.

"Nooo," he said. "No. Big time no. We'd go splat. Make soup."

She laughed and it sounded a little more human than usual. "Jakeyboy soup. Taste like poop."

"When I hit the water, I'd turn into goop," he added, which got another laugh out of her.

He dug into his pack and retrieved his binoculars. He took his time, scouring the surrounding islands, looking for signs of life. When he found none, he scanned what had to be George's Island, because it held a large, modern facility, which, unlike Boston, was still above the water, and looked maintained. It also sported a large ExoGen logo that probably glowed at night before the change, a brilliant reminder of who had murdered the world.

"That's the place," Jakob said, pointing at the island. "Keep an eye on it. Let me know if you see anything weird. I'm going to check in with Dad."

"Weird, like what?" she asked.

"I don't know. Like, weird. You know. Not normal. Not supposed to be there. Like an Apex or something."

"What about people?" she asked.

"Wait, you see people? Where?"

Val pointed a finger and angled it straight down. "You see?"

Jakob leaned his face against the glass and peered straight down. A flat-hulled boat motored between buildings, moving fast, carrying five passengers. He watched them speed between the flooded buildings—and out into the bay, where the water was already starting to swirl.

22

It was almost time for Jakob to check in, but Peter knew they'd be late. They'd gone through a lot and would need to collect themselves before reaching the roof and having enough time for a quick look around. He wasn't worried about Jakob's safety now—the boy had proved himself—and Sexton would have been the building's sole Apex. Anything else would have to enter through the fourth floor—where Peter was waiting.

Once they were on the roof, Jakob and Feesa would have to watch out for aerial attacks, but they'd be able to see thirty-five miles in every direction. It'd be impossible for anything to sneak up on them.

And that left just one big unanswered question on Peter's mind.

"Can I talk to you for a minute?" he asked Ella. She was seated at the table with Anne and Lyn.

Ella looked at him, unsure of his intentions.

"Please."

Anne lowered her head into her hands. "If you guys are going to do...Mom and Dad type stuff, can you at least go to another apartment? My dreams are weird enough already with all Mom's memories crammed in there. I don't need to add fresh details, if you catch my drift."

"Just a conversation," Peter said. "But noted."

He hated the idea that he and Ella had been...overheard. They'd only been together a few times while on the road. Traveling through a post-apocalyptic hellscape of monsters and endless crops wasn't conducive to romance, but sex was a great way to relieve stress and reforge their bond.

Peter led the way into a bedroom, and then into the bathroom beyond. It was all tile, and clean like the rest of the apartment. He eyed the shower. Felt the temptation. A shower would be sublime.

When the door closed behind him, he turned around to find a concerned Ella. "You aren't planning on Mom and Dad stuff, right? Because I don't—"

"What? No." Peter didn't know how to broach the subject.

Are you dying?

Do you have cancer?

Coming right out and asking wasn't exactly compassionate, but he didn't really know how else to do it.

"Is there...anything going on with you?" he asked. "Like...something you want to tell me, but aren't sure how?"

She squinted at him. "Are you asking if I'm pregnant?"

His eyes widened. "You're pregnant?" Peter felt like he might pass out. They'd been careful. Really careful. This wasn't the kind of world you'd want to have a baby in. They were loud. And they smelled. A baby would increase their chances of being eaten, and no matter how hard they tried, he doubted they'd be able to keep it alive.

"Deep breaths, Pete," she said with a smile. "I'm not."

Peter put his hands on the sink. Leaned his head down. Let out a sigh. "Just...is there anything? Anything I should know, but don't? Something that Anne might notice, but I might—"

"Ah," she said, understanding. "Should have figured Anne would notice."

"Notice what?"

"I'm not sure it's my place to—"

"Ella, it's my job to keep everyone alive. Everyone. That means I need to know exactly what's going on with my people. If someone is—" It clicked. There was only one person Ella wouldn't have told him private details about.

"Lyn is sick," he said. He didn't wait for confirmation. It made sense. "Don't make me play twenty questions. Please."

"Cancer," Ella said. "Severe and widespread."

"Nothing we can do?"

"Probably not even before the change."

Peter squeezed his fists. Few things made him angrier than an outcome that couldn't be avoided. "How long?"

Ella shrugged. "Weeks. Months. Honestly, there's no way to tell without medical equipment."

"The kind they have at ExoGen?" he asked.

"Yeah...but all it would really do is give us a better idea of how long she has. I know you don't like absolutes, but there is nothing we can do to save her, aside from...but that's unthinkable."

"Aside from what?"

"Unlocking her junk DNA," Ella said. "Let her eat the crops. Maybe sneak some into her food. The first thing her changing cells would adapt to is the cancer. After that...well, you know what happens."

"But it could extend her life?"

"In theory," Ella said. "It could also drastically shorten ours."

"Mm." He wanted to punch something, but just said, "Let me know if you think of anything else we can do, short of making her a bloodthirsty killing machine."

"Sorry I didn't tell you," Ella said.

Peter shook his head. "If she wanted me to know, she'd have told me herself."

"I think she didn't want to worry anyone about it." Ella hugged him, holding him tight. He knew she'd grown comfortable with death years ago, but since forming this new family with him, the thought of it terrified her.

"Yeah," Peter said, "well, Anne is observant like her mother."

"The kids know."

"Suspect," Peter said. "Pretty sure I was the last one to have any clue. Aside from Feesa."

"About Feesa..." Ella said.

Peter leaned back to look her in the eyes. "She's not sick?"

"Changing," Ella said.

"How?"

Ella shook her head. "Wish I knew, but so far it's innocuous."

"How so?"

"Hair loss, mostly. And...she's remembering who she used to be. Small things, but for an Exo, it's significant. I've never seen it before, but I suspect she's evolving...forward this time. Closer to human. It's not impossible. The ExoGenetic crops just unlocked junk DNA. It doesn't guide the adaptations that occur. Those are determined by the environment, confrontations, survival instincts. For social creatures like the Riders, community has a big impact. And right now, we're Feesa's community. It could be that her genes are reverting simply because she has a better chance at surviving if she's one of the pack."

"She's one of the pack, no matter what she looks like," Peter said.

"Really? You think a DNA strand is going to understand a concept like loyalty? More likely, it's changing because Feesa has an intense desire to be human again, and the more her memories return, the stronger that urge becomes."

"Huh..." Peter said. Genetics and cancer were so far out of his wheelhouse that he didn't have much to say, and he didn't even know what questions to ask. "Anything else about anyone I should know about?"

"I don't think so," she said, looking into his eyes. She smiled and kissed him.

"Hey!" The door burst open. It was Anne. Her face morphed from frantic concern to slack-jawed betrayal. "Oh c'mon! You said— You guys are full of shit. Two minutes alone and you're—"

"Anne," Peter said.

"I'm surprised you even have your clothes on. Another minute and you'd have been jaunting around like Jakob—"

"What's that mean?" Peter asked.

"Anne!" Ella said. "Why did you come in here?"

Anne's eyes widened. "Right. That."

Before the girl could answer, Peter heard the problem. A motor. Propellers chopping through the water. The rhythmic whump of a boat bouncing over waves. A boat was cruising past.

Peter moved Anne out of the way and ran to the living room just in time to see a Boston Whaler bounce past the windows. There were six bedraggled people inside. Dirty, cut up, bruised. The way people look after just a few days in the wild, when they don't know what they're doing. Ella joined him at a broken window just after the boat passed. They leaned out over the water.

"I know them," Ella said. "Recognize them, at least. They're ExoGen. Scientists. Not sure what they're doing out here."

An Asian woman seated on the right side of the Whaler made eye contact with Peter. And then Ella. Her eyes showed surprise, and then she just casually threw herself overboard. Peter watched her. The way she moved. The way she fell. She was bound. A captive.

When the woman hit the water, the people inside the boat reacted with surprise. The engine slowed, but then one of the men said, "Keep going!" and the boat accelerated.

Lost in the Whaler's wake, the bound woman didn't surface.

"You know her?" Anne asked, standing beside her mother.

Ella nodded. "Maggie Woo. She's…brilliant."

"She good people?"

Ella nodded again. "A friend."

"What was that?" Lyn said from the table, perhaps too tired to get up and look for herself. "Maggie is here?"

"I'll hold onto the M4," Anne said, holding a hand out toward Peter. He looked at the girl. She'd read his mind. He handed her the rifle and his pistol, whispered, "God-damnit," and dove into the ocean.

23

It had been a long time since Peter had swum in the ocean. He'd forgotten how cold water felt. An electric shock of chilled Atlantic swept over him, compressing his veins, lowering his core temperature, and sucking the air from his lungs.

He pushed against the torment, dragging himself through the waves. He was normally a strong swimmer, but his clothing added drag and weight to his body, and his boots made kicking inefficient.

That's what Anne imagined was happening. She couldn't quite feel it all herself. She didn't share a psychic bond with her father, but thanks to her mother's memories, and her own, she knew him as well as anyone could. How he thought. What he could do. What drove him.

Right now, fighting the water and the cold, he'd be focusing on Maggie Woo, overboard, bound, and helpless, in an ocean that was full of man-eating creatures long before ExoGen changed the world. He'd be imagining how much worse off she was. How desperate she felt. And he'd push past his own fears.

Through the water.

Eyes open despite the sting of salt and small creatures who hadn't changed much since life began and would remain unchanged by RC-714.

Deeper and deeper, until he saw her through the murk, bucking against her bonds, sinking steadily into the depths. He'd swim to her. He *was* swimming to her. Catch her. Calm her. Lift her.

Toward the warbling light of the sun.

And their heads would break the surface, together, both of them taking a breath, like the first breaths of newborn babies, satiating and torturous.

And their heads would break the surface...

Why aren't their heads breaking the surface?

"Anne," her mother said.

She turned her eyes up to her mother, annoyed at the interruption.

But Ella didn't return the glance. She was focused on the distance. On the boat. It had cleared the city and entered the bay.

That alone wasn't unusual. It was the water around the boat that was strange. It had gone flat and swirly. A footprint. Like from a whale's tail. But huge.

Too huge.

It didn't make sense.

The creature would have to be immense to create a footprint so large. It would displace so much water that tidal waves would be crashing through the city. And the water in the bay wasn't deep enough to fit something so large.

"It's not one Exo," Anne said to herself.

"What?" Ella asked.

"That's not one creature," Anne said. "It's *hundreds* of them. Maybe thousands. Some kind of...shoal. They're swarming the boat."

The water surrounding the Whaler began to froth. The boat bounced over the suddenly rough seas, the *whump, whump, whump* of its hull and engine rising and falling became uneven and strained.

Unbalanced by the strange seas, the boat jounced back and forth, tipping further and further until a passenger was flung out. There was a yelp, a splash, and then the water exploded with frenetic energy.

The frothy water turned red and settled just a moment later.

It took just seconds for the unseen shoal to dismantle and devour the victim.

A second scream.

Then a third.

Two more passengers hit the water and were eradicated. The sea behind the boat was more red than blue. But the blood wasn't just from the victims, it was also from the shoal, as they battered the Whaler's underside and were struck by the propeller.

The wounded among them were then set upon by the others, triggering a feeding frenzy with the boat at its core. There were two people left on the boat. The first—a man—was behind the steering wheel. The second—a woman—sat beside him, clinging to a rope stretched out and bound to the front of the boat.

It wasn't much but it seemed to help her stay in the boat...for about ten seconds longer than the others.

The Whaler hit something hard and bounded into the air, leaving the water. When the vessel dropped back down, the woman remained airborne—until that rope yanked her back down. Problem was, the motorboat hit the water at an angle and had taken off in a different direction. The woman hit the water, still holding onto that rope.

She skipped over the surface on her back, swinging out wide until something got ahold of her.

With an explosion of water, she launched into the air, her body severed in half at the waist. As she was swung wide by the rope, her insides fell out like she was chumming the water with her organs.

She's dead already, Anne thought. Had to be. But her hands clutched onto that rope in a death grip.

The moment her top half returned to the water, it was pounced on and yanked away. The sudden pull altered the boat's course back toward the island. The motor's pitch shifted. The driver had the throttle pegged, hanging on to the steering wheel with all his strength, the ocean around him alive with frantic energy, throwing itself against the hull.

And then...

All at once.

It stopped.

A half mile out from George's Island and the ExoGen facility there, the boat leveled out and returned to normal, untouched by anything below the surface. The lone survivor stayed on course for the island's coast and empty dock.

Anne wanted to watch, to see if the man would make it all the way there, but the momentary distraction the boat and its doomed occupants provided were exactly that—a distraction.

From her father, who was currently in the same waters as the agitated shoal.

"Dad needs help," Anne said.

"He'll be okay," her mother replied, but Anne didn't believe her. Her father was good at staying alive, but he wasn't perfect. There were some circumstances that were unpredictable no matter how prepared you tried to be. A single monstrous creature wouldn't have been as concerning because it wouldn't fit between the buildings. But a swarm of smaller creatures...for all they knew, the aquatic Exos populated the submerged apartments around the city.

Ella didn't notice Anne unbuckling her protective vest. Didn't say anything when she stripped out of her shirt and pants. Her mother was focused on the water below, face twisted in concern, unsure about what to do.

But Anne was sure. Because she was doing what Peter would do. What he had already done.

"What are you doing?" Ella asked, when she finally noticed Anne stripped down to her sports bra and underwear.

Anne's flair for the dramatic fueled her response. She chambered a round in her FNX pistol, said, "What needs doing," and then dove into the water. The sound of her mother's protest was drowned out, replaced by the bubbly gurgle of water enveloping her.

Being new to life and then on the run, Anne hadn't really spent much time in water. She shouldn't know how to swim, but she did. Ella had been an excellent swimmer in her youth, and the ability had transferred to Anne as though she'd taken all the lessons herself.

She let air trickle out of her mouth, descending to where the light from above began to fade. Then she kicked in the direction Peter had been moving—toward where the woman had fallen. That was where they'd be, both of them close to drowning.

Question was why.

The answer emerged from the murky darkness below. A swirling body followed by a large, fanning fin. Anne dove toward it and into the darkness. For a moment, she couldn't see. Then her eyes adjusted, and she got an eyeful of something that should have only existed in the stories of ancient sailors.

The creature had two arms and the upper torso of a deformed human being, reimagined for life in the sea. Its head was both bald and feminine, sporting a singular, mohawk-like fin that ran down the neck and expanded up over the back, like a Dimetrodon, tapering down to a long, sleek body and flowing tail.

Under different circumstances, it might have been beautiful. But it was currently fighting Peter for control of his knife, which he'd already used to stab the creature once. Behind Peter, the bound woman clung to his belt, unable to save herself or escape during the fight.

Anne closed the distance, not rushing, not making a sound, letting her heartbeat remain calm and steady. She had no idea what kind of senses the creature had, but there were plenty of modern species that could detect her presence without ever seeing her—like sharks.

Peter was thrashed to the side. The beast clutched his knife hand while attempting to stab him with its long, swordlike claws. During the scuffle, Peter caught sight of Anne and gave a subtle nod.

It was time.

She was the predator.

She'd have taken a deep breath if there was air. Instead, she kicked harder, came in behind the ugly mermaid, wrapped her free arm around its throat, and squeezed. The creature reacted instantly to her presence, thrashing about. It released Peter and spun in circles, reaching back for her.

Anne watched as Peter kicked for the surface, unable to help because he was about to suck in a lung full of water. He held onto the woman with one hand, dragging her now-unconscious form toward the sun's light. When she was sure he'd make it, Anne pulled herself in close to the mermaid, placed the FNX pistol against its temple, and slipped her finger around the trigger.

She had no idea if the gun would fire. Some guns could fire underwater. Some couldn't. But all of them were far less effective, rounds traveling only a few feet before all their kinetic energy was sapped by the water.

So, she pressed it down hard, and pulled the trigger three times. With each squeeze, she felt a vibration in her hand, but nothing else. The .45 caliber rounds were powerful enough to enter a skull and exit the other side. But there were no exit wounds, or brains floating around.

She wasn't sure she'd done anything, until the creature's body went still.

The fight was over.

Anne watched the trail of blood ooze out from the Exo's head as it sank into the abyss. *Got what was coming,* she thought, and then she realized something else would be coming. Drawn to the blood and the conflict.

She looked toward the bay, lit by daylight. The ocean was a greenish blue haze. But it was alive with movement. A fluid wall of writhing bodies swam toward her.

The shoal was coming.

24

"Oh," Jakob said. "Gross."

The other people being dragged under the water, followed by pools of frothing red water was bad enough. But then the woman holding onto the rope was torn in half, her insides yanked out by centrifugal force. He was relieved when she was finally yanked free and pulled under. It was a gruesome death, full of terrible fear and pain, but it was quick.

"What in water?" Val asked. "What do that to them?"

"No idea," Jakob said, scanning the ocean with his binoculars. He saw bits and pieces of the creatures beneath the waves—fins, hands, flashes of colorful scales—but not enough to put together a clear picture of what he was seeing. All he really knew was that the water between the skyscraper and the island was populated by a school of very violent and hungry Exos.

They'd seen social Exos before, but the sheer number of creatures below was new. In a strange kind of way, it made sense. Boston was a city on the ocean, and when it flooded, adapting to the water would be a requirement. Once that happened, they must have naturally started gathering in large groups, like fish, whose massive numbers ensured that the species would continue because there were simply too many of them to gobble up. A whole made up of thousands of individuals.

He wished someone other than Feesa—than Val—was around to tell. Anne was always showing off what she knew, but Jakob knew stuff, too. Not nearly as much, but still.

"Man still going," Val said, pointing at the boat.

The Whaler bounced back and forth as it was pummeled from below. Jakob doubted it could take much more abuse before cracking apart. When that happened, the man's death might be even more dramatic than the woman who had clung to the rope.

Jakob wondered if they were friends. Maybe more than friends.

Maybe the man down there was crying. Was thinking about just jumping in with the others and ending it all. Love made people do funny things.

The possibility of the man's lost love struck a chord with Jakob. Made him feel compassion for the man. "C'mon... You can make it."

"Me no think he make it," Val said.

Jakob looked ahead to George's Island. The boat was closing fast, but there was still a good distance between them. That was when he spotted something in the water. It was out of place and strange, but not alive. Not an Exo. It looked like a floating cable, just beneath the surface. It was pale blue, which probably meant that it was white and colored by the water and the reflected sky. Jakob followed its path in both directions, as far as he could. The cable-thing wrapped around the island. Maybe all the way around.

But why?

The answer came a moment later when the boat bounced over the cable and continued onward undisturbed. Just under the water, flashes of blue erupted from the cable, deep beneath the water.

They're being electrocuted, Jakob thought. *The cable is a barrier, designed to keep them out. And it has power.*

The footprint in the water grew larger as the mass of creatures beneath the waves reversed course before they were all zapped.

The people on the boat knew, he realized. That the cable was there, that all they had to do was reach it. The boat they used had a relatively flat hull. It sat on top of the water. Could go right over the cable without triggering it. But it was loud. Fast, but loud. The moment it cleared the city, the churning propeller rang the dinner bell.

Jakob wondered how many people had run this gauntlet, attempting to reach the safety of George's Island. Was it really safe? Power or not, it was occupied and run by ExoGen, who had purposefully unleashed Ella's discovery on the world.

Why would anyone want to go there?

Maybe they were trying to undo the damage, too? Like Ella and Lyn. There had to be other ExoGen employees who hadn't gone all in with the worldwide extinction of the human race. But it seemed unlikely. Most everyone opposed to ExoGen had left the company before the end, or they left with Ella when she escaped the facility in San Francisco—and then died out in the wild.

These had to be ExoGen people, but why were they showing up here in ragtag groups?

Why had others been eaten by the bulbous flying whale?

"He make it!" Val said.

Jakob refocused on the boat, finding it sliding up to a dock on the island's coast. He lifted the binoculars to his eyes, getting a closer look. There were three men greeting the man, all dressed in black, all of them armed. Two wore masks. The third did not, and Jakob instantly recognized him.

"Kenyon."

"Kenyon?" Val reached for the binoculars. "Let Val see."

Before Jakob could comply with the request, Val took hold of the binoculars and pulled them to her eyes, which yanked Jakob against her chest. He slid the strap up over his head and pulled away.

"It's him," Jakob said.

Val moved the binoculars around, trying to find the dock through the zoomed in lens. She'd used binoculars before but wasn't very good at finding her target. To be fair, most people weren't. But she eventually found the dock, and the men on it.

"If you're going to break something, can you put the binoculars down first? They're the only ones I brought."

Val grunted. Could have been agreement. Could have been, 'Fuck off.' Only way to know was to wait and see.

"Is Kenyon," she said, letting out a low growl. "I kill Kenyon."

Jakob wasn't a proponent of straight up murder, but the man had tried to kill every member of their family. And if he wasn't taken care of, he'd do it again, maybe more successfully. "If you get the chance, he's all yours."

"Good," she said, offering the unbroken binoculars.

Jakob looked through the lenses again and was happy to find them uncracked. There was a time when she definitely would have broken them, even before she got angry. But she was getting a handle on understanding her own strength, and her temper.

She could be driven to great violence still, but she was more focused. Had pure motives driving her.

Jakob wasn't sure how, but she was becoming more and more human as the day progressed. In terms of ExoGenetic change, he knew that was quick. Maybe a record. Adaptations in nature took millions of years. For Exos, weeks or months.

But a day?

More than that, she was shedding adaptations she'd taken from the past. Apexes layered adaptations on top of each other, becoming horrible, twisted conglomerations. But Val was headed in the other direction.

And that gave him hope. That there was a future for the planet—for humanity—even if they failed.

Jakob scanned the island again. Aside from the men on the dock, pulling the survivor up, there was no movement. Everyone was inside, and Jakob didn't blame them. A roof over your head was always safer.

The four men moved quickly, retreating through a solid metal door built into the island's stone wall. It looked heavy and sturdy, but also old, like something built long ago. Peter had told him a little about the island, about how it had been home to a U.S. Military fort where soldiers were trained, and where Civil War prisoners were held. Eventually decommissioned, the island had become a tourist destination where people could explore the pitch-dark subterranean tunnels and keep an eye out for ghosts. Honestly, it sounded cool, but not anymore. ExoGen had erected a modern building right on top of the fort, occupying most of the island's 39 acres of land.

"Well," Jakob said. "I guess we just kick back and chill, right? Keep an eye on the island and update Dad with the info until the sun sets."

"Relax sounds good," Val said, taking hold of a couch with one hand and casually dragging it over to the window, facing the ocean. She sat down, leaned back, and put her feet up against the glass.

"Hell, yes," Jakob said, and plopped down beside her, "So, what's new?"

"You know. The usual," Val said with a funny shrug. "All hair fall out. Teeth, too. Just another day."

Jakob burst out laughing. Val could be funny, often unintentionally, but that was funny because she was trying, because she was making fun of her situation. Maybe even being self-deprecating. It was exciting to think that they might be able to get to know her better. She'd always been surface level with her wants, desires, and needs. But now... She had been Valerie Wood, whose songs were deep, moving, and thoughtful. Rarely funny, but that didn't mean she didn't have a sense of humor.

She rolled her head lazily in his direction. "How about y—"

Val went still, head cocked to the side. She was hearing something.

"What is it?" Jakob asked.

"Gunshots," she said.

Jakob stood, picking up his weapon and slinging it over his shoulder. "I don't hear any—"

"Far away." Val lowered her feet to the floor. Leaned forward.

"Out there?" Jakob pointed to the island, and then looked through his binoculars. "I don't see anything."

"Not island." She leapt from the couch and hurried to the wall of windows on the north side of the building. She pressed her face against the glass, looking straight down. "Outside. At bottom. In water. Hear voices. Shouting." Her eyes locked on Jakob's. "Is family! Are in trouble!"

Jakob was about to ask what the problem was when he noticed the footprint left over from the conflict with the boat was growing again, and it was headed toward the city.

"Oh shit. Oh shit."

"We need help," Val said.

"How? We're all the way up here."

She looked out the window again, this time scanning the surrounding buildings, doing some kind of mental calculation. "How much Jake trust Val?"

"A-a lot. Why?"

She took him by both shoulders. Gazed into his eyes. "Val go help. Jake stay here. Complete mission. Val comes back for Jake. Okay?"

"What? How?"

"You no worry about that," she said. "You trust. I go. Okay?"

She was waiting for permission, even though she didn't need it.

"Okay," he said. "Help them."

She grinned and punched the window beside them. The thick double-paned glass shattered from the impact and fell away. Val leapt out after it and dropped from sight.

25

"Sometimes you just need to step up," Peter had told Feesa. It was late at night. Neither of them could sleep. Each of them had a feeling that something was stalking them, despite a lack of evidence. They'd gotten to talking about how Peter, the day prior, had faced impossible odds when caught unprepared by an Exo-Mole that had come out of the ground while he was...indisposed.

Literally caught with his pants down, he hadn't attempted to scurry away, or scramble for his nearby rifle. He drew the knife down by his ankle and waged a one-man war against a much larger and ferocious Apex...that turned out to not be nearly Apex enough to save itself.

Feesa didn't see it happen, but she heard it. And when she arrived on the scene, she understood exactly what had happened. Feesa respected his choice to fight. She would have done the same. But she didn't understand it. Feesa was strong. Feesa was fast. Had claws and sharp teeth. Peter was human. Soft and breakable.

He could have died.

So, she had asked him about it. "What is step up?"

"Means you have to move past the fear and plow straight into action. If you can do that quickly, before your opponent has time to adjust from offense to defense, you can turn the tide of an impossible situation."

"Too many words," Feesa said.

Peter laughed and patted her shoulder. "Be unexpected."

"Surprise...in way...that is...different?"

"Yeah," he said. "Even Apexes have expectations of how things will play out."

She huffed a laugh. "They attack. They eat."

"Exactly," he said. "Disrupt that, and you'll catch them off guard."

"Do unexpected..." She had liked the sound of that. Had attempted to employ the technique a few times, but brute strength and ferocity had always served her best.

This time, when Feesa, reborn as Val, jumped from the window, six hundred feet above the ocean's surface, the unexpected would serve her well.

She was sure of it.

For about two seconds.

The moment she missed grabbing hold of the abandoned window washer platform, she was the one caught off guard.

She reached out for the building, hoping to find a handhold she could grasp, but she was several feet away, and the building's exterior was flat and shiny.

A reflection caught her attention. For a moment, she was confused by the hairless woman looking back at her. But she recognized the clothing Jakob had picked out for her, the open shirt fluttering up over her head like a cape.

Like a superhero cape.

Visions of old movies slipped through her memory. Made her smile. She was powerful. Much more than an ordinary human being. She could endure things they could not. Jakob seemed to think falling from the tower would kill a person.

But Val was not really a person.

She was an Exo.

Instead of screaming and flailing in fear, Val leveled out her body and pointed her toes downward.

A quick glance beyond her toes revealed the current situation—Peter was struggling to get a dead woman into the building with Ella, and Anne was under the water, trying to surface. Val wasn't sure, but she didn't think Anne was going to make it.

And Anne was important. Everyone said so.

Val didn't understand why or how. Anne mostly made people laugh, or angry. She was a good fighter, like Peter, but very small. Val wouldn't like being little and weak, but Anne didn't seem to mind. And it never prevented her from 'stepping up,' like her father said. The strange creature sinking away beneath her was proof of that.

She had saved Peter. Had risked her life to do it.

Val would do the same for her. That was how family worked.

She wasn't sure why, but just before impact, Val cupped her hands over her face, arms rigid over her chest, body vertical, like a spike.

The water slapped against her skin, stinging every part of her, all at once. But the pain was bearable. Next came the pressure, squeezing against her body, against her ears. It felt funny and disorienting until her feet touched down on the hard surface of what once was a street.

Val looked up. Could see Peter kicking at the building's edge, and Anne swimming to the surface. The girl was still moving up but was now looking down. Could she see Val in the depths?

Didn't matter. She still had stepping up to do.

She'd survived the first phase of her plan, now she had to see it through. A quick glance revealed the danger. The Apexes she'd seen tearing apart the boat, and its occupants, were returning from the bay. Despite the gloom and distance, Val could see them—their claws, hideous smiles, large teeth, and eel-like bodies built for moving through the water. They wriggled quickly, sliding through the ocean with effortless, crazed grace.

They wouldn't be long.

Val shoved off the submerged street and rocketed up through the water. She might not have adapted to a life beneath the waves, but her body was now sleek and her feet still broad. Every kick propelled her faster and higher. When she heard Anne choking, she fought against the water, climbing toward the girl.

Just as Anne's body went limp, Val scooped her up, kicked twice more, and broke the surface.

It took just a second to swim to Peter, take the woman from his hands, and lift her up to Ella. Instead of taking the woman, Ella shouted in surprise, stepping back. Annoyed by the delay and motivated by the oncoming wave of sharp-toothed carnage, Val shot the woman through the window like a basketball.

When she turned to do the same to Peter, she found him looking strange, knife in hand, like he was about to attack her.

"Peter," she said, feeling confused. "Why you attack?"

"Fee...Feesa?"

She remembered how different she looked. He didn't even recognize her.

"Val," she said, "me help. Me stepping up. Stop being stupid."

His mystified expression didn't fade, but he did lower the knife. Val placed her hand under his backside and hoisted him up out of the water. He wasted no time in turning around to haul up Anne. Val took one last look toward the bay. They'd escaped with time to spare. "Val did a good job," she said to herself, and then pulled herself up.

But instead of moving up into the open air of the apartment building, she found herself dragged back down into the ocean.

Pain exploded from her calf. It was a familiar sensation. Blades cutting skin and muscle, grinding against her bone. The intense pressure. The writhing of a tongue against her flesh.

She'd been bitten and yanked down into the abyss.

Unfazed by the predicament, she leaned forward to get a look at her adversary. It was one of the creatures that had destroyed the boat. It moved through the water with ease, propelled by a large fishy fin and guided by a long sail along its back.

It looked at her with large, yellow, hate-filled eyes.

The creature didn't just want to consume her, it wanted to eradicate her, like she represented something detestable.

It thinks I'm human, Val thought.

Her memories as a Rider were shaky. Each day melded with the others. But she remembered how she felt when she fought an Apex, and when she hunted and killed humans. The first was a fight for survival. The latter...her only pleasure. At the time, people were detestable because they reminded her of a life she could barely remember but longed for. Always out of reach. It drove her near to madness, and the rage only subsided after having torn a human being to bits and chewed on their flesh.

And now it was happening to her.

Only this Apex had made a very severe mistake.

While the creature thrashed at her leg, it paid no attention to the rest of her. Lost in bloodlust, it didn't see her reach down. Didn't notice her hands reaching out. Didn't expect anything beyond a quick meal.

Instead, Val crushed the creature's eyeballs in her hands.

She was immediately released. The blinded Exo swam wildly away, headed straight toward its mass of brethren, closing in like an angry storm.

Val looked up. She was forty feet down and ten feet from the bottom. To get a good push up, she'd first have to swim down. That would take time. And there was blood in the water. Even if the others didn't see her as human, they'd be coming for her. She spun around in the water and found herself just a few feet from the broken windows of the building's second floor.

As the blind Exo was set upon and torn apart by the swarm, Val pulled herself into the building and out of their immediate line of sight. Their blind meal wouldn't even slow them down, so she kicked hard into the shadowy realm of water, looking for her only chance of escape.

For a moment, she was lost in confusion, unsure of where to go.

Then it all just clicked. She remembered the layout of the floor above and used that memory to navigate this floor. They were exactly the same. Feeling excited about this new mental ability, she pulled herself around a hallway corner and saw what she was searching for.

She couldn't hear her pursuers, but she was sure they were in the building, zipping through the maze of halls and rooms, gnashing their teeth. As Val's lungs began burning, she felt a new sensation, something born from her changing self: fear.

Not of pain, but of death.

She wanted to live.

Was excited to live. To see where her life led. Before, every day was the same. She just existed. But now, she felt hope. And terror.

Val swam to the set of double doors and hauled them apart. She slipped inside the elevator shaft, spun around, and—

The creature approaching was a blur of motion, cutting through the water like an arrow shot through the air. She yanked the doors closed, slamming them together...a moment too late. The doors shook as the creature slammed into them, its neck lodged in the middle, its jaws snapping at Val's chest.

Val roared back at the creature, venting her anxiety, and grasped the creature's head on either side. She twisted. There was a moment of resistance, then a crack. The Exo stopped fighting, but Val kept turning the head until flesh, bone, and sinew gave way and the neck separated from the body.

She closed the doors all the way and then pulled herself up the long cable that stretched all the way to the penthouse.

Her first breath sounded like a roar. After three more, she hauled herself up a few more feet, parted the doors, stumbled out, and fell to her knees.

Peter came running, M4 in his hand, not quite aimed at her, but ready. He was followed by Anne, alive and ready for a fight.

Val smiled at the sight of her. They were what...? What were the words?

Kindred spirits. Fighters both.

"Oh, good," she said. "Anne safe."

Val dropped the severed Apex head onto the floor and collapsed beside it.

26

"You're sure?" Peter asked, pacing, weapon in hand, on edge. The creatures living in the seas around Boston hadn't come inside the building. Yet. Ella thought they might have adapted too well to life in the water that they could no longer breathe air.

They'd clearly once been human. RC-714 unlocked past genes. If an adaptation wasn't in the rearview of your species, it wasn't available. Since homo sapiens were a recent addition to the gene pool, the only Exos with human-like features were the ones that used to be human.

They might not be able to breathe on the surface now, but that could change.

Feesa was proof of that.

"It's her, Dad," Jakob said through the radio. "It's Feesa. All her hair fell out when she was in the shower."

"Feesa took a shower?"

"Uh, yeah..." Jakob sounded like he'd been caught stealing rations. "We both did. *Not together.*"

Peter heard the embarrassment and guilt in his son's voice. He screwed up and he knew it. All things considered, it was a pretty innocent mistake. Peter had been tempted as well. Had he succumbed to that desire, he might not have given a second thought to where all the water would go and how much noise it could make.

There was no need to extend the lesson for Jakob.

Everyone had survived, and Feesa had paid a price.

Peter chuckled for Jakob's benefit and then asked, "Have you noticed anything about her behavior that's changed?"

"You mean aside from being willing to jump six hundred feet to save Anne?"

"She might have always done that," Peter said. Feesa would do anything and risk anything for her family. "I mean, anything...emotionally. Mentally?"

"Oh, right," Jakob said. "She's remembering. Who she used to be."

"She is?"

"She is," Ella chimed in. She was in the next room, leaning over Feesa, who was unconscious on a king-sized bed and taking up most of it.

"Like what?"

"You'll never believe me," Jakob said.

"There's a lot I believe now that I wouldn't have before all this."

"Valerie Wood," Jakob said.

"What about her?" Peter asked. He remembered the singer. Wasn't an avid listener but enjoyed her music.

Mostly because of her voice.

"That's Feesa," Jakob said.

"What?"

"Feesa is...was...Valerie Wood." Jakob sounded like he still had a hard time believing it, but he couldn't deny it, either.

"You're shitting me?"

"She confided in me," Ella said, "before we reached the city. Told me her name was Val."

"I heard her sing," Jakob said. "She's remembering who she was. Wants to be herself again. At least *some* of her. More human, but also not. She likes being big and strong, but not...ugly. And she wants to sing."

Peter's first thought was that singing could be dangerous. Then he looked into the bedroom, at the hairless woman dressed like a 90's grunge band singer—who'd risked her life to save his daughter's. If she wanted to sing, he'd build her a soundproof mansion.

Ella left Feesa's bedside and approached Peter, snapping her fingers, and reaching for the radio. He handed it over.

"Hey, Jake," she said, and immediately shifted gears to professional Ella. "You said she wants to be herself."

"Yeah. Desperately, I'd say. And I was thinking about that... What if our desires can guide ExoGenetic change? I mean, everyone is hungry, and back when the change happened, it was at the tail end of a worldwide famine, right? So, like, everyone was worried about food. And when there was tons of it, everyone just scarfed it down. Fell into a mindset of endless hunger. Maybe that's what fueled all the killing. And the Apexes.

"But some people, like Val, and the other Riders, still had a strong sense of community and retained it when they changed. So, for them, the change retained...what do you call it?"

"Social bonds," Ella said.

"Right, that. And now that she's been around us for so long, her desire to fit in is allowing her to adapt forward through her genetic code, rather than just backward. Or something? I don't know. I'm not the scientist."

"Couldn't have said it better," Ella said, "and I think you're right."

"So..." Jakob said, "do you think it's possible to—"

"Don't even say it," Peter blurted, trying to interrupt the thought. But Ella wasn't transmitting, and Jakob couldn't hear his father.

"—eat ExoGenetic food and not change, or maybe only change in ways that you want?"

Ella gave Peter a 'calm down' look, pressed the transmit button, and said, "I wouldn't dare answer that conclusively without a lot of testing."

"Human testing," Peter said.

"But...Feesa's—Val's—condition suggests it's a possibility. And if that proves true..." She glanced into the apartment's living room. Anne was laid out on one couch, exhausted. Lyn was on the other, sound asleep, fighting a battle of her own.

Ella turned from them to Peter.

"Might be the only way to save her."

Peter grimaced. Purposefully exposing someone to RC-714 was unthinkable. Odds were that Lyn would turn into a monster and Peter would have to put her down. *She's going to die, either way,* he thought, *but if I have to shoot her...*

He turned his thoughts away from the possibility. He'd carry the guilt for the rest of his life. But he wouldn't stop her if she made the choice to try. They'd done some crazy things to stay alive. Eating ExoGen crops as a cure for cancer would just be one more insane option in a long list.

"We'll talk about it another time," he said and held his hand out for the radio. She handed it back and returned to the bedroom.

"Jake," he said into the radio. "Tell me what you're seeing up there."

"Right. Well, the island is definitely occupied and operational. Pretty sure those people on the boat were ExoGen. They knew the island was safe and were trying to reach it."

"What makes you think that?" Peter asked.

"There's a boundary," Jakob said. "About a half mile out, around the whole island. The boat could go over it, but the mermaid-things... They got fried. Killed everything that touched it."

"And they were going so fast because they knew about the mermaids," Peter added.

"That's what I was thinking," Jakob said. "Which means they're in contact with the facility somehow."

"Maybe," Peter said.

"I'm pretty sure. There was a security team waiting for the man who made it through." Jakob paused for a moment. "Dad...Kenyon was leading them."

Peter gripped the radio. Aside from the constant threat of ExoGenetic predators hunting them down, Kenyon was the greatest threat to their lives. Peter knew the ExoGen security chief might be here, might be waiting for them, but he'd hoped the man had met his end on the journey north.

Imagining him in the belly of some monster helped Peter sleep at night.

"Doesn't change anything," Ella said, coming back from the bedroom. "He's just one more guard, and we expected it." She spoke plainly despite having had a relationship with the man. For her, it had been less romantic, born of necessity. Kenyon was a dangerous man and his affection had helped protect Ella and Anne in San Francisco. He hadn't taken the revelation well and had tried to kill both Peter and Jakob. Eventually, there would be a reckoning, but Kenyon wasn't the reason for their journey to Boston.

All they needed to do was access the lab and let Ella work her magic to finalize a vaccine against the negative effects of consuming RC-714.

"Copy that," Peter said, hiding his anger.

"Hey, Dad..."

"Yeah, Jake."

"I'm sorry the woman died. How do you deal with it? When you try to save someone but can't? Do you, I don't know, feel like you've let them down?"

"Sometimes the best you can do is try," Peter said. "Failing is a part of life. Learn from it, and it's not really a failure. It's a lesson. And...in this world...sometimes the best we can do is not try at all. In hindsight, none of us should have gotten in that water. I put our entire mission in jeopardy. What we're doing is bigger than any one person. Except for you, of course, big man."

"Ugh. Dad. Please never call me 'big man' again. Moving on. How am I going to get down?"

"For now," Peter said, "you're not. You've got rations for a few days, so you're on overwatch duty until we figure out a solution or Val recovers enough to bring you back down. We've found another elevator down here, but it doesn't ascend to the penthouse. There's a second stairwell, too, but it's blocked off ten floors up. In the meantime, we need to push forward."

"You're going without me?"

"Without you, without Val, and without Lyn." Losing Val was a blow, but not having to worry about Lyn was a weight off his mind. Ella could have used her help in the lab, but she was also sure Anne was up to the task. "We're going in small and quiet. Try to avoid a confrontation."

"Even if you have a chance to take out Kenyon?"

Peter imagined putting a bullet in the man. "Even then. Yes. We'll all be safer with a cure."

"We'd all be safer if we could do what Val is doing. Change how we want."

"At the risk of going mad and eating your family?"

"Well, yeah, I guess there's that."

"Listen, Jake. I know being alone for a few days is going to be rough. You're going to worry. Going to be lonely. But you got this. You can help us get to the island unseen. And there is presently no way for an Apex to reach you."

"Unless they fly," Jakob said.

Peter hadn't thought about that. "Well…stay away from the glass."

"That's what I'm doing," Jakob said, but Peter could hear him pushing furniture, probably away from the window.

"When the time comes, we'll coordinate our island approach with you."

"Great," Jakob said, oozing sarcasm. "I'll get to watch my family get eaten, too."

"Won't happen," Peter said, though he really wasn't sure. The people in the Whaler weren't able to move fast enough to avoid the mermonsters. And he had kayaks.

"Kenyon…" A raspy voice from the bedroom said.

"Val's awake," Peter said. "I'll be in touch. Contact me if anything happens."

"Will do. Out."

"Love you," Peter said. "Out."

Peter strode to the bedroom and paused at the door.

Val was awake and looking a little groggy.

"Me hear Kenyon name." She shifted her weight like she was about to get out of bed.

"Val," he said, catching her attention.

She looked up at him. Smiled at his usage of her human name.

"Hey," he said, placing a hand on her shoulder. "Thank you for saving Anne. For risking your life."

She grunted in response, humble about what she'd done. "Family."

"Right..." Peter added. "But your job is done. For now."

"Why?" she asked.

Peter motioned to her wounded leg, hidden by the sheet. "You're injured. Going to take time to—"

Val reached down and yanked the sheet away, revealing her bandaged stub of a leg, cut short from the mid-shin where the mermonster had shredded muscle and shattered bone. Val looked from Peter to Ella, eyes wide with surprise and fear. "Where...where leg?"

27

"I had to remove it," Ella said, "to stop the bleeding."

Val looked stymied, rightfully so. "I heal fast."

She was right about that. All Exos healed quickly. It was an adaptation they shared. But they weren't invulnerable. Val's leg had been so shredded that she'd have bled out long before the wound could heal. The only way to save her was to remove the limb and cauterize the stump, all of which she had been unconscious for, which was a blessing. She wouldn't have made a very good patient.

"It will still heal," Ella said. "Will grow back."

Val squinted at her. "You lie to Val?"

A few days ago, Val would have taken Ella's statement as gospel truth. Now she was savvy enough to spot Ella's lack of conviction.

"I'm not lying," Ella said. "I'm just...I'm hypothesizing. Some of Earth's earliest and most primitive creatures had the ability to regenerate limbs, or even duplicate themselves. I see no reason why your body wouldn't unlock that ability now." She motioned to the bandaged limb. "It's possible the regrowth has already begun. We just can't see it."

"Val want to see," she said, and reached for the bandage.

"No, no, no," Ella said, "You're not immortal. Some things, like infection, might attack faster than you can adapt. I saved your life, Val, but it's up to you to stay alive."

"Why up to Val?" she asked. "You here."

"We're heading to the island when the sun goes down," Peter said, using his authoritative voice.

"Without Val..." She leaned back and crossed her thick arms. "You all die."

Peter shook his head. "Without Val, we're small. Hard to see. Sneaky. And if we get caught, you'll be alive to rescue us, right? Once your leg regrows."

"I can hop," she said.

"You can fall." Peter lifted his leg and did an imitation of Val toppling over.

She huffed her distinctive laugh. He knew how to talk to her. How to get through. Truth mixed with humor. Given the circumstances, it was impressive she could laugh at all. In fact, she didn't seem to be in much pain. Her ability to endure injuries was shark-like, carrying on despite wounds.

"What about nasty sea monsters?" Val asked. "They eat you without Val."

Peter shook his head, much better at feigning confidence. "I don't think so. They've been hunting all day. They'll be sleeping tonight. Plus, clouds have rolled in. The moon and stars will be blocked. The sky will be dark. We'll be invisible."

Val grunted. She was understanding. "And no sound from small boats. Sneaky."

"Exactly," he said. "You get it."

She grunted again. Understood the plan but didn't like it. Still, Peter had defused her primal instincts and managed to calm her down.

"What Val do here?"

Ella was about to lay down some doctor's orders. Tell her to rest. To stay in bed. To not pick, or scratch, or any of the other things someone with a grave wound might be tempted to do when boredom set in. But Peter beat her to the punch with a very different set of instructions.

"Protect," he said, and then pointed out to the living room. "Lyn is sick. Having trouble moving."

"She not go to island, too?"

Peter shook his head.

"That was the plan, but now...she won't make it."

"You mean won't help," Val said. "Maybe slow down. Or make obvious?"

"All of that is true, too," he said. "But mostly, she needs to rest. If we can get her to the island later, we will. Until then, you protect her." Peter looked toward the ceiling. "And Jake."

"Nothing get past Val," she said. "If fishy people try to fight out of water, I crush."

Peter smiled. "I'm sure you will. But, only move if you need to, okay? The faster that leg regrows, the faster you get back in the fight. Understood?"

"Okay, Peter..." She wasn't thrilled, but her reaction to Peter's command went down a hell of a lot better after he'd entrusted her with protecting Lyn and Jakob. "What do if family no come back?"

Peter's forced positivity faded. "Protect Jakob. Run. Find someplace to live. But we *will* come back."

"Peter sure?"

"I promise." He held out a fist and she bumped it with hers. They'd done this before, like a pact between warriors, but it was the first time Val's hand almost looked human. It was still twice the size of Peter's, and strong, but it was hairless with more slender digits.

He motioned for Ella to follow him with a tilt of his head and then exited the bedroom. Ella was jealous of the way he communicated with people. The no-nonsense, but casual way he laid out reality was easy for people to swallow compared to her blunt, straightforward appraisal of facts. She was tempted to add a last bit of advice to Val, about changing bandages, about not trying to walk on the stump, but she might undo all the progress Peter just made. So, she just smiled and nodded at Val as she left the room.

Before she was out of earshot, Val started humming.

It sounded good.

Valerie Wood. A singer.

Ella shook her head.

ExoGen had taken some of the most beautiful things in the world and turned them into monsters. It was time for things to be set right.

She found Peter squatting beside Anne on the couch, silently rousing her from sleep. She couldn't hear their conversation, but Anne was fully awake in thirty seconds, and it ended with another fist bump and a nod. Then Peter reached out with his hand, placed it on the back of Anne's neck, and kissed her forehead. She hugged him in response.

He's thanking her, she thought, *for saving his life.*

She smiled.

They were a pair.

Nothing had gone to plan since she'd escaped ExoGen with Anne, but reuniting with Peter and giving Anne a father...Ella wouldn't change the past few months if she could.

The three of them met at the dining room table, which was covered in the limited supplies they'd be taking along. Mostly weapons and ammo. Anne had her FNX pistol, which had proven itself in combat both in and out of the water. Peter has his M4 and a Sig Sauer M17 sidearm, and Ella had an MP5 and a Glock 19. All of it was sound suppressed. And each of them carried a knife. Peter carried three. Two were identical Marine Raider Bowie knives, which seemed awfully close to being machetes. The third was a folding SOG Seal XR. All of them was chosen, not just because of their lethality, but because they were quiet.

The goal was to get in and out without confrontation. Ella didn't think that would be possible, but if they could get the job done without an alarm being set off, that would be preferable to all-out war.

They had enough ammo for a war, though.

There was an armored vest for each of them, loaded with ammo and first aid items. Ella didn't know how many people were in the facility, but given the number of ExoGen people they'd seen eaten by the whale, and the four killed just off the island, she suspected she had enough bullets for everyone on the island.

But that wouldn't be necessary. ExoGen had a security force. The rest were scientists, who knew Ella, who would likely be sympathetic to her cause once she explained what was possible. That was the hope. With Lyn too tired to continue, it would be good to find help inside the walls of ExoGen.

And if things went 'sideways,' as Peter liked to say, he was bringing along a full auto Fostech Origin 12, which was something between a shotgun and an assault rifle, loaded with Frag-12 explosive rounds. Peter called it a 'force multiplier.' It wasn't silent, not even close, but it could change the balance of power in combat with a single squeeze of the trigger. She'd seen what it could do against an Exo, and she felt sorry for any human on the receiving end of its 12-gauge pellets.

She hoped they wouldn't need it, but was glad they had it, especially with Val staying behind. She'd given Peter a hard time when they stopped at Fort Bragg, and he'd gathered enough guns and ammo to require a trailer. But she was glad for it now. Mushrooms and dandelions could be foraged, but bullets didn't grow on trees.

She'd argued that they'd be plentiful in gun shops along the way, but the few they'd come across had been ransacked in the early days of the change.

"So, scale of 1 to 10," Ella said. "What are our chances?"

"Of crossing seven miles of open ocean, at night, in a kayak, with hungry Exos beneath us, an electrified shield that will fry us if we touch it, and armored guards patrolling the island and inside the facility? Then finding the lab and using it long enough to change the course of human history, escaping unseen, returning in said kayaks, at night… et cetera, et cetera?"

He looked at Anne and smiled. "Piece of cake."

"Fuck, yeah," Anne said, punching her father's shoulder.

"Seriously," Ella said.

"It's not impossible," Peter said. "Let's leave it at that."

"None of those words were numbers," Ella pointed out.

"Yeah," Peter said, picking up the smallest vest and putting it over Anne's head. "Well, I've never been very good at math."

"Pff." Anne shook her head. Thought her father was hilarious.

Peter turned to the window, looking out to sea. The sky was dark purple. Wouldn't be long before it was black. "Soon as it's dark, we're leaving. Going to need as much time as possible in the lab, and then we have to get out before light."

Ella looked out at the view. It was...peaceful. But she knew better. They were about to paddle straight through a watery hell...in a god-damned kayak.

28

Eddie Kenyon couldn't sleep. He needed to be awake with the sunrise, and went to bed early, but something was nagging at him. It wasn't an uncommon feeling, and a lack of sleep was the norm, but this felt different.

Since arriving at the ExoGen's Boston facility he'd been troubled by the events that had unfolded in San Francisco while he and Viper Squad had been chasing Ella across the country.

Wouldn't have happened if he'd been there.

He was convinced. He'd replayed the security feeds in his head, inserting himself into every grisly situation, imagining how his presence would have turned the tide.

But it was a useless fantasy.

ExoGen had been overrun by a horde of tribal Apexes. Those with power and whose lives were important to humanity's future were evacuated first and flown to Boston. The rest were making the journey on foot, led by a small security detail who hadn't been trained in surviving in the wild. Thousands of people had set out on the journey as the facility crumbled and burned. Hundreds had completed it.

More arrived every week, but their numbers dwindled, and Apexes followed in their wake. Some of the creatures had followed groups of fifty people across the country, protecting them from other Apexes, while slowly picking them off, one by one. Carnivore shepherds.

The man they'd plucked from the ocean today—Shawn Fuller—was the sole survivor of a group that had started with seventy-three people. He'd managed to lead them across the country to Massachusetts, where they'd encountered an Apex that Kenyon had dubbed the SOS—not because it made those it encountered distressed, but because it was a flying Sack of Shit. It had been a whale, once upon a time, but had taken to the sky, using an adaptation no one on the science team could identify. Turned out a lot of Earth's natural history wasn't recorded in the fossil record. Survivors have observed dozens of adaptations that humanity had no knowledge of—lost to time but stored in human DNA—including what might have been intelligent ancestors capable of self-awareness and even civilization.

But the SOS was just an eating machine, bent on noshing on as many people as it could before shitting them all out, partially digested. It'd been a little more than a week since he'd seen it, probably because it was busy consuming Fuller's crew. But he'd see it again. He was sure. When it ran out of people to eat, it would come back.

He and the new Viper Squad had fought it off twice, unleashing a barrage of bullets that had injured the beast, but had failed to puncture its thick hide or pop its bulbous body. To do that, they'd need something with a little more punch.

Unfortunately, Lawrence's priority at the time of evacuation had been to preserve the science. The glorious work. It trumped all other concerns, so while they had data galore and hundreds of scientific minds, they had far less in the way of weapons, ammunition, and people who knew how to use them.

Lawrence was a strong and charismatic leader who had excelled in the old world. In the new world, that he'd helped create, he was a coin toss. But his vision kept them all on the same path, and that was important. Without his guidance, alliances would form and the unity binding ExoGen would fracture. Kenyon did his best to advise the man and was listened to far more now than in San Francisco, but mistakes happened, including not allowing Kenyon to pick up Fuller's people in a chopper.

Forcing them to take a Whaler was a huge risk. The creatures surrounding the island were a force of nature on par to SOS. The electric barrier kept them away from the island, but it was nearly impossible to cross the bay and survive. That Fuller made it was something of a miracle.

Lawrence called it survival of the fittest, but Kenyon knew better. Most of the people here had been saved because of their minds, whisked away in choppers and then planes. Very few of them would last a day in the wild.

That would change when the eggheads finished their work, but Kenyon wasn't sure that could happen without Ella. Or Anne. One of the two. He didn't care which, anymore. Ella had made her bed. She could sleep in it now, dead or alive. And if he had to kill one to get the other, so be it.

He was tired of this fucked up world.

Was ready to 'ascend.'

To become more than human.

That was how Lawrence put it, and the others ate it up like a shit buffet at a dung beetle symposium. For them, it was going to be a religious experience. Metaphysical metamorphosis. But it was just science. Unlocked and guided genetics. There was no mystery about it. No touch of the divine.

Just Ella Masse, a fallen angel leading the rebellion against Lawrence's divine will.

Kenyon sighed, rolled out of bed, and landed on his hands and feet, dropping into a push-up. An impromptu workout would do nothing to help him sleep, but it might release some of the tension knotting his back.

Aside from Fuller's dramatic arrival and the loss of more people, there had been nothing special about today. A man thought he saw a glint of light coming from one of the skyscrapers back in the city, but they were surrounded by ocean, looking at a city full of glass walls. On a sunny day, glints were common.

But Kenyon couldn't shake the feeling that something was off.

Wasn't the first time he'd felt this way. He'd been waiting for Ella to show up with her motley band of protectors, in the dead of the night, throwing a monkey wrench of ass-fuckery into everything they were doing.

It was a foolish fear.

They were unlikely to survive the journey north, even if they had allied themselves with the remaining Chunta. Feesa was fierce, but he'd seen Apex predators roaming the wilds that would inhale Riders like popcorn.

Odds were, they were dead and no longer his problem.

And if they did manage to make it to the rocky shore of George's Island, they'd be in rough shape and greeted by night guards, spotlights, motion sensors, and hundreds of people desperate for Ella to unlock RC-714's full potential.

It was also possible that one of their people might eventually crack that nut, but Ella's mind was different. She could think in ways other people couldn't. Was one of the reasons he'd fallen for her. Her brain was exceptional. Now, he wouldn't mind putting a bullet through her skull. Some people think that love fades, but in Kenyon's experience, it usually just turned to hate. Faster than the change made people into monsters.

A knock at the door stopped him at seventy-four.

"I'm awake," he said, and resumed his workout.

The door slid open like they were on the Starship Enterprise. Kenyon had warned against the facility's more extravagant features. Sliding doors weren't super useful when the power went out. There were manual options, but they wouldn't be convenient in the dark, or when something was trying to wrench your head from your neck.

"Sir." It was Hutchins. His presence meant that something had either gone wrong or that Lawrence had summoned him. Since Hutchins didn't seem agitated, Kenyon assumed it was the latter.

"What's he want?" Kenyon asked.

Hutchins adjusted his new glasses. "No idea, but it sounded urgent."

"Business urgent or personal urgent?" Lawrence was something of a drama queen. Kenyon assumed most cult leaders probably were at their core, but Lawrence needed therapy. Since no one with a Psych degree had survived, their unflappable leader used Kenyon as a sounding board. Sometimes for legitimate problems. Other times to discuss the complicated inner workings of his relationships with three of the women.

"Business, I think. He's with Fuller."

"Fuller?"

"Yeah, he debriefed him."

Kenyon groaned and stood.

Debriefing new arrivals was his job. Fuller had been in shock after his ordeal. Had all but passed out after giving Kenyon an overview of their cross-country journey. Should have waited a few days before making Fuller relive the details, but Lawrence was impatient, and he was a busy body. With no big breakthroughs on the science front, he was getting in other people's business.

Kenyon was already dressed. Was *always* dressed—always ready—unless he was showering. He picked up his sound-suppressed Alexander Arms .50 Beowulf. When it came to the size and weight of its rounds, the Beowulf was hard to beat, and its hollow point rounds created a wide wound channel. In layman's terms, it was like getting impaled by a five-foot-long rhino's horn—or whatever the hell rhinoceros had become. He gave Hutchins a nod and the pair set out on a ten-minute walk, through winding tunnels, up several flights of stairs, and then to the facility's core.

Lawrence had thought bringing Fuller to the massive, domed greenhouse at the center of the island would be a place the two of them could relax and talk. Probably never crossed his mind that Fuller had been fighting for his life, for months, surrounded by ExoGenetic crops. Last thing he'd want to do is have a chat in a greenhouse full of fruits and vegetables.

Of course, their crops weren't ExoGenetic. Like Ella's greenhouses, they only grew heirloom crops, which were harmless to eat.

Kenyon found Lawrence and Fuller seated in old chairs, on either side of a small table, sipping lemonade…in the dark.

"That was quick," Lawrence said on their arrival.

"Couldn't sleep," Kenyon said.

"That makes two of you." He motioned to Fuller, who was noshing on a carrot like their food wasn't carefully rationed.

"Why am I here?" Kenyon asked.

"Always straight to the point," Lawrence said, patting his lap. He was an older man, pushing sixty-five, with a trimmed white beard and spectacles that made his eyes large and intense. He could look like a friendly grandpa one moment and Charles Manson the next. "Well, Mr. Fuller here has something he'd like to tell you. Something you might have already known had you questioned him right away."

Kenyon ignored the dig and turned to Fuller, waiting.

"I—I... When we were on the boat. When... Leaving the city..." He swallowed, his leg bouncing now. "Before the...water... I...I looked back. Thought I, thought I h-heard something." He looked up and met Kenyon's gaze. "I-I saw her."

"Saw *who?*" Kenyon asked.

Fuller gripped his knee, stopped it from shaking.

Then he looked up at Kenyon again, and with the weight of the world on his shoulders, he said, "Ella Masse."

29

Lyn woke with a start but couldn't sit up. Everything hurt. The cancer was consuming her from the inside, and there was nothing she could do to slow it down. Even if the world hadn't fallen apart, at this point doctors would just try to manage the pain and wait for the end.

Her predictions had been off by months. She didn't blame herself for it. Life was a peculiar thing. Hard to give a date for when someone will arrive in this world, and when they will exit.

But it was clear her time was fast approaching.

She opened her eyes and saw nothing. For a moment, she feared she'd gone blind, but the view out the window was just a touch lighter than the absolute darkness of the apartment.

She listened for the others. It was night, so they might be asleep. She hadn't been able to take part in the day's excitement, but she'd heard it and been told the story. They'd be exhausted. Probably sleeping just a few feet away.

But she didn't hear any breathing. Didn't hear anything at all.

Aside from the couch supporting her, she felt like she'd awoken in a sensory deprivation tank.

She didn't like it. Felt too much like how she pictured the afterlife would, or the lack thereof. Infinite blackness. She hoped she was wrong about that. A white tunnel would be welcome, Bob waiting for her in the light. Until the curtain was lifted away from that mystery, or she simply ceased to be, she was stuck on the couch, in the dark. The idea of spending her last hours alone vexed her. She didn't want to wake the others, just to keep her company. That would be selfish. They needed their rest for what would come next.

She closed her eyes, which made no difference at all, and she tried to breathe.

It would be easier for everyone if I just drifted off right now.

In hindsight, she should have stayed in Hellhole. Been buried beside Bob. Let the women there care for her. She'd been a burden during the trip, always in danger, rarely useful. She thought she'd be able to help Ella end this mess, that she'd get the chance to give a parting gift to the world, but all she'd managed to do was put everyone in jeopardy.

She took two more deep breaths, letting them out slowly, attempting to contain her emotions.

Then reality washed over her, a merciless tidal wave that drew a hiccupping sob from her. She held a hand over her mouth, weeping into the couch cushion.

It's too much, she thought, waiting for death to take her. There had to be a better way.

The water. She could throw herself in and either drown or be killed by the monsters she'd been told about. It would be quick, and the others wouldn't have to worry about what to do with her body. She wasn't sure she could make the journey from the apartment to another where the windows were broken. Especially in the dark. She was more likely to trip, break a bone, and increase her pain until the end.

A slap and a grunt interrupted her malaise-fueled ruminations.

It repeated, strange and inhuman.

"Hello?" she said. "P-Peter? Ella?"

Slap, grunt.

It was getting closer.

"Peter! I think something is—"

"Peter not here. Ella not here. Anne not here."

The slap came again. Louder, just feet away. It was followed by the soft sound of a body collapsing into a chair and one last grunt.

"Feesa?"

"Not Feesa. Val."

"You sound like Feesa." Lyn wondered if one of Feesa's sisters had caught up to them and joined the group.

She grunted. "Val is Feesa's real name. I remember. Am Val now." She grunted again. "Val...is...my name."

Lyn was impressed. Sentence structure wasn't Feesa's strong suit, but she was making an obvious effort, at least when it came to her name.

"You've gone and changed your name while I was sleeping?"

"I did not change name," Val said. "I remember name. Remembered...self. I am Val...erie Wood. I was singer. Was famous."

Lyn rolled onto her side, facing Val though she could not see her. "You're shitting me."

Val huffed with quiet laughter. "You like Val's singing, too?"

"Loved it," Lyn said. "Still do."

"Maybe I sing for you. Voice changed, too."

Lyn felt her intellect waking up. The changes Val was describing were unprecedented among ExoGenetically altered humans. Memory retention was one of the first things to go when the change set in. It was part of what made Exos so dangerous. Even if you hurt them, they'd keep coming back for more, in part because they were driven by hunger and instinct, but also because they lacked the ability to remember the pain you'd inflicted just moments before.

But for her voice to have changed, that meant a physical change had occurred. A step forward in her evolutionary process, rather than back ward.

"Tell me, dear," Lyn said. "What else has changed?"

"Everything."

Lyn felt a gentle pressure on her arm as Val lifted it up. Then she felt smooth skin beneath her fingers. It was an arm. Val's arm. She ran her hand over the hairless limb, caught off guard by how soft it felt. That was when she realized she couldn't smell Val, either. She was clean.

"How much hair fell out?" Lyn asked.

"All of it," Val said, "and my skin is black. Also, big teeth fell out. Holes in face gone. Am beautiful now. No one else tell me that yet, but I know Jakob think so. And see?" She lifted Lyn's hand and placed it on her rolled up sleeve. "I wear clothes now because I naked without hair."

She's becoming more human, Lyn thought.

"What about the rest of you?" Lyn asked. "Your height. Your strength. Have you lost any of your beneficial attributes?" She realized her wording might have been too complex. Communicating with Val usually meant a reduction in syllables was required. So, she was surprised when the big woman answered.

"Things I don't like, go away. Things I do like, stay. Am still tall. Am still strong. But I no have hair, I soft, I beautiful, I can sing. And…and I am remembering self. Life. Family from before. I…I am not monster now. I am person, but…better." She huffed a laugh.

"Oh, I believe it," Lyn said. "You were better than most before."

Lyn grunted as her insides cramped.

"Lyn is in pain?" Val asked.

"Lyn is dying."

"Mmm… Dying is dumb." Then, as though just remembering, she added, "Val is in pain, too! My leg is missing."

"Missing?"

"Was bit. Was amp..u..tationed."

"Amputated. Heavens. I am sorry to hear that."

"It okay," Val said. "Not like dying. I Exo. Leg growing back."

"That quickly?"

"I think it happen fast because…because I want it. Like I want no hair. No be ugly. No tusk."

"You're suggesting that ExoGenetic change can be guided by personal desires…" It was outlandish, but here she was, hairless and calling herself Val.

"Some desire," Val said. "Some…what Ella call? Ext…extra–"

"External factors."

"Yes. That. But also what I learn from Peter, about controlling urge. To kill. To eat. The hunger. He taught me about will."

"Like will power?"

"Will power can overcome genes," he told me. "He wanted to teach how to control emotional self, but he also teach me how to control *whole* self. I forget to tell him that, though."

"Fascinating..." Lyn turned toward Val but couldn't see her any better now. "Where is Peter now? And Ella?"

"They go to island. But Jake is here. Well, Jake up high still. He keep watch on island. I keep watch on you."

"How are they traveling to the island?" Lyn was worried about how much she'd missed. Last she heard, the ocean was full of horrible creatures, one of which must have taken Val's leg.

Had they been found and taken to the island via helicopter?

"On little boat."

"They took the *kayaks?* The water is infested!"

Val grunted. "Peter think monsters no hunt at night. They go small and quiet on one kai-yak. Peter. Ella. Anne. Sneaky."

"And Jakob is..."

"What I said. Way up high."

"Can you take me to him?" Lyn asked.

"Is emergency?" Val asked. "One foot make climb harder and need both hands."

Lyn gave Val's arm a pat. "I'm dying, Val. There isn't time to waste."

"Mmm, me not know..."

"What if you could stop me from dying?" Lyn asked.

Val grunted. "Val takes Lyn to Jakob. Lyn...lives?"

"Maybe," Lyn said. She didn't think it would be right to lie. She was asking a lot of her large, wounded friend. Her proposal wasn't without risk to both of them, but in the still darkness before Val arrived, sobbing out her soul, Lyn realized that she was not ready to die. Not even close.

"Maybe is better than 'no?'"

"Much better," Lyn said. "If you're the one dying."

"Then we go. Take to Jakob. Save Lyn."

"Splendid," Lyn said, fighting the pain to stand up. She steadied herself for a moment, took a deep breath, and added, "And then the rest of this bullheaded family."

30

It took a lot of self-control for Anne to not sing *Row, Row, Row Your Boat* as they paddled out of the city and into the bay. She didn't like having nothing to do. Didn't like sitting still. Sure, she had a gun in her hand, and she was looking out for the mermaid douchebags of doom, but until they showed up, her job was basically to look around in the dark.

Which was dark.

And boring.

There weren't even stars to look at. Only reason they knew which way to go was because the ExoGen sign on the facility was lit up. Seemed like a stupid idea to her. Like broadcasting the fact that people were there. But Ella disagreed. Certain insects were drawn to light, but at night, animals avoided it. And most Exos weren't smart enough to understand the connection between light and people.

Anne's father was seated behind her. He was doing most of the work paddling. Her mother was in the front, helping occasionally, mostly adjusting their course. She didn't have as much experience on a kayak, and since even one thump of a paddle on the hull could be like ringing a dinner bell, Peter had insisted on being their primary method of propulsion. He didn't say it like that, but it was what he meant. There was a time when both Anne and Ella would have called him sexist, but he entrusted them with important tasks so often that he was clearly just making the best choices. Besides, who'd want to paddle across seven miles of wavy water, in the dark?

No one.

Except for Anne, whose leg was beginning to bounce. Too much time sitting still was hard for her.

She got ten bounces in before a gentle hand touched her shoulder.

Peter.

Telling her to hold still.

She gripped her leg with her hand, squeezing it tight.

She didn't like disappointing her father, especially in matters of life and death. He probably couldn't even see her in the dark, but he was so in tune with his surroundings that he felt her shaking.

'If I can feel it,' she imagined him saying, *'an Apex can, too.'*

Focus, she told herself, and she went back to scanning the void surrounding them.

Boredom reared its fidgety head ten seconds later. She ground her teeth and let her imagination provide the stimulation required to stay on task.

They were floating above hundreds of feet of water, filled with sharp-toothed, really ugly mermaids. She'd killed one, but she got lucky, and then was saved by Val. She was lucky to be alive, and she still felt tired from drowning—even if it was just for a few seconds. Peter didn't even need to do CPR, which was good, because all her ribs would be broken.

The water around them, which she could only hear, gently lapping between tides, teemed with mermaids. She pictured them swirling just beneath the surface. Hell, they could be right next to the kayak, looking up at her, watching.

When her heart started pounding, she realized her imagination might be a little too vivid to give it total freedom in this moment.

How did Peter focus so easily? He could just switch it on and off. She'd gotten better at it, thanks to him, mostly from mimicking him, but that was in stimulating circumstances. This was...

...still boring.

Like fishing, if you were the bait.

Maybe.

Being impaled by, and wrapped around, a hook was probably agonizing, but she doubted it was boring, Floating around in the water, writhing around, watching fish pick you apart until all that was left was a pale sliver of your former self, which was finally chomped on by a too small sunfish. The worm's last moments on Earth getting plucked from the fish's mouth, peeled off the hook and discarded while one of your brethren—Marge, or Stephen, or Jennifer—took your place.

Anne decided she didn't like fishing anymore.

Of course, now the fish ate *you.*

Her thoughts shifted to the creation of ExoGenetic creatures that she felt partially responsible for. She knew the feeling didn't belong to her. It was her mother's, but even Ella wasn't fully to blame. Yeah, the technology was hers, and ExoGen wouldn't have pulled it off without her, but Ella thought she was helping the world. Thought she was feeding people.

In a way she was feeding people—to each other.

But she'd never have been a part of it if she'd known the truth. It had been eating at Ella since the change and, as a result, it was a mental thorn in Anne's side as well. She closed her eyes for a moment, seeing the human genome in her thoughts, navigating it to RC-714 and then to everything it unlocked.

The totality of evolution, over 3.7 billion years' worth, locked away in every cell—every flake of skin and hair follicle.

But not in Anne. The door opened by RC-714 remained locked. All of that...potential locked away. She was glad she could eat anything, but there were times she wished she could be more than human.

A lot of times.

The real question, in Anne's mind, was what mental or biological process directed change in the bodies of ExoGenetic creatures? It boiled down to a desire to live. To thrive. And when that wasn't accomplished, the host DNA reached down into the scrabble bag of A, G, C, and T and found something that got the job done. But it wasn't through trial and error. The RC-714 didn't seem to make mistakes.

She wasn't sure how that was possible. Nature evolved over time through trial and error. Some adaptations failed over time, and those with the trait died out. It was a process of constant refinement.

But RC-714 doesn't have time for that. It adapted the first generation to its surroundings on the fly, and over time. It seemed...intelligent. Or at least guided by the intelligence of its host. That could have been why human Apexes were usually the worst to encounter. Others were big and freaky and violent, but they didn't normally have the mental capacity to strategize or work in packs.

There was something there, but Anne couldn't put her finger on it.

She wondered if her mother had. If she'd been holding out on them. Ella wanted the world to go back to how it had been, but Anne wasn't sure that was possible. Regular people were worms on hooks now.

If they didn't evolve or adapt at a pace faster than evolution could manage, Homo sapiens would follow the path of Neanderthals, Homo erectus, and Homo habilis. Not short and hairy. Extinct.

A gentle touch on her shoulder pulled her from her thoughts.

She hadn't moved. She was sure of it.

Then Peter leaned forward, his head beside her ear, whispering. "You're up."

Anne blinked. All she could see was darkness, but they weren't moving anymore. She could tell because the breeze of forward momentum had faded. She could hear waves lapping against rocks, not far away. The plan was ten feet, but how could Peter judge the distance in the dark?

She decided to trust him, holstered her pistol, and took hold of the rope beside her. Then she slowly lowered herself over the side of the kayak. She felt relief when her feet touched down on a sandy bottom. In chest deep water, she guided the kayak closer to shore, trying not to think about what might be lurking in the dark. She'd argued against this part of the plan. Didn't want to go in the ocean ever again, but Peter said they couldn't risk the kayak bumping into a rock, and some of their weapons needed to stay dry.

So here she was, in the water, guiding the small boat to shore, around a maze of rocks, until she stepped onto a small patch of sand and the kayak slid to a silent stop. Her parents joined her, carrying their gear.

Peter divided up their weapons, judging what was what by feel. Then he patted them each on the shoulder. She wanted to ask how he was seeing them, but she knew he couldn't. He just had a really good sense of his place in the world, and those around him. Like he could feel pressure changes in the air. Maybe he could smell them. Feel the shift of their weight in the sand under his feet. Could hear them breathing. Probably all of it. And he'd say she could do it too, if she just focused hard enough, if her will was strong enough.

Strength of will. That was what Dad credited his survival to.

Apparently, it was strong enough to keep all of them alive.

And they were about to put it to the test again.

They were pretty good at fighting Exos. Even the Apex ones. But people? With guns? That was different. Not just because they could shoot back, but because they were people, and killing people felt different.

But she'd do it, without hesitation, if it came down to it.

The math was easy—a human life versus all human existence. If they survived this, there'd be statues of them in future human cities. If they failed, well, there wouldn't be cities.

Anne followed the plan, hooking two fingers around her father's back belt loop. Ella placed a hand on her shoulder. Peter led them like a little train, blind leading the blind, for five minutes. Then he stopped, turned around and crouched. "I think we're close, but we're not going to find it, or open it, without light."

Anne understood that. Knew every step of the plan. Because she'd helped develop it over the past several months. They'd gathered information about George's Island from libraries along the way and had put together a notebook full of photos, diagrams, and descriptions. There was an old metal door on the shore, above the tideline. Once upon a time, a dock extended from it, allowing prisoners, or soldiers, or whoever was occupying the ancient fort to unload cargo directly to the underground storage rooms. It hadn't been used in a hundred years. Their hope was that it was so old and insignificant that it would have been overlooked by ExoGen, and so rusted that it would look like just another rock formation.

Peter's red light winked to life, aimed into his palm. In the absolute darkness it felt like a beacon that would be visible even to Jakob. But it was quite dull and muted by Peter's hand. More than that, they were surrounded by a wall of tall stones. Anyone on the island would have to be standing on the edge of a twenty-foot drop, staring straight down to see them.

Peter peeled his hand away from the light, revealing the island's rock wall—and the horrific snarling face of a mermaid.

31

"Where are you?" Jakob asked, scanning the water below for some sign of his father, Anne, and Ella. He'd tried everything to find them, including using night vision goggles to look through his binoculars. Didn't work well. His father was too good at being invisible.

Or they'd been set upon the moment they left the city behind and were already dead. There was no way to know. The night was impenetrable. With the heavy cloud cover, the only thing visible was the top of George's Island, thanks to the light provided by the ExoGen sign.

He couldn't think of a good reason they'd leave the lights on. Sure, they might be able to see some intruders on the island, but it could attract Apexes...

The truth settled on Jakob with the crushing pressure of miles-deep water. The lights were on to protect them against a predator more dangerous than an Apex—his father.

Kenyon was on the island, and that meant they were prepared for the eventuality that Peter and Ella would try to infiltrate.

Are they paddling toward a trap? he wondered. *Or are the mermaids the trap?*

He wanted to contact them via radio but resisted. It would be a quick way of getting them all killed. Peter wanted him to remain radio silent until the next night. If they hadn't returned by then, Jakob could reach out if he wanted to, but he needed to be ready to run when he did. If his father and the others had been killed or captured, calling on the radio would put Jakob and Val in ExoGen's crosshairs.

But not Lyn, Jakob thought with a frown. They'd explained the situation before setting out. Val was missing a leg. Lyn was asleep and dying. And Jakob was stuck alone in a dark penthouse, six hundred feet up, with no way down. He had enough food for a few days, if he rationed it well. The water would last a lot longer. But he wasn't getting down without Val, and who knew how long it would take her to regrow a limb.

She healed faster than a person, but a missing limb? Ella seemed to think it would, or at least *could* grow back, but Jakob couldn't count on 'could.' When the sun rose on the horizon, he'd figure out how far down he could go, and then find a way to slide the rest of the way down.

He didn't like being stuck.

Felt a bit like a princess in a tower, just waiting to be rescued. It was embarrassing and not a part of his adventures he'd be regaling Alia with when he saw her again. Anne might, though, and that was enough to drive him to find a way out of this mess.

Until then, he watched, waiting for some sign that his family was still alive.

Pacing in the darkness became dizzying. His whole world, inside and outside the apartment—other than the ExoGen sign—was a black void. He wanted to put on a flashlight or even just light a candle, but in this all-consuming darkness, it would shine like a beacon, visible to anyone on the island that might look in his direction. And if he was discovered, the others would be, too.

"This sucks," he said to himself, finding the couch in the dark and sitting down. He remembered the days of endless entertainment. Of TV, movies, video games, and friends. What he wouldn't give for a handheld game system. Or a working DVD player. A bag of microwave popcorn. Some Cherry Pepsi.

He shifted mental gears when he began to salivate.

Dwelling on the past, and the comforts it provided, was torture. Even in a best-case scenario for the future of humanity, life would never be what it once was. The remnants of modern society would crumble with no one around to maintain them. In his lifetime, existence would slowly degrade to a primal state of living, until the population recovered, and the skills developed over the past few thousand years were relearned and put to work once more.

Even if ExoGen was stopped, they'd already managed to hit the pause button on human development.

Jakob leaned his head back and closed his eyes, which didn't change the view, but let him relax. He felt sleep's grasp on him just a moment later, resisted it for a few seconds, and then gave in.

He jolted and gasped.

He'd heard something but couldn't quite remember what.

Was it part of a dream? He didn't remember a dream.

But I was definitely asleep, he thought, aggravated with himself for not keeping watch through the night. Then again, he had no concept of how much time had passed. Might have been just a minute since he'd leaned his head back. Or hours.

The sound repeated, a familiar metallic jangling.

Jakob wished he was still sleeping. Because he knew the sound. The elevator's cables were shaking. Something was climbing up.

Ella seemed certain that the mer-things couldn't breathe on the surface, and they would probably take a few days to adapt lungs again. But that didn't mean another monster hadn't been attracted to the scene and was now following his scent trail to the penthouse.

He fumbled in the dark for his MP5. Smacked the barrel with his hand, knocking the weapon to the floor. He dropped to his knees in the dark, searching until his hand touched cold metal again. He found the handle, picked it up, and noticed his hand was shaking.

"Chill out," he told himself. "Focus up. You've been alone before."

But not like this, he thought. There was no chance of help arriving, and he was at a severe disadvantage. Most Apexes could see in the dark. As far as adaptations went, it was very common. But Jakob couldn't see shit.

So, I'll listen, he decided. *I'll wait for it to get so close I can't miss. That's what Dad would do. Stay calm. Wait for the right moment. And then strike in a way that doesn't leave the outcome in doubt.* That meant draining his magazine and loading the next while he listened for a body hitting the floor. If he didn't hear it, he'd spray an arc of bullets guaranteed to hit whatever was in the penthouse with him.

He crouched atop the sofa, leaned against the back, and aimed his weapon into the hallway, where the elevator doors were. At least, where he thought they were. He might shoot up the wall instead, but he could adjust his aim, using the muzzle flash to see by.

He hoped no one on the island would see the burst of light. It would be dulled by the weapon's suppressor but could be noticeable if someone was watching.

Keep it short, he told himself.

Get the job done fast.

The rattling grew louder, and then stopped. Right at the penthouse doors. Definitely here for him.

He listened as the doors slid open.

There was a grunt, a hiss, and then the sound of feet on hard tile floor.

Jakob pulled the trigger.

Staccato light lit the penthouse, revealing the living room, which Jakob was shooting to pieces, and the hallway where Lyn crouched, hands over her head, shouting, "Don't shoot! It's us!"

Jakob took his finger off the trigger just as his weapon swiveled into the hallway. A moment later Lyn would be dead. Panicked that he'd hurt someone, Jakob removed a small flashlight from his pocket, threw caution out the window, and flicked it on.

When he saw that Lyn was unharmed, anger overpowered relief. "What the hell? I could have killed you! How did you even get up here?"

"So many questions," Lyn said with a sigh, picking herself up.

Behind her, Val swung out of the elevator shaft, landing on one foot. He couldn't see her injured limb because she had her knee bent, probably to avoid smacking the raw stump on something.

"Seriously," Jakob said. "I could have killed you."

"Me sorry, Jake," Val said, hopping around and closing the doors behind her. "Lyn had idea to save her life."

"But I need your help," Lyn said. "In case things go wrong."

"I'm not sure what any of us can do, in a penthouse, to help with your cancer."

"Mm," Lyn said. "That's what I thought, too. But now...now I'm not so sure. What I *do* know is that I don't want to die. Not yet. So, I'm willing to take a risk."

Jakob squinted. Risks were not something Peter taught them to take unless they were out of options...which, he supposed, was Lyn's situation. "What kind of risk?"

"This kind," Lyn said, holding out a package of instant oatmeal taken from her pocket. She gave it a shake. "Banana nut. I've been saving this for years."

"What are you going to do with that?"

Lyn waved him over. "Help me to a seat."

Jakob got under Lyn's arm and was surprised by how much of her weight she gave to him. She could barely walk. Behind them, Val hopped in the dark. When they reached the couch, he helped ease Lyn down. Then he dimmed the light with his hand and stood with his back to the window.

"Now," Jakob said, pointing to the oats. "What do you think you're doing with that?"

Lyn smiled. "Oh, you already sound so much like your father." She held up the package. "If I'm right, it'll be a breakthrough. If I'm wrong, it will be my last supper."

"Last supper?" Jakob said, eyeing the oats. "You can't—"

Lyn tore open the package and poured most of it into her mouth. She followed it up with a swig of water from her canteen. She slowly chewed and crunched, never breaking eye contact with Jakob. Then she swallowed, licked her lips, and smiled. "Would have let it soak for a bit, but you'd have stopped me."

Jakob was dumbfounded. Didn't know what to say, and it was too late to do anything about it. She'd already eaten the oats. Lyn...was dead. Then again, she was already on her way out. So why turn herself into—

His eyes widened. "You want to become an Exo? To cure your cancer."

She lifted her eyebrows twice and poured some more oats into her mouth.

"But...what if—"

"I become a raging, bloodthirsty monster?" Lyn finished. "Let's hope it doesn't happen. But if it does...I want you to kill me."

32

Peter put two sound suppressed rounds in the monster's forehead. Anne put two in its chest. He was pleased with their reaction time and aim, but they'd wasted four rounds. The mermaid was already dead, twisted into a gnarled rigor of pain that was easily mistaken for rage...

Because it was ugly.

Really ugly.

That didn't stop Ella from crouching down beside it, performing a quick medical exam, and whispering her findings. "Definitely started as human. The upper torso's musculature and bone structure haven't changed all that much. But the gills. The long needle teeth. The tail. All adapted for life in the water. But..." She moved up and down the creature's torso, searching for something.

"Ella," Peter whispered. "We're exposed here."

She ignored him, shaking her head, continuing the search.

He placed a gentle hand on her shoulder. "Ella."

She gave a nod and stood, abandoning her search.

Peter led the way again, creeping to the rock ledge and following it along the coast. Hidden by the twenty-foot rise, he uncapped his red light again and let its hellish glare guide them through the jumble of large slippery stones. It was a short but precarious journey that would have been longer if not for Anne's keen eye.

"There," she said, overtaking him and scrambling toward a slab of rough brown that looked just like another rock, until you got close. Its flat surface and flaking rust revealed it to be manmade, ancient, and crumbling. Unfortunately, the once massive door was blocked by a pile of large rocks, some of which Peter wouldn't be able to lift. This was how they sealed the door, way back when, before the age of welding torches. It was a problem, but he wasn't close to giving up.

Not remotely.

Peter pressed against the exposed metal.

His finger indented it. He dug in and pulled a flakey layer of metal free. The salty ocean air and surging tides had done their work over the decades, turning the solid metal into something more closely resembling a puff pastry.

He lifted several thirty-pound stones aside, clearing a larger section of the door's top. He didn't need much more than that because there was no way in hell this door was actually going to open.

The swollen metal was lodged tight. But it was also fragile.

"How are we going to get through there without making much noise?" Ella asked.

"Won't be loud," Anne said, hefting a large stone and hurling it at the door. It punched through the metal with a dull thud. Then it landed with a distant sploosh. There was water inside the tunnel.

Encouraged by how easily the door came apart, Peter started shoving the metal. It felt like when he was a kid, pushing snow out of a tunnel he'd just dug. Didn't take much, and within a minute, the hole was big enough to crawl through.

He looked at Anne. "You're on point."

Her face lit up, and then sank with a realization. "What if there are rats?"

"Don't shoot them," Peter said, and then he realized what she already had—if there were rats, they'd be Exos. "Scratch that. Shoot them or come right back out."

She gave a brave nod and scrambled up the stones to the hole.

"Why is she going first?" Ella asked.

Peter wasn't thrilled about all the conversation but down at the bottom of a cliff, with the waves lapping against the stones, hearing them would be impossible for anyone above.

Should be.

Some things have really big ears these days.

"Because she can get out quickly, if she needs to, and it's far more likely—while we're exposed—that a threat will come from behind."

"Duh," Anne added and slid easily through the hole. After a moment, there was a click and the tunnel beyond filled with light. Then Anne's hand extended up from the entrance and gave a thumbs up.

Ella entered next, followed by Peter, who had to remove the shotgun from his back to fit. The tunnel reeked of mildew, stale seawater, and shit that had been languishing since the Civil War, but it was free of rats, or anything else that might want to eat them. The arched stone walls and ceiling looked solid enough, built during a time when things were made to last. There was a foot of water on the floor that sloshed when they walked, but all things considered, everything had gone according to plan.

He knew it wouldn't last.

No plan ever survived contact with the enemy.

Especially when that enemy could adapt to whatever you threw at them. Luckily, ExoGen was made up of fallible human beings who were prone to overconfidence and exhaustion, both of which led to mistakes. The weakest link in any military or security force wasn't the hardware, it was the people using it.

"Lights out," Peter had seen enough of the tunnel ahead to know it was straight for a long time.

Ella looked displeased. "How are we supposed to—"

"Hand on the wall," Anne said, before demonstrating. Hand against the slimy stone surface, she closed her eyes and walked ahead. "Blind people do it all the time. Well, they used to. Probably aren't any blind people left alive."

"Anne," Ella chided. "That's morbid."

"I didn't mean they were all killed," Anne said. "I meant that they probably turned into horrible monsters that could see and ate their neighbors." She smiled at her mother. "See, not morbid at all."

With that, Anne closed her eyes again and started down the tunnel.

Ella grimaced and placed her hand against the wall. Peter gave her an encouraging nod and then turned out the light.

Peter thought he'd experienced pitch darkness before, but nothing compared to the absolute darkness of the underground tunnel beneath George's Island. It had a weight to it. Like it was alive and consuming their souls. Maybe some vestige of the fort's past still hung in the air. The desperation of prisoners.

The pressure increased as they pressed on. Every slosh through the water echoed around them. A silent approach was impossible. But he was confident no one would be guarding this tunnel. It would be a waste of manpower, and the subterranean tunnel system beneath the old fort was a maze.

"Stop," Anne whispered.

Peter froze in place. "What is it?"

"Laser ahead," she said.

Peter found Ella with his hand and stepped around her.

He moved up the wall until finding Anne fifteen feet ahead. She'd been moving a little faster and was able to see what he hadn't from behind. A faint red spot on the wall, nearly impossible to see, since it was positioned behind a protruding stone block.

"A trip wire under the water, tied to a grenade would have been better, don't you think?" Anne asked.

"That would be effective," Peter said, "but when you have money to spend..." He leaned down and huffed air from his lungs toward the laser. His breath fogged in the chilly air, revealing the beam, four feet from the floor. Short of an Oompa Loompa spec ops team, it would catch anyone, human or Apex, coming down the tunnel. "A grenade might not kill everyone. Best guess, this laser would trigger enough C4 to bring everything down and seal the tunnel. That's what I would do, anyway."

"So, let's avoid it," Ella said.

"Just need to get a little wet," he said, dropping to his hands and knees, putting him a foot lower than the beam. He crawled forward slowly, shuffling his hands and knees over the floor, careful not to lift his head. He did that for a full ten feet, until there was no doubt that he'd cleared the trap. Then the others followed.

Dripping wet, and getting colder by the minute, Peter decided to take the lead and pick up the pace.

Trouble was, the tunnel started to bend—down. Every few steps, the water rose an inch. Wasn't long before he was standing in waist-deep water, which meant it was up to Anne's chest.

"Hey," he said, reaching back for her, fumbling until he found her. "C'mere." He hoisted her up out of the water, holding her on his hip while holding his M4 with one hand. This worked for a few minutes—until the water rose even further.

"Peter," Ella said. "We might need to rethink this."

He hated to agree. This was their best chance at getting inside the facility undetected. But the water and cold were becoming an insurmountable problem, and he suspected Ella had come to the same conclusion he had.

"Might as well turn on the light," Anne said, revealing she'd figured out the situation as well. "Not like anyone is going to see it."

"Go ahead," Peter said.

Anne dug into a pocket and a moment later, her small flashlight illuminated the tunnel and the path ahead. Thirty feet farther, the tunnel was flooded right to the ceiling.

"Well," Anne said. "Fuck."

33

Ella let the language go. She had grown accustomed to her daughter's penchant for using four letter words, and admired the girl's conclusion that bad words were only bad because society said so, and right now there was no society. But mostly, Anne's summation of the situation was spot on.

"Now what?" Ella asked.

Peter glanced at Anne in that knowing way she always seemed to understand.

Anne shook her head. "No way. Uh-uh. I try to limit my near drowning experiences to once per day."

"Wouldn't ask you to do this." He slid through the water, back to Ella and handed Anne over. It had been a while since Ella had held her daughter like this. She was a lot heavier now.

Peter dug a tightly wound ball of climbing rope from his backpack. He unspooled a length, handed the wad of rope to Anne and then tied it around his waist.

"You're not..." Ella said.

"Only way forward is...forward. Going back means kicking in the door and shooting it out with a security team of unknown size, without Val backing us up. Odds are better down here." He cinched the rope tight. "If the rope goes slack for more than a few seconds, haul me back and do what you can. If I don't make it...abort."

"And if it doesn't go slack?" Ella asked.

"When I make it to the other side, I'll tug on the rope two times. Tie the rope to Anne. I'll pull her through." He placed his hand on Anne's cheek. "You'll move faster than anyone can swim." He turned back to Ella. "Let the slack out as she goes. When you feel two more tugs, tie yourself off, and I'll pull you through."

Ella didn't like the plan at all. The logic was sound. If Peter could clear the distance without help, it stood to reason that they'd be able to clear it with him pulling them along, doubling their speed. But Peter could hold his breath a long time. Even before he joined the military. She used to time him when they were younger, in his family's pool. He would try to impress her with handstands and dives, but nothing impressed her more than how he could just sit beneath the water for minutes.

"Good?" he asked, facing them both.

"Good," Anne said, doing her best to look and sound brave, but falling just short.

"Trust me," he told her, kissing her forehead. "Both of you." He kissed Ella on the lips, a gentle goodbye, just in case, which meant Peter wasn't that sure about his plan, either. Then he slid deeper into the water, took three quick breaths to saturate his lungs with oxygen, and slid beneath the surface, which then billowed blood red from his light.

They watched the light fade into the distance and then disappear altogether.

While Anne held the bundle of rope between two fingers, letting it unwind, Ella held the line, letting it slide between the fingers of her free hand. As long as it kept moving, Peter was alive. But if it moved too long, the distance might be insurmountable for her and Anne, even with Peter pulling from the other end.

"Scale of one to ten," Anne asked, "how dumb is this?"

"We were at ten when we got in the kayak," Ella said.

"So, like twenty?"

"At least."

"Whole world is a twenty, though," Anne said. "Even if we get through here, and find a cure for you guys, all that really changes is that you all don't have to worry about food, right?"

"Us and everyone else we can reach," Ella said. "Recovery is going to take time."

"Longer than I'll live," Anne said.

Ella didn't need to nod. They came to the same conclusions on such things because they shared the same knowledge and memories of Ella's life experience.

"So, I'll never get to go to a movie. Or like, date a guy without carrying an assault rifle. Or, I don't know, swim in a river without worrying about being eaten."

"All true," Ella said, "but those were only part of the human experience for the past hundred years. Movies. Electricity. Living without fear of man-eating predators. Those are all modern experiences and weren't even shared by everyone on the planet. Life, now, will be more in line with all of human history than the recent past was. Try to see it like that. Getting back to our roots."

"Or getting eaten."

Ella grinned. "Hey, plenty of our ancestors were eaten."

That got a laugh out of Anne, which felt good. Her daughter rarely found her funny, in part because that was how mothers and daughters could be, but also because their shared memories made most of what Ella said predictable to Anne. Catching her off guard was difficult.

"Umm," Anne said, looking at the bundle or rope between her hands. "This isn't really moving anymore."

Ella focused on the rope in her hand. There was a slight jerking motion, but it definitely wasn't moving forward.

He's drowning...

"Get on my back!" Ella shouted, moving Anne around into a piggyback position. While Anne clung to her, Ella hauled the rope back. One, two, three pulls. His weight seemed to increase with each tug. Then he wasn't moving at all.

He's stuck on something!

Ella wrapped the line around her arms several times to prevent it from slipping. Then she held on with both hands, leaned back, and put everything she had into it. She fought with the rope, grunting and shaking, hauling with all her strength.

Then the rope pulled back.

At first it was just a tug. And she waited for one more. Maybe Peter had made it after all? Maybe he was on his feet and ready to pull?

The line snapped tight, pulled on her wrist, and launched her and Anne into the water with the acceleration of a speedboat yanking a water skier from a dock.

Ella's instinct was to let go, surface, and take the breath she didn't get a chance to before she was pulled under. But Anne's preference was made clear when she held on tight, latching to her mother's back. She was in for the ride, because Peter was in trouble, the bait on a hook, taken by something large. They might be his only chance at survival—if they ever reached the other side.

Lungs already burning, Ella kept her hands wrapped around the line. It was beginning to slip through her grasp while tightening around her arm, cutting off circulation and scraping away a spiral of skin. When the pain became intense, she let out an errant scream, expelling the last of the air from her lungs.

Anne must have heard the bubbly cry, because she held on tighter, encouraging her mother to stay the course, despite the pain, despite the unknown, and the looming threat of unconsciousness.

Ella was freezing. Her vision black. There would be no tangible sign of losing consciousness before she faded away. Aside from drowning, of course. No one could hold their breath until they passed out. It was biologically impossible. So, at that very last moment, when her body's demand for air overrode her mind's control, she would fill her lungs with water. Then lose consciousness. And soon after, die.

At least my arm is bound, she thought, lungs screaming. Anne could hold her breath longer than Ella. Might have managed to catch a breath before they were pulled under, too. She'd be pulled along for what—another minute? It might be far enough...

It might be...

Ella's mouth opened. She fought the urge to breathe even as water surged between her cheeks. Fighting against her own instincts, she forced her mouth shut, compressed her cheeks, and expelled the water out. It was a momentary victory. One second longer of life.

But a second was all she needed.

Her head broke the water's surface. She coughed and heaved air three times before she could think straight. She whirled around, lifting Anne up, ensuring that the girl was above water and breathing.

She was. Calmly. But the expression on her face was sour.

"We're moving to Arizona. I'm sick of water."

Ella smiled, but it didn't last.

The line had gone slack. Peter was…what? Gone? Eaten?

She took hold of Anne's hand, planted her feet on the floor, and heaved her way through the water. The level dropped quickly as they walked up a steep grade.

Ella's legs wobbled beneath her as she stepped out of the water. She had to run, but she barely felt like she could walk. Anne, on the other hand, was still on task. She drew her pistol, leveled the flashlight next to the barrel, and searched the tunnel for threats.

"Here," she said, aiming the flashlight toward the old stone tunnel floor. A tangle of rope laid limp. "Stay close. Weapons hot."

Anne led the way and Ella followed without debate. Her daughter was a fighter. Trained by the best. She trusted Anne's instincts, and both of them wanted to find Peter alive.

They trudged uphill, pausing when the line tied to Peter stopped at a frayed broken end, lying in a pool of dark red blood.

Peter was gone.

34

"How long does this take?" Jakob slapped a card down on the bed. Val did the same and then took both. They were in the master bedroom, which was lit by a flashlight. Val had found a deck of cards and had insisted on playing War, a game from her childhood which she had suddenly remembered.

Since Jakob couldn't see anything on the island or do anything to help, he agreed to the distraction. Lyn was in the other bedroom, the door locked and barricaded from the outside. If she went Apex on them, the obstacle would slow her down enough to...

...to shoot her.

How was he going to explain this to his father?

Lyn hadn't given him much of a choice. But shooting her? In the head?

It made Jakob sick to his stomach. At first, he thought his father might be angry or disappointed in him, but the more he considered the man's reaction, the more he realized his father would be proud. Because there was no other choice. It would be the right thing to do. Lyn wouldn't want to be an Apex. Wouldn't want to kill people.

But she also didn't want to die. So, she took a risk. She'd live, or Jakob would kill her.

Or, the cancer would do her in first. For all Jakob knew, she was lying in the other room, dead already.

"Jake," Val said. "Put card down."

"Right. Sorry." He put down the ten of diamonds.

Val placed the five of spades.

Jakob just stared at the two cards.

Val sighed. "Jakey-boy is distracted."

He smiled. "Good word."

Val counted the syllables as she said, "Dis-trac-ted. Three sibels."

Jakob nodded. "You're beating me at War. Next, you'll be able to write better than me."

"You...write?"

"Yeah, like pen and paper." He pantomimed writing. "Words on paper."

"I wrote songs."

He smiled. "Great songs."

"What you write?"

"Letters, I guess. To Alia. It's more like a journal, though. So, I can tell her about everything we've done without having to remember it all."

"Remembering is hard."

"Sure is," he said. "Especially when every day is basically a fight for survival. They kind of blend after a while, huh?"

Val nodded. "Lots of fights." She looked up at Jakob. "I see letters?"

Jakob pulled a small notebook wrapped in a sealed Ziploc bag from his back pocket. He peeled it open and said, "In case it gets wet." Then he handed the notebook to Val.

The small journal was intended for Alia. As such, it was also full of teenaged pining he didn't want anyone but Alia to read. Thankfully, Val couldn't read.

Jakob collected the two cards and flipped over his next. The queen of hearts.

Without looking away from the journal, Val flipped over her next card. King of spades. She swept both cards into her pile and flipped over her next.

Jakob squinted. What... He looked at her eyes. They flicked back and forth, down, down, down the page. Then she turned it. "This is very sweet, Jakey-boy."

Hand like a striking cobra, Jakob snatched the journal away. "You can read?"

Val shrugged. "I know the words. That reading?"

Jakob threw his hands up and fell back on the bed. "*Yes,* that's reading! Man, I'd never have let you—"

"It okay, Jake. Your words are very nice. Alia is lucky girl."

"She probably already has a new boyfriend."

Val scoffed. "No boys in Hellhole. Feel good, Jakey. She has no choice, but you."

She huffed a short laugh, getting a big kick out of his melancholy.

He tried to hide his smile and wallow in teenage angst for a moment, but it was impossible.

Val snatched the journal back. "Page about my boobs in book?" She flipped through the pages.

"Hey!" Jakob said, laughing and reaching for the journal. "No, I didn't write about your damn perky boobs!"

Val dropped her jaw open. Looked down at her chest. "Perky boobs?"

Jakob caught hold of the journal and retreated with it, quickly securing it in the bag and tucking it into his pocket.

When he looked up, Val was cupping her breasts, hefting them up and down. "Is perky good?"

"Oh god," Jakob said, averting his eyes. "I'm a teenager, how am I supposed to know?"

In the silence that followed, Jakob glanced at Val, who had one eyebrow raised and a knowing smile on her face. "You are...teenage boy. Makes you expert...on boobs."

"Ugh," Jakob said. "Fine. Yes, perky is good. You happy no—"

A thump interrupted. It was muffled and distant. Didn't carry the weight of urgency, but it came from Lyn's direction.

"What did that sound like to you?" Jakob asked. Val's hearing was far more sensitive than his.

Val closed her eyes for a moment. Lifted her hands and placed them on an imaginary surface. "Shhh." She moved her hands to the side with the sound. Then adjusted so she was standing beside the bed, hands on the blanket. She made the sound again, "Shhh" sliding her hands over the blanket and then over the side, slapping down to the floor. "Thump."

"She fell off the bed?"

"If that is what falling off bed sounds like," Val said.

Jakob got to his feet. Started pacing. "Should we go in there? I mean, what if she's hurt?"

"Probably dead," Val said.

"Can you hear her at all now?" he asked.

Val shook her head. "No sound."

"Not like her heartbeat or something?"

Val scrunched up her face. "From here? I have good ears. Not super ears."

"Well," he said, hands on his head. "We should get closer, then."

"But not inside room," Val said. "Inside room is dangerous."

"Right. Right. We'll just stand outside the door, okay? You can listen. You can—"

Val stood and took Jakob by the shoulders. "Breathe. Slow down. Val and Jakob are okay. Deep breath. *Deeep* breath."

Jakob did as he was told and felt his panic wane some.

"Besides," Val said with a shrug, "Lyn is old. Was going to die soon anyway. If she dead, it not our fault, and it just...the world. Death...is part of life, ease through the pain, let go the strife."

Jakob laughed.

"I say something stupid?" Val asked.

"No. Not at all. What you said about death and life? Those are lyrics, from one of your songs."

That made her happy, until Jakob added. "Didn't care for it much, though."

She gently slugged his shoulder, but it hurt more than he'd admit.

Val waved for him to follow her to the door. "Let's go listen to dead Lyn."

When she exited, he rubbed his shoulder and rotated his arm. "Oww..." He fumbled through the dark, following the sound of Val's thumping movement on the tile floor.

"Here," Val said. "Here."

"I can't see you," Jakob whispered. He flinched when she took hold of his arm and guided him through the dark, then stopped him. "You hear?"

"I don't hear anything."

"Heartbeat, like you said."

"You can really hear that? Can you hear mine?"

She was quiet for a moment. "Uhh."

"Uhh, what?" he asked. "What does 'uhh' mean?"

"Lyn's heartbeat louder than Jake's heartbeat."

"*Louder?* What does louder mean?"

"Maybe...bigger?"

"Bigger," he said. "And stronger. Val, she's changing. Becoming an Exo."

"That was plan," she said, and then more hopeful, she asked, "Plan is working?"

"I—I don't know. Can you hear anything else?"

In the silence that followed, Jakob doubted every decision he and Val had made since she and Lyn had climbed up into the penthouse.

"Scratching..." Val said. "...something tearing...and dripping."

"That's enough. I get the idea." Lyn was changing. Becoming a monster.

Jakob slid his MP5 from his back to his hands.

But he had no idea where to aim it.

There was a major flaw with their plan.

Jakob couldn't see in the dark.

"We need light," he said.

"I see fine," Val said.

"Not for you. For me. I need to see."

"Why you need see?"

He sighed. Didn't want to say it aloud. "So...so I can shoot her."

A loud thump punctuated the sentence.

"I'll get my flashlight from the bedroom," he said, kicking himself for not remembering to bring it. Fumbling through the dark, he found the door, then the bed, and finally, the flashlight. He flicked it back on, illuminating the room and the figure standing directly across from him. The very human scream that erupted from his mouth coincided with an inhuman shriek from Lyn, followed by the sound of cracking wood and a roar from Val.

35

"Hurry up!" Anne hissed at her mother, who wasn't really moving slowly. Anne just didn't know how else to express her frustration about the limitations of her small body. She was running as fast as she could, but the uphill grade stole her energy, and the slippery stone floor made each step forward a half step back.

Ella didn't reply. She just kept moving, same as Anne. Their feelings about Peter weren't the same but were equally intense. If he were to die, not only would the mission be compromised, but they'd both be crushed. Maybe enough to just give up. Let the human race go the way of the Dodo.

"Fuck this slippery god-damn floor," Anne said, and she promptly slipped, landing hard on her elbows.

The pain and desperation drew tears to her eyes.

She was about to pound the floor in frustration, but when she lifted her hand, the slick floor clung to her arm. Tendrils of clear goo stretched out like pizza cheese, snapping as she pulled the arm higher.

"Up," her mother said, grabbing hold of her body armor and hauling her back to her feet.

Anne held a hand up to her mother. "It's not water." She separated her fingers, letting the goop stretch between them. "On the floor. It's some kind of slime. Like an excretion."

Ella nodded and urged Anne onward.

They found the top of the rise twenty feet higher. On level ground, the slippery footing was manageable, but the tunnel evened out for just a few feet before descending again. It was like an underground roller coaster. Anne couldn't figure out if the men who'd dug the tunnels had been addicted to opium or if the island's topography had shifted things around.

She discarded both theories when she thought of a third. Much of the island, like most of New England, was solid granite. It was hard to break apart. So, they'd followed the path of least resistance. Up, down, left, right, left, right. All they'd cared about was getting from point B to point A without having to start hand chiseling granite.

Ella stood beside her, looking down into darkness. Anne's flashlight did little to reveal the path ahead. What it did show was a continuing layer of slime covering the floors, walls, and ceiling. Whatever created it either filled the tunnel or was spraying the stuff like a hippo with explosive diarrhea.

"Path of least resistance," she said, glancing back at her mother.

"Wait, Anne, don't—"

There was no time to waste debating the safety of what needed to be done. Action was the only thing that would help Peter.

Moving down the tunnel was much easier than up. Anne managed to stay upright as her feet slid over the stone. She shifted her body sideways, like she was riding a skateboard, and she aimed her weapon down into the tunnel ahead, flashlight illuminating her path.

Behind her, Ella yelped as she followed, staying on her feet, but far less agile. Her mom was fit. A fighter. A survivor. But she wasn't exactly an athlete.

Over the sounds of her feet carving a path through the gel, Anne heard a sound echo up from below. A kind of gurgling, viscous motion, like a pair of hands working eggs into ground beef.

They were closing in.

"Get ready!" Anne shouted.

"Ready for what?" her mother replied.

"I don't know! For anything!"

And then 'anything' emerged from the dark, caught in the dim illumination of Anne's flashlight. At first, it was like a mirage. A shimmering surface, like a vertical wall of water. But then it undulated.

It was alive.

Anne pulled her trigger three times.

The bullets punched into the rippling translucent flesh, carving three paths before deflecting in multiple directions, like cracks in ice. The creature didn't flinch. Didn't burst. She'd hoped it was like a balloon, but it was more like a...

"Jellyfish!" she shouted. "It's an Exo-Jellyfish!

She saw it clearly now, as she slid closer, the pattern of veiny lines through its surging flesh. The creature's wiry tendrils snaking back up the wall, and at its center, Peter, struggling to escape, locked in place without air to breathe.

Anne acted with a combination of desperation, knowledge, and muscle memory that was not her own. She holstered her gun, unclipped two flashbang grenades from her chest armor, activated them, and threw them with everything she had. The canisters punctured the jelly flesh but didn't make it more than a few inches—far shallower than the bullets had penetrated.

"Close your eyes!" Anne shouted, and then she followed her own command. A muffled whump filled the air, coupled with a flash bright enough to temporarily blind anyone looking at it. The explosive was designed to be loud and bright, but it still packed a lot of energy, and if something attempted to contain all that released pressure, like a body... or a jellyfish, the results were gelatinous.

Anne opened her eyes in time to see a wave of clear internal goop burst out of the body, coating the floor. The deluge of jellyfish that followed deflated the body of its fluids and sent the long arms into a frantic spasm.

Peter's body, still at the core of the beast, was even easier to see now, but he was still trapped in the thing's intact gut, where he'd be slowly digested if he wasn't freed.

Reduced in size, the Apex was no longer squished into the tunnel. Like Anne, it started to slide—much faster than Anne could. She tried to run, but nearly fell.

"No!" she shouted, as Peter was pulled farther away.

She pulled her pistol, took aim, and dug in her feet, sliding to a stop. Arms steady, she was about to pull the trigger when Ella pushed her arms down.

"Wait," Ella said, "look."

Inside the belly of the beast, a glint of metal.

Peter was alive. And fighting.

A blade slipped out of the clear flesh and slid downward, unzipping the creature's gut.

Peter spilled out, hit the hard floor in a heap, and slid ten feet before coming to a stop. Anne and Ella crouch-walked to him, careful not to coast past him and follow the jellyfish to whatever watery den it called home.

"Peter!" Ella shouted, rolling him onto his back. Checking for a pulse. "He's alive!"

"Probably has fluid in his lungs," Anne said. "Roll him onto his side."

"I know how to—"

"Do it!" Anne shouted with such ferocity that her mother listened and rolled Peter onto his side.

"What are you going to—"

Before Ella could finish the question, Anne drove the side of her foot into the armor covering Peter's back. It was a perfect kick, just the way Jakob had shown her to kick a soccer ball. And the effect was exactly what she'd hoped for. Peter coughed and then vomited a fountain of clear fluid onto Ella's feet.

He rolled onto his stomach, rising to his hands and knees, back arched up, as he continued coughing, gasping, and puking some more. When it was all cleared, he opened the canteen on his hip, drank some water, and threw up one last time, this time on purpose.

Short of drowning himself, he wouldn't be able to rinse his lungs out, but they'd fully clear and heal in time.

While her mother held him, rubbing his back, and saying, "I got you," Anne kept her flashlight and pistol aimed down the tunnel.

When her father was able to breathe normally, she glanced back and asked, "You okay, Dad?"

"Prouder than hurt," he said. "Saw what you did with the flashbangs. Good thinking."

"Wasn't really thinking," Anne said. "I just...did it."

"Best kind of thinking there is," he said and took Ella's offered hand. She helped him to his feet, but they were all unsteady. Heaps of disgorged gel slid past them, threatening to knock them off their feet and drag them down.

"We need to get out of this tunnel," Ella said.

Peter gave a nod, hands on his knees. Then he pointed back up the tunnel.

Anne redirected her flashlight, illuminating a round side tunnel that she'd missed during all the action.

"Huh," Ella said.

The climb to the side tunnel was slow. Every step precarious. Peter took the lead, and if he went down, they'd all go down. Staying close to the wall helped, using the rough stone and groves between slabs as handholds. When they reached the branching tunnel, Anne was relieved to find it not barred off.

"ExoGen must have put the jellyfish in the tunnel on purpose," Peter said. "A subterranean guard dog. It might have been down here without a meal for years, kept alive through its starvation by its ExoGenetic DNA, perhaps in some kind of hibernation."

He entered the tunnel first, then helped Anne and Ella inside. It was round, more like an ancient drainage pipe, and blessedly level and free of anything slippery. Anne got to her feet. She was just short enough to stand in the tunnel. Peter and Ella were forced to crouch, low and awkward.

Anne turned off her flashlight and led the way through the dark, straight tunnel without being asked or told. A hundred feet in, she blinked. Thought she could see something, but it was hazy, or her eyes were playing tricks. The patter of water falling echoed from the tunnel ahead.

Peter came to a stop beside her. "I see it."

"Looks like a hole in the ceiling," Ella said.

Anne pushed onward, approaching the light as quietly as she could. She stopped just a few feet away from the rectangular light source. Water poured from it, hitting the tunnel floor, and draining away from them. Light from above made her squint as she leaned forward and looked up. She caught just a glimpse and leaned back, eyes wide.

"It's drainage," she whispered. "For a shower room."

"Shower room," Peter whispered. "Are you sure?" He shuffled forward, looking up. The sound of falling water grew louder, but so did something else. Voices. Human. A man and a woman. He looked up through the grate and caught the same eyeful Anne just had—a man and woman of mediocre attractiveness engaged in an almost acrobatic display of carnal sex.

Peter returned with a smile on his face.

"Should we let them finish?" Anne asked.

Peter shook his head.

"Best time to catch someone by surprise is with their pants down."

Then he headed back to the grate, took hold of the bars, and shoved.

36

Val wasn't sure what to do. During Jakob's brief absence, she'd listened to Lyn's body contorting, growling, and then walking. When the room's door handle shook, Val took hold of the other side and held the door tight. Lyn had yet to attempt exiting, but had shrieked in frustration—at the same moment Jakob had screamed in the other room.

Val had nearly left her post to check on Jakob, but that would have surely allowed Lyn to exit the room.

On top of that, she couldn't hear or smell anything other than Jakob and whatever Lyn was becoming.

He hadn't screamed again, and his breathing was slowing down.

Something had frightened him, but it wasn't serious.

Val didn't remember what it felt like to be that scared. She had memories of moments when her old self was afraid. A car accident. An injury. But none of it compared to everyday normal life now. The only thing that made Val's pulse quicken now was concern for her family, and the thrill of the hunt.

And she wasn't sure how to feel now. On one hand, Lyn was family, and possibly lost to them. On the other hand, there was a fight coming and Val excelled in combat. Delighted in it. Not just for the adrenaline rush, but because protecting her family made her feel good, despite the life that she'd lost.

Protecting Jakob from Lyn…was confusing. If Lyn didn't remember them…if she tried to kill them, she would be killed. That would make Val feel bad, even if saving Jakob would make her feel good. All she really knew for sure was that she needed to kill Lyn. Because she could handle it. Because while it would make her feel bad, it wouldn't last. Jakob would carry that wound for the rest of his life. He was sensitive like that.

"Lyn," Val said. "You okay?"

It felt and sounded like a dumb question.

Lyn was dying, had eaten ExoGen oats, and was now an Exo, maybe even an Apex. She was definitely not okay, and probably didn't even know her own name. But Val couldn't think of another way to address her.

"Lyn, if okay, please say it. I don't want to hurt—"

The door rattled from an impact.

The knob started to turn, but Val held it tightly.

A low growl shook the air. It was followed by another impact that knocked Val back but was easily compensated for.

Lyn had changed, but she wasn't yet strong.

She was hungry.

Her body had changed, but it couldn't grow, couldn't become powerful, without a meal. She wouldn't be strong, but she might be mindless.

Out of control.

Savage with unceasing hunger.

Val remembered what that felt like. In the early days of her change, she'd had to fight so many people. They had changed, too. All were hungry. They fought, killed, and consumed. Over and over until at last, her thoughts cleared enough that she was able to not kill the next woman she came across—Jakob's mother. That was how the Chunta began.

But she had eaten so many to get to that point.

The only meal available to Lyn was Jakob...and Val. And even that wouldn't be enough to free her from the hunger-fueled rage. Anne called being angry from hunger, 'hangry.' Lyn was beyond hangry.

Four bony blades punched through the thick wooden door, narrowly missing Val's face. She nearly grabbed hold of them, but noticed how sharp they looked, and held back. As though to demonstrate the fine edge of her new fingertips, Lyn shoved them downward, cutting through the wood.

It didn't matter how long Val could hold the door closed. Lyn would cut her way free in minutes.

"I'm back," Jakob said, winded and holding his flashlight. He pointed the light on the claws as they drew back inside the door. "Whoa. Shit."

"Big shit," Val said. "She Exo, she small, but she also hungry. Savage. Why you scream?"

Jakob rolled his eyes.

"Stupid mirror. New subject. We don't have anything for Lyn to eat but a bunch of mushrooms and weeds."

"All the mushrooms in whole world not enough," Val said. "She want meat. She want you and me and then everything else she can find. Her brain not work right now. I remember."

"You remember eating...people?"

"Many people," Val said and then shrugged. "It okay. They tasted good."

Jakob looked at her, shocked.

"At least I no scream at reflection," she said.

"*Hey.*"

"I no eat people now. My hunger is normal. Like you."

"Do you know why?" he asked. "I mean, I get that changing a body so dramatically requires energy, but I don't get why you had to change so much."

"Body is…chaotic at first. Many changes. Come and go. Off and on. I remember having tail. Having horns. Thick skin like rhino. All changes happen before, during and after fight to death. Each time Feesa got a little stronger. A little faster. Now I Val. Now I choose changes."

"But maybe you could do that from the start," Jakob said. "Maybe you just needed someone to explain it to you.

"I would eat them before they had a chance to speak."

"But right now, we have that chance with Lyn."

Val leaned back just before the long claws punched through the door again. "Not for long." The claws swept downward, opening up four new fissures in the wood.

"Lyn!" Jakob shouted, aiming his weapon and flashlight toward the door. "Don't give in to the hunger. You're still yourself. Still in control. You can direct the adaptations. Make yourself not need to eat. I don't know, give yourself a small stomach."

A moment of silence followed Jakob's speech.

It was nice, Val thought, but it wouldn't be enough.

Jakob sounded convincing, but she remembered how insistent the hunger felt, wrapping itself around her mind, constricting until it was satiated with blood. With flesh. With the wails of her victims, most of whom were trying to eat her as well.

She remembered losing a finger to a man, early on.

It grew back—after she ate him.

The memory reminded her of her missing appendage. She glanced down at the limb, still regrowing. The bandage had fallen away during her struggle with the door, shoved off by the lengthening bone and the small foot bud at the end. It wasn't enough to support her weight, but she was able to use it for balance, which let her hold the door closed.

The claws swept through the door again, severing three horizontal sections and creating a hole large enough to see through.

Jakob aimed his weapon at the gap.

Lyn's long, gray arm reached out, swiping at Val, forcing her back.

She could open the door if she chose to, but Val suspected Lyn was too far gone to think about using a doorknob. She would finish carving her hole in the door, would bound out, land on Jakob, and attempt to make off with him. If she managed that, Val would be next.

Jakob gave Lyn a reason to think twice about it, pulling the trigger on his MP5. Three rounds spat out of the sound suppressed weapon. Two of them punched holes in the wooden door. The remaining round slipped through Lyn's emaciated and stretched out limb.

She yanked her arm back with a yelp.

"Please!" Jakob shouted, tears in his eyes now. "I don't want to kill you, Lyn! Just...control yourself, for God's sake! You said you could do this. You said we could trust you!"

A raspy voice responded from behind the door. "Hun...gry..."

Val was surprised by the voice. It had taken her a long time to remember how to speak. She still struggled with it. Maybe Lyn really was fighting the urge. Maybe she could control it from the beginning?

Claws punched through the top of the door and swept to the right. The center panel fell away, leaving a large, rectangular hole.

Jakob aimed his weapon and light, revealing nothing. Lyn was still smart enough to not get shot again.

"If you come out here," Jakob said. "I *will* kill you."

"Hungry!" Lyn shrieked in the darkness.

"I don't care!" Jakob shouted. "You can't eat me. And you can't eat Val."

Growling was followed by a string of muttered words that might have just been guttural sounds.

"I can't eat you..." Lyn hissed. "I eat something else."

Lyn dove through the hole in the door faster than Jakob or Val could react. Her body had lengthened, grown thin—and quick. Her hooked talons locked on to the wall for a moment, then she sprang into the air, toward Jakob.

He pulled the trigger of his MP5, but his aim was off. Bullets trailed Lyn's path through the air, chewing up the ceiling and keeping Val from taking action.

Jakob hit the floor, the air knocked from his lungs and the weapon from his hand.

He was helpless.

Val shouted, "Jake!" but her concern was misplaced.

Lyn's leap took her clear over Jakob. She careened across the apartment, toward the window Val had broken earlier.

"Don't!" Jakob shouted. "You'll die!"

Lyn's claws dug into the floor, screeching as she slid to a stop on the precipice of a six-hundred-foot drop. She looked back, hideous face cast in the dramatic flashlight beam. Her eyes were big circles, for seeing in the dark. Her skin was stretched tight over a distorted skull. Nothing of her former self remained, including the cancer. But there was one exception.

Her mind was still there. Her will. She was fighting for control but couldn't deny the hunger.

Lyn said nothing.

She just backed away, sliding out of sight. The shriek of her claws over glass continued outside the building, fading as she dropped away.

Jakob dashed for the windows, slid to a stop on his stomach, and looked over the edge. Lyn was already fifty feet down, slowing her descent by carving deep grooves in the building's side. A moment later, she slid out of the beam's reach and disappeared.

Jakob clicked the light off.

The shriek of claws on glass stopped a moment later.

During the silence that followed, Val and Jakob looked at each other.

"Is working?" Val asked.

Jakob gave a slow nod and a smile. "I think it's working."

The silence was ended a moment later, by a splash.

37

Peter Crane was in Boston. Kenyon was sure of it. Ella too, and her little asshole kid. They were persistent, he'd give them that. But they were also predictable. They knew he'd be waiting, and he knew they'd come. Whatever happened next was inevitable, like an asteroid drawn into Jupiter's crushing atmosphere. Inexorable.

The island's security forces, including Viper Squad, were on high alert, watching the city, monitoring security feeds and sensors, ready to shoot and kill anyone who wasn't part of the San Francisco team. There was no way to know if Peter and Ella had made more friends along the way, or somehow managed to recruit the traitorous Chunta.

It was unlikely anyone could cross the bay unseen and untouched. The Exos hunting in the waters around the island were a fluke. The remnants of Boston's human population had taken to the ocean of which they were so proud. *One too many lobster rolls*, Kenyon thought. Lawrence had wanted them eliminated at first. But since the electrified barrier kept the creatures off the island, Kenyon argued that they be allowed to remain in the water as both a security measure...and a test.

Lawrence believed in survival of the fittest, and that humanity, in a new form, would ultimately claim that mantle. It only made sense that the best of their people—the strongest or smartest—be the ones to ascend.

It was bullshit. Kenyon made the point just to get out of having to find a way to rescue their people from the far reaches of New England. He'd get killed eventually. No matter how prepared you thought you were for any Exo surprise, something always managed to catch you off guard. The lucky survived, but eventually everyone's luck ran out. And Kenyon had pushed his luck as far as he wanted to.

He lowered his night vision binoculars and sighed. "Nothing."

"You really thought someone would try to approach the island from the ocean?" Hutchins asked. "I mean, who *knows* what lives out there now."

"Let's hope we never find out." Kenyon let the binoculars hang from his neck. "But you've seen this guy in action. He likes to be unpredictable, which also makes him predictable. To a degree. The path of most resistance is the one we'd never expect."

"No offense," Hutchins said, "but I think the path of most resistance is probably the water between here and the mainland, filled with man-eating freakshows and an electrified submerged fence."

"Freakshows?" Kenyon said, feigning offense. "How dare you speak so crudely of the ascended."

"Ascended 1.0. Random adaptation to shifting micro conditions. It's chaotic. Unpredictable. We'll get the good stuff. Remain in control. Our minds intact."

Hutchins was a good man. Smart and loyal, too. But he believed Lawrence's promise of ascension. He might stop short of regarding Lawrence as a new god or mystical guru, but all his hopes were pinned on the idea that humanity needed to be purged and evolved by force to become more.

No one had a clear idea of what 'more' was. Lawrence kept that vague, probably on purpose, because it allowed people to use their imaginations. 'More' looked different to everyone. And that was the key. Defining 'more' would mean some people didn't want any part of it. In the same way Lawrence had never explained that the purge would cause the violent near-extinction of Homo sapiens.

But here they were, the last survivors of an apocalypse they caused. For anyone to question their actions now...would be unthinkable. How many of them would just end their lives if they felt the full weight of what they had done? Believing in Lawrence's message gave them absolution and hope that they had made the right choice, that they hadn't destroyed the human race, but had brought it to the next stage of its evolution. The golden age of humanity had yet to arrive, and ExoGen would usher it in. "The good stuff only exists if Ella Masse, or her daughter, unlocks it for us."

Hutchins grunted. "Think she'll do it?"

"She's a wildcard," Kenyon admitted. "But she's not immune to leverage. And at the end of the day, she wants humanity to survive. Same as us."

Hutchins gave Kenyon a sidelong glance. "Not *exactly* the same. She'd save all of them. The insufferables, out there, living in squalor. ExoGen was meant to transform the best of us, not the riffraff."

Riffraff was a silly word. Kenyon never liked it, but Lawrence used it in many of his grand exhortations.

What Hutchins—and Lawrence—had yet to understand was that the people out there, surviving in an ExoGenetic world...they *were* the fittest. The people at ExoGen had been protected and fed this whole time. Some of them had made it across the country and to the island, and that was impressive. But most of the science team, including Lawrence, had been whisked across the country by air. Some of them hadn't seen a day of struggle since the change, and most of them had no idea how truly monstrous the world had become.

Kenyon didn't buy into the bullshit.

He was here for one reason—he wanted to ascend, to become more than human, not because of devotion or belief, but because he didn't want to be a mindless monster. He wanted to keep his mind, to become powerful in a way Lawrence had yet to imagine. Lawrence saw only advancement. The unlocking of the human mind. Maybe immortality and travel to other worlds. But Kenyon... He wanted to rule over the world that came next.

He could do it now, but then he might be stuck in a world of monsters as just a man, and he was getting damn tired of that. So, he played the role of acolyte, biding his time, and after the ascension, he would claim his throne—violently if need be. He'd learned a lot while living among the Chunta. Carnage quelled any challenge, current or present.

He just needed god-damned Ella to show her face and get on with it.

Or did he?

Ella would pursue her goal until she succeeded or died trying. That meant she'd find her way onto the island. And eventually to the lab, where she would complete her work—and maybe even plug her daughter in.

"Huh," he said.

"What?" Hutchins asked.

"An epiphany." Kenyon lifted the radio to his mouth and held down the call button. "This is Kenyon. If our targets are spotted, do not engage, do not let yourself be seen. Back off, let me know, and track them. Do *not* engage. Are we clear?"

A series of confirmations came in from the teams patrolling the island. When they were done, he said, "Out," and clipped the radio back onto his belt.

Hutchins squinted at him, attempting to suss out the apparent change in heart. Then he said, "Lawrence isn't going to like that."

"He will when he sees the results."

"You don't think you should have at least checked with—"

"Hutch," Kenyon said. "We've known each other for a long time. Most of that time spent in one hell or another, out there in the world, making decisions for ourselves and getting the job done. Being inside a fortress built on top of an older fortress doesn't—"

Kenyon froze. "Do we have schematics of the old fortress?"

"I would imagine so."

"Find them for me."

Hutchins gave a nod and was about to leave when Kenyon's radio crackled to life. "Edward." It was Lawrence, the devil dancing on his tongue. He only referred to Kenyon by his first name when he was displeased. The timing couldn't be a coincidence.

Hutchins gave him a pat on the shoulder and said, "Told you." Then he set about the mission Kenyon had given him.

Kenyon picked up the radio. "Sir?"

"Come have a sit with me, will you?" Lawrence said. He knew well enough to not chew Kenyon out over the radio. It would make him look bad, not because of his anger or righteous indignation, but because it would confirm what several people would already be wondering: Kenyon made his own decisions, without checking in with Lawrence first. In truth, they all did. But not one of them had any kind of true power. It all belonged to Lawrence.

Or did it?

One day they'd all find out the truth of the matter. But until then, Kenyon was happy to play the game, to placate the mad genius who envisioned a new future and made it happen, not through his own mind, but through that of someone even smarter.

Kenyon had nearly told Ella the truth. Once. When his feelings for her had shifted toward love. He didn't like lying to her, especially about something so monumental. But he knew she wouldn't see things through if she knew the truth, and he wanted this world, even more than he wanted her.

"Where are you, sir?" Kenyon asked, keeping any trace of dissent out of his voice. He could sound as innocent as he was guilty.

"In the library," Lawrence said. "Please do hurry. Time is of the essence, *my boy*."

Lawrence had a habit of using terms of endearment to lower people's positions, to make them smaller while at the same time endearing them to him. It was a subtle manipulation that slammed into Kenyon's psyche like a bullet into a brick wall. Aside from wearing away at Kenyon's patience, though, it had no real negative effect.

Kenyon looked out to sea and saw only infinite darkness. He could hear the waves. Could smell the ocean. But right now, anything could be sneaking up on them—even far worse than Peter Crane. Kenyon shivered. He'd be glad to get back inside. "Right away, sir. I'm on my way."

He made it two steps before his radio crackled to life again. "Uh, sir. Mr. Kenyon." Whoever was speaking was afraid of delivering news that might subvert his savior's orders.

"Spit it out," Kenyon replied.

"Uh, we've spotted someone. A flashlight in the distance."

"Where?"

"In the city. Top floor of a skyscraper overlooking the bay."

A perfect place to observe the island, Kenyon thought, and it matched Fuller's account of seeing someone as they passed. But Peter wouldn't be that careless. That meant it was someone else—which seemed unlikely—or something had gone wrong.

"Copy that," Kenyon said.

"Mr. Kenyon," Lawrence said, "send someone to check it out, and *then* come see me."

Well, he knows how to save face, Kenyon thought, and said, "Yes sir," and then laid it on thick. "Of course, sir." Then he headed for the helicopter pad and called out on the radio again.

"Viper Squad. I want you ready to be airborne in five mikes."

"Copy that, sir," Manke replied. "If there are rats in the city, nothing like a bunch of snakes to root 'em out."

38

The element of surprise, coupled with the shock of being confronted by something unexpected, could throw the human mind into a kind of mental reset. Depending on the level of shock, it could last from a second to a minute.

Anne knew that as well as Peter did. And it was why he agreed to her plan.

Because it was ridiculous.

Ella had complained, but it was short-lived. Her daughter was capable of taking down Apex predators. A couple engaged in a…private moment…would be easy in comparison.

And fun, Anne had argued.

As they prepped beneath the open grate, the girl bounced from foot to foot, a smile on her face. That the couple hadn't noticed Peter shove open the rusty grate, or pull it underground, confirmed that they were fully lost in the throes of passion.

The woman shouted a moment later, her voice echoing in the shower room above. "Oh, Funderburk. Yes! Yes! Oh!"

Anne clapped a hand over her mouth, laughing into it. Even Peter and Ella had a hard time maintaining their composure.

"You like that?" Funderburk said, as their wet bodies clapped together. "You *like* that?"

"Yes! *Yes!*"

Anne buried her face into the crook of her arm and Peter had to do the same. It had been a long time since he'd laughed. Felt great. Too bad they needed to ruin the good time.

He was surprised to see Ella laughing as well. With a hand over her heart, she waved the other at Peter and then pointed to the ceiling, mouthing the words, "I know him!"

Funderburk let out a series of grunts, followed by the man shouting his own name. "Fun–der–burk!"

It was too much. Peter could feel an honest-to-goodness belly laugh building inside him. And if that happened–if they were detected because they were laughing at the wonderous Funderburk, his initial reaction would be shame, which in most people was quickly followed by rage. It wouldn't serve their plan.

So, he squelched his sense of humor, leaned forward, and whispered to Anne. "It's time. Focus up."

She stopped laughing. Set her jaw. Gave a nod.

Peter returned the nod, positioned himself beneath the opening in the ceiling, and linked his fingers. Anne stepped into his hands, and when he lifted her up, she pushed off.

She rose out of the hole like a launching javelin missile and landed in a puddle of water. Her handgun came up in a two-handed hold. She'd gone completely unnoticed.

The couple had their backs turned, the man's backend to Anne, the woman pressed up against the shower's tile wall. Peter eased himself up out of the hole. It was a tight fit, and it took some squirming, but he made it without too much noise.

The shower was part of what appeared to be a locker room. It was wide open, the kind of communal shower used before jumping in a pool at the YMCA. These two must have thought they had the place to themselves, probably because it was the early morning hours when most non-security personnel would be sound asleep.

Peter glanced at Anne. Her face had soured at the sight, but she was still on task.

He gave her a nod.

She took a deep breath and barked, "Stop the fuckin' and get to duckin'!"

They hadn't discussed what she would say, only that it would be loud and angry. That alone would be enough to throw most people, but when the couple separated and spun around, sputtering with surprise, and came face-to-face with an enraged young girl dressed in tactical gear and aiming a pistol at them, their minds simply froze.

Neither of them covered up.

They just stared.

Dumbstruck.

"I said, Get. To. Ducking!" Anne aimed her pistol just above their heads and squeezed off three rounds.

The couple dropped down, hands clutching their heads in fear. "Wh-who are you?" the man asked.

Peter crouched down beside Funderburk. "We'll ask the questions."

The man's head snapped toward Peter. He yelped and pushed away, all but clambering over the woman.

"Hey, don't be a douche," Anne said, pointing her weapon at Funderburk. "Geez lady, I think you could have done better. I mean, I know the world is trashed, but there's got to be someone better than the glorious Funderburk."

"Anne," Peter said, attempting to slow her down.

"The guy is a jerk," she said. "Just let me shoot him once. In the leg."

"If he's not honest," Peter said. He had no idea if Anne was manipulating the man into talking, but that wasn't how Peter wanted to play it. If she had to shoot him in the leg, though...well, he *was* a jerk.

"What do you want to know?" Funderburk asked. "I'll tell you anything."

The woman looked at Funderburk, aghast that he gave in so quickly. She pulled away from him, now repulsed, perhaps seeing him for the first time as they did. He was weak. Had clearly been flown across the country. Hadn't had a day of squalor or suffering throughout the change or the world's end.

She had been like him, before, Peter surmised. A well-fed scientist behind the security of ExoGen's walls. But this woman...she'd crossed the country the hard way. Had lost her extra pounds and replaced it with muscle. She'd returned to her past lover, and now saw him as he really was, perhaps for the first time. She saw her old self reflected back, and she didn't like the view.

"What do you want to know?" the man asked again.

"I don't have any questions for you." Peter hitched his thumb back over his shoulder. "She does."

"Hello, Funderburk," Ella said, stepping up behind Peter, looking down at the pair with a smirk. She turned to the woman next. Gave a slight nod. "Kerrigan."

"E-Ella?" Funderburk gave a nervous smile. "Are you here to ascend? Is it time?" He started standing, arms outstretching toward Ella like he might give her a hug.

"Who told you to stand, chunk-a-love?" Anne said, and she fired another shot over his head.

He dropped back to the hard tile floor, clutching his head. "Fuck!"

Ella reached out for the shower knob and twisted it until it shut off. She crouched down in front of the pair. "I've got questions. You two have answers. Tell me what I need to know, and we'll be on our way. Don't, and you'll be dealing with the kid."

Ten minutes later, Ella knew her way to the labs and as much about the facility's security as Funderburk could remember. Kerrigan had only been there for a week and had just been let out of medical the day before. This was the first private moment they'd had.

That they were still alive was a mercy.

Peter understood that some of the science team might be here unwillingly, but these two struck him as true believers. When Funderburk first saw Ella, he looked excited and spoke of ascension. Sounded culty.

Peter pulled the last zip-tie tight and stood back.

"You can't leave us like this," Funderburk said. He was on the floor hogtied. It wasn't a great way to leave a person, but they couldn't risk these two sounding the alarm. If they were lucky, someone would eventually find them. If they weren't, there were worse ways to die than starvation—which was pretty much the status quo for people refusing to eat ExoGenetic crops. If you were good at foraging, the process could be slowed. But not prevented entirely.

Peter had been fit before the change. Two hundred ten pounds of muscle. Now, he was one sixty on a good day. He didn't feel bad for Funderburk. The woman, Kerrigan, was a different story. She'd been out there in the world. Knew what it was like. She was tied up beside her lover, but she didn't complain. Didn't struggle. This, for her, was just another day of discomfort.

Ella crouched beside her. "You know what it's like in the wild. You've seen what we did to the world."

Kerrigan nodded. "Wish I had found you on the outside."

"I'll come back if I can," Ella said. It was a promise she wouldn't be able to keep. They all knew it.

"Don't worry about us," Kerrigan said. "Do what you need to do. But... don't give him what he wants."

"Eliza!" Funderburk said, revolted by her betrayal.

"Lawrence was wrong about *everything*. And *we* were wrong to help him. He's not remaking the world to save humanity. He's corrupting it to make himself a god." Her eyes flicked to Peter, and then to Anne. "Kill him if you get the chance."

"Don't need to worry about that," Anne said.

Funderburk was flabbergasted, blundering through a series of snorts, scoffs, and lip smacks. Then he filled his lungs and was about to scream for help when Peter's boot slammed into his skull, knocking him unconscious.

Ella placed a towel over Kerrigan, and then another, covering her nakedness and keeping her warm.

"Good luck," Kerrigan said, then she closed her eyes and leaned her head on the floor like she might fall asleep. Had probably learned to sleep in less comfortable positions on her cross-country trek.

With Funderburk's lab coat over his tactical gear, Peter led the way, followed by Ella, similarly disguised, and finally Anne, whose short stature and black clothing were her only chances of not being spotted. She closed the shower door behind them and switched off the light.

"Toodles."

39

"Well," Jakob said. "Is there anything else I can screw up today?"

Val grunted at him. Didn't have the patience for teenage angst and self-loathing at the moment. The day had been overwhelming enough already. "There is no need for you to place blame on yourself and then spend the next thirty minutes bemoaning your role in how things played out."

Jakob couldn't see her in the absolute darkness, but his head whipped toward her like he could, his mouth hanging open in shock, revealing the half-chewed mushroom inside it.

"What?" Val asked. "And finish chewing first."

Jakob did as he was told, but mostly just swallowed the big chunks of fungus whole.

Then he said, "You just spoke."

"I speak all the time."

"But you really spoke. And you sound...you sound like you. I heard interviews with you when I was younger. You sound like *her* now. Like yourself."

Val wasn't impressed. Her voice had been changing along with the rest of her.

"Val," he said, fumbling in the dark until he found her shoulder. He squeezed her muscle, maybe just for emphasis, maybe checking if her body had shrunk. It hadn't. "You spoke in a complete sentence. You said, 'is.' That's a...what do you call it?"

"State of being verb," Val said.

"You see! State of being verb!? Who even knows that? You also said, 'bemoaning'. *Bemoaning.* What? Hello. It's like another part of your brain has been unlocked. The part that wrote songs. That had a big vocabulary. Can't you feel it?"

"I...I don't know..."

Jakob was right, but she hadn't noticed the shift. There was so much going on around them all the time that she hadn't really had time to self-reflect.

She smiled. Self-reflecting was definitely a part of her former life. Along with therapy, yoga, and mindfulness. Being famous was more stressful than most people realized, mostly because every encounter with a person who knows you requires a small sacrifice. Of your time. Of your energy. A simple walk to get a drink could become a circus if the paparazzi saw through her disguise.

No one would see through her current disguise, though, unless they got to know her. Or heard her sing. Jakob had been good about the revelation. He was happy about who she'd been but didn't treat her any differently. They were kin first, warriors of the new world. Who they'd been before was intriguing but didn't define who they were now.

"I can feel it," she said.

"That's so cool." He shifted in his seat, so he was facing her, again, without being able to see. "Are your thoughts, like, the same? Do you feel any differently?"

"Thoughts and feelings haven't changed. I'm still me. The new me. I just remember more...including how to speak well, I guess."

"Cool," he said. "That's cool. Maybe you'll be better at Hangman now?"

She whacked his arm. "The gallows are going to have a few less—"

She held her breath.

"What is it?" Jakob whispered.

"I hear something."

Jakob picked up his MP5. "Is it close? Is it Lyn?"

They hadn't seen Lyn since she slid out of sight. There was no way to know if she was alive or not. But the rhythmic thump she heard was definitely *not* Lyn. Wasn't even organic.

She stood to her feet and approached the window, looking out toward the island. "It's a helicopter."

"I see it," Jakob said, stepping up beside her and looking through his night vision goggles and binoculars. "Doesn't look like it's coming this..."

The helicopter banked over the island and set a course straight for Boston.

"Scratch that, they're definitely coming this way. But are they coming for us?"

"Assume the worst," Val said, quoting advice Peter had given them.

"Right," Jakob said. "The flashlight. With Lyn. They must have seen it."

Val nodded. Made sense.

"Okay," Jakob said, lowering the binoculars and readying his weapon. "What's the game plan?"

"We wait," Val said. "Then we attack."

"Right," Jakob said. "You weren't a tactician in your former life. By the way, that's called an 'ambush.'"

"Don't be a smartass," she said.

"Sorry. I'm just nervous. Can we just hide?"

Val hadn't considered that option. They'd always just fought. And she'd always been the first to charge right in. But hiding...it might be the safest way to survive an all-out assault against men with guns.

"Right. Let's hide." She started to move, but then froze. "Where?"

"We should assume they know what floor we're on," Jakob said, "so another floor might work, except we don't really know what might be on the other floors, including Lyn. So familiar territory might be best. But we can't just hide in a closet and hope for the best. They'll find us for—"

"What?" Val asked.

"The tunnels," Jakob said.

"On the island?" Val didn't understand how Peter and Ella's plan could help them here.

"What? No. Not those tunnels. The ones here. Behind the walls. If they exist on the lower floors then they could be up here, too, right?"

"I suppose," Val said.

"Suppose is great," Jakob said. "An hour ago, you didn't even know that word." He stood up. "Now take me to a closet."

"Use your night vision goggles," Val said.

"Right. Duh." Jakob put the goggles back on. "Okay. I can see."

The chop of helicopter rotors grew louder, erasing any lingering doubt about where they were headed.

Jakob picked up his gear and scurried for a bedroom.

She followed him while listening to the chopper's approach. They'd kept all the lights off, flying invisible in the darkness, but the amount of noise they made...

Anything with sharp teeth and a pair of ears would likely be headed in their direction, from miles around. Even if they survived the human assault, they would need to relocate before the building was turned into a buffet where the meals had jaws and tried to eat you first.

"Here." Jakob opened a closet door and crouched inside. He crawled beneath the hanging men's clothing. "It goes way back." He shimmed back out. "You first. Make a hole in the wall just big enough for us to fit through."

"I'm not very small," she said.

"Well, yeah. But there is a suitcase in there. Keep the hole smaller than the suitcase and we'll pull it in front of the hole."

She gave a nod and crawled inside. For a moment, the close confines of the closet made her feel safe and cozy. Like a womb. A memory of hiding in a closet came back to her, playing hide and seek, with her brother and sister. Both gone now. With the rest of her family.

She found the suitcase, and the wall. Breaking through was easy. She just pressed, and the wall gave way. No punching. No sound. Not that anyone would hear her at the moment. The helicopter was landing on the roof, just above them. Time was short.

The wall crumbled beneath her touch, allowing her to carve a large clean hole. Once done, she put her head inside the wall and smiled. Jakob was right. The tunnels filled the entire structure. But why?

Didn't matter, she decided, and crawled back out of the closet. "Tunnel's open. You first."

He gave a nod and crawled into the darkness. She followed him into the closet and then the tunnel. Then she reached back into the closet and pulled the suitcase over the hole. From the outside it would just look like a suitcase against the wall.

"I thought it was dark out there," Jakob said, removing the goggles.

Val was about to complain, but then remembered Peter explaining how they worked to Jakob. They amplified light. A lot. Outside, the night might appear to be absolutely dark, but there was moonlight filtering through the clouds. Human eyes couldn't see it, but she could, and the goggles could. But in here, there was no light for the goggles to amplify.

But...she could still see. It looked different. Not like day, or the green from the night vision goggles.

It was more like...

She held a hand up, moving it back and forth in front of her eyes. She could see little waves rippling away from her skin.

It's heat, she realized. "Cool..."

"What?" Jakob whispered. The chopper had gone silent.

"I can see heat. I can— What are you doing?"

"Huh?"

"You're...dancing."

"What? No. I...I have to pee when I'm nervous. When I'm hiding."

"Oh no," Val said.

"What, can you see them?"

"No," she said, "I have to pee when I'm hiding, too."

"Means you're still human after— What is...that sound?"

"I'm peeing," she said. "Before they get here. You should too. It will be hard to fight if you have to pee."

Jakob sighed. "Fine."

But he was too late.

Before he could lower his zipper, the sound of breaking glass filled the apartment.

40

"This is never going to work," Ella said over her shoulder as she led the way through the facility's hallways. The layout was similar to the ExoGen headquarters in San Francisco. Kerrigan's instructions were easy enough to follow—first left, second left, stairwell on the right, up four flights and voila, they were in the laboratory. That was just the first step, though, as the lab itself occupied two levels of the entire facility. What they really needed was a sub-lab. Someplace private. That was a roll of the dice, but still easy compared to the hurdles they needed to leap every time they passed someone.

Ella's hair was still shaved, like Peter's and Anne's, and anyone else concerned about contaminating a biodome. That helped, since people at ExoGen would remember her with long, straight brown hair. But her face was recognizable to everyone on the planet. Rather than make eye contact, she kept her eyes on the floor and rubbed her temples like she had the mother of all headaches.

Peter walked just behind her and to the right. Unlike Ella, no one would know who he was at first glance, and since Peter made very direct and aggressive eye contact, they all just looked away. Peter insisted it would work. That people would assume he belonged, that they would believe they knew him, but didn't recognize him after his time crossing the country. "Human psychology is predictable," he said. "They'll wonder who I am but will be too embarrassed to ask."

So far, he'd been right.

But the moment just one person looked back and spotted the pint-sized commando wedged in the blind spot created by their bodies, the ruse would be exposed.

They successfully passed five people.

Ella had no idea who they were because she never saw their faces. Just kept her head down and plodded forward like she knew exactly where she was headed, and why. Just another day at the post-apocalyptic office.

When they entered the empty stairwell, Peter said, "You're doing great. Both of you. Just keep doing what you've been doing, and we'll be fine."

Ella nodded. "Four flights up."

They started up the stairs in the same triangular position, but the staircase was narrow. If someone came down the other direction, Peter would have to shift to the left.

Three flights later, the door above opened. Someone was exiting the lab, and that increased the odds of Ella being recognized. Whoever it was started down the steps, meaning Peter would have to move.

He shifted inward, but there still wasn't enough room for someone to get by. The newcomer thumped his way down the stairs and bounded around the landing ahead. He swung around the bend, hand on the rail, and said, "Whoa there!" when he narrowly avoided barreling into Ella. He bumped her arm away from her face for a moment—just enough to make eye contact.

It was just a moment, but a moment too long.

He stopped beside them. "Ella?" His eyes flicked to Peter and then down to Anne. He was putting the pieces together, eyes widening.

"Hello, Dr. Norris," she said, trying to sound casual. Ryan Norris was a kind man. Had been a friend in the lab—not the close type you tell your life story to, but always cheerful, always hardworking, and never one to argue. "Good to see you again."

"I didn't know you were back..."

"Just arrived," she said.

"That's...great. But I thought... Never mind." He looked at Anne again. "Your daughter is still alive. That's great." His brows furrowed. "Why is she dressed like a ninja?"

"Ninja?" Anne said. "I guess that's cool, but I was going for Mission Impossible saboteur. Not that I've seen Mission Impossible. I just remember her seeing it. You know, because we share the same memories. But you didn't even know that, did you? And yeah, none of this matters, but I'm adorable, right? And you just can't take your eyes off me. *That's* called a distraction."

"A distraction?" He looked to Ella. "What are you—"

"Sorry, Ryan," Ella said just before Peter punched the side of his head.

Norris's body went limp, like he'd been shot.

Peter stopped him from toppling over the rail. "Seemed like a nice guy."

Ella nodded. "He is, but...I don't know what he really thinks about all this."

"He's a lemming," Anne said. "A happy-go-lucky lemming."

"Should we have asked for his help before knocking him unconscious?" Peter asked.

"We can ask him when he comes to," Ella said, and then motioned for them to follow.

Peter hoisted Norris over his shoulder and started up the stairs behind Ella and Anne. If anyone spotted them now, the jig was up. Peter might be able to subdue one or two more, but there was a limit to how many unconscious people they could drag around.

Below them, a stairwell door clunked open, and three voices echoed up.

Ella double-timed it up the last steps, opened the door, and peeked through. The hallway on the other end was brightly lit, maroon, and completely empty. She waved the others through and closed the door behind them.

The hallway ahead was full of long windows. Some were clear, others were dark, like the glass itself had changed colors.

"What's with the dark glass?" Peter asked.

"Electrochromic," Ella said. "The glass turns dark when a voltage is applied. The technical explanation, which involves things like lithium cobalt oxide and polycrystalline tungsten oxide will put you to sleep."

"Got it," Peter said. "Fancy shades."

Anne snapped and pointed at him. "You see, Mom, he's not as dumb as you said."

Peter nearly laughed but contained it and stayed focused.

Ella took a slight lead as they approached the first window that wasn't shaded. Three scientists were hard at work, their backs to the window, but there was no reason to take chances.

"Three inside."

Anne dove to the floor and crawled beneath the window. Peter lowered Norris to the floor, held his hands and dragged him just below the glass. If the scientists glanced out, he'd look funny, but equipment was moved around the lab all the time. They'd think nothing of it.

Ella saw one of their computer screens and did a double take, pausing in the hallway. "What the hell..."

The display showed familiar work. *Her* work.

Or at least a crude reproduction of it. But they were missing pieces, like a color printer that had yellow and magenta but was missing cyan.

Why are they working on it now?

It was still early morning.

In fact, they'd seen far more people at this hour than they should have.

Ella sucked in a breath and whispered. "They know we're here."

Peter paused. "What?"

"There's no other reason they'd be working at this hour unless it was in preparation for something."

"For us," Anne said.

"I don't think they know we're here," Peter said.

Ella agreed. Everyone they'd encountered had been subdued, and she hadn't seen any security cameras or security personnel.

"But they know we're nearby," Ella said.

Peter grimaced. "We need to warn Jakob."

Ella took the lead again, moving quickly. They passed several more labs, some blacked out, some lit up. All of them occupied. The science department was burning the midnight oil.

Toward the end of the long hall, Ella spotted a laboratory that was dark, but had not blacked out. The lights were just off. "Here," she said, headed for the door. She paused at a keypad beside the door. "Moment of truth."

They hadn't been able to get Sexton's keycard from Jakob, so rather than using the scanner, she just punched in her old security code on the adjacent keys and nearly shouted with joy when the light turned green, and the door unlocked.

They slipped inside the room. Ella turned on the light with the push of a button and then darkened the glass with the push of another. The door locked behind them when it closed.

Peter lowered Norris to the ground and carefully bound him with zip-ties. While Anne inspected the computers, Ella moved around the room, looking at what they had to work with—centrifuge, raw refrigerated elements, gene sequencers, and more.

She turned at the sound of Anne tapping keys, bringing up the software they'd need to get the job done. "Good to go over here."

Ella's hands were shaking. Life had been so hard for so long, and she was out of practice. The fate of humanity—and her family—rested on what she did next, and it terrified her. Feeling jittery, she searched through a line of drawers looking for the last thing they needed.

"I can do it," Anne said. She was holding a USB cable already plugged into the computer. "I'm not afraid."

"Anne," Ella said, unsure. She didn't know what would happen when her daughter plugged in. The USB embedded in her body and mind was meant to be a haven for Ella's own memories. But they had leached out into Anne. There was no telling what would happen to her when the information was accessed again.

Would it be removed?

Deleted? Duplicated?

Would Anne's mind be left intact?

This had never been done before, and now that their goal was finally within reach, she wasn't sure she could go through with it. Wasn't sure if saving the world was worth losing Anne.

She looked at Peter, but he was equally concerned. They'd all talked about the big picture but had avoided discussing what sacrifices might need to be made.

"Ugh," Anne said with a roll of her eyes. "You two are wimps." Then she plugged herself in, said, "You see?" and collapsed to the floor.

41

Jakob didn't pee. He should have. Now he'd be uncomfortable and afraid at the same time. And that meant he wouldn't be able to think clearly.

Val, on the other hand, felt like she was thinking clearly for the first time in many years. And not just because thoughts were complete sentences, but because she could remember who she was, as well as who she wanted to be in the changed world.

And it wasn't a singer.

As much as she loved music, and would continue to, belting out a tune wouldn't help anyone survive. Raw strength, speed, and killer instincts on the other hand... She'd retained all of that from her time as Feesa. Remembered how to hunt and kill as much as she did the lyrics to her hit single: 'Bold.'

Muffled voices inside the apartment shouted, "Clear!" one after the other. The men were sweeping through each room, searching for their prey. They were easy to imagine, dressed in black, armored, carrying assault rifles. Professional killers.

But not predators.

Not like her.

A man shouted, his voice closer. "Search everywhere! They're here somewhere."

The men weren't quiet now. They pounded through the apartment, overturning furniture, kicking open doors, breaking just about everything in a primitive display of machismo probably meant to intimidate.

"We should move away from the hole," Jakob whispered. "Just in case they—"

"In here!" a man shouted, his voice clear and just outside the closet, which he'd opened without them hearing.

"What is it?" another man asked.

"Drywall dust. Beneath that suitcase. You see it?"

"They're in the walls..."

Val's eyes widened. She sensed what was about to happen.

"They're in the walls!" the man shouted so everyone could hear. "Light 'em up!"

Val dashed toward Jakob, scooped him up, and charged down the dark tunnel as gunfire erupted from the bedroom, punching holes in the wall where they'd been just a moment before. Other men, spread around the apartment, opened fire on the interior walls, some of them distant, some much closer.

A fusillade of bullets tore through the wall in front of Val. To stop in time, she was forced to punch a hand through the wall and hold on.

The gunfire stopped for a moment.

"Here!" a man shouted. "They're here!"

Val dove forward, clutching Jakob in her arms. Bullets chewed through the wall all around them as she ran toward a junction. *Left or right?* She was trying to remember the apartment's layout when bullets slipped through the wall and then the meat of her shoulder. The insertion did minimal damage, but then the round exited and it took a chunk of flesh with it.

Val roared in pain and fell forward.

She hit the dusty floor hard, but kept her body rigid, both protecting Jakob from the impact and preventing herself from crushing him.

"Uhh," a man said from the far side of the bullet ridden wall. "Manke! You sure these are people? Sounded more like an Exo."

"Jake," Val whispered. "Are you okay?"

He didn't respond.

His body was limp. His eyes closed.

She checked his body for bullet wounds and found none. Must have struck his head while they were running. Knocked him unconscious. She checked his pulse and confirmed it. Not dead.

But he would be soon, if she didn't do something.

Boots clomped over the floor as Val pushed herself back to her good foot and her nearly fully regrown new foot, leaving Jakob lying on the floor. So far, the men had been firing at waist level. She hoped he'd be safe down there, but she also intended to give them something else to shoot at.

Val bounded away from Jakob, landing ten feet away with a purposeful thump that shook the floor. She let out an inhuman shriek at the same time.

"You see?" the man said. "I think it's one of them sea-people."

"They don't breathe air," another argued.

"They're Exos, asshole. They can breathe whatever they want!"

One of the men fired into the wall, and the rest joined in, forcing Val to turn right at the T junction, putting her in the wall of another room. She wasn't sure which.

The men, realizing she'd gone deeper into the maze of walls, stopped firing, and spread out, searching for signs of her passage.

Val moved on all fours, disbursing her weight, and reducing the impact she had on surfaces, allowing her to move silently. She could hear them nearby, in the doorways of rooms she was passing, breathing heavily, weapons raised, just waiting for the slightest hint of her location.

She rounded another corner and saw something ahead. A weapon. A...sword? She crouched over it and searched the area. The wall here wasn't ruined. Whoever had left the weapon behind had moved through the wall's tunnels, entering from some other location.

A handwritten note lay atop the sheath.

To whomsoever finds this, I wish you good tidings. Though I do not think human eyes will ever gaze upon these words, I feel compelled to write them. The world is beyond saving. I and my kind will return to our home. Humanity must find its own path to survival. May this faithful blade serve you well, as it has those who wielded it before.

—Helen

The note didn't make much sense to Val, but she knew what to do with a sword.

Only, it wasn't a *sword*. She drew the blade, revealing a black machete with a partially serrated edge and the word 'Faithful' laser etched into the metal near the handle.

She smiled.

Val didn't need a sword, or a gun, to kill.

She had her strength, speed, claws, and teeth. But she understood the visceral intimidation a blade imparted on the human psyche. No one wanted to be cleaved apart. It was debasing. Reminded the victim that they were just another animal, easily slaughtered.

Val had no idea who Helen was, or where she'd gone, but she assumed the penthouse had been hers. An eccentric rich woman with an escape plan, maybe sipping hot chocolate in some secret Antarctic base where there were no animals to mutate into killing machines, waiting for the world to sort itself out.

She couldn't guess.

Also, she didn't care. She'd use the weapon and hopefully do its previous owners proud.

Val closed her eyes and listened.

Some of the men were getting close. Others were distant, randomly shooting into walls, trying to flush her out. But she would exit the wall on her own terms, not as prey, but as a hunter.

"I'm a beast," she told herself. "Ruthless. These men don't stand a chance."

Footsteps on the far side of the wall triggered a nearly automatic response. She sprang forward, crashing through drywall.

The man in front of her spun around, trigger already held down, spraying an arc of bullets in her direction.

He stopped firing when his head came off and his limp body collapsed to the floor.

"Who's firing?!" another man shouted. The moment he stepped into the room, looking down his rifle's sights, the first man's head collided with the barrel, knocking it up. Then the weapon toppled to the floor, along with the man's severed hands and forearms.

He tried to scream, but the machete's blade slid through his open mouth, the back of his throat, and up through his skull before any sound escaped. She flung him back into the room and scrambled out into the hall, clawing her way up the wall to the ceiling. When a third soldier emerged from a room, she split his head down the middle, from above.

He toppled forward, faceplanting on the hard floor. His already split skull cracked open, and his brain spilled out.

It was...revolting. But Val didn't give the gory sight a second thought as she leapt forward and–

A bullet ripped through the air, striking her thigh, and throwing off her trajectory. With a shout of pain, she fell to the floor, sliding on her back before rolling to her feet.

Beside her, a shotgun roared. The pellets struck her side, pocking her arm, leg, and ribs. Before she could get back up, three men stood over her, weapons trained on her skull. She was lit up by their flashlights, exposed, wounded, and at the mercy of the men sent to kill her family.

"What the hell are you supposed to be?" a man asked.

Val snarled, but then remembered she could talk, and that these men might actually know who she is.

"Me is Feesa," she said. "Me is Kenyon friend."

Only one of the men reacted with recognition. "Holy shit," he said. "You're one of Kenyon's jungle buddies? He told me about you all, but I thought you were hairy and had tusks."

"They fall out," she said.

He was about to ask another question when a fourth man interrupted. "Manke. Found this one in the wall."

The man tossed Jakob onto the floor beside Val. The jolt stirred him from unconsciousness. "Ugh... What..."

The man named Manke crouched in front of Jakob. "What's your name, kid?"

Jakob looked up at the four men dressed in tactical gear. "Suck it, McFuck'n'Stuff."

"Funny," Manke said, standing and taking out his radio. He pressed the call button. "Kenyon, you copy?"

"I'm here," Kenyon's voice said from the radio.

Val bristled at the sound of it.

"I got two tangos here. One is an asshole teenager. Probably seventeen. Says his name is 'Suckit McFuck'n'Stuff.' And we got one of your old pals. Name's Feesa. Doesn't look like anyone else is home. What do you want us to do?"

There was a pause, and then Kenyon came back with, "Bring me the kid. Kill the bitch."

42

"Mom," she said. "Where are you? Mom?"

The department store was a well-lit maze. The towering shelves, stacked high with pink dolls that didn't hold her interest, loomed on every side. She felt trapped. Disoriented. Her mother had been with her just a moment ago. She'd been distracted by a toy. An action figure for boys, with blue skin and a skeletal face.

The bones interested her the most.

It was why they were at the store in the first place. Mom wanted her to pick out and play with frilly girl toys—and stop dissecting roadkill.

She'd go home with a doll, there was no doubt about that, but she wouldn't play with it.

Toys were a distraction. She had work to do. She didn't know what it was. Not really. But she understood two things about herself: she wanted to help people, and her intellect was uncommon, even though her parents' were quite average.

The doll could be her assistant at best.

At the moment, picking out a doll was the last thing on her mind. Because she was alone. Abandoned in a department store.

She began to cry, quietly at first, as she walked up and down the aisles, searching for her mother. "Mom? *Mom?*"

"You need some help, kiddo?" The man wore overalls, had gray hair poking out from under his hat and his nose. She back-pedaled, knocking over a row of Barbie dolls, and then retraced her steps, only twice as fast.

Where are you? Why did you leave?

"MOM!"

"*What?*" her mother replied, irritated by the volume of Ella's voice. She was standing in the doll aisle as though she'd never left.

"Where...where were you?" Ella asked, hiccupping with emotion. She didn't want her mother to see her like that. She didn't share her personal life—including sadness—with anyone in her family. Because she didn't trust them. It wasn't gossip she was worried about, it was the quality of the advice they'd give, like, 'The girl needs a doll,' or 'The girl needs a friend.' But the tears came despite her efforts to conceal them.

Because Ella didn't like being alone. Didn't like feeling lost. Even if she didn't like her family, either.

"Ella smella likes a fella, when he pees it's Mello Yella." Amanda Sims crossed her arms and looked down at her prey, waiting for a reaction.

"You've been saying that for eight years, Amanda. Forgive me if I don't react the way you're hoping." Ella looked up from her AP Biology textbook. She was about to graduate a year early, and wanted to ace her final test, despite having already been accepted to Caltech. "So, if you could just scoot along, that would be great."

Ella motioned Amanda away like she was a stinky breeze.

Amanda leaned over Ella, blocking her sun. They were outside, in front of the school, plain as day. But that wouldn't stop Amanda. Once she set her sights on you, she was nearly impossible to shake.

"We all know you think you're better than us," Amanda said, glancing back at her boyfriend, Michael Chatman, aka, Chatterbox, on account of how much he liked to hear himself talk. He was keeping watch like they were part of a bank heist.

"I don't *think* that," Ella said.

"Don't try and weasel your way out of—"

"I *know* it," Ella finished.

The insult took a moment to sink in, but once it did, Amanda leaned back and motioned toward Ella.

"Can you believe this bitch?"

Mike looked from Amanda to Ella and then back again. He was disinterested. "Right. Total bitch."

Amanda slugged his shoulder.

"Oww!" Mike said. "What the hell you want me to do about it?"

"I don't know," Amanda said, "how about show some god-damn fucking support." She turned to Ella, a grin on her face. "Kick her in the teeth."

"What?" Mike said. "I can't—"

"You said you loved me." Amanda's crossed arms were now directed at Mike. "Or was that just to get my panties off? If so, that's rape. And I'll tell—"

"Okay, okay. Holy shit. But I ain't kicking her in the teeth."

"Fine," Amanda said. "Punch her in the kidneys. Make her piss blood."

Mike winced. He hadn't seen this side of Amanda yet. The psychotic violent side. Probably because he'd been more interested in her curvaceous exterior side, and still was. Like many teenaged boys, he was willing to compromise his morals for the promise of intimacy.

"Sorry, Ella," Mike said. "Mind standing up? It will be easier for both of us that way."

Ella just looked up at him, face screwed up. Mike wasn't a genius, but this was beneath him.

Testosterone must really be kicking in hard, she thought. *He might actually go through with it.*

"I'm not getting up," she said. "And you're not going to hit me. Because you're not as stupid as she is."

Mike paused, unsure.

Amanda slapped his shoulder three times.

"Do it. Right. Now!"

Mike's hesitation was beaten long enough for him to make the wrong choice. He hauled a leg back to kick Ella instead. As his foot swept forward, it was struck from the side. The kick swung left, and struck the back of Mike's other leg, which sent him to the ground in a writhing tangle of pain.

Sounded like it broke, Ella thought, smiling up at her rescuer. He'd been nearby the whole time, listening in, waiting for the right moment to make himself known.

"What…in the hell?" Amanda spun around to confront Ella's tag team partner, but sucked in a breath when she saw who it was. Peter Crane. Kept to himself mostly. Spent a lot of his time just watching people. Observing. Girls thought he was mysterious, but weren't brave enough to approach him, and most boys couldn't stand him—for the same reason girls didn't like Ella.

Because he was better than them. That was Ella's opinion, anyway.

Peter was mostly known for having never lost a fight, and he'd been in enough to guarantee no one would mess with him during his final year in high school. And now that dome of protection fell over Ella.

"The fuck?" Amanda said, stepping away from Peter, who just grinned back and stood his ground. She gave Mike a kick and then stormed away.

"I think my leg is broken," Mike groaned.

Peter ignored him and offered a hand to Ella. "Can I walk you inside?"

She took his hand and was pulled to her feet. "Every day."

He smiled. "That's the plan."

As they walked off, Mike called after them. "C'mon man, I didn't know she was your girl!"

"Shouldn't have mattered," Peter said, followed by, "I'll send the nurse."

"Ella, can you take a look at this for me?" Jeff Sexton asked.

She leaned back from her computer screen. Had been staring at it for hours, attempting to confirm all her findings before bringing it to the board for review. They were nearly there, and if she wasn't so tired, she'd be elated.

They were about to feed the world. She was about to save humanity by unlocking the unlimited potential hidden away in the DNA of every plant. Billions of years of adaptation that allowed plants to grow in nearly any environment, no matter how inhospitable.

Ella pushed her rolling chair across the lab, spun around, and then waddled the rest of the way, dragging the chair beneath her. "What am I looking at?"

"Uh, well, it's a birthday card for Laurie."

Ella paused her momentum. Raised her eyebrows. "A birthday card... I'm over here saving the world, and you're making a birthday card?"

"Hey, we're just about done, right? You've tripled checked everything about five times now."

"We can't mess this up, Jeff."

"That's impossible," he said. "You don't know how to mess up."

She smiled. "Let me see it."

Jeff stepped away from his computer, allowing Ella to roll right up to it. The screen displayed a card designed in Paintbrush, featuring a two-page poem.

"I wrote it myself," Jeff said, "so be gentle."

"Gentle? You forget whose help you just asked for?"

Jeff chuckled and walked away.

Ella focused on the poem. She'd never say it, but reading words instead of genetic code was a nice break. Her eyes slipped back and forth, reading each line. "Mind if I make corrections? Your spelling is horrible."

"'Course not," he said.

She glanced to the side, seeing his reflection in the monitor, standing at her station, scrolling through her findings, which included formulas, recommendations, and the DNA code for RC-714, which would revolutionize agriculture and end hunger, in spite of a global drought.

She returned to the poem, made a few more corrections before leaning back, fingers locked behind her head. "The bad news: it's god-awful. The good news: she'll love it."

"You think so?" Jeff asked, scurrying back.

"Just...get a few drinks in her first." Ella laughed.

"Always do," Jeff said, with a strange kind of gleam in his eyes—

Anne awoke with a gasp. Her mother and father leaned over her, panic in their eyes. "How long was I unconscious?"

"Just a few seconds," Peter said. "What happened?"

"When the computer accessed the drive in my head, it unlocked everything that hadn't yet filtered into my consciousness."

"Everything?" Ella asked.

"Everything." Anne's straight face confirmed the worst for Ella. There were no secrets between them now, aside from those kept during the past few years. "But I'm good at ignoring the gross stuff. Been doing that for a while now. But none of that is important."

"How is it not important?" Ella asked. "There's no way to predict—"

"I know what went wrong," Anne said. "With RC-714. And it wasn't your fault."

43

Jakob fought against the man holding him, but it was no use. He was outmuscled and groggy. "I'll kill you," he said to Manke, as the man lifted his rifle toward Val's head.

"Doubt it," Manke said, holding his aim steady. He paused. Glanced at Jakob. "You know you don't need to watch."

Felt strange. That small act of mercy, coming from one of Kenyon's lackies, was out of place. But he wasn't being kind out of concern for Jakob. He was trying to make the burden of his own bad life choices a little easier to carry.

Jakob stopped struggling. "You don't need to kill her. She's probably going to bleed out anyway, and it's not like she can go anywhere outside this building without being eaten by those mermaid bitches."

"You're right about that," Manke said. "But...orders are orders. You all just picked the wrong side of this fight."

"The side of humanity," Jakob said.

Manke scoffed. "We're *saving* humanity. Once we ascend, there will be nothing—nothing to stop the human race ever again. Hunger, feast, or famine, we will adapt."

"Sounds like someone's in a cult," Val said.

Manke squinted at her. "Thought you were stupid."

"People change," she said, "and you might be right about the future of humanity, but here's the thing—it's already happening without your cult. The Chunta adapted to live together, like the beasts in the sea, but we can become even more."

"You did have hair," Manke said, relaxing a touch.

"And tusks," Val added. "And I was stupid. But now, I'm just...evolved."

"Holy shit," the man holding Jakob said. "She's already ascended."

"Is that possible?" the third asked. "That's not possible, right?"

"Tell them who you are," Jakob said. He sensed a shift in the men's resolve. If they became convinced that Val had already become what they revered so much, they might not kill her after all. Though she really might bleed out if her wounds weren't tended to. Her body healed quickly, but there was a limit. He didn't know where it was but didn't want to find out.

Val pursed her lips and let out a remorseful sing-song tune that reverberated through the apartment and helped Jakob tune out the smell of blood filling the air. It was the opening to her most popular song, which was also a heartbreaking account of her father's death.

"I know that song," the man holding Jakob said. "Why do I know that?"

Manke blinked twice and stepped back. "You're Valerie Wood?"

"The singer?" the third man asked.

"Just Val now," she said. "And I am what you hope to become."

She spoke the words almost peacefully, like she'd ascended both body and soul.

"We can't kill her," the third man said. "We need to tell Lawrence about this. He'll want to know."

Manke shook his head. "We have our orders." He didn't sound convincing.

"Kenyon isn't in charge," the man holding Jakob said, "and this place has been a shit show since he got back. He's paranoid, and you know it."

"He was right about people being here," Manke said. "And he's probably right about Ella. He knows her better than anyone."

Jakob knew that wasn't true. Not remotely. But he wasn't about to argue the point. Their fate had been sealed but now it was in question. That was an improvement.

"If she dies," the third man said, "and we're the ones who killed her... and we find out later that she was ascended... Lawrence will never accept us back. The last few years... All of this shit... Will have been for nothing. Let's tie them both up. Take them to Lawrence. For all we know, she might know how the rest of us can ascend. She might have the answers the science team has been looking for."

"She's a singer," Manke said. "And a savage. She doesn't know anyth—"

"Not in her head, man. In her DNA."

Jakob thought they had a chance.

He didn't know what 'ascended' meant, but it seemed to be something to which they all aspired. Did they want to become Exos...but retain their intellect? Their humanity? Val had done that, but the process took a lot of time and likely wouldn't have happened at all if Feesa hadn't adopted them as her family.

But she did prove it was possible. *Controlled* ExoGenesis. Adaptation through sheer will, rather than chaotic responses to exterior influences. Hell, even Jakob would be interested in that. Ascension sounded like a good thing in this new world. Lawrence was right about that. But he was also the guy who killed the world, who took Ella's work and made it an abomination. If Jakob had anything to do with it, the only thing Lawrence would ascend to was a casket, before it was dropped into a deep hole.

"Shit," Manke said, lowering his weapon. He turned his back on Val, hand on his head. "God-damnit..."

Val tensed, about to take advantage of his distraction, but the other two men were still focused. Attacking now would seal their fates. Jakob gave her a slow shake of his head and was relieved when she relaxed. And then took it a step farther—appearing to pass out in a pool of her own blood.

"Look, man," the third said. "She's unconscious now. Probably going to die if we don't get her back to the island. I don't want that on my head, you know? I've given up too much to get this far, to let Kenyon's personal vendettas keep us from doing what we know to be right. We might be Viper Squad still, but we're not *his* Viper Squad. We're yours."

Manke sighed. "Tie them both up. Put them in the chopper."

"What about our dead?" the man holding Jakob asked.

"We'll come back for—what's that?" Manke cocked his head to the side, listening. The room went silent, and they all did the same. For a moment, nothing. Then a rhythmic scratching filled the air.

From outside the broken window.

And it was getting louder.

"Incoming!" Manke shouted, turning his weapon toward the oncoming sound.

Jakob's and Val's eyes met. He shook his head.

If something was scaling the outside of the building, it wasn't human. These three men and their guns might be their best chance of surviving the encounter. He mouthed the word, "Wait," before being tossed aside.

"Move and die," said his captor, "Got it?"

Jakob gave a wide-eyed nod, trying to look more frightened than he actually was.

A shriek cut through the air. It was just beneath the window, but had stopped short of coming in. Manke inched his way toward the glassless gap in the outer wall, one of three. Two were made by Viper Squad's dramatic entrance. The third, by Feesa's earlier exit—the same window Lyn had crawled out of.

Holy shit, Jakob thought. *Lyn!*

Manke leaned out the window, weapon aimed down. After a moment he relaxed. "Nothing there."

The response to his relief was anything but—a scream, a staccato burst of gunfire lighting up the hint of something monstrous, and then silence once more. Jakob's captor lay dead at his feet.

"The hell was that?" Manke shouted, shining his light on Jakob and the body. The man had three large holes in his chest and a fourth through his skull.

The scramble of claws tapped in the apartment's dark shadows. Manke shined his light back and forth, desperate to find a target. A wet, "Hrck!" gave him one.

His beam of light struck the third man's body, hovering three feet over the floor, blood pouring from his feet. Eight spear-like claws extended out from his torso. Then they separated, four pulling one way, four the other. The filleted man toppled to the floor, revealing the monster who'd crashed their party.

Its hands were tipped with long claws akin to a sloth's, but they weren't curved like talons for grasping prey.

They were straight.

Made for stabbing.

How did it scale the building with those claws? Jakob wondered while looking for any sign that the Apex standing before them had once been Lyn. He didn't see it in the insectoid eyes, in the black carapace covering its body, or in the long, muscley limbs that twitched with energy. It hissed at Manke, causing the man to piss his pants.

He stepped back, nearly fell through the window, and then lifted his weapon to open fire.

It was at that moment that the creature did something very human. It defended itself, bending forward into a squat and lowering its head, turning its body into an armored orb.

Manke fired, unleashing an entire magazine. The bullets impacted the carapace but didn't punch all the way through. They just pancaked and fell to the floor, leaving nothing but dents.

When the magazine ran out, Manke surprised them by leaping from the window. He caught hold of a line hanging from above and started climbing.

"He's getting away!" Jakob shouted.

The Apex unfurled its carapace, careened toward the window, and tackled Manke from the line. They fell out of sight together.

"Holy shit," Jakob said, pushing himself up. "Holy shit!"

He helped Val stand. She was bleeding and hurt, but shooed his concern away and said, "I'll live."

Jakob recovered his MP5 from the dead Viper Squad member who'd taken it. Then he inched toward the window, despite it being dark outside. Before he reached the edge, a loud buzzing sound pushed him back.

The Apex rose up outside the broken window, a set of wings extended from beneath its shell, vibrating, keeping it aloft.

Did it have wings before? he wondered. *Were they hidden beneath the armor?*

He raised his weapon but didn't fire.

The creature scurried away from the window and stopped. It wasn't threatening or moving in an aggressive way. Then its face began to contort. The tiny lenses making up its eyes flaked away as the bulbs shrank down.

A human face resolved, eyes clenched shut, face grimacing—but recognizable.

"Lyn?" Jakob said.

"In the flesh," she said, "such as it is."

"You can control it?" Jakob asked.

"Hurts. A lot. But yes. Evolution. Devolution. Whatever you want to call it. For whatever reason, I can control the change. The only real difference between me and Val, I think, is that she stumbled upon the discovery while I went into the change believing in it."

"I can do...this?" Val motioned to Lyn's new insectoid body.

"I believe so," Lyn said, then turned to Jakob. "But not right now. If these men were here for us, then it's likely they know about your parents."

"We need to go help them," Jakob said.

Lyn nodded. "And unless either of you can fly a helicopter..." Lyn opened her arms, which were armored on the outside, but still human on the inside. Her insect wings snapped open and fluttered. She smiled. "I suggest you come give me a hug."

44

Anne sat at the computer console to which she was still connected. She worked the keys unnaturally fast, like they were an extension of herself. Ella wondered if that was how it felt to Anne, the bridge between human and computer a closed loop. The girl had multiple software suites open at once, and was opening, changing, and saving files before Ella could see what they were.

"Don't worry about all this," Anne said. "This is just the background stuff, so we can easily generate a serum." She saved several files and switched to X-ACT, a gene sequencing program created exclusively for ExoGen under Ella's direction.

"This is where things really went wrong," Anne said, starting to scroll through pages of data.

"I checked this a hundred times," Ella said, leaning over Anne's shoulder, watching the code scroll by. How long had she spent staring at these pages? How much longer did she spend developing them? Her life's work. The end of the world.

Could it have been her fault? Was she somehow negligent?

"Here we go," Anne said, stopping on a page of what would look like gobbledygook to Peter, but was a language Ella read and wrote fluently. She was out of practice, but it didn't take her long to see the subtle change in the gene sequence.

She pointed to it. "This is wrong."

"I know," Anne said, changing, tapping in new letters on the keyboard, correcting the code. "And this." She scrolled some more. "And this."

"But...I checked every line. It was all right. It was..."

"It wasn't you," Anne said.

Ella's head snapped up. "What?"

"Do you remember the last time you checked this code?" Anne asked.

Ella thought back. It was a long time ago, but when you wrap up work on a project that destroys everything everyone loved, the moment tends to be etched in your mind. "I was in the lab. Same station I always used. Spent the day going through the code. Over and over."

"Uh-huh. And then?"

Ella couldn't remember. But Anne had full access to her memories, even the ones sifted out by time.

"Who was with you?"

The memory surfaced. "Jeff Sexton."

"Sexton?" Peter asked. "The guy from—"

"The pervy secret tunnel guy that had a penchant for bone marrow," Anne said. "That's the one. Only he wasn't just pervy. He was working for Lawrence. I mean, you were *all* working for Lawrence, but he was a collaborator. A believer in the vision of a world remade."

"But when did Sexton—"

"The birthday card," Anne said. "The horrible poem. He was changing the code while you were distracted. Only I...sorry, only *you* were a faster reader than he was expecting, and he didn't get to finish. His fiddling opened the RC-714 floodgates, but he only got to add a control to a narrow subset of crops. If he'd finished, the transformation of humanity might have been less violent...but no less horrific."

"Holy shit," Peter said to Ella. "None of this was your fault."

She staggered back, gripping the desk behind her. "My code would have worked."

"Like a champ," Anne said, still working. "Exactly how you planned it. Food for everyone. But your boss had other ideas and recruited people with the right access. The problem was—"

"Jeff was incompetent," Ella said.

"And negligent," Anne said. "Rather than tell Lawrence that he'd failed to fully execute the plan, he allowed it to go forward, allowed the world to burn to hide his mistake. That's the trouble with cults. The leader might be certifiable, and a genius, but the people who buy into the bullshit being slung are usually a few turds short of a satisfying evacuation.

"So, RC-714 was unlocked, but only a few crops got the control, which I believe filtered down to people who were either exposed to the finished crops first—or ate substantially more of that crop, the most common of which was oats." She looked at each of them, and then continued. "Now, oats are in and on a lot of things, especially at breakfast, but they're by far not the most common ExoGenetic ingredient. Corn and wheat top the charts and would easily overpower the effect of oats. This is all a hypothesis, by the way, though I'm fairly certain, based on the information at hand, that it's accurate. Anyway, the ability to control the change—which is what Sexton was attempting to accomplish—could have passed down to people who...I don't know, ate a bowl of oats every morning, or added oats to their smoothie, or whatever. Point is, more oats, more control. Val probably had a dietician, which generally means oats up the wazoo. I'm assuming. I've obviously never met a dietician, but that's how *you* feel about them." She glanced toward Ella.

"And what are you doing to the code now?" her mother asked. The text on the screen was moving too quickly for her to make out now. The whole time Anne had been talking, she'd been working, not even needing to see the screen. It was amazing. Impressive.

Ella felt jealous, but at the same time worried. The human mind wasn't meant to work like this.

Then again, Anne had been engineered. She was, in many ways, flawless. The best of Peter, the best of Ella along with all her knowledge.

"How are you feeling?" she asked Anne. "Is this taxing your—"

"Never better," Anne said. "In fact, it feels natural, I guess. Like when you're in the zone on a hunt." She looked to Peter. "And everything just kind of slows down. You hear more. See more. Smell more. Your heart rate slows. It's like some kind of primal state of mind. Feels like that... though I don't think our ancestors were using advanced technology to make cave paintings." Her eyes widened. "Unless they were. Never mind. Subject for another day. I'm nearly done."

"Nearly done with what?" Ella asked.

"Plan A," Anne said. "And plan B."

Around the room, machines whirred to life. Whatever Anne had made, she was already synthesizing it. Working too fast.

"What is plan A?" Peter asked.

"Mom's original plan. Me, basically. The ability to eat ExoGenetic crops without changing into an Exo. It locks the door. Those changes were easy because Mom already did them and tested them on me. The harder part was finishing Sexton's work. He did a sloppy job the first time around, but it's good to go, now."

"You did what?" Ella asked.

"Okay, okay, okay," Anne said, raising her hands. "I know what you're going to say. Or at least I have a pretty good idea, because, you know—" She motioned to the USB cable plugged into the back of her head. "So just hear me out."

Ella clenched her teeth but didn't say anything.

"I know your vision was, and is, to have humanity eating the bounty you created, but humanity is on the brink and is kind of...outgunned. Outnumbered. Out everything. This whole island is surrounded by Merpeople I'm willing to bet liked to eat oats. Same with the Chunta. Same with the Stalkers. They were able to maintain some of their humanity thanks to Jeff's fiddling, but they don't have the will, or the knowledge, to direct it. So, they're evolving communally. But—they're still hungry, and violent, and *eat normal people*. And since there is nothing in these genetic changes that prevents copulation or pregnancy, you better believe there will be future generations of all communal Exos, and the smattering of normal people won't be able to handle them—without help."

"You want to give people the ability to...what? Change into—"

"Into anything they want, while maintaining their intellect, and the ability to change back. Like a werewolf, or the Incredible Hulk, or Jekyll and Hyde without the, you know, whole being pure evil in the ranks of mankind thing. Think of them like humanity's new special operators. Warriors who can defend human settlements, or...kill Exo populations that aren't able to be rescued."

She turned to Ella and pointed her finger. "If you're serious about saving this world, we're going to have to get our hands dirty, and I don't just mean today. People are going to have to make sacrifices. Are going to have to do things they don't want to do. Do you understand?"

Ella couldn't answer.

It was too much. To come all this way. To stop the change. To undo the damage she'd done only to find out it was never her fault. Regret billowed. It *was* her fault. She should have checked her work one more time. Should have made sure it was right. Sabotage or not, she should have noticed.

Which left her mission unchanged.

But what Anne was telling her... It was unthinkable. To ensure the success of her vision for the world, of humanity rescued, safe and fed, she would also have to embrace Lawrence's vision.

A world full of monsters, of twisted, corrupt, abomin—

"I understand," Peter said.

"Good," Anne said, unplugging herself from the computer. She bustled around the room, opening compartments, taking out supplies, working fast.

"What?" Ella said to Peter. "What did you just say?"

"She's not wrong," he said. "People, on their own? We don't stand a chance. Only reason we made it here was because of Val. If I had a few more like her, this would have been easy."

Ella paced, hand to her head.

"I can't believe I'm hearing this."

"Well, I can," a familiar voice said. "And it's music to my ears."

Ella whirled around to find Lawrence standing behind four masked security guards at the door.

Anne finished whatever she'd been working on, palming something in her hand before spinning around. She ducked behind Peter.

"No need to hide, dear," Lawrence said. "You have proven yourself to be this company's most valuable asset. Congratulations on completing our work, by the way. We appreciate it so much."

Horror seeped into Ella's bones. She glanced back at the computer. The *networked* computer. "You knew... You knew this whole time that we were here. You let us in. You let us..." She kicked a trash can across the room. "God-damn you, Lawrence."

"Your anger is misplaced. It always has been. The time to ascend, to inherit the Earth, has come, and you will be here to witness it. I will not bestow that gift upon you, but I can't think of anyone more deserving than your daughter."

"You son-of-a—" Ella charged but was stopped by a rifle butt to the head. Peter was stopped in his tracks when the rifle's barrel came up to his chest. The man wielding it pulled off his mask.

Kenyon.

"Hey, babe," he said to Ella, who was groaning on the floor. Then he nodded to Anne. "Kid."

Kenyon leveled a glare toward Peter, greeted him with, "Asshole," and then pulled the trigger.

45

Pretending to be unconscious while lying still on the floor was a trick, especially if you've just been shot point blank. Peter was wearing body armor, and it had done its job against the bullet, but the impact, directly over his sternum, felt like a wrecking ball and knocked the air from his lungs.

Mind and body urged him to breathe deeply. To suck in air. But he resisted, feigning unconsciousness. It wasn't a stretch. The bullet impact to the chest, and his subsequent impacts with the wall and then the floor, had nearly done the job.

There was no point in getting up. In letting them know he could take a bullet and keep on fighting. The primal male part of his brain wanted to show off his machismo, but it was overruled by the desire to stay alive and keep his family alive.

So, he laid still, eyes closed, breathing regularly.

It took all his discipline to pull it off, but when no one hurried to subdue him, it was clear they all bought the act—including Anne.

"I'll claw your god-damn eyes out," she shouted and threw herself at Kenyon. One of the other guards caught hold of her shoulder and paid for it with a pointy elbow to the groin. The man doubled over, releasing Anne.

Despite being outpowered by everyone in the room, Anne threw a punch toward Kenyon's crotch. She'd nut-shot each and every one of them until they were curled up on the floor—if given the chance.

She wasn't.

Kenyon caught her wrist, lifted her off the ground, and tossed her as casually as someone throwing laundry into the drier. She bounced off the wall and fell to the floor, catching herself.

That was when she remembered her pistol and drew it.

"Uh, uh, uh," Kenyon said, kicking the pistol from her hand. "Play nice. I need you alive. Uninjured is up for debate."

Anne started picking herself up, glancing in Peter's direction. They made brief eye contact. He gave her a wink, which he hoped was enough to fill her in on the game plan: feign defeat.

Fighting back right now meant death. There was no way around it.

Well, there was one way.

It was tucked in Peter's hand.

At first, he wasn't sure what Anne had slipped into his grasp. Felt like a pencil at first. But now…now he had identified the slender object, capped on one end, cylindrical in the middle, with a slightly elevated plunger on the far end.

She'd given him a small syringe. The kind used to deliver vaccines. But he didn't know what it was. The actual vaccine, meant to stop the unlocking of RC-714? Or something more...transformative.

Anne winked back and let out a groan. She pushed herself up and came face-to-face with four raised assault rifles.

"Tut, tut," Lawrence said. "I want her alive."

"Can she be paralyzed?" Kenyon asked.

"Just so you all know," Anne said, gun at her side. "I understand now why you all want to change your bodies so much. You have itsy bitsy tiny little dicks." She dropped the gun to the floor.

Peter tried not to sigh with relief.

Lawrence clapped his hands together. "Well done, girl. Well done."

"Yes," Anne said, imitating Lawrence's voice. "Bravo to me." She held out her hands. "You going to zip-tie me, or what?"

One of the men lowered his weapon and produced a zip-tie as though taking orders from Anne.

"Nonsense," Lawrence said. "She's just a girl."

"Just a girl?" Anne said, anger brewing. Then she caught herself, and said, "That's right. What am I going to do to anyone without a gun, hmm?"

"Gag her at least," Kenyon said, "or she won't stop talking."

"I will take her," Lawrence said, and then tilted his head toward Ella. "Take those two to the brig and Norris over there to the infirmary."

"The brig?" a guard asked. "We don't have a—"

"This facility sits atop a fort that was used to house civil war prisoners. I'm sure you can figure something out." Lawrence was about to leave, his hand guiding Anne by the shoulder, but then he paused and gave Kenyon a nod. "It appears you were right, Edward. Well done."

"Thank you, sir," Kenyon said, but Peter detected a hint of stress in his voice. They didn't like each other very much.

"This way, girl," Lawrence said, leading Anne out into the hall where he addressed a group of scientists. "Your work has been completed for you by this young girl. I trust you can manage the manufacturing of enough serum to test in an hour? And then enough for the ascension at noon tomorrow?"

A man answered with a hushed, apologetic voice.

"Yes, sir. Of course, sir."

While eight scientists bustled into the room, Peter and Ella were disarmed, their weapons given to Kenyon. Then the four guards picked the two of them up and followed Kenyon into the hallway.

Feigning unconsciousness was even more difficult when being held by the wrists and ankles, bumbled down a hallway. Any expression of discomfort or twitch of a muscle could give him away. Luckily, no one had noticed that one of his hands had remained closed.

"This will work," Kenyon said after a five-minute walk that took them through three doors and down a single flight of stairs.

"But Lawrence said—"

"Any of you have keys to the old fort's rooms? I know I don't. Lawrence was being dramatic. Trying to freak out the kid." There was an electronic beep and the sound of a door unlocking. "And since I can open this door…it will work."

The four guards shuffled into the room, depositing Ella and Peter on the floor.

"No one opens this door but me," Kenyon said. "Understood?"

"Wait," one man said, "You want us to stand guard?"

"All four of you," Kenyon said. "Yeah. And if he tries anything, shoot him…because if you give him a chance, he'll do the same to you."

As they moved back out into the hallway, one of the guards said, "He doesn't look like he'll be able to do all that much."

Kenyon chuckled. "Your powers of observation are as keen as ever, Munch."

"What…I don't…"

"He's awake, asshole," Kenyon said. "Been feigning unconsciousness."

Ruse over, Peter opened his eyes, which made all four guards flinch back. They were definitely not cut from the same cloth as Kenyon, or his Viper Squad. If they didn't have guns, he'd make short work of all four of them.

"Chat soon," Kenyon said, closing the door and locking it.

They were in an empty room, identical to the labs on the floor above, but devoid of equipment or shelving. The four guards watched them through the long window for a moment.

"They gone yet?" Ella asked, still not moving.

"Watching us," Peter said. "Through the window. No point in pretending to be unconscious."

"Wasn't pretending at first," she said, pushing herself up with a grunt. She had an egg on her forehead but it wasn't bleeding. "How'd they get you?"

Peter turned his chest toward her, revealing the bullet lodged in his armor.

She winced. "That must have hurt."

"Mm," Peter said, climbing to his feet. He approached the window and took a moment to look each of their guards in the eyes, communicating a threat without speaking a word. The first blinked a lot. The second swallowed. The third furrowed his brow. The fourth man took a step back and made a joke that Peter couldn't hear, but no one laughed at.

Then Peter stepped to the side and lifted his hand.

One of the guards understood what he was doing and shouted, "Stop!" Peter couldn't hear him, but his lips were easy to read. He gave the guard a smile and pressed the button, turning the window black.

"Where's Anne?" Ella asked.

"Lawrence has her. Plans to test the new serum on her. Make a display of it, and then ascend with the rest of them."

Ella climbed to her feet. "You have a plan, right? Please tell me you have a plan."

Peter nodded. "But you're not going to like it. At all."

Ella scrunched up her face. "Tell me."

Peter opened his hand, revealing the syringe Anne had snuck into it. "We're going to test the new serum first."

46

"Listen, bitch," Anne said to Hutchins behind her. "Shove me again and I'll bite your jugular."

"You got a mouth on you," Hutchins said. "Your time in the wild turned you feral."

"Just you wait," Anne said, shrugging away from Hutchins as he pushed her onward again. Lawrence led them through the facility like he was giving a tour, like Anne was there to pick out an apartment and needed to be impressed. He sounded proud of everything they'd done. A true believer in his own bullshit.

"She was purified in the fires of the change," Lawrence said. "I can think of no better person to lead us through the ascension, foul language or not."

"As long as you're not using that garbage code that your man inserted into my mother's work," Anne said.

"You're...okay with this?" Hutchins asked.

"I welcome it," Anne said, "with open arms. It's my work, after all. If I were freaking out right now, you'd have a reason to be worried. I mean, you have a lot of reasons to be worried, but if you want to jab me with the good stuff, I'm ready for it."

"You see?" Lawrence said, pausing by a door and swiveling around to face her. "She is a delight. A willing test subject. The first of her kind."

Not sure about that, she thought.

Lawrence motioned to the door. "Now, if you don't mind, please change your clothing in preparation for the ceremony." He unlocked the door, and it slid open.

"We're doing this now? Also, if you've got some kind of skimpy outfit for me, you can forget it. You don't even want to know what I did to the last perv I met."

"I'm sure you will appreciate the clothing," Lawrence said. "And yes. Our people are gathering in the atrium for the demonstration now. If all goes well, we will ascend this evening, when enough of your serum has been produced. They have waited for this moment long enough. Delay is not something I will tolerate, so do be quick. Unless you need someone to dress you."

Anne rolled her eyes, and mimicked Lawrence to Hutchins. "Do be quick." She stepped inside the room, and the door closed behind her. She closed her eyes, leaned against it, and let out a sigh.

She was naturally snarky, but maintaining her practiced lack of concern was difficult when she was freaking out. Her parents had been captured. Who knew what was happening to them. And as much as she trusted her own work, the only real way to know she'd been successful was to inject someone.

Her turn would come soon enough, but if Peter trusted her, he'd be first. *He'll go through with it,* she thought, and she hoped his belief in her ability wasn't misplaced.

Anne looked around the room. It wasn't decorated at all.

A vacant bedroom. With all the ExoGen people not surviving the journey east, there were probably a lot of bedrooms like this. The design was retro modern, orange and beige. The bed rested on a legless platform extending from the wall. It was barren of sheets and blankets but held a neat bundle of white fabric. She picked it up. The clothing unfurled to reveal a conservative white dress with little knit floral patterns. The kind of thing you have a virgin wear before she's sacrificed.

"Cliché," Anne said, looking it over. "If this thing is see-through, someone is getting a kick in the teeth."

When she put the dress back down, she noticed dirt smudges from her fingers. She was filthy, covered in months of grime and whatever ancient crap was floating around in the water inside the fort's tunnels.

"Shower would have been nice," she grumbled, and was about to undress. Then she paused and turned around. The bedroom had the same long window as the labs. She walked up to it and looked out. Lawrence and Hutchins were waiting for her.

When Hutchins noticed her and made eye contact, she flipped him the bird, and blacked out the glass. They hadn't been looking in at her, but they could have mentioned the window.

"Should have changed the code to make dicks fall off," she grumbled and then set herself to the task of changing. Her clothing was caked on.

Almost part of her skin, which stretched as she peeled the fabric away. Beneath, she was pale enough to see veins where she shouldn't. Her body was strong and fit, but she didn't really like what she saw.

"And now *I'm* the cliché," she said, and put the dress on.

It fit well enough. She wouldn't be winning any beauty pageants, but she didn't look like a sewer-dweller anymore, either. She leaned forward and rubbed her hands over her shaved head. Dirt and leaf litter flaked away and fell to the floor.

The dress made her feel like the rest of her should be presentable. She wasn't sure why. She'd never worn a dress before.

But my mother has, she thought, a memory of her grandmother rising to the surface. Seeing through her mother's eyes, she watched the woman, who looked a lot like her mother, smooth out her dress, tsk, and then fiddle again.

"I don't think I'll ever get this straight on you," grandmother had said.

"I don't care," Ella had said. "About dresses or photo day."

"I'll be sending these photos to your aunt and uncle in California. I want them to know you."

"If you want them to know me, let's go to California. Or at least send them a photo of my science fair project. I *did* win."

Grandmother had rolled her eyes, the same way Anne liked to do. "This is the real you. You'll grow into her someday." With one last tug, her grandmother had leaned back, looked her over, and said, "That will have to do."

Anne blinked out of the memory. It came and went like a breeze, like it was her own. She'd never known her grandmother. The woman had died before the change, but Anne knew the woman as well as her mother had.

When a twig fell out from behind Anne's ear, she said, "Well, that's embarrassing," and she gave up the effort. She really didn't care what she looked like, and cared even less if her grandmother would have approved.

She went to the door and opened it.

Lawrence turned to her with a big smile. "You look lovely."

"Dresses are weird." Anne stood awkwardly, like she'd been riding a horse. "Guess I don't mind airing out my business, though."

She smiled when both men squirmed.

"I know," she said. "I'm a lot. You'll get used to it."

"Yes, well, follow me." Lawrence started down the hall and Hutchins nodded his head for her to follow.

She did as she was told, unconcerned about what might happen next. Because for this part of the plan, she was on board. If they hadn't been interrupted in the lab, she was going to use the syringe on herself. She understood how the modified RC-714 would work and what it would allow her to do.

Killing people wasn't like killing Exos, but if she didn't stop the guys with guns—at the very least—her family was in a lot of trouble. She meant what she'd said, about humanity needing protectors from the changed world. She aimed to be the first, and Lawrence was giving her exactly what she wanted.

"So," she asked. "What's the plan? I mean, post ascension. You're all Exos, can become what you want, and...then what?"

"A purge," he said, "of my failures."

"Exos in the wild," she said. "I'm down with that. They're pretty much all assholes. What next?"

"We repeat the story that has marked the evolution of humanity's rise from the apes." He paused and grasped a door handle. "Join us or die." He pulled the door open to reveal a massive circular room laid out like a theater in the round. There was even a stage—encased in a cylinder of thick glass. The floor glowed white and sterile.

The atrium wasn't exactly packed, on account of so many people being missing, but this was the most people she had seen in one space in her life. For a moment it was disconcerting, then a flash of her mother's memories, speaking in front of audiences, on television, in front of the press, reassured her. She was a younger—and tougher—version of her mother. She could do this.

The crowd hushed, all eyes watching her descend the stairs behind Lawrence.

Ahead, a woman who was trying to look pleased and presentable, but still had a bedraggled air about her, waited with a syringe.

"I thought you'd be making a big show of this," Anne said.

"We are scientists," Lawrence replied. "We applaud results. Until then, we're all business."

"Makes sense, I guess," she said, and paused before the woman, who said nothing. She just rolled up Anne's sleeve and wiped her shoulder down with alcohol. "Won't need to worry about infections, you know."

The woman flashed her a shit-eating grin and then looked to Lawrence.

He asked Anne, "Are you ready?"

"Pretty sure, I was born for this," Anne said, and then she turned to the woman. "Stick me."

Lawrence gave a nod, and the woman injected the serum into Anne's shoulder. Hutchins opened the door on the cylindrical containment space. The glass was a lot thicker than she'd thought. Maybe too thick.

"In you go," Lawrence said, "before you get any foolish ideas."

Anne scrunched her face up at him and stomped up the stairs. She turned around inside the tube, about to vent her anxiety with a bold declaration when Hutchins closed the door on her and snapped its six locks into place.

Well, shit, she thought. *Guess I'll just have to wait and—*

Anne spasmed and fell to the floor, her mind and body consumed by agony.

47

"No way," Ella said. "No fucking way."

Peter didn't blame her for being reluctant. If Anne had made a mistake, he would turn on Ella and eat her. But if the serum worked...if he was granted access to billions of years of evolution, he'd have everything needed to stop Lawrence and Kenyon, and to protect their family and friends for generations.

The alternative was to sit in this cell and wait for Lawrence to ascend with his new master race, after which Ella and Anne would become expendable. This was the only way, and Peter trusted Anne. She was young, but far from stupid and had the same skills as her mother. She knew the stakes. Knew that she'd be putting her mother at risk. Anne wouldn't have done that if she wasn't confident in her work.

"We don't have a choice," Peter said. "They have Anne."

"That is untested, created by my daughter, in a matter of minutes. Injecting it into your body would be the height of stupidity."

"She's a lot more than your daughter, Ella. She's…you. In all the ways that matter regarding RC-714. If this was going to turn me into a monster, you'd have never given it to me. And neither would she."

"You could eat me," she said.

He forced a smile. "Better me than Kenyon, right?"

She soured. "Not helping."

"Look, you're used to dealing in absolutes. I get that. Measure twice, cut once and all that." He waved her confused look away. "You know what I mean. Test, test, test, and test again. That's why RC-714's failure bothered you so much. You did your due diligence. You perfected it. Would have saved the world, and I love you for that, but this is a second chance. To save what's left. And to do that, we need to do things my way.

"We need to trust the people who've been in the trenches with us.

"We need to take risks.

"And we might need to sacrifice something to get the job done."

He held the needle up.

"Your humanity…" She shook her head. "It's not right."

"Or," he said, "it's the most right choice left in the world. And, if this is what Anne envisioned, my humanity will be intact. Risk isn't the same as reality. It's more like a branch, veering off in different directions with a multitude of outcomes, only one of which includes me eating you."

"That's some bullshit Schrödinger logic," she said.

"Well, he sounds like a smart man to me." Peter looked at the syringe. There wasn't a lot of liquid inside, but when it came to DNA-altering RC-714, a single nugget of contaminated Captain Crunch was enough to get the job done. "Any idea how long this will take to affect me?"

"ExoGenetic change is different for everyone. Some people respond within minutes, others take days, most take months."

"Is there a way to guarantee it's faster acting?" he asked.

"Well, yeah, you'd just have to—" Ella stopped herself. Understood the ramifications. "She'd have made that change, too. But there's still no way to know, for sure, if it will work the way we want it to, or at all."

"Risk and sacrifice," Peter said. "Nothing good in this world is ever achieved without those two things."

She smiled. "So noble."

"I'm a god-damned American hero," he said, holding the syringe over his arm. He looked her in the eyes, taking a deep breath.

Before he could do the job himself, she closed the distance between them, kissed him hard on the lips, and put her hand over his. Together, they injected the serum.

She stepped back, looking him over. "How do you feel?"

"Well, it stung a little."

"Baby."

He held a hand out to her.

She took it and he pulled her in close. "Just in case," he said, and this time he kissed her.

Lost in the moment, he focused on the feel of her lips, of her body against his, of the comfort her presence gave to him. This was worth fighting for. Worth dying and killing for. He'd fight the whole planet if he had to.

He leaned back, wiped some grime from her cheek with his thumb, and then—

—arched his back in pain and toppled to the floor.

Pain consumed him, shooting jolts of electricity burning through every nerve in his body. His limbs contorted, out of control. An inhuman sound came from his mouth, equal parts scream, and involuntary spasm of the lungs.

His vision flickered. Mixed with flashes of light, he saw Ella standing over him, maybe shouting his name, or just shouting. There was nothing she could do. The change was happening fast, that much was clear. The DNA inside him was being rewritten in a cascade of violent change. Every cell modified, able to become not just something new, but anything new. And it hurt.

More than anything he'd endured before.

He'd been writhing for seconds, but it felt like an eternal hell, burning his core until, for a moment, he longed for death.

Then, it was over.

He heaved a breath and slapped his hands on the ground, body back under control.

"You're okay," Ella said, kneeling beside him. "You're okay."

"That..." he said, panting for air. "That was horrible."

She helped him sit up. He slow-blinked his eyes a few times. Peter's vision felt different, but he couldn't identify exactly how. He stretched his jaw next and then checked in with the rest of his body, making sure it was all still there and normal.

"Still me," he said.

"Not feeling hungry, are you?"

He smiled. "I'm always hungry, but no more than usual."

"But...can you change?" Ella asked.

"How does it work?"

She shrugged. "Not entirely sure. I've never been an Exo, but normally adaptations occur with environmental challenges ranging from temperature change to attack from a rival... But with this, it should be guided by your intellect, at least partially."

"So, I just...think it."

"More than that," she said. "You need to will it, same way sprinters do when they pump their legs faster than other people can manage. It's as much about their will power and ability to visualize than it is physical ability."

"You just make that up now?"

She smiled. "Sounded good, though, right?"

He held out his hand. "Okay...what first?"

"Something simple," she said. "Claws. Just try...I don't know...try to see them on your hands. Imagine them extending."

He took a breath, let it out quickly and then did as he was told. He wasn't a stranger to the concept of visualization. It was a useful aid in combat. The ability to see what you were about to do, accurately, increased the likelihood of success. He put it into practice whenever there was time.

And if there wasn't, he let instinct and muscle memory take over.

Despite all that, he was still shocked and somewhat horrified when his fingernails rose up and fell away, pushed by five long, black talons that took their place, like molars replacing baby teeth.

"It worked," Ella whispered. "Holy shit, it worked. Does it hurt?"

Peter said nothing.

He just looked at his hand.

His hand—

With claws.

"Peter?"

He blinked. "What? Sorry. This is ahh, this is going to take some getting used to."

"Best way to get used to cold water," she said. "Jump right in."

He got to his feet, psyching himself up for something big. Something really different. But what? An ape hand? A bear paw? He shook his head.

Think big, he told himself. *Think old.*

He took another steadying breath and said, "Don't freak out. Don't freak out."

"I'm fine," Ella said.

"I'm talking to myself," he said, and then willed a change that didn't seem possible until he witnessed it with his own eyes. His hand grew wider. His index and middle fingers fused together. So did his ring and pinkie fingers. He felt the flesh joining, the bones merging.

Extending.

His thumb did the same, and inside twenty seconds, he had the three-fingered hand of a dinosaur. He wasn't sure which one. Didn't have a name in mind. He just had the image in his head, and RC-714 reached back into the treasure trove of junk DNA contained in the human body and pulled out all the elements needed to make it happen.

He laughed, curling his now long fingers.

Then he approached the wall and dragged his talons over it, peeling away three long curls of metal. "Okay, I think I've got the hang of this." He lifted his left hand and watched as he changed it—not into the hand of a dinosaur, but into the faceless head of one—a Pachycephalosaurus—which he did know the name of, thanks to Jurassic Park.

He smiled at the battering ram limb. "I was going to have you pound on the door. See if they'd open it." He lifted his arm so she could take in its awesomeness. "But I think I'll try knocking first."

48

Kenyon watched as Anne collapsed to the floor of her cylindrical cell, writhing in agony. If the process was really that painful, he doubted everyone would go through with it. But that was kind of the point. Ascending was transmogrification. You start out one thing, you become another. There was nothing in the universe that could pull off something like that without more than a little pain, or destruction.

That was exactly how Lawrence justified the human race's near destruction.

And that was why he kept Sexton's mission a secret. Why he didn't allow anyone to check the work.

Because he knew.

Sexton hadn't made a mistake. He'd done exactly as Lawrence had asked him to do, ensuring a brutal end for most of the human race. Sexton's mistake was purposely sewing some of Lawrence's code among the corrupted crops, resulting in tribes of more advanced Exos forming, retaining some of their humanity. If they only knew they could control their adaptations, the Stalkers, the Chunta, and the creatures now surrounding the island would have been more human than monster—and a lot easier to kill.

Kenyon hadn't known all of this.

Lawrence revealed the truth to him while Viper Team was sent into the city. He'd sensed the tension brewing between the two of them and wanted to make it right. It was a noble gesture, but Kenyon knew that was all it was. A gesture. A fragile peace offering to ensure this moment went smoothly.

His thoughts shifted to Viper Squad for a moment.

He hadn't heard from them yet, which could mean trouble, but he currently had his radio off for the ascension. Peter, Ella, and the kid were here.

That left Jakob and Feesa as potential threats. Viper Squad could handle them.

He watched Anne spin and squirm, curling up into a ball, and then spasming outward. He stood from his chair and descended the stairs, stopping just outside the containment unit beside Lawrence, Hutchins, and the doctor who'd administered the shot.

There were a few more on a nearby metal tray.

Those were for the chosen few. Those most loyal to Lawrence. They would ascend first. Kenyon had no idea who they were meant for, but he doubted he was on the list. The moment these people could become living weapons, the protection he provided them would no longer be necessary.

"Is this supposed to happen?" Hutchins asked, adjusting the shotgun hanging over his back. He'd claimed the powerful weapon after Peter had been captured. The other men took his blade, pistol, and M4, but Hutchins had chosen the best for himself. The fully auto shotgun was an Exo killer...and he was wondering if he needed it now.

All around the room, people were whispering, horrified as Anne frothed at the mouth, rolling back and forth, slamming into the walls.

"Radical change is never easy," Lawrence said, but there was an edge in his voice. Doubt.

Kenyon chuckled.

Lawrence turned to him, irate. Hutchins turned as well but looked closer to horrified. Lawrence didn't publicly fail often. When he did, those he was angered with at the time tended to have accidents or suddenly develop deadly allergies.

But Kenyon wasn't concerned.

"If you'd gotten to know her better, the truth of what's happening in there would be as clear as your vision for this planet."

Lawrence waited, his pale blue eyes wide and enlarged by his glasses.

"She's faking it," Kenyon said. "Probably not at first, but..." He motioned to Anne, who now looked like she was speaking in tongues on the floor of a Pentecostal church. "...she's definitely hamming it up right now, trying to frighten us away from trying the serum ourselves."

"Trying the—" Lawrence looked him in the eyes and told him what he already knew. "You are not one of the chosen few. Your job is to keep us safe while we—"

"Don't worry, Lawrence," Kenyon said. "I know exactly what my job is. Now..." He knocked on the glass container. "Kid. Hey, kid! You can knock it off. We know you're pretending."

She thrashed and arched her back, a regular contortionist.

"You're not fooling anyone," he said.

She glanced in his direction, and he saw just a hint of a smile.

He'd gotten something wrong.

She was definitely putting on a show, but he'd gotten the motivation wrong.

She wasn't trying to frighten them away from trying the serum, she was buying time.

Figuring out how it worked. What she could do.

Looking at her, it was hard to remember that she shared Ella's intellect, while at the same time having the capacity to be ruthless.

"Step back," he said to Lawrence.

Hutchins listened immediately. Had learned to trust Kenyon's orders. But Lawrence was accustomed to giving orders, not following them. He needed a reason why.

Kenyon shook his head. "She's not trying to scare us. She's buying time."

"Time?" Lawrence asked. "Time for what?"

Anne answered the question herself by springing to her feet, cocking back a fist that changed into something resembling a Stegosaurus tail, and smashing it against the glass.

Kenyon had lived in the wild long enough to not be shocked by the transformation. He'd seen far more dramatic adaptations.

What did surprise him was the crack left in the glass. Lawrence had assured him it was thick enough to contain an elephant. Without resources to convert to new flesh and bone, Anne wouldn't be able to grow larger. But she'd changed her physiology on the inside, thrashing around so no one would see the subtle changes on the outside—the tightly coiling muscle, the reduction in height.

She'd tapped into some small, but powerful ancestors, and with a few more swings—she'd be free.

Worried shouts turned into panic. The audience came to their senses and realized none of them would be safe when Anne escaped. They scrambled for the doors, tripping and shoving, all loyalty to each other lost to desperation.

Lawrence's vision for the future would never succeed. Human nature would never allow it.

Kenyon turned toward the female doctor holding the remaining syringes. She'd begun to back away and was about to follow the lemmings out of the atrium.

Lawrence saw what was about to happen and stood in front of him. "No! It is not for you."

"Never was," Kenyon said, "but you've never really understood who is in charge here. Loyalty can't be demanded. It has to be earned." He glanced at Hutchins and then nodded to Lawrence.

Even if Hutchins was a true believer, he knew who to follow when the shit sprayed sideways. He stepped behind Lawrence, pulled his hands back and zip-tied them behind his back.

"Sorry, sir," Hutchins said. "We'll set you free when all is said and done. This is for your own good. Kenyon knows what he's doing."

Lawrence cursed and struggled but was unable to prevent Hutchins from guiding him into a seat.

Kenyon hurried toward the doctor as she continued to back away. "Drop those and I will break your neck."

The threat shocked her into standing still long enough for Kenyon to snatch the tray from her hands. He plucked one of the syringes up and turned to Hutchins. "Hey." He tossed him the syringe. "No more fucking around."

Kenyon kept a syringe for himself and placed the tray on a front row seat. "On three," he said to Hutchins.

A loud crack turned their eyes toward the containment unit. Spiderweb cracks expanded. Anne was nearly out.

"Release me!" Lawrence shouted, the pitch of his voice rising. "You fucking morons! I will have you–"

"Three." Kenyon said, and he injected the serum into his arm. Hutchins followed his lead. For a moment, nothing, then Kenyon wondered how he'd fallen to the floor. That was when the pain started, bringing on convulsions powerful enough to make him doubt his assessment of Anne.

She hadn't been faking the raw anguish. She'd just been using the time to focus, to get a handle on the change, so that when the time came to strike, she was ready. Kenyon closed his eyes and attempted to do the same.

He could feel the change roiling through him, like river rapids, churning through his cells, outward from the injection site.

"Faster," he shouted through grinding teeth. "Faster!"

Glass cracked and clattered to the floor.

Kenyon forced his eyes open. The containment tube had broken, but the hole wasn't large enough for Anne to fit through. However, she'd already reared back for another strike.

He had seconds.

He needed to focus on adapting. On changing. Ascending.

An explosion of glass burst from the center of the atrium as the cylinder containing Anne finally gave way. Lawrence shouted as a shard lodged in his skin, drawing blood. Beside him, Hutchins climbed to his feet, somehow adjusting to the change faster than Kenyon.

Because he's not actually changing, he realized.

Hutchins lacked the imagination to alter his body while the change was still in progress. A moment later, he paid the price. With a roar, Anne leapt down from the elevated platform, a triangle of glass held in her hand. She threw the shard at Lawrence. Hutchins, foolishly, did his job, putting himself between the deadly projectile and his supposed savior.

The impact was hard enough to punch through Hutchins's sternum and launch him back. He cleared three rows of seats, landing in the fourth, now upside down, his legs up in the air.

It was a noble end. Dumb, but noble. And Kenyon had no intention of joining him.

"Do what you want with him," Kenyon said, stepping backward, giving himself a little more time. "I have what I wanted."

Anne looked at Lawrence, her skin growing thick and rough as she reached into the past and turned herself into a weapon. "He's not going anywhere," she said, and then she pointed her Stegosaurus arm toward Kenyon. "And neither are you."

With a roar too deep for such a small girl, Anne charged.

49

Anne put all her strength into striking Kenyon.

Problem was, he put all his into being fast and agile, leaping out of the way. Anne's Stegosaurus fist-tail crashed into a chair, demonstrating the effect it would have on a human ribcage, folding it inward and punching several large holes.

She shrank down the spikes and pulled the limb free.

Changing her body felt natural. Maybe because she'd been grown in a lab, or just because she was a kid. But it was also taxing. Every time she changed, she felt a little more tired. Not like a muscle burn kind of thing, but like groggy. Like a nap would be nice, or a meal.

This was why the Exos were so ravenous, she realized. Adaptations used energy. Used resources. They needed a massive intake of calories to fuel the constant changes triggered by their environment. Without it, they would die out, consuming themselves from the inside out.

The secret to humanity's survival wasn't all-out war on the Exos, it was hiding until they all starved to death. It might take years, but every human out in the wild just gave them an opportunity to feast again, to extend their hunger until the inevitable famine returned.

And because they're dumb, she thought, *they don't realize they can just be vegetarians!*

During her moment of thought, she forgot that Kenyon was an asshole who wouldn't hesitate to attack a little girl. She didn't really blame him. She had just killed his friend with a shard of glass, but still. His counterstrike nearly succeeded, feigning a punch and then a kick, both of which were followed by a tail that she hadn't seen sprout from his backside.

She sprang out of the way, narrowly avoiding being bludgeoned by the club at the end. After scrambling over the tops of several chair backs, she spun around and shouted, "An Ankylosaurus tail? Really? Are you just copying me now?"

She looked at both of her arms. They shrank back down, returning the material to her body. Her fingers grew anew, each ending with a razor-sharp claw. "You can crush. I'll cut deep."

"Works for me, kid," he said, and his body expanded, bursting open his body armor and revealing large upper body musculature. But all that mass had to come from somewhere.

His pants are still on, she realized. Kenyon had done the evolutionary version of skipping leg day. He would hit hard, but he wasn't going anywhere fast.

Then he opened his mouth and began convulsing like he was going to throw up. With a gag and a cough, he shot a wad of green mucus—the size of a baseball—toward her head. She leapt out of the way and was about to comment on how gross it was when she noticed the chair she'd been on was now melting.

She also noticed Lawrence, inch-worming along the floor, trying to escape.

She lunged to the side, extending arms and legs as she moved, focusing on keeping her muscles strong and fast-twitch. She wanted to be a switchblade, to cut through the air, and then Kenyon, in a way that was hard to follow.

He roared in frustration and charged after her.

It was the moment she'd been waiting for. With her new body, changing course was easy. She bounded one way and then sprang back the other. When Kenyon tracked her and tried to match the move, his top-heavy body began to topple. He adjusted, but not fast enough to stop her from swiping his side as she passed.

He shouted in pain, arching his back.

She'd cut him. Four times. And deep. But he wasn't stupid. He'd heal quickly and adapt again.

The thing was, Peter had taught her that the key to successful combat was adaptation. Plans were great, but if you couldn't change them on the fly, you might as well just lie on a grenade, because no plan ever worked out how you expected. And Exos were completely unpredictable.

So, her next attack would need to be something new.

He'd try to do the same.

Kenyon was no fool.

But he was also older and thought things through. Anne, she was young and followed her gut, which led her on a collision course with Kenyon. He lifted his arm, which was now covered in spikes, intending to end the fight with one solid blow.

Instead of trying to gut him, she spun around, offering her back, which was now covered in a hundred two-foot-long sea urchin spines. She struck him like a pin cushion in reverse, puncturing his body a dozen times.

He howled in pain, the sound of it no longer quite human.

Then he made her pay for the attack, using his now armor-plated arm to slam down on the spines, breaking through them like they were brittle branches.

Every broken spike sent a jolt of pain through Anne's body. She stumbled free, released from his body, but trapped in agony. Being an Exo allowed the body to transform in marvelous ways, but pain was still pain, and it felt like her back had just been flayed away. She was so occupied by that flash of bodily loss that she missed Kenyon closing the distance and kicking hard.

He had yet to make any leg enhancements, but he knew how to kick and managed to put his foot right into her twelve-year-old gut. The air left her lungs as her stomach contracted, spasming from the impact. She rolled onto her back as the broken spikes retracted inside her body. Her claws shrank away, too, the physical resources redirecting to heal her injuries.

But that wasn't all.

Breathing was a weakness, and not everything needed to breathe. The change to her physiology was impossible to see, but she was now absorbing oxygen directly through her skin.

Kenyon stood over her as she continued clutching her stomach and gasping for air, realizing that she no longer required it.

"Didn't have to be like this, kid," he said. "If you and your mom had just stuck to the game plan, all of this could have been over months ago. You'd be safe. She'd be safe. And—"

"—I'd have to look at your ugly-ass face every damn day," Anne said before lifting her chin to reveal a small sphincter that had grown there. Kenyon winced at the sight of it and then again when a jet of black ink sprayed into his face.

She wanted to think of something more sinister. More deadly. But squid ink was the only thing that came to mind. It did the job though. Kenyon stumbled back, turning his hands human again to wipe away the liquid. "Fuck!"

Anne backed away and collected herself. How could she attack Kenyon in a way that would kill him? He was bigger and stronger and understood that RC-714 allowed for accelerated healing as even broken flesh could be remade. So, she needed some way to put him down—for good.

Kenyon wiped the last of the ink from his face, and spit some from his mouth. He turned his full attention to Anne, too angry to speak. He would tear her in half if she gave him the chance.

"Edward," Lawrence said, still struggling on the floor.

Kenyon glanced at the old man but said nothing.

"Listen," Lawrence said.

There was a moment of silence as all three fell silent. Anne wanted to hear what was happening, too. The sound reverberating through the facility brought a smile to her face.

Guns firing, people screaming, and something else, something a little less, or more than, human roaring behind the din.

"Better make it snappy," Anne said, giving Kenyon her best bratty kid grin. "My dad's going to fuck you up."

Kenyon kicked a syringe across the floor. It slid to a stop beside Lawrence who immediately started twisting around, reaching for it. Then Kenyon kicked another to the doctor who'd administered Anne's shot.

She was crouched down behind the front row of seats.

Looked from the needle and up to Kenyon.

"I don't know if I want to—"

"Do it!" Kenyon said, "or I will use your flesh and blood to strengthen my own."

With a shaky hand, she reached for the syringe.

Anne had seen enough. She now needed to take out Lawrence and the lady before they could inject themselves, or at least before the change finished. Kenyon was hard enough on his own.

C'mon, Dad, she thought, *hurry up.*

Speed, she thought, *agility.* That was what she needed. What she focused on. Rather than trying to piece together a collection of ancestors on her own, she let the gene adapt on its own, making a myriad of small changes to her body, both inside and out.

An armadillo-like armor formed over her skin. She became lithe and strong, more comfortable on all fours than upright. Then she hissed like a cat and sprang into action. Leaping one way and then the other, juking her way past Kenyon, headed for Lawrence, who'd just managed to inject his own wrist. Still bound, he couldn't defend himself.

But he didn't have to.

Kenyon had jacked up his speed, too, and he caught Anne by the foot. Using her momentum, he spun her around and flung her high. She crashed into the ceiling fifty feet above and was knocked unconscious for a moment. When she came to, she was falling. Feline instincts guided her limbs back toward the ground and had no trouble absorbing the second impact.

The doctor flopped to the floor, spasming, as RC-714 worked its way through her body. This was Anne's best chance, so she picked up a shard of glass the size of a dinner plate and frisbeed it at the woman's head, hoping to take it off. But the woman shook like she was being electrocuted. The sharp edge sliced her cheek deep enough to make a second hole to the inside of her mouth, but it missed her neck entirely.

"Shit," Anne said, and then she spun toward Kenyon again.

And he was smiling.

Because Lawrence was already back on his feet, his body contorting as he dove headlong into the ascension without any apprehension.

"Shit..."

To Kenyon's right, the doctor stood up. She still looked frightened, but she understood the science. How things were supposed to work. And all her fear melted away when a pair of wings tore from her back and unfurled. That was when she began to laugh.

Anne squared off with her trio of enhanced foes. "Annnd shit. You know this is totally unfair, right?" Then she charged toward an impossible-to-win fight for the second time in as many minutes.

50

Peter held the man in his hands, long claws sinking into his flesh, the smell of blood filling the air. The kill had been righteous. He had protected Ella from being gunned down by the guard, but the urge prodding him to consume—to eat—felt unholy.

It was the same craving that drove the world mad. The difference was that Peter recognized it for what it was—a depraved, cannibalistic craving for energy. For protein. For raw materials. He was like a potter in need of more clay. Every time he'd altered his body, the craving grew more intense.

But his resolve and self-discipline never wavered.

He withdrew his long claws from the man's back and tossed him to the side.

Dozens of ExoGen employees ran through the hall, fleeing with abject terror in their eyes—until they saw Peter, covered in blood, waiting for them. Most slid to a stop, screaming, unsure of where to go.

Peter considered killing them.

It would be easy.

And they were part of the cult that had ended the world. But it was also likely that they hadn't known the full scope of Lawrence's plan. Like Ella. They just hadn't been brave enough to leave with Ella, and they were now trying to survive by any means necessary—including worshiping a madman.

"It's okay!" Ella shouted to the crowd, standing in front of Peter. Some did a double take at Ella, recognizing her. Others glanced at the assault rifle in her hands and then scurried past as Ella waved the people around Peter, ensuring them it was safe.

He certainly didn't look safe. In addition to the blood from the guards he'd killed, his body was covered in thick prehistoric skin, and a tail whipping back and forth behind him. He moved on all fours and had long talons at the end of his hands and feet—half human, half velociraptor—with an armored back that had protected him from a few bullets fired by a guard who'd met his end moments later.

"We need to hurry," he said through two rows of sharp teeth.

She looked back at him and winced. "You couldn't pick anything that was both deadly and cute?"

"I'll practice in a mirror," he said, "after Lawrence and Kenyon are dead, Anne is safe, and this place is burning to the ground."

A trio of guards emerged from a hallway in front of them.

"Twelve o'clock," Peter said, unable to attack them himself with Ella in the way.

She swiveled the rifle around, unleashing two, three-round bursts—just like he taught her. Two of the men dropped, but the third brought his weapon around toward her. He hesitated for a moment when he saw Peter, unsure about who to shoot—the monster or the woman with the rifle?

He chose the assault rifle.

Normally, it would have been the right call. As frightening as Peter was, there was nothing about him that suggested he could cover the distance faster than a bullet.

But there was nothing normal about Peter anymore. Before the man—or Ella—could fire again, a bone sprouted from Peter's arm. He grasped hold, yanked it free, and in the same motion tossed it at the man. It struck the man's throat, knocking him back, choking on his own blood.

More screams rang out as a fresh wave of fleeing ExoGen employees filled the hallway. "Go, go, go!" Ella screamed at them, pointing around Peter.

He heard a mixture of reactions ranging from blind fear to curiosity. "Is that Ella?" "When did Ella get here?" Some of them even sounded hopeful. But none of them stopped.

They just kept on coming. A flood of fear.

Peter used his tail to sweep a man off his feet. He caught the man by the ankle and lifted him up. Then he leaned his face down to look at the man in his upside-down eyes.

"What are you running from?"

The man screamed in high-pitched horror.

Peter poked his talon into the man's shoulder. He wasn't trying to torture the man, simply focus his attention. "What. Are. You. Running. From?"

The man whimpered and quivered but managed to answer. "They-they changed her. She b-broke free. I th-think she's k-killing everyone."

"Who is she?" Peter asked.

"The girl," he said. "The kid." He glanced to the side and saw Ella. His eyes widened. "I-I'm sorry."

He was talking about Anne. They'd changed her and were paying the price.

Peter threw the man behind him, sending him sliding down the hallway until he crashed into a wall and swept the legs out from two other people on the way. It was overkill, but Ella didn't seem to mind. The mention of her daughter had brought out Ella's inner beast as well.

She put an arm around Peter's neck, and said, "Get me there now. Clear a god-damn path if you need to."

Peter picked her up in one arm and lunged forward. He ran on three limbs, charging toward the onrushing stampede. He could have plowed right through them like an ice cream truck through a marching band. Instead, he had mercy, leaping up toward the ceiling and spinning around while simultaneously shifting Ella onto his chest. With all his limbs available, he ran along the ceiling, keeping one foot and hand embedded at all times. It was awkward at first, but once he figured out the mechanics, they moved along the ceiling faster than they would have careened through the fleeing people.

A heavyset woman crashed through a set of double doors at the end of the hallway, heaving for air as she tried to keep up with the crowd. Peter thought two things upon seeing her; the first was that it had been a while since he'd seen someone overweight. She must have been with

ExoGen from the beginning and then flown across the country. Separated from the change. This might be the first time in her life that she had experienced the horror they'd unleashed upon the world.

The second was that she might taste delicious.

While he put the second thought out of his mind, despite his growing hunger, the first triggered him into action.

He bounded down from the ceiling and landed in front of the woman, who had only just seen him. As she screamed, he roared, putting all his anger into the sound. Abject dread guided the woman into a 90 degree turn that ended two steps later when she collided, head-on, with the wall.

Peter stopped, put Ella down, and looked at the woman in surprise.

Ella swatted his shoulder.

"I wasn't trying to do that," Peter said.

"You haven't looked in a mirror yet." She sprinted toward the door, just ahead.

Not knowing what was on the other side of the door, Peter scrambled ahead of her, lowered his head, and barreled through. Rather than opening, the doors were sent flying—along with two security guards in the wrong place at the wrong time.

Both men were dead on impact, but their bodies sailed through the air. The first struck a row of chairs, pin-wheeled once, and then fell between rows of curved seats surrounding a stage. The second man slammed into the backside of a woman, who coughed in surprise, but didn't fall from the impact, or the man's weight. Instead, she shrugged the body off her and turned to face Peter.

Her eyes were round and yellow, her nose pushed in and up, and her ears pointed. There was bat in there, but her skin was scaled. She was nasty looking, and understood how to change her body, but she lacked the tactical knowledge or imagination to come up with a truly dangerous combination.

She was a threat, but one Ella could handle.

It was the other three combatants in the room that held Peter's attention.

For a moment, he wasn't sure who was who, but then the smallest of them leapt away from a strike that ripped a bolted-down chair from the floor and sent it flying. That had to be Anne, built for speed and sharpness now—a good combination for the girl, but she lacked the power to put down the two much larger beasts closing in on her from either side.

When she spotted him and shouted, "Oh *ho*! You two are in trouble now!" she confirmed his suspicion...

And destroyed his element of surprise.

As the two monsters framing Anne turned toward him, Peter pressed the attack, heading for the creature he presumed was Kenyon. He'd be the most dangerous adversary—human or Exo.

Like Peter, Kenyon was a mishmash of creatures, utilizing RC-714 to create the perfect fighting body, rather than emulating identifiable creatures. The other man's natural sampling was a little more obvious, with the body of an ape, paws of a lion, and the face of a bear. It was a hairy mess, but large, imposing, and deadly.

Peter caught Kenyon off balance, grasping a chair back and swinging his leg around. He drove his foot in the back of Kenyon's knee, hoping to snap the limb, but Kenyon adapted quickly, adding a layer of thick skin to the back of his leg, absorbing the kick. He could reduce the impact, but he couldn't break the laws of physics.

Kenyon was knocked off his feet and pulled to the floor by gravity. Before landing, he flipped around and caught himself. He smiled at Peter and greeted him with "Asshole. I'm glad you're here. You can watch me gut your test tube baby—" He glanced at Ella, who had her rifle raised and was tracking the Exo woman around the theater. "—and that backstabbing bitch."

With a hiss, Kenyon lunged, and with claws lengthened while he spoke, he stabbed Peter in the sides and lifted him off the ground.

51

Ella fired the rifle, again and again, but Alexandra was moving too quickly. They'd been colleagues, but never really friends—mostly because Alexandra Madurn was honest to a fault, full of herself, and before the world went to hell, had a penchant for seafood so profound that her breath smelled of prawns.

Ella didn't wish the woman dead, but the moment she injected herself with the serum and went all in on the current plan, which called for the death of her daughter, Alexandra's fate was sealed.

If Ella could just make the shot.

The woman bounded around the atrium, leaping between seats, flapping her wings. They propelled her along, lengthening the distance of her jumps, but she hadn't figured out how to use them properly. She was a competent geneticist, but when it came to real world biology, she was closer to Pee Wee Herman than Albert Einstein.

Unfortunately, RC-714 didn't need a genius to be effective. Alexandra's chest was slowly expanding, responding to her desire to fly. Wouldn't be long before she was soaring around in circles rather than leaping.

Clip the wings, Ella thought to herself, relaxing into the rifle, the way Peter had shown her. He was almost metaphysical when it came to aiming a weapon. Become one with the steel. Feel the bullet's trajectory. It all sounded good, but Ella preferred a more straight forward, point and shoot technique. It wasn't serving her well, so she held her fire and tracked Alexandra around the room, trying to feel one with the weapon.

Oneness never came, but she did notice Alexandra was moving in a pattern—two leaps in the middle seats, a diagonal jump up, and then out as she tried to fly again. The pattern was bringing her around the massive room, straight toward Ella.

Was it a feint? Was she just closing the distance?

Across, across, up and out, Ella repeated in her head, tracking the woman, and then—leading her. Alexandra was close enough now that leading her with the rifle wasn't necessary. But Ella didn't want to miss again and wasn't going to count on her reflexes to pull the trigger fast enough.

Across, across, up and—she fired.

The bullet buzzed through the air, punched through flesh, and embedded itself in the wall.

Alexandra plummeted from the air with a shout. She landed atop a row of seats, and rolled over them, falling between rows and out of sight.

A familiar grunt of pain pulled Ella's attention across the round theater.

Anne was on the chair backs across the atrium. She leaped back as a monstrous Lawrence swiped a massive claw at her. It looked like Anne could evade him all day if she needed to. But she wasn't the one in trouble.

"Help him!" Anne shouted, pointing down to center stage.

Ella's attention snapped to the side, where Peter was being held in the air by Kenyon. It was a disturbing sight for two reasons. The first being that neither of them looked remotely human anymore. Had she come across Peter in the wild, looking like he did now, Ella would have gunned him down without a second thought. Even more disturbing was that the only way she could tell who was who now was by Kenyon's smile. He was enjoying the other man's pain. Peter wouldn't do that, not even to an Exo. He was a warrior with the heart of a poet, even if he hated poetry.

She swiveled her rifle around and fired.

Kenyon twitched from the impact but didn't drop Peter. He looked back over his shoulder, meeting her gaze. "Going to have to do better than that, my dear."

She fired again and again, but the skin on his back had already thickened to absorb the rounds.

Center mass had been the safest place to aim without risking hitting Peter, but it'd had no effect. So, Ella aimed higher, hoping her aim would be true, and she pulled the trigger.

The impact with the back of Kenyon's skull didn't breach his thick flesh, but it did hit him hard enough to sprawl him forward. As Kenyon fell, Peter fell free of the blades, shouting in pain.

Ella lined Kenyon up and prepared to continue the barrage when a shriek spun her around. Alexandra was mobile again, lunging at her. Her chest was bloody, but larger now, wings spread wide, carrying her the distance.

Ella fired, striking Alexandra's chest again, this time with far less effect.

Moving faster than Ella could compensate for, the she-beast didn't let her get off a second shot. Instead, she grasped hold of two seatbacks, pulled herself forward, and kicked out with her feet.

Alexandra's feet were no longer human. They were more like a giant eagle's, with long curved talons. And they were propelled by two powerful legs. The impact poked six holes in Ella's armor and body, and sent her flying. She landed hard on her back, ten feet away, the air knocked from her lungs and the rifle from her hand.

It took her three seconds to catch her breath and make sense of where she was and how she got there, which was exactly how long it took Alexandra to appear above her, long teeth extending from her mouth, eyes turning black. She clung to the seatbacks above Ella, snarling as she said, "You shot my tit!"

"In my defense," Ella said, "your chest is really big. Like a turkey."

"Speaking of turkey..." Alexandra smacked her lips. "I am famished. And you, bitch... You are finally expendable."

Ella wondered if most people at ExoGen viewed her as the enemy, after she had robbed them of their ascension. Then she decided she didn't give a shit and fired a throat strike up at Alexandra. It was a part of her body that was still mostly human, and the blow had the desired effect.

Alexandra reeled back, clutching her throat and gagging.

Ella reached up, took hold of the base of the chairs farther down the aisle, and yanked herself away. Then she got to her feet and looked for her rifle. It was nowhere to be seen. But she did see a pair of legs extending out from a row of seats closer to the stage. It would be a risky move, going closer to Kenyon, but the man was distracted by Peter, who was back on his feet, one arm clutching his torso, the other growing longer and splitting.

What is he doing? Ella wondered, and then she understood. Peter wasn't a biologist, but he knew and understood the world's hunters. He'd also made notes on the deadliest adaptations they'd come across—including a squid-like creature that could regenerate quickly.

He was healing himself, and arming himself—literally. But instead of two arms, he now had eleven. One hiding his healing wounds. The other ten were those of a squid, long and writhing, two of them tipped with hooked claws.

Ella scrambled down the row of seats to an aisle, banking hard to the right and down the long steps. She found breathing hard and worried a lung had been punctured, but she tried not to dwell on the worst case scenario. She'd landed on her back and probably had several broken ribs, not to mention a whirlwind of anxiety swirling through her.

This wasn't how she'd pictured the end of their journey. Peter and Anne transformed into monsters, battling for humanity by giving up their own. It was unthinkable, and so very...*them.*

Four rows from the bottom, uncomfortably close to the battle of modern-day Titans, she ducked into the row where Hutchins lay upside down in a chair, his chest impaled by a large piece of glass.

She glanced to her left and nearly stopped to watch. Peter used his tangle of limbs to slap and scratch Kenyon's back.

It wasn't enough to win the fight, but it had given Peter room and time to recover. Kenyon fought back, slicing off Peter's limbs, which either grew back, or quickly reattached to the severed flesh before it could fall away.

Behind them, Anne threw her hands up in the air, frustrated with Lawrence's new, brutal tactic. He wasn't pursuing her into whatever trap she had planned. He had stopped.

To eat.

During the mass evacuation, a man Ella recognized as Robert Jones had fallen and been knocked unconscious. He awoke now, dangling upside down, lowering toward Lawrence's unhinged jaws. His scream split the air for a moment before being muffled by his killer's throat, and then snuffed out entirely when four-inch-long dagger teeth closed over his neck and severed his head.

Ella did stop now, watching as Lawrence drank the pouring blood until it slowed to a trickle. Then he took another bite and began to laugh. His back bubbled and expanded. Two extra arms burst out, hulking and strong, visually human but with the muscle tone of some ancient predator.

He was more than a match for Anne, and he understood how to change. How to grow. She'd need help, but first Ella needed to take care of Alexandra.

"Shit!" she shouted, realizing she'd paused and left herself an easy target.

She spun around just in time to see the woman swooping down toward her, wings spread, chest muscles now large enough to put them to use. Talons reached down and hooked into Ella's body armor. Alexandra banked upward and tossed Ella.

This is it, she thought. The moment of her death.

After surviving the impossible in the wild, she was going to be killed by a bitch with crustacean breath.

It was humiliating.

She fell between seats. Her tailbone hit hard, sending shockwaves of pain through her body, but the impact hadn't knocked her unconscious, which she'd seen as a best case scenario—not being awake for her death.

Something broke my fall, she thought, and turned her head to the side. Her eyes went wide when she found herself just a centimeter away from the massive glass shard in Hutchins's chest. She'd nearly been impaled by it.

Her eyes shifted down and focused on the weapon lying beside the dead man. She reached for it, grabbed hold, and stood defiant as Alexandra swooped around, aiming to repeat the same attack.

Repetition was dangerous.

Gave people time to adapt strategies.

And Ella's new plan was pretty straight forward. She lifted the shotgun, looked down the sights, said, "Adapt to this," and held down the trigger. Fully automatic Frag-12 explosive rounds pounded the air with rapid fire thunderclaps.

Alexandra's inhuman face folded inward and then burst in every direction. The shotgun blasts reduced her body to pulp with each impact, stopping her forward momentum and disassembling her body, until her arms and wings fell away, leaving only a pair of legs behind.

The weapon ran out of shells and Ella took her finger off the trigger. She caught two breaths and then turned toward the sound of Lawrence's ferocious voice shouting, "Stop this foolishness—"

He was hairless now, and massive, his body built like an ape-shaped dinosaur. He lifted Anne by the throat. She was limp, but still breathing. Unconscious. He lowered her toward his mouth, oozing bloody drool.

"—or your child dies."

52

It took all of Peter's waning self-control to not press the attack. His tentacle technique had thrown Kenyon off balance and blinded him to Peter's most recent adaptation. His next strike could have ended the fight. Instead, he forced himself to back off. Lawrence would kill Anne—would eat her—if he didn't.

So, he lowered his fighting posture and stepped back.

Kenyon was just as unhappy about the development as Peter. "Why spare any of them?" His voice was hardly human now. More demon.

"Can't you see?" Lawrence said. "They have ascended. They are blessed. Killing them, without providing an opportunity for atonement would be—"

"Fuck atonement," Kenyon said, a long horn growing from his forehead. "I'm going to impale this asshole and drink his blood as it drains over my face."

Lawrence tsked and shook his head. "I always knew you would make a mockery of the ascension."

"Says the man about to consume a child," Ella said, crouching down and recovering a pistol from Hutchins's corpse.

Unfazed by Ella's comment, Lawrence lowered Anne closer to his mouth. "This is your last chance, Ella. You, above all, have earned a place in the new world, despite your...insolence. Despite the pain and suffering you have caused. None of this would have been possible without you."

"I would rather all of us die than live in your version of the world." Ella lifted the pistol toward Lawrence. "Either way, neither of you are leaving this island alive."

Lawrence's open mouth spread into a wide, toothy grin. "I will miss you, Ella."

It was at that moment that Anne snapped back into consciousness. She bucked and flailed, unable to free herself from Lawrence's grasp.

She was built for speed, not power, and like Peter, her ability to continuously transform was limited by her need to fuel the change, by consuming.

Lawrence lifted her up a little higher. "And what of you, child? Will you give yourself to the ascension? Will you lead the next generation?"

"I'll lead a ten-foot pole straight up your ugly ass," she said, swiping at his face, but missing.

"Don't try to overpower him," Peter said, offering advice he hoped she would understand. "Fight smart."

"What's the point?" she said. "He's going to eat me no matter what we do." She looked down into Lawrence's savage face. "I hope you choke." Then, contrary to Peter's advice, Anne stopped struggling and closed her eyes, resigned to her fate.

"Well," Lawrence said. "I tried. My conscience is clear." He turned to Kenyon. "Kill them both."

Then he lowered Anne toward his awaiting jaws.

"No!" Ella shouted, firing the pistol. The rounds struck Lawrence's back but had no effect.

Peter's tail snapped up, the stinger at the end stabbing toward Kenyon's side. But Kenyon was ready for the strike and severed the tail with a swipe of his now praying-mantis arms, which could strike with the same blinding speed.

Peter seethed with pain and staggered back, focusing on the end of his tail for a moment, healing the wound. He wouldn't be able to take his eyes off the man, even for the slightest moment, which was difficult given Ella's shouting and the gunfire. She wasn't having any luck, and Anne was still descending into Lawrence's mouth.

But Peter couldn't help her if he was dead. And that meant killing Kenyon, which was easier said than done.

Peter had lost a lot of blood, and parts of his body. All of that gave him fewer raw materials with which to work. Exhaustion sought him out, climbed on his shoulders and weighed him down.

Fight smart, he told himself. Fight—

Kenyon's long mantis limbs snapped out faster than Peter could register. The prongs drove into his back hard enough to puncture armor.

He tried to resist, but Kenyon pulled him closer.

"I'm going to eat you," he said. "And then the bitch. After that, I'm only going to think about you both one last time—when I shit you out."

After speaking the last word, his lower jaw and mouth grew a light green carapace, his teeth fell out, and a pair of mantis mandibles emerged.

He's going to eat me alive, Peter realized.

He willed his body to change, to form a defensive skin Kenyon couldn't chew through, but he lacked the strength.

Peter had seen a lot of people die. Recognized the look in a person's eyes when they realized the end of life was inevitable. If he could see himself, he'd see that same look. He'd endure a minute of pain, and then...nothing. He'd fight it the whole way, but his fate was sealed.

A moment later, the situation grew even more hopeless. ExoGen's security forces had regrouped. They re-entered the atrium in formation, heavily armed with assault rifles and shotguns.

Exo or not, if the small army opened fire, they were all dead.

"Pick a target!" a man shouted, and weapons came up.

The distraction forced Kenyon to turn away from Peter and change his face back to normal. "Hold your fire!"

There were a few shouts of surprise, and Peter heard the word 'ascended' a few times, but the overall effect was obedience. They recognized Kenyon and followed his command, along with the next. "Kill them!" He pointed toward Lawrence and Anne.

Kenyon turned back to Peter. Smiled when gunfire erupted. "Where were we? Oh, right. I was about to eat your face." Kenyon's face transformed again, the lower half becoming a mantis once more.

They were done.

Lawrence was taking the gunfire for now, still lowering Anne into his mouth, apparently savoring the moment. Ella fired back at the guards but was quickly pinned down between rows by return fire. And Peter... he was about to have his face eaten.

Kenyon's mandibles scraped against Peter's cheek. The razor edge carved a line, drawing blood. A long straw-like tongue emerged, sucking up the blood.

He was going to draw this out, make Peter suffer.

"Mother…fucker…" Peter said, struggling to transform himself into something useful, but his energy was sapped.

Peter allowed his body to return to its human form. He was finished.

He was—

The ceiling above exploded inward, sending debris in all directions. When the dust cleared, a large black ball the size of a Volkswagen Bug was revealed. It was round enough to be man-made, but crisscrossed in organic lines, and seams where a shell came together.

It was an Apex.

From outside.

Kenyon's face snapped back to human. "What now?!"

The armored ball began to unfurl, revealing the body within. It was a powerhouse of insectoid limbs, with the muscular body of a hundred different creatures. Four wings snapped out, buzzing as they recovered from the impact.

"What the f—" Kenyon's expletive was interrupted by the last voice Peter expected to hear—

—his son's. "Heads up, you son of a bitch!"

When Peter and Kenyon looked up, it wasn't just Jakob they saw. It was Val, careening down like a missile, feet aimed toward Kenyon's face. She arrived faster than he could react, with the kinetic force of a rail gun.

Peter was released and dropped to the floor. Jakob knelt beside him as Val picked Kenyon up and tossed him across the room. "Dad! Are you okay?"

"I don't understand," Peter said. "What…is *that?*" He glanced to the insectoid Apex still righting itself.

"Question isn't what," Jakob said with a grin. "It's who."

Jakob laughed at Peter's incredulous expression.

"That…is Lyn. We figured it out. How ExoGen crops work. Or maybe just some of them. Same thing that let Val change let Lyn save herself."

The monster that was Lyn flipped over, wings snapped out and buzzing. She soared across the room, her thick carapace absorbing the guards' gunfire. The men quickly realized it was hopeless and attempted to retreat, but Lyn was fast, and set upon them with merciful ferocity. Every strike was an instant kill.

She wasn't venting anger. Wasn't unleashing her hunger or eating anyone. But she'd clearly eaten a lot—of something.

Peter noticed the MP5 slung over Jakob's shoulder. "Can you help your sister?" He looked toward Lawrence and furrowed his brow. Anne was still in his grasp, still inhuman looking, still dangling over his mouth, but they were frozen in place.

"Are...are they frozen?" Jakob asked.

"Not sure..." Peter said, struggling to stand. He'd lost a lot of blood... and had to use cells from his body to regrow his hand. He was diminished and would stay that way until he ate something.

Jakob helped him to his feet, and together, they started up the stairs, slowly getting a view of Lawrence's frontside.

"Who is *that?*" Jakob asked.

"It was Lawrence," Peter said. "Head of ExoGen."

"He's an Exo?"

"A new kind," Peter said. "He can control the change. Just like your sister."

Jakob seemed to fully notice Anne at that moment, hanging still in Lawrence's grasp. "Wait. *That's* Anne? She's an Exo, too?"

"And me," Peter added.

"You...can do *that?*"

"Could," Peter said. "I need to eat something before I can—"

"You're not...like, hungry, right?"

"Not like that," Peter said, starting down the row of seats that would lead them beneath Anne.

Movement drew his gaze to Lawrence's face. It was twitching. His eyes were moving, tracking Peter. He was paralyzed, but alive, and maybe recovering. Peter looked Anne over and noticed a change. Her skin beneath Lawrence's hand was smooth, green with orange spots, and slimy.

She fought smart, Peter realized. *Excreted a neurotoxin through her skin.* But the effort either exhausted her, or the toxin was working on them both.

"Shit..." Jakob said. "How do we get her down?"

Peter sighed. He knew how. But he didn't like it.

"Gonna need you to look away, son," Peter said.

"But—"

"Now," Peter said, growing a single, razor-sharp claw on his fingertip. When Jakob relented and looked away, Peter reached up and sliced open Lawrence's wrist. Blood seeped from the wound, flowing like a spring from the Earth, straight into Peter's mouth.

Peter was both revolted and delighted by the blood meal. He wanted to retch it all back up, but he could also feel his body rejuvenating, his cells expanding, his potential for growth—for change—increasing beyond anything he'd experienced so far. And he'd already developed a resistance to the neurotoxin in the viscous liquid.

As he continued to drink, Peter's arm grew longer. A large bony blade extended out. He didn't know what part of the fossil record the limb came from and didn't care. Feeling stronger, Peter swept his arm up in an arc. The bone blade sliced through Lawrence's immobilized flesh, severing the hand.

"What the fuck..." Jakob whispered.

Peter turned to his son. "I told you not to watch!"

"But that...that was awesome."

Peter grimaced, reducing the blade back into a hand, which then became a single, large talon—along with his left hand. Using the hooks, he carefully pried the dead hand's fingers away from Anne.

The moment she was released, her eyes popped open, and she sucked in a breath. She was groggy, but conscious.

"Are you paralyzed?" Peter asked.

"What? No! Do I look like an amateur to you?" The green skin on her belly had been replaced by a coating of hair.

"You look like a little werewolf or something," Jakob said.

"Jakey-boy!" Anne said. "You're alive!"

"Hey!" Ella said, hurrying down the aisle. She reached Anne first, wrapping her arms around the girl, despite her current Exo form. "You're okay?" She looked at Jakob and Peter. "You're all okay?"

"Fine," Jakob said, "but I think the big guy is recovering?

They all turned toward Lawrence. Jakob was right. His muscles were twitching, limbs starting to move, hand regrowing.

"He's my problem," Ella said. "I'll take care of him." She held her hand out to Jakob and he understood the ask, placing his MP5 in her hands. She racked the slide and aimed the weapon up at an angle, toward Lawrence's face. Then she pulled down the trigger, unleashing a stream of bullets, punching small holes in his large face, but completely missing her target.

She released the trigger, sighed, and handed the weapon to Peter. "You do it."

He took the weapon, aimed almost casually, and pulled the trigger three times. All three rounds slipped through Lawrence's eyeball and punched into his brain. When he didn't immediately fall, Peter shifted his aim to the right and fired three more times, destroying the other eye and the rest of Lawrence's mind. All at once, the massive, paralyzed body collapsed.

"It's done," Ella whispered.

"Not quite," Peter said, watching as Kenyon's body sailed across the atrium again and collided with the stage at the center. He was wounded, but not dead.

The family, including Val, converged on the stage. Kenyon tried to move, to heal, but his body was tapped. He slowly returned to his human form, defenseless.

"Bitch," he said, spitting blood at Val's feet.

Peter reached down to his son's waist and drew the knife sheathed there. He stepped up onto the stage and knelt beside Kenyon.

"Couldn't finish me yourself. Had to—" Kenyon coughed blood. "Had to rely on your monster whore—"

Peter stabbed the knife down directly into Kenyon's forehead, burying it to the hilt. "Guess I *am* an asshole."

"Umm," Anne said. "I think we should probably leave now." She pointed up to the hole in the ceiling. A shadow fell over the room. High above, a bulbous body floated past overhead, and then unleashed the ear-splitting call of an ExoGenetic whale.

53

Anne let herself revert back to her human form, to conserve energy and to help Jakob and her mother not freak out. They were handling it all okay, but their sidelong glances revealed that it would take some time to trust someone who looked like an Exo. Made sense. Aside from Val, they'd been trained to kill Exos on sight.

Now, she, her father, and apparently Lyn, could turn into monsters.

Then again, Jakob seemed to trust what Lyn had become.

Maybe because he was there when it happened, and she hadn't eaten him.

But Anne was also exhausted, and like her father, hungry. She didn't want to find out if there was a limit to how much they could change before the craving to eat overwhelmed them.

She didn't think they'd turn cannibal, but even normal people resorted to munching on a human limb when hungry enough. And if she wasn't wrong, her father had just drunk some of Lawrence's blood to save her. So...it wasn't a super far-fetched idea.

Hands to her ears and eyes to the sky, Anne watched the floating whale glide overhead. When its blaring call finally ceased, the sound of screaming people took its place. At least some of ExoGen's people had fled the atrium and gone outside, perhaps hoping to evacuate on a helicopter or a boat.

"Man, did they make the wrong choice," she said, watching as the massive whale's jaws opened up. Where once there had been baleen for filtering the world's smallest prey, there was now what looked like a wriggling lump of massive worms.

The mass of slithering bodies lolled to the side and fell out of the whale's mouth. It unfurled and untangled as it descended toward the ground, snapping open overhead as a blossom of pale tendrils, each one wriggling around, seeking out prey.

And finding it.

Screams grew louder as people were yanked up into the sky, drawn up into the whale's mouth, and shoved back into its gullet. One by one, the creature plucked the residents of George's Island into the air, stuffing them into its maw, snuffing out one scream after another.

When the whale descended and the facility shook, Anne knew it was breaching entrances, seeking out tasty treats with its long appendages, using them like an anteater's tongue.

It was carnage. And about to get worse.

While the first whale feasted, a second cried out. Then a third.

"It's a pod," Jakob said. "We need to get the hell out of here."

"We can head underground," Ella suggested. "Same way we got in."

Peter shook his head. "They've adapted to plucking their prey out from under the ground. There's no way to know how long their reach is. We need to get the hell off this island."

"We need Lyn," Val said, yanking the knife out of Kenyon's head, wiping the blood off on his corpse, and then handing the blade back to Jakob. He took it without wincing, which impressed Anne—he'd gone through something while they were gone.

Jakob sheathed the knife and nodded. "Lyn can get us out of here."

"I believe you," Peter said, "but I don't see her."

"She can hear us," Val said with a grin.

Peter squinted at her. "What did she eat?"

"You know the Exos surrounding the island?" Jakob said. "There aren't as many of them now."

"And how do you know she can hear us?" Ella asked.

Val shrugged. "I can hear her." She pointed to a wall, tracing a finger, following an invisible path. Her eyes widened. "She definitely heard us! Get down!"

Val stood in front of them, her back toward the wall—which exploded a moment later. A ferocious looking Apex insectoid creature burst through the wall. Concrete and metal shrapnel was flung around the room.

The creature that was Lyn was about to collide with them when its four transparent wings snapped open and unleashed a fluttering buzz that stopped her in her tracks and kicked up a hurricane force wind.

Anne's instinct was to put a few rounds in the thing's bug-eyed, mandibled face, but then it began to change, revealing hints of its original, human form. It *was* Lyn.

"All aboard," she said, her voice a rattling hum. She glanced down and saw Kenyon's body. "And good riddance."

She lifted the front of her body and opened four of her insect limbs, as if she was coming in for a hug. "Got room for four. Val you can ride on t—"

"Don't worry about it," Peter said, stepping back. "I'll cover your exfil."

His body expanded, growing stronger, chest enlarging. His arms lengthened and stretched a thin membrane out between long spines that used to be his fingers. At the end of each wing, a bony blade grew, as did a line of spines that looked like a serrated knife.

"Unlocked the secret of ExoGenetic change?" Lyn asked. "Makes two of us."

Ella gasped. "Wait! We can't leave without the formula, without making more serum for other people."

"No choice," Peter said, his voice a baritone now. "There are other labs in the world—"

"—and I have the formula," Anne added, tapping her head. "Up here. But not if we get eaten!"

Ella relented, stepping up to Lyn along with Jakob, Val, and Anne. The long limbs wrapped around them like safety bars on a roller coaster, hugging them close.

Anne had a front row seat and was excited for what came next. Sure, there would probably be screaming and near-death encounters, but she didn't mind them much—as long as everyone made it through.

And she had no doubt they would.

Because they were awesome at surviving the end of the world.

"Let's go!" she shouted, pointing toward the hole in the ceiling.

Lyn's wings buzzed and kicked up a plume of dust, the wind growing so strong that Kenyon's body was rolled off the stage and dropped onto the floor—one last, well deserved insult. Then they rose up fast, an out-of-control elevator like the one in *Willy Wonka & the Chocolate Factory*—a movie she'd never seen yet remembered—straight up and out of the ceiling.

They were spotted the moment they crossed the threshold from the facility's interior to its exterior. Fleshy tendrils snaked down toward them from the whale above, but also from two sides, where another two whales floated. There were seven in all, descending upon the island in a slow-motion fervor, plucking people from the rooms and hallways below.

Wouldn't be long before ExoGen and George's Island were barren of life.

When Peter soared up past them, Anne let out a "Whoohoo!" as she watched her father race upward to greet the descending tendrils. Just before impact, he spun his body in tight circles, turning himself into a flying blender.

Writhing limbs came apart and filled the air like carpet bombs dropped over World War II Germany. A storm of blood followed.

Lyn spun and wove her way through the cascade of body parts and fluid, keeping them safe *and* dry.

The smallest of the whales—probably a baby when the change began—kicked its tail and followed them up through the merging tangles of flesh.

Lyn's upward momentum continued to increase, even as her movements became almost erratic, narrowly escaping one tendril after another. And then, with the same suddenness with which they had emerged from the ExoGen facility, they cleared the waves of prehensile worms and cruised up into the open sky.

Lyn banked to the left and did a happy spin that made Anne laugh, and Jakob shout, "No more fancy flying, unless you want me to puke!"

Beside Anne, Val had her eyes closed, a smile on her face, enjoying the breeze.

She had changed, too.

Anne nearly shouted in surprise when Peter flew past them, headed back the way they'd come. Lyn did a three-sixty spin without altering course. Behind them, the smaller Apex-whale was still in pursuit—not fast enough to catch them, but plenty fast enough to follow.

Peter snapped his wings open, stopping in between them and the whale.

"No!" he shouted at it. "No more!"

When it didn't stop, he flared his wings wider, expanding them and shading them with patterns that looked like a pair of massive eyes.

"Oldest trick in nature's playbook," Ella said, with a chuckle.

Anne wasn't so sure. "I think it's more than that."

Val nodded.

Lyn's strange voice buzzed at them. "She's right. They are...communicating."

Anne wasn't sure how, but it was something those with ExoGenetic blood could sense.

And the whale could, too.

It opened its mouth and let out a long sigh, slowing its forward momentum. Then the creature's mass of tendrils recoiled and slid back inside its mouth. There was a moment of connection, and then the whale turned away and descended toward its brethren, eager to rejoin the feast.

Peter glided up beside them, his face not quite human anymore, covered in hair with bat-like wings. "We're good," he said, "Next stop, Hellhole Bay." Then he soared up into the sky, curled over, and dove past before flaring his wings and gliding beneath them, leading the way south.

Epilogue

Jakob woke from a dream—a pleasant one for once, and he stretched. The winter air was just cool enough to make him want to stay in bed. He rolled to his left, wrapped in a comforter cocoon, facing the empty mattress, longing for the day when he'd find Alia lying beside him.

Reuniting with her, after everything his family had been through, was awkward. But she understood better than most, and it wasn't long before their relationship was close enough that Peter had to make Jakob swear they wouldn't move in together while he was gone.

That was three months ago, and Peter, Ella, and Anne hadn't returned. They'd only been at Hellhole for two weeks before they had announced they were heading back out. The lab in Boston was destroyed. The other ExoGen bio-domes Ella had built were far away, and their status unknown. But Ella had been sure that everything she needed could be found in hospitals and research labs dotting the country.

They set out on their quest without even asking Jakob if he wanted to join them. He wasn't insulted by it because he would have said 'no,' and he knew it was obvious. Because, for the first time in a long time, he was really happy. Not just because he was with Alia, but because he wasn't worrying something might eat him.

While they were gone, Boone had managed to expand Hellhole Bay and shore up their defenses. Turned out he was a much better leader than Mason had been. The small community was thriving with the help of the Chunta—and now Lyn and Val, who had begun teaching her brethren how to control their ExoGenetic adaptations. A few of them almost looked human now. But all of them were fierce defenders of Hellhole.

In the past three months, there had only been one attack from an Apex, and it was handled so swiftly that Jakob didn't know about it until he was told.

He was well-fed, sleeping well, and madly in love.

And today was his day off, which meant—

A knock on the door to his small camping trailer made him smile.

"Come in!"

The unlocked door swung open. Alia bounded inside, looking for him. When she found him lying in bed, she twisted her lips and raised an eyebrow at him. "Really?"

He laughed. "I just woke up."

"I can see that," she said, taking hold of the comforter and pulling it off him. He grabbed hold and pulled back, trying to yank her onto the bed. She let go, and he flopped back. "Uh-uh. I don't think so. I've been looking forward to this all week. Get your ass up."

"Ugh." He threw the blankets off and slid out of bed. He was still dressed from the day before, and since clean laundry was still hard to come by, he didn't bother changing. He put a baseball cap on his head and slipped boots onto his feet. "What are we doing again?"

"It's a secret," she said.

"Right," he said, stretching. "Code for 'something you'll hate.'"

She wrapped her arms around his back and squeezed her head against his chest. "You'll love it. I promise."

He hugged her in return.

"Can I at least eat something? I'm famished."

She rolled her eyes and checked her watch. "I don't know if there's—"

The trailer's wall shook from three solid whacks.

Then the door opened, and Val leaned in. "Almost time!"

Jakob threw his arms up in the air. "Does everyone but me know about this? How many people are going to be there?"

Val hooted a laugh and did an impersonation of her old self. "Jakey-boy wants sexy-time." She let out an exaggerated sigh and said, "Jakey-boy always wants sexy time." She gave him a wink, laughed again, and then left as quickly as she arrived.

"What's that supposed to mean?" Alia asked.

"Nothing," Jakob said. "She's just screwing with you. Let's go." He took her hand and hurried out of the trailer, hoping a change of scenery would also shift the conversation in a less embarrassing direction.

Hellhole Bay was alive with a different kind of energy. Everyone was awake, even the people who'd been on guard overnight.

Something big was happening.

"Am I the only one who doesn't know?" Jakob asked, feeling a bit stunned.

"Just shut up and move." She gave him a shove toward the gate, where the residents of Hellhole were gathering.

He thought it must be an Apex, dragged to the gate for everyone to see, study, and learn from. It was what they did with the last. Know your enemy and all that, but only a dozen people dared show up for that. Why would everyone—

A hope slipped into his thoughts.

He looked at Alia, and she must have seen the question in his eyes. She smiled, eyes watering.

Jakob broke into a run, pushing his way past the gathering throng. He reached the gates and kicked them.

"Open the gates!"

"But it's not time," a guard said.

"Open the god-damned gates!"

While Boone was still in charge, Jakob was seen as a surrogate for Peter, who Boone recognized as their true leader. But Peter had been gone for a long time.

"Open it," Boone said, standing behind Jakob and patting his shoulder. "Let the kid out."

The gates cracked open. When there was just enough room for him to fit, Jakob squeezed through and looked left and right. The dirt road leading to the gates from both directions was empty.

Motion pulled his eyes to the sky. It was Lyn, in her preferred insectoid form, buzzing around in circles, keeping watch, but not over Hellhole Bay. She was watching for something else, something still in the swamp, thick with trees, surrounding the compound.

As Alia, Boone, and Val stepped out behind him, Jakob broke into a sprint. Ahead, he heard an engine, loud and rumbling, the kind of thing that attracts a lot of attention out in the wild. The kind of thing only people who really know how to survive would attempt.

A school bus rolled into view ahead. Behind it, an eighteen-wheeler. He could hear other vehicles, too, still out of sight. It was a caravan. And the sight of it approaching made Jakob stop in his tracks. What it promised shocked him into stillness.

The bus pulled up beside him, its brakes squeaking as it stopped.

The door slid open, and a blur leapt out and tackled him to the ground.

Anne pinned his shoulders, her eyes sparkling and wide, smiling down at him. "Broseph!" She flattened herself on him as he hugged her tight. "I see you still have the reflexes of a slug."

"Missed you, too," he said.

"Son."

Jakob looked up to find his father stepping out, a thick beard surrounding his smile, and more hair than he'd had on his head in years. Anne had longer hair, too, blonde and glowing in the morning sun. It was almost like they weren't worried about contamination...

Jakob's eyes flared wide. "You did it..."

Peter offered him a hand. Anne rolled off, allowing Jakob to be pulled to his feet. Peter wrapped his arms around his son, hugging him for a full ten seconds before kissing the top of his shaved head and leaning back to look at him.

"Things okay here?"

"Going great."

"Good," Peter said, glancing at Alia, who was approaching with the rest of the compound's occupants. He turned back to Jakob, squinting. "How great?"

Jakob laughed. "Hey, I followed the rules. Most of the time."

Peter chuckled and put his arm around Jakob. "C'mon. I have something to show you." He turned back to the growing number of people. "We have something to show all of you!"

They walked past the bus, to the back of the eighteen-wheeler. The back had already been opened. Ella smiled down at him. He barely noticed her. The high-tech mobile laboratory built into the trailer was stunning...and functional. "What..." He looked at Ella. "How?"

She smiled and reached down to him, helping him up into the trailer.

She kissed his head, and said, "We started as we intended, collecting everything we needed, but after coming across a few other communities with skill sets of their own, we were able to build a mobile lab with everything we needed to create more of the serum."

"Needed?" Jakob asked.

"We can make more, but we have enough to treat everyone in Hellhole Bay, and then some."

"How many is everyone?" Jakob asked.

Peter hoisted Anne up into the trailer and climbed up behind her. Outside the trailer, the residents of Hellhole gathered around the open doors, Val, Alia, and Boone at the front.

"But..." Jakob whispered. "...is it the kind that lets you eat everything, or the kind that makes you able to, you know?"

"We have both," Anne said. "The good stuff, for people we really trust. And the other stuff for wussies like you, who just want to eat and make babies or whatever." She glanced at Alia and was pleased to see her embarrassment.

"Well, you haven't changed," Jakob said to Anne.

"You love me just the way I am." She stuck her tongue out at him. "And for the record, I change all the time. I just didn't want to scare you."

He smiled. "Thanks."

"What's important," Ella said, "is that we can make as much as we need, can transport it around the country, and the world. We can inoculate everyone that's still alive. As the Apexes die out—and they *are* dying out—we can take back the planet."

"What about the Apexes living in packs?" Jakob asked.

"They face the same challenge as all Exos. If they don't realize they can eat plants, they're going to die out. But if we encounter them, we can communicate."

"Like Dad did with the whale?" Jakob asked.

"A little more than that," Peter said, and he pointed toward the back of the convoy. People he didn't know were exiting the vehicles, including some who were clearly not fully human, or perhaps had been far from human before, like Val. But they were peaceful, walking among humans.

Jakob was overwhelmed by the sight. He'd have cried if he wasn't sure Anne would tease him. "How many people do you have with you?"

"Just under three hundred," Peter said.

"Combined with Hellhole's population, that puts us just a hundred shy of enough," Ella said.

"Enough...for what?" Jakob asked.

"Repopulation," Ella said. "Of the planet. It will take a few thousand years to get back to where we were, but we're on our way to undoing the damage I—that ExoGen did."

"So," Peter said, opening a brown cardboard box. Inside were dozens of small syringes, all lined up, all pre-loaded. "Who's hungry?"

"I'm famished," Anne said, smiling.

"Peckish," Ella added.

"Getting hangry," Val said.

Jakob smiled. This was a big moment for everyone, and as a representative of his family, and as someone the people of Hellhole Bay trusted, he didn't want to screw it up. He rolled up his sleeve, exposing his shoulder for an injection, and gave a casual shrug.

"I could eat."

AUTHOR'S NOTE

Well, this author's note has been a long time coming! In case you didn't know, I released HUNGER and FEAST, books one and two of the Hunger Trilogy back in 2015 and 2016 under the pen name 'Jeremiah Knight.' It was around that time that the way people consumed books (mine, at least) began to change, shifting from e-books to audiobooks.

The result was that sales in both mediums, for the new Jeremiah Knight, suffered, and book three was shelved. Meanwhile, the Jeremy Robinson name continued its upward sales trend. But, thanks to my love for this concept, the story, and the characters, along with my hatred of leaving things unfinished, I decided to find a way to complete this trilogy.

So now, after all this time, we've released all three books as one mega-novel, with book three, FAMINE, being a completely new grand finale, and under the Robinson name. And I am thrilled with how it came out. Despite the time gap between writing the first two books and the third, I had no trouble slipping back into the chaotic and almost limitless world of HUNGER. I also realized that Anne was the blueprint for the character of Bree in THE DARK.

I hope you enjoyed HUNGER: THE COMPLETE TRILOGY as much as I did returning to it. If so, please consider writing a review on Amazon or Audible. Every single one, even a really short one, helps the AI-overlord algorithms recommend me to other readers and make each release a hit.

If you want to be sure you don't miss all the books to follow, and news about upcoming comic books, movies, TV series, etc., you can visit:

bewareofmonsters.com

When you do, be sure to sign up for the newsletter. Or, you can join the Tribe at facebook.com/groups/JR.Tribe. It's an amazing group of fans, the first place that cool stuff gets announced, and it's where I interact with readers every single day. Also, we give away free stuff every week!

Hope to see you there.

—Jeremy Robinson

ABOUT THE AUTHOR

Jeremy Robinson is the *New York Times* and #1 Audible bestselling author of over seventy novels and novellas, including *Infinite, The Others,* and *The Dark,* as well as the Jack Sigler thriller series, and *Project Nemesis,* the highest selling, original kaiju novel of all time (which is in development for TV with Chad Stahelski, director of John Wick). Robinson is known for mixing elements of science, history, and mythology, which has earned him the #1 spot in Science Fiction and Action-Adventure, and secured him as the top creature feature author. Many of his novels have been adapted into comic books, optioned for film and TV, and translated into fourteen languages. He lives in New Hampshire with his wife and three children.

Visit him at www.bewareofmonsters.com.

Made in United States
North Haven, CT
23 July 2023

39384103R00450